HUSBANDS
for HIRE
TRILOGY

HUSBANDS *for* HIRE TRILOGY

3-in-1 Collection

Kelly Eileen Hake

BARBOUR
PUBLISHING

RUGGED &
RELENTLESS

DEDICATION

Every good gift comes from the Lord—and writing this novel was a gift to me. Perhaps because there's a lot of myself in Evie, the heroine. So, first and foremost, this work is for Him.

But after Him come a lot of wonderful people in my life without whose support, encouragement, and reality checks things just wouldn't come out the same. For my writing accountability partner, Steve, who put in the long hours writing with me even a country apart. For Julia, my best friend, who good-naturedly puts up with postponed girls' nights out. For Aaron, my copy editor, who listens to my character questions and always suggests something to have me heading for the keyboard again. . . .

And this one is, most of all, for Tracie, the editor who bought my first novel and came to be a cherished family friend. You'll never know how much your mentorship and love have meant over the years—this book, and all the growth I think it represents, is thanks to you.

Hugs and Blessings,
Kelly Eileen Hake
Mistakes, Love, and Grace!

KEY SCRIPTURES:

Man looketh on the outward appearance,
but the Lord looketh on the heart.
1 SAMUEL 16:7

There is nothing covered, that shall not be revealed;
and hid, that shall not be known.
MATTHEW 10:26

A false balance is an abomination to the Lord:
but a just weight is his delight.
PROVERBS 11:1

PROLOGUE

Maine, April 15, 1886

Y ou don't have to do this, Jacob!" Mama wrung her hands from the doorway to his bedroom, where she hovered a respectful and appropriate distance. Appropriate and distant—amazing how two words could almost sum up a person's life.

"Someone has to." He shoved clothes into the satchel, fistfuls of hardy work material and not fancy churchgoing stuff or business wear. "Why not me?"

"You have a place here! Responsibilities! The business. . ." Mama ticked off answers to what he'd meant as a rhetorical question.

Women. Jake shook his head and stuffed in a pocketknife and his shaving kit and looked around the room for other essentials. With his pistol holstered at his hip, his favorite boots on his feet, and his saddlebags bulging with enough food to see him through a few days, he didn't need much else.

Except. . . He strode over to the bureau, opened his top drawer, and reached until he felt the cool piece of metal he'd thrust back there three months ago. Now he shoved it into his pocket without giving the object a glance.

"Your father needs you to help run the mill," his mother's

litany continued. "Now more than ever with Edward gone—"

He could tell the instant she recognized her mistake. That she stopped talking was a dead giveaway in and of itself, even if her hand didn't flutter toward her mouth as though to capture the name and stuff it back before it could do any damage.

"Yes, Mama." Jake paused to look her in the eye. "Edward's gone." *Good to hear you noticed.* He swallowed the sarcastic comment but couldn't bury the bitterness at its root. "Four months since his death, but no one acknowledges it."

"It doesn't honor his memory to—"

"Remember him?" Laughter, raw with rage, scraped his throat. "But it honors him to pretend he flitted off to another state, leaving Pa in the lurch? It *honors* him to let his murderer go free to live a long life?"

"The way he died. . . Jake, the scandal of it would smear his memory." She shrugged as though in supplication.

"You mean it would smear the Granger name." He swung the satchel from his old bed and went to the door. "I have to go, Ma." Something in him softened at the misery he saw in her face.

"But. . ." Tears filled her eyes and began to spill down her cheeks. It seemed as though the sudden desertion of her only remaining son allowed her to mourn both of them at once, finally crying for the firstborn who'd never come home.

Jake caught his mother in a long hug, not saying he had to go but would come back with Edward's name clean enough to display on the family tree again.

Jake didn't make promises he couldn't keep. And he knew a hug didn't promise anything, but he hoped it gave his mother some small comfort when she'd finally—*finally*—shown sorrow for the things that mattered most to her.

"But. . ." She sniffed, clutching his coat. "What will people *say?*"

Words. Always words, with his parents. *I should have known that's what mattered.* He brushed her hands away. "I. Don't. Care."

"What about this family?" She made a final plea as he slapped his hat on his head. "What about honoring your parents?"

"We have different definitions of honor, Mother." With that, he headed out the door. West, to begin his hunt.

ONE

Charleston, Virginia, May 5, 1886

S ell it." Her sister's voice cracked on the second word. "Tell Lacey to sell it all and be rid of the accursed place forever."

"Tell her yourself." Evelyn Thompson thrust a handkerchief at her sibling but offered no other solace. "Lacey promises some exciting news, and you've hidden inside too long, Cora."

"Mourning, not hiding."

"Lacey mourns for her brother but honors him by pressing on." *But here is another matter. Lord, I can't allow the tragedy of the mines to bury my sister along with her fiancé.* "We must change our plans and see to our futures."

The sodden handkerchief plummeted to the floor in Cora's first show of spirit in weeks. "I told you—sell it. Sell every inch of Hope Falls we own. I'll never set foot in the town that took Braden, and no profit will be made from a ghost town. Tell Lacey to take the offer and not look back."

"You can tell your opinion to Lacey and Naomi in person."

"I can't." The fire in her eyes dimmed. "Evie, please."

The whisper tore into the very foundation of her relationship with her sister. For as long as she could remember, Evie'd sheltered, raised, and comforted Cora. Streams of mopped tears, scores of tended scrapes, hours of hugs invested demanded that she do the same once more. But their lives hung on the outcome of today's meeting.

If I can just get her there! "You can." Evie picked up the soiled handkerchief and thrust it into her sister's hands. "You must."

With that, she summoned the carriage and headed Cora off when she made for the stairs. Instead, Evie thrust a black bonnet atop her sister's head and all but hauled her out the front door and into the waiting conveyance.

The Lyman house sprawled only a few short blocks away—a simple walk the sisters had made hundreds, perhaps thousands of times. But not today. Today, Evie didn't trust her own ability to force her sister through a walk. Today, those few blocks yawned before her, stretched beyond recognition and filled with peril. Thus, the carriage. It wasn't until they sat safely seated inside that either of them spoke.

"I haven't stepped foot in that house since his memorial." Cora's quiet words held no accusation, only resignation.

Evie's stomach wrenched—and not only from the jostle of the carriage, although that would not have been surprising. Any sort of sustained motion managed that unsavory effect. No, this time the sensation traced back to her own insensitivity in forcing her sister to face a lifetime of memories filled with her recently departed fiancé. *It isn't the meeting Cora has been avoiding—it's the house! That should have been obvious.* She gave herself a mental kick. "Forgive me. I hadn't realized the reason you hesitated—"

"Nor did I, to tell the truth. It wouldn't have occurred to me if you hadn't forced me out of isolation." A rueful smile played about the corners of Cora's lips for a brief moment before tightening into grim determination. "We're here."

Fashioned of stately brick and built along Georgian lines, Lyman House graciously watched over the end of a curved street facing an open park. It had, for at least three previous generations, watched over Lymans and seen them prosper. Until Braden and

Lacey broke the delicate pattern. They first bore the misfortune to be orphaned—albeit after reaching their majorities. But the real trouble seemed to be their disregard for more traditional British customs in favor of a thoroughly American spirit of curiosity and adventure.

A spirit Evie and Cora shared. A spirit that led to an impulsive investment in a promising mining town and, ultimately, Braden's death in a catastrophic cave-in.

So the flags flew at half-mast around the grand residence, and the servants wore black and, as they habitually wore black or gray, added a black armband to signal the household's loss. Solemn quiet completely unlike the usual hustle and bustle of the big place shrouded the building.

Too much change in too little time. As she climbed the front steps, Evie fancied the house hibernated; the windows of its eyes and ears no longer flung open to catch the rhythm of the world around it, it slept. She shivered at the notion that it seemed to be waiting for something—much the same way her sister had been ever since word of the Hope Falls tragedy arrived.

Mr. Burk opened the door before Evie so much as raised the knocker, disproving her theory that the house slumbered. "Miss Lyman and Miss Higgins await you in the morning room."

They made their way past the grand staircase, to the left, down the second hallway, and into the third door on the right without any further guidance. The Thompson sisters counted as family, and all the servants knew it. Not one of them would say a word about how, with Braden gone, Cora would never become a Lyman in truth. Not the way everyone always expected.

And if anyone dares show such insensitivity, I'll step on his toe. That should be enough to erase any thoughtlessness until the fool's foot heals. Evie's eyes narrowed. *Slowly.*

"Evie! Cora!" Lacey rushed to greet them, a froth of black fabric swirling about her feet as she sprang from her chair to flood them in hugs.

If the ponderous weight of grief seemed absent in Lacey's effusive embrace, it etched its burden upon her companion. Miss Naomi Higgins, who boasted a mere five years more than her charge, made her way across the room at a more sedate pace. Her thick muslin skirts dragged at her steps, the harsh black of mourning making the premature streak of pure white at her crown even more startling than usual.

"Naomi." Evie placed her hands on her friend's shoulders, exchanging an understanding glance before drawing her close. Although the slightly older woman seemed disapproving, the two of them shared a special bond. Naomi's propriety kept Lacey's exuberance in check much in the same way Evie looked after Cora.

"Evie." Naomi sank into the hug as though allowing herself a brief respite before putting the starch back in her spine. "It's good to see you." She turned to Cora for a somewhat awkward embrace. "*Both* of you."

"Come." Lacey grabbed Evie's and Cora's hands, pulling them to a plush sofa and settling herself between them. "Have some scones or tarts—Cook knew you were coming." Her smile may have fooled a casual acquaintance, but Evie saw beyond the brittle facade erected around a long-standing joke.

The Lyman cook constantly worried that Cora—with her unending energy and impossibly tiny waistline—needed to eat more. At the same time, she respected Evie's position as a restaurateur and never missed an opportunity to impress her. So the great joke at Lyman Place was that if they wanted to eat well, they need only invite a Thompson for tea.

Evie put as much warmth as she could muster into her answering smile and selected a scone—although her stomach still roiled from both the carriage and the difficulties she couldn't keep from her sister. "How could I resist?"

From the look Cora shot her, at least one person knew she could have resisted easily. Evie didn't mind—anything that made amusement flash across Cora's features was well worth the price.

She nibbled at the edge of her scone before putting it down with undue haste. *Really, daily carriage rides might do much to improve my figure. . . .* She shoved the thought back. Now wasn't the time.

With pleasantries out of the way, silence usurped the place of comfortable conversation and laughter. No more would their afternoons be filled with sharing updates from Hope Falls, poring over catalogs for their businesses, and making plans for their eventual trip out West to join Braden.

Wedding plans for Cora's big send-off evaporated like so much spilled milk, and no matter how old the adages about crying being no use, the sense of loss seeped into every niche of their lives. Everything left seemed soured, though Evie refused to say so. *No. We'll make the best of things, just as we did when Pa died. . . .*

Now there was land, interest in a mine to be partitioned off. Decisions to be made about Evie's café and Lacey's general store out in Hope Falls—the businesses in which they'd invested so much on the promise of their new lives. The businesses that now lay fallow in a soon-to-be ghost town. Those dreams kept company with men who'd never made it out of the mines. Lost forever.

"Well"—Naomi cleared her throat—"we can't sit here all day and hope the situation changes." She gave a slight wince at the word "hope."

They all did.

If Naomi could be counted upon to break the ice, that left Evie to keep chopping away at the frigid barrier surrounding their futures. "She's right. We need to discuss what we're going to do, ladies. Where do we go from here?"

"Not Colorado." This from Cora, who looked as though she would have leapt from her seat if Lacey weren't still clasping her hand. "I'll tell both of you exactly what I told Evie—sell it all and good riddance!"

Evie knew the others awaited her response to this outburst, but she held her tongue. This couldn't be her decision. Not only because Lacey held the principal investment, and they'd made promises to their friend, but because Evie felt torn between the two choices herself.

Part of her agreed with Cora. The venture had cost far more than they'd foreseen, wiping out her inheritance and savings. Then it took the ultimate price in Braden's life. Hope Falls. . . even the name, which once seemed whimsical, now sounded a sinister warning. A dark part of her mind, the part that whispered superstitions and imagined phantasms when tree branches scraped windows in the dead of night, urged her to protect her sister and wash her hands of the place once and for all. *Not to be secretly melodramatic,* she chided herself.

Evie focused on the more practical, and thus important, aspects of the situation. With the businesses not up and running and the town defunct, the chances of recouping even a reasonable percentage of those investments were all but nonexistent. And without Braden, Evie needed to think about how she'd support not only herself, but Cora as well. Could she afford to sell out? If they couldn't revitalize Hope Falls, could she afford not to? That's what it all came down to. That's what she'd come to find out. Evie returned Lacey's gaze in silent question, noting the barely perceptible shake of her flaxen head.

"My solicitor assures me that if we sell, we'll lose almost everything we've put into Hope Falls." Lacey bit her lip—most likely thinking about how buying into the town so they could move with Braden and Cora had been her idea. "He also assures me that, with everyone leaving, the chance of recognizing a profit is negligible."

"What does that leave?" Heart thumping, Evie crumbled her scone into a fine powder, where at least it wouldn't cling to her waistline.

"Keeping the land until it becomes a more marketable asset is what Mr. Slurd suggests." Lacey's eyes narrowed. "I disagree. If selling it means we lose everything, and leaving it fallow means the same, we simply must find another way."

"How?" Naomi spread her hands in a fatalistic gesture. Her involvement more limited to a supportive role by virtue of her lack of personal investment, she didn't offer any outright opinions. "I don't see another option, unless another mining company would buy up the entire area."

"There's been an offer, but it's ludicrous."

Evie's fists clenched at the sum Lacey revealed. It wasn't even what she'd paid to begin the café, much less enough for her, Lacey's, and Cora's stakes. Not to mention what Braden left in his will—why, he'd been co-owner of the mine itself. "Shysters!"

"Is there any way to bring the town back?" Naomi's question surprised Evie, who thought her friend would be more in favor of selling out and staying in Virginia.

"No. It floated loose from hell and needs to go back." Cora's voice sounded oddly flat. "There's no saving it."

Or us.

∞

You shouldn't pace. A voice that sounded suspiciously like it belonged to Lacey's mother echoed with her steps. The habit would surely give away her lack of confidence in the plan she was about to propose.

Lacey expected resistance from Naomi but knew she could win over her companion if Evie joined her. Cora, on the other hand. . . She shot a worried glance at her closest friend. Cora would be dead set against the idea.

But we need a solution to our troubles, and this is all that's come up. How can I convince the others to trust in this vision for the rebirth of Hope Falls, when they see it as a place of death?

"We need to redeem it." Lacey reached one end of the room and marched resolutely back toward the settee, where the Thompson sisters watched with wary expressions. Naomi, if it were possible, looked even more leery.

"Do we have some sort of vouchers for the land?" Cora faltered. "I'd thought there'd be more official documents but didn't ask Braden many questions when I signed over my dowry. I trusted him to make the right decisions for our future."

"We all did." Evie patted her sister's knee. "But no one could have foreseen the mine's collapse. No one."

Naomi steered the conversation to less emotional waters. "There are no vouchers to redeem."

"I meant Hope Falls." Lacey fought to keep still. "We need to redeem the town. It's what Braden would have wanted—for us to help Hope Falls recognize its potential and become the success he planned. We owe it to his memory, and to ourselves, not to give up on everything we prepared for."

"It's a town, not a person." Evie's gaze held a measure of calm Lacey envied. "It cannot be made whole again with the mine collapsed and unable to reopen—there's no longer a reason for it to exist. There are other train stops nearby, with Durango and the like."

"We can save it!" Enthusiasm burbled up, threatening a tide of words to drown out the sense of anything she said. Lacey took a deep breath. "It can be saved."

"Towns don't have souls, and even if they did, Hope Falls would be the exception." Cora all but spat the words. "There's no redeeming it. No making it wholesome or eking anything worthwhile from it now."

"Without the ore, there's nothing to sustain the locale." Naomi's response typified the woman herself—cool and logical.

Perhaps Lacey miscalculated. Naomi's analytical mind could be swayed by the economics, and then Evie's practicality might follow.

She curled her fingers toward her palm, thumb picking at her cuticles in a habit her mother would have deplored. Lacey marshaled her points and continued her argument. "That's not true. What Hope Falls now lacks in ore, it still more than makes up in another valuable natural resource with a high demand in today's market." For once in her life, she held her tongue at the right moment, letting that startling tidbit provoke interest. Actually, Lacey bit her tongue to keep from explaining everything all at once, but she wasn't one to quibble about minor details. The main thing was it worked.

All three of the other women—even Cora!—were exchanging quizzical glances and baffled shrugs. Eventually they all focused their attention on Lacey, silently waiting for her to continue.

She couldn't blame them. She always continued, never failed to speak whatever happened to cross her mind. But not this time. This time Lacey would make them ask. Make them invest such simple assets as time, thought, and words into discovering her scheme. It would bring them one step closer to taking part in it. Lacey rather suspected she wouldn't be able to taste anything for a month, but resolutely kept her tongue between her teeth.

"What resource?" Evie—not Naomi, as Lacey expected— broke ranks to ask the question on all their minds.

"Trees!" She almost bounced in her enthusiasm. "The San Juan Mountains are absolutely covered in trees!"

"Lumber," Naomi breathed, understanding instantly. Lacey could have hugged her.

"Precisely. Lumber is in high demand with the supply in New England depleted from centuries of logging. Hope Falls has the supply, and it's situated right on the railroad."

"You're proposing to turn a mining town into a sawmill?" Disbelief tinged Evie's tone, but a spark of interest lit her eyes. "How?"

"We'd need to buy up the surrounding land, but if looking into selling our property has shown anything, it's that we can get it cheaply. Then it's a matter of labor." Lacey hesitated. *This is the part where things get tricky.*

"Hire men, you mean." Naomi raised a brow. "Buying the land and gear to set up a sawmill and hiring men is an expensive venture. You'll need investors."

"Or husbands." Lacey winced. *And I'd done so well up until now!*

"Never!" Cora jumped to her feet. "We won't travel there and make our home without Braden. I won't have it!" Tears blurred her next words, but the meaning remained clear.

Lacey was at her friend's side in an instant. "We'll be closer to him this way, Cora. I want to go."

"No!" She sobbed. "It's too hard. I won't go without. . ."

"If we don't go"—Lacey tried to be as gentle as possible as she spoke the truth—"we're leaving him behind. Not just in the mine, but in our hearts and dreams. Let Hope Falls die, and we've lost the last part of Braden we could have kept alive."

"But marrying another man—it's a betrayal." Cora shook her head. "I can't."

"I anticipated that. But if the rest of us do, we should be able to make a go of it." Lacey's hopes faded at the shock painting Naomi's and Evie's features. "Come now, ladies. Husbands will provide protection, bolster legitimacy to our claim to the land, and, if we do it right, offer the know-how and some of the labor to start things properly."

"It's. . ." Naomi blinked, words apparently failing her.

"Preposterous. Absolute lunacy." Evie stood beside Cora. "Finding investors, perhaps. Jaunting out West to try our hand at converting a mining town into a sawmill? A distant possibility, if only to recoup our investment. But binding ourselves to absolute strangers on a whim? Never!"

"Never say never." Lacey chirped her standby refrain, hoping for a chuckle. Hoping for it to hold some truth.

The Thompson sisters headed for the door, Evie shaking her head. "We'll find another way."

TWO

Three weeks, endless miles, and dozens of cities populated by hundreds of unhelpful citizens after he started out, the gnawing hole in Jake's gut became a churning chasm. Instead of bridging the gap between himself and his prey, every step he took widened the distance.

He'd made a conscious decision not to travel by train, certain that too many stops and too many opportunities would pass him by. Now, however, Jake's scheme to follow the mysterious Mr. Twyler by taking the personal approach seemed doomed. Sure, talking to people eventually pointed him in the right direction. Eventually. But by the time he got there, Twyler was long gone. Another train stop ahead of him. Another opportunity lost. So this morning he'd parted company with the horse he'd raised from a colt.

Wonder what it says about me that saying good-bye to Honk made me feel worse than leaving home. He pushed the morose thought aside and bought a ticket for Charleston—the best lead he'd wrangled from an uncooperative cardsharp back in Baltimore. When barkeeps didn't remember Twyler's name and local authorities hadn't detained him for a night or two, petty criminals managed to cough something up.

Which just goes to show I've been right all along. Edward didn't get himself killed by some self-righteous drunk he'd cheated at poker. A criminal set him up, then fired a bullet when Edward turned out too smart to swindle. Somehow the vindication didn't seem so satisfying without the proof to show the world. Jake needed proof to still wagging tongues and flapping gums before he could go home.

Soon. He leaned back in his seat and tilted his hat over his eyes. Maybe he'd catch a little rest before he reached Charleston and started the latest round of cat and mouse. *Soon...*

Sooner than Jake thought possible, the porter shook his shoulder and stiffly informed him that they'd reached Charleston. The uniformed man's gaze raked over Jake's dusty clothes and trusty satchel, silently accusing the unkempt passenger of angling to ride farther than he'd paid.

Just for fun, Jake pressed a walloping tip into the man's hand as he departed the train. *Why not give him something to tell his family about?* He gave the dumbfounded porter a jaunty wave from the platform before disappearing into the crowd. Who knew? Maybe next time the man wouldn't be so quick to judge by appearances. *And the moon is made of cheese.* Jake snorted.

Appearances, as his parents demonstrated since his early childhood, made the world go 'round. And appearances were part of why Twyler kept evading him. The criminal looked like a gentleman, whereas he—Jake wouldn't call himself a gentleman any longer—looked less than reputable.

Fair enough. Jake didn't feel very reputable as he headed toward the center of town. Main streets were always a good place to find a jailhouse or, at the very least, directions to one.

His latest tip about the poker playoff—sure to draw an inveterate gambler like Twyler—was out of date by a week or so by now. All the same, local police would have had a presence around the big game. Whether they acknowledged it or found it more profitable to look the other way, it served their best interests to make sure no one lost his temper. Or his life. The police were his best chance for meeting someone who'd interacted with Twyler firsthand or who could point him to someone who had.

He ducked into the jailhouse, narrowing his eyes until they adjusted to the dim light inside. Jake made out two cells to the left, one to the right. The right sat empty. Two drunks took up the spots on the left. One snored fit to bring down the building while the other amused himself by alternately twirling his hat atop his index finger and glowering when it fell off.

Promising. Jake headed for the desk pressed against the far wall, where a deputy made an unconvincing show of pretending he hadn't been napping before the interruption. *Men like this are part of the reason why Edward's dead and definitely to blame for Twyler still running free. How many crimes does a man have to rack up before lawmen start recognizing a wanted criminal right under their noses?* Jake eyed the man before him. *Supposed to protect the public, but sleeping on the job.*

Something of his thoughts must've translated into his expression, because alarm flashed in the deputy's eyes, and his hand groped for his holster before coming up empty.

"Looking for your paperweight?" Jake nudged the firearm toward its rightful owner. If it hadn't been such a prime example of modern justice hard at work, he would've smiled. As things stood, he didn't bother to hide his contempt while the other man scooped up the pistol and shoved it back in place.

"What can I do for you?" He slicked back his hair in a futile and far-too-late attempt to look official.

Your job. He swallowed the truth, as he had so many times before. But this time, it wouldn't stay down. "Your job." His words sparked anger in the other man, but it sizzled into shame. *Good.* "I need information about someone who probably came through here for the poker games."

"Lotta men for that, and it's all settled and done with." His hand twitched over his weapon. "Good riddance, I say. We don't need any more of that sort of crowd."

"Greed makes the best men unpredictable." Jake eased his stance to make the man more comfortable. . .and coax more information from him. "I'll bet you had more than your share in here. No town needs extra gamblers sleeping off a few too many or cooling their heels after a disagreement."

"No two ways about that. Which one were you looking for?"

"Twyler's the name. Smart. Well dressed. Average height. Brown hair. Brown eyes." Jake could have rattled off the nondescript list in his sleep. Except for the name, it could describe any number of men, but it was all he had. For now.

"Can't say the name Twyler rings a bell." The only help Jake got from the man was to rouse the snoozing drunk to ask him, but the jailbirds knew nothing more than their keeper. With a shrug, the deputy plunked down and began rummaging through a drawer. He didn't seem the type to keep reliable records, but maybe someone above him kept a tighter ship.

Jake didn't wait long before the deputy surprised him and pulled something worth his time out of the desk. He crossed the room in two swift strides, unable to tear his eyes away from the improbable find now sitting so proudly atop the scarred surface of a desk made from ponderosa pine.

The suddenness of his movements startled the other man, who grabbed the prize and yanked it up against his chest with the fiercest glower Jake had ever seen. And he'd seen many. "Get your own sandwich."

"I'll pay." His hand inched toward where a sizable cookie still lay on the desk, but his eyes never left the work of art the other man held. Generous slices of soft bread—sourdough by the tang scenting the air—lovingly cradled thick slabs of marbled ham and cheese piled nigh unto infinity. Mouth watering, Jake swallowed before speaking again. "Name a price."

"Not for sale." Cruel, he sank his teeth into his lunch with a muffled moan of delight. "Ookin gofu coffee yerself," he mumbled

around his mouthful instead of chewing with the appropriate
appreciation. He did, however, slap a protective hand over the
cookie. So the man had some brains, after all.

"What?" Envy made his question sharp.

"You can go to the café yourself," the hat-twirling drunk
translated. "Lucky man, if you do."

"Where?"

"Thompson's Café. One block up and to the north." His hat
stopped twirling as he watched the jailer finish his sandwich. A
gusty sigh chased Jake out the door. "Wish I could join you."

∞

"I'm going to have to fire that girl," Evie admitted to Wilma as
they ran around the kitchen. "But I don't know when I'll have
time to find another to take her place."

"She only shows up half the time," Wilma agreed. "With Cora
out, we're already shorthanded!"

Evie plowed through the swinging doors back into the
dining room, arms loaded with dishes. Unloading them posed
no problem—the moment she stepped up to a table eager hands
relieved her of her burdens with smiles all around.

Praise the Lord for a booming business. Her own smile rarely
flagged, bolstered by those of satisfied customers. *If things keep
going so well, we might be able to make ends meet despite the disaster
of Hope Falls.*

"Hooo!" Caught up in her thoughts, Evie hadn't paid close
enough attention to her surroundings. Even she couldn't say which
knocked the breath out of her more—the chair back lodged into her
stomach or the stranger who'd stepped through her doors. Not that
it mattered much, since either way left Evelyn Thompson standing
certain of one thing: *I knew I should have laced my corset tighter!*

But a woman needed to breathe, after all, and her corset
couldn't truly control her overly exuberant curves. She had what
she privately referred to as an ongoing case of the "sqwudgies,"

24

a terrible affliction of squooshy pudginess no man-made device could cure.

So here she stood, squashed between the chairs of two customers who'd simultaneously decided to scoot backward, as the most gorgeous man she'd ever clapped eyes on strode into her café. This sort of thing, she'd noticed, never happened to Cora or the other girls who worked in the dining room.

It was one of the reasons she stayed in the kitchen. *And,* she fumed, tugging herself free and refusing to consider what color her face must be turning, *yet another reason why I have to hire another girl. My dignity can't survive this on a daily basis.*

Somehow she'd pasted a smile back on her face by the time she reached her new customer. "Good afternoon and welcome to Thompson's Café. What can I get you?"

He didn't sit so much as sprawl into ownership of the one vacant table. With a knapsack on the seat beside him and long legs stretched past the table to bracket the chair across from him, he should have looked tired.

He didn't. Everything about him shouted of coiled intensity, from the rigidity in his shoulders to the strong line of a jaw stubbled with at least five days' worth of a beard. One hand seemed nonchalantly half tucked into his pocket, but it was the pocket closest to his holster. His eyes scanned the entire room before coming to rest on her with an absolute clarity she couldn't remember seeing. "Everything."

"Oh." Her mouth went so dry she licked her lips without thinking, and still his penetrating gaze didn't waver. "We aren't the typical café, with only one option. We have roast chicken and potatoes, onion soup and biscuits, ham or meat loaf sandwiches, sugar cookies, and berry cobbler today." She finished the recitation with pride. "So what would you like?"

His brows rose, what might have been a sigh from a less robust man passed through his lips, and his eyes narrowed as though measuring her.

Kelly Eileen Hake

Evie caught herself fidgeting with her apron strings at the thought. Measurements—aside from cups and teaspoons—were the last thing she wanted to think about. But he didn't need to know that, so she put a hand on her hip in what she hoped was a nonchalant fashion. "If you can't decide, I recommend the chicken." It cost most.

"I already decided." A smile broke out across his face. He leaned back and folded his hands across his chest before closing his eyes and practically purring his order. "Everything."

Evie gaped at him for a moment before gathering her wits—and several empty dishes—on her way back to the kitchen. Luckily, the lunch crowd started thinning out about then, and her only other dining room helper—a girl by the name of Lara—had things fairly well in hand.

"Next pot's almost ready," Wilma promised when Evie found the soup tureen dangerously low.

"Perfect. Looks like the rush is slowing down anyway." She filled one of the crockery bowls full of the thick soup, topping it with crumbles of leftover corn bread from yesterday and some of the sharp cheese that went so well with the sweeter flavor of the onion. Grabbing a basket with four biscuits, she tucked a crock of butter inside. "I'll be back in a minute for a plate of chicken and potatoes. . .and I need one each of the ham and meat loaf sandwiches wrapped up." He must want them to go.

Wilma cast a perplexed look over one shoulder and kept working. "Thought you said we were slowing down?"

"We are." Evie elbowed her way through the swinging doors and called back, "It's all one order!" She wished she could see Wilma's expression but chuckled at the thought.

Skirting tables and the more treacherous chairs, Evie reached the stranger. She set down what she'd consider to be his first course, gratified to see him lean forward and pick up a spoon almost before the food hit the table.

"Hat off while you eat—house rules." A thrill ran through her

26

when she set a warning hand on his shoulder. She quickly moved back to gesture at the sign posted on the wall.

"Hats off to the chef," he read aloud, amusement quirking the left corner of his mouth. He slanted a glance toward her. "What if I don't like the food?"

"Then you can take it up with her." Evie fought a smile of her own. "Or the owner."

"Fair enough." He thumbed his hat back until it slipped off an unruly crown of brown hair in sore need of a barber, then placed the article on the chair beside him.

As much as she wanted to wait, wanted to watch him eat his doubts to find them as delicious as anything else she'd mastered in the kitchen, Evie went back to fetch his chicken. And his sandwiches.

Mere minutes later she set them before him with a flourish, smug to see a now-empty bowl and basket strewn across the table.

As Evie reached to collect them, his callus-roughened hand closed around her wrist. "I'll have a talk with that cook now."

It'd been a mistake to touch her. Jake knew it the moment his fingers slid across skin so soft he suddenly resented the fashionably proper, tight cuffs concealing her wrists. The startled widening of her remarkable eyes—gold like the sweetest honey—warned him he'd gone too far.

He could have released her quickly, but that would be akin to admitting his faux pas. Instead, he reached over her arm with his free hand and picked up the now-empty biscuit basket before giving up the warmth of her hand nestled beneath his. "I'm not satisfied." Jake plunked the basket back down as though to punctuate his comment, biting back a grin at the astonishment flitting across her features.

"What!" With the lush grace of a serene Madonna and the

rosy flush of a woman tamping down indignation, his waitress held more appeal than the food she'd brought him. *And that's saying something.*

"You heard me." Jake manfully ignored the smells of herbed roast chicken and potatoes in favor of watching her. He could eat any day—he'd only be in Charleston tonight.

"Dissatisfied, my left foot!" She snatched up the basket, turned it upside down, and shook it as though making a point. "Nary a crumb left to pity a pigeon."

"Yep. I'll discuss it with the chef." He put his hat back on, to really get her goat. "Or the owner."

"You're speaking with her." Her fingers twitched as she eyed his hat, obviously itching to swipe it from his head.

"Chef or owner?" As if he didn't already know. *Owner. No ring. If she's the cook, she'd be married. No way a pretty thing like that with a way around a stove would be unwed.*

"Both." Never had such a sweet smile carried so much grit.

"In that case"—Jake removed his hat in a heartbeat—"you can fix the problem right away."

"The only problem I see is a man who's bitten off more than he can chew." She gestured to the bounty of food before him. "And is trying to talk his way out of paying for it."

"Um. . .Miss Thompson?" the other girl piped up in a thin voice. "He paid while you were in the kitchen."

"Oh." The waitress/cook/owner visibly deflated, curiosity replacing her ire as she focused on him once more. "Then what was wrong with your biscuits, sir?"

"Lots." Now that he knew the identity of the cook, his original plan to compliment her flew out the window.

"Such as?"

"For one thing"—he leaned back, drawing out the time he'd spend sparring with her—"the texture needs fixing."

"Hogwash!" The denial burst out of her with enough force to send the wisps of hair framing her face dancing. "People love my biscuits—they aren't hard, burnt, lumpy, nor doughy. That batch came out the same as they always do—the way my customers like them—light and fluffy."

"Exactly." As intended, his agreement snapped the wind from her sails. *Bewilderment doesn't suit her half so well as exasperation. She's not the sort of woman who's often confused.* Strange how much that pleased him. "Your light-and-fluffy biscuits all but melt in the mouth and leave a man wanting more."

"It's why we serve four per customer!"

"Which brings me to the second problem. In all fairness, it's related to the first. More biscuits in the basket would take care of both." He lifted the basket to emphasize its sorry state—which was, as she'd pointed out, absolutely empty.

"Hear, hear!" A man from a nearby table added his support.

"More biscuits!" another seconded.

Miss Thompson closed her eyes as though gathering strength, and Jake abruptly realized how much his teasing would cost her. *I should have known others were listening—Ma had reason to worry about what others thought.*

"I say you offer a 'bounty of biscuits' option—for an added fee, of course." He raised his voice to make sure this proposition carried. "I'll be the first to take you up on it, Miss Thompson."

"It's not every day I'm served patrons telling me how to run my café."

Jake respected any man who stood his ground, and he'd just found that went double for a woman. They both knew she'd be foolish not to take him up on the offer, but she claimed her territory with aplomb.

"Me, too!"

"Same here!" Three other men took up the chorus of rattling baskets.

It wasn't until she pursed her lips—he suspected to trap a smile—that he noticed their fullness.

Which I have no business noticing. Everything about Miss

Thompson, from the polished toes of her boots, to those tightly buttoned sleeves he'd deplored earlier, to the proud fire in her eyes declared her a lady.

And Jake had left behind his life as a gentleman.

THREE

Evie eyed the stranger causing so much chaos in her orderly café and tried to hide her amusement. Before her sat a tall, rangy example of why that old maxim, "The customer is always right," hadn't made it up on her wall.

But at least he knew when he did wrong and moved to fix it. For that matter, the entire battle of wills led to an extra way for the café to expand its profit. *Thank You, Lord.*

"I'm a patriotic woman," she declared, "so in the spirit of democracy, I'll add the bounty of biscuits to what we offer." With that, she collected baskets and orders, otherwise ignoring the man who'd instigated it all.

"Already have more in the oven," Wilma greeted her when she reached the kitchen and headed for the baking table.

"Conversation carried all the way in here, did it?"

"Bounty of biscuits and all." The two women shared a laugh. "Took me a moment to realize they were shaking their baskets like tambourines though. Wish I could've seen that."

Evie's chuckle went alongside those extra biscuits until she reached the stranger. Then she schooled her features into a completely blank expression as she surveyed the now-clean plate in front of him. Well, almost clean. A few chicken bones littered the surface as he dove into his second basket of bread. "Any complaints about the chicken?" The challenge shot out before she could stop it.

"Just that I ate it so fast, if the bones didn't stay behind, I'd swear it flew by me." He slathered butter on a biscuit, his easy grin nowhere in sight. "I think I'll be changing my order now."

"The cookies are wrapped one with each sandwich," she clarified so if he decided he didn't want them he wouldn't be surprised if she reached for them.

"I figured." One bite demolished an enormous amount of food, but he didn't seem to be enjoying himself as much as before. "I'll need another two cookies—and change my order to a double serving of cobbler."

He didn't look at her the way he had before the bounty-of-biscuits exchange. If Evie didn't know better, she'd say the man outright avoided looking at her at all. Certainly the teasing tone of his conversation switched to all business.

Why? And why didn't I realize how much I was enjoying the way he talked before, until it changed? Evie couldn't very well ask the man, so she set about serving him in this newly constructed silence she found so unsettling.

He ate every bite she brought him—save the sandwiches, which she'd been right in assuming he intended to take with him—without another word. And when he was done, he stood and left with a gesture she'd remember for the rest of her days.

The tall stranger strode to the door, opened it, and turned around. He stood in the frame, silhouetted by the setting sun, and when his gaze met hers, he pointed to the sign on the wall. He made a show of stepping entirely outside before placing his hat back on his head and letting the door close behind him.

Hats off to the chef. Such a small sign of respect, an acknowledgment she'd never thought to see—and it touched her more than it had any right to. Evie was very much afraid she froze in place and stayed that way for an indecent amount of time, staring at the door as though addlepated.

The remainder of the day blinked by, and in no time at all, she'd made it home for the night. Before dark—always before dark. For her own well-being and reputation, as well as those of the women who worked alongside her, Thompson's Café closed earlier than some of her patrons would like. But Evie wouldn't budge on that. *I might not be able to afford losing the business, but I can spare it more than I can spare our safety.*

Regret warred with relief when she reached the boardinghouse where she and Cora lived. Taking rooms with Mrs. Buxton had been meant as a temporary measure. Now, the place she thought of as home would most likely remain such for a long, long time.

When their father died three years before, Evie'd been forced to use her own dowry to keep the household going until she couldn't avoid selling their home. But those proceeds wouldn't last forever, so Evie took her one skill and turned it into her investment. After two years, the café proved itself enough to have garnered a modest savings account and flattering mortgage deal with the bank to fund Evie's part in Hope Falls.

But the grand plan for Wilma to run things in Charleston while Evie went to Colorado vanished in a heartbeat with Braden's death. The bright future of Cora happily married to a wealthy mine owner with Evie and their closest friends living nearby had all been fool's gold. Which wouldn't pay off the mortgage on her restaurant, or even keep rented rooms over their heads.

Just entering their home wrapped a cloak of concern around her thoughts. Worry pressed away the joy she'd found at work, robbing her of any ability to coax Cora back to the world outside these rooms.

It is, she thought, *almost as though where we are becomes a part of us. At home, I mourn for Cora and the promising lives we've lost. In the café, I'm cheery for the customers and proud of what I accomplish.*

So what if we went to Hope Falls? How much worse would things be for both of us, with Cora surrounded by the reminder of what she should share with Braden and me without customers to cook for? The thought made her temples ache.

Even without Lacey's ludicrous mention of hasty husbands, the plan spelled disaster—which was why she and Cora hadn't so much as discussed it in the week since. They'd been right to walk away. *Here, we may not have much, but at least we know its value.* Bolstered, she swept up the stairs and into their suite—to find their rooms filled with visitors.

The small couch held Lacey and Naomi, with Cora—her pale face showing signs of strain—in the only chair. Evie would make do with the ottoman, she supposed, although—

Thud.

With a seat now readily available, the women in the room did the only natural thing—they immediately surrounded Cora on the floor.

"She fainted!" Even Evie couldn't explain why she bothered to remark on something so obvious, aside from the surprise of it. She chafed her sister's cold hands in her own warm ones as Naomi smoothed back Cora's hair and loosened her collar. "She's only ever fainted once before, when—"

Lacey caught Evie's look and nodded, her eyes solemn. "When I told her of Braden's death."

"What did you tell her this time?" No matter she counted Lacey Lyman as one of her closest friends, Evie battled an urge to shake the girl for whatever shock she'd foisted upon Cora.

"Evie?" Cora's voice sounded weak, but her grip would most likely leave bruises on Evie's arms as she struggled to sit up—no mean feat for a woman lying prostrate on the floor in a corset. Little wonder she seemed breathless. "You don't understand."

"Ssshhh, dear. Rest a moment."

"No!" Cora gave a sudden lurch, eyes glittering with a fierce light. "Don't you see? Braden's alive!"

Seems I'm not the only Thompson sister with a secret penchant for

34

melodrama. Evie shook her head.

"No, Cora—you fainted. Things will clear up in a moment." She motioned to Naomi. "We'll get you a drink of water." As she spoke, she maneuvered her sister onto the sofa and propped her against one of the arms, where she'd be less likely to fall.

"Lacey!" Cora all but shoved Evie away in a bid for the other woman's attention. "Tell her!"

"She's right." Naomi's voice whispered in her ear, her closest friend putting a hand on her shoulder as though to brace her for news that would turn their world upside down yet again. "Perhaps you'd best sit down."

Call her silly, but one glance at Cora's wild-eyed expression made Evie reluctant to hear them out. She shrugged away Naomi's hand, using the scant moment it took to reach the ottoman and pull it toward the tea table to seek peace.

Lord, my prayers for Your provision never specified what path You'd choose—it wasn't my place. More than that, it seemed we'd learned that lesson the hard way when all our carefully laid plans for Hope Falls fell apart. But now it's plain to see my sister and I will be swept into something unbelievable. Grant me the faith and strength to see it through and the heart to do so with good humor!

She situated herself on the ottoman, pulled one of Cora's hands into hers, and declared, "All right. Tell me everything."

$$\infty$$

"I don't know nuthin'." The man shook his head hard enough to bruise his brains. If, that was, someone assumed the down-on-his-luck gambler possessed any in the first place.

Jake didn't assume. Resisting the impulse to get better acquainted with the delectable cook had left him too surly to bother. *The time is long past for me to find Twyler and finish this so I can get back to the things that make life worth living.* "Yes, you do." Jake intentionally widened his stance, an unspoken threat. "Not much, but you know something about Twyler. Spill it."

The barkeep at the saloon where those poker games had been held couldn't tell him much that afternoon, but he'd pointed the way toward the entrenched gamblers who might remember more. From there, persistent questioning and more rounds of whiskey than Jake bothered to count pointed him to this sad excuse for a man.

"Nuh-ugh." A nervous swallow. "He was a mean cuss, but that's all I know. Bad news, but old news, if you catch my meaning."

Seemed Twyler'd been smart enough to cover his tracks, this time. But intimidation wore off in time—and for once, the lag between Jake and his prey might pay off.

"You shared a room with him—where'd he say he was headed?" He casually pulled back the flap of his duster, revealing the holster sitting on his hip. If intimidation worked, he'd beat Twyler at his own game. *I have to.*

"Dunno." A shifty glance from Jake's gun to the street behind him, where no one wandered after dark. No one to interfere. The grizzled gambler started to wheeze.

If the man were younger, in better health, or boasted more fight and less fear, Jake's conscience wouldn't set up a fracas. *But at this rate, I'll be no better than the murderer.*

"Sorry to waste your time." Jake shifted so his coat closed then took a step back to give him more room to breathe. He eyed the man, unable to give up altogether but unwilling to bully the old fellow. *Wonder if cold, hard cash would wipe away the memory of Twyler's threats.* He'd just decided to give it a try when the other man spoke up.

"Durango." Seemed he'd gotten some of his courage back along with his breath. "Dunno where it is, don't care, and don't want to see either one of you again." With that, he pushed back into the saloon, ignoring Jake's muttered "Thanks" with all the dignity of a dethroned king.

For his part, Jake wasted no time heading back to the train station, where he'd leave on the first ride heading toward Colorado.

He settled onto a bench, a man with a ham sandwich—and a purpose.

Twyler was a dead man walking.

∞

"He's alive." Lacey verified Cora's outlandish claim in a single breath. "Braden and two others were pulled from the mines. My brother—" Here, her voice broke. "Is a survivor."

So why aren't you smiling, Lacey? A frisson of foreboding tingled up Evie's spine. *Why isn't Cora leaping for joy? What am I missing?* She looked to Naomi to fill in the gap.

"Along with this happy news, we've received a few other, less joyous revelations today." Naomi seemed to be searching for words. The thoughtful, tactful nature Evie'd always admired chafed today while she waited. "Mr. Lyman's lost the use of his left leg—perhaps permanently. He's also suffered head and back injuries and a broken wrist and can't be moved."

"But he's alive?" Evie remained flabbergasted by the lack of celebration. "Everything else is secondary! This is wonderful!" She turned to her sister. "You still have—"

"He sent word he's dissolving the engagement." Cora's voice had gone strangely monotone and hollow, as though traveling over a great distance. "After his experience, he's reevaluated our situation and decided this is"—she consulted a piece of paper Evie hadn't noticed she crumpled in her hand—"best for all."

"What? That can't be right. . . ." Evie trailed off as Lacey and Naomi nodded that it was, indeed, the case. *Now it makes sense. They're relieved he's alive but stupefied by his foolishness!*

"First I say good-bye because we plan to reunite. Then I get news of his death and struggle to make peace with it." Cora's eyes reddened, but no tears fell. "Now I hear he is alive—but doesn't want me." She didn't make it a question or even an exclamation of disbelief. It sounded almost as though she were making it real by speaking the words.

"That's not true." Evie didn't know how or why she was right; she just knew it with everything inside her. "Braden loves you and that can't have changed." Then it clicked into place. "Head injury? He's not thinking straight and he's been through a terrible ordeal."

"Exactly." Lacey's eyes widened with understanding—and obvious relief. "In fact, with his legs crushed, he might think you want a different husband. It would be just like Braden to want you to be happy, no matter the cost." She all but bounced next to Cora as she convinced herself.

Evie wasn't convinced entirely. In fact, that ordeal and head injury were all that stood between Braden Lyman and her righteous fury over his treatment of her sister. But now was the time to look after Cora, whose color began returning.

"That could be it." Cora blinked a few times, glancing at Evie in something akin to apology before turning to Lacey. "We must go to him."

"Yes. Lyman Place will be put up for sale. Naomi and I will leave before the week is out to oversee Braden's recovery." Lacey looked as though she might say more but stopped herself.

"My engagement still stands, no matter what Braden has to say about it." Cora's chin lifted. "I'm going with you."

Evie's mouth went dry. *Here it is, then. With Braden alive and in need, everyone is going to Hope Falls despite the fact the town will fail. But there's nothing for it. . . .* "Where Cora goes, I go." She answered the unspoken question hanging about the room like the sword of Damocles. "Wilma will hire help and run the café here while I'm in Colorado, as we planned."

"We're in this together." Lacey's smile demanded one in return. "Which is a blessing. There's so much to do, so many things to oversee, supplies we'll need to make this work—"

"Starting with the most important item on our list." Naomi's usually quiet voice rose with a determination demanding their attention. She paused to draw in a deep breath before clarifying. "Husbands."

Silence reigned for a good, long while.

"No, thank you." Evie kept her tone polite. *Perhaps if I treat it as something inconsequential, it will become so.*

Lacey burst out laughing. " 'No, thank you?' " she parroted. "Evie, you sound as if someone offered you liverwurst!"

"Liverwurst, while unpleasant, is fleeting. Marriage binds you to a man for life. It's not something to be undertaken on a whim or with an eye to free labor." Evie shook her head.

"The Bible calls a wife a helpmeet, a partner. These days, women are viewed as secondary. Why don't you think of this as an opportunity to find a man who would be a true partner in all the areas of the life you'd share?" Lacey's words tattled that the heiress had been waiting for a chance to reopen the discussion. More dangerously, her argument struck a chord.

Haven't I given up on the idea of marrying simply because I know it would be the end of my independence, the end of being respected for what I've accomplished through hard work and prayer? What would it be like to share my life with a man, instead of be expected to fit into his?

"We can do so much more than you give us credit for, Lacey." She turned the tables. "You've run a household here and set up a mercantile in Colorado. I've a café awaiting me. Cora will see to Braden, and Braden's claim to the land won't be challenged by the mining company for fear of legal reprisal. Hire a solicitor to see to gathering workers for the sawmill, but don't throw your life in with a stranger!"

Unbidden, an image of the stranger from the café strode into Evie's memory before she shook it free. Now wasn't the time to reminisce over a handsome customer with mischief in his eyes.

"Braden's in no condition to look after us." Cora added her thoughts for the first time. "It must be why he tried to keep me from going at all! With his legs healing, he won't be able to guard and protect us in an untamed land with several men to every woman. It won't be safe for us to live alone, and hiring guards poses the same problem."

Fear bit into Evie at the mere mention of Cora and her friends being unprotected in the wilderness, possible prey to lonely, unscrupulous men. "And Hope Falls is a railroad stop." There'd be no avoiding any passengers—indeed, such passengers would be their only hope for revenue until the proposed sawmill began to turn a profit.

"If any of us had a father, or another brother or two, or even a close male cousin, things would be different." Lacey spread her hands in a gesture of helplessness. "I considered all of this. Husbands aren't something I would suggest except as a last resort. And with Braden in need, I'm more than willing to take this leap of faith."

Of course Lacey would. She'd been the one to dream up this zany scheme! Evie looked to Naomi's better judgment.

"I don't see an alternative. Husbands will offer the personal and financial security we need." The words rang with confidence, but a shadow of pain held out against the hope in Lacey's gaze. "Think of it this way, Evie. In this circumstance, as a landowner and investor, you're in the position to choose your husband instead of waiting for one to choose you!"

Here lay the cause of the shadow haunting Naomi's green eyes. At three years older than Evie's own twenty-two, Naomi ranked as a spinster. So far as any of them knew, she'd never received an offer of marriage before becoming Lacey's governess, then companion, and certainly had not since.

Even now, Naomi didn't own a business or land, nor did she bring a significant dowry to a prospective husband. For her, the notion of choosing a man instead of waiting—always waiting—to be chosen would be appealing.

Evie knew, because she felt the same way. *No man ever chose me, either.* For a moment, she let herself be swept away in the fantasy of choosing a business partner for a husband, standing on the closest thing to equal footing that a woman could enjoy with a man. It had benefits, but somehow left her cold. Still. . .

"I'll do it." For Cora. For herself. For all of them. And as for the husband? *I'll just not think about the fact he didn't choose me and may never have wanted me in the bargain.* She shoved the thought away. No sense anticipating heartache. "Now the real question is how do we find these husbands?"

"Now that I've planned for." Lacey bounced out of her seat. "We'll go about selecting husbands the same way we'd fill any other position."

"Spread word around town?" That was how Evie'd always found girls in need of respectable work when she needed help at the café. The very thought of asking around after eligible men brought on a queasiness on par with riding in a carriage for long distances. A closed carriage. On a bumpy road.

"We can't put it about we're looking for men!" Naomi sounded scandalized. "You'll be ruined."

"That's not what I meant. We won't ask around for husbands." The smile sliding across Lacey's face made Evie's stomach plummet. "We'll hire them."

FOUR

W hat can you be thinking, Lacey? That's akin to. . ." Naomi's voice dropped to a scandalized whisper. *"Prostitution."*

"Pishposh." Lacey waved away her companion's worries. "It's nothing of the sort. Marriages of convenience and arranged marriages make society go 'round, after all. The only difference here is we'll be making the arrangements ourselves."

"To portray it as hiring someone implies he'll be compensated for what he provides. In this case, the groom provides himself." Evie, not surprisingly, took up Naomi's perspective. "So he would be, in effect, selling himself. You can call it whatever you like, but Naomi's right to object."

"By that logic, you're calling Braden some sort of. . ." Cora groped for the words before managing, "Unsavory sellout. He received a sizable dowry upon our engagement."

"That's different!" Evie spluttered.

"Not really." Lacey seized on the opening, throwing a quick smile at Cora. *I knew I could count on her!* "In olden days they demanded a bride price. Money has bought more marriages than love ever could have managed alone. Why not decide what we want from a spouse, gather options, and make our selections?"

"Because no matter how you twist social convention to suit your argument, you cannot buy a husband." Naomi lost enough of her reserve to roll her eyes. "And you cannot simply choose what you please and send away for a spouse!"

"Yes, we can." Lacey dug around in her reticule and withdrew the folded paper with a flourish. "If men can send away for wives, there's no reason we can't apply the same principle. Out in Hope Falls, there'll be no one to judge us."

" 'Mail Order Brides.' " Cora beamed in triumph as she read the advertisement. "If that's not sending away for a spouse, nothing is! Better yet, no one calls it prostitution."

"Are you proposing we pen an advertisement to catch the attention of available bachelors?" Humor and curiosity laced Evie's question—far better than the scandalized outrage she'd shown earlier.

"Precisely." Lacey maintained her decorum. Hopping about in victory wouldn't make the others confident about their plan, after all. "We'll telegraph it to all the major papers, who'll run it immediately upon receiving the wired fee. I'll take care of everything once we've written the ad itself."

"So we'll state what we're looking for, and they'll write letters or telegraph us back." Thoughtfulness softened the worry in Naomi's eyes. "We'll read them, choose our favorites, and arrange for meetings. Although. . .what if it doesn't go well?"

"If you don't want to marry the man, send him back." Lacey wanted to be absolutely clear on this point. "Any sign he'd be abusive, any hint that makes you uncomfortable, don't choose him. We need to be mindful of time, but these are our lives. I'd never forgive myself if you rushed into wedding the first bachelor you met simply because you felt forced."

"No—none of us will do that." Evie slanted a hard glance at Naomi, as though demanding agreement.

"Of course not."

I'm glad. Naomi's the one I'm most worried about accepting the first proposal to come her way. She thinks she has nothing to offer—and I don't have long to change her mind. But she'd start that project soon enough. "So, ladies," Naomi mused aloud, tapping her forefinger against her chin, "what does each of us want in a husband? What makes a man the sort you'd want to live with?"

"Or, at the very least, *be able* to live with." Evie's joke shook loose their laughter. "No man's perfect, after all."

"Braden's taken."

"Nice of you to prove your sister's point," Lacey teased Cora. She, of all people, knew her brother to be far from perfect. Cora knew the same—she just needed some time with Braden to remember it! "Let's each list three qualities we'd like to find in a husband. No repeating. Naomi goes first."

"God-fearing, strong character, and appreciation for the little things," Naomi suggested without even needing to think.

"Sharp mind and an easy smile—no, make that a sense of humor. The smile follows." Evie's own smile made Lacey wonder what man her friend was thinking of. "And cares about others."

"I'd say curious with an adventurous bent." Lacey watched Cora add it to the list. "And hardworking. We'll need that."

"But as nice as these sound, they aren't practical enough. Well, most of them." Evie frowned.

"She's right. We'll need to have an age requirement—say, twenty-four to thirty-five?" Naomi shrugged. "Old enough to take it seriously, at least, but not so old they won't work."

"Perfect! We should ask for sawmill experience, too. Someone needs to know what needs to be done to get things started." Evie shifted in her seat, obviously uncomfortable with the idea of beginning a business about which she knew nothing.

Lacey patted her shoulder. "I bought several books about sawmills and logging—even scientific treatises about the types of trees we'll find. At first, we'll need to look after Braden and make more finite arrangements while creating a transport system to the mill site. All that gives us time to learn the ins and outs before the mill goes up and becomes operational." She paused, welcoming the surge of hope and confidence filling her at the thought. "Time we'll also use to meet and marry the men we've asked for!"

"You asked for good things"—Cora tapped her pencil against the table—"but overlooked something rather important."

"What?" All three of them chorused the question at once.

"Something we take for granted until it's gone."

"We can't take anything for granted until we have it," Lacey pointed out. She couldn't let anything ruin this now, when they'd come this far. *We're so close to the greatest adventure of our lives, and there's nothing I take for granted about it!*

"Husbands among them." Evie's wry smile didn't seem to lighten Cora's mood. "Though I don't see how we can take for granted someone we select so carefully. What more could we need?"

"Just one thing." A tear trickled onto the paper as Cora blinked, obviously thinking of Braden as she added one word to their list. "Health."

Braden thrashed against the straps binding him to the bed, fighting against the warm, floating haze of the morphine as it beckoned him back to sleep.

"No!" The protest came out as little more than a feeble croak, rasping past his dry throat. *Confound them!* Didn't they know the waking pain could be borne until he lost consciousness without the drugs? Better that than the fog of the medicine, where memories waited to ensnare him the moment he slept.

Licking his cracked lips, he tried again, but the doctor already seemed far away, the room blurred around the edges. Now the sharp streaks of agony racing from his legs began fading to the bearable ache Braden knew signaled unbearable dreams—but he couldn't stop them any more than he could stop the cave-in. . . .

Hushed voices, words he couldn't make out but understood anyway, brought Braden around the corner to the newest offshoot of the mine.

Known only to himself, Owen, and a handful of others, it promised to be the biggest strike Hope Falls had ever seen. Even in the muted glow of lanterns sulking for fresh air, the vein sparkled with the promise of dreams made real. He lifted the light so Eric could see that golden stripe continuing on into the wall—where they'd not yet excavated.

Safety first. Always.

The geological surveys hadn't been completed, and until they were, Braden wouldn't give the order to proceed. He grinned. We can afford to wait.

Besides, it wouldn't be much longer. He expected to hear back any day now—though Owen urged him to wait until they hired security and half a dozen other unnecessary measures he argued were vital to safeguard the site. Once things went public, his partner insisted, they'd be dealing with claim jumpers.

"*All the more reason to get started as soon as we're cleared.*" *Eric's assessment matched Braden's, though he kept his voice low. One tunnel over, workers mined as usual. No need to attract attention to the offshoot.*

Approaching footsteps spurred Eric and Braden to move forward, blocking the vein of gold ore from view, until they saw Owen's flushed face. It wasn't unusual for his face to turn red from the exertion of climbing into the mine and traipsing around in thin air—Owen held up more of the business end of things—so Braden thought nothing of it.

"*Why are you here?*" *Dismay sharpened the question to a cry.* "*Both of you! You shouldn't be here!*"

"*You're the one who'll attract attention, Owen.*" *Braden tugged the furious man deeper into the tunnel.* "*Calm yourself.*"

"*No. You didn't listen to me—*" *Whatever else Owen planned to say was drowned out by an incredible roar as the mountainside was torn apart. Wooden supports buckled, stones tumbled, and dirt rained until it gave way to clouds of dust coating Braden's face, mouth, throat. . .and his very soul.*

Cave-in.

While it lasted, he prayed for it to end, but in the silence, he heard the screams, shouts, and cries of injured men the next tunnel over. Oh, Lord. . .what have I led them to? *It wasn't until he heard a moan but couldn't move toward the sound that Braden realized his legs were pinned beneath something. His hands told him it was a wooden support burdened by rock and earth.*

I can't feel my legs. *It didn't seem to matter. He lay, time measured by ragged breaths and unrelenting thirst. His men grew quiet. Braden strained to hear them, but silence steadily won until he prayed for even the screams and sobs from before. . . .*

Light assaulted his vision the moment he opened his eyes, flooding him with reassurance that the nightmare had ended. Braden gasped. He felt his heart thudding from the strain of the ordeal. Felt the leather straps holding him to the bed—tangible proof that the nightmare may be over, but it had been real.

The harsh glare of day taxed his eyes, the only admissible cause for the tears he couldn't wipe away. The doctor ordered his arms bound so he didn't convulse in his sleep and perhaps damage his spine. Or so he said.

Braden knew the real reason. They'd trussed him so he couldn't free himself to begin the work of rebuilding his strength until they deemed him healed enough. He'd heard them talking—confident that the morphine pulled him under long before he'd stopped fighting it—saying he'd never have use of his legs.

But they're wrong. His fists clenched, because if there was one certainty in his future, it was that Braden Lyman would walk out of Hope Falls. *For every man who didn't.*

Even so, he'd never be whole again. He didn't harbor any illusions about that—which was why he'd set Cora free. Braden closed his eyes, refusing to picture her.

She needs better than a cripple who'll at best always have a limp and a chip on his shoulder, he reminded himself. *Cora deserves a man who didn't lose everything when his investment collapsed on top of him. Someday she'll appreciate the choice I made for us both. Now she can have any man she wants.*

∞

Wanted:
3 men, ages 24–35.
Must be God-fearing, healthy, hardworking single men
with minimum of 3 years logging experience.
Object: Marriage and joint ownership of sawmill.
Reply to the Hope Falls, Colorado, postmaster by May 17.

Jake stared at the ad in disbelief for a good minute before giving in to the chuckle trapped in his chest. A second read, and the chuckle expanded to a full-blown guffaw. Obviously, someone with a well-developed sense of humor had far too much time on his hands. Satirizing the way miners and lonely settlers mailed away for brides provided a good laugh.

He flipped through the rest of the week-old paper he'd unearthed from beneath the seat, searching for an addendum to reveal the real reasons behind the ad. The first time, Jake assumed he'd missed the explanation. By the second time he scoured the rag, he'd drawn an altogether different conclusion.

He threw back his head and howled long and hard at the realization the paper somehow left it out entirely. *Without the addendum, there'll be fools who buy into the idea and respond.* The image of the mysterious debutante deluged with marriage proposals made Jake wish he had time enough to track down the printer and discover the author's identity. *Then again, the thing's old enough they most likely printed a retraction in later issues. It'd be interesting to find out. . . .*

The shrill blast of the train's whistle as they pulled into Durango reminded him of his true purpose. *I'll have time for entertainment after I find Twyler.* He set the tattered paper aside and headed for the door long before the train screeched to a halt. He ignored the scroll-worked metal stairs. Why wait when a jump would do just as well?

Jake started walking the moment his boots hit the dirt and

didn't stop until he hit the saloon. The area swarmed with the frantic activity of a booming town—all hurry and hustle with no way to sort things out.

The perfect place for a man like Twyler to lose himself when he got word I'd been tailing him. A grudging measure of—not respect, he'd never respect anything about the man who'd killed his brother and stolen his good name—acknowledgment set Jake's jaw. *The more difficult the prey, the sweeter the victory when I bring him in. Better yet, it reaffirms that Edward wouldn't be taken in by anyone easily. It took a master.*

Jake strode into the saloon, not looking right or left, simply making his way to the bar and plunking his knapsack down. To the casual eye, he'd seem unconcerned and oblivious to his surroundings. Few would suspect he'd taken in the entire place as he opened the doors. He knew which tables were filled, where the piano stood, and which end of the bar he could find the barkeep's shotgun under if he needed it. This last he'd learned from the way the man's gaze often strayed there.

No one would guess—and that's just the way Jake liked it.

FIVE

"I don't like it," Evie announced. "I don't like it one bit."

"We know, dear." Cora patted her hand. "You might have mentioned it a few times this morning already."

"You saw the way they handled it!" She knew she should stop worrying. *Or, at the very least, stop making the others listen to it!* But Evie couldn't help herself. Her fists clenched into balls so tight her knuckles ached. "It was all I could do to keep from marching over there and—" She caught the looks on her friends' faces and amended, "All right, all you three could do to keep me from marching over there." A smile tugged at her, and she gave in. "Thank you, all, for that."

"You're welcome." Naomi answered for the group. "When they dropped your stove, my heart fell right along with it."

"They make it hard work to damage cast iron." Now Evie hastened to reassure them. Her worrying was one thing; her friends' fretting was quite another. *I won't think about the crack in the enamel facing. There's nothing to be done now.*

"Do you know, Evie"—Lacey eyed her as though studying something new—"this is the best you've looked through the entire trip. You've got fire in your eyes and even the color back in your cheeks. Fury becomes you!"

The moment Lacey mentioned it, Evie's color fled. She knew because the clammy sensation that had plagued her throughout their journey replaced the heat of her indignation. For a brief while, the incident with the stove distracted her from the motion of the train. . .and its unfortunate effect on her stomach.

"I do wish you hadn't mentioned it, Lacey." Cora's frown made it clear she'd noticed her sister's improved health and most likely deduced the reason for the change. "She might have not thought about the movement for a bit longer."

"Oh dear. The stove distracted you, and I retracted you. Retracted. . . No, that's not the word. Got you back on track?" Lacey's words tripped over one another and her eyes went big, as they seemed to do whenever something upset her. "On track thinking about the train. . . Oh, I'm making it worse. I'll hush."

"The trouble isn't with you," Evie protested. Although, truth be told, the sudden nervous chatter made the churning worse. Extra anxiety, even someone else's, had that effect.

But the real blame for her internal somersaults lay with the motion of the train. She'd anticipated that it would move forward when she agreed to this venture, but Evie'd convinced herself that modern locomotives would otherwise prove steady and secure. Instead, the rocking from side to side, the tilting turns, and the ever-present assortment of creaks emanating from the train joints and cars themselves churned her as though she were butter. And that wasn't even mentioning uneven tracks, steep climbs uphill, and occasional slants downward.

Hope Falls must be a dream come true, she'd decided early into the trip, *because we live through a nightmare to reach it!*

"We're slowing down." Naomi's announcement put everything else out of their minds in an instant.

Lacey's nervousness disappeared, anticipation making her glow with delight as she peered through the grimy train car window. "Welcome to Hope Falls, ladies!"

The shrill blast of the train whistle punctuated her exclamation as though the conductor waited for Lacey's remark. The train slowed, the slightly choppy tugging of the engine replaced by the stubborn resistance of brakes against metal rails.

Evie's stomach jumped toward her throat at the shift. She tightened her lips as her belly threatened to lose the dry bread she'd forced herself to nibble on for breakfast. When they lurched to a stop—more accurately a long, lurching slide—it took several swallows before she trusted herself to so much as draw a breath.

That she'd bent over as far as her corset would allow escaped her attention until she felt hands smoothing her hair back and more hands rubbing her back as everyone sought to comfort her.

The corset, of course, dug into her hips in a pressing demand that she improve her posture. Immediately. She settled for straightening up as quickly as her testy stomach would allow. In a word, slowly.

How is it that Cora falls off the chair, to the floor, prostrate in a dead faint, and manages to rise easily and with some semblance of grace? Even after days of the "Evie Travels West Diminishing Diet," I so much as lean forward and begin gasping like a landed fish!

She shook her head, rejecting both her thoughts and various offers of help. One deep breath—or at least as deep as her corset and stubborn stomach would allow—and Evie edged into the aisle. Blessedly, the floor didn't move beneath her feet as it had so often over the past days. That made it much easier to smile as she gathered her things and prepared to exit the train car.

She'd made other decisions during the journey—one of them being that, no matter what they found in Hope Falls, she'd smile and find something to be thankful for. After all, Evie believed in living out the fruit of the Spirit. . .and this venture had "lesson in perseverance" written all over it.

For now, though, she needn't look far to find the blessing in the day. *Blessings. . . Surely the fact I haven't disgraced myself by losing any of my meals counts as a minor miracle!*

"Ladies, before we disembark. . ." She paused for a moment at the stunned expressions on their faces. Then she realized everyone must expect her to be overeager to leave the train behind. Evie's smile grew as she continued, "I think it'd be a wonderful idea to pray—thanks for thus far and seeking guidance for what lies before us."

She felt Cora grasp one of her hands and reached out the other to Naomi, who didn't hesitate. They all bowed their heads as Lacey made their circle complete.

"Thank You, Lord, for bringing us here safe and sound." She gave Cora's hand a squeeze, the signal they'd chosen long ago and never abandoned.

"Now we ask for the strength to see this through," her little sister added, joining their prayers together. A brief pause—Evie almost completed the prayer, assuming Lacey hadn't responded to the hand squeeze because it was unfamiliar or she didn't want to—and then Naomi spoke.

"And the wisdom to make the most of the choices You put before us. In Your name. . ." They all joined in saying, "Amen."

"I—I'm sorry. I've never prayed aloud before, and I didn't know you'd want me to." Lacey turned to Cora, still holding her hand, squeezing without noticing. "That's what the squeezing meant, wasn't it? That it was my turn to join in? Such a lovely idea, for all of us to pray together, and I ruined it." Her eyes had gone big again, bright with an unmistakable sheen.

"You didn't ruin the prayer!" Evie took Lacey's hand away from Cora's. "We should have explained, but even if we had, prayer is always a choice. It's never something you do because you're expected to. It's between you and the Lord—and those you pray with or for, depending on the situation. Don't worry."

"But Naomi caught on!" A forlorn sniff followed this.

"We're all here, together. The prayer was about and for all of us, with all of us hoping and loving and thanking. Next time—say, when we begin sifting through the responses to our ad—you can start the circle," Evie suggested. "We'll make it a regular practice. All of us are in this together, after all."

"Oh." A tremulous smile chased away the doubt. "I'd love that. Just think. . .we most likely already have a slew of responses filling the postmaster general's office, just waiting for us!" With the anticipation lighting her face, Lacey led the way out of the train car, into mountain air Evie could almost taste with each breath, now that the doors had opened.

Strange how she'd never noticed how the air hung heavy over Charleston—thick and pungent. Here, the air whispered through the tops of the trees, light and fresh and almost crisp. *If air were something I could bake, Charleston would be dense brown bread, and Hope Falls would be delicate wafers.*

This first impression lasted only so long as it took for the others to disembark. Evie was last to step off the train. Last to set foot in Hope Falls. Last to face the truth of what her new home—what her new life—would be. She looked around.

Closed her eyes. Tight.

Opened them just the tiniest sliver until she realized the only thing she could see were her own eyelashes then flat-out gawked at what lay before them.

It was a mistake to sit in the aisle seat. The others didn't seem as floored as she—and Evie realized why. Watching the scenery pass by only made her more aware of the motion, so she never looked. Even when they stopped or got out at a town, she'd not paid much attention to the surroundings. Hiding her misery seemed far more important.

But the others had. They'd been watching as the train carried them farther and farther into the mountains. Miles away from civilization they'd traveled, deep into the untamed wilderness until they came to that awful, lurching stop in the middle of this. . . breathtaking place Evie was supposed to believe they owned.

As though we could be so presumptuous as to assert ownership over anything so magnificent and powerful as this land. The very idea would be laughable, if it didn't call to her.

Trees peppered mountains mixed with a sky so blue Evie could hardly believe it was the same one she'd lived under her entire life. Clouds the consistency of lovingly whipped cream floated above treetops before disappearing into the distance. The sound of a river rushed nearby, promising refreshment and the ability to make everything they'd need in the kitchen. Well, water along with what she'd brought, at least.

That made her look less to the horizon and more to her immediate surroundings. Which were...somewhat less promising. The mountainside abutting the area beside the town bore silent testament to the collapsed mine in its sparse trees and the way it appeared almost...crumpled. Dust and neglect coated the town. Buildings stood unused. No one broke the tomblike stillness with movement or sound. All in all, it looked exactly like what it was: abandoned.

Until now. No matter what had come before, they were here now. *And we're going to change things.* Evie lifted her chin. *No matter what anyone thinks.*

"I think you're looking in the wrong place, mister." The barkeep swirled a stained rag in a grubby mug. "Looking for any one man in a place like Durango is like trying to find a particular tick on the hide of a mangy stray. Too many of the same kind to try and tell 'em apart. You won't have anything to show for it." He gave a significant pause. "Neither would I."

"I appreciate you taking the time to share your observations." Jake kept his expression impassive, reached into his pocket, and pulled out more than his drink was worth. He slid it across the bar, the smooth glide of gold the most eloquent speech he could give in a mining town. *Could have guessed that, but no use throwing money away.*

"Glad to hear it." The money vanished in an instant, along

with the man's dismissive manner. "Not everyone recognizes the. . . *value*. . .of what I can tell them. Never know what you might see or hear in a place like this, if you know what I mean."

Jake gave a nod in answer, patting his pocket with wordless promise. "Brown hair and eyes, probably better dressed than most in these parts." He kept his voice low. "Goes by the name of—"

The barkeep plunked down the mug he'd been wiping with such force, a crack splintered its way up the side. A warning. "Funny thing about those observations, stranger. They're best received at night, when men are tired and relaxing. Otherwise it might make some folks uncomfortable, you see, to take a good hard look around and realize others can do the same thing."

"I understand." *I understand the trail could go cold by the time you work up enough nerve to spill your guts.* "But I'm short on time. Just point me in the direction—"

"Come back tonight, when you can enjoy yourself." His voice sounded too hearty, too loud.

The barkeep had outmaneuvered Jake. If he stayed, it'd look suspicious. More importantly, he'd never get any information from the man who seemed able to provide it. Left with no other option, Jake tipped his hat and sauntered out into the street. If anyone read frustration in the tense line of his jaw or shoulders, he'd ascribe it to a poor haul in the mines.

Half a day would be unacceptable if Jake had anything to say about it. Losing even an hour chafed. But Dad's business lessons held true, and this afternoon Jake would employ his least favorite: tactical retreat. His old man called it diplomacy, but Jake always thought of it in terms of battle. Let his father hide behind suits and smiles, handshakes and shams over coffee or lunches. Better to be honest about things from the start to his way of thinking. Business, full of strategies, negotiations, and victories, made for a battlefield of brains instead of brawn.

Defeat wasn't an option. "Failure," as Dad called it, would not be acknowledged. He didn't fail, didn't invest in failing ventures, and most important, he didn't raise "failures" in his sons. To the world, Montgomery Granger upheld that. The three of them ran an extremely successful lumber business, held their heads high in society, and you'd best believe any Granger got whatever he put his mind to. Nothing less would ever be acknowledged, and nothing more need be said.

That is, until Edward went traveling after a supply contract for a new shipping company, and word of his death came to them a solid month after the fact. Dad had something to say to that. "No son of mine got himself killed over a crooked poker game." With that, he turned his back on his weeping wife, leaving Jake to comfort his mother.

His mother collected herself enough for a few choice words of her own. "It's a lie. We don't repeat lies." Jake held his tongue about his mother's penchant for gossip as she thrust the letter at him. "Burn it—make it disappear. This was not our Edward."

Jake took the paper but hadn't destroyed it. At the time, he'd foolishly believed his parents to be in denial over Edward's death, outraged over the implications in the letter. In time, they'd acknowledge the death of their golden boy.

During that time, Jake would investigate the scurrilous accusations against his brother. No one who knew Edward would believe for an instant he would cheat at cards, much less move to pull his gun on the man he swindled.

Problem was time passed. His inquiries turned up no new information—save that the man who'd fired a shot point-blank into his brother's chest hadn't even been arrested—and his parents showed no signs of accepting the fact that Edward would never walk through the front door. Grief could do strange things, and, granted, his parents long ago mastered the fine art of fooling even themselves. But after a month, it became eerie.

As gently as possible, he pressed his mother for when she'd begin making arrangements for Edward's memorial—questions she dismissed as "unnecessary" and "macabre." Broaching the subject with his father resulted in stern censure: "You know better."

Another month of this sort of thing, and Jake decided even his parents couldn't believe Edward hadn't passed on. With the lag in time before they were informed, an entire business quarter had gone by without so much as a telegram from him. More telling, the company he'd gone to negotiate with contacted Granger Mills to implement production as based on their agreement. They had, apparently, paid a full half of the contracted fees to Mr. Edward Granger. Cash.

The day of his brother's death, Jake noticed. He also noticed there'd been no mention of any money on his brother's person at the time of his death, nor had any deposits been made to company accounts. The sizable sum vanished into thin air.

Dad noticed the same—he noticed anything to do with money.

Jake made the only natural assumption. Dad was making investigations of his own into Edward's death, preparing to seek justice for the son who'd never let him down. Meanwhile, mourning would wait. There were too many unanswered questions. Too much to smear Edward's good name when he deserved better.

Jake might have been wrong about his parents' motivations, but that fact remained. If word got out now, people would think Edward to be a cheat, a swindler, and a violent drunk.

Not my *older brother.* Jake clenched his teeth. *Edward truly lived by the convictions our parents pretended. If I'm forced to practice one of his virtues in order to clear his name, I'll be patient. For now.*

SIX

I t's now or never." *And never doesn't cut it on my menu.* Evie smiled at the thought as she gathered her traveling bag, where she'd tucked her courage alongside the family Bible.

Train workers scuttled about, busy loading water into the steam reservoir or—and this managed to be the far more ambitious undertaking—unloading everything the women had brought with them. Although Evie and Lacey had started establishing their businesses early on, efforts had been abandoned and then redoubled. Mr. Draxley, the mine representative who'd stayed on in Hope Falls and negotiated the sale of the remaining property, helped them send supplies ahead the moment they'd hatched the new plan.

All the same, they were four women with two modest, if solid, businesses and one grand, risky venture to prepare for. That didn't even take into account their plans for marrying and setting up their individual households.

"Packing light" wasn't possible. "Packing light enough not to stall the train engine" seemed a noble goal, to Evie's way of thinking. One they'd accomplished, no less, despite moments of grave misgiving when the locomotive strained up steep inclines.

Only once had their "bare necessities" caused issue—when something with the freight car holding everything snapped and caused it to wobble precariously on the tracks.

Despite dirty looks from some of the men who'd been enlisted at the last stop to transfer the "freight," it seemed this type of thing happened often enough. That realization hadn't settled Evie's nerves—or stomach—much.

Evie kept a close eye on the men as they unloaded her stove this time. True, most of the men were different, but that didn't matter. In fact, the half dozen or so who'd appeared from various places in town struck her as polite and respectful, judging by the way they tipped their hats. What mattered was. . .

"I thought most of the men were. . .gone?" She addressed this to Lacey, whose business contacts made her the expert. Evie was careful not to say "dead." How tactless it would sound to mention the town was supposed to be as abandoned as it looked when they'd first pulled in.

"They were—they are." Perplexed but not concerned, Lacey shrugged. "It looks as though Mr. Draxley started hiring loggers already. I mentioned to him that we'll need several for the initial stages, though I hadn't expected them so soon." As she spoke, more men made appearances—each one offering a friendly wave and a smile along with a dip of his hat.

"I've never seen such bold workers." Naomi gasped as one fellow threw a saucy wink her way. "Mr. Draxley will need—" She hushed as a pale fellow with a twitchy blond mustache bobbed to a stop in front of them and adjusted his spectacles.

"Oh dear, I'm late," a reedy voice fretted. "I'm also afraid I do far better with lists, but I will strive to remember whatever it is you mention, miss." His mustache gave another twitch just before he sank into an overblown bow more befitting a foreign dignitary. "Mr. Draxley, at your service, at all your services. I'm rather afraid I cannot deduce which name belongs to which lady, at this point, but surely that can be forgiven until proper introductions are dispensed?"

He reminds me of someone. Evie pondered who it could be while Lacey made formal introductions. *I can't put my finger on who though.* It tickled at the very edge of her mind but shifted away when she got close.

"Mr. Draxley, would you mind overseeing the unloading of our things? You'll know what to do—everything is labeled either 'mercantile,' 'café,' or 'house.' We've come a long way. . . ."

"That's the house, down there." Mr. Draxley made a vague gesture toward a two-story building closest to the crumpled mountain, obviously too polite to point. "You must long to rest and refresh yourselves. Forgive me for not seeing it sooner."

"I'd like to see my fiancé," Cora broke in, her patience worn to a frayed edge after months of believing Braden to be dead then days of travel. "Immediately."

"You're overset by his experience, but I don't believe you understand the particulars of his. . .condition." The mustache twitched so rapidly Evie began to wonder when it might fall off. "Mr. Lyman wouldn't want to be seen this way. 'Tis unseemly."

"She asked where she could find him." Evie kept her tone even but firm. "I should think it apparent we aren't women to cavil at breaking a few social niceties." She fought to keep a stern expression at the massive understatement.

"I intend to see my brother, so we'll go together." Lacey's declaration brooked no argument. "If you'll just point us to the doctor's office, Mr. Draxley, we'd much appreciate it."

Lips compressed into a thin line, he bobbed his head to indicate a small single-story structure close by.

"Perhaps it's best for the two of you to go the first time," Naomi suggested, as discreet and thoughtful as always. "It's to be expected Braden will tire easily, and he'll be overwhelmed to see you both. Best to keep it to family."

At the word "family," Mr. Draxley's shoulders unhunched, showing him to be less compact than he seemed. "Until Miss Higgins here mentioned it, I didn't consider the matter thoroughly, but Miss Thompson—the other Miss Thompson, that is—does boast some sort of family tie with the Lymans."

"Lacey certainly accepts her as a sister. Cora and Braden would be wed already if not for recent tragedy. A slight delay changes little." Naomi soothed the man's ruffled feathers. Something Evie foresaw would need doing quite often in the coming weeks.

"Of course! I should have seen it right away—Misses Lyman and Thompson would naturally want to see Mr. Lyman directly, after believing him dead and crossing the country to be by his side. Quite romantic of her to show such bravery."

"Thank you, Mr. Draxley." Evie seized the break in his monologue to end it. "It seems they've unloaded everything." The real meaning behind the reminder went unspoken. *Talking doesn't move crates, barrels, boxes, chests, sacks, nor cases to their proper homes. Overseeing and instructing your men does.*

"Excuse me for a moment while I organize things." With another odd little bow—this one not so deep as the first—Draxley hopped to work. The moment he reached the dozen or so men, he straightened his shoulders, raised his voice, and apparently began issuing orders en masse.

The other men slid glances at each other. Eyebrows raised. Gazes shifted to where Evie and Naomi stood watching the tableau unfold. Some men shrugged and looked about to set to it. Others responded to Draxley in low tones, even going so far as to nod in their direction. It looked, Evie decided, like a mutiny about to break loose.

"What is it about men and luggage?" She huffed the question to Naomi, recalling her ire over the stove that morning. "These are big, strong men who'll gladly swing sharp blades at massive trees threatening to crush the life from them, but a few boxes and bags inspire revolt?" *And they claim men are more logical.*

"Not to suggest anything but complete agreement with your sentiment," Naomi murmured, eyeing the colossal heap of baggage they'd hauled along, "but in all fairness, it's more than a few."

"Many hands, Naomi." Evie grinned. "Division works wonders. But where mathematics fails to persuade, a woman has her ways." With that smile still in place, she swept toward the men, adding the last part under her breath so only Naomi could hear her. "After this evening, Draxley will have to fire the whole lot."

"Agreed. They lack a proper work ethic." Naomi beamed and raised her voice as they reached everyone. "Good afternoon."

The transformation almost stunned Evie as, to a man, they straightened up. Literally. Gone were the slouches, sullen glances, and idle hands shoved in pockets. In an instant, grins appeared, shoulders went back, and chests puffed out for all the world as though imitating prize peacocks. Expectation lit their gazes, which remained absolutely riveted on herself and Naomi.

"Good afternoon, ladies." A rumble of voices responded with a haphazard chorus to make even the strictest schoolmarm proud.

Evie blinked. She looked at Naomi, who looked back, as disconcerted as she. They looked again at the men, just to check and see if they were all staring in the same transfixed, expectant fashion. *Yep.* She blinked again—and suspected Naomi did the same, though she couldn't tell. *Maybe I'll ask later.*

Dedicated workers were hard to come by—*devoted* workers almost indescribably rare. Here, before her, stood a dozen men looking at them with the sort of regard she'd only seen reserved for. . .supper. *Or possibly dessert, if a man harbors a sweet tooth.* Her plans to bribe them with the information that some of these boxes held what *could* be a spectacular dinner evaporated in the face of this strange turnaround. Things grew more awkward every moment they stood without speaking. *What on earth is going on here?*

"We sure is glad to see ya," one of the horde spoke up.

"No' expectin' the lassies yet, aye?" another added.

"Leastways, not till the seventeenth," one man said finishing the thought so that the picture began to grow clear.

"But, as someone first mentioned, we're mighty glad you ladies came early!" This reiteration set off a round of nods.

"You're—you're not loggers?" The squeak came from Naomi, but Evie almost would have believed it sprang from her thoughts.

Why wouldn't my thoughts sound squeaky? They'd almost have to right now, since my brain's all but screeched to a halt, and any thought worth its salt would have to be squeezed out. . . .

"Most of us are loggers, some buckers, and Bob and Dodger back there"—the huge man speaking jerked a thumb over his shoulder—"are even high climbers." Hearing his name, one waved as the spokesman completed his recitation. "But we're timber beasts, one and all—just like you asked for in that ad of yours."

Somewhere amid those nonsensical terms lay one simple truth Evie grasped. She hadn't wrestled it into submission yet—most likely never would—but the fact remained fairly obvious.

"Mr. Draxley didn't hire any of you?" She verified, "Everyone came in response to the advertisement we placed, asking prospective grooms to reply *in care of the postmaster general*?" Surely she could be forgiven for placing emphasis on that last part. She'd refrained from adding, "and not in person!"

"He don't seem to care too much, but that were a good way ta give the locale." A bulge in the man's cheek tattled of a wad of chewing tobacco. "We came early to up our chances."

"I believe that's because he—and I'll have to admit we, as well—were expecting written responses to that ad." Naomi didn't shy away from being more blunt. God bless her. "We never imagined you might travel all the way here before we responded."

"Best way to pick a man is to look him over in person," one of the better-looking candidates insisted. "Only natural."

"Well, now that you're all here"—Evie decided to make the best of things—"would you be interested in saving us the trouble of hiring other loggers to do the preliminary work? You'll have room and board and all the food you can eat."

"Evie!" Naomi caught on in a flash. "You're not promising *your* cooking? That's outrageous. You'll work yourself to the bone with those creations of yours."

"They'll work hard, too." Evie beamed at the men then allowed her smile to fade. "Or if not, we'll hire men who will. Besides, I'm going to marry one of the loggers. They should all sample my cooking. It's a fair reward, I think."

"More than fair." The twinkle in her friend's eyes belied her grumble. "Though maybe we should hire others just to have more prospects? I hadn't even considered that, but—"

"Now, now!" Mutters and murmurs among the men exploded into outright protest. "A deal's a deal, missy!"

"You don't lay an offer on the table then yank it away before a man decides whether or not to accept it."

Another frowned at them. "That's not honorable business practice."

Evie made note of him. She liked the sound of his values.

"Especially not if it involves the *dinner* table!" Outrage colored that exclamation, and it evoked the biggest round of agreement yet. "You never mess with a man's meals."

As though I don't already know that. She gave in and grinned. *Looks as though my plan to bribe them with supper wasn't too far off the mark. Meals work in any situation.*

"Should I take that to mean you're accepting the offer?" She widened her eyes as though unsure and waited for the nods.

"We aren't fools, are we, boys?" The spokesman started off the round of verbal agreements, and in no time, they had a deal.

"I'd be happy to make a fine supper for you this very evening, but I'm afraid your first meal will have to wait until we're unpacked, and my stove"—she ran a loving hand along the top of the largest crate—"is in place in the café."

The one who'd mentioned the dinner table volunteered on the spot. "We're more than happy to see to it, ma'am."

"You seemed. . .hesitant. . .when Mr. Draxley made the request." Now was the time for Evie to establish him as their mouthpiece. He may not be much, but with Braden ill, he'd have to do.

"We don't work for him," the burliest one explained. "But we're more than happy to take care of anything for you ladies."

"Anytime." The men hurried to add their assurances.

"Just ask and it's done." They played right into her hands.

"Mr. Draxley might ask on our behalf sometimes." Naomi spoke the words, sliding a glance at the anxious man and then looking back to the others with an almost helpless shrug. "If we can."

"You can do anything you want, ma'am."

"At the moment, we need to discuss our bargain with the other ladies so we can arrange proper introductions with all of us present." Evie didn't want to overlook good manners, but they needed to talk to Lacey. Now. "And then I'm going to fix something special for our first supper together!"

∽∽

It was, Jake decided, a meal he'd never forget.

He speared what the cook tried to pass off as a green bean with the tines of his fork just to watch the limp, grayish thing slide back to the plate with a faint sucking sound. A glob of cold potatoes congealed beside them—slightly more appetizing than the yellowed meat loaf taking pride of place.

He thought it was supposed to be meat loaf. At least they called it meat loaf. Never mind the fact he'd never seen yellow meat loaf in all his born days—never hatched any desire to do so, either. More off-putting yet, the offensive thing boasted a sort of springy texture when he pressed the fork into it.

Fighting food. By that, Jake meant it was the kind of meal a man fought to swallow, and the kind of meal that returned the favor by fighting for its freedom once he'd downed it, then stuck around to grumble about its defeat for days afterward. He pushed the plate away in favor of the biscuits.

Bounty of biscuits. The memory of fantastic food prepared by a plucky woman made his mouth water. Jake slathered butter atop the biscuit, hoping for something even vaguely reminiscent of that previous perfection. He bit into it, chewed, swallowed, and reached for his mug.

He wasn't one to judge cooking. Jake couldn't make biscuits himself, so he could understand if they came out a bit burned or underdone or whatnot. *But how in thunder did anyone manage to make one hard as a rock on the outside, lumpy on the inside, and practically the batter itself in the middle?*

Strike one: No edible food. Strike two: No pretty cook—though, in Jake's opinion, that counted as two strikes. If Miss Thompson served this mess to him, he'd have downed it just for the sake of the company. Strike three: The place overcharged.

His hat wasn't budging.

The only thing this place had going for it was the quiet—which first tipped him off the food wouldn't be worth ordering extra. Memories of meaty sandwiches wrapped in brown paper, with sugar cookies tucked atop like sweet greetings, made his stomach growl. He cast another assessing glance at the table before him and ignored his belly for its own good.

Strong coffee and a place to read the papers he'd picked up earlier kept him in his chair—that, and the time he needed to kill before going to get answers from the squirrelly bartender. The man's yellow belly probably matched Jake's meat loaf.

Cracking his first smile since he'd walked into the place, he unfolded the paper and started reading. Then stopped. Jake flipped back to the front page of *Durango Doings,* a two-bit town newsletter he suddenly suspected to be at least a week old.

Today's date stared back at him in smudged black on grayish paper of obvious poor quality. He turned the page to reread the advertisement that caught his eye, certain it couldn't be the same one he'd chortled over from a week-old paper on the train.

"'Wanted: three men, ages twenty-four to thirty-five. . .'"

He read the first line aloud before shaking his head. Same ad all right. Durango might be out of the way of civilization, for the most part, but with telegraphs transmitting words and the train carrying everything else, nothing could excuse being an entire week behind—even when it came to a joke.

Jake snorted, tossed the rag aside, and reached for the more reliable publication.

He scanned through it, waiting for something to catch his interest. When it did, he just about choked on the grit from his coffee. There, in a prestigious paper, the same cheeky ad stared up at him. No need to check the date this time—he already had.

When an ad ran for several days, in numerous publications, across several state and territorial lines, it wasn't a joke missing its retraction then reprinted in a Podunk town. No.

Jake gaped at the words marching before him, considering them seriously for the first time. *"Object: Marriage. . ."*

"Unbelievable." He didn't realize he'd muttered it aloud until chair legs scraped over the floor.

A fellow diner—who seemed only too glad for a reason to abandon his food—looked over his shoulder and caught sight of what he was reading.

"You just now seeing that?" He poked the paper with a grimy finger. "It's been running in all the papers for a solid week now. At first everyone had a good laugh over it, but now seems like these gals mean business—and some men are planning on trying to take them up on the offer. Strange days, eh?"

"Strange, indeed." Jake set the paper down—atop his plate, so he wouldn't have to look at it. "Makes a man wonder."

"Wonder what the world's comin' to, or what kind of hatchet-faced Methuselah shrews would try to hire husbands?"

Jake chuckled at the way the fellow put it. "Both."

"Way I figure it, they're desperate old maids with tongues sharp enough to cut a man off at the knees. Must be, putting an ad like that in the papers, bold as brass and twice as cheap."

"It's unfair to judge women you've never met." *I suspect he's more right than wrong, but that doesn't make it right to say so.* "There's no way of knowing what they're like."

"Oh, there's a way." The fellow leaned forward far enough to be balancing on two chair legs. "I aim to go and meet 'em face-to-face and see what they have to say."

SEVEN

G et out!" Braden roared the order when his sister and fiancée ignored him the first time. *No, not my fiancée.* His lungs closed, cutting off his breath the way they seemed to do whenever he overexerted himself. *They have to leave. Now.*

"Braden, we've come all this way to see you." Cora—beautiful, incredible, muleheaded Cora—stepped close enough to place her hand over the sheet covering his. Sweet torture.

Thank God for the sheet pulled up to his chin. They couldn't see the straps holding him helpless as a newborn or a lackwit. And, if he had his way, they never would. He drew deep breaths, fighting for air so he could fight for his dignity.

"We've so much to tell you!" His sister flitted around the room, touching everything, not holding still for an instant. "Why, you'll never guess half of it, absolutely never believe—"

"That you're *still here?*" He needed them gone before they realized the extent of his shame. Before he saw pity and sorrow replace the joy and love in Cora's eyes.

"No, not that." Lacey pshawed. "Stop worrying about that. We're real enough. Not some dream because of what they give you for the pain. Cora and I won't disappear. We promise!"

"I won't leave you. Ever." Cora reached over to smooth his hair from his forehead in a gesture meant to be maternal.

She didn't realize the effect her very nearness had—that the movement brought her close enough for him to catch the scent of lilacs and summer so uniquely Cora. She couldn't know that the merest brush of her soft hand against his forehead made him shiver, or that the shiver sent streaks of pain shooting from his wasted legs. *She'll never know. I won't let her.*

"Don't touch me. Just leave." He gritted the words from behind clenched teeth, behind the pain he wouldn't show them. "I don't want you here. Go back home and don't come back."

Cora recoiled as though he'd shot her.

The moment her hand stopped smoothing his hair, his pain doubled. *Coincidence.*

Lacey paid him no heed. "Don't be such a bear, Braden. You've put your fiancée through a lot these past few months."

"She's not my fiancée." He refused to look at her—saying the words was hard enough without seeing what he was giving up. *Yet another reason she has to leave. If she's near, I won't be able to let her go.* Her gasp pierced through him, but he held firm.

"We thought you were dead!" Tears wavered in Cora's voice. "The news devastated me, Braden. When I learned you'd survived, that was all that mattered. Don't worry about whatever else you said. You've been through a harrowing experience. In time—"

"I won't change my mind." He wouldn't turn his head to face her, either, for fear she'd see the truth. It would be all too easy for him to change his mind, to claim her as his own and ignore the fact that she deserved a whole man. *A real man.*

"Neither will I."

"Now isn't the time to be discussing the particulars of your engagement, really," Lacey broke in, hands fluttering as though warding away worries. "We need to discuss our plans."

"The plan. . ." Braden's clenched fists began to ache as he

reiterated, "The plan is for you to *get out of here!*" He raised his voice to a shout on the last four words. *"Now!"*

"No need to yell, Mr. Lyman." Evelyn Thompson swept into the room, Naomi Higgins close behind her. "Our hearing works quite well, thank you. Besides"—she bustled over to lay a bracing hand on Cora's shoulder as she spoke—"we just arrived."

Good. Her sister will take care of her. Braden's hands relaxed a little. *Evie's the practical one. She'll listen.* He'd made a mistake in watching Evie cross the room to Cora, because it let his eyes fall on his fiancée. *No. Not my fiancée.*

Her eyes—her glorious, mismatched eyes that saw straight through him—shone with tears. Her lips, usually curved into the sort of smile a man felt all the way through, pressed together tight, as though damming up a torrent of words. But her hands nearly broke him. He'd ordered her not to touch him, so she'd stopped. Now he saw her hands rested on the edge of his bed, long fingers splayed atop his sheets, stretching as close to him as possible without making contact.

Braden groaned and slammed his eyes shut. *She has to go, Lord. There's a limit to my strength. To any man's strength.*

"It's good to see you, Braden." Naomi's voice pulled him.

"You've all seen him now." Pompous as always, the doctor pushed his way into the crowded room. "That's enough visiting." Choice phrases like "tiring," "overtaxed," and "setback" promised dire consequences if Braden wasn't left to rest and heal in peace.

Strange how the same ominous warnings he'd disregarded, barking orders at the mutinous little man to unstrap his arms, now made perfect sense. Better yet, they shooed the women from the room.

When they left—with every intent to return, despite Braden's orders—the doctor took one look at him and advanced with the morphine. Braden didn't protest. For now, the memory of the mines couldn't be half so wracking as thoughts of Cora crying because she wouldn't listen. . .

72

"I couldn't have heard that right." Lacey sank onto a sofa and scarcely noticed the sudden poof of dust. A clear sign of duress, that the fact their current home needed thorough cleaning ranked so abysmally low on her list of priorities.

Somehow she'd thought everything would fall into place once they arrived in Hope Falls. So why was it that, all of a sudden, everything seemed even more complicated? The town seemed far emptier and more dismal than she'd imagined, which meant setting up the café and mercantile and even the mill would be a greater challenge than expected. Mr. Draxley, whom she'd counted as a resource, clearly wouldn't provide much help.

Braden looked worse off than she'd hoped. Worse yet, he'd not been happy to see her. *Ingrate.* She scowled at the thought of all they'd gone through for such an ungracious reception. *My brother needs more than medical attention—he needs to relearn several lessons in manners!*

Because, as disappointing as everything else may be—and there was no "may" about it in Lacey's book—the absolute worst thing about their first day in Hope Falls was Braden's callous treatment of Cora. If Lacey's heart broke at his harsh words and clear wish to never see his fiancée again, she could only imagine how her best friend felt.

Though, judging by the stiff way Cora moved, the absolute lack of expression on her face, and the way she kept blinking, it didn't take too much imagination. Shock, sorrow, and a desperate will not to dissolve into tears seemed about right.

If my brother weren't crippled, I'd tell Evie and let her wallop Braden until he remembered himself!

With all that swirling around in her head, it didn't leave much room for dust balls to loom large. Especially not with Evie telling her how all the men unloading their luggage were going to be trying to marry them. Which made no sense. None at all.

I need a nap. A good lie-down will help sort things out.

"You heard it properly," Naomi chimed in. "Be thankful you weren't there when we heard it from the men themselves."

"Draxley didn't hire them, then?" Cora bestirred herself—a good sign. "I must admit that part makes some sense. He doesn't seem the most effective sort of business manager, does he?"

"In all honesty, he puts me in mind of a rabbit."

"Naomi!" Evie's gasp at the other woman's statement made them all jump. She began to laugh. "Thank you! It's been bothering me the entire time—I couldn't decide exactly who it is that Mr. Draxley puts me in mind of, but that's it. It's as though the White Rabbit from Lewis Carroll's *Alice's Adventures in Wonderland* sprang to life as a man and hopped here!"

"My word." Lacey went into peals of laughter. "Now that you point it out, the resemblance is uncanny. The spectacles. . ."

"Something about the twitchy mustache." Cora chuckled along with them, beginning to rally from the encounter with Braden.

"Weren't his first words something about being late?" Naomi's observation set them off in a fresh round of titters.

There's only so much a woman can endure in a single day without a bracing bout of giggles. Lacey decided that the four of them had been overdue, but the timing couldn't have been better. When they caught their breath, they were far more ready to tackle the situation at hand. Well, situations, but one at a time would simply have to do until they'd settled in.

And cleaned. She beamed as she noticed how the dust had gained importance now that her vexation over Draxley eased. Dust could be done away with, which meant even more progress.

"So the men currently carrying things to the café and mercantile aren't workers. They're prospective grooms." Lacey brought the conversation back to the most pressing topic.

"Both," Evie corrected. "Once they'd clarified their intentions, Naomi and I struck a bargain. Our erstwhile suitors will also be doing the initial work clearing the mill site and so forth in exchange for room, board, and meals."

"And the chance to cut out the competition they might face if other loggers came in to do the job." Naomi sighed. "It seems our earlybirds already expect another influx of men."

No, no, no! This wasn't the plan! The men were supposed to write their responses, and then we'd choose. She grappled with this displeasing sensation of being thwarted for a few moments. *Think, Lacey. What do you do when things don't go your way?*

The answer to that was startling. *Why have I never realized before how rarely things don't turn out as I'd like?* Most likely because she'd never needed to think about it. So she'd think about it now until she came up with a solution. *Ah. . .there. I'll simply turn it around again to work for me.*

"What an excellent stroke of luck!" Her interpretation stunned them all. She understood. Lacey would have stunned herself with such a declaration mere moments ago. "Yes, the unexpected is unsettling, but look at all the benefits of having so many men already here! We won't have to wait to meet them, already have several options, and don't need to feel guilty over those we don't choose, as we didn't send for any of them!"

"Yes, but selecting our husbands was supposed to take several steps and a certain amount of time," Naomi protested. "And, while I'm not saying these aren't fine, upstanding, hardworking men, it's belatedly occurred to me we didn't mention anything about education, refinement, and the like."

"Refinement isn't a requirement to make a life out West," Evie pointed out. "As far as education goes, yes, I noticed their coarse speech, but they know what we do not about the business of lumber. That's what we need—and what we asked for."

Lacey wanted to cheer Evie's speech, but a small corner of her thoughts whispered doubts. *Coarse speech? Lack of refinement? Little or no education? Why didn't I consider that would be the case when we asked for working-class men!*

"Ingenious of you to elicit their help while they're courting.

That way, you don't have to rely on Mr. Draxley to hire workers."
Cora raised a single brow. "Better still you bargained for room,
board, and meals without any mention of wages!"

"Better yet, they have motivation to work hard to impress us."
Evie'd been thinking about this in great detail, it seemed. "And
when others arrive—if any other men arrive—they'll have to
abide by the same bargain or be forced to leave, having lost face.
The men won't stand for anyone not pulling his weight."

"It's obvious which of us is the businesswoman!" Naomi
gestured toward Evie with obvious admiration. "I only thought of
the basics when you started enlisting them as our workers!"

"There's nothing basic about any of this." Sorrow drew across
Cora's face. "This place makes everything convoluted."

"We'll sort it all out." Lacey drew her into a hug. "Braden
hurts and his pride put his nose out of joint when you saw him
lying there. Give him time. . . And if that doesn't work, you have
my permission to do whatever else you feel necessary." *He already
deserves it for acting like a fool!*

"I might take you up on that," her best friend warned.

"We all might." From the grim note in Evie's tone, she'd
already surmised what sort of reception Braden had given her
sister. "But for now, I promised those men supper, and I'll need
your help to get it done in time. Besides. . ." Her glance shifted
toward the window as she added, "We promised the men proper
introductions, so we can all get a better look at them."

"You know you want to get a gander at 'em yourself." The other
occupant of the diner waggled his brows in what he clearly
intended to be a persuasive manner. The effort failed.

"Doesn't make a hill of beans' worth of difference to me what
the three ladies look like." Jake shook his head, suppressing a
sudden swell of curiosity. If nothing else, witnessing this strange
event would be entertaining—the sort of detour he would've

easily made in happier times.

"Ya never know. Could surprise us all and be real lookers. Then you'd regret not tagging along to find out what's what."

"That's a turnaround from 'hatchet-faced Methuselah.'" Jake didn't bother to hide his amusement. "Why the change of heart?"

"Dunno." He scratched his head. "Can't stop thinking it might be a buncha widows with more land than they can handle, not bothering to look for love or money the second time around—just a strong arm and a steady smile. Then I'd kick myself for a fool for not finding out." The fellow suddenly seemed to realize he'd let his inner romantic out in public. "Though it's most likely they've got hairy lips and squinty eyes, o' course."

"Of course." His coffee mug hid his chuckle until Jake knew he wouldn't offend the other man. "But you misunderstood. I meant they can be bucktoothed or beautiful—it doesn't matter."

"In it for the money, then." The flat statement, devoid of any humor, tattled of the other man's disapproval. "Or getting the land out of trust or whatever sort of arrangement must tie things up. Reckon on there bein' plenty of those sorts."

"No. I'm not in it at all. I already told you, Mr.—"

"Klumpf." His companion shoved out a hand for a friendly shake. "Volker Klumpf. Glad to hear you say you aren't after riches. I hadn't pegged you for the mercenary sort."

Let's hope you never have cause to see just how mercenary I can be, Mr. Klumpf. An unlikely concern. True, he'd looked him over with a keen eye at first—same as he did most men. Klumpf seemed about the right height, right age, with brown eyes and shaggy brown hair to loosely match the all-too-vague description Jake worked with. But Klumpf's eager conversation, blithe revelation of his plans, and the gap-toothed smile giving him the air of a good-natured puppy pointed to a conscience so clean it would squeak if anything rubbed it wrong.

Just like when he'd thought Jake might be after the mystery women's money. . .

If Volker Klumpf's a scheming thief and cold-blooded murderer, I'll eat my hat. He shook the man's hand without reservation. *It might taste better than the meat loaf, anyway.*

"Jake Creed." He'd repeated the lie so often it didn't strike him as false anymore. Jacob Granger didn't exist anymore—traded his family and birthright for a chance to hunt a killer. Jake Creed, the hunter whose belief in justice drove him all the way to Colorado, took Granger's place the moment he left home.

"Glad ta meet ya, Creed. I like the sound of that. . .Creed. Most folks call me Clump. Ain't noble-sounding like yours, but it serves well enough." He shrugged. "Sure you aren't interested in catching the train in an hour and heading up to Hope Falls? We can sneak a peek at the women tonight and see what's what."

"Sounds like an adventure." Jake slapped Clump on the shoulder. "I won't join you, but I wish you all the best."

"Train leaves in an hour if you change your mind." Clump got to his feet, plunked some change on the table behind him, and—there was no other honest word for it—clumped toward the door. Black boots with some sort of heavy sole weighted the man's gait to a distinctive series of thuds. "And if you don't, I hope someday you'll find the woman of your dreams, Creed."

The sudden image of tawny eyes filled with laughter made Jake shake his head. *Not for me.* The comely cook with her mouthwatering dishes and saucy smile could take her pick of men. *I'd have a better chance with one of the hatchet-faced, buck-toothed wantwits who placed this advertisement!*

He eyed the ridiculous thing one last time. A sour smell from the meal buried beneath it made the cream Jake had swallowed in his coffee curdle in his stomach. *A sad day,* he mused, *when a man finds himself plenty of time to kill—and no murderer near at hand to make the work fulfilling.*

The doors to the diner swung open with the sort of shrill creak to make anyone within hearing distance wince. Since Jake now claimed the dubious honor of dining entirely alone, he ignored the sound and focused on the man edging his way into the room.

A slow, nervous shuffle, empty sack bumping against his shins every step, chin tucked low against his chest as he moved in a straight line toward the kitchen in the back, the man's posture screamed that he had something to hide—or something to tell.

Jake's feet hit the floor the instant he recognized the man. An instant before the barkeep's eyes widened and his pace picked up in a bid to reach the kitchen before Jake reached him.

Not something to tell, then. Too late. Jake blocked the broader man's path long before his quarry could hope to evade him. He set himself a wide stance and waited while the nervous barkeep eyed the rest of the room. Once. Twice, to make sure no one else could be watching. Or listening.

The other man relaxed enough to offer a smile as watered down as the whiskey Jake had watched him serve earlier. "I see you found the Down 'n' Out Diner. Hadn't thought to run into you here." Another swift glance around the abandoned place finished the thought—he hadn't expected to run into anyone here.

"I'd never passed through Durango before—didn't know the local spots." Which, of course, translated to: *didn't know to avoid the Down 'n' Out Diner.* "You come here for lunch?" Jake's raised eyebrow left little room for misinterpretation. Having sampled the fare, he knew no sane man would eat here.

"Meat loaf day." A grin broke out across the man's face. "Best sober-up in the world is to force a man to swallow Bert's meat loaf. I stock up on it every week, and let it be known."

"Less trouble on meat loaf day." Jake didn't ask. One glance at his newspaper-covered plate reminded him full well what lay beneath it. The threat might well make men less apt to break saloon rules. "You can have the piece under there."

"Not just meat loaf day." The man snagged the piece from beneath the paper and shoved it into the sack. "Strangest thing about Bert's meat loaf. Keeps same as the day he made it for as long as I've seen. Same sort of bouncy feel but turns white around the edges and darker yellow in the middle. Of course"—he leaned closer as though unwilling to offend a potentially eavesdropping Bert—"smells even worse the longer it sits."

"Glad to give you an extra helping." Jake spared a moment to hope it didn't end any young miner's life. "Now that we're out of sight of prying eyes, what say we talk business?"

"All right, but seems to me you already got—"

"Man goes by Twyler. Average height, brown hair, brown eyes. Would've come through here earlier this week." Jake patted his pocket meaningfully. "Any information you could give me would be well rewarded. Especially where he headed next."

"Wish I could tell you something you don't already know." The barkeep gave a gusty sigh and gestured toward the paper he'd nudged aside. "But you already saw the ad, so you know about as much as I do. Every stranger who's come through these parts and not stayed to mine has gone on to Hope Falls, you see."

"Have any stayed on who fit the description?" He shoved aside the idea Twyler would answer the ad. No self-respecting criminal would follow such a ludicrous course. "Well-spoken sort of man, more educated. Even if he went by another name?"

"Miners come through here all the time, but it's hard work. They're either experienced in mining or they quit in a minute. Someone well spoken and educated would stick out like a sore thumb, and I'd remember him." He gave a shrug. "Best tip I can give you is to go on and try Hope Falls, mister."

Frustration closed Jake's throat. *Twyler won't go to a logging camp to win a bride. It's a fool's mission, and no fool got the better of my brother and evaded me this long. I can't expect to find him there.* He cast a fulminating glare at the paper, the benighted ad mocking him as the know-nothing barkeep sidled around him and into the kitchen. No help there.

It's a dead end. I pack it up and go home in defeat, as good as admitting Edward's a cowardly cheat, or I head to Hope Falls. Maybe someone there will know something worth hearing.

"Seems to me it'd be a good place to lose yourself if someone was searching." The barkeep bustled back through, sack bulging and a sly smile stretching his face. "No one would think to follow a man on such a goose chase. Might be just the thing."

"That's—" Jake swallowed the word "harebrained." *So out of the norm it might work—just the sort of thing Twyler might do.* "An interesting notion. Thanks for those observations of yours." He tossed the man a token of his gratitude as he headed for the door, not bothering to acknowledge the man's thanks.

The barkeep—and the sour stench of 'meat loaf' more powerful than should be legal—followed him out the door and down the street a ways. Other people, spotting the sack and obviously knowing what it meant, gave them wide berth.

Morbidly fascinated in spite of himself, Jake had to know one last thing before he left Durango in the dust and boarded Clump's train: "Ever killed anyone with that meat loaf?"

EIGHT

I think I've died and gone to heaven."

The groan following the statement sounded anything but heavenly as Evie wrapped the intruder on the knuckles with her wooden spoon. Hard.

At least this one didn't yelp like number three, or howl like two and four. Compared to those, the groan sounded downright manly. Or, at least, the manliest of the four. The first troublemaker didn't count—Naomi actually gave the swindler a biscuit, setting off the entire problem of loggers popping into the kitchen like so many hopeful ground squirrels.

"No fair!" A distinct note of wheedling entered the fellow's voice while he backed away with one eye on Evie's spoon and one eye on the biscuits. "Kane got one."

"My mistake!" Naomi rushed forward, wringing her hands. "I didn't know the rules of the kitchen, you see, and he asked so nicely, and I didn't realize it would mean all of you would come filing through, wanting to eat before mealtime. I'm so sorry!"

"Don' you be frettin', lassie." The sixth sniffing hopeful poked his head around the door frame. This time Evie recognized the huge redhead. A man of his size couldn't help but make an impression. "Not a one of us have eaten anythin' halfway decent in at least a week, and it's been a good sight longer than that for most. Keeping a dozen strapping men away from a kitchen smelling so fine as this would take a minor miracle."

"Please, missus." Sensing which woman would be weakest to his plea, Number Five zeroed his smile in on Lacey. "I won't tell none of the other guys iff'n you can see your way to sparing another one of them biscuits. You can trust ole Dodger."

"Dodger, you need to learn to take a lady's first answer." The redheaded giant's rumble inspired a flash of alarm, swiftly replaced by determination once Dodger looked at the biscuits one more time and took a deep breath. "I'll leave with you."

"You leave, Bear. I'll keep the ladies company."

"We don't have room for company. We've work to do!" Evie'd gotten caught up watching the byplay for long enough. It was time to reclaim her kitchen. "No men are allowed in my kitchen unless by express invitation. Spread the word, please. Mr. Dodger, I'm a businesswoman, so I'll make you a deal. You're more than welcome to take a biscuit with you on your way out the door." She saw his face light up as he edged toward his prize. She also noticed that the one he called Bear stayed in the doorway, arms folded, shaking his head. *Smart man, that one.*

"Hear the lady out before you take the bargain, Dodge." His warning cemented her good impression of his intelligence.

"What?" Dodger froze, hand hovering over the biscuits, where he'd been trying to decide which looked largest. "She said I could have one, so I'll take one. That's the deal, ain't it?"

"That's the first part. You see, it's a choice I'm offering you." Evie saw Cora's grin as she nudged Naomi with her elbow. "You may take one biscuit now, or you can have supper later this evening. Whichever decision you make, you abide by."

"Or supper?" Dodger asked it the first time. At the round of nods, he exploded. "*Or* supper, she says! I'm not trading an entire supper for one measly biscuit. That ain't fair."

"Neither is you getting something the other men don't." Evie pointed toward the door with her spoon. "Now that you've made your choice, I'll be happy to see you at the supper table. If you'd kindly extend my offer to the others, we can be through with these interruptions once and for all, I'd assume."

"We've been dismissed, Dodge, me-boy." The redhead reached into the kitchen and snagged the smaller man's shoulder. "Let's not hold up that fine supper any longer." With a surprisingly boyish grin, he hauled a still-spluttering Dodger out of the café. "And we'll be sure to pass along the message, ma'am!"

Ma'am, he called me. Evie couldn't help but notice that the first man who caught her eye called her "ma'am" but reserved the more appealing and feminine "lassie" for Naomi. *I should expect more of that. Lacey's so pretty and lighthearted, the men will swarm around her. The only reason she's not already wed is she wanted more adventure than becoming a society wife.*

She chopped carrots while she evaluated the situation. *After Lacey's taken her pick, the men will look to Naomi and me. Naomi first—she's more soft-spoken and would make a better bride than I would.* The mound of carrots grew before her, the series of chops busying her hands and giving ease to her heart as she confronted the plain truth with no frosting. *Not to mention her trim figure. I'm too bossy and loud and plump. I'll be the last of the women left to hire her husband. So as long as there are three I could live with, things will be all right.*

"You're brilliant, Evie." Lacey scooped away the carrots and plunked them into the massive pot boiling atop the stove—far too soon. "That generous 'offer' of yours will keep the men from sticking their noses in your kitchen again tonight!"

"Tonight?" Naomi harrumphed, carefully browning the second round of chopped beef then adding in diced tomatoes to the mixture of meat and onions, as Evie instructed. "That's the sort of threat we can reuse every meal to keep scavengers at bay."

"Scavengers." Cora giggled. "You make them sound like

crows, skulking about, waiting for us to drop something so they can swoop in and snabble it up. Or fight over it."

"Snabble?" Evie pulled the carrots off the stove then pushed more potatoes toward her sister. "You made fun of my word when I made it up, and now you dare use it?"

"Joking about the words you make up is a sister's privilege. Besides, I like the ones you create. They're so expressive and vibrant—just like you are." Cora put down her paring knife to reach over and give Evie's hand a fond pat.

"We can always tell when Cora's repeating an Evie-ism." Naomi's smile took the sting away. "You have a flair with words, the same as you do in the kitchen. Creativity always shows."

Evie shook her head and went to rescue the next batch of biscuits from Lacey's overexuberance. So far, Lacey had committed just about every crime known against biscuitkind. She'd left the batter lumpy then overstirred to correct it. She'd rolled them too thick, then too thin. Left them in the oven too long, and not long enough. This time it looked like overdone batter combined with thin rolling. In truth, the entire scavenger issue hadn't been Naomi's fault. Entirely.

The other three women had been sneaking ruined biscuits out of the kitchen for a while now, and Naomi simply got caught ditching the duds. The bribe she'd used to purchase silence—one of Evie's own biscuits—brought the man sniffing around for more. With others trailing in his wake when he left empty-handed.

"I think snabbling scavenger has the right ring when they first show up," Lacey mused, almost not noticing when Evie shooed her away from the biscuits and set her beside Cora to peel potatoes. She certainly didn't catch the glare Cora shot Evie as her sister pried an already-peeled potato from Lacey's fingers and replaced it with a runty one still wearing its skin.

"No!" Evie swiped the paring knife she'd just put in Lacey's hand and demonstrated again. "Like this. Never move the blade toward yourself. Always keep your thumb out of the way."

"I see." Lacey reached for the knife again and merrily began slicing the skins off half her runty potato. Meaning she took off half the potato along with its skins, of course. "I also see that the scavengers turn to beggars awfully quick."

Evie watched for another moment to make sure Lacey wouldn't lose a thumb or do herself any other sort of injury. She couldn't let her friend near the stove, they didn't have time to waste any more rounds of biscuits, chopping carrots would be far too dangerous, and besides, Evie hadn't planned to feed a small army of men right from the start. Potatoes she'd brought aplenty for Lacey to mangle. It would have to do for tonight.

"You could sell predinner biscuits and make a fortune." Cora's suggestion made everyone stop whatever she did and stare.

"Cora, I've never heard something so absolutely—"

Mercenary, manipulative, downright shameful. Evie finished Naomi's exclamation a dozen different ways even before Lacey beat her to it. *Maybe even a little bit funny, but mostly—*

"Brilliant! I say propose the idea to the next scavenger."

"That's dishonorable. We agreed to meals as part of their payment for the hard work these men will do." Evie rationed the browned, seasoned meat into pie pans as she rejected the plan. "Although I might as well mention we'll need a far sight more food than I brought along—especially if more men show up. Mr. Draxley will need to put in an order as early as tomorrow for an entire array of supplies if I'm to feed a logging outfit from the first day. We already have two stoves, but I'll need the room and storage we discussed right away, too. The café wasn't designed to accommodate the quantity of a log camp cookhouse."

"The men can build on an extra room tomorrow, I'd think."

"Naomi's right—the mercantile is supposed to be stocked with lumber so they can start right away." Lacey added her second potato to Cora's enormous pile and announced with a great sense of accomplishment, "We've finished the potatoes!"

"Great job." Evie winked at her sister, sharing the joke instead of letting it become a sore spot. By then, she'd rescued her carrots from the pot and set the water a-boiling once again. "Now those can boil while you start to mash the others!" Because, of course, Evie saw to it the first ten pounds of potatoes Cora peeled—minus their skins—stood alongside condensed milk, butter, and salt for mashing. She hastily added the other ingredients and toted the still-hot pot over to the worktable for them. *Thank You, Lord, that I brought an extra masher. Even Lacey can't do worse than make a mess of her apron with this task!*

Meanwhile, Evie kept a watch on the minced beef, onion, and tomato mixture as Naomi finished pan after pan, laying it into pie tins to cool and form the thin skin signaling their readiness for the mashed potato topping. Shepherd's pie, alongside the biscuits Evie whipped up in such a frenzy she had already planned on ways to use leftovers the next day, should make those men more than glad to hold up their bargain.

The peas and carrots she'd steam last, to avoid that dreadful cold limp vegetable phenomenon she'd seen too often. Peas and carrots, steamed slightly soft and bathed in butter with a hint of brown sugar, never failed to please her diners. Better still, they cooked quickly and went with almost anything.

With everyone busy and things progressing, Evie sifted a good amount of flour onto a clean wooden surface then put over a third again as much sugar alongside it. With her fingertips, she rubbed butter into the sugar until thoroughly mixed then lightly added in the flour bit by bit, working it until it formed a rather loose dough. She lifted it onto a baking sheet she'd greased beforehand and shaped it into a long oval about a quarter inch thick and three inches wide. Her fork pricked even holes all around before deft strokes of her knife separated the mass into long strips she sprinkled with more sugar.

She readied two batches of the shortbread before the time came to finish assembling the shepherd's pies. Evie set Naomi and Lacey to beating eggs while she and Cora spread fresh mashed potatoes atop the cooled minced meat and vegetables.

A sister could always tell when her sibling had lost patience, and Cora's acceptance of her best friend's inexperience in the kitchen fared far better when both of them stayed outside it. For that matter, it seemed everyone fared better when Lacey stayed away from the kitchen. Evie heard the splat of a dropped egg and reconsidered. *Make that far, far away from the kitchen. Any kitchen, really, but* especially *mine!*

Within moments, the dropped egg forgotten, they had no fewer than twenty-one shepherd's pies ready to brown in the oven. They had the dozen loggers, Braden, the doctor, Mr. Draxley, and themselves. The ladies wouldn't eat one each, but Evie held it was best to make a little more than they expected to need. They glazed each with beaten egg for that glossy sheen Evie considered her signature then sprinkled cheese on top for extra flavor and color.

Naomi kept an eye on the pies, rotating and removing them when ready. Cora steamed the peas and carrots, the sugar Evie'd already browned in the pan adding sweetness so she need only dab butter atop the vegetables afterward. The biscuits stayed warm in covered baskets near the oven, much like they had back home.

"I'll make tea for everyone, if you like." Lacey's offer took Evie by surprise. "Coffee for the men, I'd suppose."

"Have—" Evie groped for a diplomatic way to ask, couldn't come up with one, and simply blurted out, "Have you ever made tea, Lacey? Or coffee? It's not as simple as most think."

"Oh, I know!" Apron filled with more stains than the other three would see in the entire week, Lacey nodded with great confidence. "Tea, chocolate, and coffee were the only things Pa insisted I learn to make for myself. It was useful when we traveled. Particularly if Pa took meetings—I could replenish the coffee without waiting an age in an uncivilized place." She beamed at the evidence of her independence. "If worse comes to worst, I can also drive a team of horses and shoot a pistol. It's all part of being a modern, self-reliant woman, you see."

She's invaded other kitchens? Evie took a deep breath. *Even if only to make tea and coffee, I pity the cook who returned to the carnage Lacey left in her wake.* The other women gave voice to their reactions, too stunned to stay quiet.

"Self-reliant?" Naomi echoed in what Evie knew to be disbelief, but apparently Lacey interpreted it as admiration.

"Your father let you shoot a gun?" Cora's horrified gasp came closer to Evie's own reaction. "A *real* one?"

This elicited a matching gasp from Evie. *When did Cora's priorities become more organized than mine? And, really, what could Mr. Lyman have been thinking, to let Lacey lay so much as a finger on a firearm? She can't handle an egg without chaos.*

"I'm a dab hand with pistols." Lacey's nonchalance could have been comforting, but Lacey managed to be nonchalant about everything from butterflies to a dozen hungry loggers. While she spoke, she took down the grinder, selected coffee beans, and began grinding with an expertise lending credit to her claim. "As a matter of fact, I didn't want to mention it for fear of frightening anyone, but I brought one along for each of us."

Silence filled the kitchen. The familiar backdrop of the stove burners and oven didn't count as noise to Evie as she joined Naomi and Cora in gaping at Lacey. While she gaped, she nudged Cora out of the way and took the carrots away from the heat before they burned, but otherwise, she'd ground to a halt.

"I knew your father took you shooting, Lacey, but he never confided in me about your proficiency." Naomi, as Lacey's live-in companion for the past five years, obviously felt she should have known about this. "Nor did you ever mention it before."

"We agreed it wasn't the sort of thing to make Charleston society look upon me more favorably." A blithe shrug as she took the grounds and began measuring them into drip percolator pitchers Evie herself only recently learned to use. "Our own business ventures, my friendship with a female businesswoman"—she shot a conspiratorial grin at Evie—"and the proposals I chose not to accept already served to make me something of an…oddity, shall we say? We thought it best not to make it known I carry a pistol around in my reticule whenever I travel."

"There's a pistol in your purse right *now*?" Cora's curiosity began to overcome her disbelief and outrage.

"Of course! To be honest, I'd hoped to have the chance to teach you each some level of competence and a degree of comfort with your own before we invited any suitors to Hope Falls." A frown twisted her pretty features. "Perhaps tomorrow, while the men are building the storeroom onto the café, we can start?"

"Absolutely," Evie answered almost before she thought it through. She knew what Cora and Naomi were thinking—the way their jaws all but hit the floor told her they worried she'd lost her mind. "With this many men around, we should avail ourselves of every type of protection at our disposal. If Lacey claims proficiency, I believe her. She's quick to admit when she lacks experience in cooking. I want to learn, and I'd sleep easier knowing you both did, too. Won't you agree?"

She watched their faces while she spoke, but the distinctive aroma of shepherd's pie had her opening the oven, grabbing a dish towel, and pulling out the golden-brown pies the moment she finished. She waited a beat as Lacey set the percolators atop the stove to come to a boil. They exchanged a brief nod—a silent agreement Lacey would teach Evie even if the others didn't agree to join them the next day. Evie then busied herself sliding the sheets of shortbread into the oven.

"Someone should point out the danger of this little scheme. I suppose, as the oldest, I should be that someone." Naomi's eyes sparkled. "Instead, I'm going to be honest and say it sounds like great fun. Learning to handle a firearm should be one of the benefits of moving out West, and there are the safety concerns Evie pointed out to consider. I'll join both of you."

"By now you should all know better than to think I'd miss something like this!" Competition glinted in Cora's gaze. "When else would I get the chance to become a crack shot?"

"There's something deliciously. . .masculine. . .about it, isn't there?" Lacey carefully checked the color of the coffee, judged it too light, and set the percolator pitcher back on the stove.

"Liberating, I imagine, to know you can defend yourself." Evie had reason to be glad she'd put warm bricks in the base of her pie safe—they would keep everything toasty until the shortbread finished. Usually she'd simply send supper out ahead and stay in the kitchen. Tonight—and every night hereafter—she needed to dine with the men to become better acquainted.

"Not to mention invigorating. It's a wonderful thing to have a secret, I must say." Lacey blanched. "Not that I regret telling you three. You're all becoming a part of it, making it an even better secret than I kept before. I love that! I promise!"

"Calm down, Lace." Cora tweaked one of her friend's curls. "We understood what you meant and didn't take any offense."

"Impossible to refuse the chance to learn something men believe only they can master." Naomi's laughter caught on. "Someday, if we have cause to reveal our secret, it will most likely be for no better reason than to wipe a smug, superior smile off a man's face or warn him not to underestimate us."

"Is there a better reason?" Evie kept her reply light but hoped they never ran into a real threat causing them to draw their pistols. *But if we do, at least we'll be ready.*

As Jake somehow knew he would, Volker Klumpf spotted him at the train station and affixed himself like an extra appendage. And also just as Jake knew he would, the man called Clump yakked nonstop from the time he plunked himself onto the train seat to the time it came to a rough halt in Hope Falls.

At least, Jake assumed Clump kept talking. He'd caught a nap an hour in and woken four hours later to find his new friend midsentence. *Call me crazy, but I doubt it's the same sentence I fell asleep to.* Not that he could remember either way, mind.

Twilight bruised the sky as night bullied its way forward, its bluish-purple glow silhouetting a town eerily empty. Lights shone in only two buildings, leaving the rest of Hope Falls to encroaching darkness. Jake frowned. Whatever he'd been expecting, a ghost town hadn't made the list.

He headed toward the closest light, which also happened to be the larger building. Clump's distinctive tread tailed him, but Jake noted at least two other sets of footsteps. He threw a casual glance over his shoulder. *Yep. The two others I marked on the train as heading for the Hope Falls free-for-all.* Good. One of the men matched Twyler's description. It didn't mean much—about one in three managed that—but Jake would keep an eye on him all the same. *Not a bad start for a wild-goose chase.*

With every step he took, his conviction Hope Falls harbored secrets worth uncovering grew. And grew. By the time he opened the doors to the building he now saw marked as CAFÉ, nothing could convince him he'd made the wrong decision in coming here.

Not the dozen or so men glowering at him as he stepped through the doors, muttering about do-nothings who swooped in for supper. Not the strangely familiar sign hanging on the wall: HATS OFF TO THE CHEF!

Motion at eye level drew his gaze toward an opening door in the back left corner, where women bustled through. Each carried platters of food—much to the delight of the men seated at the long tables lining the dining room.

Jake's stomach rumbled its own homage to the mouthwatering steam rising from the savory dishes. The food smelled so good, it almost kept his attention away from the women. Almost wasn't good enough, though he wished he hadn't noticed that the women filing through the door were pretty enough to make the air heavy with competition.

Beautiful women, good food, and an offer too good to be true. It spelled trouble.

The ladies made their way into the room one at a time until four formed a neat row. Finding each lovelier than the last, Jake wondered if this wasn't a terrible idea, after all. Until his gaze followed the line, snagging on a pair of golden eyes wide with recognition.

Then again...

NINE

Evie gawked. She gaped. She was very much afraid she down-right ogled the stranger standing in the midst of her new dining room, looking for all the world as though he hadn't done the exact same thing in her old café back in Charleston.

She scarcely remembered to snap her mouth closed as he lifted a sardonic eyebrow, motioned toward the sign she'd brought all the way to Hope Falls, bowed his head, and swept away his hat just as he had before.

Oh my...

"Dibs on the last one." Clump elbowed Jake in the ribs.

"Not on your life." Jake's growl sent the shorter man's eyebrows shooting toward his hairline, but Clump didn't back down. "She's not up for grabs, Clump. There are three women in that ad, and four women standing up front. She's last because she's the chef, not one of the brides-to-be." As he spoke the words aloud, they gained enough weight to send the lump in his throat tumbling back down to his stomach, where it could settle. *That has to be it. Miss Thompson doesn't belong here.*

"How would you know?" Clump's jaw stuck forward. "I like the looks of that one, and you didn't want to come along in the first place. I said dibs."

"If anyone's layin' dibs on any of the women, it's one o' us what got here first." A lean man buried in far too many layers of clothes for a logger rose from his spot. "You four hop back on the train before you think to claim what you've no right to."

Cheers and cracked knuckles encouraged them to take that kindly advice. It also made a set of tawny eyes narrow— something Jake knew instinctively boded well for no man. Or, more importantly, his stomach. And his stomach wasn't having the promise of Miss Thompson's food carried out of sight.

"If it comes to that, we were the first four to get here." A swarthier man with an incongruous top hat perched jauntily atop his balding pate rose to his feet and gestured toward his companions. Rumbles of discord couldn't swell to a roar before the fellow held up his hands and continued. "But every gentleman knows that it's the ladies"—here he paused and tipped his hat toward the women before continuing—"who make the final choice. We'd all do well to remember that, before taking it upon ourselves to make others unwelcome where we stay by invitation."

"Well said, Gent!" One of his friends pounded an empty tin mug on the wooden surface of the table, and others swiftly followed suit. In a few moments, even the most hostile loggers nodded their agreement, outdone by their own logic.

"Well said, indeed." Miss Thompson laid down the heavy platter she held on a sideboard while exchanging a knowing glance with the other women. She selected one of the fragrant pies—potpie, he suspected—and made her way over to where the first man tried to muscle them out of town. A man, Jake noted, who numbered among at least half a dozen to bear Twyler's not-so-distinguishing hallmarks.

"Mr. Dodger, did I hear you say a man shouldn't lay claim to something he has no right to?" She held the dish beneath the lucky man's nose, so close he practically salivated atop the golden mashed potatoes Jake recognized meant shepherd's pie.

"Yes, ma'am." He donned an air of wounded dignity.

"Do you know, Mr. Dodger"—Miss Thompson slowly moved the pie back and forth, pretending not to notice every man's eyes following the motion as she spoke—"I absolutely agree with you." With that, she turned and handed the pie to Clump. "Welcome to Hope Falls, sir. Mr. Dodger admits he won't attempt to claim what he has no right to, so you're more than welcome to his supper." A dimple appeared in the recess of her left cheek.

Jake swallowed his laughter at the bereft look on Dodger's face as he mourned the loss of his perfect pie and regrouped.

"Here, now. The deal says I'm supposed to get my meals!" His demand earned him glares from the other women, grins from the men as he dug himself deeper, and the undeserved attention of Miss Thompson as she turned to face him once again.

"We made another deal, Mr. Dodger. When you invaded my kitchen, I told you if you took a biscuit then, you'd forfeit your supper tonight. If you don't recall, I'm sure the man you called Bear will be happy to speak up."

Or lose his own supper. Jake's satisfaction slipped a notch when he realized Bear must be the brawny Irishman seated nearby whose nodding response sent a smile to her face.

"Aye, lassie, that I do. You're free to call me Bear, but just so you know me proper, Rory Riordan is my Christian name."

"I recall saying I wouldn't swap supper for a biscuit!" Righteous indignation colored the response. "I want my pie."

"What a man says and what a man does can be two very different things." Miss Thompson's words struck straight through Jake, almost making him miss what happened next. "Please empty your left jacket pocket, Mr. Dodger, then turn it out."

"That don't make no sense." The man's face went purple.

"The more quickly you humor Miss Thompson, the more quickly we'll serve supper." The woman dressed in the frilliest gown called out this encouragement, prompting the other men to add their demands and yells until Dodger turned out the pocket.

"No, not that one." Her tone brooked no argument. "I didn't say your overcoat, but your jacket. That's the pocket to empty."

The man gave a sigh of resignation and plunged his hand between layers of garments to hold out a blue pocket. Along with a few coins and an impressive amount of lint, a shower of crumbs scattered across the tabletop beneath his jacket—clear evidence.

"As I suspected. You tried to have your biscuit and eat supper, too." Miss Thompson shook her head. "I expect more from any man who works here—and still more from any man who intends to court any of my friends. God-fearing, the ad said. It meant men of character and honor."

Friends, she said. Jake raised an eyebrow at Clump, who didn't spare him a glance. His attention stayed divided between the pie in his hands and the woman who'd handed it to him. Jake couldn't blame the man, but something inside him growled at Clump's all-too-obvious appreciation of Miss Thompson. *Lucky for him it's only my stomach.*

"A man's got to honor his stomach when it growls." Desperation for a fine meal made idiots out of better men.

"Say what you mean, and your stomach won't argue." Jake decided to support the spunky chef's decision. Before another man could beat him to it. "A man's word is his bond."

The Gent and Bear were quick to back him up. Clump was quicker, but then again, he had the pie to protect. Dodger looked ready to lunge for it, but the man next to him grabbed his arm and held him in place, the other men at the table muttering dire warnings about holding up their own meals until it got through his thick head he'd have to abide by the cook's decision. At last he gave a grudging nod and hushed.

"We'd like to welcome you all to Hope Falls." The blond in the fanciest dress spoke on the women's behalf. "First, I'd like to make introductions. I know you're all waiting to eat—which means we have your full attention." They all smiled.

"Ain't that the truth," came one good-natured reply. A few other, more restless murmurs agreed.

"You'd have our attention if you brought nothing but your pretty selves," one slick fellow swore, his smile oozing charm.

Jake decided on the spot that one meant trouble, no matter his blond hair ruled him out of *his* manhunt.

The second in line—a regal lady whose raven hair bore a shock of white—spoke in a low, melodic voice. "Gracious of you to say so."

"Before we share our names, we want to clarify that the ad was correct—only three of us seek husbands." The frilly one spoke again. "My brother claimed Miss Thompson long ago."

Discontent surged through Jake. *I knew from the start she'd be spoken for, at the very least—a woman like that.*

"I'm Lacey Lyman," she continued. "Sister to Braden Lyman, who owns the now-defunct mine and town of Hope Falls—in name only. My brother holds portions of the land and businesses in trust for myself and my friends. The ad mentioned a sawmill. With the mine collapsed and inoperable, we seek to plumb the other treasure of these mountains. That's why you're here, gentlemen, to begin the Hope Falls Sawmill. Three of you will become husbands. It's our hope the rest will stay on as members of the company. Time will tell."

"I'm Naomi Higgins—cousin to the Lymans." The black-haired beauty kept her words short. Something a man could appreciate.

"I'm Cora Thompson." Probably the youngest of the four and third in line, the last name of the ginger-haired woman caught Jake's attention.

Thompson? Did she say Thompson? If he could, he would've perked his ears to hear the rest, on the off chance she was the—

"Fiancée to Braden Lyman, and sister to. . ."

Jake didn't know if she actually trailed off or not. He'd stopped paying attention when relief surged through him. *Another man hasn't laid claim to the feisty chef.* Then reality hit him like a felled sugar pine. *So she wrote the ad along with the other two women—and not a single hairy lip nor hatchet face to be found among them.* Sudden, unfounded rage darkened the room and folded his fists. *What was she thinking?* Well, that much seemed obvious. Nothing. None of them recognized the danger they'd placed themselves in. Four comely women alone in a town full of men they'd *advertised* for?

"Evelyn Thompson." His incomparable cook flashed her dimple to the crowd of men. "It seems silly to say I'm Cora's sister, so I suppose that's all for now. We'll be getting better acquainted in coming weeks. For now, we'll serve your supper. Each night we'll sit at the same table and a different group of you will join us." She gestured toward one of two empty tables, where Jake planted himself without further prompting, putting his back against the wall so he could face the room. "Tonight, we hope each of you will stop by and chat with us for a while."

Jake eyed the men in the room—fourteen of them, all looking pleased as punch. Except the one who'd done himself out of a fine supper by filching a biscuit, of course. None would leave willingly—even if Jake could convince the women to abandon their scheme. *Which would also mean losing my only chance at Twyler.* The evaluation he came up with became more grim by the moment as everyone around him carried on, supremely unconcerned.

Clump reverentially set his pie atop the table and lowered himself in front of it as the women spread throughout the room, distributing pies to each man. Pitchers of hot coffee sat atop each table, alongside sugar bowls.

The engaged Thompson sister placed dishes of carrots and peas on each table for the men to help themselves once they'd dug enough room into their pie tins. She also slid familiar baskets, heaped with fluffy biscuits, onto the tables for the men to pass around. Good thing she doled out four baskets per table of six, or fights would've broken out on the spot. As it was, it came to a near thing. The younger Miss Thompson—the one clearly labeled as "taken"—finished first and joined them at the table first.

Wish the others would hurry up. Jake eyed where a burly logger held up the other Miss Thompson—and her pies—with conversation. Apparently the table with the ladies would be served last, and see the women last. He understood the reasoning behind it. He understood the fairness of it.

I also understand the others will be finished and invading the table the minute the women sit down, and we won't get a moment's peace. Jake squelched a surge of irritation. By the end of the evening meal, he'd know who to look at more closely and which husband-hopefuls couldn't possibly be Twyler.

He couldn't have manufactured a better scenario to scope out the men—or stay close to the women. *Because that's the only thing I can do. I can't stop the foolishness now it's been set in motion, but I can stay here and protect them from the worst of the danger.* Jake cast a glance at Miss Evelyn Thompson, who walked toward his table at long last. *Even if they never notice.*

Aside from those first few moments when she first spotted him, Evie made special effort to ignore the stranger from Charleston. Well, he'd been a stranger in Charleston instead of a regular, but he'd visited her café, so that's the only way she could think of him for now. *I need to stop thinking about him!*

Then Dodger showed the nerve to try to oust the one man she knew she wanted to stay. Evie didn't know why she wanted the tall, rangy stranger with his easy smile to stick around. She didn't have to. All she knew was that the weasely man who'd dared snitch a biscuit and think she wouldn't notice also dared to act like he owned Hope Falls. Her eyes narrowed in preparation to set the upstart in his place—the men needed to know who ran things and respect it. From the very beginning.

Rabbitty Mr. Draxley made it painfully obvious he wouldn't

speak up on their behalf, as he hunched in a corner. The man visibly shrank. Evie noticed that, in his fear that he might be called upon, even his mustache seemed to have lost the will to twitch. A sad sight, to be sure.

The genial Gent spoke up, wisely making the point for her and earning himself an extra piece of shortbread later. Pity for Dodger he didn't take the words to heart—the slight troublemaker still sneered at the late arrivals.

Evie had thought to turn a blind eye toward Dodger's offense. Creating a confrontation on their first night, before they'd established order and the men had a taste of their incentive to make the deal work, seemed a poor idea.

I shouldn't have forgotten this is business. Meals for logging and even courting count as transactions. The others look to me as the businesswoman, and we can little afford to leave a single loophole or let anyone else take a stronger position to negotiate. We're already outnumbered.

So she caught him in his lie and gave away his pie. But not to the stranger. Evie kept very busy being unaware of his presence at the head of the newcomers. She didn't even think about him— thinking about not thinking about him didn't count—until they'd introduced themselves to the men, served supper to everyone else, and headed to their own table.

Where he sat. Directly across from the only seat left.

Cora. Evie narrowly avoided elbowing her sister in payback for the nudge Cora served her earlier. The one that effectively nudged her out of her gaping and brought her back to her senses. *Cora knew about the stranger from the diner, saw my reaction to this man's gesture. Even if she doesn't suspect he's the same one, she's still meddling. Little sisters have no right to meddle.* She took a deep breath and slid onto the bench. *That's reserved for big sisters!*

"The men wanted to wait for you," Cora said, explaining the untouched, cooling plates Evie eyed with some concern.

"Now we can pray together." The somewhat nondescript man

she'd given Dodger's pie to gave an undeniably sincere smile.

"We'd be honored to have you bless the meal, Mr. . . ." Naomi groped for a name and came up empty-handed.

"Klumpf." Without further ado, he bowed his head, signaling the others to follow suit. "Dear Lord, we thank You for everyone's safe arrival and ask Your blessing on the food before us smelling so good and the hands that made it. Amen."

"Amen," Evie chorused along with the others. She'd taken note of which men bowed their heads before picking up their forks and which didn't bother. Though she allowed some might have prayed before she reached them—particularly the last few.

"Thank you, Mr. Klumpf." Cora passed Evie the vegetables.

"Thank you, Miss Thompson, Miss Thompson, Miss Higgins, and Miss Lyman." Mr. Klumpf raised his fork, heavy with seasoned beef and mashed potatoes, to his mouth and paused in appreciation before chewing. He gave a sigh. "Thank you."

"You're more than welcome, Mr. Klumpf." *I like him.* Klumpf showed a wholesome appreciation for the Lord and good food—qualities she looked for in a potential husband. *He also,* she acknowledged, comparing him to the enigmatic man at his side, *isn't so handsome he'd look for great beauty in his bride.*

While she considered the two men occupying the bench on her half of the table, the other two introduced themselves. Evie heard and forgot them both just as quickly. She'd ask the other women to remind her later that night, when they compared their impressions of the men. To be honest, most of the names hadn't stuck with her so far. Her memory, so fine for recalling the finest details of any recipe she read even once, always failed when it came to putting names to faces. Almost always.

"Now, sir, you have us all at a disadvantage." The way Lacey eyed the stranger from Evie's café didn't sit well.

"Jake Creed." The same slow smile she remembered crept across his face, softening a jaw too strong for most faces. "I'd tip my hat, but I already took it off in honor of the chef. Miss

Thompson—the elder, that is—made it clear she expected a man to bring his manners to her table the first time we met."

So he remembers. Not overly surprising—the female owner of a restaurant was enough of a rarity to stick with most people, and she'd encountered Mr. Creed a scant week ago. *But he also remembered to take off his hat, and his decision that I'm worth it. Or,* she allowed, *that at least my cooking is worth that respect.*

Either way, that fact overshadowed being labeled "elder." Mostly.

Only one thing bothered her. *Creed.* The one thing that saved her when it came to her abysmal memory for names was that, more often than not, people somehow fit their names. Long ago, Evie came up with a theory that, since people couldn't change the names given them at birth, they grew into them. Much the way muffins or jumbles baked into the shape of the tin or mold they were poured into, people adjusted to reflect their names.

So as Evie got to know a person, she knew the name. Take Klumpf, for example. With a broader build, he boasted a low-slung walk, distinctive for its heavy tread. She'd noticed it in the few steps he took to the table and attributed it to the thick-set soles on his heavy boots. Klumpf clumped. Evie matched the man to the name and wouldn't struggle for it again.

Creed? A sense of purpose emanated from him, but the name didn't fit. *After all, aren't creeds statements of belief? The sort of thing usually handed down by those in positions of wisdom or authority?* Chills prickled down her arms as his gaze met hers with the intensity Evie convinced herself she'd misremembered. Somehow, the man before her seemed the sort to create his own system, not wait to be given what he wanted.

TEN

J ake wanted to throw all the other men in the room into a freight car and lock it. Didn't really matter when the train left, so long as the men couldn't get out and tempt him to knock their fool heads together. The lot looked ready to fight over who got to sit in the empty chair at the head of the women's table.

Evelyn Thompson tilted her head, the soft contours of her profile a taunt to any man, forcing Jake to consider the idea he may be just as much a fool as any other sap in the building. If he wasn't already sitting here, he wouldn't have waited in line. Then she smiled at something one of the other men said.

Not the dimple. Jake stopped just shy of cramming an entire biscuit into his mouth to stop a groan. *Protecting the daft woman will be next to impossible if she keeps smiling like that. I'll need more bullets than an army regiment to keep the men away. Even worse once they figure out she's the cook.*

Maybe he'd do better to just snag her and jump aboard the next train himself. Jake pushed aside a twinge of guilt over the thought of the other three but swiftly reasoned it away. The younger Miss Thompson had a fiancé to look after her, who happened to be Miss Lyman's brother and Miss Higgins's cousin. Let him worry about the other three. From where Jake sat, it seemed like they'd hatched the entire crackpot idea and swept Miss Thompson along with them into the lunacy.

He shoveled another bite of shepherd's pie into his mouth, creamy mashed potatoes blending with heartily seasoned beef in such a way as to make a man believe in miracles. *Yep.* Jake eyed the woman sitting across from him, sharing one of those miraculous dinners with her sister. She—and her cooking—was the only thing in this fool town worth saving.

Too bad he'd be up against fourteen—no, fifteen—lumberjacks the moment he tried to take her. Even Clump would fight him tooth and nail. Jake shot a glance at his traveling companion to find the man making calf eyes at the cook. *Especially Clump.*

Even worse, Miss Thompson didn't look like a woman who wanted to be rescued. Which meant he might've been wrong in judging her a woman of good sense. Jake hated being wrong under any circumstance, but for some reason, this rankled more than most. Evelyn Thompson wore the face of an angel, whipped up meals to make a dying man smile, and ran a business of her own with spunk and grit. A woman like that wasn't allowed to plant herself in the middle of the most harebrained scheme ever hatched.

He should haul her out of Hope Falls to prove it. But somewhere in this mess of men sat a murderer. *And I'm not leaving until I find him. Miss Thompson made her choice, and I've made mine. Twyler's who I came for, and Twyler's who I'll leave with. Justice before—*

"Move, mister." Men crowded behind the row of women and glowered at him, interrupting his train of thought. And more to the point, his supper. "You've sat there long enough."

"Excuse you?" Thunderclouds gathered in Miss Thompson's gaze, while the other women merely seemed amused by the show.

"Don't you worry 'bout a thang, miss." A voice near the back piped up. "We figgered out how to make it so's we all get a chance to get ta know ya better, without goin' one by one."

"I ain't movin'." Clump crossed his arms, uncrossed them to snag the last biscuit, and crossed them again. "I'm eatin'."

"You chose your seats before we arrived." Jake set down his fork. "You were served first. We're going to finish our meal."

"You four can finish at another table." A demand.

"We could," Jake agreed, "but we won't." He picked up his fork and started eating again, sending a smile to comfort the now-nervous women. Not that they deserved it. They should've known this sort of thing would happen when they paraded themselves in front of a dozen lonely men, with no rules.

"Then you won't finish at all." A man whose swift movements labeled him a high climber darted forward to grab the smallest man from the train by the collar. His fingertips barely brushed his target before he hit the floor. He sat there for a moment, stunned, before rising to his feet.

"That does it!" Miss Thompson slapped her palms on the table and stood, drawing all attention to herself. "There will be no brawling in my café. There will be no fighting over which men sit beside us, or we won't take our meals with you at all. There will be order, or giblet stew and liverwurst will be the only items on the menu. Do I make myself understood, gentlemen?"

"Oooeee, she's a spitfire, thatta-one is!" Someone with more admiration than brains whistled. "I like that in a woman."

"Seems a mite bossy to me," another muttered.

"I don't care. See how her eyes flash? She's right purty when she's riled," the first one said, defending his choice.

Magnificent describes her better, Jake decided, watching a vibrant rose flush climb her cheeks, her eyes indeed flashing.

"We thought it would be a simple matter for everyone to share a meal then have each of you men stop over and say hello for a moment." Miss Lyman stepped over the bench, the other women following suit until all four stood at the side of the room, in varying postures of disappointment, worry, and anger.

"She's the one I like," a nameless fool evaluated. "Women should look like that—girly and poufy and so forth."

"Poufy!" Miss Lyman patted her sleeves—which, Jake suddenly noticed, were kind of poufy. Apparently she didn't like the term much, though. "I'm not 'poufy.' This is fashionable!"

"I never liked the frilly, fussy sort, m'self," another judged. "But that one in the corner's got possibilities."

"We assumed you could behave as gentlemen!" Miss Higgins scolded, wagging her finger at every single one of them like an irate schoolmarm. "You should all be ashamed of yourselves!"

"That one," another scoffed, "seems kind of priggish."

"Nah. A woman should be prim and proper." The one who'd pointed to Miss Higgins shook his head and grinned. "In public."

"Oh, I see what you mean." Knowing chuckles spread through the room as every man caught the implication that a woman who was prissy in public might be a lot less controlled in private.

Thankfully, the women didn't seem to understand the joke. They were plenty overset, each one blushing and angry.

Good. Maybe they'd rethink the wisdom of their plan. But for now, the men weren't showing proper respect, and it needed to be checked before things got further out of hand. Tonight would set the tone for the rest of this farce, and Jake couldn't let the women be endangered—no matter they'd done it to themselves.

"That's enough." He stood between the women and the crowd almost before he'd decided to move. "These are ladies." Jake emphasized the title and made eye contact with a few particulars whose comments had set up his back. "If you can't treat them as such, I'll be more than happy to escort you to the train."

"Aye, and I'll be doin' the same, d'ye ken?" The giant redhead didn't stand beside Jake. He stood a few paces away so they bracketed the women. His speech wasn't as easy to understand as before—his thickened accent a sign of his ire, most likely—but not a single man could mistake his meaning.

"You don't talk that way about ladies, and you don't act that way around them." Clump plunked himself between the two of them so they formed a semi-solid barrier. "I won't let you."

"Ribald jokes offend delicate ears." His top hat marked the Gent's progress through the crowd as he took a place alongside Clump. "And aggressive postures disrupt peace. It will not do."

Before any others could detach themselves from the fold, Jake decided to put the force of their conviction to use. "Each man who wants to stay, and work, and respect these fine women, sit back down. Anyone else goes to the train. Tonight."

To a man, every single one took a seat. Some grumbled, some looked embarrassed—as though they'd only just remembered their manners—but most seemed amused and even relieved to have order established. Only Jake, Clump, the Gent, and the redhead they called Bear remained standing.

∞

"Do you think. . ." Cora's whisper drew Lacey's attention away from the men standing and, from the sounds, sitting before them.

She couldn't really tell about the ones who might be sitting down, because the four who stood in front of them did an excellent job of blocking her view. *Which isn't what we hired them for.* Lacey let loose a disgruntled little huff.

"They've entirely forgotten we're standing back here while they decide how to run our town?" Evie's whisper carried just far enough for Lacey and—Lacey assumed by the way her cousin sidled over—Naomi to hear. "Yes, I do believe that."

All four of them took a moment to look at the backs of the four men forming a human blockade between them and their beaus. Not a single one turned around or even looked over his shoulder. They just kept glowering at the others—or at least that's what Lacey imagined they did. The backs of their heads didn't really tell her all that much about their expressions, after all.

Funny how all four, different as they were, stood the same way as they took control of the unruly room. Boots planted a little wider than shoulder width apart, jaws thrust forward, arms crossed over their chests in a sort of instinctive male posture that screamed of take-charge masculinity and authority.

Of course, only two of them really managed it with any aplomb. The men on the ends—the great big Irishman and the rangy Mr. Creed whose presence obviously made such an impact on Evie—exerted the power that made the others listen. The one in the top hat, for all his fine manners, couldn't exert enough primal influence to keep a bunch of working men under control. Neither could the stockier Mr. Clump, for all his good intentions.

"They can't forget us!" Lacey whispered back. "Please tell me why are we whispering when we don't *want* to be forgotten?"

"Because those four are taking over our town, and we need to set everyone in his place," Naomi hissed back, her explanation eliciting nods from the others. "We need a plan."

"Mr. Draxley should come to our aid at a time like this." Lacey craned her neck, searching for the businessman in what she already knew to be a futile attempt. Even if she spotted him, the squirrelly fellow wouldn't take a stand for anything.

"We need to just walk up there and start listing rules." Evie's brows lowered in determination. "First rule: We invite who dines with us, and there is no changing that arrangement. I'll go up and say it while you three each make up a rule of your own, and we'll keep on going from there until we're done." With that, she headed toward the line of men still firmly planted in their way, bound to uproot them.

Lacey exchanged startled glances with the other two and scurried to keep up. In a moment, they'd slipped past the men to stand directly in front of them. If they turned around to face the four fellows, they could perform a rollicking Virginia reel. As it was, they stayed where they stood, with the women in front and the men right behind, waiting to follow.

But where are we leading them? She slid a glance at Evie, who'd burst up there with more outrage than solid planning but somehow managed to take her place last out of all of them. *And where is Evie leading us with this little maneuver?*

Evie didn't know where to go. If she went to the right of Mr. Creed, she'd most likely wind up shimmying against the wall. If she attempted to make her way to his left, she'd be squeezing past both him and Mr. Clump—which would be worse for two reasons. First, she'd brush against both men and give either a chance to halt her progress. Second, if Cora tried to go to Clump's right, she'd block her sister. Which left her the wall.

This would be so much easier if I were a slender wisp of a woman, but the element of surprise works wonders, Evie assured herself, striding behind Mr. Creed, darting right, and sliding past. Make that *almost* sliding past.

A fraction of a step, and he stopped her midslide, his shoulder lightly pinning her against the wall for the merest moment while he dipped his head and murmured something for only her to hear. "Stubborn woman." As quickly as he said it, he'd shifted away to let her through, leaving only the memory of the words and the heat where his arm pressed against hers in his wake.

She shrugged it away to stand squarely in front of him—where she could best ignore the man. Besides, her friends already stood in front of the other three, waiting for her to begin taking back control of *their* town. None of them encountered the slightest trouble slipping through. *Naturally.*

"Now that you've each made the decision to stay," she began, "it's become excruciatingly apparent we'll need to establish a few ground rules for how we'll be running Hope Falls. Anyone who can't follow these simple laws is welcome—"

The man behind her cleared his throat in a meaningful, manly sort of way, as though to punctuate her comment.

"No, make that *encouraged* to catch the next train." She gave a bright smile to the assembled men. "I'm certain you can each find it yourselves, but should the need arise, the fine gentlemen behind me are more than willing to...assist...you in departing."

"Aye, that we will." Rory Riordan's agreement burst from his massive chest with no further prompting, an angry growl showing one and all why he'd been given the name Bear.

Evie couldn't be certain if it was her words or the men who supported them that made the impact, but heads nodded around the room in agreement. Some more willing than others, but she wouldn't quibble about it for now. Results were results.

"First and foremost, there will be no fisticuffs in the café, the mercantile, or on the job." She held up one finger to signify this as the first rule. "Do I make myself clear?"

Another round of nods, peppered with yeps and all rights and even a few why nots, told Evie that she'd made her point.

"Next rule." Cora spoke up. "After tonight, each of us will invite one man to share the evening meal that day. One chair will be open at either end of the table—for two of the four men behind us. This is not negotiable and cannot be changed."

Evie held up a second finger, despite growing grumbles from the men. "If you take exception to our choices, you may leave town or, at the very least, the café for that night. Any squabbles or rudeness, shoving, or other such behavior regarding seating will result in loss of the next meal. No exceptions will be made, and no such behavior tolerated. Understood?"

"The same holds true if you refuse to work or the other men report you are not pulling your weight," Lacey added.

"Or if you lie about your fellow worker in an attempt to belittle him in our eyes or cost him his meals," Naomi finished.

Evie held up one hand, palm open, all five fingers outstretched. "Do we have an agreement thus far, before we continue, or does the crowd need thinning already?" She felt rather than saw the men behind them take a half step forward.

Mr. Creed's breath warmed the back of her neck, the toes of his boots bumping the back of her own in a silent challenge.

She refused to skitter away, instead holding her ground.

No men stood up, protested, or otherwise demonstrated a need to be removed from her café. They were learning. Quickly.

"No disrespect will be shown to these ladies." Mr. Creed started talking behind her, a rumbly reminder that not every man had learned something—and this one needed to stop trying to fight her battles for her before something awful happened.

Like I get used to someone else taking care of things. Evie swallowed a lump in her throat at the thought, horrified by her own reaction as he kept speaking in that low, gruff tone with just enough of a rasp to make it distinctive even when all the men spoke at the same time.

"Unless you offer an arm while walking alongside one or some such reason, not a one of you will lay a finger on any of them." Creed's voice lowered an octave as he issued this directive, the raw intensity sending chills down Evie's spine.

ELEVEN

Och an' ye be touchin' so much as a hair on any lassie's head I'll be seein' to it ye canna dance a fankle agin fer certain sure." Rory Riordan's booming oath all but shook the rafters. His accent became so thick, it would take Evie's butcher knife to cut through to the English beneath it, but no one doubted he'd sore regret finding out the particulars of the Irishman's threat. He sounded so irate by the very idea of any one of the men daring to sully one of the lassies, it made Evie want to smile. Rory seemed the finest of the lot to her.

She bit her lip to keep from ruining the fine impression he made on the other loggers and, after a swift glance, ignored the expressions on Cora's, Lacey's, and Naomi's faces. Cora beamed fondly at the giant redhead. Obviously blood ran thicker than good sense when it came to her sister. Lacey's eyebrows winged to meet her hairline. Naomi couldn't seem to stop blinking.

Creed, for all his faults—never mind that Evie couldn't think of any truly grievous ones at the moment as she knew she could come up with them some other time—saved them. He simply kept on spouting rules as if he owned the place. "You'll not take an insulting tone when speaking to them, nor will you discuss them with anything other than the proper respect. If any one of them takes exception to something you say, or the way you say it, an apology won't be enough."

"Not hardly," Clump added, cracking his knuckles.

"I daresay we should add that, even if the ladies don't hear something, but any of us"—the Gent gestured toward the four Guardians, as Evie dubbed them—"take exception to what you say, the same will apply. Gentlemen are gentlemen at all times."

"That should be so," Lacey agreed before she must have realized what the men maneuvered to do.

Evie stepped in immediately. "Be that as it may, no men will be made to leave Hope Falls without our agreement." She gestured to the other women and looked the Gent, then Mr. Creed squarely in the eye to show she wouldn't let them push out the others based on their own judgment. "That won't do at all."

"Of course not!" Naomi seconded her immediately.

"But ye need be sheltered when men forget themselves and act like bluidy savages, aye?" Mr. Riordan's speech started clearing up more—a reflection of the lessening tension.

"We'll decide what measures need be taken for what offense." Evie looked around the room, letting her gaze rest on a few particular faces. She remembered which men made the comments to initiate this entire fiasco. *They already think I'm bossy—and I thought the same thing earlier. Why not show them the worst, so only the ones who are truly willing to live with it will bother courting me? At least I'll make sure the others are protected.*

"Normally a lady doesn't point, but since I don't know your names, I'm afraid I'll have to resort to using some sort of gesture to indicate who I mean. Please step forward if you're included." With that, Evie raised her entire hand and dipped her fingers in the direction of the men whose boorish comments had incited this ruckus to begin with.

First, the one who called her a spitfire who looked pretty when angry. *I refuse to be swayed by the fact he called me pretty.* Nevertheless, she found it far easier to single out the man who'd called Naomi priggish, as well as the logger whose incomprehensible joke about public prissiness set off a round of hoots and hollers earlier. The fellow who'd admired Lacey's "poufy" muttonchop sleeves joined the growing group as well. But Evie could easily admit, if only to herself, she took a special satisfaction in calling forth the observer who'd dared judge her bossy before one and all. The slight fellow she'd heard others label a "high climber," who'd tried to muscle the other man out of his seat, rounded out the ranks of those she judged guilty of creating chaos.

"You want us to take these rascals outside?" Clump's voice, just another way his name matched him, came out in low, almost guttural syllables—not unpleasant, but certainly noticeable.

"No, thank you, Mr. Klumpf." Evie had to remind herself to add the *f* at the end of his name, since he'd volunteered his nickname and, worse, Mr. Creed referred to him as such. "Tonight, as the first night with the Hope Falls rules, we'll take a first-step misbehaving measure." She caught Cora's smile as she remembered her childhood and knew what was coming. "My sister will be happy to tell you the cost for your actions."

"Mother died before I left the nursery"—Cora shared more than Evie intended her to—"but I was blessed to have an older sister who helped raise me. Misbehaving brought penalties, but the first numbered among the harshest." She cast a commiserating glance toward the men about to be sentenced. "No dessert."

Poor dullards—it would've been kinder to take them to the train. Jake couldn't help but pity the fools. The hangdog looks on their faces showed they possessed enough sense to recognize what they'd lost. It seemed Miss Thompson hid something of a cruel streak, to make them stay and watch others enjoy whatever she'd baked. *I hope it's those cookies.* His mouth started to water.

"No dessert!" one of them mourned in a low moan.

"Can't we just apologize? This one time?" Another—the one who'd called Miss Thompson pretty when riled—attempted to bargain. That one would bear close watching from here on out.

"What is it? No, wait—don't tell me." The overeager big-mouth who'd commented on Miss Lyman's sense of fashion clapped a hand over his eyes. "I might not be able to bear it."

Jake noticed a satisfied smile tugging at the stern expression Miss Thompson wore. She wouldn't give an inch. *Good. If she backs down, they lose all hope of corralling this group.*

"Tell us!" One of those who'd not lost his share piped up.

"It will be waiting for you when you return," Miss Higgins promised. "Along with fresh coffee for every table."

"Return from what?" Clump asked the question a breath before every other man in the room voiced some variation of it.

"Washing your dinner dishes." Miss Lyman favored them all with a beaming smile. "If you'll step outside, you'll find two barrels by the water pump in the back. The first with soapy water, the second with rinse water. Wash your tins and forks clean and bring them into the kitchen, if you please."

"You want us to wash our dishes?" Someone not-so-bright scratched his head and squinted. "Ain't that woman's work?"

A few grumbles of agreement sounded, but no one outright agreed.

Jake figured no one wanted to lose out on dessert.

"There are twenty people here tonight, and you all believe more will arrive in the next few days. We didn't anticipate so many mouths to feed, and there are other things demanding our attention." Miss Lyman squared her shoulders. "There are men who were injured in the mine's collapse to look after, and other business matters to attend to. The ad asked you to respond in care of the postmaster, and we expected letters rather than men."

Burying his face in the palm of his hand wouldn't do any good, Jake knew, but the sudden explanation for the situation made too much sense. These gently reared women placed that ad naively believing they'd weed through letters to select a small group of prospective grooms, and found a heap of timber beasts waiting for them when they stepped off the train. The mention of men injured in the mine collapse sat heavy in his stomach—it certainly wasn't the excellent supper he'd eaten.

They're trying to save a dying town and ease Mr. Lyman's guilt over the mine collapse. Anger sparked. *No matter his guilt, no matter the men injured, Mr. Lyman belongs in this room watching over his sister, cousin, fiancée—and her sister.*

"My sister struck a bargain to feed you, and we're happy to abide by it." The younger Miss Thompson rubbed the back of her neck. "But we haven't time to take care of everything, and cook, and wash up after all of you. We can either cook or clean, so we assumed you'd all be more than happy to pitch in so you could enjoy real meals and even dessert instead of soup every day."

"I'll do it!" The one who'd first protested was all but drowned out as over a dozen men stampeded toward the door.

Jake beat them all. The way he figured it, Bear and the other three could keep an eye on any stragglers. He'd be in the best position to watch everyone file through the kitchen, past the women. He didn't plan to let a single man alone with them.

It worked. Jake stepped through the back door to the kitchen mere seconds after the women entered, their arms loaded with baskets and carafes. He set down his pie tin and started sweeping stacks of baskets out of their arms and setting them onto the massive wooden worktable dominating one wall of the kitchen. He gave a nod to each of the women then busied himself taking the small butter crocks out of each container and shaking biscuit crumbs into one catchall basket. There weren't many crumbs, but it gave him a handy pretext to stick around—and a reason for the women to let him.

Other men filed through in what became a patterned march. In the back door with a clean, wet pie tin, they stumbled to a halt. Then came the blink 'n' sniff to take in the cheery warmth of the kitchen, layered with the smells of fondly remembered dinner fading beneath a rich, buttery scent Jake couldn't quite place.

Miss Lyman's welcoming smile as she handed them a dishcloth provoked a dazed grin before the fellow dried his dish and handed it to a waiting Miss Higgins, who stacked it neatly on a shelf and tucked his cutlery into a wooden drawer in orderly rows. At that point, the younger Miss Thompson would direct him toward the swinging doors to the dining room and ask that he stand near the entrance to wait for the others.

The elder Miss Thompson laid out bowls on the surface beside him, eschewing any contact with the men as she went about preparing what must be dessert. She spooned a healthy dollop of blackberry jam into the very center of each bowl, working steadily alongside him. The woman most likely didn't realize she'd chosen the safest position, but he appreciated not having to look around to see where she'd flitted off to.

All the while, Jake tucked the crocks of butter into a nook at the side of the door, giving every man a good once-over as he walked through. A few, like those who'd stood up alongside him, or the ones who'd let their mouths talk over their good sense, he recognized. Some passed initial inspection immediately. Several loggers would be too broad in build or too tall for the average height and appearance that thus far protected Twyler. One or two fell by the wayside for red or blond hair or blue eyes.

By the time he'd looked over the entire crew, Jake counted only half a dozen men who might fit the bill. Shame he couldn't number only six on the list of men he'd have to keep an eye on when it came to the women. Jake didn't trust a single, finger-lickin', goofy-grinnin' one of them.

Riordan's sheer size made him a valuable ally, but the man showed signs of being possessive and territorial—which might make him the worst of the bunch later on. The man tried to hang around the kitchen, jeopardizing Jake's position, but without a task to perform and his bulk obviously in the way, he had to leave.

Gent put on pretentious airs, with that overly formal language and silly top hat of his. Jake suspected the man used the hat as a means to further camouflage his thinning hair—telltale smudges around Gent's scalp, ears, and fingertips tattled of careful application of shoeblack. The man must be in his forties to take such measures, Jake figured.

Even Clump presented more problems than help. His friend from back in Durango looked ready to follow Miss Evelyn Thompson around like a besotted puppy, ears perked and tongue hanging out as though begging for the smallest scrap of—

Shortbread? Jake shoved stacks of baskets up against the wall as the chef headed his way with sheets of golden cookies pulled from the pie safe. So *that* explained the rich, buttery aroma wafting through the room. Fresh coffee, which the women put on before the men began filing through, promised a solid counterpoint to the sweetness of dessert. Strong coffee usually swallowed anything else in the air, but even it had the sense to savor Evelyn Thompson's fresh-baked shortbread.

If the men still wandered through, they'd refuse to leave. Jake knew, because he didn't plan on budging from that warm, heaven-scented room until all the women exited before him. Even then, he'd be following to protect his share of that shortbread as much as to oversee the treatment of his makeshift wards.

A man had priorities, and Jake well knew he only boasted three. First, hunt down Twyler and bring the murderer to justice. Second, ensure no bystanders got hurt in the process. This is where protecting the women came in and things got complicated. Their ad gave him the chance to catch Twyler, but it left them in far more danger than that. And third, eat as much of Evelyn Thompson's cooking as possible.

Admittedly, he'd only tacked on the last one tonight, but its recent addition didn't lessen it. On the contrary, he'd given up everything for those first two priorities—it took something mighty important for him to make room for a third. And right now, those fingers of shortbread, made airy by fork holes and delectable by shining crystals of sugar dusting each piece, held his complete attention. Well, almost.

He'd never thought about it, but if someone asked, he'd probably have said such a talented chef would have graceful hands with long, delicate fingers and a light touch. Jake couldn't help noticing Miss Thompson's hands, smaller than he'd realized before, nails trim and neat as she deftly arranged four cookies around the dollop of jam in each bowl. Swift, capable hands used to hard work. They suited her spunk and grit.

The same spunk that brought her out West with a wild plan to find a husband. Suddenly the shortbread didn't smell so sweet. *The same spunk that made her leave safety, slide past me, and lay down rules, taking control of a group of scoundrels. . .*

"Who's that one for?" He spotted a bowl with double the shortbread when she spooned more jam into the center of it.

"Mr. Dodger." She didn't say another word about the matter. Miss Thompson didn't need to. After taking away the man's shepherd's pie—no matter he deserved losing it for thievery and hypocrisy—obviously the woman's soft heart worried the man would be hungry. With a little extra after some of the men had forfeited their dessert, she'd found a way to be kind and stay firm.

Yep. Jake shook his head as he followed the women back into the dining room. *That spunk's going to cause trouble.*

∞

"Braden?" Cora's voice came to him, the same clear memory that helped him through the darkness before. This time, the promise of her tugged him from the mines more easily than ever before.

He struggled from the clutches of drug-induced sleep, fighting through the murky fog beyond the blackness of the mine to crack one eye open. Light pierced his vision, but that wasn't the shock to slam his eyelid shut.

Braden took a ragged breath. And groaned. *It's not enough that*

I have to send Cora away, Lord? Must she bring her sister's cooking?
Hunger panged through him at the thought of something other
than the gruel and soup the doctor foisted on him for weeks
on end—not, Braden suspected, because he shouldn't be eating
heartier meals but because the doctor couldn't cook anything else.
So whatever lay under that tea towel almost tempted Braden to
put his plan to run her out of Hope Falls on hold.

Regret already swamped him for the way he'd treated his
fiancée earlier. *It didn't work.* Braden's jaw tightened. *She should
have listened. Should have left.* The surge of anger saved him.

"What are *you* doing here?" He barked the question, refusing
to open his eyes and witness the look on her face. Refusing to see
anything that would edge away the rage and submerge him in the
desolation of his current situation. "I don't want you."

Liar. His conscience bit into his battered pride.

"You look at me when you say that, Braden Nicholas Lyman."
Tears trembled in her voice, and most likely in her eyes, but he
wouldn't look. Cora could be a myth sprung to life, the very
opposite of the ancient Gorgon whose glance turned men to
stone. Those mismatched eyes of hers, one blue, one brown, held
the power to break through the walls any man erected.

If Braden looked, he'd crumble. And if he crumbled, she'd see
the pathetic excuse for a man he'd truly become. *Never.* "I don't
want to look at you. I don't want to see you."

A strangled gasp, all but inaudible, warned him Cora wouldn't
give in easily. "What do you want, Braden?"

*To be whole again. To be able to hold you. To know I didn't kill
my men.* He swallowed. *But I can't have any of that, so I'll settle for*
"Your leaving." *So your life won't be wasted, too.*

"You can't have that."

Her words so closely matched his thoughts, he almost smiled.
Cora always came close to knowing what was on his mind, if not
managing to guess exactly. Any smile died a swift death at the
idea of her knowing. . . "Yes, I can!" Braden shouted the words,

head turned so he wouldn't see her. "I say you don't belong here. Get out."

"No." She set the tray—which he'd forgotten until then despite the smells still lingering in the room—on some table or other. The thud told him before her footsteps rounded the bed.

"Yes." His hands fisted beneath the sheet, twisting in what he already knew to be a vain attempt to break the bonds holding him. Before Lacey left, he'd have her hire another doctor. That way, something good would come from this mockery of a visit.

"I won't go anywhere until you look me in the eye. You haven't done it once, Braden. Not yesterday afternoon, not now." Her words rushed out in a flood. "You left to come here, and I agreed to it although I missed you. I believed you dead and grieved terribly. When I heard of your survival, I rushed to your side, and by all that I have in me *I will not leave* until you look at me and I believe you don't want me anymore."

Consigning himself to the monster he'd fought since the mine's collapse, Braden opened his eyes. Then opened his mouth. . .

TWELVE

And then"—Cora gulped in a great big breath, gathering strength for another round of sobs—"he looked me straight in my eyes and ordered me to leave. To make it clear, he said out of his room, out of the building, and out of Hope Falls. He just stopped short of demanding I leave Colorado entirely!"

"Oh no." Lacey patted her shoulder. "I'll talk to him."

"No." Evie caught Lacey's eye and shook her head. "The three of you go on ahead back to the house. I'll have the doctor walk me back. . .after I have a word with your brother."

Lacey considered for a moment—probably torn between wanting to shake sense into her brother on her own and wanting to protect him from Evie's wrath—before giving a short nod. Not one of them argued as she and Naomi steered a tearful Cora toward the dusty house they'd yet to fully explore.

Evie watched their progress, all too aware of the men currently rushing back and forth between the café and mercantile, hauling supplies.

Breakfast went well—partly because they hadn't joined the men for the meal and partly because last night's rules remained fresh in everyone's memory. Today marked the first time their workforce would earn their keep.

Evie only hoped they were worth the staggering order for eggs, meat, vegetables, and cooking supplies she'd placed with Mr. Draxley. The nervous man balked when she requested dairy cows, but she'd prevailed in the end.

They simply couldn't purchase ready-made butter, cream, buttermilk, and bottled milk to be transported daily on the train, and Evie needed the milk and cream for cooking and baking. Besides, they had plenty of sheds that could be emptied to house some livestock. It would prove a sound investment.

As would the "conversation" she intended to have with Braden Lyman. Evie's eyes narrowed as she watched the other three women disappear into the house—too far away to interfere. She didn't bother to hide her ire as she practically stomped into his room. He'd made Cora cry; now he'd face the consequences.

"I said, 'Go away.'" Braden's words lashed out but missed their target. He didn't open his eyes to see who arrived, only lay beneath the covers, gritting his teeth even after he spoke. The muscles in his jaw worked hard enough to show even beneath the unfamiliar beard now covering the lower half of his face.

"What kind of man can't look a woman in the face when he tells her to leave?" Evie shooed away the doctor, who'd cracked open his study door a bit, and waited for him to close it before advancing into Braden's room. This conversation needed no other participants. Just her, Braden, and his missing conscience.

"Evie." His eyes snapped open, his scowl mirroring the fierce rage she held trapped inside. But not for long.

"You remember me, then. Good." She took two long steps to reach the foot of his bed. "Now you can start remembering yourself, your manners, your promises, your responsibilities—"

"What of your responsibilities, Evelyn Thompson?" His roar cut her off mid-recitation. Well, not quite. She'd hardly *begun*, which made his interruption both rude and poorly timed.

"I'm taking care of them." *Don't ask me how.* Evie knew Lacey hadn't discussed the sawmill scheme with her brother yet.

"You're supposed to look after Cora!" The words exploded from him with enough force to send Evie back a step. "What were you thinking, dragging her to this forsaken place with no one to protect her? I trusted you to keep her safe!"

Oh, Lord. . .he's right. We've bitten off far more than we can chew. Worst of all, now Braden tells Cora he doesn't love her. I can't raise a fallen soufflé, and I can't mend a broken heart, Jesus. . . . Please help.

Fury faded into apprehension—the far more unsettling emotion. Anger had a way of bracing one, powering a person through a storm of troubles with righteous zeal. Unease crept more quietly, filling small spaces between solid plans with doubt and worry.

I've ignored too many possibilities—that Braden might truly not want Cora as a fiancée, that men might respond in person, even Draxley's incompetence. We can't afford not to consider such things or overlook the obvious signals.

Still, some things held true no matter the circumstance. "No." Evie drew a deep breath. "We relied on each other to look after Cora. You trusted me to bring her to you safe and sound; I trusted you to keep her that way once we arrived. I kept my part of the deal, Braden Lyman, and you know it. You know it the same way you know you've broken both your unspoken promise to me and your spoken words to my sister. Your fiancée."

"Not my fiancée!" His head thrashed side to side in vehement denial. "Not mine anymore. You have to take Cora home, Evie."

And suddenly she knew. Evie looked at Braden Lyman's face, eyes wild with a sort of desperation she'd never seen, and felt it as sure as she'd ever known anything. Plain and simple—"You still love her." Her words made him freeze, almost as though the very act of drawing a breath would confirm them.

"I don't want her." When he finally spoke, Evie watched closely, carefully. . .and noticed what she'd overlooked before.

God, grant him the strength to lean on You in his suffering. I can't imagine what it's like to be so trapped. And I have to confront him with the truth, for Cora's sake.

"Here. You don't want her"—Evie took one step with each word, stopping just beside him, where his head rested on the pillow, watching her finish the sentence properly—"here."

His breath hissed in as though she'd hit him. "No."

"Yes." Evie made a broad gesture to include the expanse of the bed. "And this is the reason. I didn't notice at first, but now that it occurs to me, I can't believe I missed it. I'm so sorry, Braden. I can't imagine what it's like to be paralyzed, but Cora will learn of it whether you send her away or not."

"I'm not paralyzed."

He'd been silent so long and muttered the words so low, Evie almost asked him to repeat them. Then decided that would be foolish. "You used to use your arms and hands when you spoke, Braden. Now, no movement at all."

"Straps."

"I beg your pardon?" Evie refused to blush, but the direction of the conversation headed toward the indiscreet.

"With both legs broken, the doctor decided casts weren't enough, so he strapped them down." Braden's words came out curt, as if forced from his chest. He wouldn't meet her gaze. "I dislocated my shoulder, though that went back in place well."

"But. . ." No matter she regretted beginning this conversation, Evie couldn't let the matter drop. "Your arms as well?"

The doctor appeared in the doorway. "So he won't fall while he sleeps and do further damage. There's some concern over the position of his spine. The arm bands are a necessary measure, as otherwise Mr. Lyman always removes the lower constraints."

"He's not a child." Evie rounded on the man. "After being trapped in a cave-in, the last thing anyone needs is to feel trapped by anything else! It's simple common sense."

"Initially we tried rails around the bed, but that was the reason he gave for tearing them off," the doctor spluttered.

"I won't live in a lidless coffin." Braden all but snarled at the man, winning Evie's admiration. *She* would have snarled.

"Surely now his shoulder's healed sufficiently to remove any…" Evie searched for a delicate way to phrase the request and came up with a serviceable "*Upper* restraints, at least?"

"Mr. Lyman has proven he will undo the others, once able. I can't jeopardize the welfare of my patient to suit his whims."

"With all the *visitors* Mr. Lyman can *expect* now"—Evie emphasized the words so he'd know good and well she included Cora in those visitors—"I'm sure he'll find the strength to leave well enough alone in exchange for the use of his arms."

They locked gazes in a silent battle for what seemed like hours, but most likely lasted mere seconds.

Finally, Braden gave a short nod—tacit agreement to leave the lower restraints alone. Evie bore no illusions he'd agreed to their continued presence in Hope Falls, nor did she envy Lacey. His sister was welcome to the task of explaining the grand plan they'd already put in motion—without Braden's permission.

"Cora need never know," was the only promise she made as she left. Evie knew Braden would continue to act beastly in an attempt to run Cora out of town…for her own good. She also knew her own stubborn sister better than to believe he'd succeed. Either way, now that she knew Braden still loved her sister, she'd leave what lay between them just that way. Between them.

If I convince Cora to go home, she'll always pine for the Braden she lost and wonder if she could have nursed him back. If I drag her to Charleston, she'll hate me and run back to Hope Falls the moment my back is turned. Either way, I'd be going back on my promise to Lacey and Naomi, who are relying on me.

The weight of it all pressed into a lump at the back of her throat. *Braden Lyman isn't the only one trapped in Hope Falls.*

∞

Jake caught her coming out of the doctor's office—which took a fair bit of planning, absolute use of the authority he'd stepped into the night before, and above all, a good sense of timing.

He'd kept an eye on all four of the women the entire morning, but especially Miss Thompson. The sassy chef flaunted an independent streak that showed why she shouldn't be left alone.

After a breakfast of sweet buns and bacon to leave any man too contented and agreeable for his own good, the women began making requests. Jake admired their strategy. He even admired the requests. Adding a large storeroom onto the café seemed the order of the day—requiring the men to knock out a door in the only wall not already graced by one to the dining room or outdoors or taken up by the stoves. It also meant utilizing supplies from the mercantile and making the men work together in town, where the women could see if anyone wandered off or caused trouble.

From where Jake stood, it looked like a brilliant piece of planning. Not only did it ensure the women could keep the town stocked and the men fed; it made sure they knew it. A man liked knowing his stomach rated as a high priority.

But as soon as they'd cleaned up after breakfast, the women headed to the doctor's office. Where three waited outside. Only the younger Miss Thompson—the engaged one—went in with a tray of breakfast.

Jake measured off the dimensions of the storeroom, outside. He kept tabs on the situation with the ladies, letting the Gent measure and direct the cutting of the doorway, while Bear directed men in the mercantile, digging out tools, nails, lumber, rope, and other sundries. Clump kept busy emptying the kitchen of anything that might get in the way.

Which meant Jake—and maybe a few of the more shrewd suitors—was the only one to see the fiancée fly out of the doctor's to cry all over the other women in a fine show of feminine hysterics. He got the others working on minor details when he caught some showing too much interest in the spectacle a few buildings over. Jake didn't want them noticing only three women walked back to the house they shared. One stayed behind.

Alone.

Foolish, headstrong woman. Jake bit his tongue and mentally reeled in more colorful concerns for what could happen if one of the rougher fellows caught Miss Thompson wandering on her own. Anyone with the ability to add one to one and come up with two could see the younger sister's distress ruffled the mother hen's feathers. She'd marched right in to cluck at the offender, and she'd find herself in a stew if no one looked after her.

Jake proposed a door on the outer wall of the storeroom, facing the train station, for easier transport. A blithe announcement that he'd get the women's agreement and make sure nothing else needed to be cleared from the path gave him the pretext to hover close to the doctor's office. He managed to walk around the corner just in time to surprise Miss Evelyn Thompson as she exited the doctor's. Alone again, with not even the sense to have the doctor escort her to the house where she'd join the other women.

"Miss Thompson." He offered her his arm before she could recover from the way his sudden appearance startled her. As he expected, she automatically accepted it, slipping her hand into the crook of his elbow almost before registering the action. "Allow me to escort you to the house? I'd hoped for a word."

"Presumptuous?" She muttered the riposte on a breath so low Jake knew she didn't intend for him to hear her.

Laughter shook him as he contained his mirth to paltry chuckles. If he let loose, the other men would head over. "Not the word I had in mind, Miss Thompson." Jake grinned anew over her blush when she realized she'd been caught.

"I should not have said that," she admitted, a rueful smile tilting her lips. For once, her dimple didn't peek out.

"But you don't apologize for thinking it." Jake waited for her to deny it or tack on a hasty addition to her apology.

"Absolutely not. My thoughts are my own, and I won't apologize for their existence." Her dimple sprang into view as she flouted his expectations. "I only regret their escape."

"You surprise me, Miss Thompson." Already shortening his stride to match hers, Jake slowed his pace still more.

"In what way, Mr. Creed?" Her use of the name struck him. After her refreshing honesty, it rang more false than before.

"Few show such candor." Jake debated his next move, reluctant to prove her right, then added, "Or such foolishness."

"Your very comment proves I'm not foolish at all to call you presumptuous." Her hand, which had nestled so agreeably in the crook of his arm, became stiff and somehow hostile. "Merely observant. While I'm grateful, to an extent, for your efforts on our behalf, you take too much upon yourself, Mr. Creed."

"Miss Lyman told us last night the four of you hadn't planned on dealing with prospective grooms showing up in person. The four of you as good as said you can't handle the situation." Jake kept his tone even. "The men took things too far, and it would have gotten worse if someone hadn't stepped in."

"Presumptuous! We didn't say we couldn't handle it!" She gave a little huff. "Nor did we ask you to interfere, as I mentioned before. Reminding the others to behave as gentlemen is something we all appreciate. Taking it upon yourself to create rules for our town is most certainly not!"

"Yep." His agreement threw her off balance for a scant second before he added his final assessment, "Foolish, all right."

She started seething again, her fingers curling into his sleeve like a harmless creature trying to develop claws. Which, in Jake's estimation, didn't land too far from the truth.

"Words don't hold up without action behind them. Same with rules, Miss Thompson. They can't make a difference if no one enforces them. What does it matter who makes the rules, if they're good ones and will be enforced for your safety and the good of the town? I'm going to be blunt here." He stopped, pivoting to face her and tightening his arm against his side so she'd stay put and hear him out. "You four can spout laws until you're blue in the face, but if all you have is cooking to keep a crowd in line, you'll run into trouble sooner or later. Men want things other than food, and out here, there's places with five men to every woman. Why do you think they're all here?"

He paused to let that sink in, to let it register that she stood, alone, with a man she didn't know. "Placing that ad and coming here was foolish. Not admitting you need help now you're all here is foolish. And yes, Miss Thompson, I'm presumptuous enough to warn you about it." *So you can stop the foolishness.*

"It seems, Mr. Creed, that we've reached an impasse." Evie drew herself up to her full, if unimpressive, height. "You want me to stop making my own decisions; I want you to start apologizing."

Never mind the fact I'm very much afraid your assessment is dead to rights. She couldn't really tell if it was guilt over not agreeing with his good sense about the ad and their position or worry over the safety of her friends, but a sharp pain jabbed her side, a sort of stitch beneath her ribs.

"You misunderstood, Miss Thompson. It's not that I want you to stop making decisions." He started walking again, covering the last few steps to the house before leaving her with his final, parting shot. "I want you to start making better ones."

THIRTEEN

T here's nothing worse than letting a man get the last word,"
Cora fumed, prying open another packing crate as the four women
stood in the midst of the parlor. "Nothing at all."

"I couldn't agree more." Evie nudged a traveling case toward
the pile they'd designated for "upstairs." "First, there's the matter
they think they've bested you." *Insufferable, arrogant dictator, he is.
Handing out orders right and left.*

"And once you know precisely how you want to respond, to
put him in his place, it's too late." Naomi scooted a box toward the
narrow door leading to the woefully inadequate kitchen, where
two large stewpots already simmered away for dinner.

"Couldn't you both simply. . .oh, I don't know"—Lacey's voice
came out a bit muffled, what with her head half buried in a
steamer trunk clearly belonging in the "upstairs" section—"simply
pretend not to have heard the last little bit?" She emerged with
a triumphant sound, waving an airy scarf at them. "Or let them
know you ignored it, as beneath your attention?"

"No." Evie and Cora answered as one, with emphasis.

"Oh." Lacey blinked. "I, for one, ignore most of what Braden
says to me. I find it makes life much more pleasant."

"Well, Mr. Creed isn't the sort of man a woman can ignore," Naomi offered. "There's a certain quality about him...."

"Arrogance." Evie didn't like the look in Naomi's eye. "The quality Mr. Creed possesses is arrogance. Can you imagine the nerve, telling us all we need to be making better decisions?"

"I don't know, sis. He only said something to you." Cora's amusement didn't douse the anger still burning beneath it, fueling her abrupt movements and keeping her from more tears.

Some things, an older sister knew all too well. Mostly because Evie learned, after years of failure, there were some things she couldn't fix. There were times when words offered little comfort, and logic could only make things worse. Time, prayer, and love were the only way to wear away deep hurt.

But laughter smoothed away the ragged edges. *If nothing else, I'll forgive Creed's interference because it gives Cora something to think about, a way to tease, a reason to smile.* Evie fought her own smile at a sudden, ironic realization. *Maybe that's the first of my "better decisions"—to not resent them. Actions over words...*

"I'm the first one he found the opportunity to speak with," Evie shot back. "Seems as though he could've made the same comments to any one of us, from where I'm sitting. I took the insult personally, but I'm also offended on your behalves!"

"My behalf feels wholly fine." Cora thumped a box onto the ground as though to squash her own terrible pun as they groaned.

"Oh, that wins as worst of the trip." Naomi shook her head. "For what it's worth, although I dislike Mr. Creed's high-handed manner, I'll admit to a nagging sense there's some truth behind his observations. We can't handle this on our own, ladies."

"That's why we advertised for husbands!" Lacey stretched the scarf between her hands. "We knew we'd need help with the entire sawmill venture, or it would fail before it began."

"But now we need help with hiring your husbands. I know I'm not really in any more of a position to say anything than your Mr. Creed, Evie, but—" Cora's comment ran into a delay.

"He isn't mine!" Evie protested immediately. "Don't try to pawn him off on me, as though I should be the one to deal with the one man so headstrong he tries to take over an entire town the very night he arrives! I don't claim Mr. Creed."

"Not yet," Naomi teased. "But you have to admit, he knows how to surprise you. I knew the moment he pointed to your sign and swept the hat from his head that we were looking at the stranger who'd made such an impression on you in Charleston."

"That's another thing!" Evie tried to push a crate of books into the corner and failed. It was one of many—not one of them had been willing to part with a single work of literature. "How on earth did he show up here? No one knew of our plans!" *Not that he would have followed me, in any case.* She'd considered the glorious, far-fetched notion and discarded it the moment she'd seen him the night before. A man like that could take his pick of women. *And he wouldn't pick a foolish one.*

"You won't claim Mr. Creed." Lacey helped her wrestle the books out of the doorway, where they'd hitched on an uneven floorboard. "Perhaps he's come all the way here to claim you."

Evie's heart thumped in her chest, a result of moving too many heavy boxes, to be sure. *Only ninnies go giddy at the idea of opinionated men striding into town to sweep them off their feet.* Unfortunately, the stern reprimand did nothing to quell her inner ninny, who chose now to make her presence felt.

"Like Evie said, he wouldn't know who placed the ad, which puts paid to the notion he followed her to Hope Falls. Honestly, so many men trickled through her café it would be a wonder if she never ran into any." Cora walked over, frowning.

"Even if he didn't know Evie placed the ad," Lacey insisted, "anyone could tell he was pleased to see her here!"

"That's true." Naomi joined them, looking at the stacks of crates holding their assorted volumes with something akin to awe. "I don't remember bringing quite this many books."

"When she had to give up the house after Papa's death, Evie

refused to give up any of his books, even if they crowded our rooms." Cora shrugged. "So there will be more than you brought."

"Naomi refused to leave behind a single volume from Lyman Place," Lacey commiserated. "She packed up every tome from the study to bring out here. Added to your books, and the novels we purchased to read on the journey, we could start a library."

"Precisely!" Naomi's exclamation made them all jump. "Ladies, these crates contain the Hope Falls Library! A bit of knowledge, education, and culture to civilize the wild."

"That's a wonderful idea." Evie caught on to her friend's enthusiasm. "We'll simply choose a building and have the men move the books there. After things settle and we've time, we can go about unpacking and organizing the library."

"Good—at least that's one section of crates that won't be underfoot!" Lacey peered around. "We've boxes and luggage all through the parlor and study down here, creeping into the kitchen, and nothing but our carpetbags in the bedrooms. Have you three sorted out what you'll need in your rooms, and what you'll put in the third as storage until. . .needed?"

Even Lacey, the originator of the entire Hope Falls scheme, faltered at putting the end result into words. She and Naomi would share one bedroom, Evie and Cora the other one that was outfitted with a bed. The third, they'd designated as storage for all the household goods they'd brought to set up their homes—once they each chose a husband and married him.

"Now that we're here, and the men are already here, it's going to be much faster than we planned." Naomi's voice lacked the enthusiasm from when she talked about the library.

Which just goes to show there's something very wrong—or very foolish—about all of this. Evie sighed. *We can make the best decisions possible from here on out—not because Mr. Creed wants us to, but because it's what's best, and the Lord bids us to seek out wisdom.* She sighed again. *No matter the source.*

"Plans change. So do people." Cora snatched a hatbox from

one pile and shifted it to another. "We can adjust accordingly."

"We agreed no one would rush into any wedding," Lacey reminded her cousin, "and that much stays the same. If he's the right man, he'll wait until you're certain of it, too."

"I think we should wait until we've all chosen our grooms and then share one big wedding." Evie seized the opportunity to propose the idea. "With so many men here, it's not safe for us to leave this house one by one, and it sends the message we aren't going to be in a hurry." *By then, hopefully, Cora will have gotten through to Braden, and they'll join us!*

"I like that idea!" Naomi's agreement came a breath before Lacey's but several beats before Cora's slow nod. "But I'd like to add something on to it—we should have the approval of at least two of the others in whomever we choose."

"Absolutely." Cora supported the suggestion almost before Naomi finished giving it. "That's the best decision yet."

"We haven't made it a decision!" Lacey's brows came together. "While your opinions matter to me, I didn't escape the strictures of society and travel all the way out here to require anyone else's *approval* or *permission* regarding my choices."

"But that's exactly what you've done, Lace. Your husband will have more of that sort of power than society ever did. Since we know you better than any of these men possibly could in a couple months and have only your best interests at heart, why not see it as a precaution against choosing some sort of tyrant?" After five years as her companion, Naomi knew how to best soothe Lacey's nerves and coax her into listening.

"What if only one of you will agree to the man I choose?" Lacey saw them exchange amused glances. "It's best to prepare for such contingencies! Look what happens when we don't think ahead." She peered out the window, where she could see their workers already fashioning walls for the storeroom.

"Don't borrow more trouble than we've already found, Lace. If he's the right one, you'll fight to keep him until you win."

Everyone knew Cora didn't just refer to Lacey's future love. "If he's the wrong one, we won't regret it when he catches a train."

"So long," Evie grumbled as she caught sight of a familiar lean figure heading toward a cluster of three men she couldn't make out, "as you don't let him have the last word!"

"Then there's nothing more to say." Jake uncrossed his arms—the better to reach his pistol, should the need arise. "I'm sure you three can catch the train before it pulls out if you hurry." He judged it worth the odds to send them out of Hope Falls. Only one of the men before him fit the description of Twyler, and that just happened to be the one who talked too much.

"I've plenty more to say." Williams proved him right. Shorter than his companions, with thinning brown hair and a bristling demeanor, he had the look of a man used to giving orders. His speech marked him as intelligent and possibly educated, but despite that and the coloring, Williams didn't match up with the depiction of a nondescript man who faded into the background and vanished into the night. If this was Twyler, the man mastered disguise to a degree Jake hadn't prepared for.

"We don't need words here." *Unless they're confessions.* Jake scrutinized Williams more closely, trying to discomfit the stranger. When shows of confidence faded, the real man stood for evaluation. "If you won't pitch in like everyone else, the rules are you get back on the train and ride on."

"I want to talk to the ladies who wrote the ad. It was an open invitation, and I don't see how you have any authority to retract it." Williams's confidence might not be a facade, or if it was, he'd built it high and strong. "Where are they?"

"Have you found troubles this fine morning, Mr. Creed?" The brogue sounded pleasant enough, but the newcomers' expressions showed that Rory "Bear" Riordan didn't look very welcoming.

"These three men came in on the train. I offered to show them to the bunkhouse before they started working, but they refused." Jake didn't bother to glance behind him. He knew when Bear reached his side. "At that point, I suggested the train."

"Work or leave—that's the law of the ladies."

"Where are the ladies?" Williams repeated, this time directing the question to Bear, whose size apparently didn't intimidate the smaller man enough for him to shut his mouth.

" 'Tis no' your concern." Bear's ham-sized hands folded into fists. "As you won't be working to win your keep nor their hands, you won't be needin' to make their acquaintance."

"I work hard when there's something to work for." Williams took an ill-considered step forward. "But I don't work for nothing. How do we know this entire scheme isn't a hoax?"

"Do you think over a dozen men would work for nothing?" Jake kept his tone amused but his hand near his holster. This Williams character had enough brains to make him suspicious and enough pride to make him dangerous—a volatile combination. *The sort of man who might hold a grudge or seek revenge.*

The irony of that judgment pinched at the sides of his jaw, where Jake clenched his teeth against finding himself guilty of the same. Yes, he hunted a man he'd never met, but this was no petty offense. A thin line divided justice and vengeance, and it all depended on which side the murder fell. Jake knew where he stood. Question was, where did Williams?

His assessment cost him the man's response, but Bear's reaction told Jake all he needed to know. Either he'd overestimated Williams's intelligence or Twyler would go to any length to keep his identity hidden. Even anger a giant.

Bushy brows slammed together, forming a furious red curtain. "Just turn those boots an' meet up wi' the train."

By that point, most of the other men noticed the disturbance and circled around. Speculative murmurs and hostile glares made no impact on three strangers standing their ground.

"What'd they do to rile Bear?" someone wanted to know.

"We asked where the women are." One of taller men spoke up before Williams, suddenly keen to keep the peace.

"I asked what kind of gargoyles these women are, to have to hide away when men come calling." Williams's challenge both explained Bear's ire and incited the same in several others.

"Don't you talk about our women that way!" someone yelled.

"Now, Bob," another talked over him. "If they're so smart, let them hop back on that there train and ride the rails more."

Kane. Jake dredged the name from his memory. The man lobbying for the loggers to go along with their assumptions so others left town wasn't above manipulating circumstances to rid himself of competition. He also happened to be one of the half dozen men sporting brown hair and brown eyes.

"It's never smart to insult a lady," Gent intervened, his ever-present top hat skewed to the left. "If a man can't think of a kind word, he speaks none." He cast a sweeping, meaningful glance at what Jake began to think of as the "regulars." "No matter how stooped, old, spotted, or hideous the woman in question, a gentleman never remarks upon it."

"Hush, Gent." Dodger caught on quickest. "Such talk would hurt their delicate feelings, and you know it."

"We've seen enough tears this morning," Jake added, beginning to enjoy the new strategy to route the interlopers. "Seems the doctor couldn't improve their situation."

"Situation?" Williams, whose belligerence wavered in the face of rising doubts, asked with something akin to dread.

"Yep, Craig here was joking about the women being gargoyles," one of the others explained, glancing back toward the train. "That was before all this talk. What situation?"

"Deafness," rang Miss Thompson's too-sweet reply, "so that twenty men somehow manage not to hear four women approach them."

Jake's shoulders tensed, but he wouldn't turn his back on Williams, whose gaze turned right-down predatory as he realized the trick they'd played. . .and why.

"Finding yourself surrounded by men determined to frighten off any other would-be grooms could count as a situation." A second feminine voice carried above a cacophony of groans.

"We been caught right an' proper," someone confessed.

"There's nothing proper about what you men just did." He couldn't be sure without looking, but Jake pegged that as Miss Higgins. "You ought to be ashamed of pulling such a stunt."

"They ought to be ashamed for making these men think we're gargoyles!" Indignation dripped from Miss Lyman's exclamation—the same indignation from when she'd defended her poufy sleeves.

"They should be ashamed for making light of those in need of medical care." The quiet outrage had to belong to the younger Miss Thompson, who'd been distressed after visiting a patient in the doctor's care. Her tears gave way to dignity now, at least.

"But most of all"—the cook's voice gathered strength for the final feminine invective—"they should be ashamed of their own hypocrisy!"

FOURTEEN

Bull's-eye. Evie bit back a triumphant grin when Creed's shoulders, already tense, went completely rigid. *Good to see he knows that was aimed at him, judging other people's decisions. Humph. At least he can't argue with my evaluation of him in return! A more presumptuous man never drew breath before me.*

But he still didn't face her. He and Mr. Riordan kept their backs turned while every other man in Hope Falls—minus Mr. Draxley, whom they'd left placing orders with someone on the train, and, of course, occupants of the doctor's or post offices— changed positions the moment she spoke. That they did, indeed, feel shame didn't seem enough of a reason to explain their odd behavior. Evie pondered it as she made a path through the other men, her sister and friends following.

She reached the new arrivals with an apologetic smile, as any woman would. Or at least, she came close to reaching them. Evie found her way blocked by none other than the maddening Mr. Creed, who somehow collaborated with Mr. Riordan to make things difficult. The two guardians didn't block her entirely, merely angled their bodies so the group had to form a large circle—the new men on one side, the women on the other, with the guardians slightly inward so they didn't form simple rows.

They're being protective. The realization drained away some of her indignation. *Only Creed and Riordan refused to turn their backs on the unknown. While every other man sought to placate us, they made sure we stayed safe.*

Gratitude on behalf of her sister, Lacey, and Naomi won out over the obvious logical conclusion that strangers wouldn't get to them before the others intervened.

Because now, if these two men hadn't interposed themselves, Evie and her friends would stand toe-to-toe with the newcomers, with the men who'd already accepted their terms too far behind to step in. She'd fully planned to storm up here, have the women introduce themselves, and establish the town rules fully under their own power. *Pride makes poor decisions. . . .*

"We are the women of the ad," she began, sliding a glance at the others and raising her right hand to rub her forehead. They'd established a few signals last night before turning in—a glance before rubbing one's forehead meant "wait and listen," to be used in case someone planned something unexpected.

"In usual circumstance, we'd introduce ourselves and welcome you to Hope Falls," she continued only after seeing faint nods of understanding. "But these circumstances are most unusual, and so we'll be doing things a bit differently."

"I'm Craig Williams." The man she pegged as the leader of the three stepped forward in what she instinctively recognized as a territorial move. When he came forward, Mr. Williams all but closed his men from the circle, upsetting the balance.

He wants to see if Mr. Creed and Mr. Riordan will step back, giving up ground to let his men in. It's a test!

Women played the same sort of game with seating arrangements. For the first time, Evie wondered what other subtle rules dictated interactions among men—and if all of them were so complex and nuanced as polite feminine rituals.

"Step back, Williams," Creed growled, reclaiming his territory and ending Evie's nonsensical notions. Men were blunt.

"What if I don't?" The shorter, more muscular man didn't seem concerned. "Seems I traveled here to be near the ladies."

"If you don't, the pleasantries end here." Evie made a show of turning toward her cohorts. "We'll return to the house and let these gentlemen return you to the train, where you'll be more comfortable until you find a town more to your liking."

Cheers sounded behind them, reminding Evie of the more than a dozen ornery men who hung on every word. She'd all but finished the job of running the newcomers out of town for them.

A great, bellowing laugh sounded over the cheers as Mr. Williams threw back his head in a show of mirth Evie suspected was more show than mirth. But respect shone in his eyes when he looked at her and took a step back—a smaller one than he'd taken forward but a concession nevertheless. "Very well, ma'am."

"What made you change your mind, Mr. Williams?" Naomi's voice, usually throaty and full, sharpened with suspicion.

"Things might not be usual here in Hope Falls," he explained, "but at least they're interesting. I don't plan on leaving until I learn more about it—and about the beautiful women who rule it." Somehow he managed to include all four of them in an admiring glance while his men nodded their agreement.

Grumbles and mutters sounded from behind them as the men realized they'd been thwarted—newcomers would be welcome. Evie wondered how many of them realized they'd all forfeited dessert that night—a boon, considering she'd be cooking from the house kitchen, which simply wasn't equipped for mass baking anyway.

"In that case, allow me to introduce"—Evie raised a brow in silent acknowledgment as she named their champions—"Mr. Creed and Mr. Riordan. Should you have any questions, they're the ones to ask. Direct any requests regarding supplies to them, and they'll bring the matter to our attention if need be. They'll also instruct you in town rules. And, should you decide not to follow those rules, they'll escort you from Hope Falls."

"With our assistance," the Gent swiftly seconded, with rousing support from the remaining men. No one wanted to be left out of the opportunity to toss someone else out of town.

A grudging nod from Williams preceded two more congenial ones from the pair behind him, who seemed almost like a set of matched horses. Perhaps they worked as a team? Less pleasant were the measuring looks given Mr. Riordan and Mr. Creed.

She refused to look at Mr. Creed, refused to let him think she'd admitted defeat in accepting his help, refused to seek any support for her decisions from the man who'd belittled them. His opinions on what was best for the other women mattered. His opinion of her did not. *I won't let it.*

"We've set things up as follows." Lacey took over, as she should. The town belonged to all of them, and every man who wandered through needed to esteem them equally. "We'll provide room, board, meals, and the opportunity to further our acquaintance until we've chosen our husbands."

A glower from Mr. Creed silenced a swell of hopeful murmurs about lunch when Lacey mentioned meals, making Evie glad she'd baked ten pans of corn pone that morning while the men ate, then set two massive pots of Brunswick stew to simmer at the house. Better still, she'd had the foresight to lock the pie safe so none of the men might try to steal a snack before dinner.

Once things quieted down, Naomi added the final stroke. "In return, we ask you to help lay the groundwork for the Hope Falls Sawmill Company. Every other man knows these conditions and has agreed to them. The question is. . .will you?"

The pair behind Williams glanced at each other, shrugged, and each gave a single nod, but Williams took longer to make his decision. His gaze ran over everything in town and evaluated the trees beyond before taking stock of the people around him. The men didn't seem to concern him much. The women did.

"Four women standing here, so why do only three of you want

husbands?" It seemed he'd noticed a lack of wedding bands during his scrutiny. "And which woman isn't available?"

"One of us"—Cora lifted her chin as she answered—"already has a fiancé and thus isn't looking for a husband. Which one of us that happens to be shouldn't make a difference to you."

"It matters very much, ma'am—you'll forgive me for not using proper address, as we've yet to be introduced. No man wants to set about courting a woman when she's taken." Craig Williams shook his head. "And some men know right away which women they're willing to court and which they won't be." His eyes ran down the line of them once again. "I'm one of those kinds of men who knows his own mind and doesn't change it."

Incredible! He's saying that if the woman he most likes the looks of isn't available, he's not interested in any of the other three. Evie stewed, refusing to name Cora. *Doesn't he realize it's not for him to waltz in and choose but for us to wade through and select which man we'll accept? He doesn't deserve Naomi or Lacey!*

"In that case, it's best you move along." Clump stomped forward, his irate appearance causing her to wonder where he'd been before. "Mr. Draxley's still talking with the conductor, so the train's still here. I know 'cause I went to see about getting you some milk, Miss Thompson. I remembered what you said last night about making shortbread instead of somethin' else on account of having no milk. Hoped they might be carrying some, but they didn't have any on board today. Sorry 'bout that."

"Thank you for your thoughtfulness, Mr. Klumpf." Evie favored him with a smile, hoping to ease his disappointment. "And for mentioning Mr. Williams has time to catch the train."

"Oh no." A wolfish smile gleamed her way. "See, *Miss Thompson,* Mr. Klumpf over there wouldn't be trying to bring you any gifts if you already had a fiancé."

"Miss Thompson does have a fiancé!" Dodger—Evie could already tell it was Dodger—shouted that bit of information. No one added a single word of clarification either.

Evie couldn't stop a smile over his clever phrasing—a smile that made Mr. Williams's brow furrow as he began to rethink.

"My brother proposed before we journeyed out here." Lacey jumped in, making it obvious that, for all her words about independence, her friend wasn't above meddling. "Braden Lyman? He's the principal investor in the mill, you see."

"I see. Your brother, Miss Thompson's fiancé, and. . ." Williams turned a questioning eye to Naomi, then Cora.

"Miss Higgins, cousin to the Lymans." She offered no other explanation or attempt at conversation. Then again, Naomi didn't approve of falsehoods in any form. Leaving out the relationship between Evie and Cora in an attempt to fool a man into thinking the wrong sister was engaged counted as one. Somehow. . .

"And you're related to all this in what way?" Now less than amused, Mr. Williams's tone took on a demanding tinge as he spoke to Cora. He suspected something, and Evie almost respected him for possessing enough intelligence to discern that much.

"I'm Miss Thompson's sister." Cora's eyes narrowed.

"Yes, that makes all of us related in some way," Evie agreed. "But that's as it should be. Family supports each other and stays together. No matter where it leads."

❧

Her words struck him with the force of a falling redwood. Jake closed his eyes to lash down the memories jarred loose, but one tumbled free in spite of his efforts:

"Why don't you come with me this time?" Edward invited, flipping his favorite good-luck talisman in the air. "It's a good-sized profit we stand to make if this contract goes through, but the company owner's skittish. Someone double-crossed him on the last deal, so he'll need persuading."

"You're the persuasive one," Jake joked. Eyes on the copper piece as it spun upward, he waited to snatch it out of the air just before it

hit Edward's waiting palm. "That's why you stick with the business contacts, and I handle operations."

"So why is it you're the one who's made a fortune of his own in side investments?" Ed watched as Jake removed the matching piece from his own pocket and began juggling the two small squares until they blurred into a single streak. He reached forward, but not to make a grab and see which one he wound up catching, as they'd done since their school days. No, this time Ed jostled one of Jake's hand's, neatly seizing both pieces and examining them before tossing one back.

"You cheated!" Jake plucked it from the air and checked the side not embossed with a crown and fleur-de-lis. Sure enough, nothing but a surface worn smooth from centuries of use stared up at him. "You never cheat. Hand over the lucky one as forfeit."

"Sometimes you try a new trick to get what you want." Edward shrugged and tucked the lucky coin weight, its blank side marred by the gash of an axe blade, into his pocket. "You won't come with me, and I've got a feeling I'll need all the luck I can get on this trip. Besides"—his brother grinned—"we're family. You can win it back the next time you see me."

"All right, but you won't keep it for long. Good-bye. . ." Jake couldn't resist throwing one last jab at the older brother whose virtues so far outweighed his vices. "Cheater!"

The last thing he'd said to his brother, if only in jest. And now, thanks to Twyler, the way Edward would be remembered if Jake didn't find justice for him. Only one part of Jake's taunt that day had been true—Edward didn't keep the piece long. The scarred metal square, passed to the firstborn Granger through generations, hadn't been found among his possessions.

And now, here stood Miss Thompson, reminding him that family stayed together. *I didn't go when Edward asked. I waited too long with Mother and Father, making pointless inquiries while the trail went cold after his death. "No matter where it leads," she says, and she has no idea how right she is.*

Craig Williams's eyes slitted as he looked from one woman to the next—too clever to be allowed near them and too much of a suspect for Jake to let out of sight.

Family. . . Miss Thompson said it herself. There wasn't really a choice to be made. Jake could have kicked himself for how close he'd come to putting Williams on that train—and betraying Edward in doing it.

"So there are not one but *two* Miss Thompsons." The man read people well and thought too fast on his feet to be trusted.

"Yep." Jake slid a glance at Evelyn, who stiffened.

"And only one of them's spoken for," the intruder prodded.

"We've already explained that, Mr. Williams." Evelyn—Jake thought it suited her better than "Miss Thompson," which belonged to her younger sister—made a dismissive gesture. "At this point, you've managed to insult three of us and are still speaking in circles. Don't you think it's time to move on?"

Jake knew why a lot of the regulars began clapping. Her ability to avoid an outright lie and still address the pertinent issue deserved applause. More to the point, he itched to set Craig Williams on that train, where he couldn't so much as look at any of the women. But Jake couldn't let that happen.

"Yes, I do. I think it's time to move to the point of all this, Miss Thompson." Brown eyes gleamed with anticipation. "I notice everyone here's very careful not to mention which Miss Thompson happens to be engaged, but they're mighty eager to see the back of me. I'm thinking it's your sister who's taken."

Jake could see the battle between her conscience and her will as she stood there, silent. Defiance flashed in her amber eyes, consternation showed in the way she nibbled her full lower lip, and pride kept her chin up as she made her decision.

"But you won't lie. I like that." Williams leaned forward—too smart to take a step but too brash to do nothing. He stayed put even when Jake shifted farther into his path. "And I like a strong woman who needs an even stronger man. You're worth accepting the terms. I'm staying."

"No, you aren't." Braden rubbed a hand over his eyes and stifled a groan. "You can't stay because I won't allow you to."

"Well, at least you've moved on from the asinine nonsense about not *wanting* me to stay." Cora leaned over to balance the tray across his lap then removed the plate she'd set atop the soup bowl—most likely so nothing spilled while she carried it.

If I had even one good leg, I'd kick myself. Braden groaned. *No matter how long I live, I'll never understand women.*

"I won't allow you to stay because I don't want you here. They're connected, but if one won't oust you, the other will." *So help me, heaven. Because, to be honest, Lord, I think I'll need all the help I can get if I'm going to convince Cora to leave me behind and move on. It's even harder than I thought.*

"No, it won't." She cheerfully—*cheerfully*—dug a spoon from her apron pocket and handed it to him. "Because you do want me. You just don't want to admit it because you're too stubborn."

That hit close enough to make Braden bend the spoon handle. *Not quite, but what can I say? "Actually, Cora, I don't want you here because I want you here too much?"* He snorted. Loudly.

"For pity's sake, if you want a hankie, just ask for one." She pulled one from another pocket and pushed it toward his other hand. Then the daft woman picked up what looked to be corn bread, split it in half, and began slathering it with butter.

When Cora drizzled honey on top, he reached for it. "Hey!" His jaw dropped when she smacked his hand.

"Fix your own." She nodded to the three other pieces sitting on the tray before sinking her teeth into hers. "You don't want me here, you should pretend I'm not. In fact"—she gave the tray a considering glance—"you shouldn't eat that at all. Evie made it and I carried it in, so it should be part of your protest. If you don't want us, you don't want our food."

"Lunch can stay." Braden held the sides of the tray in a death grip, silently daring her to try to wrestle it from his hands. "You can't. And this is *my* tray."

"Very well." Cora set down her piece of corn bread, stood up, and dusted her hands in a show of supreme unconcern that didn't fool him enough to relax his grip one bit. "Keep your tray, Braden Lyman." In a flash, she grabbed the soup bowl and plate of corn bread and flounced toward the door. "Enjoy it!"

FIFTEEN

I changed my mind." Lacey saw Cora come stomping out, sloshing stew from one hand and trailing corn pone from the other, and made an instant decision. "Telling Braden isn't something I should do alone. Truly, it isn't." *Especially when he hasn't been softened up by a good meal first, like we planned.*

"We're running out of time, Lace." Naomi waved her hands to encompass the entire town. "Look at this place—men everywhere! The doctor may be prudent enough not to say anything to Braden for now, not wanting to overset him until we explain, but he's bound to notice all this activity and begin asking questions."

"I know. Twenty men do make an awful racket." Lacey felt surrounded by noise and eyes. Men in the house moving boxes, men in the diner knocking doors into walls, men outside the diner building on rooms, and men in what used to be a saloon, of all things, carting in crates of books for the library. "We're dreadfully outnumbered, though it pains me to say such a thing."

"Five men to every woman," Evie mused. "That's what Mr. Creed mentioned to me as part of the reason we've so many responses. With the three arrivals today, and if you count Mr. Draxley and Braden, that's twenty men to the four of us."

"Don't count Draxley and Braden," Cora directed. "Draxley isn't courting anyone, and Braden's already taken. So am I." Her eyes widened. "That leaves eighteen men to three of you."

"Six men to each woman." A giggle crept from Naomi before she stifled it and gave a penitent shrug. "I'm sorry, girls. I just never thought an old spinster like me would see such odds!"

"You're twenty-seven, Naomi." Lacey dropped into the familiar scold with ease. "Hardly ancient. Besides, you know you look far younger than your years. Don't ever call yourself a spinster."

"None of us will be spinsters, and any man would be blessed to have either of you. Now, Cora"—Evie changed the subject—"may I ask why you brought back Braden's lunch? With no tray?"

"He spouted some hogwash about not allowing me to remain, then got testy when I pointed out at least he wasn't pretending he didn't *want* me here." Cora rolled her eyes. "So I told him if he didn't want us, he didn't want our food. Braden said I couldn't take his tray and held on to it like a drowning man."

"So you took the dishes." Lacey began to giggle at the image of Braden clutching a suddenly-empty tray as Cora left.

"Of course she did." Evie patted her sister's shoulder, the show of closeness sending a pang of regret through Lacey.

Braden was a good brother, usually, but still a brother. *Worse, my only sibling acts like an utter heel from the moment we arrive in Hope Falls. Braden may be a man, but that's no excuse for his boorish behavior.*

Lacey remembered comments about poufy sleeves and Mr. Williams's bluntness over how he only cared to court Evie. *Well, it's a very poor excuse at least.*

Besides, Braden hadn't always been such a cad. Back in Charleston, they'd gotten on quite well in most circumstances. He'd treated Cora as a priceless treasure, an amusing and charming way of showing his affection. It would have driven Lacey mad to be treated as a delicate china shepherdess. Indeed, many suitors made that mistake back home, forcing her to refuse them. A pretty face didn't erase a healthy curiosity after all.

But it did tend to put a woman in danger, her brother often pointed out—the very reason he'd insisted she, Cora, and the others wait until he'd established Hope Falls more fully. Braden wanted the town to be not only prosperous but far more civilized before they arrived to take their rightful places.

Which was why he'd been so put out when they showed up. Now, more than ever, Hope Falls lacked any sort of order or civilization. *And he doesn't even know the half of it.*

"He's not going to handle this well," Lacey warned in what just might be the greatest understatement of the century.

"He doesn't get a choice." Cora's lips compressed into a thin, determined line. "Braden can't give orders all his life."

"We'll all go in." Naomi clasped Lacey's hand in hers. "Together."

Alone, Braden stared at the empty tray he grasped. It still held a small pot of honey, a butter crock, and the spoon he'd set down to stake his claim on the tray. So really it wasn't empty. It just didn't have anything worth keeping anymore.

Useless. His hands were clenched so tight his knuckles went pale. *Like a man who can't walk or provide for his own bride.* He had more in common with that almost-empty tray than Braden ever would have believed possible.

"We both need Cora back to make us complete again," a treacherous voice whispered.

"No!" He shouted the denial as his tray slammed into the wall, shattered crockery sticking to globs of honey as everything else clattered to the floor. *I don't need her.*

"What on earth is going on?" Lacey plowed through the door, drawing up short as she caught sight of the mess to her left. Cora, Naomi, and Evie raced in right behind her, until all four clustered around his bed wearing expressions of shock and anger.

"I take it back. It's not that I just don't want any of you here."

He directed his gaze at Cora, refusing to wince when her eyes widened in hope. Braden wouldn't change course now, not when gentler means failed. "I don't want your food either!"

"Oh, you. . .you. . .insufferable. . ." She started spluttering at him, searching for words vile enough to describe him. "Lout!"

"I'm much worse than that, sweetheart." He tucked his hands behind his head and forced a sneer. "Want me to sully your ears with a few more colorful descriptions, or will you *leave?*"

"You should slap him, Cora." His own cousin turned on him.

"If you don't, I'd be happy to." Evie's hand twitched, and Braden hoped she'd go ahead and do it. Maybe it would ease some of the guilt he felt and help hasten this entire process.

"We can't hit him. He's injured." As they so frequently did, Cora's eyes showed two different emotions. The left, brilliant blue, blazed with the heat of anger. The right, a more faceted hazel, swam with sorrow, hurt, and resignation just before she reached out and yanked the pillow from under him.

Braden's shoulders and neck jerked back without the familiar support, only the cushion of his hands keeping his head from smacking against the mattress. It didn't matter. The move jostled his still-healing shoulder and jarred him clear down to his legs, sending shooting pains upward. He sucked in a breath and held it until the room blurred—and so did the intensity.

This is why they can't stay. A pillow. A single blasted pillow moves, and I'm down for the count.

As the pain cleared, so did his thoughts. No more worrying about their feelings or even considering them. As far as Braden was concerned, Cora, Lacey, Naomi, and Evie no longer owned emotions. They owned only themselves—and he'd pay whatever price it took to pack them up and ship them home to safety.

"I think that might've been worse than slapping him." Evie's quiet comment reached him now. "Did you know he dislocated his shoulder, too, Cora? We can't jar him like that."

"He deserved it." Again, his fiancée's eyes showed separate

emotions—conviction she'd been right warred with horror at the unexpected severity of her punishment. "But I didn't mean it."

You should mean it! he wanted to yell at her for daring to look overwrought at giving him *less* than he deserved for treating her so terribly. She didn't know it was for her own good. *I'm not worth your tears.*

"One of us means what he says. Get out. All of you. Wire me a telegram when you're back in Charleston, and don't return."

"I mean everything I say." Cora glowered at him afresh.

That's my girl. He bit back his smile. *But not anymore.*

"I didn't mean to cause you so much pain when I moved your pillow. All I wanted was to give your brain enough of a thunk to knock some sense back into it!" She railed at him; the entire time she tenderly tucked his pillow back beneath his head.

"Try that little maneuver on your own selves," he barked. "Let me know when the four of you combined manage to scrape together enough common sense to match what I already possess. You don't belong here, this is no place for women, and you need to pack up what I'm sure is too much stuff and head home!"

The jibe about packing too much hit pay dirt, Braden could tell. Evie bit her lower lip, Lace inspected her nails, Naomi cleared her throat, and Cora harrumphed in the sort of way she did when she couldn't deny something but really wanted to. He'd give them this much—they rallied in a blink.

"We belong here as much as you do, Braden!" His sister made an expansive gesture he took meant Hope Falls. "Each of us owns a part of this town, same as you, and that makes this our home."

"And our livelihood." Evie raised a brow. "Lacey's mercantile, my café, and Naomi's mending shop all represent substantial investments we can't afford to see lost or sold for the ridiculously low current market value, Braden."

"The low market should tell you any business situated here will fail, and you're better off concentrating on the café in Charleston. Lacey and Naomi are well taken care of with Lyman Place and other investments, so you're not choosing wisely."

"You're here." Cora's simple statement cracked the foundation of his defenses. "So we came to be with you."

Me. He pinched the bridge of his nose. *That's the bottom line. They discovered I survived and couldn't be moved, so all four of them packed up their lives and moved out West. For me.*

It humbled him, the strength of their devotion. It also made him want to yell until his voice went hoarse.

"I'll join you as soon as I'm able to travel." He gave the last-ditch, polite concession they absolutely couldn't ignore.

"You won't have to." Lacey's chipper assurance made a muscle in his jaw begin to twitch. "We already came to you."

"But you're leaving," he insisted. "End of story."

"No, we aren't." Now that he'd left behind tray-throwing, shouting, and offering to instruct them in vulgarity, Naomi seemed to have regained her typical regal composure.

"I won't allow you to stay." Braden sucked in a dry breath. "If it comes down to it, I'll have the doctor telegram the authorities, and they will remove you from Hope Falls."

"You can't do that." Lacey looked completely unconcerned, but then, she'd mastered the art of ignoring anything unpleasant long before she'd started putting her hair up for company.

At least the others seemed uncomfortable, shifting about.

"Yes, I can. Half the mine and surrounding land belong to me. Even the properties you call 'yours' are under my name." Braden knew he'd sunk lower than a snake in a ditch, but without his normal abilities, fighting fair wouldn't yield results.

"You wouldn't." His fiancée grasped the corner of the pillow, thought better of it, and released her hold. "No."

"I would." He leaned forward slightly, in case she changed her mind and decided to rob him of his headrest again. "I will."

"Legalities pose the only reason your name holds our properties." Evie spoke as though biting off the words. "Ethically, you know they belong to each of us, and would on paper if single women bore the right to own property."

"Lawmen uphold the law, not murky morals. Names on paper mean more than a pathetic protest. Make it simple and leave under your own steam, or earn yourselves an escort." Braden set his jaw. "Either way, you will leave Hope Falls and not return."

"I don't think so." Naomi eyed him. "You won't do it."

"Try me."

"No need." Lacey's smile could have dripped syrup, so sweet was the look she gave him. "You won't have to waste your time."

The words should have filled him with relief, with even a hint of regret, but suspicion pooled in Braden's gut. He knew that sugary smile. Lacey wore it whenever she planned to spring something so incredibly devious, the victim never suspected the trap until he or she fell headlong into it. *Not good.*

"Don't let that worry you, sis." He gave her the smile she knew promised retribution should she pull anything out of line. "I don't have much else to do with my time."

"Fixing your attitude looks to be a Sisyphean task." Evie folded her arms. "That should more than keep you busy."

Cora gave the little snort that always escaped when she tried not to laugh but couldn't quite manage to keep it inside. His sister and cousin both grinned, though whether at Evie's saucy comment or Cora's reaction to it, Braden couldn't say. It didn't matter. The point was they weren't taking his threat seriously, if the four of them could smile and joke.

"I'm finished with this conversation." An all-too-familiar weariness crept over him. "And I'm having you four removed."

"You can't." This time Lacey reached out and clasped his hand. "I know you would if you could, Braden, but you can't."

"I've already explained—it's my right under the law." He didn't pull his hand away—he knew it would be a long time before he felt a caring touch again. "I can, and I will. So go."

"No, you can't. You were declared dead. Your assets shifted to me, held in trust by the family solicitor." Lacey's grip tightened in response to his own clench as her words sank in.

"Upon news of my survival, Mr. Rountree would have cleared up the matter, Lace." *He had to. The old fool may be wrapped around my sister's little finger, but he dots every* i *and crosses every* t. "It reverts back to me. Don't fool yourself."

"It reverts to you, yes." Her gaze hardened. "But the physical limitations and emotional trauma of your experience have persuaded Mr. Rountree to recognize me as head of the Lyman fortunes. While I used my position to buy the rest of the mine so you do own the entire town, and not just the majority share, you can't act on it. Until your doctor agrees you've made a full recovery, you don't have the right to order anyone from Hope Falls."

SIXTEEN

The string of curses pouring through the open window of the doctor's office stopped Jake in his tracks. If not for the vulgarity of it, he might have admired the sheer variety of colorful phrases as a stranger vented some rage. Jake usually bore a healthy respect for creativity. Not this time.

Oh, he'd worked alongside loggers for too many years for coarse language to shock him any. A man shouting such things in reaction to the sudden pain of a broken arm or the like happened fairly often. Such things, in the midst of a forest, with none but other lumberjacks around to hear, could be accepted.

A man yelling words like that around women absolutely could not. And from the gasps and reprimands flowing between and around the fellow's litany, he'd chosen to indulge his vice around none other than the four women of Hope Falls.

Too bad it didn't sound like Craig Williams. Jake wouldn't mind a chance to haul the cocky fellow off to the train. . .and wrangle the answers to a few key questions out of him. With a man like that, the blunt approach would probably work best. Blunt meant straight questions paired with right hooks.

For now, he needed to find out whose temper needed a trip down an icy flume before it burned any of the ladies. Two steps, a hand braced on the sill, and Jake vaulted through the window.

He landed on his feet, knocking into one of the women. Reaching out to steady her, he ignored the softness beneath layers of clothes and the curtain blocking his view and his hands. When blows began raining about his head and shoulders, Jake moved to free himself from the curtain caught on his belt. "Stop that!" He barked, batting the fabric from his face.

"Oh, Mr. Creed." Miss Lyman stopped pummeling him to put a hand to her heart. "What are you doing, jumping in windows?"

"At a guess"—Evelyn's voice held a note he couldn't place, but suddenly he knew which woman he'd almost bowled over—"I'd say he heard your brother's tirade and our displeasure over it, and assumed we were in danger." She didn't look any the worse for wear, almost amused at the entire incident. Only a shadow of apprehension dimmed her smile.

"Who are you?" The reason for her apprehension—at least Jake thought it a safe assumption—lay in bed, bracing himself on one arm and glowering as though *Jake* were the threat.

"Your brother's tirade. . ." In an instant, it all came crashing together. The tension that left when he knew the women weren't in immediate danger came rushing back. Hadn't he wondered what type of man let the women of his family wander out West alone? *A man injured in a mine collapse, of course.*

"Jake Creed." He reached out to shake the man's hand. "I'm going to go out on a limb here and say you're Braden Lyman." *Please tell me I'm wrong. Please say you're another brother.*

"That's right. What's it matter to you?" Pride and suspicion didn't cancel out Lyman's need for information. "Why are you in Hope Falls? How do you know my sister?"

Oh, this keeps getting better. Jake ran a hand over his face before looking each woman in the eye to make sure he hadn't gotten it wrong. *Nope. They haven't told him what's going on.*

"It matters to me because these women made it all the way out here and are flitting around without any sort of protection." He met Evelyn's gaze, remembering the moment when she'd named him and Bear, establishing them as their protectors. "Except me and another man. Riordan." Truth was truth. "We knew Miss Lyman's brother and Miss Thompson's fiancé owned most of this town and wondered when he'd make an appearance."

"I won't be appearing anywhere but this bed for weeks yet." Lyman's scrutiny ended. Apparently the man judged him an ally, because he relaxed against the pillows. "Which is why I've ordered the women to leave Hope Falls and return to Charleston. I'll pay well to see they make it safely, Mr. Creed."

What a mess. Even if the others would let me take the women, I couldn't be the one to do it. I have to find Twyler.

"We aren't going anywhere." Miss Higgins put one hand on her hip. "Braden doesn't have the right to send us away."

"Doesn't sound like he agrees with that, ma'am. And if he owns the town, the law won't take your side either." Jake decided to stick with the facts and make no enemies either way.

"He might not agree, but he knows it's the truth." Miss Thompson's grin could've rivaled that of a cat in cream. "Lacey's in control of Lyman properties until Braden recovers."

"She informed him of that pertinent detail a scant moment before you jumped into the conversation." Evie's tongue-in-cheek explanation brought him up to speed on Mr. Lyman's behavior.

"Hence the explosion of obscenities," Jake deduced.

"It's a technicality," Mr. Lyman spat out. "It's beneath them to abuse the situation to overrule my wishes."

"The same way it should have been beneath you to claim ownership of the town to have the authorities run us out." Evelyn showed the man no sympathy. "You would abuse the fact our land and businesses are registered under your name, which was done solely because single women cannot own property!"

"That's different!" the bedridden man protested. "I'd make you leave for your own good. It's not safe for you women here."

"It's no different." Miss Thompson fussed with her fiancé's

pillow for a moment. "We decided to stay, and you would have manipulated your position to overrule our right to Hope Falls."

"I'm thinking clearly and should control my assets. You women don't have the sense God gave a goose and need someone else making decisions for you. *That's* the difference." Braden Lyman turned his gaze to Jake. "Get them out of here, safe and sound, and I'll make you a wealthy man, Mr. Creed."

"I appreciate your confidence, Mr. Lyman." Jake slid a glance around the room. "But it's not a simple situation."

"Yes, it is," Lyman ground out. "Ignore whatever qualms you may have. You'd be ensuring the safety of four henwits who can't plan beyond the next day. You can take them back to Charleston. How could it be any less complicated than that?"

"Well, Mr. Lyman, for one thing, these women have planned a lot farther ahead than tomorrow." Jake let out a long breath and let the truth fall. "For another, there's the eighteen men they invited here to try and win their hands in marriage."

SEVENTEEN

"Tattletale!" Lacey's hiss faded beneath her brother's renewed vigor for words Evie had never heard before.

She blocked out another string of invectives from Braden, pushing back an urge to rush around the bed and clap her hands over Cora's ears. Cora needed to see the worst in her husband-to-be before she stepped up to the altar, and Evie wouldn't shield her from that. *Sickness and health. . .*

The news of Braden's death painted her sister's memories with the golden glow of treasured moments and dreams left forever perfect. Now, the reality of his life—and lack of health—would tarnish her image of him back to the truth. Worse than the truth of the old Braden, it would be the man she'd live with when things went wrong and days wore long. *'Til death. . .*

Of course, some men meet their Maker sooner than others. Evie looked at Jake Creed, who still stood between her and Lacey. *There's a man who's angling for an introduction quicker than most—challenging entire crowds of men, insulting the woman who cooks his meals, jumping through windows—all in less than twenty-four hours. Not to mention the way Lacey's looking at him right now for spilling the beans to her brother.*

"Not with ladies present, Lyman." Creed's voice cut through Braden's rant. "Throwing a tantrum won't get you what you want."

Braden stopped cold. So did everyone else, waiting for him to order Creed from the room, start yelling again, or something of the sort since he couldn't reach anything more to throw. "What will?" His quiet response, when it finally came, took them all aback. "What will it take to get the four of you home?"

"It's too late, Braden." Lacey put a hesitant hand on his shoulder, as though bracing her brother for the worst news. "Cora and Evie gave up their rooms, and Lyman Place has been sold. There's no place for us in Charleston now. Hope Falls is where we all are, and now we've brought everything we need."

Including future husbands in a passel of loggers willing to create a sawmill you know nothing about. Evie kept her lips closed tight around that comment, knowing the coming conversation would reveal everything as it unfolded. No sense rushing it with blunt statements sure to cause panic.

Mr. Creed missed the accusatory glance she shot him. *Not that he'd admit he shouldn't have blurted out anything about the men, anyway.*

She bit back a sigh as Braden groaned and raked a hand through his hair. *Why is it men enjoy the luxury of flat rolling-pin conversation, when women must resort to cookie-cutter comments? If something could raise hackles, we sort out the least offensive scraps and attempt to mold them into a more pleasing shape. It's a bothersome way to communicate.*

Just look at Lacey, trying so hard to tell Braden about the sawmill scheme. She couldn't overset him last night, and this afternoon she parcels out unpleasant bits of the story so it doesn't overwhelm. Mr. Creed no sooner jumps through the window than he spews out the worst in a single, uncensored sentence.

"So I cannot send you back, and even if I could, there's no place to send you?" Braden began tugging at his beard. "Do I have that much right, before I go any further?"

"Yes." Four women chimed the single word.

Joined by a "Sounds that way" in Mr. Creed's complementing baritone.

"And they've invited men up here to court them?" He directed this new line of questioning at the other male present.

"We didn't precisely invite men to come here," Lacey hedged, ignoring her brother's grammar to try to guide the conversation toward a more flattering perspective.

"When are the suitors supposed to arrive, Creed?"

"The seventeenth." Creed showed enough discretion not to offer more information than Braden requested. "Tomorrow."

"I can't send the women away, and it's too late to stop the men from coming here." Braden pulled so hard, Evie began to wonder how he kept his beard at all. "So I'll have to ask for your help, Creed. We'll send the men away as they arrive."

"You can't do that either." Cora tugged his hand away from his abused beard. "Even if you had the power, Mr. Creed wouldn't agree to it. He's one of the bachelors, you see."

"All the more reason he'd want to get rid of the others." Braden rose up to address Creed. "What do you say?"

"It's not for him to say at all." Evie couldn't quell the objection. "Neither of you make the decisions here."

"We can stop new men from coming in, but that won't do much." Creed shrugged. "Besides, the men here came for the women. No one wants to get on their bad sides, Lyman." The half-smile he sent her did nothing to ease Evie's indignation.

"No one." Braden fell back against his pillow. "That means more than just you and that other fellow you mentioned are already here. How many of the eighteen sit in town right now?"

"Eighteen." Naomi rubbed the back of her neck. "And they aren't going to escort themselves to the train, Braden."

"What kind of men did you invite that they all showed up early?" Braden began yelling again. "Where did you even meet that many men who'd be willing to come out West? Evie's café?"

"Don't you go insulting Miss Thompson's café." Creed's warning took her by surprise. "It's a fine establishment."

"Lacey already told you we didn't actually issue invitations." Cora shared a glance with her best friend. "And Evie's café didn't have a single thing to do with it, except Mr. Creed stopped in a few days before we left Charleston."

"So you just let it be known you'd be waltzing out West, and any men interested in you and your property could follow along?" Braden began knocking his head against his pillow in a series of rhythmic, muffled thumps. "You four need keepers."

"We do not!" Evie refused to take any more of his skewed assumptions and derogatory comments.

"Some might disagree." Creed's interference reaffirmed Evie's earlier thought about his meeting his Maker early. *Very* early.

"Evie's right. We don't need keepers. What we need," Lacey proclaimed, sticking her nose up in the air, "are husbands!"

"Oh, Lacey. . ." Evie groaned at that brilliant declaration as Cora and Naomi made similar sounds of frustrated disbelief, and Creed, reckless fool that he was, began to laugh. So she did the only thing a refined woman could to control the situation and discreetly demonstrate her pique. She elbowed Creed between the ribs.

He stopped laughing. Creed pivoted just enough to look down at her, his blue eyes somber. "You have my attention."

"I don't want it!" Evie snapped, unaccountably disconcerted by his perusal. "All I wanted was for you to stop laughing."

"I see." Creed raised a brow. "Someone mentions three women in the room needing husbands, and you're the one to nudge me. Does that mean you want to be serious, Miss Thompson?"

"No!" The gasp wheezed from her before Evie could blink.

"Serious suits me just fine." Braden's irritable voice spared her any further taunts. "Would someone tell me how it is that eighteen men came here if no one invited them?"

"We asked for responses care of the postmaster," Naomi began to explain, "expecting letters from interested men. From there we wanted to correspond and then perhaps invite a few."

"But things didn't quite go as planned," Lacey blithely tacked on, "and so here we are, with six prospects apiece."

"You mean to say you arrived in town to find eighteen lonely men you don't know from Adam?" If Braden looked any more grim, the reaper would get jealous. "Men who came here in response to something you sent out. What, exactly?"

"Nothing, really," Lacey assured him. "A simple ad."

"An ad," her brother echoed. "You placed an ad for prospective husbands?" His volume increased with each word.

"That's what it boils down to, yes." Evie spoke over Lacey's convoluted explanations and Naomi's elaborations.

"And what, may I ask"—he obviously tried to control his yelling, as he gritted out the words—"possessed you four to come up with such a harebrained, far-fetched piece of idiocy, much less *follow through* with it?"

"We need men to protect our claims and help save the town." Evie summed it up as best she could without making Braden feel guilty for being unable to help protect those claims.

"It was my idea," Lacey confessed with some pride.

"Who else?" Braden's lips compressed, his color an ashen sort of gray with a thin line of white around his mouth. He wouldn't admit that he was tired and hurting, but Evie could see it as he extended a hand. "Show me this ad you placed."

"No." Lacey shook her head. "It'll make you angry, and it's not important. All you need to know is we placed one, and men came, and we have things completely under control."

Dumbfounded, Evie could do nothing but stare at Lacey. Until Creed began to laugh again, pulling a piece of paper from his pocket. He handed the creased square to Braden, and Evie lost what little was left of her composure.

This time she stepped on his foot.

Jake didn't stop the laughter springing up at Miss Lyman's confident declaration that the women had "things completely under control" for more than a few reasons. First, it'd been too long since he'd laughed so much, and it felt good. Second, if someone didn't throw a distraction or two his way to keep him afloat, Braden Lyman would drown in anxiety over his women.

It didn't take a doctor to see the strain of the situation showing around the wounded man's eyes and mouth. He needed rest, and instead all he got were more worries. The Good Book said laughter did good like medicine.

Now, I may not think much of a lot of folks who claim to follow the Word, but that doesn't mean it's not good in and of itself. People agree to take sound advice every day, then go back on their decision and ignore it. Give their own word, and don't follow through...

But the final reason clinched it. Jake knew his laughter would provoke Evelyn Thompson. Evie, they all called her.

I knew it. It suits her spunk. In fact, he liked that spunk enough to want to see what it would do when he laughed at another one of Lacey Lyman's naive comments. Last time, after Evie had bemoaned the comment with a small, disbelieving cry, she'd gone ramrod stiff. Without a word, without a glare, without moving so much as an inch, she'd simply lifted her elbow and jabbed him in the side with unerring aim. Right where it hurt.

Then she lowered her arm and, with great dignity, set about pretending she'd never done any such thing. Until he'd called her to the table for her sneaky maneuver and she'd blushed that rosy color he liked so well. Evie's impulsive streak intrigued him enough to bait her with his question about getting serious.

Almost a pity she said no, but she needs to learn to be less impetuous around other men. The thought stilled his laughter just as her heel came down on the toe of his boot.

The boots he ordered special-made from a cobbler he'd known

for a decade. The boots with two layers of leather hiding a thin piece of steel between them to guard his toes. Jake witnessed too many ax accidents caused by carelessness or an unforeseen back-strike not to take any precaution he could dream up.

So he felt her stomp on his foot, but it didn't hurt any. Worse, he couldn't make a joke about her trying to bring him up lame because Braden Lyman lay in the bed before him. Lyman's hands, arms, shoulders, and neck all seemed in working order, but Jake hadn't seen the slightest movement of the sheets to indicate the man could use his legs. Which meant Jake didn't say a word about Evie's second attempt to curb his amusement.

And from the gleam in her eye, she'd known he wouldn't.

Clever minx. A realization jolted him. *It's not the first time she's shown discernment. She knew Dodger would steal a biscuit when she made that deal, and she took Williams's measure in a few moments. That's why she named me and Riordan and went along with the "Miss Thompson" gambit—she didn't like Williams. Evie has good instincts and the ability to read people.*

He eyed her with new respect. Now that Jake knew about Mr. Lyman, the entire situation made far more sense. He'd been right about her following her sister to her fiancé's side but wrong about the necessity of them moving out here. He sided with Lyman in believing the women belonged back in Charleston and had landed themselves in a heap of trouble. But now he respected Lacey for coming to her brother, Naomi to her cousin, Cora to her fiancé, and Evie for staying with her sister. Family first.

I'd do the same, and would expect no less from any man. Jake looked down at Evie's oh-did-I-do-that? smile, that dimple as bewitching as ever. He fought to forget how soft she'd been when he almost knocked her over through the window. . .and failed. And that right there was the entire problem in a nutshell.

She's a woman. Worse, she's a pretty woman. Worst of all, she's a pretty woman who cooks the best meals I've ever eaten. No wonder

Lyman's desperate to get them back to civilization. Out here, single women like this will start riots.

"Get out." The first words he spoke since seeing the incredible ad, and Braden Lyman sounded as though he expected defeat before he fought the fight. Well, maybe he should. He'd already lost this battle a few times over. "All four of you, get out but don't go far. I want a word with Mr. Creed. Alone."

"Absolutely not," Evie squawked, the first of dismayed clucks all around. "He shouldn't have barged in here at all!"

"No," Miss Higgins fretted. "Mr. Creed doesn't have a say in how we run Hope Falls. You should talk with us, Braden."

"We haven't even discussed the plans for the mill!" Miss Lyman's plaintive wail hit a shrill note. "You'll want to—"

"Speak with Mr. Creed," Lyman reasserted. "Now."

"You can talk to him with us present." His fiancée set her jaw. "We've set this in motion, we know the plans, and we're the ones who will see it all through. Speak with Mr. Creed if you like, but you won't try to make decisions without us present."

"Seems to me you four made a few decisions without him." Jake wanted to know what Lyman had to say. Besides, he upheld that ancient, unspoken code to stand alongside his fellow male when the so-called "gentler" sex started to run roughshod. "We all know it, so none of you can argue the point now."

"You obviously don't know them very well." Lyman snorted. "They'll argue anything."

"That's not true, and you know it!" His sister reached out and pinched his upper arm. "You take that back, Braden."

The man on the bed dissolved into laughter. "Are you arguing to try to prove you're not argumentative, Lace?"

"You tricked her," Evie broke in. "If she said nothing, she agreed she argues anything. If she disagreed, she proved she argues. It's like flipping a coin and declaring, 'Heads I win, tails you lose!' Either way, *you* come out ahead."

"There's always another option." Jake found the one-sided

piece in his pocket, rubbing his fingers over the familiar squared edges. "She could tell him he's entitled to his own opinion and leave him to talk it over man-to-man."

"Or"—Evie reached behind and pulled back the curtain—"you could hop back out the window and work with the other men. Please notice that we are willing to compromise, Mr. Creed, so if you fancy a change, you're welcome to try the door."

EIGHTEEN

"Looks like someone attacked that door earlier." He'd noticed the tray and broken crockery, coated in clumps of butter and globs of honey, heaped at the base of the wall by the door.

For now, Jake found it difficult to keep his eyes off Evie. *She's not going to forgive me for this anytime soon.* He realized he'd overstepped his place with their earlier conversation, but she'd been wise enough to listen and take his advice to heart. *Somehow I don't think lightning will strike twice. One livid woman's bad enough, but now I've got four on my hands. And the best of the bunch looks in the worst temper.*

"I wanted my lunch, and she stole it." A guilty grumble confirmed Jake's suspicions that Lyman didn't confine his tantrum to shouts and profanity. "Rotten thing to do to a man."

"Oh, I forgot about that!" Evie's sister sprang forward to start cleaning the mess, righting the tray and placing broken bits atop it to be carried away. "It'll be gone in a moment."

"Here, Cora, let me help." Miss Higgins abandoned her post by the bed, pulled a towel from her apron, and began scrubbing the wall until it became evident she'd need stronger measures.

"Lyman, I know they've tried your patience, but you and I need to have a talk about the way you act around women." Jake curled a hand around Lacey Lyman's elbow and pulled her forward, trading places so he stood at the head of the bed. "I won't let any of the other men use foul language or violence." As he spoke, he placed his hand at the small of her back and nudged.

"That's right, Braden. You've forgotten your manners!" his sister twittered at him, either unaware or uncaring of the steps leading her toward the door until Evie halted their progress.

"Yes, Miss Lyman, your brother needs some time to consider all the news and collect himself before he's fit company." Jake put his free hand at the small of Evie's back and tried to guide them both toward the door. One of them resisted.

"I need some water," Miss Higgins murmured and slipped out the door, presumably to go wet her towel and return.

"It's not safe for her to wander alone," Jake directed Miss Thompson, who already stood with the tray in hand.

"Right. I need to dispose of this anyway." With that, she bustled after the other woman, leaving the room half empty.

"Stop pushing me toward the door." Evie dug in her heels.

"You women need to stay together, and Mr. Lyman wants a word with me before he passes out from exhaustion. Don't make it any harder on him or anyone else than it has to be." He knew the whisper carried to Miss Lyman, because she threw a glance over her shoulder as though surprised by her brother's fatigue.

"It's Lacey's place to speak with Braden, Mr. Creed."

"That's true." Miss Lyman looked torn. "But he's tired...."

"And you yourself put me in the position of answering any questions the men had, bringing requests before you, and taking care of problems," Jake said, reminding Evie of her previous trust, then lowered his voice. "Let me answer his questions, so he'll be more comfortable, and bring his concerns back to you."

"All right." Miss Lyman headed for the door. "Braden, we'll let you two alone this once, but if your behavior doesn't improve, you won't be allowed any other visitors until it does."

"I'm not a child asking for a tea party, Lace." Lyman nearly ruined Jake's victory by snarling at his sister.

"You've got your work cut out for you, Mr. Creed." With that, Miss Lyman sailed from the room.

"Now you're stuck, Evie." Lyman laughed. "If your position is that Lacey owns Hope Falls until I heal and it's her right to inform me of how it's run, you have to respect her decision."

When cornered, animals become most dangerous, and Jake knew firsthand humans could outdo them all. Since Evie boasted more fight than most, he braced himself for her reaction to hearing the trap spring shut. *This should be interesting.*

She went still. "You're entitled to your opinion," she said, parroting Jake's advised response for when someone found herself in an impossible conversation. "I'll leave you to discuss it." With that, she raised her chin and swept from the room in the most dignified exit Jake ever had the privilege to witness.

He followed in one step—and shut the door behind her.

⟳

The man had the nerve to shut the door. Evie whirled around to find wood blocking her view of the room. More importantly, the thick barrier blocked her plans to eavesdrop.

Her fingers crept toward the handle as a plan formed. *Maybe I'll open it a crack, so slowly they won't even notice a difference.*

The snicking of lock tumblers sliding into place stunned her. *How low will that man sink? What does he plan to discuss that he's so determined not to be overheard? And what sort of suspicious mind expects to have someone listen in at all?*

A rather brilliant one, Evie begrudgingly admitted. Then plucked a hairpin from her bun and set about trying to coax the lock open. But really, the last thing she planned to do was admire anything about the devious, double-crossing Mr. Creed.

"What are you doing?" Cora's question made her jump, snap her hairpin in the lock, and lose all hope of opening it.

"Sssssshhhhhhhh!" Evie straightened up. "Lacey's defection after you two went for cleaning supplies forced me to leave or admit Lacey didn't have the right to make decisions for Braden. Then Creed shut the door on me." She paused for Cora and Naomi to take that in before adding the *coup de grâce*: "And locked it!"

Naomi gave a satisfactory gasp. "The nerve of that man!"

"Lacey, you didn't agree to leave them alone?" Cora took up the most important issue, if not the most timely.

"Braden's tired and Creed will explain the town rules," Lacey faltered. "So I went after you two to wait for them."

"Leaving Evie alone to stop their plotting, until they forced her into the hallway," her sister moaned. "Where they shut the door and locked it, adding insult to injury."

"The sheer gall"—Lacey recovered from her regret to indulge in righteous rage—"to assume we'd eavesdrop!"

"Presumptuous men," Evie agreed, and promptly set about trying to retrieve the other half of her hairpin from the lock. "Now be quiet so we can hear them better, will you three?"

Giving up the hairpin as a lost cause, and furthermore deciding it served Creed right if he had to jump back out the window if the lock jammed, Evie pressed her ear near the doorjamb. The other three joined her until they lined up almost like a show in the circus, with her crouching at the very bottom and the others leaning over her to try to catch any hint of the ensuing conversation. She hoped they had more success.

When Lacey disentangled herself and tiptoed down the hallway to the doctor's study, her murmurs to the doctor further canceled out any chance of hearing Mr. Creed or Braden. She tiptoed back with two water glasses. She set one down and promptly leaned the drinking side of the other against the door panel, pressing her ear against the bottom of the glass. "That's better," she mouthed, then covered her other ear as though to better concentrate on the conversation only she could properly overhear in this thoroughly improper spying attempt.

A brief tussle ensued over possession of the other water glass. Evie made a grab for it with one hand, pulling Cora's arm away from the prize with her other in a bid for victory. Her sister used much the same tactic in return, leaving the field open for Naomi to swoop in and claim the piece instead. A smile bloomed across her features as she copied Lacey's posture, apparently with the same results.

When her smile faded, Cora jabbed Evie between the ribs in silent retribution.

"That was your fault!" Evie hissed. "I stayed in the room the longest and tried to listen in first. That glass was mine!"

"Sssshhhhhhh!" Three women shushed her before two went back to their glasses, no longer smiling. Apparently the conversation had taken a turn for the worse.

That does it. Evie rose to her feet. She'd sunk from her crouch into a kneel once the others joined her, and now her knees ached, anyway. *Creed closed the door, but I doubt he'd go so far as to shut the window. With those curtains, they won't even see me so long as I'm quiet.*

She headed out of the building and around the corner, finding the window wide open, the low timbre of male voices carrying the conversation to her ears. *No water glass needed.* Evie inched closer until she stood beside the window. She stooped slightly. Her eyes peeked over the frame. One never knew when a stiff wind might blow back the curtain.

Thanks to Mr. Creed's dramatic earlier entrance, the curtain slid back, revealing a slice of the room. When she shifted, she could almost make out Creed's profile as he spoke to Braden. A foot to the left, and she'd have a better view, but the office was built on a hill. The top of her head would bump the sill, but she wouldn't see anything at all over there.

Hmmm. . .perhaps if I scoot a bit forward and step on this muffin-shaped rock. Ooops! She hopped off, looking at the now-sideways stone before gingerly pressing her toe on it then testing it with more weight. *I'll just grip the windowsill with my fingers and raise up on tiptoe, like this, and—*

"This is much better!" Cora's murmur ended in a muffled *oomph* as Evie landed on top of her sister, whom she hadn't noticed follow her outside. "Get off me! We're missing everything!" The barest breath of sound, Cora's voice lost no urgency as they struggled to their feet.

As usual, it took her sprightly sibling less time to recover. Cora didn't bother to brush off the dust coating her skirts, merely glanced about to make sure they hadn't been spotted and hopped into place atop the rock where Evie so precariously perched the moment before Cora startled her.

"That's my spot! Find your own!"

"I like this one, and you lost it!" Cora peered into the room. "Now be quiet, Evie, or they'll hear us and—"

Her sister didn't get the chance to finish that sentence, as Evie grabbed Cora's apron strings and tugged her off Muffin Rock, leaving her standing beneath the window while Evie reassumed her rightful position. Smug smile still playing about her lips, she turned to look through the window.

And found herself eye to eye with Jake Creed.

∞

Her exclamation of outrage when he shut the door made Jake smile…and decide to lock it before beginning his discussion with Lyman. They didn't say a word before the other man pointed to the base of the door, where shadows played and a thin scrap of green flirted with the floorboards. The same green Evie wore.

Jake stopped wondering if he'd become overly suspicious. The women were spying. At least, they were trying to. He and Lyman watched and waited, and sure enough, the faint sounds of footsteps and even what sounded like a small scuffle pushed through the barrier to their ears.

When it became clear they'd not hear anything, Jake turned to his unlikely ally.

"I've got a few questions of my own, Mr. Lyman." He kept his voice low. Not a whisper, but low enough that it couldn't carry past the room. "But you go ahead and ask yours first."

"Can you and this Reary fellow you mentioned keep them safe?" Lyman kept his priorities in order at least.

"No one man can watch over four women, Lyman. Even two won't manage that task every hour of the day, and it'll be worse once we start heading into the timber, and I can't account for all the men at any given time." Jake didn't hold back. "Then we'll be splitting into about four teams. Riordan and I can only monitor half. If any from the other crews double back to town. . ."

"Can you enlist two men you trust to lead the other crews?"

They know me as Granger. Jake hesitated. *They're smart men; they won't slip up. If they do, better my identity is lost than one of the women.* "I can. We need to choose the site for the mill and clear it, from what I can see. That will buy us time. Wouldn't hurt to have a day or two of rain to hold things up."

And speed up my hunt for Twyler so I can give this more focus. When the rain falls, trees and mud aren't the only things to make a man slip. Boredom loosens tongues like little else.

"I'll pray for rain then." A muted thump outside the window halted Lyman's next words. The men exchanged glances.

Not even a peep for the next moment, and then a muffled cry and thudding bump, accompanied by a series of not-so-quiet whispers. Finally, a stifled *oomph* before scrabbling at the windowsill.

Lyman turned his head, trying to hide his chuckles. *If the government employed these women as spies, we'd still belong to the British.* Jake crouched and pulled back the curtain, not surprised to find a pair of golden eyes staring back at him. They widened in surprise before darkening in irritation long before either of them said a word. "Next time you decide to take up jumping through windows, I'd be happy to teach you better technique, Miss Thompson."

"Why, you lousy—" She reached for him, only to lose her purchase on the windowsill and make a hasty grab for it.

Curious, Jake leaned out the window to see the cause of her troubles. Aside from Cora, who gave a sheepish wave, the construction of the building left too much distance between the window and the ground for such a petite woman to cover. Evie balanced precariously on an uneven stone, clutching the windowsill to maintain her perch. He guessed she'd slipped twice and downright fallen at least once, if the dust coating her and her sister's skirts was anything to go by.

"Lousy what?" He moved back into the room and gave her a grin. "I make a far better spy than you and your sister here."

"I'd expect that, from a double-crossing sneak." A lock of brown hair, threaded with cinnamon strands and dusted with, well, dust, escaped from her pins. She tried to puff it away from her vision and failed, looking adorably thwarted.

"Double-crossing?" Jake wouldn't protest the sneak part of her insult. He'd let everyone believe he'd come to Hope Falls to win a bride. "How have I double-crossed anyone?"

"Despite your presumptuous, arrogant, high-handed summation of my choices, I listened to you." Her chin jutted out. "I took your advice to make better choices. Not because of you, but because I'll do whatever it takes to do right by my sister."

"Even yank her by her apron strings to take her eavesdropping rock." Cora's mutter explained the thump.

"Reclaim her rock, more like." Evie spared a glare for her sister before turning back to Jake. "But when I decided to accept your assistance and set you in the position to help us, you turned right around and sided with Braden instead."

She thinks I've betrayed her trust. It stymied him. "You entrusted me with your protection, Miss Thompson. Have I done anything to endanger any one of you?"

He waited for the reluctant shake of her head.

"In that case, perhaps you need to reconsider your concept of trust. Look to what I do—not what you think you hear."

With that, he closed the window. And the curtain.

NINETEEN

Have you done anything to earn it?" Lyman started talking the moment the window hit the sill. "Their trust, I mean."

"Has the doctor done anything to stop the epidemic?" Jake countered. "Eavesdropping seems to be spreading like butter on Miss Thompson's corn pone." His stomach rumbled at the memory, but he ignored it. Another line of fabric peeked under the door.

"Corn pone?" Lyman perked up. "Is that what it was? I guessed corn bread. Did it taste as good as corn bread?"

"I'd say it's about the same." Jake lowered his voice a bit with each step he took toward the door, so the women wouldn't catch on. "Seems Miss Thompson's making do without milk, but we'd never know it by the meals she sets on the table."

He set a hand on the doorknob and one on the lock, turning both at once. Something snapped inside the mechanism, but it worked regardless. The moment he opened the door, Miss Lyman and Miss Higgins tumbled into the room in a heap of cotton and blushes.

Jake helped the women to their feet before reaching down and plucking two water glasses from the floor. *Impressive.* "Which one of you knew this little trick?" He held one up, the light catching on a hairline crack spidering down the side.

"An old friend taught it to me at boarding school," Miss Lyman admitted as the two Miss Thompsons edged their way into the room behind everyone. "Though I never expected to use it."

"You shouldn't have needed to," Evie defended her friend.

"Nor should you have had to lurk outside windows, only to have them slammed shut in your face," Miss Higgins commiserated.

"Lurk? I did not lurk," she objected. "I. . .hovered."

"Until she fell on me," her sister helpfully chimed in.

"One o' the lassies fell?" His shadow preceding him, Bear filled the doorway as though unsure which woman to help.

"All of them," Jake informed him. "Two toppled into each other beneath the window, while the other two met the floor when I opened the door they'd been eavesdropping against."

The women spluttered—though they didn't deny it, Jake noted. Lyman began demanding to know the name of the giant, and Riordan looked at them all as though they'd sprouted antlers.

For his part, Jake judged Riordan to have the best grasp on things. "Rory Riordan, meet Braden Lyman." Jake didn't say more. Let Riordan work out the connection for himself.

"Ahh. . ." Riordan caught on quick. "Miss Lyman's brother and Miss Higgins's cousin what owns the bulk o' Hope Falls. We didna know you been injured in the mine collapse, Mr. Lyman."

"We didn't think it best to mention that detail until we had the situation more settled." Evie stepped closer to Mr. Riordan to confide that fact. "It seemed prudent to wait."

"Indeed." Green eyes searched the room, lingering on Lyman as though to note that the man didn't rise from the bed. "Though I'd go so far as to say it would hae been still more prudent for you lassies to wait to come here a'tal. 'Tis no safe when your man canna watch o'er you proper in these parts."

"We'd been told Braden died. When we heard he'd survived but couldn't travel, we took the only choice." Miss Lyman's sudden anger took them all aback as she defended her position at her brother's side. "What else could we have done?"

"You could have hired a caregiver and corresponded," Lyman burst out. "You could have waited for my recovery. For heaven's sake, you could even have made a trip out here with armed men accompanying you to protect your safety and then returned to Charleston. You could have done *anything* other than sell our home and advertise for a horde of strange men to descend upon the town with no way to manage them or protect yourselves!"

"Aye." Riordan nodded. "Any one o' those would hae done."

"Corresponding is what left us believing you dead, Braden." Miss Thompson slipped past Jake to stand by her fiancé's side. "And we had no way to know. . ." She fished around in her apron for something as she spoke. "Had no way to know if you'd recover at all or if you'd contract some wasting disease and truly"—a deep breath steadied what Jake strongly suspected shaped up to be sobs—"died before we saw you even one more time. Oh, where is my handkerchief?" She apparently gave up searching for it.

"Here." Lyman pulled a folded square from his sleeve. "You gave it to me when you brought lunch—just before you stole it." The fact he'd saved his fiancée's hankie before hurling the remains of his lunch tray at the wall spoke volumes. "Now you see I'm recovering and plan to stay among the living."

"Thank you." Miss Thompson accepted her hankie to dab her eyes before glaring at her beloved. "Though I begin to suspect you hang on to your life simply to make mine more difficult."

"A worthy cause." If Evie's smile seemed strained around the corners, it didn't stop everyone from joining in. "Don't deny the man whatever motivation keeps him among us, Cora. It'll brighten his days when you find ways to get even with him."

The hairs on the back of Jake's neck prickled. Not from Evie's words, but from the fact she looked at him when she said the part about getting even. *And I'm about to make her angrier.*

A smart man stops while he's ahead. Any fool knows to quit when he's behind. So what does that make me, when I'm not only behind but plan to stay there and enjoy watching the sparks fly?

"I was wantin' to know what the lassies want done with their furniture and such," Riordan was saying. "Another train's come in, and things won't fit in the ladies' house."

"Sounds like something the women need to oversee." Lyman grinned. "Mr. Creed and I need to discuss a few things, but I think I can trust Mr. Riordan to watch over the ladies."

"O' course." Riordan gave Jake an arched look—quite the accomplishment for a shaggy lumberjack the size of a mountain. "Not a single lass will fall on my watch, Mr. Lyman."

"I don't mind falling, Mr. Riordan," Evie mentioned as he ushered them out the door. "So long as I take a stand first."

Jake Creed let out a low whistle as he shut the door for a second time. "Rare to see a woman with that much spunk."

"Cora's one in a million," Braden agreed, looking at Creed with narrowed eyes. *Who's this stranger to notice? He's only known her for a day. Not nearly long enough to appreciate her. Maybe I should wait and talk to Riordan instead.*

"I meant the other Miss Thompson." Creed sauntered back toward him. "Not that your fiancée isn't a rare woman, but her older sister beats her for spirit and sass."

She's not my fiancée. You're wrong about her spirit. And I'm not enough of a fool to tell you so, with nearly twenty men running loose in town. Braden shook his head. *Besides. . .* "Evie's caught your eye, has she?" As though he needed to ask. He'd seen it in the way Creed looked at Cora's sister, spoke to her more than anyone else, waited for her reactions.

"She's a pretty woman." Creed's noncommittal response told Braden everything he needed to know. "Any man too blind to see it can still taste her cooking and figure some of her worth."

Some. Braden would have laughed if he hadn't been in the same predicament over Cora a couple of years back. A man who met a Thompson sister and couldn't get her out of his head qualified as walking wounded. But the man in front of him couldn't yet guess he'd been dealt the blow to bring a man down...on one knee.

Wish I still qualified as walking wounded. He stared at his legs, encased in casts and strapped down so they wouldn't move. *Instead, I'm worthless. Unable to keep Cora safe from her own choices or other men, I have to sit here and do nothing.*

No. Not nothing. He eyed Creed, deciding not to press him about Evie. It wouldn't do any good, and he had bigger problems. "You were saying you could enlist two other men to lead the timber crews, after they cleared the sawmill site. Men you'd trust to look after your own sister or wife?" *Or Evie, at least.* Braden couldn't say how much Creed's interest in her put him at ease when it came to Cora, Lacey, and Naomi. When it came to Evie herself, well... *Evie's the strongest, and Creed strikes me as honorable. This, and prayer, is the best I can do.*

"Yes, I would trust Lawson and McCreedy. They're good men and better bosses." Creed sank down into the high-backed wooden chair beside the bed, steepling his fingers. "There's something I need you to know before they arrive, Lyman. You're trusting me with your family, so I'm going to be straight about mine."

Braden didn't say a word. Didn't make any promises. If Creed revealed something that made him a danger, he'd have to be removed from Hope Falls. One way or another.

"My name isn't Creed. It's Granger. I had a falling out with my family—my father in particular—about four months back. I left the name and family business behind, but these men will know me as Granger. They're smart, but if they slip up, I don't want it to take you by surprise." His piece said, Creed stopped.

"Granger." The name floated through his mind like a dust mote, catching a beam of light but fading before Braden could catch it. Then, "Like in Granger Lumber? Montgomery Granger?"

"My father."

"I'm sorry to hear about your falling out." The loss of his own father, a five-year-old wound, gave a sudden ache. *Dad would tear his hair out if he knew I'd gone out West and left Lacey alone. If he knew Lacey sold Lyman Place and broke our legacy. . .* Braden winced at the thought. "Never easy to break ties."

"Sometimes a man has to walk away." Creed's stoic shrug hid a world of pain and reasons Braden could only guess at. The only reason he knew they existed was because he'd told himself the exact same thing about letting go of Cora.

"I'll want to meet each of the men, put names to faces, learn where they're from, what they do, and which woman they're interested in." Braden set his jaw. "If we both agree he's no good, I want you and Riordan to see him out of town."

"The women should be here for those interviews, Lyman. They have a say in who goes and in who they're willing to have court them. Besides"—Creed started to chuckle—"I don't see how we can chase all of them from the room whenever you meet with someone. You'll need to discuss the idea with them before planning it, but I'm glad you're asking me to be present if the meetings occur."

"They'll occur." Braden shot him a look. "You want to size up the competition or just hope they make fools of themselves?"

"Size them up." Something flashed in Creed's eyes, a sort of determination too intense for the situation. It left in a blink. "Not just as competition, but as workers for the outfit."

"That's the last issue." Braden leaned forward, unable to conceal his interest. "A man of your background and experience wouldn't be wasting his time if he didn't see at least a possibility for success, which is more than I would have believed if my sister approached me with this scheme. My question is how slim are our chances of making it work?"

"To be honest, Lyman, I can't answer that." Creed rested a boot on his footboard. "You've got the land, you've got the forest, and you've got a snake-off of the Colorado River to help you transport trees to the mill. The railroad already runs through town to carry lumber to buyers. Pretty much an ideal setup if you've got the capital to get it up and running."

"So, aside from the start-up investment, you're saying Lacey's dreamed up an entirely plausible business proposition?"

"And a lucrative one, at that. Lumber's at a premium, with New England forests suffering over a century of harvesting. A lot of places out West run into trouble with the transport. That's why the river and the railroad put you in an optimal position." Creed gave a slow nod. "I don't know about your finances, or how much of that the ladies managed to plan. The figures run high, but a lot of that is the land. If you run dry in start-up, you could consider taking on investors."

"After the failure of the mines, none of my contacts would invest in another venture associated with my name." Braden rubbed his forehead. "We don't have contacts in lumber."

"I do." Creed paused. "And I say it's a sound investment."

"It relieves my mind to hear you say so." The streaks and shoots of pain starting in his legs couldn't be ignored much longer, but Braden needed to finish this. "As much as it shames me to admit it, I don't know the state of our finances. I don't know what all Lacey's done in the past month...aside from sell the house and buy the rest of the mine. I couldn't say what price she paid for the mine, or how much it takes to begin a mill or pay the workers. Lacey and I will have to talk."

"For now, your workers are taking their meals as payment. That and the chance to court your sister, cousin, and Miss Thompson. They'll eat a mighty amount of food, but that's always included aside from pay, so you're coming out far ahead." Creed appeared to think for a moment. "Then again, considering the cooking, everyone's coming out ahead in the bargain."

"So they're lounging around town, eating like horses, doing nothing until they're organized?" The headache that hadn't completely left came roaring back. "That can't last, Creed."

"It seems like the mining company emptied the cookhouse and the sheds before selling the land, so they weren't functional. The diner wasn't equipped for supplying and feeding a logging camp, so today the men are building a storeroom onto the back. They're also redistributing the goods the women brought along."

"No need to tell me they brought enough to sink the Ark." Braden almost smiled at the thought. "Or overburden a train."

"They made it here yesterday just fine, by all accounts, but had been sending things ahead for a few days. Today's the last of what they sent from Charleston, but they have Draxley making orders right and left for the mercantile and diner."

"Any other men should arrive tomorrow, you said?" Braden saw the nod and dared to ask, "Think any more will arrive?"

"I'd stake my claim on it, Lyman. Spring's the slow season for logging. Rains make it worse than foolhardy to work with saws and axes, and mud ups the danger for days afterward. Even during dry days, running sap makes for harder work and lots of cleanup and wear and tear on tools. There'll be loggers available to come."

"We have long winters here. Spring doesn't show itself until May. That's why you're finding sap a problem so late in the year," Braden agreed. "So even though we're coming up on summer, that means eighteen would be a low number? Will we need more workers at this point, or is this a viable reason to send some away in the first few days before they eat us dry?" *Fewer men make it easier to watch over the women, safer for everyone.*

"It depends on the finances, Mr. Lyman, but I can tell you there'll be enough work for two dozen men to clear the site, construct a working flume, and build the mill itself."

"Building a mill doesn't take that long, Creed! I've seen it done by two men in a matter of weeks with brick and mortar."

"A small, rural mill, perhaps. An industrial sawmill, built from lumber hewn from your own trees, as it should be, will take longer." Creed's boots hit the floor. "You'll lose standing if you order precut lumber from another mill, Lyman. If you don't stand by your own product, your competitors will broadcast it."

"Understood." Braden leaned back, more relaxed than he'd felt since he spotted his sister the afternoon before. "So we can actually turn Hope Falls into a sawmill town."

"Those women got in over their heads with that ad." Creed got to his feet. "But the mill could keep you afloat."

TWENTY

Sinking into a nice, soft feather bed—the dream dogged Evie's every step after the busiest week she'd ever spent. She'd thought the time after Father's death would rule as the most hectic time of her life. Moving herself and sixteen-year-old Cora while Evie struggled to set up the business took every ounce of energy and ingenuity she scraped together.

This time, it isn't simply Cora, the move, or the business. It's the men. Evie gave a bone-weary sigh. *If Mother had survived, she would have warned me about how exhausting they are, always needing something, constantly wanting attention and praise.*

And food. Merciful heavens, the amount of food these men packed away boggled the mind. She'd run through the supplies she'd brought along and almost half of the first order she'd put out the day after their arrival. Worse, the dairy cows had been held up in a freak spring storm, leaving Evie fantasizing about all the recipes she'd create if only she had milk and cream.

You'd think I'd find better things to dream about, with prospective husbands around every corner. But somehow, hard work and compromise pushed any hint of romance from the air. Even with two dozen would-be grooms underfoot, they'd accomplished more than she'd imagined possible in the past eight days.

Her diner now boasted a storeroom twice the size she'd envisioned—which she now feared would still be only half as big as she'd need. They'd gone tramping up mountains and through forests to survey trees and sites for two days before choosing ground for the mill. Erstwhile suitors provided steady arms at every turn, while others cleared their paths of any obstacles.

Light rain showered them throughout the second day, but none of the men's protests could convince them to let a little water wash them back to town and leave such an important decision to be made by others. The perfect uphill spot, it sat within sight of town, near both the river and the railroad. Best yet, Cora pointed out, Braden would be able to watch the progress from clearing to construction through his window.

Mr. Williams insisted on another area, which seemed equally advantageous, but Mr. Creed and Mr. Riordan stayed firm on their choice, to the unanimous approval of the other men.

She still hadn't determined whether the men voted to be closer to the food or to thwart Williams. The man proved Daddy's old advice, "A man who shares many opinions keeps few friends." To be fair, Creed held easily as many opinions as Williams, and the other men seemed to respect him. Not necessarily like him, but still recognize him as a man of honor and intelligence.

Much the same way I do. His superior attitude and assumption of power never failed to irk her, but Evie couldn't say where they'd be now without Jake Creed. He kept the men in line, worked with Riordan to oversee labor, and, most importantly, alleviated the worst of Braden's worries. *Though I doubt I'd approve whatever else he does on Braden's behalf.*

Today she'd find answers to some of the questions she and the other women carried about Creed's collaboration with Lacey's brother. They already suspected he reported on the other men and the progress made so far with the mill, though when he found the time Evie couldn't imagine. Creed kept just as busy as she did.

"All right, ladies." Evie dried the final pan and set it on the proper shelf. "Before we meet with Creed and Braden, I need to find Draxley and set up a standing order for foodstuffs."

"He keeps himself well hidden in the telegraph office," Naomi reminded. "We've precious few telegrams, but coaxing him from that room is nigh unto impossible since that first night."

"We need to speak with him about other things, too." Lacey frowned. "Do you know he went to Braden to discuss an 'increase in salary due to onerous demands placed upon his time and as befits the change in business practice and his position'?"

"That's absurd." Cora gaped at her friend. "When the mine operated, he received and sent far more telegrams and spoke to the train conductor daily. I kept all of Braden's letters describing the town. He's keeping his room and board, and now that we arrived, Draxley eats meals the same as our other men."

"He asked me just yesterday if we'd be so kind as to take trays to his office, so he wouldn't need to 'abandon his post' any more than necessary," Naomi threw in. "I hesitated to mention it, as I told him he was welcome to come fetch his meals and bring back the tray if he felt uncomfortable spending time away from his desk, but we couldn't bring it to him."

"He's not given me the lists of suppliers I requested, nor the ordering catalogs for the latest season." Lacey frowned. "Evie, what would you say would be the cost for his food?"

"Twelve dollars a month." Evie heard the women gasp and knew the tabulations running through their minds.

"But. . .with thirty people, and thirty days, that's five hundred dollars in food every month!" Cora went pale at the sum.

"It's more than worth it." Evie and Lacey said almost the same words at the same time. Evie looked at Lacey in surprise.

"Their labor is worth more than three times that," Lacey elaborated. "Some of them are worth nearly nine, depending on their position, experience, and skill. Mr. Riordan, Mr. Creed, Mr. Williams, Dodger, and Bobsley would be some of those."

"I knew that they'd earn forty-five dollars a month, but how do you know the rest, Lacey?" Evie asked the obvious.

"Before I ever suggested this idea, I read up on the industry. What types of trees would be there, whether the wood would work, how much it takes to build a mill, what the pay scales for workers are. . ." Lacey blinked at their expressions. "Well, you didn't expect I'd suggest we uproot our lives and hie off with no specifics to ensure our success, did you?"

"Of course not, Lace," Cora hastened to assure her. "We simply had no idea you'd gone so far in depth as all that."

"How is it the men you listed are worth more than the others?" Naomi's curiosity matched Evie's on that point.

"Riordan, Creed, and Williams are camp bosses, crew leads, whatever you want to call them. They know every job and can do most. Dodger and Bobsley high-climb to the tops of tall trees to saw off the upper portion and make it safer to chop down the rest. Bobsley also does rigging up there for mechanized engines."

"I wouldn't have guessed that," Evie mused. "Dodger swims in so many layers of clothes tailored for a larger man, I'd think he'd find it dangerous to scramble about so high."

"Lacey Lyman, are you telling us you actually understand all that blather the men spew about beasts in the timber and felling bucks without hunting?" Cora planted her hands on her hips. "And you didn't mention it before or explain?"

"They've explained what they do when we've asked them." Lacey blinked. "Every single one we've asked to join us at dinner."

"But it hasn't made any sense! It's nothing but a bunch of nonsense nicknames and such to us, Lace. And you can explain." Naomi beamed. "What, exactly, is a timber beast?"

"They're all timber beasts. It's a silly term for any man who works in the woods, felling or hauling lumber. Fallers are men who chop down the trees. Buckers take a felled tree and cut it into more manageable lengths for transport. Bull of the forest is the nickname for the bosses like Riordan and Creed."

"That fits. He's stubborn as an ox," Evie muttered.

"Mr. Riordan's quite amiable!" Naomi protested immediately, making Evie wonder whether her friend liked the same man she herself felt something of a partiality toward.

"She meant Creed," Cora interjected. "Not Riordan."

"Mr. Kane"—Naomi moved on to mention a man quick with a compliment and flattering smile—"he's a faller?"

"Why?" Lacey's eyes narrowed. "Are you falling for him?"

"Worst pun goes to Lacey, now Naomi." Evie saw the light of battle in the sudden tension lining Lacey's chin.

"No." Naomi blushed. "I'm wondering if fallers work in teams. Those two who came with Mr. Williams—they're fallers, and Mr. Kane has that other fellow who follows him about like a shadow. They're roughly the same height and size, though Mr. Kane somehow seems larger than Mr. . . . I can't recall."

"Fillmore." The name sprang to Evie's lips. "I noticed it, too. He's the same size as others but seems to shrink around the other men. I keep thinking he should fill more space."

"Yes, fallers work in teams. It takes two to fell a large tree, trading off for rest periods." Lacey must have memorized several articles on logging. "It's best if they're roughly the same height and strength if they man a whipsaw together."

"That makes sense. In fact, a lot of things make sense now." Evie added lemons to her list and tucked it in her apron pocket before heading out the door. "Let's go find Mr. Draxley."

With that, they headed for the telegraph office to find the door closed and no one answering their knock. Evie pushed it with her fingertips until it swung open to reveal the office.

Two neat piles of paper, edges perfectly squared, bracketed the telegraph machine. A breakfast tray—plate clean, napkin precisely folded, and cutlery crossed neatly over the top—lay on a side table. If one thing could be said about Mr. Draxley, it was that he possessed a penchant for order.

Or, Evie added to herself, *that he didn't wash and return his dishes.* But both of those faded next to the significance of the sight monopolizing the middle of the room.

"Do you know," Naomi whispered, "I do believe he's asleep."

"Do you know"—Cora giggled—"I do believe his mustache twitches even while he sleeps. Yes, there it goes again!"

"Do you know?" Lacey didn't whisper. On the contrary, she raised her voice a few notches. "I don't find it amusing when a man who asks for an increase in salary due to his hectic schedule is found sleeping in his tidy little office."

"Hmm? What? What, now?" Draxley didn't startle awake so much as hop to his feet. Adjusting his spectacles, he blinked to find all four of them crowded before him. "Oh, I say. Er. . .well, yes, madam. In the normal way of things, I'm quite alert. I can assure you of that. It's only due to the increased demands on my time and abilities I find myself somewhat drained, in spite of my valiant efforts on your behalf. I'll endeavor to improve."

"What efforts would those be, Mr. Draxley?" Naomi lifted the edge of the tray with her forefinger then let it fall back to the desk with a small clatter. "Certainly not your dishes."

"Nor overseeing the men or helping organize the mill," Cora observed. "In fact, I've only spotted him during meals."

"It's an interesting question, Mr. Draxley." Lacey tilted her head as though confused. "Would you enlighten us as to what extra tasks you've taken on with our arrival? Aside from placing orders, which falls under typical telegraph duties, of course."

"The luggage and seeing the men settled." Peeved, his mustache stopped twitching, showing more personality than the man attached to it. "Coordinating with the conductor. . ."

"Those were either before or the day after our arrival," Evie objected. "What of the week since that point? Unexplained fatigue is a matter of medical concern, Mr. Draxley."

"I'll rally, madam." The mustache bristled. "This will not happen again, I promise you that. Now, is there a particular reason for the unexpected pleasure of your visit this morning, or did the four of you ladies merely drop by on a whim?"

He would have to imply we've no reason and operate purely on whim. After we find him asleep at his post, no less. And I'd planned to be gracious about the entire issue.

"We've a few matters to discuss. I'll leave the matter of your salary to Miss Lyman to address, as that decision rests in the hands of herself and her brother." Evie didn't smile, simply met his gaze with a steady one of her own. "My opinion happens to be that a man who sleeps on the job should consider himself fortunate to still be in possession of it, but perhaps you won't be in possession of it at all. That's why she'll go first."

"You won't be receiving an increase in salary, Mr. Draxley. If you find this unacceptable, please tender your resignation and we'll hire someone to fill your position." Lacey waited.

"In light of the most unusual and humbling circumstances this morning, I cannot argue." Though his still-bristling mustache told them all he'd like to. "What may I do for you?"

"We'll need to place a standing weekly order for these items." Evie slid the list from her pocket and passed it to him. "Please quadruple the first order, so we've laid in a good supply against inclement weather or railroad strike, et cetera."

"I say." He peered at her list. "Is this the quadrupled order, then a quarter of the same for each following week?"

"No, Mr. Draxley. That's to be the weekly order, with four times those amounts ordered for this first shipment." Evie didn't blame the man for his mistake—it made an enormous order.

"You are aware, Miss Lyman, that Miss Thompson requests" —Draxley adjusted his spectacles and began to drone in a reedy voice—"twenty-seven pounds of flour, twenty of cornmeal, eighteen of sugar, six of butter, ten pounds each of venison, beef, and chicken, five of pork, fifty in fruits and vegetables, and no fewer than seven dozen eggs?"

"Oh, Evie." Lacey drew in a deep breath. "That much?"

"Per week," she affirmed. "Though he left out coffee. I've

included a section at the bottom I'll be reordering periodically, separate from the rest, but it needs doing now. An assortment of spices, various preserves and airtights, condensed milk, molasses, raisins, peppermint sticks and honey. . ."

"How much will all of this cost?" Even Cora, who'd helped in the café, seemed staggered by the sheer volume of the list.

"Somewhere in the neighborhood of five hundred dollars a month. Perhaps more, considering transportation costs." Evie drew a deep breath. "Which is what I told you—twelve dollars a man, apart from the cost to lay in a supply against contingencies."

"That's true. Very well, Mr. Draxley. Place four times the order, plus the additional requests today, then work out a standing weekly order for everything else." Lacey sighed.

"Thank you for your time," Evie called to Mr. Draxley, ushering the others out the door and down the single step. "We'll be back regularly!" She shut the door behind them.

"So later we can check on his nap time, but for now we can join Braden before he and Mr. Creed plot anything without us." Cora knew her far too well for comfort.

"Does anyone get a sneaking suspicion they already have?" Evie couldn't point out anything in particular, but she somehow knew Creed wouldn't be content ordering around the workers. *No, that man wants to know everything that goes on here.*

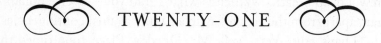 TWENTY-ONE

He needed more information. Jake needed time to ferret out the information. But somehow this week kept him the busiest he'd ever been in his life. He'd worked ten-hour days alongside logging crews since he graduated. It wasn't the work, the town, or even the time of year. It was the women. *Dad warned me not to let a pretty face get in my way, but he never prepared me for anything like this.*

In all fairness, Jake figured no man could have prepared another for a situation like this, even if it had a precedent. And he was all but sure nothing like Hope Falls existed before.

None of the complaints he'd heard about women seemed to fit the ladies who'd decided to carve a niche out of these mountains. They didn't complain about circumstances or pout to get their way. Jake could have handled that. *Instead, I find what no man bothers to warn others about—a woman who works hard and doesn't bother pouting when plotting serves her much better.* Which meant, of course, he had to watch her even closer.

Jake struck the final undercut blow into the trunk of a proud old Douglas fir and stood back to judge his own work. The angle, the depth. . .just right to let Robert Kane and Chester Fillmore team a whipsaw to bring her down. He motioned them over, mind working full-steam ahead.

With all the work to be done and the women to watch over, he'd done precious little fact-finding. Thus far, he'd narrowed the suspects down to ten men—which made nine too many. Jake's best hope lay in convincing the women to agree to Braden's scheme about interviewing the men one by one and asking questions.

After a cool drink of water and a swipe of his bandana along the back of his neck, Jake consulted his pocket watch. *Perfect.* He started walking, reaching the doctor's office a solid ten minutes before the appointed meeting time—the better to steal a word with Lyman before the women arrived.

He'd planned to show up even earlier, but that last tree proved more stubborn than most. He'd needed to clean the resin from his ax twice before carrying on. In most areas, spring came around about March, but the San Juan Mountains held a longer winter season. Running sap meant slow going. Not that it mattered. Women always showed up late.

Except "always" didn't always manage to be the case. All four women sat around Braden Lyman's bed in a cluster of chairs. Those chairs hadn't been there when he'd poked his head through the window to say a good morning earlier that day. Once again, they defied his expectations and set him at a disadvantage. Evie's smile as he entered the room told him who planned it.

I wonder if I'd grow accustomed to her, and she'd become as easy to read and anticipate as everyone else. Jake shook away the thought. Nothing about that woman, from her tiger eyes to the tips of her toes, managed to be mundane. *How could it? She's one of the first women to try to run a sawmill.*

He gave her a genuine smile in return for her smug one, before realizing they hadn't brought in a chair for him. Not that he expected women to haul furniture around for his benefit, but Jake didn't intend to stand around while everyone else sat back and chatted. He held up a forefinger and left the room.

A swift search of the doctor's study turned up no extra chairs. Neither did the other patient room. The best Jake found was a curious wheeled stool. It'd have to do. He wheeled it into the room and maneuvered to be near Lyman's side. Men stuck together. . .especially against a quartet of troublesome females. Most especially when wedging his stool up there edged Evie into less prominence, eliciting an irritated little huff.

He liked that huff, and he liked sitting next to her. *She smells like cinnamon and warm woman—the kind of smell a man could get used to.* If he planned to stick around. Jake shifted so he sat farther away from her and her tempting scent. He had other things to focus on, things that meant he'd be leaving.

Something in him stalled at that idea, but this wasn't the time to consider it. Jake could buck that log after he felled the tree. For now, he'd undercut the troublemakers and chop away suspects until the time came to take Twyler down. Hard.

In the meantime, the women would need a softer approach. "It's good to see everyone in this room with no one glowering, arguing, or refusing to let others pursue a conversation." He grinned, seeing tight smiles in return.

Only Evie refused to play along, her eyebrow shooting upward. "I'd say it's good to see everyone in the room without anyone trying to push them through the door and lock it." Her rejoinder told him he'd hit the right note. They accepted each other's presence, but she stayed on guard. *Smart girl.*

"Let's not dredge up the past." Miss Higgins stood and shuffled around another chair toward a side table bearing a teapot, pitcher, and now-familiar mugs. She poured some coffee, added sugar, and passed it to Lyman. "Coffee, Mr. Creed?"

"Thank you." He held completely still as Evie got up to help pass cups around. When she stood, her skirts brushed his legs in a sudden caress—an unconscious retribution for his decision to force his way between her chair and Miss Lyman's.

He didn't breathe easy until everyone was served and seated.

"First order of business," Lyman started in, "is a frank discussion of finances. Creed tells me it takes about twenty-seven thousand to build a sawmill, but that's taking into account lumber, labor, and land, which we already hold in hand."

"The labor isn't entirely free," Evie spoke up. "Lacey asked me before I placed a standing weekly order this morning. It comes to twelve dollars a man, per month. An excessively low price for the work, but something to take into account."

"Five hundred dollars a month," Miss Lyman clarified.

"Negligible compared to typical wages," Jake approved. "So what you're looking at is hardware materials and the machines."

"Wait," Miss Lyman reminded. "I've read that the costs to build an operational flume can be staggering. Those men building the Sanger Flume estimate costs of over five thousand dollars per mile. Even if we start short, that's a large investment."

"Smith and Moore's costs run so high because they're buying their precut redwood. Right now they're building at a decline of over three hundred feet per mile. That's steep going and slows things down considerably." Jake alleviated some of her concern. "You won't need to buy your wood or deal with inclines of that grade, and you'll only need to build enough of a flume to carry the logs to the river in any case. Much simpler."

"This sounds like it will take time," Evie pointed out. "We can't rely on free labor indefinitely or even beyond a few weeks at best. We'll choose our husbands and need to pay the rest of the workers good wages to keep them in Hope Falls."

Something in his chest began to snarl while the other women nodded their agreement. Jake drained his coffee in one gulp, the hot liquid a slight distraction. That Braden didn't look pleased either did nothing to quell his rising irritation.

"You three don't need to get married to make the sawmill work. It's foolish to chain yourselves to men you hardly know, who don't match you. Pay the men decent wages, and they'll stay on for the food, I guarantee it. If the outlay looks to be a problem,

I'll help you rustle up investors." *I'll invest.*

"We aren't getting married to save on labor, Mr. Creed." Evie's glower could have burned through a sequoia. Twice. "I, for one, am offended you think we're marriage mercenaries."

"The ad called for written responses," Miss Higgins corrected him. "When the men showed up in person, we adjusted. The four of us couldn't route them from town, nor could we leave them loitering about, idle and underfoot and causing trouble."

"You set out to hire husbands," Lyman broke in. "If that's not mercenary, I'd like to know what you'd call it."

"Practical." Evie all but pounced from her chair with the answer. Jake felt her tense and lean toward the bed. "Logical. We came out here to begin new lives and establish a business, and sought partners for both ventures. We're offering a lot, and any man who wants a chance should bring something to the table."

"Gingersnap?" Miss Lyman passed around a plate of crisp, spicy cookies, starting with her brother and ending with Jake.

"This isn't the type of thing I meant when I said bring something to the table." Evie's dimple made a shallow indentation, but he spotted it as she passed him the plate. While everyone else munched, she didn't take any cookies.

That's when he noticed it. The sharper angle of her jaw, the more pronounced hollow at the base of her throat. "I'm not taking one unless you join us." He held the plate out to her. *She's either not been eating enough, or not sleeping enough, or worrying too much, or all three.* "Take one, please."

"No, thank you." Her dimple vanished, and Jake suddenly wondered if it would leave forever when her cheeks lost their beguiling, cheery roundness. "I'm not hungry, Mr. Creed."

"You should be." He pushed the plate into her hands. "Take more than one, Miss Thompson, because I'm only having as many as you do, and I've got my heart set on a minimum of three."

"Then take them all." She pushed the plate back. "There's no connection between whether I partake and how much you enjoy."

"But there is." Jake scowled at her. Surely she wasn't one of those namby-pamby females who tried reducing regimes to be fashionably thin? Evie had more sense. "I can't properly enjoy your fine baking when I see you looking like that."

"Excuse you?" She rose to her feet. "If the sight of me so offends your delicate appetite, perhaps you should leave the room, Mr. Creed." Her offense made him realize his mistake a moment too late. "Better yet, why don't you leave Hope Falls?"

"I meant I can't enjoy it when I see you not eating with us, woman." He stood to look down at her. "Don't look for offense when there's none to find. So sit down and eat up."

"You don't tell me what to do or when to eat, Mr. Creed, and I'll thank you to remember it. Furthermore, I didn't look for an insult. You flung one my way with your ill-considered words. Next time, be more clear about what you mean."

"Fine!" He scooted her chair forward so it nudged behind her knees, forcing her to sit; then he shoved the plate into her hands again. "I'll be clear. I don't like it when a woman stops eating. You're working too much not to need the strength."

"Are you saying I look sickly?"

"You aren't sickly at all, Evie, considering you can outwork most men I've known. But Creed's observant." Lyman shook his head. "He wants you eating more, and now that I look at you, I can see what he noticed before any of us. Eat a gingersnap."

"I don't want to." She set the plate on the bed and folded her arms. "But tell me what you think you see, Braden."

"You know, Evie." He stared at his fiancée's sister, who stared back in complete incomprehension. Then Lyman shot a glance at the other women, whose wide eyes and silent smiles offered no assistance. "It looks as though you. . ." He waved a hand up and down as though to indicate her frame. "That is to say, the work up here seems to be taking something of a toll on you."

Creed watched as Evie's hands flew up to check her hair. She looked down as though to make sure her clothes were in order.

None of the other women spared her the uncertainty. Instead, all three kept their gazes locked on him, heads cocked to the side as though encouraging him to enlighten their friend.

"Oh." Understanding flickered in a normally sunny gaze, clouding it over with a foreign sadness. "I believe I know what you're all too polite to say. It's true there's been more work to begin than I expected, but that's no excuse for my poor temper or being quick to take offense. My apologies to everyone. No need to press sweets on me to improve my disposition."

"No!" Three women and Lyman burst out their denials.

But Creed had had enough. Delicate manners caused the misunderstanding and hurt in Evie's eyes, and he wanted them gone. "You're not a fool, so stop acting like one, Evelyn Thompson." He held the plate out to her one last time. "Truth is everyone's too polite to be blunt, but I'll do it. You're losing heft and I don't like it. Now eat your cookies."

∽

"Heft!" Evie could only be thankful her friends' cries drowned out her own screech, or at least relegated it to part of a chorus instead of a full-fledged solo. It wouldn't have flattered her already paltry share of feminine graces.

Then again, she decided, *I'd really rather not hear that word. Ever. For as long as I live. Having it surround me doesn't minimize its impact at all.* Then she realized two terrible things. First, Braden started laughing and hadn't stopped since Creed uttered the loathsome word. Second—and far more unforgivable—she was eating one of the accursed gingersnaps.

Why, oh why, do I always eat when I'm upset? She pushed the plate at Creed, who refused to take hold of it until she let go, forcing him to catch the entire thing. *And I was doing so well with ignoring my sweet tooth. It's all his fault!*

"I can't..." Braden wheezed between hoots of laugher. "Can't believe you, Creed." He drew in a deep breath only to start off on another round again. "As good as call a woman. . .hefty."

"*Yes, dear*"—Evie fantasized about the conversation she'd have with her sister later—"*it's a terrible thing to lose your fiancé again. But we both know he more than had it coming.*" Then her sister would sigh and completely agree that smothering Braden Lyman had been a necessity. Not even Lacey would argue.

"Lyman, I know you've been through a lot, but if you ever say something like that about Ev—Miss Thompson again, I'll make sure you regret it." Creed's low growl interrupted Evie's reverie. "Even if I have to be tied down to make a fair fight."

"You said it first." She poked him in the chest with one finger. "Don't threaten Braden." *If anyone gets him, I will.*

"I did not!" Creed's blue eyes went icy. "But if you're going to hitch on exact words, I said you're losing heft, not that you're hefty. And I said I don't like it." He surveyed the plate, selected the biggest cookie, and held it out to her. "Here, eat this one next so you don't get scrawny."

"Scrawny?" This time the echo came out in a sort of squeak. *Did a man just say I'm in danger of being* scrawny?

"That's what he said," Cora yelled three feet away.

"I heard it, too!" Lacey and Naomi verified the event.

"Don't you start getting your feathers ruffled over being called scrawny," Creed warned. "You're not that far gone, and I aim to make sure I don't have to see it happen, but even a woman can't get her dander up over being called two opposites." He brandished the cookie at her in both threat and invitation.

"My feathers are fine and don't need you evaluating them." Perversely, now that she knew she looked thin enough to eat a cookie, she didn't want one. In fact, wouldn't touch it.

Contrary as she felt, Creed had her beat. He raised a brow then looked her down and up in a slow, assessing glance that left her feeling the blush from her ears down her neck. An appreciative smile tilted higher to the left of his face. "I've reevaluated, Miss Thompson." His words sent her mood plummeting. Of course it'd been a mistake for him to think she needed feeding up. "I was selfish, claiming three." Creed moved so he handed the plate to her. "Let me keep this one instead."

"Oh no, you don't." Evie couldn't believe the way the rascal dared to tease her in front of everyone. "Mr. Creed, you take that back right now." She waggled the plate.

"Yes, ma'am." A hangdog look crossed his face. Quick as a flash, he dropped his one cookie atop the mound on the plate. "You're right. The way you're wasting away, you need every one." With that, he sat back on his stool, which somehow turned to leave her staring at nothing more than his back while he resumed conversation with everyone else as though nothing had happened.

Leaving her standing there with a plate of gingersnaps. And the memory of a man who'd said she looked almost scrawny. If she wasn't very, very careful, Evie realized, she might just end up liking Creed.

And then where will I be?

TWENTY-TWO

Facing the same conversation she'd started three weeks previous, Lacey fought the urge to bury her face in her hands. Giving in to frustration over everyone's doubt in her grand vision wouldn't win any confidence from them, she reminded herself.

Why is it that men are the ones credited with common sense and good instincts, when they're completely incapable of the most basic daily tasks? She watched as Braden ignored Cora and Creed smothered Evie with orders, both of them too obtuse to carry on so much as a decent conversation. When Braden and Creed both insulted Evie, Lacey almost left the room in disgust.

How Evie withstood it, I'll never know—unless she secretly returns Creed's interest. That kept Lacey in her seat. *For all his domineering ways, at least Creed's protective and kind underneath. He shouldn't have said "heft," but how many men would notice that Evie's dropped weight? He's only known her a sennight! Better yet, he liked her the way she was.* For that alone, Lacey would approve Creed if Evie chose him as her husband...despite his inexplicable loyalty to Lacey's own brother.

As for Braden's own behavior toward Cora...well, that would be Cora's dilemma. Not that such a technicality stopped Lacey from wondering and watching. Nor would it stop her from involving herself if Braden didn't shape up. In a very real way, Cora's presence in Hope Falls was Lacey's fault.

In fact, all of their presences in Hope Falls could be laid squarely at her door—a circumstance Lacey hoped she'd one day be proud to proclaim. For now, she had her hands full trying to keep it from devolving into a catastrophe. At least she had it figured out what to do if this endeavor became a spectacular failure. After all, she'd been doing it since she was old enough to talk. *Blame Braden.*

And this time it wouldn't even be a lie. Braden chose to invest a healthy portion of his own inheritance and all of Cora's dowry into the mines, then encouraged Lacey, Naomi, and Evie to do the same. Braden insisted on moving out here alone to oversee things, insisted on personal involvement with the business. Braden's own decisions led to his being trapped underground in that terrible mine collapse, breaking his legs. That's what pulled them west to the ghost of a town they'd planned before.

If the sawmill succeeded, that meant Lacey's glorious ambition saved the town and provided for them all. *My dream.* She held that close to her heart. *Not Braden's, mine. Not Evie's café. My mill will be the way to redeem Hope Falls and renew Braden's spirit.* She could already see it working. He had more color and vitality than even the first time he'd yelled at her.

Well, the first time he'd yelled at her since she'd come to Colorado. Lacey couldn't really remember the first time he'd yelled at her back when they were both children. It's part of what made her so good at ignoring him whenever he disagreed with her. Years of practice afforded a woman a great degree of skill in defusing unpleasant situations. An increasingly useful skill, Lacey found, when one was surrounded with uncouth men.

Especially men who didn't appreciate how incredibly fortunate they were to enjoy her presence. Braden pestered her and Cora about coming here. Creed took it upon himself to irritate Evie over the same matter. And neither one bothered to consider the fact he wouldn't be enjoying the opportunity to harangue anyone if the women didn't brave the wilds of Colorado.

With appreciation in short supply and men in overwhelming numbers, Lacey was almost tempted not to defend her entire idea to advertise for husbands. Almost. If it weren't for the basic, unchanging principle that Lacey was always right, and Braden always wrong—unless, of course, he wisely agreed with his sister—she would let the matter rest.

But Lacey Lyman had undergone more than enough change in the past week. So this two-way conversation between Braden and Mr. Creed about simply paying her suitors instead of allowing them to work for meals and the chance to court them would end now.

Lacey waited only for Evie to reclaim her seat before breaking in. "We advertised for husbands instead of workers because we need husbands instead of workers." She kept her tone even. "It isn't a matter of money but because women are, as you two have taken every opportunity to point out, vulnerable in Colorado."

"Yes, you're vulnerable." Creed's habitual scowl returned as he warmed to the subject. "And even more so with your brother unable to get his feet under him for the next few months. But with me, Riordan, Lawson, and McCreedy, you'll be looked after well enough you needn't rush into wedlock anytime soon."

"Lawson and McCreedy?" Naomi's brow grooved into deep lines Lacey hoped never showed up on her own forehead. "Why don't I recall those names? Are they any of our workers?"

"You haven't met them yet." Braden brushed away her concern. "They should arrive today. One's an engineer to help design and construct the building and flume and operate machinery, and the other will make the fourth team boss."

"What?" Lacey yanked the coffee mug from her brother's hand. "You two went behind our backs and hired additional men?"

"Give that back." Braden made a swipe for his drink and

missed. "We sent for extra eyes Creed can trust, and who fill specific positions we need. Did it the first day we met."

"You didn't tell them?" Creed showed the decency to look displeased. "So they don't know about Martha or Arla either?"

"They're bringing wives?" Cora perked up. "More women can be nothing but a blessing in this town, to tell the truth."

"McCreedy's bringing his wife, Martha. Lawson's bringing his newly widowed sister, Arla Nash." Creed's hesitation warned Lacey she wouldn't like what came next. "She's in the family way, with the child due within the next month or so."

"This is no place for a woman with child!" Naomi's wrath made Lacey jump. She'd never seen her cousin so angry. "She shouldn't be subjected to the journey, much less the harsh realities of Hope Falls as it stands. What of the child?"

"It's too late to object," Evie pointed out. "If they arrive sometime this day or the next, we make the best of it."

"Lawson wouldn't leave her behind, with no other family to speak of." Creed's explanation accounted for the decision. "Same reason the four of you came out here to be with Lyman here."

"No, it's opposite. We came to him. He's making her come along." Lacey refused to be lumped along with such selfishness.

"Whatever the case"—Cora pushed aside her objection— "we'll need to make arrangements for their housing. Ms. Nash will need the third room in our house, and the McCreedys should take one of the homes abandoned by a mining family. You would tell us if they planned to bring any children, wouldn't you?"

"They've no children," he assured her. "Just themselves."

"Mr. Creed, after this discussion, we'll need men to empty out the final upstairs room and move the second bed from the first room to the third, so there's one bed in each." Evie's direction made it so she'd share a bed with Cora—a selfless act, in Lacey's estimation. She knew Cora kicked in her sleep.

"The four of us will find and fix up a house as best we can this afternoon, given the short timetable." Naomi didn't waste a glare, and Lacey wondered if it was because they did no good. "We will welcome these four, but you two men may not invite anyone else into our town without our agreement. Understood?"

Creed and Braden exchanged looks as though reluctant to make any such vow. As though they had a choice, really.

"Either that, or we send the McCreedys back." Lacey mimicked the steel-and-starch tones of her former headmistress. "We'll do to them what Braden threatened with the four of us. Give us your word that you'll pull no more of these quick changes, and we'll take you on your honor as gentlemen."

"Agreed." Creed made the decision for Braden, but Lacey took it. He gave the right answer, which was the important part.

"You also need to stop sending men away from town without our consent." Evie's addendum shocked Lacey and the other women.

"What?" Naomi's and Cora's disbelief assuaged her pique. At least they'd all been left in the dark about this little trick.

"Haven't you noticed that no new men have arrived since the seventeenth?" Suddenly, Evie's observation was painfully obvious. "Men step off the train but never stay in town."

"The ad itself listed the seventeenth," Braden defended. "The men who arrived on time have the right to send latecomers packing. Otherwise, you'll have trouble among your workers."

"Besides which, we don't need more men right now, and you four are stretched to feed us all and keep things going." Creed's logic couldn't be refuted. "We've two dozen workers, and that's men aplenty for clearing the site and starting construction. Any more and they'll get in each other's way so much that you won't be able to control the fights and such."

"The issue isn't whether or not the decision makes sense. The issue is you made that decision without us." Cora frowned.

"Every one of your workers made that decision," Creed revealed. "I couldn't have naysayed them even if I wanted to." The look on his face clearly said he hadn't wanted to.

"If that's the case, what makes you think they'll accept these men you two have hired, Mr. Creed? They're bound to protest some sort of favoritism. Particularly as I assume you've promised them competitive wages to convince them to uproot burgeoning families and come here. None of the others are paid."

"The men will accept them for the sake of the women." Evie answered Miss Higgins in a blink. "McCreedy isn't bound by the same deal as he's already married, and no one would oust a woman in the family way. That ensures Lawson's tolerated presence. If he's the engineer, they won't be able to object his salary."

"Well done, Miss Thompson." Creed's nod told them Evie assessed the situation correctly. "Those are the reasons I chose McCreedy and Lawson before I knew about his sister."

"That, and to increase your pack of watchdogs," Lacey accused her brother. "It doesn't change the fact we need husbands. The security I spoke of isn't just for ourselves, Braden. It's to hold our property and defend against claim jumpers who'll try and take what we build once it's of value."

"Not to mention expansion," Cora tacked on. "More men mean more claims, and married women are allowed to own property now. The more land we hold, the stronger our position against those who discover our success and seek to move in on it."

"Besides"—Naomi waited a breath behind Cora to speak her piece—"there's the issue of propriety. If we aren't married, people will assume that the only sort of single women to live in a logging town are of. . .loose morals. A house full of us won't be secure indefinitely with dozens of men around—particularly as time wears on and the business grows to include more workers."

"That leaves only one option." Evie made up in certainty what she lacked in enthusiasm. "A husband."

A wife. Corbin Twyler couldn't believe he'd sunk so low as to need a wife. Worse still, he'd returned to his roots in logging.

He'd sworn never to come back to this sorry, scrape-bait existence. Little more than a boy, he'd seen no opportunity in the muzzle-loaded bunkhouses of the lowest logging outfits back in New England nor in the flasks of cheap ale passed around to pass time.

Until the Game.

At first, he'd ignored even its call, blind to the beauty of battered cards dealt and flipped until their marks faded to fond memories. The young Corbin lost his pay and his pride with capricious dice he now knew had been weighted against him. But the Game didn't take luck so much as patience. And skill.

The annoying habits that so irritated him about his fellow loggers suddenly served a purpose other than to send him straight to a book after supper. Tapping fingers, a blink too many, a red nose or itchy neck—they signaled a change in fortune when Corbin tried his hand at the Game. Winning too often raised suspicion, so he lost occasionally, enough to placate the roughest workers. A few beatings taught a man awfully fast.

All the while, he saved his cache in a hinged flask. Men searched his boots, his bunk, his bedroll, and his laundry, but none found his freedom flask. Then one payday, he left to try his luck elsewhere. Without the familiar mannerisms, against other cardsharps, he fared worse. Better bluffs, more experience, marked decks, and his own desperation stacked against him more than the cards themselves ever could.

For a good bit, he steered clear of other inveterate players of the Game. Corbin could read common folk and fleeced them regularly while he cultivated the skills used against him. It worked its way into his dreams, his very soul. The Game called to him. The thrill of the stakes, pulse pounding as he turned a card, the exhilarating fear of being caught with a marked deck. . .nothing pumped the blood like the Game.

Nothing made the Game better than a worthy opponent. That's why he needed the stake for big games. He couldn't test his worth anywhere else. Without the shared passion, the consuming drive to win at any cost, the honed senses precisely tuned to determine the other player's thoughts and moves. . .the Game withered. And without the Game, Corbin had nothing.

So what were a few petty thefts, a minor robbery here and there, if it kept a chair open for him? Cheating didn't count as a matter of dishonor but as the best sort of bluff, the ultimate level of conning another player. Either they knew the score when they sat down, or they'd learn. Even when a man suspected he'd been cheated, he usually had too much pride to announce the fact. Corbin counted on it when he underestimated a mark. That didn't happen too often now.

It happened just over five months back. He chose the wrong mark, in the wrong place, at the wrong time. If the Granger boy hadn't caught on, or had kept his mouth shut, he'd have lost a bit of walking-around money and that funny coin he flipped around. No more harm done. But he did catch on, showed every sign of raising Cain right in front of the men Corbin fleeced two nights prior. From there, things went bad. Real bad, real fast.

He'd been running ever since. And when he ran out of funds and friends, he found that ad and headed for Hope Falls. Corbin Twyler could live through logging for a little while. He'd survived worse for less. After all, who needed Dame Fortune when a man nabbed a wealthy wife?

The Game waited.

TWENTY-THREE

Evie needed a miracle to keep up with the ravenous appetites of two dozen hardworking men who put away enough food to feed a small city, and enough coffee to wash all of it down. Sure, Cora helped out as she'd done ever since Evie judged her old enough to boil water, and Naomi could manage basic tasks and even a few more complicated skills, but that wasn't enough.

So she prayed for a miracle—and God sent Martha McCreedy. A sturdy Irishwoman whose lilting speech patterns closely mimicked those of Mr. Riordan, Martha no sooner rode into town on the iron horse than she took a post behind one of Evie's iron stoves.

God bless the Marthas of this world, Evie rejoiced time and time again over the next few days as Martha's name proved no mistake. Not that Mrs. McCreedy in any way lacked a heart for resting in the Lord's will and teaching, but Martha's busy hands and servant's spirit made her a welcome addition in Hope Falls.

Mrs. Nash, the grieving widow expecting her firstborn, made for a more cumbersome, if no less welcome, addition. She stepped from the train with a watery smile and gracious, "Thank you for your kind welcome. I'm so pleased to be here," before subsiding into the sort of gut-wrenching sobs best indulged in private.

Of course, it made the transition far easier for Mr. Lawson and the McCreedys. One whiff of a weeping woman and almost every timber beast made for the forest. Or, at the very least, the luggage. In either case, they swiftly maintained a wide berth between themselves and the new arrivals. By the time the men realized a single man had been included in the bunch, even the most curmudgeonly didn't bother to grump about the situation.

Evie highly suspected Mr. Creed threatened them with spending time looking after the good widow if they made trouble, which would have been a violation of their agreement not to create or enforce punishments without first consulting the women. As she wholeheartedly approved of the results, Evie made it a point not to question this particular method. It worked.

Better yet, it kept the men from upsetting Arla Nash. Or getting close enough to discover a lovely and more even-tempered young woman than she initially appeared. After a difficult day rounded off by a porter bearing an uncanny resemblance to her deceased beloved, Arla withstood a poorly timed warning from her brother about the uncertainty of her welcome in Hope Falls.

Apparently he hadn't seen fit to concern her with the detail earlier for fear of oversetting her, so he sprang the news upon her mere moments before she faced dozens of now-unfriendly faces. It seemed Braden Lyman and Jake Creed weren't the only men incapable of exercising good judgment.

In any case, Arla made herself as useful as possible. She swiftly volunteered to peel any vegetables needed, freeing Lacey from the monotonous task she so often deplored. Since Lacey proved herself adept in only two other areas, she managed beverages and baking bread. Not biscuits. Not muffins. Not corn bread nor cakes. Bread, and bread only, came out correctly when Lacey took to baking. No one could explain it, but they accepted it after a while and their days settled into a rhythm.

Evie woke up earliest, used to sunrise hours from getting up at dawn to head for the café. Once she washed up and dressed, she nudged Cora until her sister emerged from beneath the covers like a disgruntled hedgehog from the zoo, fine wisps of ginger hair spiking around bleary eyes.

By the time Evie carried the tea and chocolate upstairs, Cora had accomplished the unenviable task of coaxing everyone else awake. Cups of warm fluid braced the women before they wrapped themselves in cloaks warm enough to ward against the biting chill of each spring morning.

Mrs. McCreedy somehow managed to meet them en route to the diner. "I canna believe that Mr. Draxley o' yourn still hae not managed to obtain proper milking cows." Mrs. McCreedy tsked a familiar lament as she scrambled panful after panful of eggs.

"The men didn't mind an extra team of oxen to pull logs away from the felling site." Naomi tried to look at the silver lining. "And everyone enjoyed the fresh meat from butchering the others. Besides, it gave Evie a reason to request a smokehouse."

"We'll be ordering more condensed milk, I take it." Lacey looked up from where she diligently worked bread dough. "Those cows arrive by tomorrow, or Mr. Draxley pays for them himself."

"My babe fancies a glass of fresh milk," Arla admitted as she peeled another mound of potatoes to tax the patience of Job. "Tea and chocolate are all well and good, but some days there's nothing like a fresh bit of milk alongside your breakfast."

"I fancy some of whatever it is Evie's up to at her stove." Cora looked up from where she cut long, even slices from a wheel of cheese before dividing them into squares. "Fried corn mush?"

"That's it exactly." Evie took two loaves from the oven and slid two others inside. A few moments, and she tapped the cooling loaves from their pans and refilled them with more batter before slicing the baked mush and lightly frying each side in a hot, buttery skillet. She filled platters with them.

"Since I've never heard of it, I've never eaten it." Lacey wiped an errant strand of hair from her forehead with the back of her hand. "But I do know it takes twice as long to bake this bread with you using all of my loaf pans, Evie Thompson!"

"*Your* loaf pans?" Evie cocked an eyebrow. "How's that?"

"I use them at least three times a week." Lacey gestured toward the six loaves cooling on the windowsill. "Although, come to think of it, why is it that I bake so much bread these days? It seems as though that's all I do when I enter this kitchen."

Evie exchanged guilty glances with the other women. Truth be told, they all conspired to make sure Lacey did precious little besides bake bread. "You also take care of the coffee and help serve, same as the rest of us."

"For the most part, all I do is peel potatoes and such." Arla sounded downright cheerful. "It's good to have something to occupy your hands and ease the burden for everyone else."

"Thank you, Arla." Naomi gave the woman's shoulder an encouraging pat. "We're glad to have you and Martha with us."

"I wish I could say I'm glad to be here." Arla looked down at the lumpy, half-peeled potato in her hands. "Truth is I miss my Herbert something dreadful and want nothing more than for him to have never choked on that fish bone. He'd be such a wonderful father, and I'd still be in my own house. . . ." Her voice trailed off, eyes shining with tears she wouldn't let fall. "But since I can't have that, I'm grateful to have found friends."

Evie's own vision went a bit misty, so she nearly burned the next piece of fried corn mush. "It's selfish of me to say so, but I'm glad you and your baby are here. You'll be the one to make Hope Falls a real town, Arla. Until a place sees a baby, it's only an outpost at best." She heard the others agree with her, except the part about her selfishness, but Evie knew.

She knew how much she'd ached for a little baby, though she'd given up hope of ever holding her own son or daughter as years passed by and no man showed the slightest interest in proposing to her. Evie accepted awhile ago that Cora would be the closest she'd come to having a daughter and convinced herself to be content in her role as an entrepreneur and chef.

Lord, why is it that whenever I feel comfortable with the path You've set me on, the road takes a sharp curve? I resigned myself to the entire scheme of advertising for a husband, but it snowballed out of control before we even arrived in town. To be honest, Jesus, I'm almost afraid of what will happen when I resign myself to choosing a husband from amongst these strangers. What strange turn will You bring then? Give me faith to trust You, and some sign that the husband of Your choosing wants me for more than my property or my cooking, but myself...

"...shoot him." Lacey finished saying something Evie wished she hadn't missed. "Of course, it takes more than just aim. I'd imagine you need great courage and determination to fire."

"Don't hesitate, lassies." Mrs. McCreedy covered another platter of scrambled eggs and planted her hands on her hips. "Once Miss Lyman teaches you to shoot, pull the trigger the instant you know you're in danger from any man, you ken?"

"Yes, Mrs. McCreedy," Evie chorused dutifully along with the others, but she couldn't help thinking of a pair of changeable blue eyes. Laughing one moment, icy with rage the next...

There's more than one kind of danger to guard against.

The sound of gunfire made Jake's blood run cold. Without another thought, he dropped his end of the saw he'd been manning with Gent and took off running toward the sound.

Praise God, it's not coming from town. He barely noticed the prayer. Jake rarely prayed. He believed in the Lord, didn't believe most people bothered to live up to what He laid out in the Word, and washed his hands of paying lip service to any of it long ago. But he'd accepted the truth, and those sorts of thoughts slipped out in intense times.

Jake hoped God saw it as a good thing—that he did the best he could and handled most of what came his way as he saw fit, but didn't hesitate to call for help when he needed it. And if the women were in trouble, Jake would take any help available.

Pistol drawn, he slowed, taking cover behind trees as the haphazard shots grew louder. Closer. From the sounds of it, he'd circled behind the shooters, which meant they fired *away* from town. Good. That meant everyone might just survive this.

Then he heard it. A feminine shriek. *The only women for miles are ours.* Jake threw caution to the winds and ran toward the bloodcurdling sound, heart pumping so loud in his ears he almost missed the next sound. This one stopped him cold.

Giggles? Jake canted his head toward the cheerful sound breezing toward him. No doubt about it—girlish giggles filled the forest. Right before another shot rang out.

"Did I hit anything this time?" Evie's call made him blink.

Did she. . . Then he understood. The women were practicing their marksmanship, learning to shoot as a precaution against the many threats surrounding them. *That's my girl.*

"Wait and let me go check. I didn't see any of the cans move, but perhaps you scratched one." Miss Lyman's voice sounded farther and farther away as she presumably went to check a target. A few moments later and, "Well, I'm sure you hit something, Evie. But not in the vicinity you aimed for."

"Razzlefrass," Evie muttered. "I should be good at this."

Jake paused in the act of creeping toward the stand of trees guarding the voices, easing into a better position rather than rushing now he knew the situation. He snickered silently into his sleeve at her assertion she should be good at shooting, as though everything came easily to her. Then. . . *Razzlefrass?*

"Razzlefrass?" Miss Higgins repeated the strange phrase. "That sounds like a berry jam, Evie. A tart one, I think."

"I used to wonder why my sister can't say something simple, like fiddlesticks, when something irks her." Miss Thompson's amusement carried to him. "Now I enjoy the words she concocts."

So do I, Jake decided. *I wonder what others I've missed.*

"*Peduncle* remains my absolute favorite," Miss Lyman mused. "There's something so whimsical about saying it. You cannot help but smile when you do. Try not to...peduncle..."

"I've told you a thousand times, Lace, I didn't make that one up. A peduncle is the stem of a piece of fruit. I've offered to show you in the encyclopedia several times!"

"But that's less fun to believe, Evie. Now why don't you try again, but this time, squint at the target when you fire." Miss Lyman seemed to be the one directing firing practice.

Jake took advantage of the noise to steal forward the last bit he needed to see them all clearly. Sure enough, the four women stood in a long, clear expanse. At the end, they'd balanced several cans atop a broad rock. From here, Jake could make out more than a few holes in the beaten metal. *So at least one of the women can shoot accurately. Maybe more.*

"I'll go check for myself this time." Evie stalked toward the end of the field, determination lengthening her stride and emphasizing the sway of her hips. She was a sight to behold. Right up until she counted the number of bullet holes in the cans and a frown furrowed her brow. She counted again and let out a strange, unfeminine sort of frustrated sound.

"Don't worry, sis," Cora called out. "You'll get it."

"This is our second lesson, and Lacey had no trouble teaching you and Naomi. Shouldn't I be doing well by now?" She nibbled on her lower lip, obviously distressed over not being good at something she'd set her mind to excel in.

It's about time. I was starting to wonder if there was anything Evie set her mind to that she didn't master. Jake caught himself grinning and immediately frowned. *An imperfection in no way makes her perfect,* he chided himself. Stupid notions like that got a man in trouble. Jake watched as Evie took aim again and missed by a mile.

This time he couldn't stop the grin.

 TWENTY-FOUR

The grin abandoned him by the time he sat next to Braden Lyman for the first of the "interviews" the women agreed to. Everyone sandwiching into one room made for a tight fit, so Jake removed the dresser and washstand for the meeting and brought in a bench for the men to sit on. It took up less space than chairs and had the added benefit of seating two if the women decided to speed things along by taking them in pairs.

Jake saw the benefit in that but also wanted the opportunity to take a good, close look at each suspect individually, without having to divide his attention. If two suspects were questioned together, he'd be more apt to miss some small sign to indicate that Twyler's disguise had slipped.

Every one of Jake's instincts told him he'd tracked Twyler to the right place this time. The feeling grew stronger the less he wanted to leave Hope Falls, spurring him toward his real purpose. The proposed mill made for good cover, and nothing more. The women made for a constantly aggravating diversion.

But, ultimately, the entire setup would lead him to Edward's killer. Smiling faces hid treachery, and the longer it took Jake to find Twyler, the longer it gave the vermin to get close to Evie. Or one of the other women, he supposed, but by and large, the men paid Evie the most attention.

Jake couldn't blame them. He could see why some were put off by Miss Higgins's cool reserve when Evie's warm smile provided such contrast. And Evie's shirts with their simple lines made a far more approachable picture than Miss Lyman's fussy frills and overblown sleeves. Even if Miss Thompson weren't engaged to Braden, the men would most likely prefer her older sister. So Jake couldn't blame them. But he didn't have to like it.

He sat in what he'd begun to think of as his customary place between Evie and Miss Lyman, near Braden. Sure enough, the women all agreed they should send the men in pairs. If need be, they decided, they could always speak with one in private. For now, their main concern was speeding things along.

Robert Kane strolled through the door first, his coloring and build placing him squarely on Jake's list of suspects. Most loggers carried more muscle after years on the job. His unctuous smile and ingratiating air whenever one of the women happened to be nearby put him in another category. That one didn't reflect well on the man either.

A second man trailed in his wake. If Kane strode with an over-abundance of confidence to make himself seem taller than he truly stood, Chester Fillmore's retiring nature made the man smaller. The same height, build, and coloring as Kane, Fillmore shrank into himself. And away from scrutiny, Jake noted.

Lyman began with the basics—what jobs the men performed, how many years of experience each had, whether they'd worked with ponderosa pine or Douglas fir before, or anything larger.

"We're fallers, the pair of us," Kane answered for both. "I've put my hand to some bucking work when whipsaws will do and, all told, done about seven years in the woods. Two in Puget Sound, five farther east. Douglas fir's about the largest I've brought down." He named two lumber outfits he'd worked with.

"I'm a faller, as well, with four years. Three in Oregon, so I've gone up on springboards to take down coast redwoods fourteen feet across if they were one." Fillmore's voice came out quiet enough everyone strained to hear him. He didn't name any companies he'd worked with, but then again, Lyman hadn't asked. Kane volunteered that information, and Fillmore didn't seem the type of man to use three words when a nod would do.

"Where'd you put in this past winter?" The crucial question, from where Jake sat. It'd take some time to make inquiries and follow up whatever answers the men gave, but this provided the starting point to sniff out a liar. It came closest to the real question on his mind: *Where were you in January, when some coward fitting your description shot my brother?*

Kane named a small outfit in an isolated area, not likely to be well known or listed by any others in town. Nevertheless, his response made Jake's back tense in recognition. If he didn't misremember, that's where McCreedy had spent the season. He could verify or debunk the smooth talker's story that very afternoon. He didn't let any of his racing thoughts show in his expression, keeping it bland. *Even if Kane left for Christmas and didn't return, that's a strong sign he's hiding something.*

Loggers typically came back for another two months in the strongest season. Snow didn't stop the lumber business. In fact, cool, dry weather made for better conditions than hot summer. Snow facilitated moving the giant logs across short distances in areas where they hadn't upgraded from skid roads to the new compact steam engines for hauling. Donkeys, they were called.

Late spring through early autumn, several camps closed or greatly slowed while many of their loggers went home to farms. Late fall through the start of spring, it went full-speed ahead. If a timber beast vanished in the middle of the season, it would be noted. Twyler started running across the country in January.

"Truth be told. . ." Fillmore's hesitant opening nabbed Jake's attention. "I didn't join any outfit this past year. Heard of all the success in mining and decided to try panning for gold. I planned to come back, but an early blizzard snowed me in. Turns out I'm a better timber beast than silt-sifter any day."

"I'm sorry that didn't pan out for you." Miss Thompson's statement elicited a round of groans from her friends. More suspiciously, it earned the sort of cleared throat sound from Lyman that a man made when stifling a chuckle.

"Cora reclaims worst pun," Evie announced. "I'm sorry, Mr. Fillmore. It's something of a game amongst the four of us."

"But that one was unintentional!" her sister protested.

"I cannot believe"—Miss Lyman giggled—"you manage such an abysmal turn of phrase without any effort whatsoever."

The lighthearted banter gave Jake time to sort through his impression of Fillmore's answer. *Getting snowed in would explain his slighter build. He wouldn't have the provisions or constant workload to maintain a faller's strength.* A simple, believable reason, as so many men succumbed to the lure of gold fever.

But it's too neat and tidy. He didn't name the company he usually worked for, and Fillmore doesn't seem the short-stake type. A story about a freak blizzard can't be verified or looked into. There are too many solitary miners in too many places. It'd be the perfect cover for a man like Twyler, if he suspected someone might bother to check a false reference.

Fact was he'd walked into the room with two suspects, thinking to eliminate at least Fillmore. Instead, he'd follow the lead on Kane and keep a closer watch on the mousy man who followed him. If anything, Jake's list kept growing.

Evie's store of patience shrank as the conversation wore on. Too many things ran through her mind, too much to do for her to be sitting still. It seemed a waste of time to question the men's logging credentials when they'd all been out working for almost two weeks now. Couldn't Creed judge their competence firsthand?

Of course he can. Really, this entire exercise is more for Braden's benefit than anything else. The thought kept her from fidgeting. If being unable to get things done for a mere hour made her itch to get moving, how much worse must it be for her sister's fiancé? Suddenly, she didn't begrudge the time spent. *Besides,* she cautioned herself, *you're supposed to learn as much as possible about the men you or your friends might marry.*

Except…Evie didn't care for either Mr. Kane or Mr. Fillmore, and she rather doubted Lacey and Naomi did either. Surely Naomi's question about the pair the other day only had to do with her curiosity over the way they worked in teams. Unease crept through as she recalled Naomi's blush and the competitive glint in Lacey's gaze as she asked if her cousin had "fallen."

Perhaps I'm only halfway correct. Neither evinced an interest in Mr. Fillmore, but maybe the more forward Mr. Kane caught at least one eye. She looked at him afresh. He did count as one of the better-looking possibilities, Evie supposed—if one ignored the sense of something sort of…oily…about the man.

"When did you two meet?" She looked from one man to the other, wondering at the bond between them. Perhaps distant cousins? They shared the same coloring, if not mannerisms.

As expected, Kane answered. "En route to Hope Falls."

"From what I've seen, I assumed a long, strong friendship." Naomi admitted the surprise Evie shared.

"We get on well, match up for a whipsaw." Kane glanced at his companion and shrugged. "Fillmore makes for good company since he's not a hothead or given to talking anyone's ear off."

Fillmore gave a shrug and seemed ready to leave it at that, but rethought and added an eloquent, "It works."

Cora inquired as to age, finding them well-matched there, too. Both claimed twenty-eight years, twenty-nine in the fall.

Evie breathed a sigh of relief—that had been the last question the six of them planned to ask, unless the conversation led to others as a matter of course. Just in time. *The train with my dairy cows should pull in within the next hour or so.*

"I've one last question for you, gentlemen." Lacey rubbed her right hand over her forehead—the old signal for "wait and listen" when one of them changed plans. It didn't bode well. "At this point, we'd like you each to specify which two of the three of us you'd choose to direct your attentions toward, and why."

Evie's stomach dropped to her shoes. She entertained the brief, fanciful notion that if she stood, she'd squish it underfoot like grapes for wine. *Little wonder Lacey didn't mention this question when we planned the interviews. She knew good and well we'd never agree. It's an embarrassment!*

From the corner of her eye, she saw Naomi shoot an alarmed look her way, as though imploring her to find a way to end this dismaying turn in conversation. But Evie could think of no method to save them from hearing the assessment of their would-be suitors, straight from the horses' mouths. So to speak.

Lord, I know I fall short in many, many ways and one of them happens to be humility. But did Lacey have to ask for both names and reasons? I don't want to listen to a man explain why he'd choose other women before looking my way. Especially not with others listening, and most especially not with other men within hearing distance. If I must be humbled, and being sent into a situation beyond my control is not sufficient, could it not happen at some time when Jake Creed isn't watching?

"A man would count himself fortunate to win the hand of any lady in the room, Miss Lyman." Kane's slick response left Lacey shifting irritably and Evie hoping for a way to avoid this.

"You're right, Mr. Kane. Thank you both for your patience." The words spilled in such a hurry, Evie could only be thankful they formed coherent thoughts. "We're glad to have you here."

"Why don't you answer the question, Kane?" Braden eyed the faller with undisguised hostility, and Evie belatedly realized he wondered about Kane's evasive response. "Any lady in the room" included Cora, and despite Braden's obstinacy in insisting he'd dissolved the engagement, he hadn't suggested or allowed anyone else to suggest Cora remained free to wed.

Another time, his protectiveness would gladden Evie's heart. *But the numskull would choose now to be possessive!*

"The answer I gave happened to be sincere." The glint of battle appeared in Kane's eye. "Since you press the issue, I would narrow my selection to Miss Lyman and Miss Thompson. Miss Lyman appeals for her femininity, and Miss Thompson for her domestic abilities. I find I prefer a woman with more conversation than Miss Higgins seems inclined toward sharing."

Evie drew a deep breath, offended for not only herself and Naomi, but Lacey as well. No matter he'd pointed to Lacey as his first choice, Kane didn't see beyond her penchant for bright fabrics and dainty patterns to the woman beneath. Meanwhile, he only recognized Evie herself as a cook and housekeeper, and all but called Naomi a bore. *I won't approve of Robert Kane even if Lacey decides she'll accept his proposal. Naomi and Cora will have to be the two who allow it. As far as I'm concerned, Hope Falls could do better with another worker less self-absorbed.*

"This sort of question does no good for any man or woman involved, but as the ladies make the decisions here, I see no alternative but to answer." Mr. Fillmore showed the good taste to present a mild objection. "I'd select Miss Lyman, for her foresight in recognizing the lumber after the mines collapsed. It seems a good characteristic in a wife, that she look ahead and find the best in each situation. Although I agree Miss Thompson shows great creativity and skill in the kitchen, I differ from my friend. Miss Higgins, with her more demure ways, would make a more fitting companion for me. Still waters run deep, or so they say, and I like to believe it true." With that, Mr. Fillmore sank back onto the bench, looking as though he'd exhausted himself by speaking more words in that one speech than he'd voiced during his entire stay in town.

Much better. Evie sent him an encouraging smile. Not because he'd chosen her—he hadn't—or even noticed anything about her beyond her cooking—as far as Evie could see, men never did—but because Chester Fillmore's quiet personality hid a discerning nature. He'd understood and appreciated some of her friends' fine qualities. In particular, the well-spoken miner might make a good match for Naomi. Never mind that he, too, listed Lacey first.

"Thank you, gentlemen." Cora signaled the end of the conversation, and Braden leaned forward to shake each of their hands in turn before Mr. Kane and Mr. Fillmore departed.

"Lacey, what were you thinking to throw that last bit in?" The words blurted from her mouth the minute Evie thought the men left hearing distance. "We never discussed anything like that!"

"If we discussed it, you wouldn't have let me ask." Lacey gave an unrepentant shrug. "All those details about their work history and logging make for a fine work interview, but that part interests Mr. Creed more than it pertains to us. We need to learn more about the men themselves, and which one of us they plan to ask for. With so many about, it's difficult to guess."

"That may be, but to put them on the spot like that smacks of poor taste." Naomi's eyes remained as wide as they'd been since Lacey asked, and Evie found herself wondering whether her friend had blinked in the past quarter hour. "An ambush."

"If you catch a man off guard, you're more apt to get an honest answer." Creed's observation did little to soothe her nerves. "Notice how much more polished Fillmore made his response than what Kane scraped up. Forewarned is forearmed."

"So now the other men know what to expect, there's little to be gained in asking." Evie gladly followed his logic.

"Wrong. Those two won't warn anyone." Braden shook his head. "They're competitors and won't hand out an advantage."

"From now on, we call them in singly." Creed looked out the window, sunlight illuminating his profile. "Kane answered for both too often, and Fillmore reaped extra time to think. We'll see more of a reaction if we talk to them one at a time."

"Drawing things out seems unwise." *And painful.* Evie swallowed. *How many times will I sit here and either not hear my name or be lauded for nothing but my meals? Do any of the men see me as more than a cook? Do any of them even want me?*

❦

Jake wanted her to stop looking as though someone shot her dog. He saw the doubt in Evie's expression and wanted to tell her that not all men would be idiots. Some saw her kind smile and the brave heart behind it. He wanted to tell her the two men who walked out of the room a moment ago were nothing but fools.

But one of them might be so much more. Even if Kane and Fillmore turned out to be clean, one of the men walking so freely around town wore the stain of murder on his soul.

Seeing her hurt made him want to go find one of those sequoias he'd seen photographs of and fell one with nothing but an ax, but Jake knew he'd rather Evie stay gun-shy than moon about with stars in her eyes. Better she be wary, stay on guard against the men surrounding her and her friends than let any one of them fall into the schemes of scum.

After all, it's only a matter of time before I carry the filth away.

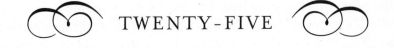 TWENTY-FIVE

T hey're here!" Clump pushed his way past the line of loggers snaking toward the washing tubs the next day. His heavy, uneven gait more pronounced than ever as he ran toward the women, he made better time than Jake guessed. "The cows is come home!"

He bellowed that last as he burst into the kitchen, Jake just behind him.

Jubilant whoops sounded before Evie came bustling out the doors, apron strings streaming behind as she headed for the train. Needless to say, everyone followed. At least, everyone who'd already washed his dishes. Those who hadn't sulked in line while faster men chased after the women.

If that wasn't some sort of commentary on the entire setup of Hope Falls, Jake didn't know what was. Nor was he entirely clear on what that commentary said about any of them. He just shook his head and kept close watch as the tableaux unfolded.

He tried to guide the women away from the train so the men could unload the livestock, but Evie insisted on seeing her cows first thing. The other women took one look at the bulk of their suitors keeping a distance and wisely accepted the arms of Clump, Gent, and Riordan. Only Evie remained resolute in her position.

So Jake stuck directly beside her as they rolled open the doors to the livestock car, took a deep breath, and held it.

"Mercy." Eyes like sunshine began to water as the stench rolled over them. Evie coughed and rocked back a step as the workers set up the unloading ramp for the cows to walk out.

"Here." Jake closed her fingers around his bandana and raised her hand to her nose to block the scent of cow patties, methane, and livestock. He held her elbow to keep her steady and led her to the other women, away from her precious acquisitions.

"Those can't be *my* cows," she moaned from behind his bandana. "Nothing as wholesome as milk could come from anything smelling like *that*. Mr. Draxley erred again, I'm sure."

"If quilts need to air before use after they sit in trunks, cows need heavy winds after being crowded in trains." Jake saw no reason to hold back a chuckle and heard a few more from the men who caught his comment. "These are no oxen, I'm sure."

"Nah, Miss Thompson." Clump gestured toward the five bovine culled from the cargo. "You can see those there ain't ox nor even bulls, but honest, live, milking cows. It's easy to see."

"How can you tell?" Miss Lyman looked at the animals with great interest. "They look much the same to me, Mr. Klumpf."

"That's easy. See, it's the ud—er. . ." Clump hit the realization he'd stumbled into an indelicate topic of conversation, and his ears began to turn red. "Small horns."

"Oh." Evie lowered the bandana to reveal that fickle dimple of hers. "I wouldn't have noticed such a slight difference. Thank you for your expertise, Mr. Klumpf. Have you had much experience with barnyard animals, or ranching, or some such?"

Suddenly, Jake saw Clump with new eyes. The compact logger with sturdy legs and an inability to keep anything to himself never mentioned his own past. *Why is that? And how is it that a logger knows anything about dairy cows and how to identify them?*

"M' family settled in Kansas, where we claim a good-sized farm. But Klumpfs believe in being fruitful. We multiply somethin' fierce, and there's only so much land to go around. I left to set up a homestead but started logging along the way." Clump shrugged. "You could say I know plenty about a barnyard."

A Kansas farm boy found logging in the Colorado mountains? Jake might find it suspicious if it weren't so ludicrous. Farmers usually remained farmers, no matter if they uprooted. They just set back down and planted somewhere else. On the other hand, Clump would be a fool to lie with five cows waiting.

Then again, he had no business making that comment to Evie about Klumpfs being fruitful and multiplying. It went too far, was too bold. The fact Clump used a biblical reference to boast of his family's virility worsened the offense. *I never thought to hear the Bible used when a man tried to flirt.*

"Let's take our cows to the 'barn.'" Miss Lyman drew a deep breath.

"We'll give Mrs. Nash a fine surprise with supper," Evie planned as they led the way to a surprisingly well-made shanty behind the café, off to the side. "She's craved milk for days."

Now partitioned with four barriers to make five stalls, the structure smelled of fragrant hay. Various men led the cows in one by one until each stall housed an antsy occupant. They lipped at the straw, slurped up water from their trough, and gave resonant lowing sounds as they restlessly moved about.

With the cows inside, Jake sent the loggers back to work digging out the stumps of trees they'd felled the week before. No need for over twenty men to loiter underfoot and gawk over the women, as they tended to do whenever given the chance.

"They don't look happy." Worry creased between Evie's brows. "Don't they stop giving milk if they're not happy?"

Miss Lyman rolled her eyes. "Whoever heard of happy cows?"

"They need milking," Clump instructed. "It pains them."

"The books say to milk in the morning and evening, not the afternoon." Evie looked surprised at the very suggestion.

"Usually 'tis so," Mrs. McCreedy affirmed. "But in this case,

Mr. Klumpf tells it true. More than likely these poor dears had no morning milking, and they're long overdue."

"Very well." Evie rooted around in a corner and emerged with three short stools. Pails hung on pegs in the wall. "I've read about the method behind milking. Now I'll practice."

"They're not looking very friendly," her sister warned. "Perhaps we ought to wait until they've settled down?"

"Discomfort makes anyone testy." Miss Higgins chose a stool after Miss Lyman took one. "I doubt they'll settle as is."

"Come along." Mrs. McCreedy took the two toward the closest animal. "I'll show you two how to go about it. 'Tis simple."

"The tracts seem straightforward enough." Evie headed for the farthest stall and began murmuring to the beast. The soothing sound of her voice carried as Jake followed to find her patting the cow's side while lowering herself to the stool.

Placing her cheek against the same place she'd had her hand, Evie reached under and began pulling. First one hand, then the other, she tugged in a rhythm that matched the sound of milk squirting into a tin pail. Only trouble was the sound came from across the makeshift barn. Perplexed, she drew back, glanced down, repositioned herself, and tried again. Same results.

Jake bit the inside of his cheek to keep from laughing as her confidence faded to confusion then irritation.

Meanwhile, Miss Lyman moved on to another cow while Mrs. McCreedy showed Miss Higgins the way of things. The sound of milk splashing into pails filled the structure. . .and none came from Evie's efforts.

She went so far as to get up, giving the cow's hindquarters wide berth, and settle on the other side. Still nothing. Finally, Evie gave an exasperated huff. "This one doesn't work."

"I'll try." Clump shuffled over, distinctive tread muffled.

Yet again, Jake noticed how thick the soles of the other man's boots must be for the entire uppers to remain visible when each step sank into so much hay coating the ground. Could Clump's characteristic stomp be an adopted mannerism? *Does he wear those boots as protection in the woods and for stabilization in the mud, or to make himself taller?* It wouldn't be the first time a short man elevated his shoes.

Clump squatted beside Evie. Oblivious to her doubtful glance, he reached in and had milk pouring into the pail in about two seconds flat. "There she goes, Miss Thompson."

Bewilderment gave way to outrage. "I talked to her, patted her side, rubbed my hands together so they weren't cold, and tugged firmly but carefully with alternating hands like all the tracts directed. That cow did this on purpose, Mr. Klumpf!"

Jake couldn't hold back his laughter anymore, earning himself an evil look. He didn't care. The expression on Evie's face when Clump succeeded had been so incredulous.

"Stop laughing this instant, Mr. Creed." She gave the order but didn't bother to see if he followed it. Instead, she watched as Clump repeated what he'd done before, protesting that she didn't see any difference. In fairness, neither did Jake.

But Evie didn't need to know that. Her annoyance whenever she didn't master something amused him. It was as though she expected to be good at something simply because she wanted to be. And on the rare occasions when determination and preparation didn't produce results, the idea anything remained beyond her control was treated as a personal insult. It made Jake's day.

Until Clump slid his hands over Evie's to demonstrate what he described as "rolling your palm while you pull." Then the entire scene didn't seem so funny anymore. Especially when she smiled that way, flashing her dimple at Clump. *At Clump.*

Jake stopped laughing.

⁂

A sense of humor was God's greatest gift to mankind, Braden Lyman decided during the dozenth interview with one of his new workers and his family's prospective suitors. Maybe he should list those the other way around, since the men came to Hope Falls for the women and worked as a secondary pursuit.

Either way, Braden figured he would've gone mad weeks ago if he hadn't been granted a keen appreciation for the ridiculous. And Lacey's ad certainly managed to attract a few improbable characters. Clumpy Klumpf and Bear Riordan were distinctive men with amusing names, but Braden had other favorites among the workers he'd met thus far.

Salt and Pepper, he nicknamed the two tall Nordic fallers who'd apparently arrived with the man now answering Creed's questions about his work history. The pair split one personality between them, but at least their dependence on each other made for a point of interest.

Dodger brightened Braden's day when the shifty fellow tried to make off with his pen. When Evie caught him at it, Dodger gave a merry wink and tossed it back, claiming he liked to borrow things from time to time. Since he possessed fine taste, Braden should have been flattered. Instead, Braden was amused. He gave Dodger the pen as payment for the entertainment he provided then told him he'd be out of Hope Falls the moment he tried anything like that again. Strange how the men who made their way through his door seemed so much more full of life than the stuffed shirts he'd known back in Charleston or even when he did accounts for the mine.

Take that fellow with the overblown manner and patched top hat who went by "Gent." Sweating from the start, Gent's brow and neck bore charcoal-colored trickles of nervousness. No one mentioned the telltale evidence that Gent blackened his hair, but Creed pressed the man about his age. Gent admitted to a stately thirty-seven, a mere two years over the request. No doubt he shaved a few years from that figure, but the man worked hard and made a good influence among the men, so Gent remained.

So a man in his forties roamed the forest, chopping trees and trying to nab a bride half his age, while Braden lay stuck in bed.

His sense of humor kept him going when hope couldn't. Time stretched thin, days passing in dark drips of unfamiliar shadows creeping over too-familiar walls.

"You know I'm a bull-of-the-woods." Bullheaded Craig Williams spoke now. "Creed knows the outfits I've worked for. I've been at it for twelve years. I can do everything from bull-whacking to falling to bucking and even make a passable engineer when called to man a donkey engine. My work speaks for itself."

But that doesn't stop him from flapping his gums. Braden wondered how quickly they could get the pompous logger out of his room. *Going to be a long time if we wait for him to pause.*

"That's not the real reason you're calling all of us into this room one by one. So why don't you skip easing into things by asking about my profession and move to the important questions?" Suddenly, Williams sounded a lot smarter.

It made Braden trust him even less. None of the other men challenged the way they chose to conduct the interviews. That Williams felt comfortable enough to do so said a lot about his character. Or lack of it.

"All right, Williams." Creed didn't shift from his chair, where he sprawled to take up as much of the room as possible. If he leaned forward, it signaled interest. If he leaned farther back, it indicated he'd given up ground to Williams. That Creed knew the rules of staking territory and didn't hesitate to use them was just one reason Braden kept the man close. He made a good ally, but Creed would probably make a far worse enemy. "If you've got everything figured out, why don't you just tell us?"

Braden arched a brow in silent challenge, relieved to notice that, for once, none of the women interrupted. His sister had a way of barging into situations without understanding them—the entire town had become a prime example of that—and his fiancée and her sister didn't do much better. In fact, Evie might just give Lacey a run for her money when it came to being outspoken, but that wasn't Braden's problem.

From the way he'd seen Creed eyeing Evie, he'd be glad to take on that burden when the time came. And when the time came, Braden wouldn't object. If nothing else, Creed could match his fiancée's sister for stubbornness. Besides—it amused Braden to watch the byplay between the two of them. They each kept so busy not acknowledging their interest, it became comical.

"You're trying to make sure I'm good enough to marry one of your women." Williams mimicked Creed's posture—knees bent, boots facing outward, and shoulders down and back as though relaxed. Only trouble was, the shorter man looked boxed in, as though keeping all his energy leashed. "I never attended a university, don't come from a prestigious family, and don't regret either one. What I do have is years of experience, a history of hard work, and the ability to protect what's mine."

Braden tensed. He hadn't imagined the way Williams's gaze flicked toward him when the cocksure lumberjack said that last bit. "The less you own, the easier it is to guard."

Williams drew in a deep breath, too smart to rise to the bait. "That's true, Mr. Lyman. And if it's easy to guard a little, it's difficult to protect a lot. You and your family here possess too much to safeguard without help. That's the reason you put forth the ad, and the reason I'm here."

"I respect honesty, Mr. Williams." *Doesn't mean I like you.*

"I'm an honest man. Ask whatever questions you want."

"My grandma always told me to beware a man who says he's honest, because he's either lying to others or lying to himself. No one manages to tell the truth about everything." Naomi smoothed her hair and gave a winsome smile. "Do you believe my granny's advice, Mr. Williams?"

Braden closed his eyes. He knew if he met his cousin's gaze, or saw Lacey's startled glance, he'd start laughing. *I never heard Grandma Lyman say that.* He shook his head. *Only Naomi would twist a moral question to trap an opponent like this. It's why I never argue or play chess with her.*

"Although no one succeeds every time, I believe a man who attempts honesty can be called an honest man." Williams gave a catlike grin. "But, all told, yes, I believe your granny."

"Now that's an interesting answer, Mr. Williams." Evie tilted her head. "By such logic, a man who attempts piety should be labeled pious, one who attempts to gain wealth would be rich, and so on until everyone on earth could be anything."

"You twist my words, Miss Thompson. That isn't my meaning."

"Do you suppose"—Cora twirled a lock of red hair about her forefinger as she speculated—"that means he was dishonest?"

"It's a moot point," Lacey broke in. "Our granny never gave any such advice, so Mr. Williams shouldn't have believed it. Naomi was giving one of those peculiar lessons of hers again, trying to show us it's a mistake to assume *anyone* is honest."

"How clever!" Cora beamed at his cousin. "But what do you suppose Mr. Williams makes of your ruse?"

"I'll tell you what I think." Williams got to his feet. "I like a woman who uses spunk to fight her battles and spirit to enjoy life. These sneak attacks and silly lessons don't work. My first decision was best. I'll take Miss Thompson."

~ ∞ ~

"And I'll take your apology, Mr. Williams, for acting as though I'm a horse for auction." Evie jumped from her chair.

"I apologize when I'm wrong, but I've not treated you as a horse, Miss Thompson." He rose from his bench. "Though I admire your spirit, I've not so much as asked to see your teeth."

She resisted the impulse to bare them at him, something warning her he'd take it as encouragement. Strange man.

"Insult the lady again, Williams, and you'll lose a few of your own teeth." Creed didn't bother to stand when he made the threat, but somehow that made it all the more ominous.

"Since when does a woman find it insulting that a man wants to marry her? Miss Thompson's a spirited woman with enough fire and wit to keep a man from slipping into boredom." Williams eyed her as though trying to piece together a puzzle. "I like what I see and chose her from the bunch as soon as I got off the train. If she doesn't want a husband, why advertise for one?"

Good questions. Even worse, Williams answered whether or not there's a man in town who wants to marry me for more than my cooking. He chose me before he knew I could make more than gruel and says clearly to anyone who asks that he admires my spirit, strength, feisty ways, or what have you. So why, Lord, does my stomach capsize at the very thought of wedding him?

"Because she wants the *right* husband." Cora began tugging on the lock of hair she'd been twirling. "My sister and friends went about selecting their spouses this way so they'd find partners. Evie chooses which man she'll accept."

"She did the choosing when she listed her requirements in that ad. I fulfill them, and I've come to claim my prize."

"She's a prize, to be sure, but not yours to claim." Catlike reflexes silent and sudden, Creed stood beside her.

Braden held up a hand to stop Williams from moving forward. "You can't pick her up and carry her off, Mr. Williams."

He could have said that some other way. Evie refused to blush as abandoned plans to wreak vengeance upon her sister's fiancé sprang to mind. *First Braden said hefty, and now this.*

"I could with strength to spare." Williams cast an appreciative gaze her way, squared his shoulders, and made the muscles in his arms jump beneath his sleeves.

She let out a squeak of horror. Firstly, the idea of a man picking her up and slinging her around like a sack of potatoes meant he'd know exactly how much "heft" she had. But secondly, the entire image reminded her too much of the Sabine women carried off by Roman soldiers and wedded against their will.

I have more will than most. Evie squared her own shoulders. *And heft, if it comes to that. It might do me good for a change.*

She also found it comforting that Creed looked ready to use

his fists if her overly determined suitor came another step closer. *No, wait. Creed's starting toward Williams. That's a mistake.*

Without another thought, she reached forward to curl her fingers in Creed's sleeve, snagging him and halting his movement before it could start a brawl. Or, if not precisely start one, as Williams' own belligerence held more fault for that, at least exacerbate the situation. Either way, Evie wouldn't allow it.

They'd made strict rules about no fighting in town, and she wouldn't let Creed be the one sent away from Hope Falls for it. Particularly not over a cretin like Williams.

"Don't make mischief, Mr. Williams. Any smart man knows you don't claim a prize like Evie." Naomi's wit defused the situation before it escalated to fists. "You have to win her."

Eyes narrowed, Williams looked from Creed to Evie and back again. "So be it. Let the game begin."

TWENTY-SIX

The Game played before him—a paltry example, to be sure, but Corbin expected no more from a logging camp bunkhouse. Not even one so outlandish as this, with its strange assortment of workmen at odds with themselves, the season, and each other.

The long room unrolled into levels of function. Two layers of bunks lined the walls, outlining the half-log deacon seat benches boxing in the center fire pit. Lanterns hung at intervals on pegs above bunks wherever occupants wanted, and none said a word about it so long as they went out at a decent hour. With generous quarters, they didn't chafe for space.

Groups of men huddled on or around the benches, telling stories, throwing dice, whittling whatnots as they passed time before sleep. Those didn't interest Corbin. High in his perch on the top bunk in the farthest corner, lamp wick pushed barely high enough for a faint glow, he ignored the pages of his book. As he'd done for two weeks, he turned an odd square coin over and over between his fingers, watching the men who played the Game. Memorizing their faces, their movements, the tells that would betray them when Corbin left his corner at last.

He never began the Game. Corbin considered it a sacrilege to demand her favor. Instead, he bided his time, tested his strength by resisting the unworthy. He stayed faithful, knowing the Game would call him once again, give him the opportunity to prove himself the accomplished player he'd become.

He'd allow himself the small pleasure of an occasional round with the men. He'd win most often but throw a few hands occasionally to stay beyond suspicion. Already he'd come close to overplaying his disguise. Too little left him vulnerable with Granger tracking him, but too much left him less desirable to the women. They'd already shown more shrewdness than expected, setting up those probing interviews of theirs.

Not that the questions posed any trouble for him—Corbin had his background set up long before anyone asked. Always did as a matter of course, and it never failed to be useful. Situations changed, stories changed, but how to play the Game never did. Because the rules of the Game were taken from life—where people like these foolish women begged to be played.

If anyone remarked on his ability with the Game, or identified him as a follower, the women would ask uncomfortable questions. The ad specifically listed "God-fearing" as the first requirement for prospective husbands, and Corbin dealt only in the solid truth of here and now. Things he could manipulate.

The Game provided means for survival, offered constant challenges, and rewarded him for success. He didn't fear some vague notion of anyone else's god. Corbin feared losing the Game. Maintaining the facade that he cared for anything else took every ounce of the skills he'd honed over the past decade.

But Corbin judged it worth the effort. By the end of this match, Corbin Twyler planned to win the richest hand he'd ever played for.

"This isn't some amusing diversion, Lacey." Her cousin scolded her as though she herself hadn't toyed with Mr. Williams two days before. "These days will shape the rest of our lives."

"I'm well aware of that, Naomi." Lacey carefully stacked three cans atop the now-familiar target rock at the far end of the clearing, also aware that all three of her friends had followed her. "Why do I have a feeling you three planned to discuss something more than shooting during today's practice?"

"High intelligence?" Cora offered the compliment as a sop.

"Or she knows us very well." Evie's dry response probably came closer to the truth, but Lacey liked Cora's answer better.

"We can chitchat at any time." She made for the other end of the clearing at a rapid pace. Not running, but not lollygagging either. If they hoped to nab her in an unpleasant conversation, Lacey planned to make them work at it.

"Not in private, with just the four of us. Men plague us everywhere we go except the kitchen or the house. Mrs. McCreedy spends as much time in the diner as Evie these days, and Arla only leaves the house in our presence." As always, Naomi wielded logic like an infallible weapon. "When can we speak alone?"

"Not now. Now is the time to practice marksmanship and ensure we can all protect ourselves if need be." Lacey darted a meaningful glance in Evie's direction, raising her eyebrows.

"Don't you do that, Lacey Lyman." Evie shook a finger at her. "Don't you look at me as though I'm the only reason we come out into these woods and fire bullets into stacked cans."

"You're right." Lacey's patience frayed like the edging of an old satin ribbon. "You're not the reason we fire bullets into those cans, Evie. How could you be, when you've never hit one!"

"That was uncalled for, Lace." Cora sprang to her sister's defense. "Every single one of us needs the practice."

"Some more than others, and Evie's the worst of the lot. Stop looking at me as though I've committed some terrible grievance by being honest about it! Right now, your sister would be lucky to hit the broadside of the bunkhouse at ten paces." She knew she should stop talking. Knew that the anger surging in her chest and venting through her words shouldn't be aimed at Evie, but Lacey couldn't hold it inside anymore.

Nothing, but *nothing*, had gone right since they arrived in this town, and something needed to change. Since Lacey couldn't magically make the men into husband material or whip up a functioning sawmill as easily as a loaf of bread, the only way to ease the pressure in her chest was to cry. And Lacey Lyman didn't cry over trivialities. She cried when her parents died, then waited five years before tears swamped her over Braden. In between, not a single salty speck marred her record.

Which meant she had a solid four years and ten months to go, at the very minimum, before indulging in another bout. Or until she had a child. Either/or. But neither one of those options allowed for standing in the middle of the woods, surrounded by friends she'd just insulted, while two dozen lonely men waited for them to hurry up and get hitched.

Maybe, Lacey considered, *I need to rethink my terms.*

In the meantime, her three closest friends all stared at her as though she'd donned a dress four years out of date. Their shock should have spurred her to make amends, but it only brought up her defenses even more. What right did they have to judge her?

"Lacey, what's gotten into you?" Cora reached out. "None of us is good at everything. We accept each other's shortcomings and pool our talents to make the load lighter for everyone."

"I'm tired of carrying so much," a voice sounding suspiciously like her own snapped at her best friend. "Who bakes bread three times a week? Lacey. Who has to keep Braden in line? Lacey. Who teaches you to protect yourselves, or thinks to ask the men what they're looking for in a wife while everyone reprimands her? Lacey!" She threw up her hands. "For pity's sake, you three can't even *eavesdrop* properly without me!"

The more things she listed, the tighter her chest constricted. Why did everything have to be so difficult?

"That's enough, Lacey Danielle Lyman." The stern note

in Evie's voice put the old headmistress to shame. "You'll stop indulging in this morass of self-pity right now."

"It's not self-pity." To her horror, she felt tingles running up her nose, the precursors to unsheddable tears. "All three of you know I'm telling nothing but the truth!"

"A very small part of the truth," Naomi chastised. "We're all working hard. Evie does the lion's share of all the cooking and planning even with Mrs. McCreedy here. Before she ran herself ragged cooking and figuring what supplies we'd need to keep the town going, I suppose you didn't notice how hard she worked to keep the men in line? Mr. Creed contributed to that success, but he's been a difficult one to rein in on his own account, and we have Evie to thank for that, too."

"That's true." Lacey gave a great big sniff. "I know you do a great deal, Evie. It's not that I don't appreciate it. I—"

"And if you think you've managed to keep your brother in line, you need to open your eyes, Lacey." Evie drew a comforting arm around Cora. "My sister never complains over the way Braden continues to treat her, but I see the way it wears. It's between them, but she takes the most care of him and reaps the worst of his temper in return. And she washes most of the pots and pans!"

Evie's outburst, coupled with the misery Cora didn't hide for a few moments, weighed heavily on Lacey's conscience. *I did this. I brought them here and convinced them to place the ad.* Sniffling wasn't slowing down the tingles very much anymore.

"Naomi's the one who steps in to keep peace or put someone in his place without starting a fight." Cora took a turn now. "She's the one to look after Mrs. Nash, and she does most of the milking, too. Even now, she pumps most of the water we need when none of the men are around to take on the task. Each and every one of us does our part, Lacey. It's shameful to hear you imply that we leave the worst of the work to you."

"That isn't what I said, and not what I meant," she protested. "It just seems as though you three don't notice what I do, or think

I fool around and don't contribute or take everything as seriously as anyone else. And that's not true!"

Evie spoke softly after a long silence. "We notice what you do. And I think you see your own plans more than you see the larger picture. Since we came to Hope Falls, you've slowly stopped involving us in your decisions, Lacey."

"I'm thinking of all of us. How can you say otherwise?"

"Small things, at first." Naomi wet her lips. "You didn't think to help us understand the logging terms when it would have helped so much, and you knew we had no chance to read the books."

"You waited until Naomi and I left the room to change your mind and allow Creed and Braden a chance to plot together." Cora's nostrils flared. "That put Evie in the position of stopping the men from scheming or supporting you. She chose to support you because we're a team, but you don't think that way."

"Of course we're a team!" Lacey looked from one upset face to another, reading the disappointment in each one.

"Then you shouldn't have asked the men to narrow down their choices when you knew the rest of us would object." Evie shook her head. "With each day, you're acting more like your brother, Lacey, choosing what you think is best for all of us instead of letting us decide how we want to proceed. We don't like it."

⌒⌒

If asked, Evie felt confident she could list quite a few things she didn't like, but Lacey's increasingly self-centered attitude happened to be one she could help change. Or at least try to.

The incredible growing laundry pile back at the house would wait until the next day they found some spare time. The four of them needed to band together again before everything fell apart. Because, loath as Evie was to admit it, Lacey and the laundry just might be the only two things on that list she could fix.

Not that Lacey needs fixing, Evie corrected then glanced at her friend. *And perhaps her nose,* she added. *I've never seen one turn precisely that shade of crimson before.* Then again, she'd never seen Lacey cry. Or even come close to crying. A sudden surge of sympathy for the youngest member of their group had Evie drawing Lacey into a hug.

"Well, I don't like it either." Lacey's nose brightened another shade. "Especially since I didn't know I was doing it."

Naomi fished one of her never-ending store of embroidered handkerchiefs from a pocket and passed it to her cousin. "We know, Lace. If you realized, you would have stopped."

"I don't even like it when"—she paused to rub her nose, adding the luster of a polished apple—"*Braden* acts like Braden. That's not the sort of thing I ever aspired to, you know."

"Everyone's tired and trying to settle into an unfamiliar place." Cora patted Lacey's shoulder. "Making the best of things sometimes brings out the worst in us, I think."

Evie stared at her little sister, who'd grown up and gained wisdom when she hadn't been paying close enough attention. Perhaps Cora could brazen out Braden's recovery, after all.

"The entire plan collapsed before it started," Lacey moaned. "It's just like the first time I visited a dressmaker's shop with Mother and wandered out of sight. I found the most beautiful gown draped over a dressmaker's doll—an absolute vision of a dress in gold and cream—and nothing would do but I try it on. They warned it wasn't finished, but I begged and pleaded and cried until Mother insisted and they agreed."

Spoiled little bratling, Evie couldn't help but think.

"The moment they put it on me, dozens of pins jabbed me and it fell apart before I got to the mirror." Remorse filled Lacey's voice. "I feel as though I put each one of you in that dress when I convinced you to write the ad and come here."

"It's not the same, Lace." Naomi rejected the comparison.

"Yes, it is. I forced you into something that didn't fit. It jabs and pokes, and it's all falling apart before any of us gets the chance to see how beautiful it should have been!" She crumpled the handkerchief, her nose fading to deep pink.

"Lacey, you're a persuasive woman, but you couldn't have forced me to take part in your plan." Evie took responsibility for her own choice. "I said no once and could have again. All of us did. Not one woman who stands here was dragged across country, kicking and screaming against the injustice of it."

"If you ever question how willing we were, just look at how much we packed." Cora's giggle sparked a round of chuckles.

"It's true," Naomi joined in. "We brought along a library and a diner, sent ahead enough to stock a mercantile, and packed up everything needed to begin four homes and families. How many women can claim they carry an entire town when they travel?"

"Only four that I know of." Lacey cracked a smile.

"So we've encountered a few obstacles and made mistakes along the way," Evie acknowledged. "That doesn't mean we can't make it right."

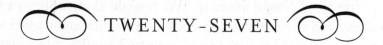

TWENTY-SEVEN

Something was wrong. Jake felt it low in his gut, the same way he'd known when Edward found trouble. The air lay thick in the room but thin in his throat when he breathed deep, his pulse thrumming in anticipation.

Sleep would elude him if Jake reached for it, but he didn't close his eyes. Tonight called for readiness. He didn't speak a prayer—God, in his opinion, was bigger than mere words. Wasn't the Creator of all a God of action? One who saw into hearts, listened to thoughts, and heard hopes? So Jake lay in wait, thinking of what might be needed—of Him. . .of the Lord who watched over His own.

He waited to see if he'd be part of that protection, if that was the reason raw energy filled his mind instead of rest. He prepared, wordlessly, for whatever would disturb the quiet of the bunkhouse. Quiet, in this case, a relative term. It may be the dead of night, but silence found no home here.

Snores and grunts punctured the peace at regular intervals, joined by assorted thuds and thumps as restless limbs bumped against wooden walls. Several slept in their boots. Outside, wind whistled through sharp branches, forcing its cold inside to tickle the flames of their fire.

When Jake could lie still no longer, he slipped his boots onto his feet and walked outside. A circle of the women's house revealed nothing amiss. No lights flickering, no cries of distress, no windows or doors flung open to indicate intruders.

But the feeling remained. So Jake did what any man of sense would. He scaled the nearest tree positioned between the house and the men's quarters and kept watch. If no trouble showed itself, he suffered no more than a sleepless night. But if—

Jake's thoughts ground to a halt as he heard the sound of footsteps. He shifted, ready to jump at a moment's notice. That's when he spotted them. Four men, bundled in jackets and hats as they crept toward the house, whispers carrying on a suddenly subdued breeze. It was as though the entire mountain listened along with Jake as the mysterious figures spoke.

"Pretty little Lacey Lyman's mine, and no switching. Once we make women out of 'em, they have to marry us."

"No need to get shackled when you can enjoy someone else's. Engaged girls know what's what, and she'll need a real man now that her fiancé's an invalid." Snickers met the crude comment.

Jake gripped the branch so hard his hands bled, but it wasn't time to leap. They weren't close enough. Yet.

"I don't think any of 'em is decent women. Only trollops prance around these parts without a man, but the best ones know we like a little chase. Prissy Higgins is mine."

"We'll know the truth after we take their hair down and let loose." The first one rubbed his hands together before he added, "Creed's not abed, so you might have to wait, Tom. Plain to see which woman he fancies, though I can't see why."

"After chopping logs all day, some of us don't want twigs in our beds. There's nothing better than a nice, soft—" The fourth man never got a chance to finish.

Jake leapt from his perch and slammed the man's head into the trunk. He crumpled without another word. By the time Jake planted his fist in another's face, the other two got over their surprise. A punch to the stomach made Jake double over, so he plowed his head into the man's gut and took him down.

From that point, he stopped thinking. Jake couldn't say how long the fight would have lasted—until they'd taken him down or he'd finished beating them so bloody they'd never touch another woman, most likely—if they hadn't made such a racket they woke up half the town. Which, in turn, woke up the other half.

Several things happened almost simultaneously. First, the windows to the house opened, and a cacophony of female shrieks and wails rent the night. Right after that began, but while it continued—because the women didn't stop caterwauling until long after the fists stopped flying—Riordan came barreling over in his bare feet to do battle alongside Jake.

Jake pulled back his arm and smashed the full force behind it into the heel of his palm, connecting with the nose of the opponent before him. As the man went down, blubbering, Jake saw Riordan simply lift the final fighter into the air and send him crashing into a nearby wall before trotting off to retrieve him. With that, the brouhaha ended as swiftly as it started.

Or it would have ended there, but every man circled around, suddenly keen to be a valiant protector. Questions abounded; boasts of how others would have handled things filled the air until not even all the knives in Evie's kitchen could cut through the bluster. Scuffles over who threw a better punch started to break out until Mrs. Martha McCreedy arrived.

"Get back in the bunkhouse, the whole lot o' ye." She assessed the situation in a single glance. "Creed and Riordan took care o' matters. Mr. Klumpf will kindly fetch the doctor."

No one moved. Jake felt fairly certain, since only one of his eyes was swelled shut. "You heard her," he yelled. "Get to bed or you'll all be worthless tomorrow, and we'll have four fewer workers as it stands. Besides"—he resorted to blackmail—"if you keep the ladies awake any longer, you'll be making breakfast for yourselves." That got them moving, if slowly.

For a pleasant change, the women didn't rush headlong into the melee. Instead, they waited until the men cleared out before bustling Jake into the house. He only went because two of the four offenders remained unconscious, one of them the man who'd had his eye on Evie. For that reason, Jake let Riordan truss up the criminals while he withstood the doctor's fussing.

Withstood, shooed away. . .what difference did it make? "I've had worse," Jake assured the women when the doctor slammed his black bag shut and stormed out the door. "Split knuckles, a black eye, a few bruised ribs—pass me some witch hazel, and I'll be fine in a couple days." *Unlike the men on the other side of those knuckles.* He indulged in a grim smile.

"I won't ask if you're all right." Evie's face entered his line of vision. "Obviously you'll be fine since you're as stubborn as ever, refusing to let the doctor look at that eye." She scolded and fussed the entire time she smoothed his hair back to lay a cool compress over that very eye.

Though she, like the other women, had donned a dressing gown over her night rail and was swathed from neck to foot in layers of fabric, there was something far too intimate about the gesture. Especially at night, and especially when her hair swung down her back in a long, saucy braid whose tip curled lovingly along her arm. Evie looked far too inviting.

Jake circled a hand around her wrist when she looked ready to adjust the compress. He thought only to stop her. Instead, the contact stopped his thoughts. Aside from the day they'd met, and the time he'd jumped through the window and gotten tangled in the curtain, almost knocking her over, he'd never let himself touch Evie. Not once.

And he never should have.

∞

She shouldn't have touched him. Evie knew it the moment her fingertips brushed his forehead to whisk an errant lock of hair out

253

of the way. The heat of him nearly burned her. But like a moth to a flame, she fluttered back, only to be caught.

And when the strength of Jake Creed's long fingers closed over her wrist, unintentionally pushing up the sleeve of her dressing gown, Evie feared she might hear a sizzle. Awareness of the contact streaked through her, scrambling her thoughts and holding her captive long after he released her.

In fact, he let go so quickly, Evie wondered whether he felt any of the same reaction. Warmth flooded her cheeks at the idea until she turned to hide the telltale blush. Fumbling, she passed him the witch hazel he'd requested, along with a towel.

It gave her just enough time to recover before Mr. Riordan and Mr. Klumpf strode through the door. Riordan looked none the worse for wear despite having joined Jake in the fight.

Everyone adjourned to the dining room, the only room with enough chairs to accommodate all of them. Evie could only be thankful Mrs. McCreedy insisted on taking Arla home with her for the remainder of the night—there'd been too much excitement for a woman in her condition already, and none of them was willing to wait to learn the details of what had happened. Before the brawl itself, naturally. They saw that firsthand.

"Where are they?" Creed directed the question to Riordan.

"Ach." The Irishman's face went thundery. "I trussed 'em good an' tight and tossed the lot in an old privy shack, then barred the privy door from t' outside. I found it fitting."

Evie choked back her laughter. *Until I know what these men did to deserve their fate, I shouldn't laugh at it.* She could almost imagine standing before an enormous blackboard, chalk in hand, writing the same sentence over and over again. *"It's not amusing to lock someone in the privy."*

Creed held no such compunction. He threw back his head and roared at Riordan's punishment. When he caught his breath, he clapped the other man on the shoulder. "That should hold them." As swiftly as it came, his amusement fled. "Though they deserve far worse. We'll need to call the authorities. Press charges."

"I dragged Draxley out of bed to send a telegram." Mr. Klumpf gave a satisfied nod. "Those men will be gone tomorrow."

"Lucky for them." A dark gleam lit Creed's eye. Only the one, since the other remained swelled shut and would for much longer than necessary since the fool wouldn't hold his compress over it. "If they stayed any longer, their fellow loggers would want to go a round or two before handing them over for lawful justice."

"I assumed as much." Riordan's voice rumbled low enough to mimic an earthquake. "When the lassies shrieked like banshees, I feared the worst. 'Tis glad I am you intervened, Creed."

"Banshees!" Lacey's screech didn't give lie to the label.

"Aye. 'Tis said they wail and scream a terrible warning." Riordan's green eyes took on a teasing light. "And can appear as uncommonly beautiful women if they take on the notion."

"Oh, well, that's not so bad." Lacey settled back.

"Irish superstitions aside"—Evie wanted to direct the conversation back to the events of the evening—"could someone tell us why you and those four were out wandering tonight, Mr. Creed? And what did they do to deserve such a sound thrashing and"—she paused, quelling another inappropriate chuckle before managing to finish—"unconventional form of imprisonment?"

"They came for you." Creed answered two questions in four words, none of them yes or no. In another situation, such a feat might have been deemed impressive. But not now. Creed seemed to sense that they awaited more of an explanation, as he generously doubled his response. "So I stopped them."

Perhaps, Evie wondered, *when a man resorts to using his fists, he temporarily loses the ability to express himself through words? It's either the visceral or the cerebral? But if he gives no reason, he's broken the law and has to leave.*

"We noticed that you stopped them, Mr. Creed." Cora gave him a bemused look. "We even assumed it had something to do with their proximity to the house?"

His nod verified the assumption but added nothing more, forcing the women to pry further.

"Did you originally make up one of their party, and something went wrong?" Naomi took a wild guess as to why, of five men strolling through the dark, only one still stood.

Or at least retained his ability to stand, in any case. The hope behind her question made Evie wince. Apparently she wasn't the only one desperate for any reason but the worst.

"Nope."

"Mr. Riordan, can you explain?" Lacey's exasperation shone through her attempt at making it a polite request.

"Well, miss, I only joined in after the wailing began, so I ken that the four o' ye saw more than Rory Riordan." He frowned.

"Oh, for pity's sake." Evie abandoned trying to be polite. It was late. She was tired. Four battered men slumped in an outhouse somewhere nearby with no explanation, and Creed needed to start talking. "Stop being vague and tell us what happened!"

Everyone's eyes went big, but smiles bloomed around the table.

"You know what you need to." Creed's jaw thrust forward. Or maybe it, too, was swelling. Either way, he wasn't talking.

"I know you and four men were involved in a brawl. I know we've given you the opportunity to explain yourself, and you've declined." Evie planted her palms on the table and stood. "I know I'm to look at a man's actions. The laws we set down for Hope Falls state that any man brawling in town will be escorted to the train, and since you've given us no reason to make an exception, it must stand." *Words are important, too.* She kept from saying this last by a slim margin.

The other women started to gasp, recognized her intent, and began setting their expressions. Nods, crossed arms, and regretful sighs circled the table as Mr. Creed looked about. If he thought he'd find a soft heart to sway, he'd underestimated their curiosity. Evie knew her friends better than he could.

Riordan and Klumpf stared at them all, incredulous, but held their peace. Whether they waited to see which side gave way, or to be given the order to escort Creed to the train, Evie couldn't say. Either way, it worked in her favor.

"Especially after an upset like this, every effort must be made to maintain order," Lacey chimed in. "You understand."

"I couldn't sleep, so I walked around to see if anything looked out of the ordinary. Nothing stood out at first, but over by the tree I heard footsteps." Creed's good eye narrowed, and the swollen one seemed to darken into a more livid bruise. "All I needed to hear were a few comments to know what they planned."

Silence reigned again as Evie, along with everyone else, waited for him to explain just what the four men planned. *Please tell me it's not what I think. Give me another reason.*

But Creed snapped his jaw shut.

"That explains why you were there," Evie prodded, "but not why the others were, nor the reason behind your actions."

"Some things a man doesn't like to mention to ladies," Mr. Klumpf broke in, darting a glance at Creed. "I suspect that's the case here, and Mr. Creed's doing right not to offend you."

"Is that the way o' it?" The question came on a breath, the answer a ghost of a nod between Riordan and Creed. "So be it." Riordan turned to them. "Those men planned to harm you ladies. Sneaking around in the middle of the night, heading to your home while everyone slept, 'tis the logical conclusion, and I lend my support to Mr. Creed. I assure you the other men would agree."

"But we don't." Lacey huffed. "What if Mr. Creed took offense at something they said, and things got out of hand?" She looked at him. "Did you overhear them insult any of us?"

"All of you." Creed's answer made Evie's blood run cold.

Four men. Four women they didn't respect, defenseless in the middle of the night. No alternate reason after all. *Braden's worst fear made real if not for Mr. Creed's vigilance.*

"The other men will suspect the cause immediately, will they not?" Evie held his gaze until he gave another short nod. "Do you believe any others think the same way, or will tonight's events abolish any doubts as to our virtue?" *Will we be safe?*

She ignored the horrified resignation on her friends' faces as Cora, Naomi, and Lacey were forced to face the cause of all the ruckus. They'd suspected as well as she but not accepted it until now.

"There should be no other doubts." Creed's assurance lent little comfort, despite Riordan's and Klumpf's hasty agreements. "But even amongst these four, they debated the issue."

"That makes no sense," Lacey all but whimpered.

"What Mr. Creed is saying"—Evie closed her eyes—"is that not all of those men believed us to be loose women. Even if they all know we're virtuous, our reputations won't protect us."

"On the contrary." Creed cracked his split knuckles as though to underscore his point. "A man knows that if he dishonors one of you, you'll have no choice but to marry him. They counted on it."

 TWENTY-EIGHT

A man couldn't count on anything these days. Corbin stalked past the others, noisy crows cawing over the night's adventure and causing enough racket to make sure anyone sensible couldn't catch a wink of sleep. He flung himself onto his bunk.

Fools. He turned his back on the lot of them, facing the unfinished wood of the bunk wall. *Cretins.* Hope Falls had been settling into a familiar, plodding routine. Wake up, eat breakfast, work, eat lunch, work more, eat dinner and socialize with the women, and go back to the bunkhouse. If it weren't for the women—and their admittedly superior food—it would have been exactly the same setup Corbin abandoned a decade ago.

He despised the routine, but it served a purpose. Routine lulled the dull-witted and optimistic into a sort of drowsy contentment. It made men lazy, and women more appreciative of small gestures designed to woo and win. Corbin had bided his time, waiting for the routine to assert itself.

And four fools undid in forty moments what had taken weeks of patience to establish. Excitement ran high tonight, but tomorrow wariness would replace the thrill. Men would eye their fellow workers with new suspicion, the women withdraw to reassess their judgment. Something shattered never became whole again. At best it mended. But Corbin couldn't wait for time's healing touch.

Granger followed him across three states to Charleston, and he'd gotten word the man came as far as Colorado. Corbin didn't know whether the tenacious hunter tracked him to Durango, but he couldn't take the risk he'd get that far. Granger was to be avoided at any cost.

Except the Game. Corbin would sacrifice anything but that. He pulled out the piece he'd lifted from Granger's brother, square copper emblazoned with a crown and three fleurs-de-lis on one side and naught but an angry slash on the other. Rubbing it between thumb and forefinger, Corbin considered his next move.

Originally, he'd thought to pursue the cook. Miss Thompson appealed to him at first for the additional revenue to be earned from her café, but he'd quickly realized she'd be a difficult woman to control. So he settled on Miss Higgins, whose more biddable demeanor suited his purposes. If worse came to worst, a widower's inheritance could be worth more than a wife after all.

Miss Lyman, owner of the mercantile and sister to the principal mill investor, would make the richest wife but also the most closely watched. She'd never been a possibility for the simple reason that a wealthy heiress involved too high a risk.

But the situation had changed, and the Game called more strongly than ever. Corbin flipped the piece, pondering his options. He'd thought marriage would be the ultimate bluff, but now things were becoming clear....

The longer the women stayed, the more muddled everything became. Before they arrived, Braden knew exactly what he had to do. He sent Eric and Owen home to proper hospitals as soon as they could be moved and wrote to free Cora. But the moment his featherbrained sister whisked into town, packing luggage to the sky and headaches to hide them, everything became a negotiation.

Battles couldn't be chosen because every single one could be the turning point, a weakness leaving Cora and his family exposed to even more danger. So Braden waged war with every word he spoke. Every pang of pain he ignored so the doctor wouldn't drug away his scant ability to protect the women.

And I failed. Braden's hands clenched into fists, nails breaking the skin of his palms as Creed summarized the events of last night. *Cora was in danger, and I slept through it. Blasted morphine.* The doctor would never force it on him again. Never.

Creed gave the bare bones of it, but they both knew the gravity of what could have been. Braden didn't trust himself to demand the details yet. He didn't trust himself to speak. If he opened his mouth, he'd yell himself hoarse before he could do anything useful. And it would scare Cora even more.

She walked into the room with the others, back stiff and chin set as she prepared for the conversation to come. But Braden knew her too well to believe her unaffected. Cora finally feared what he'd dreaded the moment he saw her in this accursed excuse for a town—that she'd need the type of protection he couldn't provide. And, for the first time, she might understand why she needed to find another man to build a life with.

But she wouldn't do it. She had to leave town to be safe, but he hadn't been able to force her from his side. Cora's loyalty ran as deep as an ocean and could drown any force but the woman's own stubbornness. Or Braden's.

There's only one way to be rid of her. Lord, forgive me for what I'm about to do. What other choice do I have?

Too many options. Robert Kane left town in a blaze of bruises, but Jake hadn't thinned his crowd of suspects nearly enough. Kane's story hadn't been cleared, but Jake could live with that. The odds Kane and Twyler were the same man sank low. For one thing,

Twyler wasn't stupid, and five suspects remained.

Even if Jake was wrong, Kane would remain in custody—safely tucked away from the women he'd planned to accost and easily within reach should word come back he hadn't worked where he claimed.

In all honesty, Jake didn't truly suspect Gent either. Despite his intelligence and the bootblack, Gent's age precluded him. All reports of Twyler put him at no more than thirty, too obvious a difference for someone not to have mentioned.

Which left four men fitting Twyler's description. Dodger, the high-climbing thief whose too-large clothing concealed more than Jake could guess; Williams, whose cocky attitude made him enough of a character it could be a disguise; Fillmore, the unassuming shadow who'd shown enough backbone not to accompany Kane the night before; and Clump, whose unusual background and raised boot-bottoms made him an oddity if nothing else.

Any one could be Twyler. Or none of them. Theories and questions chased themselves around Jake's skull until they tangled tighter than a logjam. It took him nowhere in a hurry while Evie and her friends faced growing danger. If Twyler panicked or changed his plans, the women might pay the price.

"We need to set guards to watch the house at night," he told Lyman the next morning. "I only trust myself, Riordan, and Lawson to do it. McCreedy, too, but he's got a wife to look after already, so he's out. Things can't stay as they are."

"Stand still or sit down, Creed," Lyman barked at him, obviously unable to marshal the fury coursing through him. "I can't believe I slept through the entire thing. Morphine takes away the pain but steals the time from a man's life."

"No harm done." His fiancée reached out to clasp Lyman's hand, but he pulled away. "Mr. Creed and Mr. Riordan kept everything under control, and we're none the worse for wear."

"I am." Jake gestured to his left eye, which only opened a fraction of an inch. "But keeping the women safe is all that matters." *And finding Twyler is a part of that. Edward's death deserves justice, but a crafty criminal who shows no remorse when it comes to murder needs to be caught more for the sake of the living. It shouldn't have taken a black eye for me to see it.* He cast a glance toward Evie, who didn't say much.

"A guard won't be good enough." Lyman stuck his hand beneath the sheet and glowered at his fiancée. "I was right when I said it at the start—Hope Falls is no place for a woman. You four need to leave. We'll find investors for the mill and use our resources to set you up back East, in safety."

"No." Evie shook her head. "Even if we could be sure that would work, it's too late. I gave my word to those men to make them meals while they worked here. Besides, I won't leave Mrs. Nash. She can't move now, with the babe so close."

"We can hire another cook." The moment he said it, Jake wanted to bite back the words. He made it sound as though Evie could be replaced, exchanged, or some such foolishness. Anyone who'd spent more than three minutes in her company knew better. And that was before tasting any of her food.

"Men consider it a matter of honor to keep their word." Miss Higgins looked at them incredulously. "Why would you imagine we'd go back on ours over an isolated bit of idiocy?"

"*Most* men consider it a matter of honor." Cora Thompson stared at Lyman with such intensity, Jake suddenly wondered what had passed between the two of them since her arrival. "Some make promises and become all too willing to break them."

"And some women are too blind to see when circumstances change," Lyman snapped back. "If it comes down to your well-being or being thought well of, there is no possible comparison."

"He's right." Jake threw his support behind Lyman before the women could quibble about the wording or some such. "I chose to shield you from the crudeness of what the men said, but I dislike the consequences. Words aren't actions, and I spared you both since the worst didn't reach your doorstep. But it came close—too blasted close to ignore."

"Language!" Miss Higgins fixed him with a gimlet eye.

"It's worth worse, and if that offends you, believe me when I say you'd faint dead away had your ears been sullied by the speculations made about the four of you last night." Jake refused to apologize. If one little "blasted" brought home the seriousness of the situation, he'd count himself blessed.

"You do offend, Mr. Creed." The hint of hollows pressed beneath her cheekbones, mute testimony to Evie's perseverance. And the fact she still wasn't eating enough. "Not only with your swearing but with your low opinion of us."

"Low opinion?" He was reduced to parroting her, unable to make sense of the statement. *I've never met a woman I think more highly of, and very few men.* "Aside from your determination to put yourself in harm's way, I highly regard each of you."

"They can also be bossy," Lyman added in. "But their stubborn ways overtake that. Paired with an inability to exercise critical thinking, stubbornness becomes dangerous."

"Lyman?" Jake waited for his so-called ally to look at him. "Now would be a wise time to stop talking. Before you win the ladies' argument for them." *Or I gag you for insulting Evie.*

"The one time Braden's outpouring of negativity can work in our favor, and he stops it." Miss Thompson rolled her eyes. "But the damage is done, Mr. Creed. It's foolish and dishonest to claim you hold any one of us in esteem when all you do is denigrate our decisions and order us about like children."

"All the while accusing us of selfish and shallow reasoning," Miss Higgins tacked on. Only a woman could manage to sound both triumphant and aggrieved in the same sentence.

"Selfish and shallow have no part in it. Nonsensical, I'd more than agree with." Jake searched the gaggle before him for any hint of solid reason and found only indignation. "We wouldn't bother trying to keep you safe if we didn't value you."

"Then you must value vapid fools who care only for what other people think." Evie's words hit too close to home.

All the way back to Jake's parents. "That's the last thing I value." Not that they were vapid, but the rest came within a splinter of describing his family. None of it came anywhere near depicting Evie or her friends. Or their worth.

"The Bible specifically tells us we can't speak out of both sides of our mouths, Mr. Creed." Miss Thompson fingered a golden cross hanging around her neck. "You can't claim to think both ways on a single issue, or you've ruined your own credibility."

"Would you believe he looks confused?" Miss Lyman shared glances with the others as Jake tried to dissect where they'd gone wrong, because obviously the women were the ones confused.

"I'd believe he judges us so trivial as to put the opinion of other people above our own safety." Miss Higgins furrowed her brow in mock concentration. "Yet he clearly claims he doesn't value petty people who think like that, so how can he value us?"

"They're doing that female thing again, where they ask a question with no good answer." Lyman's warning told him nothing new, only validated a long-standing suspicion that women took logical conversations and warped them into terrible traps.

"Every question possesses a good answer," his fiancée snapped at him. "It's just a matter of men not doing that male thing of refusing to admit how wrong they've been!"

"Hold it." Creed held up a palm to stop the squabbling and return to the issue at hand. "Lyman's a man who forgoes shovels to dig himself into a hole with nothing more than his mouth. That much is evident to anyone. But there's no denying you four took a solid conversation and chopped it to kindling. So instead of trying to undo the damage, let's go back and start again."

"We'll take that as an admission that men go about things backwards and graciously go along with it." Miss Lyman's capitulation—and the dig behind it—bought smiles from the women.

"Only because if men always go ahead, it means we can't look *after* you." Jake emphasized his point. "So you find danger. Now here's where things stalled. We place importance on your safety because we find you worth protecting. You four place more significance on what the men think about you than you put on your own security. That has to change."

"It's gratifying to hear you find us worthy." If a certain dry humor laced Miss Higgins's remark, Jake could overlook it.

"But far less gratifying to hear you disparage both our actions and our motives." Evie had stayed quiet since her comments about fools who cared only about what others thought. The grace period ended as she fixed her stare on him. "We don't deliberately put ourselves in danger, nor do we choose to remain in a precarious position out of a misguided superficiality. Simply put, Mr. Creed, we don't only keep our promises for the sake of the men. We keep them because we owe it to ourselves."

"You don't owe it to anyone to stay!" Lyman shouted. "Foolish decisions reflect poorly on you and your planning!"

"If a man's words are worthless, so is he," Evie threw back at him. "It's no different with women. We uphold our pledges because it respects the men we made them to and shows we value our judgment and promises enough to act on them. That you and Creed dismiss that reflects poorly on the two of you!"

"All that would be so, if not for one thing." Jake met her gaze with a fierce look of his own, standing so close his boots almost touched hers. "You're wrong when you say you didn't deliberately place yourself in danger. The moment you wrote that ad, the four of you brought this down upon Hope Falls. You set it in motion, and now you need to rectify your mistake."

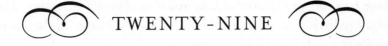# TWENTY-NINE

I t wasn't our mistake!" Miss Lyman slapped a hand on her brother's mattress for muffled punctuation. "We did not invite all these men into town in person and put ourselves in peril!"

"She's right." Miss Higgins sighed. "The ad may not have been the wisest idea, but, as written, it didn't invite danger."

"Since you've had over forty men come into town, despite only two dozen being allowed to remain, I'd say the general public disagrees with you, ladies." Jake silently dared them to refute that bit of evidence—a mistake.

"Of course they side with you. The general public of Hope Falls is male," Evie burst out. "They're the ones who misread or willfully disregarded the print and ruined our plans. Face it, Mr. Creed. This entire situation isn't because the four of us rushed headlong into danger. It's because men"—she paused as though to savor her next point—"refuse to follow directions!"

"You four are ones to speak." Lyman's roar muted to a thunderous growl. "Refusing to follow a single order since you arrived. No matter your intentions, no matter your plans, at least we can all agree that the outcome placed you at risk. Which means you need to abandon this failure and return East."

Four feminine heads gave mutinous shakes.

"Stop acting as though you need to stay. Safety and common sense overshadow some misguided principle here," Jake coaxed.

"Then we have different definitions of honor, Mr. Creed." Evie's remonstrance, a perfect echo of his parting words to his mother, robbed him of the ability to continue the conversation.

Honor is what brought me here. Honor is what keeps me spending time protecting you women. Honor is the bark that binds together the loose rings of my life. And she defines it as though I'm lacking. The irony roared in his ears until the sudden stillness of the room broke through to grab his notice.

"You don't mean that." Miss Thompson's brittle voice shattered the unnatural quiet, but no one moved.

"I do." Lyman's tones came out hollow. False. "If you won't leave, you have to marry. As soon as possible."

As Jake realized that his friend's alternative was to force the women into hasty weddings to gain the protection of husbands, his temples pounded in rage. *No. They'll marry the men they choose. Evie won't be given away to just any man so Braden Lyman can rest easy.* He opened his mouth to start objecting, but Lyman kept going.

"Even Cora."

⬯

Especially Cora. Evie leaped from her chair, intent on reaching her sister's former fiancé. *Cora will need another husband more than any of us once I'm jailed.* Her hands curved, pulling Lacey and Naomi away from where they tried to block her path. She couldn't tell whether the pair sought to protect their kin from her wrath or tried to beat her to him so they could let him have it first. They probably knew her well enough to know that there wouldn't be much left of Braden Lyman once Evie finished with him. Old adages claimed blood ran thicker than water, but Evie figured men thought that one up.

Battles didn't always leave visible bruises, friends became extensions of families when distance and time left loved ones lonely, and women knew well the wounds inflicted by words. Men shed blood together; women shed tears. Evie knew which made her stronger and believed she knew which bond Lacey and Naomi upheld now.

But it didn't matter why they blocked the bed. No matter their good intentions, her friends were in her way. So she barreled through. *I can't hit him. I can't kick him. I can't smother him with his own pillow.* She ran into the solid, unmoving obstacle that was Creed as she pondered just how she'd exact retribution on Braden for trying to throw her sister to the wolves. *I'll do worse than any of those. I'll sit on him!*

"Oh no, you won't." Creed slid to the side to block her when she tried to maneuver around, taking up far too much space.

Evie stopped. "Did I say that out loud?" Mortification swallowed surprise in a blink. Then she shrugged it away. If Creed stayed in the room, he'd see her act on the words.

"You didn't say anything." An inappropriate chuckle lightened his voice. "I could guess at a slew of possibilities by the look in your eye, but I'm not going to let any of them happen. So I don't see the use in giving you any extra ideas."

"Feel free." She leaned right then darted left, only to be brought up short by one rock-hard arm suddenly encircling her midriff. Evie gave a strangled yelp and jumped away from the contact. The heat surprised her. His speed caught her off guard. The idea that he felt, however briefly, how wide across she measured was unimaginably awful. That mortified her more than if he'd heard her plotting vengeance against Braden.

Braden, who still sat hale and hearty—or at least as hale and hearty as he had five minutes previous—in his bed. Which meant Lacey and Naomi remained behind her, most likely consoling a bereft Cora.

The man will pay. Creed can't guard him forever. Evie clenched her fists so tightly they cramped, the pulse in her fingertips matching the pounding at her temples and in the sensitive place behind her jaw. That Braden would stoop so low as to renege on the engagement, she'd suspected. That he'd throw her sister to a pack of lonely loggers without a word or any sort of arrangement for her protection, she'd never imagined.

Lacey, Naomi, and I came alone, knowing we'd find men. Agreeing to that plan. Cora came for Braden. Evie began to shake as she considered all that Cora had given up for the ungrateful brute. *He may not be able to stand, but he could have stood by his word. The simple title of fiancée offered Cora a certain measure of protection. The men didn't swarm around her equally.*

"Home or husbands." Braden started talking again. "You have to be protected, and either one will do. There aren't any other options, and each one of you will need to make her choice."

"They'll choose their husbands in their own time, Lyman." Creed's snarl jerked Evie's attention back to the man who blocked her path. "Marriage is for life, and, as you've so aptly illustrated, a woman can never be too careful about what sort of man she chooses to give her hand—or her heart—to." Blue eyes, blazing with heat, stared into her own as he said this last, making Evie almost believe Creed urged her toward caution rather than reprimanded Braden for being unworthy of Cora.

Either way, she fought a sudden, strong urge to hug him. Or bake him a pie, which was just as good and far more proper. "Thank you." She then rose on tiptoe to peer over Creed's shoulder.

The man unbent enough to champion them about not rushing to the altar, but he showed no sign of moving.

"Braden Lyman, you're no longer allowed to give any suggestions, offer any opinions, or make any demands regarding our safety," Evie declared. "Of all the men in this town, you've demonstrated that you, who should care for us and cherish Cora, Lacey, and Naomi the very most, instead value us the least. We aren't burdens to be given away."

"That's not what I—"

"Do. Not. Say. Another. Thing." Creed spoke as though each word was a sentence, a proclamation unto itself.

Lyman obeyed.

"We've arranged for Mrs. Nash's brother, Mr. Lawson, to move into the study below stairs. After last night, we all agree we'd feel safer with the added protection, and he's the only male relative any of us boast in town." She didn't tell them to assuage their concerns, merely to inform them of the decisions they—the women—had already made. "With the babe so close to term, it's wise to have him nearby in any case. These are the measures we've taken for our own security and to maintain propriety."

"Why did you four. . ."

Evie didn't listen to the rest. She spun on her heel and walked the few steps to where her sister still sat in her chair, shock freezing her in place. "Cora-mine"—she whispered the old nickname, the play on Coraline's full name—"you'll not be courted by the others. It's too soon and wasn't the plan."

"No," Lacey assured her. "We won't put about word that your engagement has ended. No one need know. Creed won't mention it, and if Braden does, he knows full well we'll move Mrs. Nash and her brother to another house. He's said more than enough, and it's time he learned to keep his fool mouth shut."

With that tirade, Evie knew she'd been right about the strength of the friendship shared among the four of them. Even though they'd faced Lacey in a sort of fight the very day before, she stood ready to deny her own brother for their sakes.

"There's nothing for him or Creed to keep secret." So strident were the words, Cora might have been marshaling troops. Or, perhaps, the formidable reserves of a woman's strength. "I'll not discuss it now beyond saying this: Braden can deny me as many times as he likes within the hearing of the four of you." Here, she gave a nod to include Creed. "Because we know that the truth of the matter is the engagement stands."

"Now, Cora," Braden tried again. "See reason. You need to marry another man to be safe. It's the only logical thing."

"I'm nothing but logical, my love." Bitter determination tinged the endearment. "You proposed, kept me to a long engagement, accepted my dowry, and invested it in this town." She gave a strange laugh, ruefulness mixed with determination as she looked at her fiancé. "You didn't think of that, did you, Braden? That I can sue you for breach of promise? That Lacey holds your estate and would support my suit?"

Evie sucked in a breath. *Lord, please don't let my sister force a man to wed her. Please look after her tender heart, and don't let her determination and the memories of the man who used to be her beau ruin her future. Please. . .*

"None of you thought of it, but I considered that this might happen. The other three placed an ad, Braden." Now Cora drew a deep breath. "But I knew, if worse came to worst and you became bullheaded, I could always point out one unchangeable truth. Out of all of us, I've already hired my husband. . . . You."

"Me?" Braden snorted, as much to keep the howl of despair jammed back in his throat as to sound amused. "I hope you realize how fortunate you are, Cora, that I've released you from a bad bargain without asking to see the bill of sale."

Stubborn, brilliant, beautiful Cora. She waits for me to reclaim her, and when I refuse, she rolls up her sleeves and comes for me instead. God, grant me strength to keep pushing her away until she stops pulling me close.

"Joke all you like." She folded her hands in her lap. "But I've not released you from our bargain and have no intention of doing so. You might as well resign yourself to your fate and make a wise decision—for a refreshing change—to be pleasant about the situation." The smile she gave him looked nothing like Cora. It looked like something with no heart wearing a tragic mask of Cora's smile.

Braden wanted to throw it away and bring back the real thing. *But I can't. Until she accepts that I've cast her aside and demand she weds another, she'll never leave Hope Falls. Cora won't be safe until they go back East. I have to make her believe. I have to make it even worse.*

"A man can't be bought, darling. Everyone knows that." Braden raised his arms and nestled the back of his head in his stacked palms, as though bored. "We're too smart for such a practice. Men use commodities and make the most of them. We aren't the goods to be made use of. The world runs on that truth, and the four of you need to accept it."

Creed made a low warning sound deep in his throat, but Braden ignored him. Now wasn't the time to explain the ploy to his odd ally. Now was the time to make sure it worked.

"You took my money; I took your hand. That's an exchange of goods." Cora pointed out the simple business. "That makes you a commodity I found to be worth a certain amount. Of course, you used to be far more pleasant, so it seems I made the common mistake of overpaying when I signed over my dowry. But all that is past, and we move onward."

His sister and hers tried, unsuccessfully, to hide chuckles at Cora's assessment that she'd overpaid. But it was no laughing matter.

Can't they see it's true? I'm no longer worth what I once was. No longer worthy of her. "Such naïveté for a budding businesswoman." Braden tsked. "It's not a matter of whether or not my worth matched your dowry, little Cora. Dowries are merely incentives. You know what incentives are, don't you?" He raised a brow.

"Lyman, I might let her sister get to you." Creed breathed the threat.

Braden knew that his friend was letting him know where he was headed. And, more importantly, that it was despicable enough to be effective. *Good.*

"When the goods are not up to par or don't match to the value being exchanged, something is added to make them more desirable. It's commonly accepted that women, in and of themselves, lack any particular value. Thus, the invention of the dowry to persuade men to part with their freedom. It helps even out the trade, so to speak. Your dowry was compensation for my sacrifice in taking you." Braden twisted the knife.

"Is that so?" The travesty of a smile took on the fine gleam of a sharpened knife.

"You've seen enough of the world now to begin to understand." He sliced away at every sweet memory they shared as he reduced their love to dollars and nonsense.

"I'm beginning to see that you admit you were compensated, and I'll hold you to the job. Better yet, I've been learning to get the most for my money." That sharp smile edged to the faces of the other three women as Cora spoke. "Since you seem so certain you'll be unhappy with me as a wife, I see no reason we should both be miserable. So I'll be happy. Which means you'll have a lot of work to do to pass muster from here on out."

"Cora, stop this." It had gone on far enough. "Lacey will return your dowry, plus interest. You're free to find another." He managed to say the words without wincing and ruining it all.

"I know I could be free." The smile vanished, leaving a grim, tight line in its place. "But you won't be. I won't accept my dowry in return, even if Lacey would give it to me. Which I'm certain she wouldn't, as her heart is set on having me for a real sister. Isn't that true, Lace?"

"Absolutely." Lacey nodded. "It'd be a shame for Braden to lose everything he owns in a lawsuit over such a thing."

"Send for the lawyer, Lace." He wasn't playing this game. "If I lose, I lose. But I'd rather lose my money than my life."

Because that's what will happen if anything happens to Cora while I'm trapped in this bed. She has to be safe. At any cost.

THIRTY

I t's not worth it!" Lacey protested but knew she could only blame herself. Whether it was a matter of speaking before she thought or a simple case of packing everything she owned—and quite a few extra purchases to supplement her possessions before traveling west—Lacey Lyman created this entire mess.

And it looked like she'd have to unpack all of it. Today. For no good reason but a persistent need to make other people happy. *Or, at least, not un*happy *with me,* she acknowledged. Unfortunately, that admission didn't make her any happier with the task before her. And behind her. And in the next room over. . .

"It's more than worth the effort." Cora started to open a crate. "The rain won't let up anytime soon, and we aren't equipped to handle another day of so-called 'courting weather.'"

"I'd thought yesterday couldn't get any worse, after that confrontation with Braden." Naomi's mutter made Lacey wince and look at Cora, afraid of her friend's reaction to the reminder.

"It didn't." Cora's lips tightened. "But while Creed kept Braden alive, I accepted a few things. I expect Braden to adjust to his situation—proverbially lay in the bed of his own making. So I can do no less when it comes to my own circumstances."

"You don't have to stay with him." Evie dropped a box with a satisfying thud. "Wait until you're ready then find someone new. There's no rush for you, sis, and you don't deserve the way you've been treated. Leave Braden to his own miserable griping."

"In any other case, I'd say my brother should get far worse than his own way." Lacey unlatched a trunk and began rifling through paper-wrapped packages. "But this time, it'd serve him right to have things his own way. There is no greater punishment than losing Cora."

"Yes, there is—being outwitted and trapped in the engagement. For me, I deserve the strain of hearing how little he wants me. He threw me over in the letter telling us he'd lived, but I dragged Evie out here with me anyway. I came for myself more than I came for Braden, and now I'll pay for it." Cora moved to the next pile. "I just plan to make him pay more."

"Then you should have Mr. Riordan drag my brother's bed in here so Braden can make himself useful. Make him dig through trunks and crates in search of a tiny little box of cribbage pegs." Lacey shut the lid of the trunk she'd just searched. "Honestly, I never imagined being courted would take such work!"

"Don't you dare let any one of those men step foot in here, Lacey." Evie craned her neck around another pile. "Then we won't be rid of them until the sky clears. You may bemoan all the goods loaded into this mercantile, but I celebrate each and every reason for the four of us to enjoy some peace and quiet!"

"It's true. I don't care how many hog pens, chicken coops, and cribbage boards we have to set those men to making. An afternoon in their company is more than enough. The morning belongs to us!" Naomi sat back with an exhausted sigh.

"I never thought to see such a thing as arm wrestling." Cora shook her head. "Much less imagine they thought we'd find it impressive or appealing to see them twist and crush each other's hands to slam their opponents' arms atop Evie's tables."

"They do all have such lovely strong muscles." Lacey couldn't help but notice. "Strange the way I never noticed how the men in Charleston seem so. . . Well, scrawny sounds unkind."

"Big arms, big appetites, big, stinking cigars." Evie wrinkled her nose. "I can't believe they dared try to smoke those inside my diner. Did you ever consider whether you'd marry a man who smoked cigars or chewed tobacco? I doubt I could."

"So long as he limits it to his study or outdoors, it wouldn't matter to me." Naomi shrugged. "Not regularly, of course. Habitual smoking leaves an odor and stains clothes."

"And I'd imagine it makes a man less pleasant to kiss." Lacey sidled through a narrow space toward a long case lining the back wall. Shocked gasps followed her progress, making her stop and turn around. Well, try to turn around, give up, and back her way through to eye her disbelieving friends once more.

"Oh, do stop gaping at me! I know it's not precisely proper to think of such things, but we're not conventional anymore. Let's not pretend otherwise." She gave a righteous sniff. . .and promptly sneezed. When she recovered, the other three wore small smiles. "Now admit it. Whether or not you can stomach the thought of kissing a man should be an indicator of whether or not you might be willing to marry him. Don't you agree?"

"I agree." Evie and Cora eyed each other as though unsure how to handle their own accord. Both blushed the same shade.

"What do you mean, you agree?" Evie planted her hands on her hips. "We've never discussed any such thing, young lady."

"Oh, stop looking so appalled." Cora rolled her eyes. "I'm engaged and have been for quite a while. Did you never think—"

"Ugh!" Lacey broke in. "Of course we didn't think about that. Braden's my brother; you're Evie's sister."

"I thought about it." Naomi's quiet declaration took them all by surprise. "You may not have given it much thought, but I endeavored never to leave the two of you alone behind closed doors for more than five minutes, Cora. Not because I doubted either of you, but for the sake of your reputation. A woman can never be too careful. And now, more than ever, I'm glad I did."

"Oh." Cora's blush returned, deeper than before. "Now that you mention it, I do recall Braden being rather short with you in the month or so before he left Charleston for Hope Falls."

"He didn't appreciate my efforts." Satisfaction laced Naomi's tone. "Kept insisting I was a companion, not chaperone."

"We're all each other's chaperones now." Lacey gave her cousin a hug. "But putting that aside for just a moment. . ." She fixed a smile on Naomi, then Evie, before asking what she'd been dying to know for days. "Now that we're discussing the men, which amongst our contenders do each of you find acceptable?"

"For marriage or kissing?" Cora's teasing widened Lacey's smile. If her friend could joke, Braden hadn't crushed her.

Which means my brother might survive the coming weeks. "Both!" Lacey thought a moment. "Though if you're only willing to admit to a kissing curiosity, so to speak, rather than proclaim men marriage material, that is your prerogative."

"Kissing curiosity?" Evie's squeak sounded less like outrage and more like guilt. "Are you trying to say we're supposed to evaluate whether or not we'd like to kiss each man and then discard him as a potential husband accordingly?"

"Not at all." Lacey frowned. "Hopefully you won't be discarding every man, or even the majority, based on that."

"I take it to mean you haven't excluded them all." Evie's eyes sparkled. "And since you've given this the most thought, you should go first!"

Kissing was the last thing on Evie Thompson's mind. Until Lacey brought it up. Then the conversation pulled her thoughts into previously untraveled territory. The sort of thinking that got a woman in trouble, when the first man who sprang to mind needed clouting—not kissing. *When did I take such a violent turn?*

Now that question had an easy answer. Evie could trace her

dismaying urges to raise her voice to unladylike levels and shake sense into dense skulls back to her arrival in town. *No. That's not true. It's not fair to blame an entire town for my sudden surge of temper. Hope Falls isn't at fault.* Evie's eyes narrowed as she mentally caught the culprit. *It's the men!*

Oddly enough, she found the explanation soothing. What woman wouldn't be driven to the brink of brandishing cast-iron cookware after an arduous journey rewarded with nothing but oblivious, ogling, or—even worse—order-spewing men just like—

"Mr. Creed?" Lacey's sly inquiry, or the very end of it, dovetailed with Evie's ruminations. Except Lacey was supposed to be listing the men Lacey wouldn't mind kissing. Could it be that her friend developed a tendre for the man who increasingly preoccupied Evie's own thoughts? And why wouldn't Lacey notice Creed, whose innate authority and commanding presence kept even the most unruly loggers in line. . .or walloped them into submission on the one night four of them tried to cross over that line.

"What?" Evie tried to dislodge the lump blocking her throat at the idea of Creed and Lacey. *It shouldn't bother me. In fact, it's almost laughable I didn't see it before. He always sits beside her, and Lacey would have the good sense to notice him before any of the other men around here.* But she hoped for another reason why Lacey mentioned his name in conjunction with kissing, all the same. If only because. . . Well, she didn't have any good reason at the moment, but it didn't feel right.

"I said that none of us could fail to notice the four men who stepped forward that first night." Mischief sparkled in Lacey's eyes. "Gent, Mr. Riordan, Mr. Klumpf, and Mr. Creed."

A bizarre wave of relief washed over Evie at the explanation, receding slightly at the implication these men had won her friends' favor. "So you're saying you've considered kissing all four of them and remained there?"

"No. Gent's age makes him a poor match for me." At eighteen, Lacey's decision made good sense. "And Mr. Klumpf doesn't seem a good match for my interests, though I think he's very good-hearted and fulfills all the requests on our list."

"I agree, although Gent's age doesn't bother me." Naomi seemed hesitant to add her opinion. "I would preclude Mr. Creed as overly forceful for my tastes. And I wouldn't take Mr. Riordan for myself. I find his strength somewhat intimidating."

"Truly?" Evie blinked in astonishment. "He's a sort of gentle giant, Naomi. The only time I've seen him utilize any of that force was when he came to Creed's assistance that night."

"You'll each find different traits appealing," Cora pointed out. "It's a good thing you won't have all the same men on each of your lists, though I expect some crossover, of course."

"Do any others catch your eye, offhand?" Evie wondered.

"I'll admit that Mr. Fillmore's answer pleased me best." Naomi blushed. "Though his taste in friends, considering Mr. Kane led that troupe of men determined to accost us, gives me pause as to his ability to read character. So I don't know."

"Consider him with caution, Naomi," Evie urged, recalling the man who'd withdrawn even more since Kane's departure. "Does another man stand out, Lacey, or merely Riordan and Creed?" *Please let there be another, or I'll be left with only the kindhearted but somewhat overeager Mr. Klumpf.*

"Not one of our suitors, so that's all," Lacey hedged.

"Lawson!" Cora crowed. "Oh, I thought so. He's smart and mannered and keeps to himself enough to make Lacey curious. Besides, he's the best dressed out of every man in town."

"Stop teasing. What I want to know is why have both Lacey and I revealed the names of three men while Evie's managed not to say anything beyond a defense of Mr. Riordan? Which is not the same as choosing him." Naomi turned the conversation around.

"Snickelfritz, Naomi!" Evie leveled a scowl at her friend. "You weren't supposed to notice, much less draw attention to that. But since you have, I'll say I think Riordan one of the finest of the lot, and Mr. Klumpf would make a very good husband." *For someone else.* She didn't speak the last part aloud, but that didn't change the truth of her statement.

"Oh no, Evie Thompson. We each named three men. Pick your third." Lacey wouldn't let her squirm away. "So long as it isn't that awful, brazen Mr. Williams, we won't mock your choice."

"There's something to be said for a man who truly wants you and is willing to proclaim it to anyone within hearing." Evie pretended to consider the notion. "Flattering, you could say. He also fulfills the requirements on the list, so. . ."

"Stop joking, sis." Cora shuddered. "It's not amusing."

"She doesn't need to name her third, in any case. We all know it without Evie bothering to admit it." Naomi laughed. "Mr. Creed caught her attention that first night and never lost it."

"If something catches on fire in the kitchen, it takes my concentration, too. Creed's much the same way—untended, he can wreak havoc." Evie shifted uneasily, realized she was shifting, realized her friends noticed her shifting, and wondered why this entire topic made her so uncomfortable in the first place.

Creed. He walked in, took on the role of our protector, and set about exasperating me so thoroughly I stopped thinking of him as one of the others. The thought of marrying him made her uneasy. This sudden curiosity about kissing made her neck and arms feel prickly. *Is that a good thing or a bad thing?*

"Fire fascinates, warms, provides a means for you to do what you love, Evie." Cora tilted her head to the side. "Any man you marry should be able to do the same, and you can't deny Creed manages to strike sparks with you. I like him, sis."

"We strike sparks because we argue. He's constantly telling me what to do or what poor decisions I make. The only thing he likes about me is my cooking." A dull ache settled in Evie's chest. *Just like most of the men.* "Creed won't choose me."

"What?" Lacey shook with laughter. "Did you never wonder why we asked every man but Creed which two women he'd be most interested in, Evie?" She gulped in air as though to speak more.

"To be honest, I stopped thinking of him as a suitor and more as a partner in the mill." Evie shrugged. "But I'd assume if, after all he's done to earn a stake, he still wants to marry one of us, he'd choose you, Lacey. Why else didn't you ask?" The ache grew into a throbbing pain, sliding down to tumble in her stomach as she spoke the words aloud. *Creed would choose Lacey.* It was worse than riding the train days on end.

"Because he already chose you, Evie." Cora tossed a bundle of material at her head. "Don't pretend you're a half-wit. Our family intellect runs far too strong for you to insult it."

"All of us noticed it, Evie." Naomi peered at her. "We took it for granted you did the same. The only reason I've held Lacey back from interrogating you about whether or not you returned Creed's interest was I thought you hadn't decided."

"What interest?" It took an effort to keep from shrieking the words. "Mr. Klumpf follows me about. Mr. Williams all but tried to stake his claim. *They* have shown interest—not Creed." *I would far rather it be Creed than Williams, for one thing.*

"He always sits beside or across from you, Evie." Cora made the first point. "But even before that, he swept his hat from his head and pointed to your sign the moment he walked into the diner and recognized you. Mr. Creed remembered and paid you a compliment before he spoke a single word to anyone in town."

"He complimented the cooking," Evie muttered. "That's all."

"Did you see the look on his face when Mr. Klumpf tried to call dibs on you?" Lacey giggled. "Pure outrage. He disallowed that in an awful hurry, Evie. Then he chose to talk with you about making decisions, so you'd be protected. Not any of us."

"But all of that pales in comparison to the moment when all three of us knew Mr. Creed watched you more closely than the rest." Naomi's smile grew wide as though savoring it before uttering the single, unforgivable word: "Gingersnaps."

"When he mentioned my *heft*?" Evie could be forgiven for one tiny, disbelieving shriek. Or even a not-so-tiny one.

"When he said you were *losing* your heft," Cora corrected. "And he didn't like it! So he wanted you to eat more. The man did everything but force-feed you those gingersnaps to stop you from losing more weight, because he *didn't want you to change.*"

"He'd known you only a few weeks, but he noticed the difference." Lacey all but bounced on the trunk she'd chosen as a seat. "Between your motion sickness for days on the train and all the running around you've done since we arrived, you'd started shrinking. We knew, but a man who didn't pay extremely close attention wouldn't see it—or care."

"Creed likes you as you are, Evie." Naomi's eyes softened. "Not just your cooking, but the way you look. And if you listened to him yesterday, he clearly values you, even when he disagrees with the decisions you make. Your safety is important to him, more than the rest of ours. It's the reason why he argues the most with you. I can't believe you didn't realize it!"

"I never imagined Creed might want me," Evie admitted. *So I never allowed myself to think about wanting him. Why borrow the pain, when I knew I'd be choosing after Lacey and Naomi?*

"You need more confidence." Lacey sniffed. "I never understood why you seemed to think men wouldn't clamor around you if you gave them the least encouragement. It's not that men won't want you, Evie—look at Klumpf and Williams if you need more proof of that—but that you made it seem like you didn't want them to! So don't doubt that Creed likes you. And it won't hurt to admit it," Lacey prompted.

Evie let out a shaky breath. *You can't make an omelet without breaking a few eggs, and I can't make the most of what's before me if I'm not willing to leave my own shell behind.*

"I like him, too."

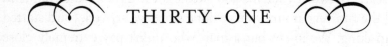

THIRTY-ONE

I don't like her much, to tell the truth." The words floated into the kitchen from the dining room, where men bored holes into cribbage boards. Unable to distinguish the speakers from where he'd just tightened the outside pantry door hinges, Jake took two steps.

And stopped.

Because, by opening the inside pantry door leading to the kitchen, he caught sight of four women. Mrs. McCreedy had left to look after Mrs. Nash, leaving only the four original females of Hope Falls to prepare the midday meal. Jake thought they'd all adjourned to the mercantile for a futile search for cribbage pegs. But before him stood the proof they'd returned earlier than expected. Earlier, it seemed, than anyone had expected.

How on earth did they manage to find such a small item amidst the epic disarray inside that store? I imagined they'd be kept busy for at least another hour before having to give up.

Reality replaced expectation yet again. The four of them clustered to the side of the swinging doors to the dining room, where the wall would hide their skirts from any man wise enough to glance back. From the sounds of the conversation going on in the next room, Jake seriously doubted any of the men speaking possessed that wisdom. Or rudimentary survival instinct, if he wanted to be particular about the entire mess.

Unfortunately for those men, the more they talked, the more particular Jake felt like getting. It hurt their case even further that he could see the women's faces and reactions to the foolish assessments spewing into the kitchen.

"What do you mean you don't like her?" One dumbfounded dummy yelled. "You've eaten same as the rest of us, and everyone knows she's the cook. Ain't a man alive who shouldn't like her!"

Jake's hands clenched, but he didn't move. If he budged an inch, he'd keep right on going and bust up the conversation before the women got to hear frank appraisals undiluted by threat of punishment. He owed it to them to allow the ladies an unfettered glimpse of the men they might choose to marry—but hopefully wouldn't.

"I like her cooking just fine, but the Lyman gal's prettier. Always took a shine to blonds, so you keep the chef."

"Don't go givin' any of the women away, now, Bob." Another speaker identified one of the fools. "I'll give Earl a run for the cook. She may be round as a biscuit, but I bet she keeps a man warm as anything she bakes fresh in the oven."

Feminine hands slapped over mouths to hold back outraged gasps, but that didn't concern Jake. Aside from a powerful fury at the thought of any man warming up next to Evie, he wanted to take away the dejection widening her golden gaze at the poorly phrased biscuit comment. The same dejection he'd seen when he'd fumbled over a way to protest how she'd started wasting away.

"She and the Lyman gal have spirit to spare," someone added in. "For me, I'd take the Higgins woman. She's more settled, knows her place, so it wouldn't take much to keep her in line."

"I like a high-strung filly." There was no mistaking Williams's strident tone. "And the rest of you can stop talking about Miss Thompson. Any man who tries to cozy up to her will have to go through me, and he won't make it in one piece."

Dodger's reedy, nasal whine cut through the jeers. "Stop your jawing, Williams. Everyone knows which woman you want—same as everyone knows she doesn't want you. Leave her be."

The first twinge of respect for the shifty high-climber niggled at Jake's mind. Even if Dodger turned out to be Twyler, at least he'd had the decency to tell Williams off—which would mean every man had at least one moment of usefulness.

"I'll gladly leave her be," someone chortled. "No appeal in a pudgy woman, but she holds true to the old adage about good cooks and housewives. The rest of you are welcome to Thompson."

Jake bit back a growl, his hand on the door before he stopped himself from barging through. Evie's horror would only be worse if she knew he'd been listening. *Never mind her own practice in the fine art of eavesdropping.* The stray memory almost made him smile. But not now, not over the rhyme of...

"It's a little too little to save,
And a little too much to dump,
And there's nothing to do but eat it,
That makes a housewife plump!"

A roar of laughter met the recitation, but tears clouded golden eyes as Evie spun on her heel and made for the door. The pantry door.

Jake stepped out of the way, pressing himself to the side of the shelves as she swept through as though determined to burst outside into the rain and keep walking until she'd left behind everything she'd overheard. Instead, he snagged her elbow, the speed of her own motion swinging her to face him.

"You!" Livid blinks kept her gorgeous eyes afloat in unshed tears Jake saw all too clearly. They hadn't built the pantry wide enough for two people, so she stood close enough to kiss, all but nestled in his arms. "Let go of me right now, Creed!"

If a man could call a squirming, arm-slapping fury of a woman the nestling type. *Wonder what it says about me that I think a woman like that's worth holding, so long as the woman is Evie.* Jake didn't take the time to ponder that thought before her elbow landed in his midsection and her heel stomped on his instep—just beyond the steel lining his boot, so it hurt.

The second he let go, she whirled out of his arms and through the door. Which she also managed to slam in his face, courtesy of those newly tightened hinges. Not exactly Jake's idea of thanks for a job well done.

I'd rather take that kiss, he decided as he jerked the door open and raced after her. Needles of rain stung his forearms, hands, and face where his hat didn't protect him. Wind pushed against him, a cold chill doing its level best to bite through his jacket. Jake bit back, his stride eating away at the distance between himself and Evie.

She didn't stand a chance, hampered as she was by long skirts and those confounded contraptions women strapped themselves into to look thinner. Men weren't supposed to acknowledge the existence of corsets, much less mention the fact they made it difficult for a woman to breathe when she laced them too tightly. But for all her good sense in other areas, Jake knew Evie didn't allow herself so much as an extra inch.

Some people never know when to give themselves some slack.

"Evie!" He bellowed her name, watching as she scampered even more quickly toward a thick stand of trees. Jake caught her in three paces, snaking his arm around her waist and tugging her beneath the protective canopy of the densely packed trees.

"Leave me be, Jake Creed!" She wriggled like a rabbit in a snare, water streaming down her face. Whether tears mingled with the rain or not was impossible to tell. Evie gave a great big sniff, the tip of her nose glowing an affronted red.

Tears, too, then. Jake scowled. "I'm not letting you hie off into the mountains because some idiot recited a nursery rhyme. Now

don't move. If I have to chase after you again, I'll carry you back."
He waited for her to gulp an acknowledgment of that threat
before regretfully slipping his arm from her waist.

Actually, he wouldn't have minded a reason to carry her back.
She felt warm and soft and needed some comforting. Maybe—

*Maybe I should hurry up and shrug out of this coat before I do
something stupid.* He whipped off his wool-lined leather coat and
wrapped it around her, frowning to feel her shivering.

"Thank you." She clutched the lapel, threading her arms into
the sleeves before wrapping her arms around herself—as much
to ward him away as to keep in warmth, he guessed. Good idea.
She looked far too alluring with her hair straggling in streams of
cinnamon and coffee around her fresh-scrubbed face, the rest of
her tucked into his coat.

It didn't quite close in the front—God made her too womanly
for that—but the leather hung far past her hips. Evie's strength
often made him overlook how small she was, but now, with her
golden eyes dimmed to dark amber, her nose red as she huddled
outside in the rain, it hit him anew how much she took on. And
how much thinner she'd become over the past month.

"You're not plump," he blurted out before thinking.

Her eyes widened, and Evie stared at him, saying nothing.
She tilted her head, looking for all the world like a curious little
owl as she blinked and waited. What she waited for, Jake didn't
know. He only knew he didn't plan to say more until he knew it
wouldn't be the wrong thing this time. *Which means I'll most likely
have to go mute around women.*

He blinked back, watching as she nibbled her lower lip the
way she did whenever she thought something over. Jake liked the
way she did that. Especially now that no other men could see it.

"Yes, I am."

⬡

"No, you aren't." Jake's—Creed didn't suit him, and Evie had never
understood why—jaw set in that stubborn way of his.

288

"Oh, but I am." She rocked back on her heels and lifted her own chin. "In a pinch, Cora, Naomi, and Lacey could exchange clothes. A few quick alterations, tacked-up or let-down hems and so forth, and they'd manage." She looked down to where Jake's coat—a man's coat, cut wide across to accommodate his broader shoulders—didn't close over her own chest. "But not me."

"So?"

Evie let loose something sounding perilously close to a growl. "So, it's because I'm plump. I'm larger than other women, far more than fashionable."

"There." Relief lightened his blue eyes to an almost crystalline shade as he reached out and flipped the coat collar up to warm her throat. "You said it yourself, Evie. You're not plump or round or anything else you think of as bad. You're more than most women ever manage, in a lot of ways. Don't regret it."

Her eyes closed as though to imprint the memory forever. Evie fought not to think, not to ruin his admiration by analyzing what it might mean. What the words should mean. But she couldn't help herself. In a moment, she choked out, "More hefty, more bossy, more difficult...yes, I'm more of a lot of things. And I regret most of them. But I'm less, too, Mr. Creed. I'm less unkind, I'm less quick to judge, and I'm less likely to ignore someone when needed. Trouble is"—she finally trusted herself to open her eyes and almost faltered when she saw the anger in his expression—"others tend to see the more instead of the less. I don't know how to change it."

"It's not your job to change the way others see you." Jake took a step forward, a step too close, forcing her to back up. "It is your job to see yourself more clearly instead of muddying things up with all your doubts. The way people see you does not matter. The Bible tells us not to judge according to appearance, that man looks on the outward appearance, but the Lord looks on the heart."

"I found the Lord when I was young, Jake." Evie snapped her mouth shut when she heard his name slip out then decided to forge ahead. "Here, in Hope Falls, I'm trying to find a man. You heard them as well as I did. They aren't looking at my heart. They're looking at my appearance and finding it lacking."

"Then choose a man who sees all of you, Evie!" When he rumbled her name, her heart beat faster. "One who sees that you're not bossy so much as protective of your loved ones. You're not difficult; you challenge others to be their best. And"—he stepped closer, eyes blazing blue fire as though he meant every word—"you're not round or plump or hefty."

She held her breath as he reached one calloused hand to tuck a soggy strand of hair behind her ear.

"You're soft and sweet." With that, he bent a breath away, sliding his forefinger lower to lift her chin.

My first kiss. Evie almost forgot to breathe. Forgot her anger at the men in this town and her distress over the one before her. In fact, she forgot everything but the one thought thrumming through her mind until it squeaked past her lips before he reached them.

"You." She swallowed. "I choose you."

He froze, hand still sending warmth from her chin down her throat. Jake's gaze searched hers, asking whether or not she was serious. A deep breath lifted his shoulders, his voice the lowest she'd ever heard as he responded to the single most important declaration she'd ever made. "What?"

Back to the monosyllabic replies. Evie fought the urge to scowl. After all, she'd just accepted a man's unspoken proposal. A man didn't want his new fiancée glowering at him. That would tarnish the memory of the day she agreed to make him the happiest man on earth or some such twaddle. So she smiled.

Which may have been a mistake, because he reached up to trace her lower lip with the rough pad of his thumb.

And her thoughts stuttered. *Oh my. . .*

THIRTY-TWO

*M*ine. Something primal roared its satisfaction as Jake waited for Evie to repeat what she'd said. Now wasn't the time for any misunderstandings or strange twists of feminine logic to rob him of what she'd just promised. *No. Now is the time for her to be sure she knows what it means to choose me. To be* mine.

He felt her swallow, though his gaze remained fixed on the progress of his thumb teasing its way back and forth across the softness of her lower lip. Soon, he'd press his own lips there.

But until then, he kept his hand as a barrier, so he wouldn't rush things. Because Jake suddenly knew one thing with a certainty he'd never felt before. *Once I kiss her, there's no going back.*

"I said I choose you, Jake Creed." Evie's affirmation doused the fire in a flash. "I'll be Mrs. Creed, your wife."

"Evie." He dropped his hand as though it turned to lead, his chest tight with the sudden realization. "You can't be Mrs. Creed." *How do I explain what I've done, and how can I make you accept that I'm the same man you trust, when I've deceived you?*

"What?" She stumbled, her back pressing against an unyielding ponderosa pine as she tried to scramble around it. Away from him. "I thought. . .I didn't. . .I must have misunderstood."

Desperate to evade him, she tripped over a rock and would have fallen if he hadn't caught and steadied her. But Evie, who'd leaned into his embrace moments before, proclaiming her willingness to become his wife, fought him like a wild thing.

"Stop!" He planted his palms against the trunk of the tree on either side of her, pinning her in place. "You'll hurt yourself if you take off again, and I won't allow it, Evie."

"Miss Thompson, to you." Her hiss told of battered pride; the redness returning to her nose tattled of something far worse. "And it doesn't matter what you will or won't allow, Mr. Creed. You have no say over me or over what goes on in this town. I'm sorry I mistook your kind words for personal interest, but I assure you I won't do so again. Now. Let. Me. Go."

Never. "No." He straightened to give her more space but kept his arms as they were. "Not until you hear me out, Evie." Jake wasn't going to give up the newfound freedom of saying her name aloud. He'd been thinking it for far too long to lose it.

"There's nothing to hear. If you want Lacey or Naomi, that's between you and them. For me, I'll go back to the diner." She shoved at one of his arms, her tiny hands covered by the sleeves of his coat. Evie's effort couldn't even bend his elbow.

"There's plenty to hear. And no matter how much you don't want to listen and I don't want to tell it, we're both going to do our part in this conversation." He made a sound low in his throat when she tried to duck under one of his arms. "Try that again, and I'll step close to keep you in line until I finish talking." *Go on,* his gaze challenged her. *Try it. I'll like it.*

"A gentleman doesn't trap a lady against a tree, Mr. Creed." Her scowl could have sizzled the morning bacon.

"Most likely not, but I never claimed to be a gentleman." Jake took a deep breath. "More important, I'm not Mr. Creed."

"Yes, you are." The fierceness of her denial touched him. Evie shook her head as though rejecting the very notion he could be anyone or anything other than she believed—and she believed he was the type of man who deserved a woman like her.

Which made him, supposedly, the best kind of man.

"No, I'm not. My first name is Jacob, but Creed isn't my real surname, Evie. I left my family earlier this year and adopted the name, but I couldn't tell you or anyone else here." Silently, he willed her to understand, to decide that the name didn't matter so long as the man behind it remained the same.

"So. . ." She looked him up and down as though surveying an unknown insect and finding it both creative and faintly repulsive. The sort of thing that might well need squashing, but she hadn't decided yet. "Not Creed? May I ask why you chose that particular name? To be honest, I never thought it suited you."

"You never thought it suited me?" Unaccountably insulted, Jake looked down at himself then at her to demand, "Why not?"

"I never could put my finger on it. The same way Dodger's clothes are too big for him, the name Creed feels too small for you." She shrugged. "The only way I remember names is by how people break them in. A good name gets worn like a favorite shawl or pair of boots, until you almost can't imagine the person without it. Most folks grow into their names that way. You're one of the few I couldn't reconcile. Now I know why."

"Is there anyone else whose name doesn't fit?" He leaned closer, urgent now. "Think, Evie. It's important."

"Step back, whoever-you-are." Ice frosted her tone. "I don't know your name, and I don't know you. You have until the count of ten before I begin screaming fit to bring the forest down and all of Hope Falls running to find the commotion."

"Jacob Granger. I'm Jake Granger." He hastily offered what should have been the first thing he told her. "Ask Braden, McCreedy, or Lawson if you need to verify the truth of it."

"Lies." She all but spat the word. "All lies. You said you couldn't tell anyone in town, but you told *Braden* your name?"

"Not initially. Only when we decided to bring McCreedy and Lawson into town for your protection. Those two worked with me for years and know me under my real name, but they keep it to themselves and will continue to do so." Jake could have kicked himself for forgetting about Braden. "I wouldn't have told anyone at all if it wasn't for the fact that keeping you safe outweighed the risk of ruining my cover."

"You tell me not to concern myself with appearances, but everything you've done, everything you've been since the moment you stepped foot in town, was lies! You said look at actions, not what I heard, but do you know what?" She started shoving at his arm again. "Words count. What you say has to match what you do, and you've said one thing and done another."

"Try to understand the reasons, Evie." Her accusation sliced through him—too true to ignore. *Lies aren't just something we say. They're something we do to others.* He looked down at the woman still pushing fruitlessly at his arm, wondering if he might have lost her. *And ourselves.*

"I don't trust that you need a false name. I don't trust you brought McCreedy and Lawson to keep us safe. And I can't believe I was foolish enough to believe everything you said about me being more than most women and thinking you came here looking for a wife! You never saw me as more than an obstacle to some sort of grand, secret plan and I don't—"

No. I won't lose her. He swallowed a laugh as her eyes crossed, trying to track the finger he placed over her nose to stop her from speaking. "You're going to be thoroughly kissed if you don't stop spluttering and start listening, Evie. That's a promise."

"You wouldn't dare." Slightly muffled, she blinked to gather herself and glare again.

"I would. In fact"—he lowered his voice to a whisper—"after you're finished listening, you still might be thoroughly kissed. But that's only with your permission, so listen."

"Either way, you'll be thoroughly slapped. And that's a promise." She poked him in the chest, but Jake noticed she wasn't sidling away. Or slapping him, which showed potential.

"You never fail to surprise me, Evie Thompson." He gave in to the grin. "When I told you I'd taken a false name, the last thing I expected was for you to tell me I chose poorly."

"Well, you did," she defended. "And I called you a liar. And threatened to scream and have promised to slap you at some point in the future when I'm still furious but not so curious."

∞

Curiosity, Evie decided abruptly, could be a curse. Because, really, any sensible woman when faced with a situation like this would— *Be honest, Evie. No sensible woman would be faced with a situation like this. How is it you just accepted a proposal never made by a man who never existed and stand trapped in the forest with a proverbial stranger about to spin his life's tale? After threatening to kiss you senseless, no less?* She gave up an inner struggle to pretend nonchalance. Especially *after he threatened to kiss you senseless.*

Well, for one thing, Evie obviously already counted as senseless since she'd abandoned good sense at some point in the past few weeks. For a few others, *he's not a stranger; he's still Jake. He's just a sorry, lying excuse for a Jake.* She harrumphed over that for a moment. *For another, it's not that I was wrong about him wanting to kiss me, after all, and that goes a long way toward mending my tattered pride.* Though if her good sense hadn't gone missing, that would most likely alarm her more than convince her she should stay. *Besides, it means I was right about Creed not really fitting him. And Braden knows about his name change, so it's not a deep, dark deception.*

Just one he kept from her. Evie started scowling again. *Good thing I kept the right to slap the man, at least. . .*

"We received news of my brother's death a month after it happened back in January. He'd been out of town on business and never returned. They kept things hushed due to an investigation into the circumstances surrounding Edward's death. He'd been accused of cheating in a poker game and drawing his gun on another player who called him on it. The other player, a man named Twyler, was a quicker shot, or so the story goes."

"Oh, I'm sorry to hear about your brother." Evie patted one of the arms imprisoning her against the tree trunk before pulling back as if he'd scalded her. Impossible, really. Despite the protection of the thick trees above them, the rainy weather permeated everything with its chill. And Jake didn't have his jacket any longer, because he'd given it to her. Her heart did an inappropriate little flip before she calmed it.

"Not as sorry as those who knew him would be." His face hardened, grief and rage blending into a heartbreaking mask.

"Would be?" Evie echoed the tacked-on phrase in question.

"My parents—great believers in appearance on earth then forgiveness in heaven—decided not to announce Edward's passing." Jake's hands fisted against the tree, fingers digging into bark until Evie winced. "I sent queries regarding the so-called facts surrounding his death, and assumed Father conducted his own investigations. All the while, they denied his death to me and never mentioned him to the outside world. By the time I did the unthinkable, looking through my father's papers for any clue about Edward I'd missed, two more months had passed. Two months in which I could have been searching for Twyler."

A chill having nothing to do with the weather crept down Evie's spine. "Never say you seek revenge on a man whose only crime was to protect himself when your brother drew his gun."

Lord, what do I know about this man? Where did I go wrong, believing his sweet words to be Your answer to my prayer for a loving husband? Have I misread everything and put myself in danger, only to dismiss the concern in favor of anger and curiosity? Give me wisdom, Father. I desperately need it now.

"Anyone who knew Edward should know he wouldn't cheat at a card game or try to swindle anyone. More importantly, he'd only draw his weapon to defend others first and himself last— never to threaten an innocent man. Never." A muscle in Jake's jaw twitched. "Edward carried a large sum of cash on him the day of his death, along with a French coin weight. The twin of one I carry." He pulled back to dig in his pocket, drawing out a square copper piece imprinted with a crown and fleurs-de-lis. "Neither the money nor the token—which has passed through our family for generations—were found on Edward after his death nor in his rooms. Twyler did it."

Evie stared at the piece as Jake pressed it into her palm, its slight weight a much heavier burden than she expected as she passed it back to him. "Twyler. Twilight. Liar. It's a name for a thief or a man who lives in darkness." She traced the small crown with a fingertip. Understanding flooded her. "Creed means belief, but it also means watchword or token. You chose the name because you believe in your brother's innocence, and you carry the token you hope will prove it when you find its match."

"Somehow Twyler murdered my brother, robbed him, and not only escaped but ruined Edward's name in the process." Jake's fist swallowed the weight. "The papers in my father's study— he wasn't tracking my brother's killer. He paid off officials and witnesses to cover up the ugly incident and pretend it never happened." Jake's voice went gruff. "My father. . . Evie. . .he even paid Twyler to keep the secret. Our father betrayed Edward by believing the lie and disowning my brother in his death."

"Oh, Jake. . ." Evie could find no words to comfort the man before her. "I see now why you left your family name." *Your father needs a few lessons in what it means to be a family, and what it means to be decent, for that matter.* But it was Jake's father, so she held her tongue.

"Not forever. Only until I find Twyler. I don't know his face, only that he's of average height, with brown hair and eyes." Determination straightened his spine. "I don't look like Edward, but the name would ruin my chances. So I became Creed. Twyler knows I've hunted him all the way to Colorado, Evie. I believe he came here."

"To Hope Falls?" Evie's hand went to her heart as though to keep it from leaping through her chest. "*That's* why you came here?" She made as though to back away from him, to find the tree behind her a cold reminder she couldn't hide her hot blush.

Was there ever such a fool? Humiliation lanced through her in hot stabs. She closed her eyes and let the back of her head thump against wet bark. *Of course a man like Jake didn't come here to woo a woman from an ad. The only man we didn't ask which bride he'd choose was the only man who would've told us he didn't want one at all, and here I went and...* Her eyes snapped open so wide she felt the strain clear to her hairline, but she couldn't blink.

"I proposed to you." Evie choked out the words, unsure if they were meant to be a confession or an accusation. "You let us think you came for a bride, and I convinced myself you chose me, but that wasn't true at all." *You never wanted me.* She couldn't speak the worst hurt aloud, but the anger poured forth easily.

"It's not why I came, Evie, but—" He reached to touch her face.

She slapped his hand away, talking over him. "You told me not to doubt myself, and you were right about that much. All along I should have been doubting you." The realization freed her from one weight even as her humiliation kept dragging at her. "People may not like what they see when they look my way, but I've never hidden my identity or my purpose."

His breath hissed in as though her words slapped him. Perhaps they did. "Try to understand, Evie. I have an obligation to my brother, and to protect others."

"Protect. . ." Now was her turn to fight for breath as his meaning dawned. She turned and hit his arm as she headed for the diner. "Let me go. I have to find Cora and Lacey and Naomi. And Mrs. Nash, now." Fresh rage flooded her. "You knew Twyler was here, and you allowed Lawson to bring Arla in her condition? How could you!"

"How could I not, when he told me after they were en route?"

She shoved at his arm and shoulder, which wouldn't budge, tried to duck beneath, and found herself hauled back up against the tree. "How could you not tell us of the danger?" She fought to get past him. To Cora. And she didn't get so much as half an inch until she made good on her threat. *Crack!* The sound of her palm striking his cheek split through the sound of rain falling and wind weaving between trees.

But still he didn't let her get past him. "I deserved that. I deserve more than that." The gruff edge to his voice grew more ragged. "But you four wouldn't leave on your own terms, and if I'd told you, Twyler would have known I'd gotten this close. Then I'd never catch him."

"But later, you should have warned us!" Even as she screamed it, Evie knew that if he'd told them, Lacey would have let it slip to Mrs. Nash, who would have told Mrs. McCreedy, and so on and so forth until Twyler slipped into the night like the criminal he was. "You disparage your parents for caring about appearances, denouncing hypocrisy when everything about you is a lie," she yelled at Jake anyway. "The Word promises there is nothing covered that shall not be revealed, Jake. Twyler's time will come, and you can't put others in jeopardy to hasten it! Now let me go, or you will regret it."

"I already regret more than you can imagine, Evie." He ignored her command, continuing to block her. "But you can't tell anyone about Twyler. He'll notice if you all act suspiciously, and he'll run away only to come back and remove anyone he sees as a threat. You have to keep it secret."

"I'll protect my own, Jacob Granger," Evie promised. Then she pulled out the only weapon left in her arsenal. She'd elbowed, kicked, stomped, scratched, pushed, shoved, pulled, pummeled, and slapped. Since she didn't carry her reticule with the tiny pistol Lacey had given her, Evie took him down the only other way she knew how.

THIRTY-THREE

She cried.

Jake froze as his strong-willed, take-charge Evie dissolved into a series of sobs and sniffles to strike fear into the heart of Paul Bunyan himself. *And it's all my fault.*

Before him stood a woman who sold her family home and began her own business to provide for her sister after their father's death. A woman who packed up and headed West for the sake of her family, agreeing to marry so her friends could be secure. Evie could rise at dawn, feed an entire lumber camp, charm a contingent of loggers, and still have enough energy and determination left to console her sister and chastise a bullheaded Braden.

But I made her cry.

It was enough to paralyze a far better man than Jake knew himself to be. So when she made a watery request for a handkerchief—and Jake couldn't give her his trusty bandana, which covered the back of his neck and already held enough rain to fill half a glass—he did what he could. Which was thrust his hands into all his pockets in frantic hope he'd turn one up.

He didn't even realize he'd been tricked until his back end skidded into the mud, the memory of Evie's hands pressing against his chest fading in the cold air. Jake didn't recover in time to stop her as she stepped over one of his sprawled-out boots and beat a hasty retreat back to the diner.

Pulling himself from the mud with a sickly slurp, Jake started after her, ready to call her out on that piece of trickery. *Of all the underhanded things a woman can do,* he fumed, stalking down the mountainside after her, *crying has to be the absolute lowest. I never thought Evie would be so treacherous, adopting a pretense to get her way when I—*

The air rushed from his lungs when Jake realized exactly what he'd done. *I did all that and more. At least she showed the decency to warn me I'd regret not letting her through. Instead of giving her some sign to be on guard, I insisted she trust me.*

Her charge of hypocrisy hung heavier than the rain beating down on him. The memory of Evie insisting they had different definitions of honor wedged into the tree of his ideals until it was stripped of its branches and ready to crash to the ground.

Jake had, indeed, told Evie not to doubt herself, but she'd never pretended to be anyone other than exactly who she was. She didn't keep secrets or hold grudges against people who made wrong decisions on her behalf or the behalf of those she loved. If Evie didn't bear the gift of forgiveness—or at least tolerance— Braden Lyman wouldn't still be drawing breath.

But she'd never doubted him—because he'd shown the arrogance not to doubt himself. He'd fallen into the same trap as his parents—living out one life before the entire town but privately hiding an entirely different person. *No more. No cause overpowers walking upright. It's not seasonal work.* Aside from keeping the name Creed until he caught Twyler, Jake wouldn't allow any more shadowed truths.

Clear Edward's name, be proud to claim my own, then offer to share it with Evie. That's the new plan. Jake straightened his shoulders as he neared the doors to the diner. . .and heard the unmistakable sounds of a brawl in progress.

In one second flat, he burst through the door, ducked out of the way as another man flew past and out into the rain, and stiff-armed some fool who came running at him for no reason. Pandemonium reigned, but it didn't take Jake long to catch the reason for the brawl as blustering boasts, dire threats, and wheezing protests flew through the air along with punches.

While Jake took after Evie, someone else took offense at the conversation and started to "handle" matters inside. From an occasional yell, he could even gather who'd been the one to stop the talking and start trying to remove the offending parties.

"Clump, what in tarnation were you thinkin'?" Dodger shrilled, air whistling through what Jake suspected was a newly broken tooth. "Cain't try to force three fools to the train on yore lonesome. Shoulda waited for Bear or— Oh, hey there, Creed!" A judicious duck accompanied the welcoming wave.

Slight change in the plan. First check to make sure the women are safe. Then come back, track down Bob and Earl, and give them good reason to want to board the next train Clump sees. After that, I'll get back to the entire Twyler issue.

Jake cracked his knuckles and headed for the kitchen, making it three-quarters of the way before Earl came blundering into his path. A smile spread across Jake's face as he eyed the other man, whose brows smashed together and head lowered in imitation of a charging bull trying to decide on a target.

Shaped like a rectangle, shoulders squaring up clear down to his feet, Earl was built like a brick, with all the accompanying agility. But for all that, he had sturdiness on his side when Clump rushed him, shouting a defense of Evie's honor and beauty the entire time it took for him to bounce off the larger man and through the swinging doors into the kitchen.

From the sounds of the worried clucks and anxious questions barraging their way toward Clump, the women fared none the worse for wear. Jake assumed they'd decided on discretion instead of venturing into the fray in hopes of restoring order.

A wise choice, Jake approved just before he jerked his chin toward Earl in unmistakable challenge. Sure enough, the fool lowered his head and rushed him. Jake sidestepped, slamming one fist into the man's gut—where he presumed Earl got the gall to call Evie plump—before bringing the force of his weight down on his elbow to the man's back. Earl hit the floor just about hard enough to bounce then showed the idiocy to rise. Jake popped him one in the nose, not bothering to watch the other man hit the floor a second time while he continued toward the kitchen.

Jake got one boot past the swinging doors when something caught his eye. A small square piece of copper lay on the ground. Directly between the door and where Clump now stood amid all the women, Edward's coin weight stared up at him.

"Put him down!" Lacey swatted at Jake's hat as though trying to dislodge a willful butterfly. "Mr. Klumpf stopped those men from saying such awful things. Don't blame him for their vulgarity!"

"Hush, Lace." Evie's warning came out sharper than she'd intended as she herded her sister and two friends across the kitchen. Away from Mr. Klumpf, who even now dangled in the air, caught by Jake's grip on his suspenders. "There are other things than just the brawl out in the dining room. Trust Jake."

Trust Jake. Now that was sketchy advice. *Why do I feel it's safe to trust an admitted liar bent on vengeance?* Evie fretted along with the others as they watched Jake interrogate the hapless Mr. Klumpf, who'd gone slightly purple in embarrassment. If the man were more round and less boxy, Evie considered the idea he'd bear a striking resemblance to a blueberry as he protested Jake's treatment of his suspenders.

"These are good suspenders, and you need to let go of 'em, Creed. Iff'n you're of a temper on account of how I decided Earl, Bob, and Mason needed to hit the train and not look back, believe you me, they deserve it. Just ask the ladies." Klumpf's babbling sounded as sincere as always to Evie's ears.

"The piece, Clump." Jake released his grip on the suspenders, dropping the shorter man to his heavy boots. He held a square copper coin in his hand. "Where did you get this?"

"That? If you take a fancy to it, you can keep it, Jake." Klumpf adjusted his collar and straightened his shoulders. "Just a trinket I won in a poker game is all. Nothing important."

Evie let out a breath she didn't know she'd been holding at Klumpf's explanation. She hadn't been able to believe the worst of the good-natured, sweet man whose signature stomp added to the rhythm of Hope Falls. Klumpf was one of their own, really.

"To tell you the truth, I most likely would've forgotten and not noticed it fell through the hole in my pocket if you hadn't picked the thing up." He put a hand in his pocket, and Evie could only assume he fingered the unraveled seam within it.

"Poker game?" Jake's throat worked. "With who? Who put this in the pot, Klumpf?"

"I don't remember who threw it in. But it was just me, Draxley, Dodger, and McCreedy who was playing." He scratched his head. "Sorry I can't recall any better than that, Jake."

"Evie? Call Dodger in here, please." Jake kept his tone perfectly controlled. Evie took it to be a sign of how uncontrolled he really felt.

Dodger scuttled inside in response to her summons so quickly it almost made her feel guilty for luring him in to face Jake. Until she reminded herself that this might well be the man who'd murdered Edward and could threaten each and every one of them. Dodger would be fine so long as he wasn't Twyler.

And if he was...well, Evie would have to wrangle pity for the man when it came down to that. At the moment, she couldn't dredge up any sympathetic feelings for such a mangy cur. So she watched, tense as could be, while Jake circled to keep himself between them and the petty thief.

"Dodger, Clump tells me he won this off of you in a poker

game." Jake held up the coin weight and lifted a quizzical brow. "You never struck me as coming from a French background, and it's an unusual piece. Where did you run across something like this?"

"It's mine." Dodger plunged his hands into various pockets, fiddling with the contents before moving to the next pocket. "Or was, until I lost it to Clump there. If someone says I lifted it, they's lying sure as the sun shines after a rain, Mr. Creed."

"Take your hands out of your pockets, Dodger." Jake's hand hovered over his own holster as Evie kept Lacey and Cora from leaning forward. Thankfully, Naomi had the wisdom to refrain.

"I took what Mr. Lyman said to heart, I did." Dodger gave a virtuous nod. "Seeing as how if I help myself to little pretties, I'll feel the boot quicker than I can snatch a farewell present. That there flattened coin-y is mine, fair and square. Especially the square part, in this case. It's why I like it."

"Why's that?" Once again, Evie's curiosity got the better of her.

"Round places got no corners, Miss Thompson. Can make a man nervous." Dodger gestured around the room. "So it's the first time I saw a square coin instead of round. Liked it better."

I imagine you did, Dodger. You're a sly one, liking dark shadows and places where sticky fingers don't go noticed for a good while. Evie tapped one finger against her chin in thought.

"It only makes a man nervous if he's trying to hide something." Clump crossed his arms from the other side of the room, apparently having decided to side with Jake again.

"I'm going to ask you one more time, Dodger." Jake flipped the weight into the air, watching the other man as he watched it fall back into Jake's outstretched hand. "To whom did this coin belong before it found its way into your hands?"

"He wouldn't put it on the table." Dodger began to babble, backing up until he bumped against a counter. "He knew I'd taken a shine to it but seemed awful put out I'd noticed it at all. Don't go telling Mr. Lyman I light-fingered the thing, Mr. Creed. It's just a little coin. I figured it can't be worth much. And, in all fairness, it don't seem like Fillmore's missed it any—"

Evie watched as Jake charged through the swinging doors and back into the mass of fighting men.

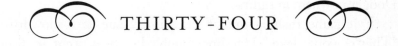

THIRTY-FOUR

*F*illmore. Jake's pulse pounded in time with his boot steps as he paced around the dining room, eyeing men slumped on benches or down on the ground, steering clear of those still up and fighting as he searched for the one man he'd traveled so far to find. *Twyler.*

His nemesis hid himself deep within the faded background of Fillmore's identity, so unobtrusive that Jake wasted the bulk of his time focusing on more obvious choices like Williams, Kane, Dodger, and the like. When all along he should have expected Twyler to be so crafty he poked about like a turtle—content in a slow, steady pace where he could observe everything and retreat to safety at a moment's notice.

Which is why Jake wasn't surprised when he didn't find Fillmore in the diner. Out of concern for Mrs. Nash and Mrs. McCreedy, he looked in on them at the house before proceeding to the bunkhouse. That's where he expected to find him, perched in the top back bunk, hunched around a book like an overgrown crow. Because that's what Twyler was, whenever he shed Fillmore. A crow. Sharp and greedy, with a wicked intelligence to get his way no matter who he hurt in the process.

But Fillmore didn't lurk in the bunkhouse either. Fingers

of dread tickled the back of Jake's neck as he raced back to the diner—to the women he'd left under the care of Klumpf and Dodger, neither of whom would manage to outwit the likes of Twyler.

He burst through the dining room doors, vaulted over a groaning bucker with a swelling shiner, and barged through the swinging doors to find Clump—and two women. Naomi and Evie's sister sat at the same table where he'd left them, with Dodger nowhere in sight.

Evie came rushing out of the pantry, pale as a snowdrift. "They're gone, Jake." Her lips trembled. "Lacey went to find Dodger a peppermint stick for his upset stomach—he claimed he's nervous about you and Braden kicking him out of town since he swiped that token from Fillmore. But Lacey couldn't find them, and he wandered over to the mercantile while she checked again..." Her voice died off as Jake rushed past her to check things while she finished explaining. "But neither came back, and now Lacey isn't in the pantry and the door's wide open."

Dodger! Tracks crossed the mud beyond the door—a clear set of footprints marred by long stripes and deep heel scuffs—the imprints of a woman dragged away against her will. Mercifully, the sun replaced the rain clouds as Jake ordered Evie back inside and began tracing the tracks back up the mountain. He hurried, knowing he'd made a grave mistake—the same mistake he'd resented his parents for making.

I erred, Lord. I judged by appearance, letting my knowledge of Dodger's petty thievery color my judgment until his flawed caricature of a cover worked in his favor. Just as he'd planned. Now he has Lacey, and I pray for her protection. I ask for peace when I confront my enemy. Let me seek justice instead of the vengeance I'd planned before. Help me see Your way rather than let my own decisions hurt Evie's friend. Let Lacey be all right....

"Here's your jacket." Evie's whisper made Jake want to pound a ponderosa into the ground with nothing more than his fists.

She panted from the exertion of running to catch up with him, swathed in her own chestnut cloak as she held out his coat.

"I told you to get back inside," he ground out. "I don't have time to send you back." A worse thought occurred to him. "Twyler might have doubled back. You can't go alone." He snatched the coat from her outstretched hand and shrugged into it.

"You'll notice I went inside to fetch your coat and a few of my own things." She patted her reticule with a smile. "Now hush and do keep going. Lacey wouldn't be in danger if you'd handled things differently, and griping about me going along to help the pair of you will only slow us down, Jacob Granger!"

Now wasn't the time to notice she'd said his real name. Jake noticed anyway, even as he twined her right arm into the crook of his left and plowed ahead as swiftly and quietly as possible, following the disturbed mud, moss, and ferns underfoot. It looked as though Lacey hadn't gone easily. Quietly—Twyler must have gagged her to avoid any ear-splitting screeches to sound the alarm—but not docilely.

Good girl. She's spent a lot of time with my Evie. The thoughts fled as he heard a male voice a few yards ahead.

"Don't test my patience." Less nasal and lacking the whine, Dodger's thin voice resonated through the forest. "I said I'd tell them your location. I did't promise you'd be alive. So you can climb on in and they can find you snug and spitting mad, or I can waste a slug and cram you down there so they find whatever the bugs leave behind."

An angry murmur responded, too muffled to be made out. Jake shared a glance with Evie and nodded. That had to be Lacey.

"Let her go, Twyler." Jake edged out from behind the uneven row of trees concealing him from view. "She's no good to you." The sight that greeted him wore his considerable store of patience very thin indeed. "You can't shove a full-grown woman into a hollow tree stump, Twyler. And there's no reason to anyway. Drop your gun, set her free, and we'll go back to town."

"I'm not going back to that place," Dodger snapped, all hint of mischief abandoned. "Miss Lyman here is going into this empty stump—it'll make for a tight fit, but we both know how large ponderosas are, and luckily she's a tiny thing. You and Miss Thompson will be tied around the same while I catch the next train from Hope Falls."

"We can't allow that, Twyler." Evie edged forward, standing level with Jake. "There's nothing to be gained by it, in any case."

"Ransom, my dear." An evil smile spread across the face Jake once considered simple-minded. "I'll reveal your location, as well as the location of Miss Lyman, after a substantial sum is wired to me. By then, I'll have the means to move on, and the time in which to do so before Mr. Granger decides to follow me yet again. Pity it's unwise to kill him outright, but after the unfortunate incident with his brother, it's a risk I'd rather not take. I'm more than happy, however, to take the additional ransom the two of you will provide."

"That's not going to happen." Jake shook his head. "We both know you won't leave us to be found in the woods so near town, so easily. And we've only run across one large hollowed-out tree stump for you to use, Twyler."

"Ah, ah. Dodger, now. I must say, I'm pleased how well my little ruse worked. What better explanation than that I'd stolen the piece, should Granger show up and discover me? Simplest thing in the world to get 'caught' swiping other trinkets. A smart trickster is always one step ahead with a solid contingency plan behind him. Like this." With that, he hauled his hostage against him, pressing a sharp blade against her delicate throat. With his free hand, he pointed a pistol at Evie.

Jake struggled against the hot rage surging inside him, urging him to do something to protect Evie. *But not at the expense of Lacey. Not in anger. . .* A small measure of calm steadied him. *It's not about my vengeance. It's in the Lord's hands now. He can't play upon my weaknesses.* "One ruse worked, Twyler. No more. Give up—now."

"This is no ruse." A thin red line inched across Lacey Lyman's throat, though she did nothing but wince. "I suggest you drop your weapon, Granger, if you want both—or either—of these ladies to see another sunrise. Your one shot might just as well hit Miss Lyman as myself, but I'm guaranteed success with at least one of my targets." Satisfaction oozed from his voice. "And I'm quite likely to survive, if not go entirely unharmed. So let's get on with it, shall we? A stacked deck is a gamer's greatest ally."

"I wonder"—Evie's nonchalance warned Jake that she planned something outlandish—"whether that's not something like a woman with a well-packed purse. Because I do find, Mr. Dodger or Twyler or whichever you prefer"—she chattered on brightly as she rummaged through her reticule—"that it's best to be prepared for anything." In an instant, she pulled out a familiar dainty pistol with inlaid mother-of-pearl handle. "Don't you agree?"

Besieged with memories of Evie's complete inability to so much as wing a metal can at ten paces—memories she had no idea he possessed—Jake could only stare at the spectacle with something approaching awe. He noted, too, that Lacey made an abortive attempt to struggle, brought up short by the knife held to her throat.

Jake knew Lacey didn't want to be anywhere near the direction where Evie chose to fire, but Twyler would read her movements as an attempt to give her friend an even better shot. Despite her complete inadequacy when it came to shooting, everything about Evie's conversation and bearing indicated an intimidating level of expertise.

"You've proven more perceptive than most, Miss Thompson." A gleam of appreciation lit Twyler's gaze, inciting further fury from Jake. "A rare and resourceful woman could be a great asset, but I find myself unimpressed by your show of fashion accessories. Wield your toy as you please, Miss Thompson. This is between

Granger and me."

"Then let the women go." Jake jumped on the idea.

"We've come too far for that, I'm afraid. And time ticks away while you make idle chitchat. Throw down your gun, Mr. Granger, and admit that the woman at your side wouldn't be able to hit a target if I drew one three feet from her nose."

"Oh, that's absolutely true, Mr. Dodger." Evie's smile widened. "It used to be that I couldn't hit the. . .what's the expression my mentor used? Oh yes, I couldn't hit the broadside of the bunkhouse. But it's such a cunning little piece."

"Listen to her." Jake opted for honesty. "She won't be able to hit you, Twyler. There's no threat in letting her play along. It's not as though she'd shoot you." He gave a convincing scoff at the idea. Convincing more thanks to reality than his acting ability.

"No." Twyler's self-satisfied ooze dried up in a hurry. "You want me dead. You want me to ignore her purse pistol in hopes she wields it as well as she claims and ends my life." He darted glances around himself, edging farther out of reach. "She changes the game. Changes the cards, different value. . ." He degenerated into strange rambling mutters.

"Why did you kill my brother, Edward?" Jake needed to know the truth before the man in front of him slipped beyond the edge of sanity forever.

"He noticed me cheating and started to raise a fuss. Two men I'd fleeced a few nights prior sat just one table over, so I couldn't allow that. And I'd already marked him for carrying a large amount of cash." Twyler clicked his teeth together repeatedly. "So I fired first, paid off the other players, and pocketed the profit. Double the windfall when your old man started paying off people to not besmirch dear Edward's memory."

Twyler's mocking laugh made Jake's trigger finger itch.

"And then you came after me, and I did more and more paying off of my own until I ran dry and needed a rich wife." Twyler's eyes narrowed. "But here you are again, forcing my hand. With two skilled shooters against only myself, I can't hope to make it out alive and carrying off my plan." He looked right at Evie. "So I can either take revenge on Granger here, before leaving this earth, or hope your misguided sense of feminine kindness precludes you shooting a man to death in the back."

With that, Twyler shoved Miss Lyman so she stumbled, falling downhill and forcing Jake to catch her. He halted her progress, sat her down, and took off running after his prey.

One shot. I only get one shot, Lord, and I can't shoot a man in the back no matter how despicable he is, or I become an opportunist like the man I chase. Justice over vengeance—let my aim be true.

He followed, waiting until Twyler hit an open area before Jake sank to one knee, steadied his hand, and took the shot.

A shot echoed in the forest, followed by a terrible cry. Then silence.

Evie huddled with Lacey, whom she'd unbound after the men went hurtling off through the trees.

"Please tell me you wouldn't have fired," Lacey said only after the silence became unbearable—and Evie handed over the pistol.

"Have a little faith, Lace." Evie scanned the horizon, anxious for Jake to come back. It hadn't escaped her notice that Twyler hadn't dropped his gun before taking off.

"Does that mean you would've uttered a prayer and pulled the trigger, or that I should have faith you wouldn't do anything so foolish?" Lacey blanched at the thought, which wasn't precisely flattering.

"We can do all things through faith, Lacey Lyman." *Even wait for Jake to come striding back through these trees. No matter if it's taking him forever and a day to mosey his way home.*

"In that case, I have faith that you'll never fire a gun unless faced with a man like Dodger or Twyler or whatever his name was, with absolutely no one else anywhere near the vicinity." Lacey rubbed her throat, where the knife had rested. "Thank you for coming after me. I couldn't have gone into that stump."

It was then that they heard it, the snap of twigs beneath boots as someone heavy headed their way. They froze, Lacey's hand tightening on the gun, until they made out Jake, with a prone form slung over his shoulders.

Twyler.

Evie's heart sank. *I'd so hoped he'd find justice and not vengeance, but Twyler forced Jake to choose between the lesser of two evils. Shooting an evil man in the back is the better choice than letting him go free to harm more people.*

Jake slung the other man's body to the ground, eliciting a wretched moan from the captured criminal. "Oh, my leg," Twyler groaned. "Why couldn't you let me go, Granger? Or let the woman shoot me outright, at least?"

"Because I can't shoot the broadside of a bunkhouse. We told you that, Twyler." Evie couldn't smile at the sight of blood soaking the man's right leg from the knee down, but she judged him a lucky man nevertheless. He deserved far worse.

"Brings new meaning to the term 'long shot.' " Lacey shuddered.

"Worst pun, Lace." Evie nudged her friend.

"Best threat, Evie. Pity we can't use it on the rest of the men."

"You mean. . .it was true?" Twyler gasped the words, starting to wheeze. If Evie hadn't heard only the one shot, she'd have wondered whether something was wrong with the man's chest. Until a bark of laughter escaped. "A double bluff, then. I was outdone by a double bluff from an amateur?"

"And an exceptional shot from a master," Evie lauded Jake. "He could well have ended your life, but he chose not to take revenge."

"The shot didn't matter. Only the bluff. Never the hand, only how it's played. . ." The wheezes stretched and thinned into a series of wispy cackles. "An amateur! I deserve my fate, then. I held all the winning cards and threw them away."

He kept up the steady stream of incoherent babble about

games and bluffs and the ultimate loss until Jake left him with the doctor, who mercifully put Twyler into the oblivion of drugged rest. Merciful for everyone—not just the man with the shattered knee.

"Evie, I'd like a word." Jake had washed up and taken off his jacket, so Twyler's blood no longer stained him. Nor did the memory of his brother's injustice or his father's betrayal, it seemed. He stood even taller than before, the lines of worry she'd never thought unattractive lessened until Jake seemed almost free. When she nodded, he led her into the doctor's study. . .and sat her down in the wing-backed chair.

"You know the worst of me, Evie Thompson. You've seen my quick temper and penchant for issuing orders. I've lied about my name and my purpose in Hope Falls, allowing you to think I came looking for a wife when I came hunting a killer." He paced during the entire recitation, as though unable to remain still. "I'm not as good a man as you deserve. I can't go back and start things over and introduce myself as Jacob Granger, or appreciate your sense of honor before you explain it. But I can do one thing—and I hope I do it right."

Is he proposing? He can't be proposing. Can he? Evie fought the urge to hop up and pace alongside him.

But it was a good thing she didn't, because the next thing she knew, he stopped right in front of her and stared down into her eyes with the same intensity she remembered from all the way back in Charleston—when he'd first taken off his hat. Her heart fluttered as he opened his mouth and professed, with touching sincerity, his deep and abiding need to. . .

"Apologize." Jake reached out those large, callus-roughened hands of his and cradled hers between them, an inadequate anchor when her heart fell like a cake.

Of course he's not proposing, she chastised herself, blinking furiously against unreasonable tears. *We've already gone through this once today. If he didn't accept it when I all but proposed to him, what sort of wigeon would I be to think he might be doing anything more serious than apologizing?* Although, of course, to a man that might just be a more serious and difficult matter than even a proposal.

"You can stop apologizing." She tried to end the conversation by standing, but he laid one large hand on her shoulder to keep her seated.

"No. I can't. You charged me with hypocrisy, for saying one thing and doing another—and it's true. I've a long way to go, Evie, starting with the trip home to bring Twyler up on charges. Before I left, I should have confronted my father and spoken with my mother, and now I need to make amends as best I can. Even if they don't see they were wrong, I have to own up to my mistakes. But when I get back. . ."

Her breath hitched as he dropped to one knee.

"Proverbs tells us that 'a false balance is abomination to the Lord' "—Jake pressed one of the copper squares into her palm as he spoke—" 'but a just weight is His delight.' With you, I find my balance, Evie.

"I'm asking you to be mine to delight in for the rest of our lives. Once, you were willing to take Jacob Creed. Now I'm giving you the only thing I can offer, besides myself. The greatest gift love ever gave was a choice." He paused, his gaze searching hers. "Could you choose to love Jacob Granger?"

"Jake, don't you know?" She clutched the square coin weight in one hand, reaching out to trace the contour of his jaw with her other. "I already do."

He stood at the same moment she did, sweeping her into his arms for an embrace to prove something Evie always hoped. *For every woman, there's a perfect fit.* Hers just happened to be a land as rugged as the mountains they covered, and a man relentless enough to convince her they belonged together.

"Although I should mention," she managed to gasp once

she'd somewhat recovered from his kiss, "you'll have to convince at least two of the other women to accept you as my fiancé. It's one of the rules we agreed upon."

"Oh?" For the first time, one of his short responses didn't bother her. Perhaps because he followed it with another searing kiss.

"Well, yes." Evie looked up at him, emboldened by the love she'd found. "But I'm sure we can do away with that. I can be rather determined when I want something."

"No." Jake tugged gently on a lock of her hair. "I'll never again ask you to break your word, Evie. You're more than worth running the gamut through your sister and friends."

"You'll win them over, Jake." She beamed at him.

"I don't mind winning them"—he leaned in for another kiss—"so long as I can keep you."

TALL, DARK, AND DETERMINED

Dedication

As always, my books are dedicated to my Lord,
who gives me words and patience when I have neither.
But this particular story is for my fellow capable, take-charge
women—and the men strong enough to love us anyway.

ONE

Colorado Territory, June 1887

Dead men told no tales, but jailbirds sang aplenty. Chase Dunstan knew Braden Lyman, victim of a mine collapse, couldn't be telling anything. Problem was, no one else gave details about the accident, leaving too many questions about how—and why—those men died. The property sold with ungodly haste.

Only a need for answers brought him to the jailbird, a man foolish enough to miss their rendezvous four days and three counties back. Getting thrown in a cell didn't excuse failure.

"What did you find out?" Chase waited while his quarry paced the small room, still not responding. He waited while the other man drank a dipperful of water and almost choked. A dry throat and slippery nerves made anything hard to swallow, and the man before him dealt lies thick enough to block a bison.

But Chase knew what all good trackers knew; waiting was the longest part of the hunt. So he tested his patience against his fellow man instead of an animal until Robert Kane faltered.

"You're not going to like it." When Kane finally spoke, Chase didn't so much as shift on the hard wooden seat he'd chosen.

"That much, I can tell you plain and simple."

"That much, I already knew when I found you in a cell." Chase allowed a thin thread of amusement to reel in his prey.

"And left me here to rot." Kane kicked the wall to vent his frustration and regroup. "You could've posted bail, us being brother-in-laws 'n' all." His grumble died out when he looked up and caught Chase's unblinking gaze. Robert Kane possessed no shame—but he boasted some degree of self-preservation.

"Your brother's marriage makes you no relation of mine." *If the scriptures say a man leaves his mother to cleave to his wife, surely that includes his no-account half brother.* Chase eyed Kane. "*He was a good man, so for both your sakes, I hope you found some information worth my time.*"

He made no direct mention of his sister. Laura had seen enough hardship at the hands of their own family without allowing Kane's oily thoughts anywhere near her. There were worse reasons to send Kane to Colorado than to keep him away, but only one better. Details about the death of Laura's husband—and the mine collapse to kill him—hadn't been forthcoming.

The settlement the mining outfit gave Laura to make up for the loss of her husband wouldn't last a year. Chase would have taken the matter to Lyman, the partner he'd dealt with when working as a guide for that same outfit early on, but Lyman went down in the collapse, too. Chase's suspicions deepened when the surviving partner sold the town in record time and vanished.

Since then the only mention of Hope Falls came through a ludicrous ad folded and still tucked in his back pocket:

Wanted:
3 men, ages 24–35.
Must be God-fearing, healthy, hardworking single men
with minimum of 3 years logging experience.

TALL, DARK, AND DETERMINED

Object: Marriage and joint ownership of sawmill.
Reply to the Hope Falls, Colorado, postmaster by May 17.

The thing must serve as some sort of code. But if the mining company was involved and covering something up, they might recognize him. Chase Dunstan couldn't go poking around Hope Falls. But Robert Kane held the anonymity and logging background to head out there and look for answers.

Kane also had the bone-deep idiocy to botch it.

"If the information's good enough, will you get me out of this cell?" No longer pretending any sort of kinship, Kane began bargaining for freedom he didn't deserve. "Because I don't have to tell you anything, Dunstan. As long as I'm behind these bars, it doesn't matter to me what happens in the world beyond them."

"You're bartering with what already belongs to me." It wasn't a question. Chase didn't ask questions he already knew the answers to unless trying to appear unthreatening.

"You don't have the information; it doesn't belong to you." Kane spread his hands in offering. "It's simple business."

"Business finished when I saved your backside from that posse stringing you up for fraud. Try again." He stood up.

"The past doesn't concern me. Right now I need to know—"

"You can stay out of reach behind those iron bars. Or I can get you out and show you firsthand my opinion of men who fail me. Either way, you'll tell me what I want to know. Your only choice, Kane"—Chase leaned forward—"is how."

"All right, all right." Kane glanced at the bars as though afraid they might vanish. "Can't blame a man for trying."

Yes he could, but Chase didn't waste the breath.

"The mine collapsed—you can see where it used to be, how the mountain sort of fell in on itself and crumpled." Words started pouring from the prisoner—and lucky for Kane, they were true so far. Chase had circled close enough to confirm the collapse for himself just after hearing about the tragedy.

"And the ad that got your hackles raised?" Kane started to get to the good stuff. "Sure enough, there were four women running that town. They dangled the line that three of 'em wanted husbands to keep control over the loggers."

"Four women run the town?" Chase ran the pertinent detail to ground. "The ad made it seem as though three owned it." *If any of them do, and it's not some elaborate hoax.*

"Four. Claimed that together, with the one's fiancé, they'd bought up the town and wanted to convert it to a sawmill. They chose a site and cleared it, brought in an engineer, interviewed everyone, and divided them into work teams. It's just like the ad said, Dunstan." Kane smirked. "Those women weren't ladies—no lady puts out an ad like that, and no man with half a brain would believe it. Course, most of those loggers didn't own half a brain, so they were fooled into hoping for pretty wives in the wild. Could almost see why—the gals meant business."

But what kind? Chase kept the question to himself and asked another. "Who's the fiancé—the man they claim owns Hope Falls?"

"Don't remember." Kane looked chagrined—or at least as chagrined as he could look, which meant he looked afraid of displeasing Chase. "But he was in bad shape—bedridden. The man giving orders went by Creed, if that helps. He arrived after most of us, and it looked like he only knew one of the women."

"No." Chase didn't know any men by the name of Creed, which was too distinctive to forget. Then, too, any man planning on being front and center running the town would have established his status from the start. Some truth ran through the old saying men were dogs—when it came to dominance, neither animal left room for questions. "The name of the fiancé. Now."

"I can't remember." Kane started talking fast. "Adam? Brian? Something like that. He was fiancé to one of the Thompson sisters and brother to the girl I had my eye on."

"Word is you had more than your eye on her, and you got caught." Chase cast a glance around. "Was she a widow?"

"No, a miss." Kane scowled. "Now there was a girl who didn't belong in the backwoods, Chase. All done up in bows and fluff, looking like a lady when she wasn't, putting on airs as though she owned the place. The type to lead a man on but kick up a fuss when he got close—she's the reason I'm stuck here."

"Her name." Not a question; a command.

"Lacey, though I doubt it was real." Kane looked ready to go off on another long-winded speech about the temptress.

"Surname, you fool. She should share it with her brother."

"Lyman."

Chase sucked in a sharp breath at the answer like a hound drawing in scent for the hunt. "The brother's name. Braden?"

Kane snapped his fingers. "Yep. That's it. Stuck in the doctor's bed."

"Why?" Chase had to be sure.

"Mine collapse, they said." Kane hadn't known any names going in, so whatever he came up with wouldn't be half-truths drawn from his own twisted conclusions.

Chase narrowed his eyes as he left the jailhouse. A rangy wolfhound abandoned its post in the shade to lope alongside him. There could be no doubt—Braden Lyman lived. This gave rise to a slew of new questions. Was the one man in Miracle Mining whom Chase had trusted involved in its collapse? Did the real Braden Lyman still own Hope Falls? And if both answers were yes—*why?*

Because despite what Kane told him, Chase knew one thing: *an attempt to conceal a sabotaged mine is still more likely than three good women advertising for husbands in the wilds of Colorado.*

Hope Falls, Colorado Territory, 1887

So this *is how it feels to be wrong.*

Lacey Lyman abandoned the laws of ladykind to gnaw on her nails. Of course she'd been wrong before—one didn't reach the advanced age of eighteen without a few token mistakes. But this wasn't always-talking-too-much wrong or even clashing-bonnet-and-dress wrong. She shuddered at the last one, but it still didn't come close to the current situation. No. *This* counted as nothing less than best-start-swooning wrong.

Creed, the man they trusted enough to make head of operations, had just dangled another logger by his suspenders in some sort of fit over a single coin then rushed out of the kitchen. Normally, that would be odd. Just now, it was ungentlemanly to abandon ladies in such alarming circumstances.

An all-out brawl was taking place beyond the swinging doors of the kitchen, where twenty or so loggers pummeled each other. Some defended the honor of whichever woman caught their eye, some tried to prove their masculinity, and a small cowardly number simply defended themselves. But there was no escaping the fact that, to a man, they clashed in competition over herself and the three friends she'd talked into coming West. The rain hadn't stopped in hours, so they didn't even take their fight outside the diner like somewhat civilized mountain men.

Even worse, it was *all her fault.*

"Oh, hush." Evie jabbed her with an elbow, although that might have been an accident. The newly built storeroom Lacey dragged them all into hadn't been made to house four women amid its shelves. "It's not *all* your fault, and you know it."

Lacey shot her friend a sharp look before realizing Evie

couldn't see it. In addition to space, the storeroom also lacked a lit lantern. Nor did it share the warmth of the stove, which had made the kitchen much more inviting until a pair of loggers came flying in from the fight and hadn't gone back.

"Then whose fault is it?" she demanded, stung by the way her friend emphasized *all* as though, indeed, Lacey bore the lion's share of guilt. *If Evie thinks I'm to blame, she could at least show the decency to be agreeable about it!*

A jumble of answers bounced around the tiny space all at once, but Lacey caught who'd said what in an instant. They'd been through too much not to know each other's voices and the thoughts of their hearts by now. Tangled together, they went: "Creed!" The loudest burst from Evie, who'd been fighting the rugged stranger for weeks—mostly because she was fighting an attraction to him. About an hour ago, Evie ran out into the rain, distressed over a callous comment made by one of the men. Creed followed, but obviously failed since Evie came back alone.

"Braden!" The most vehement came from Cora Thompson. Evie's sister and fiancée to Lacey's own brother, Cora had every right to blame Braden. He'd convinced them to invest in a Colorado mining town then destroyed everything by falling victim to its collapse. But when word of his miraculous survival surprised them in Charleston, Cora didn't think twice. They all moved to Hope Falls only to hear Braden denounce them as fools.

Lacey brightened at the fact that if it weren't for Braden, none of them would be here at all. Truly, it was all her brother's fault. The world made sense once more, and—

"All of us!" The longest and fairest answer came from Naomi Higgins. Her elder by nine years, Lacey's cousin observed, "We all invested in Hope Falls as a mining town, and nobody forced us to come here when things changed."

Three women shifted uncomfortably in tight quarters.

Whether Cora and Evie moved to ease a sense of shame, Lacey couldn't be sure. But she suspected they, like herself, found the quiet truth in Naomi's answer too compelling to ignore.

Except. . .a sort of needling sensation in her chest wouldn't let Lacey accept Naomi's answer. She wanted to. Oh how she wanted to, but Lacey had a gift most people never suspected. Not an astounding talent. She simply. . .remembered things. If she heard them or read them, Lacey could repeat them years later. Not precisely word for word, but with surprising accuracy.

Surprising because, when she most needed to, she couldn't pay attention. Life offered so much. Color and sound, textures and tales, sparkles and sensations forever calling her away from the moment. . . So people never imagined Lacey could *remember*.

But she did, and right now Lacey was remembering a conversation from when they'd still believed Braden dead. Mere weeks past, it seemed a lifetime ago.

TWO

*L*acey took a deep breath. "Hope Falls can be saved."

"Towns don't have souls, and even if they did, Hope Falls would be the exception." Cora all but spat the words. "There's no redeeming it. No eking anything worthwhile from it now."

"Without ore, nothing can sustain the town," Naomi agreed.

"That's not true. What Hope Falls now lacks in ore, it more than makes up for in another valuable resource." For once in her life, she didn't let everything rush out all at once.

This time Lacey needed them to ask. Investing time and thought would bring them a little closer to agreeing to her plans. She suspected she wouldn't be able to taste anything for a month, but kept her tongue between her teeth. Literally.

"What resource?" Evie spoke up for everyone.

"Trees!" She almost bounced in her enthusiasm. "The San Juan Mountains are absolutely covered in the lumber New England lacks. Even better, we have railroad access to meet the demand."

"You're proposing to turn a mining town into a sawmill?" Disbelief tinged Evie's tone, but interest sparked. "How?"

"We'd need to buy up the surrounding land, but if looking into selling our property has shown anything, it's that we can get it cheaply. Then it's a matter of labor." Lacey hesitated.

"Hire men, you mean." Naomi raised a brow. "Setting up a sawmill is an expensive venture. You'll need investors."

"Or husbands." Lacey winced at the way she blurted it out.

"Never!" Cora jumped to her feet. "We won't travel there and make our home without Braden. I won't have it!"

"If we let Hope Falls die"—Lacey tried to be gentle—"we've lost the last part of Braden we could have kept alive."

"But marrying another man—" Cora shook her head. "I can't."

"I anticipated that. But the rest of us can marry." Lacey's hopes faded at the shock painting Naomi's and Evie's features. "Husbands provide protection and legitimacy."

"Preposterous. Absolute lunacy." Evie stood beside Cora, shaking her head. "Finding investors, perhaps. But binding ourselves to complete strangers over a sawmill? Never!"

It took all of two moments for the scene, fluid with sights and sound, to unroll in her memory like a bolt of watered silk. Silken memories binding her to her own mistakes. . .

He'd overplayed his hand. Corbin Twyler knew it the moment he saw Creed with the square luck token he'd lifted off that body six months back. Seemed as though he'd been on the run since he shot Granger and claimed the self-righteous fool pulled his gun first.

Yes. Nothing but bad luck since then. That's why he'd put the token in the pot. After Kane's mischief made every man in Hope Falls suspect, Twyler had to get rid of any hint of bad luck or incriminating remembrances. They came through the Game, and the Game would help him pass them on to another player. Surely the time drew near for Twyler to win once more.

Why else would a man keep on playing? What use was the challenge of living if a competitor never moved ahead? The Game taught a man patience, how to read small tells and anticipate another player's next move, all for the sake of winning.

And while he'd overplayed, Twyler hadn't lost this hand yet. So he asked himself, how would Creed move next? How quickly? And how could Twyler get the goods—and the last laugh?

Funny thing about mistakes, Lacey reflected less than an hour later, *they travel in groups. Become familiar with one, and all of a sudden a girl finds herself besieged with a slew of them.*

The gun pressed to her temple brought the realization she might not have the opportunity to meet with any more mistakes. Of course, nothing less than a pistol at point-blank range would convince Lacey to let herself—or her blue worsted wool—be dragged through the muddy mountainside in a frigid downpour.

This, too, was *all her fault.*

And none of her friends were around to tell her otherwise. No, all the other women remained safe and dry in the kitchen, most likely unaware that Lacey should have returned with those peppermint sticks by now. How horrifying, the idea she might not even be missed while a crazed criminal kidnapped her.

She concentrated on breathing shallowly through her nose until he abruptly removed his grimy hand from her mouth.

"What do you want? Where are you taking me? Couldn't you have waited for better weather?" Lacey didn't waste her breath screaming—he'd obviously waited until they were beyond earshot of the town. Why bother howling when she could harangue?

"Money, you'll see, and no." The man had the effrontery to grunt, as though hauling her about required more strength than he'd anticipated. Honestly, what kidnapper expected a woman to go tromping to her doom? Sagging into deadweight slowed the man down at least. "Now shut your trap and start walking, woman."

"I'll pay you well to return me, I'll walk back to town, and I'll even be silent," Lacey offered. Guns made her generous. The mention of money made her more comfortable. A greedy man might negotiate where a man intending personal harm would not.

"You couldn't pay me to go back to town with Granger lurking about," the logger refused. "As for the others, you'll do as I say or live to regret it, missy." He jammed the pistol into her tender skin, bruising to underscore his meaning.

So long as I live. Lacey almost chirped the response, but sensed it would provoke her captor. So she stayed quiet for a moment while she thought—and shuffled her feet in a show of grudging obedience, falling back with her full weight on his shoulder with each "step" she took, as though walking backward up a muddy mountainside in sodden skirts might be difficult.

"We'll order anyone named Granger out of town, Mr.—"

"Twyler." He cut her off, coarse speech dissolving beneath a sneering mockery of cultured tones. "We haven't been properly introduced. You think me a logger, but I'm a gentleman."

"Of course. True gentlemen kidnap ladies and trudge them up mountainsides at gunpoint regularly." Lacey coughed as the arm wound beneath her ribs tightened mercilessly. "My mistake."

"I wouldn't do this at all if it weren't for Granger," the man hissed into her ear. "He's hunted me here, and now I don't have time to woo one of you women and win your fortune legally."

"That makes sense," Lacey allowed. "Fortune hunting has been an honored sport of gentlemen for generations. But I'll still pay you to release me—and we'll send this Granger from town. We don't need any new men anyway." Not so much as a twinge of conscience for all the lies she told. Twyler wouldn't get a cent, and she might not send Granger away at all because once the massive brawl in the diner ended, several loggers would be leaving Hope Falls in disgrace. But none of that mattered.

"You stupid twit." Twyler's arm moved from around her waist. Almost instantly, his hand fisted in her hair as he jerked her backward, quickening the pace. "Do you really think I'm the only man to give a false name? Ah, but I fooled him until today, just as he fooled me. The difference is my bluff wins because I fooled all of you longer. *Creed is Granger.*"

Fear, ice-cold, slithered down Lacey's spine as Twyler went on about games and bluffs and Creed. *He's not sane.* She no longer pretended to drag her feet; dread made them heavy and plodding. All hopes of reasoning with her captor or waiting for the two dozen loggers to come searching for her unraveled in an instant. Her kidnapper's plan couldn't work—he headed away from the train—and when he realized it, the wildness in his voice would be vented upon his victim. *Me.* Lacey gulped in air.

"Now you're quiet, eh? Creed's not your hero anymore? Don't you worry, Miss Lyman. You'll be nice and safe right here." He patted a large tree stump slightly downhill of them.

"What?" Lacey gaped at the nondescript logger whose dull clothes and brown hair seemed so normal until one caught the maniacal glint in his eye. "You're leaving me here to wait?"

Hope fluttered once again. If he planned to tie her to a tree, she'd be found eventually. Or she might work herself free.

"Yep. When I get the money, I'll send them your location." Twyler rocked back on his heels. "So you just hop on in there."

Thoughts stuttered to a stop as he gestured again to the hollow trunk of a massive old tree. "Did...did you say...*in?*"

"I'll boost you up, and you can't get back out on your own. It'll be tight quarters, but a bitty thing like you should fit."

"No." Lacey looked at the jagged edges, brittle at the top, which she could see from her vantage point. Rain streamed into the narrow black opening, and she didn't want to think what creature hollowed it out in the first place. Or how many types of rodents and insects made their home within now. She didn't care whether or not she *might* be able to fit inside. "I won't."

"Don't test my patience." Twyler tightened his grip on the gun. "I said I'd tell them your location. I didn't promise you'd be alive. So you can climb on in and they can find you snug and spitting mad, or I can waste a slug and cram you down there so they find whatever the bugs leave behind."

"Because you're a gentleman," she muttered, debating.

"Yes." His eyes narrowed. "That hooped skirt isn't going to make it though. You'll have to shimmy out of it first."

"I beg your pardon?" Lacey stopped debating. Surely the man hadn't just instructed her to *disrobe* before descending into the dark bowels of a forest prison? As though she'd simply cast off her best worsted wool in the middle of the day. While it rained.

"You heard me. The cage thing and bustle have to go, at the very least." He brandished the gun again, making Lacey decide there really ought to be some sort of limit on how many outrageous demands a man could make per pistol. In all fairness, Mr. Twyler had to have used up all the good threats in that one.

Which really isn't fair, when I'm probably a better shot than he is. Lacey heaved a sigh over the pearl-handled pistol in her purse. Back in the kitchen in Hope Falls. *It only goes to show,* she decided, *that of all my recent mistakes, the absolute worst was neglecting the importance of my accessories.*

∞

Evie gripped her purse, hoping she wouldn't need to use the pistol inside it. Lacey tried to teach her to shoot when she gave each one of them a matching firearm, but every woman knew that the safest thing in range was whatever Evie aimed at. It still rankled how Cora and Naomi learned to shoot so quickly.

Even worse, she knew Lacey wasn't carrying the weapon she'd ensured they all possessed. Her friend's purse, with the first of the pearl-handled pieces inside, remained on the baking table. She'd left it there when she ducked back in the storeroom in search of peppermint sticks to settle an uneasy stomach.

The women let her take an extra moment to compose herself—Lacey felt irrationally responsible for the men's poor behavior—but the man Evie now knew as Twyler announced he'd look at the mercantile for the peppermint sticks and left the room. Then Jake burst back into the kitchen, abandoning a false trail and desperate to find his brother's murderer. But they were too late. Time's slow crawl had sped, and the only sign left of Lacey were scuffs in the mud beyond the storeroom door.

Now Evie watched with her heart in her throat, following behind the man trying to save her friend and clear his brother's name. Jake Creed held more than his fair share of courage, and, she was afraid, about the same amount of her heart.

"Let her go, Twyler." Jake edged out from behind the uneven row of trees concealing him from view. "She's no good to you." The sight that greeted him wore his considerable store of patience very thin indeed. "You can't shove a full-grown woman into a hollow tree stump, Twyler. And there's no reason to anyway. Drop your gun, set her free, and we'll go back to town."

"Ah, ah." With that, Twyler hauled Lacey against him, pressing a sharp blade against her delicate throat. With his free hand, he pointed a pistol at Evie, as though threatening the women made him powerful. "I suggest you drop your weapon, Granger, if you want both—or either—of these ladies to see another sunrise. Your one shot might just as well hit Miss Lyman as myself, but I'm guaranteed success with at least one of my targets." Satisfaction oozed from his voice. "Let's get on with it, shall we? A stacked deck is a gamer's greatest ally."

"I wonder"—Evie pretended nonchalance, trying to look unthreatening—"whether that's not something like a woman with a well-packed purse." In an instant she pulled out her familiar dainty pistol with an inlaid mother-of-pearl handle.

She ignored the fact she couldn't shoot worth a burnt biscuit. Evie also overlooked Lacey's renewed struggles. Obviously her friend didn't want to be anywhere near the direction where Evie chose to fire. Not that Evie wanted to fire at all, but Twyler didn't need to know that.

"You've proven more perceptive than most, Miss Thompson." A gleam of appreciation lit Twyler's gaze. "But I find myself unimpressed by your toy. This is between Granger and me."

"Then let the women go." Creed jumped on the idea.

"We've come too far for that. Throw down your gun, Mr. Granger, and admit that the woman at your side wouldn't be able to hit a target if I drew one three feet from her nose."

"Oh, that's absolutely true, Mr. Twyler." Evie's smile widened. "It used to be that I couldn't hit the. . .what's the expression my mentor used? Oh yes, I couldn't hit the broadside of the bunkhouse. But it's such a cunning little piece."

"No." Twyler's self-satisfied ooze dried up in a hurry. "You want me dead. You want me to ignore that little pistol." He darted glances around himself, edging farther out of reach. "She changes the game. Changes the cards, different value. . ." He degenerated into strange rambling mutters.

"Why did you kill my brother, Edward?" Jake asked.

"He noticed me cheating and started to raise a fuss. Two men I'd fleeced a few nights prior sat just one table over, so I couldn't allow that. And I'd already marked him for carrying a large amount of cash." Twyler clicked his teeth together repeatedly. "So I fired first, paid off the other players, and pocketed the profit. Double the windfall when your old man started paying off people to not besmirch dear Edward's memory. And then you came after me, and I did more and more paying off of my own until I ran dry and needed a rich wife." Twyler's eyes narrowed. "But here you are again, forcing my hand. With two skilled shooters against only myself, I can't hope to make it out alive. So I can either take revenge on Granger here, before leaving this earth, or hope your misguided sense of feminine kindness precludes you shooting a man in the back."

With that, Twyler shoved Lacey so she fell downhill, and Jake had to catch her before running after his prey.

A shot echoed in the forest, followed by a terrible cry.

THREE

All was silent. Evie huddled with Lacey as time grew heavy and wore her nerves thin.

"Please tell me you wouldn't have fired," Lacey said after the silence became unbearable—and Evie handed over the pistol.

"Have a little faith, Lace." Evie scanned the horizon, anxious for Jake to come back. It hadn't escaped her notice that Twyler hadn't dropped his gun before taking off.

"Does that mean you would've uttered a prayer and pulled the trigger, or that I should have faith you wouldn't do anything so foolish?" Lacey blanched at the idea.

"We can do all things through faith, Lacey Lyman." *Even wait when it's taking Jake forever and a day to mosey back.*

"In that case, I have faith that you'll never fire a gun unless faced with a man like Twyler, or whatever his name was, with absolutely no one else anywhere near the vicinity." Lacey rubbed her throat, where the knife had rested. "Thank you for following. I couldn't have gone into that stump."

It was then that they heard it, the snap of twigs beneath boots as someone heavy headed their way. They froze, Lacey's hand tightening on the gun until they made out Jake with a prone form slung over his shoulders.

"Oh, my leg," Twyler groaned. "Why couldn't you let me go, Granger? Or let the woman shoot me outright, at least?"

"Because I can't shoot the broadside of a bunkhouse. We told you that, Twyler." Evie couldn't smile at the sight of blood soaking the man's right leg, but he deserved far worse.

"You mean. . .it was true?" A wheeze of laughter escaped. "A double bluff, then. I was outdone by a double bluff from an amateur?" The gambler's wheeze stretched and thinned into a series of wispy cackles. "An amateur! I deserve my fate then. I held all the winning cards and threw them away."

∞

Midmorning light shafted through trees, striping the ground in sun and shadow. Thirsty earth rested after a long drink of yesterday's rain, leaving puddles and slicks in every path.

Chase Dunstan strode through, keeping sure footing with a heavy step. Today, he didn't need to slide soundlessly through rock and brush and dirt. Today, he closed distance on quarry that couldn't move. Today, he traveled to Hope Falls.

What he expected to find, he couldn't catalog beyond Braden Lyman, risen from the ranks of those killed in the mine collapse months before to languish in a doctor's bed. Alternately, the bed-ridden "patient" could prove an impostor pretending to be Braden Lyman to usurp his claim to the land.

Either option brought questions regarding the collapse—reasons behind it, the way it was handled afterward, what current plans pushed "Braden" to stay in Hope Falls. And of course, what on earth any of it had to do with the incredible ad. Chase couldn't forget Kane's assurance that four women, supposedly attractive, attempted to run a town full of loggers.

All lumped together, it created the worst mess Chase came across in all his days. None of it made a lick of sense. *Which is why I steer clear of towns and keep to myself and the mountains. Bad enough men make messes. Women make woes.*

A mighty racket made mincemeat of his thoughts, spurring Chase toward the sounds of a town in trouble. He stopped a moment to take off his pack and tuck it into a small grove of Gambel oak. The low-lying, shrub-like trees made for a distinctive visual marker against the tall pine and spruce dominating the area. That taken care of, Chase broke into a jog, scarcely noting as the dog at his side did the same. He came up to the train in a matter of minutes and halted.

Decoy came to an abrupt stop at his heels, tilting his head in canine question. Chase held up a hand in the "wait" motion, allowing Decoy to sink to his haunches while Chase listened. Observation didn't always require a line of vision, and he never went into a situation without gathering any information at hand.

Angry voices tangled across the tracks, their owners made mysteries by the train. Men—no fewer than seven—yelled in a bid for respect. Shuffling steps and cracking knuckles told of glares and the advance-and-gain-ground precursor to every fight. The words themselves offered fragments of the excuse behind it.

A howl of "I'm not leaving!" vied with a plaintive, "Don't make me go, I'll miss the cookin' too much," which was almost lost beneath the bluster of "Ya cain't make us go—". All mixed together in a noisy din of men protesting being forced out of Hope Falls.

"Yes we can." A familiar voice broke through the others, comfortable in giving orders. "And we are. Get on the train as you stand, or be thrown on as we hog-tie you, but you'll go."

Granger? It took Chase a moment to identify the man he'd

worked with about three years back, working as a guide through prospective timberland higher in the Rockies. *With Granger here, the claim they're trying to build a sawmill gains credibility. Grangers know lumber like no other family in North America.* His jaw set as he realized Kane deliberately omitted the name.

"You can't hog-tie all of us, Creed," one of them argued.

"I'll have help." Granger's voice came back.

Granger is answering to the name of Creed? *Why?* Chase took a soundless step closer, plagued with more questions than ever.

"Aye, that he will." The burr told of an Irishman—the rumble could have come from nothing less than a deep well of a chest. A sort of Gaelic giant sprang to mind, matching the heavy stomp of massive boots as the speaker stepped forward.

"You don't insult the ladies and stay." A slight German accent, in an unremarkable voice made all the smaller compared to the giant's, agreed. "And no fighting was one of the rules."

"Though I'll pitch in if it comes to it." This last sounded so self-satisfied, Chase took the fellow into immediate dislike— particularly as he sounded farthest away from all the arguing.

"Four of you," sneered one of the rougher protesters, "against eight of us. Even with Bear Riordan there, you don't have the manpower to run us all out of town, Creed."

Chase heard enough. Rough customers who insulted ladies and brawled in streets, and a man he respected—albeit going by an alias—standing up to them against bad odds. He ambled around the train, taking his time to look over the men involved.

The loggers not wanting to leave looked much as he would've expected—large, unkempt, and, apparently since they'd been fighting, sporting an assortment of bruises and lumps. The four men shoving them on the train were a more unlikely assortment.

Granger, as Chase already knew, stood lead. A redheaded giant—the one called Bear, Chase assumed—flanked one side.

If they'd stopped there, things looked promising.

But a short man with ruddy cheeks and too-big boots glowered from Granger's other side, and a puffed-up logger with more mouth than muscle brought up the rear. Little wonder the outcasts thought to protest their send-off. If they fought the enforcement crew, they stood a considerable chance of winning.

"Five." He came shoulder to shoulder with Granger, not bothering to make eye contact with his old ally. "Six counting the wolfhound." Chase didn't bother to gesture at Decoy, knowing full well the dog stood almost four feet tall and six feet long.

Instead he eyed the rabble-rousers with casual interest. "Just fists?" He slid his hunting knife from its sheath with a predatory smile. The sun shone on its razor-sharp blade as he flipped it into the air, didn't watch the piece spin, and caught it by the handle again. "Or knives, too?"

∞

"You only get one vote." Lacey matched Evie glower for glare.

"Jake deserves one, too," her friend protested. "And, since he's not here, I have to represent his best interests!"

"He does not deserve a vote." If a tone of voice could convey an eye roll, Naomi's did just that. "We all agreed that when we decided on our grooms, we'd put it to a vote among the four of us, and we needed a three-quarters majority before marriage. Your vote counts as one of four, which means you still need another two. And, no, the prospective groom doesn't count."

"Particularly when you're asking us to approve two men in one." Cora rubbed out a mark in her ledger and sighed. "Hypothetically, that would mean you'd ascribe him two votes."

"Don't be silly!" Evie rebuked her younger sister. "Just one man. . ." Her face took on a dreamy look. "Jake."

"But Jake Creed or Jake Granger?" Naomi's now-gentle tone

wrapped the query in concern but couldn't quite hide its edge.

Lacey recognized that edge. She'd walked it as a sharp line of doubt since she discovered her kidnapper's crazed splutters held truth. The four of them were deceived by two men wearing false names: one a criminal and one their protector. So which man could be trusted more? Such thoughts made her stomach lurch.

"He's both!"

"No." Cora refuted her sister, much to everyone's shock. "Either he's Creed, a man all four of us admire and rely upon, who's proven himself knowledgable and trustworthy, or else—"

"He's still all of that," Evie broke in. "We've simply learned he hid his name for the noble purpose of tracking down his brother's killer. If he whipped into town as Granger, Twyler would've hied off before Jake could see through his disguise!"

"There's purpose to his plan and his actions." Naomi's attempt to soothe Evie tore through the crooked stitches holding Lacey's layers of emotions in check, unearthing ragged edges.

"His purpose, and his plan," she choked. "Things your Jake, whoever he is, never bothered to tell us while he used Hope Falls to enact them. He deceived us as much as Twyler did."

"There's nobility in clearing his brother's name and catching his murderer." Naomi's judgment leveled things for a moment. "But Lacey's right; Mr. Granger knew who we are and what we want to accomplish. His failure to repay our trust is a betrayal."

"What would you have him do? Flaunt his real name at the cost of justice?" Evie flared. "Abandon his responsibility to the people Twyler would hurt if left to roam free?"

Cora laid a hand on her sister's shoulder. "Return our confidence. Perhaps not the first day or so, but at some point he should have revealed his identity and warned us."

"He warned us about being careful and not trusting the men from the moment I met him! Every step of the way, he watched over us to provide protection. Who helped enforce town rules? Kept order? Stopped those evil men from sneaking into our house with Mr. Kane that night? Jake, that's who. And you turn on him?"

"Creed did." Lacey tried to make her see. "Not Granger."

"All right, then who's out there right now, ridding the town of the brutes who began brawling yesterday? Eight burly men who won't leave quietly, and who's protecting us right now?"

"They think it's Creed, but it's not, is it?" Lacey pointed out. "If those men knew Creed wasn't real, he wouldn't hold any sway with them either. That's why you're having difficulty getting our approval. There's a reason we implemented the vote, Evie. Remember, you convinced me of its wisdom when I balked."

"But I never imagined there would be a problem with *my* choice of groom," Evie grumbled. "The three of you practically pushed me into Jake's arms, and now you won't give me your sanction for a wedding? Seems to me you three have changed."

"Don't go admonishing me about changing my mind, Evie." Cora held ground against her older sister. "If Jacob Creed existed, I'd still agree he'd make a fine groom. But he never did. This Jacob Granger stands little more than a stranger."

"His name doesn't matter—the man wearing it does!" Evie wrung her apron into a mass of wrinkles. "Jake hasn't changed."

"Then I'm even more worried. You're willing to bind yourself to a liar." The heat of anger eased some of the ache from constant tension, but Lacey didn't welcome it. "Bad enough, his words hid his identity. His silence hid a killer."

"A killer he saved you from, Lacey Lyman! A criminal he tracked down and exposed when Twyler would have gone free."

"I wouldn't have needed rescuing if I'd been warned." Stung, she snapped the words. *I came here to prove I don't need to be treated like a china doll, and I wound up being rescued?* But beneath the rage simmered a lingering fear. "We all trusted him, Evie, but none of us will let you make the mistake again."

"We all make mistakes." Naomi's reminder held a private sorrow, and Lacey winced alongside her cousin. "Which is why I won't say nay to Mr. Granger. I feel I know enough about the man to see how he cares for Evie. He has the time it takes the rest of us to choose husbands to iron out the rest."

"We'll be watching to make sure you don't get burned." Cora's vow made her sister smile, though it died swiftly. "We'll start by finding some way to be sure the former Mr. Creed is the real Mr. Granger. Once that's certain, we can investigate more."

"Mama's old friends back in Charleston will help. There's no one like a society matron to sniff out a bachelor's background. Particularly if he's eligible, and Mr. *Granger* would fit that bill." Satisfaction starched her spine as Lacey found something to take charge of—a concrete way to safeguard her friends. *I should have done it before. Why didn't I stop to think?*

"Mr. Lawson and Mr. McCreedy vouch for his identity," Naomi pointed out. "Since he knew we approved of him as Creed, I doubt the man would trouble himself inventing a name at this point. I believe he truly is Granger, and now that he's caught Twyler, he's setting things straight. It's only good sense, after all."

Cora nodded, but added, "He brought Lawson and McCreedy, so we might do well to assume they'd support him regardless."

An exasperated sound escaped Evie, but she didn't remark.

"Stop huffing." Lacey resolved to telegraph Charleston that very day. "If there's one lesson we can take away from this entire debacle, it's that we can't trust anyone in Hope Falls. From now on, we take a hard look at every new hire."

For instance, Lacey didn't quite like the looks of the fellow conferring with Riordan, Clump, Williams, and Cree—Granger. She caught herself thinking of Evie's intended by his false name and stopped short. But thinking about fake names was the first step in a dance she'd rather sit out, so she studied the new man instead. She took in his broad shoulders. The confident stance. The sun-bronzed skin, and head of hair dark enough to drown doubts. Lacey Lyman gave a heartfelt sigh.

Of regret. After all, nothing good came dressed like *that*.

FOUR

Y ou're going with the next train."With the biggest threat safely stuffed onto the train and on their way to who-knew-where, the rooster bringing up the rear of Granger's crew bobbed his head toward Chase. "Nice of you to step in, but you weren't needed then, and you sure as shooting aren't wanted now."

Two sentences, and the man cemented Chase's poor opinion. *Yep. More mouth than muscle, and more muscle than mind.* He shook his head. Once. That's all it took to acknowledge the man's insulting order to board the train and refuse it. It also served as a silent invitation for the rooster—which was always just a chicken with a strut—to try and enforce it.

Granger stayed clear, a silent show of respect from a man whose esteem he'd earned long ago. Bear, the big Irishman, gave a growl of disapproval but otherwise held his peace. The German, whose primary concern had been for the women, ignored those cues. The man either disregarded or didn't know the Rule.

There were few unspoken exceptions having to do with protecting women and children or preventing injustice, but otherwise male interaction could be boiled down to one rule: handle your own business; leave other men to handle theirs.

Most conflict in the world could be traced to some idiot ignoring the Rule. And here stomped the German, spluttering about how the other man lacked manners. Poor sap never even saw the blow coming, just doubled over with surprise in his eyes and no air left in his lungs, the wind knocked clean out of him.

Chase waited for the rooster to turn to him before letting fly with a right hook to the jaw. Stepping over the chicken now crumpled in the mud, he offered his hand to the fallen German and pulled him to his feet. "Leave it be, next time, yes?"

"*Ja.*" A shaky nod belied a hearty handshake. "I'm Klumpf. Friends and men who knock over Williams call me plain Clump."

"Dunstan." He pulled back his hand. The rooster—Williams, he now knew—didn't stir. Perhaps when he woke, he'd crow less.

"Riordan." Another handshake, this from the redheaded giant. "Most call me Bear, but I'll answer to either, ya ken."

"Ken?" The word caught him. "Not Irish?"

"Ah, a canny one." A broad smile split his face. "Scots-Irish I be, and you'll hear the lilt and the brogue and a whole hodgepodge of phrases from me. Most never notice."

"When Riordan gets riled, no one understands him." Granger clapped him on the shoulder. "Good to see you, Dunstan."

"Likewise. Hadn't heard you were back in Colorado." Chase raised a brow but held his tongue. Whatever his old friend's reasons for calling himself Creed, it wasn't his business.

Not yet.

Why now? Jake Granger eyed the newcomer warily, doubts warring with relief. *There couldn't be a better time for Dunstan to blow into town, but that's what's suspicious. Why does he show up now, when*

I have most use for him but didn't send word for him?

"You didn't hear I was back in Colorado for good reason." He addressed the question behind his old friend's statement, glad he'd taken Bear and Clump aside earlier that morning to fill them in on his real identity. The men leaving town hadn't known. Any hint that Jake wasn't whom they thought, and their pride over being lied to would rile them even more.

"No one knew. I've been going by Creed to keep it quiet."

Dunstan's short nod affirmed Jake's memory of the man. Observant, Dunstan noted the name change. Quick thinking, but methodical, he chose not to ask in front of others.

"The others still don't know." Clump nudged Williams's arm none too gently with one overly large boot. The man didn't stir.

"With the rabble-rousers gone, the rest won't prove problematic. Worst case, they won't believe I'm a Granger. He"— Jake jerked his head toward Dunstan—"can help there. I've worked with Dunstan before—three years back. He hires out as a guide, hunter, tracker, you name it, along this stretch of the Rockies. Some of the others will have heard of him. McCreedy and Lawson will vouch for me, and Lyman always knew."

"The name Granger holds clout." Bear nodded. "Once it's established that you've finished your family business to reclaim your name, things will go smooth again."

"Hold it, Bear." Clump stepped forward, thumbs threaded protectively through his suspenders. The other man clearly hadn't forgotten when Jake dangled him by those same suspenders and interrogated him. "Just what kind of business did Creed finish? He didn't get around to explaining that part, and I want to know why he lied and why he doesn't need to anymore."

"Granger." Dunstan's amused correction marked his first, and possibly only, contribution to the conversation at hand.

"Now, I'm going to level with you three." Jake cast a swift glance to ensure Williams was out cold. "The men in the bunkhouse will only hear what I've already said. Understood?"

"Ja." Clump nodded for good measure. "This has something to do with your strange questions yesterday about the square coin?"

"My brother Edward carried that coin. A cheating gambler shot him point-blank, robbed him, sullied his name, and got away with it." Jake paused. "Until now. That piece—it's really an old balance used to check coins for weight and prevent clipping or shaved edges—marked the murderer I've been tracking for months."

Dunstan rolled his shoulders, evincing an easy readiness. He'd obviously weighed Jake's earlier statement about finished family business and decided whatever was left wouldn't be urgent or difficult. That frame of mind told, as nothing else could, Dunstan was the only man who had yet to meet the women of Hope Falls.

Good. It meant he might be talked into staying while Jake hauled Twyler in. Dunstan didn't like towns, and the less he knew about this one, the more likely he'd be to hire on awhile.

Next to him, every muscle in Bear's arms and neck strained. From the way the Scots-Irishman's breath came out in great huffs, Jake judged him ready to thrash any murderers still lurking around. Then again, the big man might be straining to hold back his rage over not being informed about the problem.

Equally good. Big Bear had a protective streak a mile wide when it came to the women and the stature to make good on it. If he got worked up over having misjudged Twyler, he'd keep an even sharper eye on Evie and the rest until Jake got back.

Clump. . .brightened. A grin split his face in a smile wide enough to look painful. "So you held my suspenders to find out who stole your brother's coin and hunted him down for justice. With Earl and the others gone, now all is good in Hope Falls, and I can return to Miss Thompson and ask her to be mine."

Not good. Jake fisted a hand around those familiar suspenders before he even decided to do it. "Listen, Clump. You're a good man, but I'm only going to say this once. Evie's my fiancée now, so you aren't going to try to court her anymore."

An outraged growl sort of strangled from Clump as he jerked his suspenders free and backed up. "I called dibs on her!"

"And I refused." Jake grinned. *Evie was mine from the start.* "So admit you lost with good grace, and tell me you'll look after her and the others while I'm gone. Otherwise I'll have to ask you along when I haul Twyler back to Maine. Doc says he'll be able to travel day after tomorrow, and I'm not letting him postpone his meeting with justice a second later."

"Who?" Bear practically choked the question. "Who is this murderer in our town, who fooled us all? How did you catch him?"

Seeing the look on the other man's face, Jake thought it best to give the short version of Lacey's kidnapping. No sense working so hard to capture Twyler and override his own need for vengeance just to have Bear kill him before the law tried him.

"Ye best be takin' him soon, Granger." Riordan's voice darkened. "Afore I decide to teach the man a lesson about how to treat a dainty thing like Miss Lyman." He cast a sorrowing glance toward the women's house. "The poor, sweet lady."

"Vile, wretched beasts!" Lacey trudged along, swatting high-rising shrubs and low-lying branches out of her way. "Should all be strung up by their thumbs until they learn common decency."

Surprising how good it felt to go for a brisk walk, exertion and exasperation driving the breath from her lungs and venting the trouble from her thoughts. Each step felt lighter, each word rang louder, and the forest seemed to welcome her.

She hugged her shawl—a light kerseymere chosen more for its soothing softness and beguiling strawberries-and-cream stripes than for warmth—around her shoulders as she muttered, "Or at least manners, which everyone knows are the pretense of common decency. Men should at least learn *that* much before being allowed in any sort of town. No matter how isolated."

At first she'd rushed to get out of sight before anyone realized she'd slipped away from the house but hadn't joined Cora at the doctor's. Lacey didn't want to face Braden just now. She knew full well what her brother would say about yesterday's events— they'd all heard it well in advance. Memories tumbled through her thoughts like buttons shaken from a glass jar.

He'd been incensed when they first arrived in Hope Falls: *"You don't belong here. This is no place for women, and you need to pack up what I'm sure is too much stuff and head home!"* Of course, Lacey knew her brother was wrong.

Until that terrible night when Robert Kane led a few men to the house where they slept, intent on ruining more than their reputations. If it hadn't been for Granger—well, Lacey couldn't stand to think about that. Neither, she knew, could her brother. The almost-attack was Braden's worst fear sprung to life. How many times had he said it, trying to run them out of Hope Falls? *"Leave for your own good. It's not safe for you women here."*

But instead of leaving Hope Falls, she and the others simply had Mr. Lawson move in downstairs, where he could be close to his sister. Granger hired him to be their engineer, not knowing he'd tow a newly widowed, heavily pregnant sister along. But it worked out well for the purposes of protection.

Inside the house at least.

Outside, it didn't guard against Braden's judgment. *"No matter your intentions, no matter your plans, the outcome put you at risk."* Which meant Lacey couldn't walk far enough or fast enough to outrun the most earth-shattering realization yet: *my* brother *was right.*

It was enough to make any woman question her surroundings, her plans, and even her own good taste. *Well, perhaps not that last.* Lacey ran a loving hand along the cheery rose of her surprisingly soft woolen skirts. After such a dismal yesterday, she'd chosen a bright new dress to lift her spirits, her resolve, and her ability to face the consequences of her mistakes.

The bonnet, with its matching ribbons trailing in a jaunty wave as she marched along, seemed a sort of battle standard for a formidable and fashionable woman. Yes, she'd planned for a difficult day full of brotherly recriminations by dressing to impress. Then promptly turned an about-face and avoided it all.

"Because, truly, after a woman's been kidnapped at gunpoint, lost any hope of her beauty sleep, and awoken to a morning without one of Evie's delicious breakfasts the first time she really needs one, she deserves some peace and quiet." She announced this to the trees and sky at large, testing her argument. "Not that I'm typically the sort to enjoy quiet, but I've not had a moment alone in weeks. 'It's not safe'."

She mimicked her brother's censorious tones then sighed. This little excursion would only earn her more scolding from everyone—but with the worst of the loggers booted out of town and half the others still abed nursing wounds from yesterday's fray, it seemed the best possible time for a little private thinking.

"Not to mention that the odds of being manhandled by another crazed criminal the very next day must be incredibly low," she informed a squirrel, which had frozen midscamper. The small creature seemed transfixed by this logic, as it didn't so much as blink, so Lacey continued. "Besides, I remembered my purse and am keeping one hand on my pistol. But you wildlife seem quite hospitable thus far. I doubt any bears lurk near—"

A massive, shaggy beast lumbered out of the shrubbery before she finished the sentence, sending her tiny friend shimmying up its tree and leaving Lacey speechless. For one wild moment, she imagined her comment conjured a bear—if for no other reason than to continue her recent streak of mistakes—but the animal now picking its way across a few boulders wasn't a bear.

Its size could give anyone a fright, but once Lacey's heart stopped fluttering along with her bonnet ribbons, she recognized the creature. She'd seen that shaggy silver-gray coat standing beside the new man in town. *A tamed wolf, perhaps?*

Lacey remained still as it came to a halt a mere foot from her skirts, nose thrust forward in a curiously impertinent sniff. *Wolves aren't described as shaggy, nor this large.* She thought back over everything she'd read, looked over the creature now wagging its long, curved tail at her. She saw a dog's wide brown eyes, perked ears that nevertheless flopped back, and rounded cast to the muzzle. *Some sort of mix then.*

"Good wolf-doggy," she crooned, ever so slowly extending one hand for a more thorough, moist sniffing. "Where's your owner? Lets you roam free? Lucky puppy." A rough slurp of approval rasped her palm before Lacey gingerly scratched between his ears. Definitely a he. No female would be so unkempt.

Besides, males always like me. She grinned as his tail wagged harder, mouth falling open in an unmistakable grin at the attention she lavished upon him, falling into step alongside her when she continued. In fact, she sped up a bit, enjoying the warm breeze and easy acceptance of the animal at her side.

Until her new friend tensed, fur rising along his spine in a long, thin patch. His nose thrust forward as he breathed deep, swiftly turning his massive head eastward to locate the source of a new scent. Growls rumbled low in his throat, a warning Lacey wasn't foolish enough to ignore.

FIVE

She pulled the pearl-handled pistol from her purse, spinning around to scan the trees for whatever upset her new friend. The dog crouched back on its haunches as though ready to spring. A blur of tawny brown flashed from Lacey's right, descending straight toward her with an unearthly howling. She barely had time to shoot before a cacophony of sounds and sensations overwhelmed her.

Everything seemed distorted. The shot had an unexpected, too-loud echo. Lacey heard a woman's scream, but would have sworn she hadn't the breath to make a sound. The animal from the trees knocked her down, but another force barreled into it before the thing did more than swipe her bonnet loose.

The dog, she realized, pushing herself up on her elbows. "Here, puppy," Lacey gasped. *It must have sprung on the other one.* Suddenly her friend filled her vision, concern clearly written on his furry face as he tried to nose her shoulder.

"I'm all right, boy. What was it?" She peered around him. *There.* A few lengths away, a large tawny animal lay unmoving.

355

"Cougar." Without warning, a man spoke from behind her, hunkering down after appearing as though from nowhere.

Lacey shrieked and would have jumped if the dog weren't anchoring her skirts to the ground. Its wagging tail gave her an inkling of the man's identity before she really saw him.

"Decoy's made grown men run in fear." The deep voice held an intriguing rasp, almost as though it went largely unused. "A cougar jumps you; you get back up. But I merit a scream?" An amused black brow arched at her over bottomless brown eyes.

Now that she'd gotten her breath back, Lacey realized a blush traveled along with it. *And he's laughing at me.* Rising to her feet without taking the hand he offered, she snapped, "Absolutely. Between a wolf-dog, a cougar, and a man, every sane woman knows which animal is the most frustrating!"

∞

When he first spotted her, Chase closed his eyes, hoping when he opened them the vision would disappear. He cracked one lid open. Nope. Everything looked the same. Blue sky, green trees, gray boulders. . .pink fluff. And this time there could be no doubt.

The pink fluff was on the move.

Which meant some foolish woman traveled alone in an area rife with wildlife, placing her in danger, and therefore under his protection. All because he couldn't pretend he hadn't seen that pink fluff ball bobbing down the mountainside.

No matter that it interfered with his plans. Chase had seen cougar tracks in the area. He started down toward her, giving Decoy the signal to go guard their target while he closed in.

Before he spotted her, Chase had two options. He could wait in the forest for Granger to take Twyler off, roaming about at will with pretty much just Bear and Clump knowing anything about him. Problem with that idea was limited access after the initial observation stage, plus the Williams fellow he'd clocked earlier would set to squawking if he somehow managed to spot him.

No, the smarter option, which Chase now had no choice but to accept, was to take Granger's offer. He'd hire on as the Hope Falls hunter/tracker, keep an eye out for large predators, and keep the cooks in as much fresh meat as possible until Granger returned. At least, in title. Granger expected him to look out for the ladies, too. One of whom roamed alone.

Which meant more time in town, more trouble, more questions from other people. But it also meant more opportunities to discover if the bedridden Braden was the true Braden Lyman, and if so—or even if not—what caused the mine collapse. Why did the Miracle Mining Company sell out so soon? What was going on with that incredible ad and this strange sawmill proposition?

Granger's presence threw him off—it meant that either a legitimate logging enterprise was going up, or they'd fooled a shrewd businessman whose sawmill expertise couldn't be beat.

Too many questions to ignore, and it all started with the man claiming to be Braden Lyman. But to get close, Chase would have to start by working for Hope Falls—and protecting the women. Starting now. He closed the distance, wanting to witness her reaction to Decoy. How people interacted with the wolfhound—and how the dog responded—told Chase more than ten conversations.

She didn't faint. The first realization brought him to a halt. He'd expected her to faint. *Or scream.* His unassailed ears approved. But when she didn't run off, Chase began to wonder about the woman. Did her lack of cowardice indicate idiocy?

Decoy butted his massive head against frothy fabric, but the woman in pink held still. By now Chase drew close enough to see she hadn't gone stiff with fright. She simply stayed put while Decoy sniffed her skirts—a literal version of what two dozen loggers must be trying with the pretty girl.

"Good wolf-doggy." Her sweet voice, with its clear, high-pitched inflection, echoed her feminine appearance.

Probably practiced.

Chase almost reached them, but she began walking again. With that bonnet blocking her vision, she wouldn't see him until the last moment, meaning he'd probably frighten her. *Not good.*

The wind shifted, Decoy tensed, and Chase spotted the cougar whose tracks he'd seen earlier. Yellow eyes fixed on wind-swirled pink ribbons. It pounced with an unearthly shriek. He fired, running toward the girl the moment after the recoil. In one of those strange mountain moments, the shot seemed to echo. The wounded cougar landed, swiping the bonnet as Decoy bounded into the cat, bowling it off the girl and to the grass.

Now seemed as good a time as any for introductions. Chase squatted over by the fallen cat, turning to face the woman when she let out a shriek and jump made futile by Decoy's weight.

"Decoy's made grown men run in fear. A cougar jumps you; you get back up. But I merit a scream?" Honestly, it amused him, but he figured it would embarrass the stuffing out of her.

A rosy blush crept across her cheeks before she answered. "Absolutely. Between a wolf-dog, a cougar, and a man, every sane woman knows which animal is the most frustrating!"

For a second Chase stared at her. Then the chuckles came, piling atop each other until they became guffaws. The woman looked like an angel, all rosy blushes, golden curls, and big blue eyes. But those big blue eyes held an unholy anger, and those petal-like lips spouted insults to make politicians proud.

Chase wanted to set her back down and take a closer look at her shoulder, where claws had caught, but knew better than to touch her. Her wariness gave way to peevishness at his teasing, which helped, but wasn't enough. Mad made a better mood than scared, but something shared would lower her guard more.

With no suave words to offer, Chase wielded humor in a return shot. "And between a she-wolf, cougar, and a woman, we both know which has the sharpest claws."

For a moment it seemed as though she'd take greater offense. Then her scowl shifted like a branch in the breeze, a reluctant smile tugging at the corners of her mouth. "I shouldn't have snapped at you like that. My nerves were worn of course, but you didn't deserve the shriek nor the snark."

"Snark?" Chase couldn't stop challenging the changeling.

"My friend Evie makes up the most marvelous words," the girl explained. "Snark is when someone is waspish."

"Ah." He leaned forward while she spoke, pressing a folded bandanna against her shoulder, where pink fabric gaped in three slim stripes. The jagged tears flashed glimpses of cream and crimson not unlike those decorating the scrap of fabric twisted alongside her. "Hold this here. You've been scratched." He frowned at a thin, darker line etched along her neck.

So this is supposed to be a dainty society darling, who suddenly places scandalous ads and heads West on a whim? The sort of woman who's kidnapped one day and wanders the woods alone the next, but knows the difference between a wolf and a behemoth gray dog and remains calm through a cougar attack. Lacey Lyman, intrepid pink fluff ball? He snorted.

"Oh, so that's why your dog was nosing my shoulder." She cautiously pressed the tips of her fingers to the edge of the bandanna in an obvious bid to avoid touching his hand. "What is his name, by the way? I'm greatly in his debt."

"Decoy." As much as it amused him to let her think the dog killed her cougar, honesty made him add, "But I shot the cat."

"Balderdash." Her finely drawn brows knit closer in a glower. "How dare you attempt to take the credit for that?"

"Check and see—the cat was shot. Decoy didn't kill him."

"I know full well the cat was shot since I shot it." She gave an indignant sniff before admitting, "Well, it only looked like a great streak of tawny brown coming at me, but I still shot it, and that's really the important thing."

Chase stared at the set line of her jaw and knew Miss Lyman truly believed she'd shot her cougar. A swift perusal of the ground turned up a small pearl-handled pistol. "With that?"

"Don't sound so disbelieving. It's a cunningly crafted piece of weaponry. Simply because something is lovely doesn't mean it isn't useful or even extraordinary, you know." The growing ferocity of her glower warned him she might apply that principle to more than ludicrously miniscule pistols.

"Explains the echo." He didn't say more, just checked the carcass. Most likely she'd fired her little toy and not hit anything. The large hole left by his shotgun would convince her, but Chase doubted he'd ask her to look. Bullet wounds were too much, even for this oddly adventurous female.

Except. . .the cougar took *two* bullets to the chest. One from his shotgun, and one considerably smaller, but no less deadly.

"I can see by the surprise on your face—which it hardly needs be said isn't flattering—that you've discovered I'm a good shot." Satisfaction laced her voice. "I thought *your* shot was the echo, so I'm glad that much is explained. But what about that awful scream? You yourself mentioned I didn't do it."

"Cougars do that unearthly shrieking howl. Even the males— though this one's young, about sixty pounds. Just over a year, I'd say." He looked it over. "Still a big kitten, too curious to resist the lure of your fluttering ribbons. Must've thought he could pounce, grab the 'wounded creature' you carried, and be off to play with his prize before Decoy moved."

"My bonnet?" For the first time, the girl went pale. "You think

I was attacked over my *bonnet*?"

"Yep." Of all the things for her to get upset about. Only a woman wouldn't mind the idea of a predator leaping for her throat until someone pointed out it endangered her headgear. Chase decided it was time to head back to Hope Falls.

"My bonnet in no way resembles a wounded animal!"

"This wouldn't have happened if you had someone with you." He ignored the issue of her hat. It didn't matter. "Even young cougars aren't foolish enough to attack something traveling in a pair or group. What were you doing out here alone?"

Becoming quite angry and trying not to show it of course.

Lacey didn't say so. Instead she stared at the stranger before her. Here stood a man daring to chide her as though she were an infant who'd wandered too far from her nurse. Why, the first words he'd spoken were a taunt over her shock at his sudden appearance. Who was this man to dictate her behavior?

Obviously, such rudeness deserved a proper dressing-down.

"What am I doing out here?" She repeated the impertinent question, raising her chin. "*I'm* enjoying a walk on *my* property. And just what, may I ask, do you think *you're* doing here?"

Aside from trying to take me to task, she silently added.

The grimmest grin she'd ever seen pulled her into his answer before she considered whether or not a grin could truly be grim. "*I'm* enjoying your walk, too."

"Of all the ridiculous—" Lacey caught herself and changed pattern. "In that case, I suggest you enjoy the walk heading that way, while I enjoy the vistas in this direction." She gestured widely to illustrate the opposite paths, but stopped abruptly at a swift stinging in her shoulder. *The scratch.*

"No." His grin disappeared, leaving only the tension stretching tightly around his surprisingly square jaw.

Surprising that Lacey could make it out through that much scruffy stubble, not surprising that the man would boast a square jawline. It seemed, somehow, the shape of stubbornness.

Rounded chins, she suddenly decided, implied better ability to compromise—both a strength and an art. That her own chin happened to be round, rather than square, simply proved it.

"Very well, I'll trade. You go that way, and I'll head back from whence I came." She made the offer with modified, less sweeping gestures to again illustrate opposite directions. But again, a sharp sting in her shoulder made her drop her left arm.

"No." Something she could only describe as fierce lightened the dark ash of his gaze. Now he stared at her through a rich burnt umber. "Let me look at your shoulder."

"No." Lacey belatedly realized she'd echoed him and hastened to add, "I'll just keep this bandanna pressed against it until the doctor can take a look, and everything will be fine."

While she finished refusing, he moved. Lacey didn't note any sway of his shoulders indicating a step, heard no scuff or shuffle of his boots. It looked as though the ground itself shifted to bring him forward because now he stood too close.

"What are you doing?" She shrilled the question, loud voice a ladylike assault designed to force him back a measure. Or two.

He didn't step back. Nor did he answer. In fact, he did nothing but take up far too much space for any single person. And even that seemed more a side effect than anything planned. No, this tall, dark stranger managed an almost unnatural stillness as he just. . .stood. Silently. Looking at her.

SIX

I t gave her a case of the woollies. *Because this disconcerting, itchy sensation can't be my dress. Doesn't the man know long silences make people nervous?* Lacey tilted her head to the side, the pretext of shifting her now-askew bonnet allowing her to break eye contact. When its bow finally gave way and the entire creation slipped to the ground, she breathed a sigh of relief. Since she'd risen from the cougar's impact, those ribbons chafed against the scab Twyler—

Lacey froze as the offhand brush of memory set her prickling anew. *I'm alone in the forest with another strange man, and absolutely no one knows where I've gone or that I might need help. Every man in Hope Falls will already be accounted for.*

It wasn't as though she'd failed to notice he was a he and they were the only two people. But he didn't seem threatening.

After all, she thought wildly, *threatening men don't save women from cougars—or try to save them, because he truly didn't know I'd already shot it—or scold them for walking alone. Fathers did that. Big brothers did that. Gentlemen with good intentions and high self opinions order women about.*

Except. . .gentlemen didn't don dusty leather and go climbing mountainsides with shaggy wolfhounds. Nor would any gentleman stand overly close to a lady and demand to touch her—no matter the reasoning. Which brought Lacey right back to the woollies.

Because every instinct God granted and every lady lesson learned warned Lacey that the man before her was no gentleman.

"A gentleman would pick up my bonnet," Lacey pointed out, trying to prod the man. Any attempt to pick up the hat—or, better still, the shawl which might better conceal her torn bodice— meant releasing her grip on the bandanna pressed to her shoulder.

And, though Lacey wouldn't have believed it in a thousand years, that bandanna now ranked as the most important part of her ensemble. It didn't match—in fact, everyone knew red clashed with pink—but since coming West she'd found that clashing, faded articles of clothing seemed almost du jour in mountain wear.

Even more important, the blessed thing stopped the non-gentleman who owned it from inspecting her wound, a process she strongly suspected might involve him coming closer and touching her bare shoulder. No man had ever touched her bare shoulder. In fact, Lacey was hard pressed to recall a time before Hope Falls when a man touched so much as her ungloved hand. Obviously a mysterious stranger couldn't be permitted the liberty.

Besides, she tried not to make a fuss about it, but—

"It hurts." The gravelly voice shook her from her thoughts as the man inclined his head toward her wound. "Let me see."

She still needed to say no, but at least he sounded nicer and as though it mattered to him that the scratches burned. Lacey could be gracious since he'd been kind enough to ask.

"Thank you for asking, but—wait." Her eyes narrowed. "You didn't ask at all, did you? You ordered me in a nicer tone!"

"I've found questions usually are just that: orders phrased nicely to make the other person feel like they have a choice." He shrugged then reached for the bandanna as though she agreed.

"Oh no." Lacey skittered backward, not even ashamed at the retreat. "I do have a choice, and you didn't phrase your request nicely enough to acknowledge it. You best try again. . .buster."

I don't know his name. She held back a groan. *I'm trying to hold him to manners when I neglected basic introductions.*

"Dunstan. It wasn't a request—now stop moving." He shadowed her in a slow waltz around the felled cougar.

The man most likely didn't recognize the steps of the dance. Counting the beats took almost none of Lacey's concentration, and the movements both avoided crushing her bonnet and kept her from his reach. Unless he lunged, which she'd be prepared for once the pattern brought her beside her pistol.

"I'm Miss Lyman. That's the problem. . . ." Lacey's comment trailed off as she darted to the side, grabbing her pistol despite her now-throbbing shoulder. "And *now* I'll stop moving."

Honestly, I'm not certain I could keep going even if I wanted to, she admitted to herself as she raised her pistol. Lacey didn't aim it at the man—Dunstan—nor release the safety. She simply held it between them in readiness, a silent message she wouldn't be ordered around.

"Plan to shoot?" He showed the audacity to sound amused.

"Careful, Mr. Dunstan." She gritted the warning from behind clenched teeth. Keeping the pistol aloft cost her, but he needn't know it. "That sounded more like a real question."

This time the silence-and-shrug combination didn't fool her. Dunstan only kept quiet when he didn't have a good answer.

That means I'm winning!

"Have you lost your wits?" Braden Lyman yelled at her.

"No, though my hearing might be at risk." Cora Thompson

neatly snipped through a stitch of her embroidery and knotted it. "Do you realize, dear, that you yell more than you speak?"

"I do not," he roared. "And I'm not your 'dear.' "

"There. You did it again." She hid a smile behind the needle she threaded with another color. "Loud and loathsome."

"Then loathe me and leave me." His grumble made her smile.

Good to know my needling still has its uses. Cora avoided looking at the mess she'd made of her embroidery. Not that her crooked stitches mattered. The past few weeks taught several lessons, but the one Cora found most practical when visiting her reluctant fiancé was to bring something to occupy her hands.

Full hands helped keep her from strangling the man.

"No such luck, sweetheart." She beamed a sunny smile and jabbed the needle back through her hoop. "I'm here to stay."

"Then you'll be in a pine box before long. All of you will." He pushed against his pillows, sucking in a sharp breath. Whether Braden braced against pain from his dislocated shoulder, his broken knee, or both, Cora couldn't guess. He wouldn't want her to ask, even if he hadn't continued his lecture.

"You sit here as though yesterday doesn't change anything, pretending the danger still doesn't exist, when the proof snuck up and grabbed Lacey. My sister could have been killed!"

"The way you could have been killed in a mine collapse?" Cora's needle dipped and rose, gaining speed as she spoke. "You don't use danger as a determining factor in your decisions."

There. She'd stopped tiptoeing about his ordeal. *Long past time we stop pretending the cave-in didn't happen, as though not asking questions or acknowledging the horror of it will somehow help him battle through the lingering effects. The light of day will shrink it, no matter if it makes him feel smaller for a while.*

"No one can predict a cave-in." Her beloved no longer spoke. He snarled. "But any twit with half a mind and half a thought to rub alongside can spark a warning against gently bred women wandering out West. If you were honest, we all foresaw—"

"That one of our hired men happened to be a deviously disguised murderer whose sick need to fund high-stakes gambling would make him kidnap Lacey and try to stuff her into an old tree?" Cora stopped stitching to gape at the man sitting stock-still in his bed. "Of course you're right. That sort of thing happens far more often than a cave-in, so we women knowingly put ourselves in the most danger simply by staying in town."

"Stop trying to make it sound as though I'm being foolish."

"I'm not trying." She shook her embroidery hoop at him like a tambourine. "There's no need, foolish as it is already. If Evie were here, she'd say your argument is meringue."

A brief battle ensued. Braden stared her down, refusing to ask about meringue but obviously wanting to. Cora stared back, refusing to elaborate unless asked. The old Braden would ask.

A sudden tightening at the base of her throat made Cora put down the embroidery. *Foolish.* A warning hammered in her pulse, advising against empty hands and heated arguments. Last time she'd yanked the pillows from beneath Braden's head in retribution for his harsh words. She hadn't known about his dislocated shoulder yet, and the resulting jolt brought him low.

And now I know. I know about the shoulder, about the deeper wounds to his pride, and the truth about why I pulled that pillow. Cora swallowed against the crest of emotion. *It wasn't just the words; I tried to punish him for not being* my *Braden.*

But that Braden died in the mine collapse as surely as the sparkling, unstoppable Lacey would have died if she'd been trapped in a hollowed tree stump for days. For now, hope kept her believing time and love—along with healthy doses of ignoring him as needed—would bring back the Braden she knew and loved.

The old Braden—her Braden—would have asked about the meringue, a whipped-egg topping Evie put on lemon pies. Cora would have explained that Evie called arguments meringue when someone clucked themselves silly, so worried that they laid an egg. Then the only thing they could do was whip it up in hopes it would be impressive enough to top everything else. But mostly it owed its size to air. No substance.

Then Braden would smile, and they would have laughed. But today Braden shrugged his good shoulder and started lecturing her about safety again, leaving her to sigh over memories.

I miss the days when he had a sense of humor.

Chase just about hooted when the fluff ball came up with that plaything of a pistol, but pegged her for the type to lose her temper first and regret her reactions later. Which meant he didn't smile at her triumphant tone, much less laugh.

His amusement died a swift death when he caught her slight wince, prompting him to catalog other signs that Miss Lyman's show owed more to bravado than substance. The hand clutching his bandanna to her shoulder pressed harder, her knuckles now faint shadows beneath pale skin. Skin that went from pale to practically translucent around the fingertips of her other hand, where she gripped her pocket pistol. The revolver dipped then righted once more, evoking another hastily hidden wince.

Swiping the gun would damage her pride more than anything, but Chase didn't want to jar her arm and shoulder. He bore no doubts about whether or not she'd fight him; he'd never met a less biddable, more contrary woman. *Or a more amusing one.*

Despite her one good point, Miss Lyman still counted as a woman. Which meant he might *not* have to take her gun away. Whistling a slow tune to warn away any nearby scavengers who might have caught scent of the cougar's blood, Chase did what any man should when faced with an irrational woman. Ignored her.

Except for keeping her in the corner of his eye, he focused on the cougar instead. Chase angled toward the fallen cat as he slid his rucksack off his shoulder. He hid a smile at her disbelieving huff when he sank into a crouch, riffling through his essentials and withdrawing a coil of tightly braided rope. But as far as any onlooker could see, Chase ignored her.

And it worked. She lowered the gun, stopping the pull against those scratches. It didn't let him examine her shoulder, but he could already hear her breathing more easily. When people braced against pain, they tended to hold their breath, exhaling almost as an afterthought when the pressure became distracting.

Women are the only creatures known to avoid attention then become irritated when they succeed. And the pretty ones were worst. Right now Miss Lyman stood, stymied by his sudden lack of interest. Any minute now she'd start chattering at him to reestablish the familiar scenario of a man focusing on her.

Chase focused on the cougar. He took his time binding the cougar's paws, so it'd be easier to sling across his shoulders without sliding to the side or back during the walk to town. With her arm no longer raised and pulling at her shoulder, he had no reason to hurry. Particularly since Miss Lyman hadn't started blithering at him yet. Come to think of it, he couldn't hear her breathing any longer, which meant she might be in greater pain than he realized. He straightened, turning to see—

His pink fluff ball was on the move. Again.

Not again, Chase snorted. *Still.* Since the moment he spotted her, Miss Lyman refused to bow to convention, much less any expectation. He should have guessed he couldn't use typical female behavior to predict hers, could have seen this one would choose to be difficult and take the opposite position. *But no one would expect her to head the opposite* direction, *too.*

He hefted the cougar across his shoulders and headed after the woman. Despite her shoulder and a disgruntled Decoy trying to corral his stubborn charge back toward Chase, Miss Lyman managed impressive headway before he caught up to her. Usually he appreciated that sort of determination and efficiency.

This time it made him want to dump the cougar in the dirt, scoop up the girl, and head through Hope Falls until he hit the doctor's doorstep. But Chase wouldn't touch her unless she looked ready to collapse. Judging by the set of her jaw, Miss Lyman would march clear to Cape Horn and back before admitting she needed assistance or accepted his help. So she'd just have to accept his company until she reached town.

Unfortunately, that meant he had to accept hers. Preparing for verbal buckshot, Chase stepped within blathering range.

SEVEN

I can always shoot him, Lacey comforted herself as the disconcerting Mr. Dunstan gained on her. *If he makes one false move or a single threat, I'll fire without hesitation.* Never mind her hand shook at the very thought of harming him.

This mysterious stranger pounced into her life with the lithe grace of that fallen cougar, but showed the snarl to match. If push came to shove, Lacey didn't intend to test the man's ferocity. Too much kept her off balance lately.

Yet here I am. Still standing. Walking, with great vigor, despite multiple attacks by man and beast. I haven't gone down yet. She squared her shoulders with pride, only to wince at the burning sensation chasing trails from her neck downward.

Perhaps she *would* lie down for a while once she got back to town. Lacey slid a sideways glance toward her unwanted companion. *Not that he needs to know I took a rest. In fact, if I can somehow lose him, then sneak back into the house and change before anyone notices my state of disrepair. . .* She couldn't suppress a shudder at the thought of how she must appear.

One sleeve hung in tatters, no bonnet in sight, and the back of her skirts were most likely smeared with alternating streaks of grass green and muddy brown. Nature set rose pink amid those shades with admirable results, but Lacey doubted her rear wore the combination well. *So much for my Battling Braden outfit.*

Now her brother had this little incident, in addition to Twyler's kidnapping and her husband-hunting advertisement, to convince his doctor Lacey shouldn't be the executor of Lyman estates. He'd persuade the doctor to declare him more competent, citing his recovery compared to her repeated "poor judgment."

She halted so abruptly that Mr. Dunstan managed another few strides on sheer momentum before recognizing her pause and returning. Not that Lacey wanted him to return, much less wanted him to accompany her back to Hope Falls, but suddenly personal pique faded. She had an entirely more important reason not to want this man making his way to *her* town. If he regaled her brother—or the doctor—with tall tales of wandering women and deadly cougar attacks, Hope Falls wouldn't be her town anymore.

No matter Braden's experience in the collapsed mine turned him into a new, but definitely not better, man. No matter that if Braden had those rights, he'd legally force all the women from Hope Falls until he deemed it safe. No matter they were in the middle of saving the town with the new sawmill.

"Which was *my* idea!" Some of her indignation escaped in that small outburst, but it didn't make Lacey feel any better. Nor did it provide any way to rid her of Mr. Dunstan.

"What was?" He shrugged his shoulders, adjusting the damning evidence of her run-in with a wild predator for the second day in a row. Otherwise, Mr. Dunstan stood eerily still, gaze fixed on her shoulder as though trying to determine how much it pained her and whether or not she'd let him examine it.

Which of course she wouldn't. Nor did she want to answer

that question and explain to such an interfering male that she was trying to thwart yet another interfering and overbearing man. Mr. Dunstan would most likely take Braden's side, sight unseen, on the sheer principle that of course men knew better than women. *That sort of principle just proves men know* less*!*

"I have lots of ideas," she evaded. The less he knew, the more room Lacey had to design a plan. "And even more questions."

"Ask later." The dratted man started to turn away, as though he'd continue on to town without her, his dog following.

"Later will be too late!" It burst out before she could swallow the sound of her desperation. Lacey leveled her tone. "You won't get another chance once we get to town, Mr. Dunstan."

"For what?" He hadn't moved back toward her, just stopped leaving. It was as if her answer would determine his next move.

What does he want? Her mind raced. *Why did the stranger come to town? Men come for two things: a chance at marrying one of the women from the ad or a job with the sawmill. He's obviously not interested in marriage—the only smiles he flashes are at my expense— so work must be the lure to bring him here.*

She shoved aside a swirl of curiosity about this man who'd been unimpressed by her looks and unswayed by her stubbornness. "A chance for a position in Hope Falls. It's what you came for, and if you don't speak with me now, you won't have another opportunity to be hired on. That much I promise, Mr. Dunstan."

Just in case her winning combination of lure and threat didn't work, Lacey began formulating an alternate plan. *I'll have Granger send him from town posthaste before the damage can be done and dismiss his stories after he's gone.* Except the afternoon progressed past the point any trains would come through, saddling her with the problematic man until tomorrow.

Tomorrow is too late if he chooses to amuse the men with his version of today's events. Word of the cougar attack—and my impetuous wandering—will reach Braden in an instant. Which meant her only hope lay in Mr. Dunstan wanting a job.

He still didn't move as he uttered, "Already have one."

Drat. Lacey would have winced, but she knew he'd notice. Then she'd either have to fend him off from examining her shoulder—which stung quite strongly now, though she refused to dwell upon it—or leave the man thinking she'd been disappointed to hear he wouldn't be staying in town. *Which is ridiculous.*

"Already have one what?" The question may be inane, but it purchased invaluable time to think. *Only it's difficult to think with him looking down his nose like he disapproves of silly, time-consuming questions from women with injured shoulders.*

Even worse, he didn't bother answering. One quizzically raised brow absolutely didn't count as an acceptable response.

The churning sensation in her stomach warned the situation slipped further from her control. Lacey always felt sick to her stomach when it looked as though things wouldn't go her way—and she had a sneaking suspicion her stomach would never feel settled so long as Mr. Dunstan remained in the vicinity.

On the balance, I suppose I should feel rather glad he won't be staying long. Her attempt to look on the bright side met with failure as the churning intensified. *Such a pity I need to convince the man he wants to stay in town for a good while.* Somehow the acknowledgment Mr. Dunstan needed to stay—because once Lacey made a decision, she inevitably found a way to carry it through—calmed her innards. Except for one trifling detail.

How do I convince him to stay in Hope Falls when he has a position elsewhere? How does one bargain with empty hands?

The answer burst from her memory, setting Lacey's teeth on edge. *Ask for help.* She drew a deep breath to cleanse away the echo of Naomi's refrain whenever the two of them did charity work. *"Empty hands ask for help; full hearts fill the need."*

No! Every iota of pride shouted against the idea. *I did not sell my family home, buy Hope Falls, and keep control from Braden only to beg favors from a stranger!* She'd come too far, and still had too far to go, to give any power away. *Naomi, Cora, and even Evie are counting on me. I brought them here; I convinced them we could advertise for husbands and choose our own mates. If I ask Dunstan to stay, I'm giving him control—even a tiny measure is too much—over the lives we're building.*

If it came to that, Mr. Dunstan would simply have to leave. Unease curdled in her midsection at the realization, but she argued it away. *After all, even if I do ask for his help, how can I know whether this stranger has the heart to give it?*

He'd given her more than enough time to gather her thoughts. Judging by the expressions chasing across her fine features, those thoughts were as scattered as chicken seed in a barnyard—and maybe they should be left to lie where they fell.

Her stance progressed from skittish to still to tense, indicating she'd wrestled with the situation before settling on a decision he wouldn't like. People only set their jaws when prepared for a fight, and Miss Lyman's looked braced for war.

All because he didn't want to discuss his position in Hope Falls with her. *Just like a woman to want to discuss things that didn't need to be discussed. And at a bad time, too.*

"We don't need to waste any more time." Chase planned to plunk the stubborn woman in front of a doctor—let another man deal with the minx. He needed to track down Granger before his old friend left town—and Chase's growing questions—in the dust.

"You're absolutely right." Her too-agreeable response started a prickle of warning between his shoulder blades. Thus far this woman reveled in causing difficulties, and the glimmer of determination in her narrowed eyes tattled that, despite her agreement, Miss Lyman didn't intend to make things simple now.

Chase shifted the cougar across his back, letting the movement distract her while he gestured with his left hand and gave the command Decoy, at least, would follow. He held grave doubts about the lady showing such good sense. "Stay close."

"No need." Her immediate refusal didn't surprise him.

Nor did Decoy's prompt obedience. The wolfhound rose from his haunches, where he'd sat at Chase's side during the entire exchange, to take the single loping step, turn, and butt his massive head beneath Miss Lyman's injured arm. He leaned a bit of his considerable weight against her skirts until the woman compensated by resting her hand atop his head. Then he calmed, looked for Chase's nod of approval, and closed his eyes to enjoy the way Miss Lyman's fingers absentmindedly ran through his fur.

Wolfhounds were hunters, but most people didn't know they had a knack for herding as well. Decoy would help shepherd the woman safely back to town, and his massive height gave Miss Lyman a place to rest her arm so it didn't pull against her injured shoulder. Best of all, she wouldn't realize the dog was following Chase's orders—she'd just assume the mutt liked her.

With her arm seen to as best as he could arrange—suspicious woman still wouldn't let him close enough to tell whether the marks were skin scratches or deeper tears—Chase started walking. Turning allowed him to let loose a self-satisfied smile. *Miss Lyman might not want to stay close, but she'll follow my lead.*

"Wait just a moment, Mr. Dunstan." She elected to talk rather than walk, as no sounds of shoes on rocks or twigs accompanied her suddenly sweet voice. Her *overly* sweet voice.

The prickle between Chase's shoulder blades expanded, raising his hackles. All the way back to a time before Christ, the Greeks wrote legends to warn of women with too-sweet voices luring good men to their doom. An ounce of sense warned that sugary tones were a womanly wile to be avoided at all costs. Especially when wielded by so skillful a warrior as Lacey Lyman.

"Since you already have a position"—she continued speaking to his back, since Chase refused to answer her Siren's call and turn around—"there's no reason for you to visit Hope Falls."

"I disagree." His own words emerged as though fighting through a pit of gravel—rough and sharp. *Good. Let her see I'm more man than manners. No amount of chitchat will sway me.*

"Of course." She still sounded pleasant as she rattled on. "I rather thought you might prove difficult. It's my growing experience that most men do, you see. Prove difficult, I mean."

"*Men* prove difficult?" Disbelief blackened his echo. "I disagree again." Partly because women, with all their emotions and mandates, were always far more difficult to deal with than men. And partly, though he'd never admit it to the pink fluff ball, because he suspected she usually managed to manipulate his gender with great ease. Beautiful women had that advantage, and Miss Lyman was nothing if not beautiful. *All the better reason not to turn around. Just start on and keep going.*

"Disagreeable is merely a minor case of being difficult." Steel now underlay the sugary tones. "Which is precisely why we don't welcome men who don't wish to take part in building Hope Falls. They have no reason to follow the rules, you see, and that makes men with their own agendas far too troublesome to be allowed entry. Surely you can understand the logic?"

Something important lurked in that barrage of words, but it took Chase a moment to separate the bullet from the babble. When he did, he turned back to look at the small woman with big orders. "Are you, Miss Lyman"—he bit back his mirth—"by any chance telling me I'm not allowed to go back to Hope Falls?"

"As owner of the town, it's my responsibility to keep things orderly." A sanctimonious nod bobbed blond curls loose from a few of their pins. "So it would be best if you and your hound—who is agreeable enough *he* can stay, but I presume loyal to his master—to keep on toward that position you spoke of."

A simple admission that his position was in Hope Falls would clear this up, but first Chase wanted to punish her high-handedness. And see if he could uncover some information about just how she claimed ownership of her brother's town.

"I'll take up my position sooner than you imagine." Relief slumped her shoulders, almost making him feel guilty for continuing. "But I'll enjoy your town's hospitality tonight." Sure enough, that produced an immediate reaction—just not the anger or irritation he'd expected. That he could brush off.

Watching as her entire small frame tensed even more tightly, her eyes widening then closing in an expression of desperation. . . that, Chase couldn't brush off. *She's scared.*

EIGHT

Of what? What could scare a woman who doesn't mind walking through the woods alone, isn't fazed by a wolfhound the size of a small bear, and bounced back from a cougar attack?

The prickles of unease started up again. It looked more and more like Granger was right about these women needing protection. At the time, Chase assumed he meant that the women needed protection from the situation they put themselves in. Now it looked like maybe there was more to it. Something worse.

What was it Kane called Miss Lyman? *"A girl who didn't belong in the backwoods. . . All done up in bows and fluff, putting on airs as though she owned the place."* And for once the oily good-for-nothing got it right. Miss Lacey Lyman belonged in high society. And Chase himself dubbed her a pink piece of fluff.

Now that's a new one. Thinking like Kane. He shook his head to dismiss the uncomfortable idea and focus on a more important one. She called herself the owner of Hope Falls, but Kane said it was her brother, and that made more sense. Braden Lyman—if it's really Braden at all—would have already owned a good portion of the land after the mine collapsed. So why was this girl, who may or may not be Braden's sister, claiming to own his town?

And why doesn't she want me going near it?

He'll ruin everything! Lacey closed her eyes and tried to think.

Strangely enough, her thoughts marched in more orderly fashion when not distracted by the sight of the unkempt man wearing a cougar carcass strung over his shoulders. Then again, that wasn't strange at all. It would have been far stranger if she could think properly with such a spectacle loping in her line of vision, heading toward Hope Falls to destroy her dreams.

If it weren't for the cougar, it wouldn't be so bad. Some part of her mind couldn't help but notice that, beneath the dust and displeasing lack of manners, Mr. Dunstan cut a fine figure. The icy depths behind his brown eyes alone gave her shivers.

No. Not shivers. Shudders. Lacey resolved to look over a few editions of *Harper's Bazaar* to remind her what a fine male figure actually was. The very notion that such a wild and woolly mountain man held any points of attraction at all just went to show how far Lacey had come from civilization—and how much she'd compromised her standards of an acceptable suitor.

Although obviously Mr. Dunstan isn't a suitor. A deep sigh let loose some remorse. *Not because I want him as a suitor—although I suppose I might be offended by his lack of interest, if I had the time or inclination for trivial pettiness—but because if he were a suitor, he'd be easier to manage.*

Because, truly, she could think of no way to manage the man. She couldn't very well threaten to shoot him if he walked into town—he'd most likely call her bluff. So she'd have to shoot him. *And of course I wouldn't, as no matter how disagreeable the man is, he doesn't deserve to be shot—or let him go into town with something even more ridiculous to add to his story of how I traipsed out alone and got mauled by a cat.*

She opened her eyes to find him still staring at her in that disconcerting manner and realized she'd been lost in her wandering thoughts far too long. Even worse, they hadn't brought her to any plan. Which meant, short of threatening him with her pistol, Lacey didn't have any recourse but to accept the fact Mr. Chase Dunstan fully intended to stroll into town, cougar slung across those broad shoulders, and show the world she'd gotten herself into more trouble than she could handle. Again.

Except it wasn't true. She'd killed the cat and come this far, after all. Therefore the cougar could be used as proof that she, Lacey Lyman, could look after herself. A smile pulled at the corners of her mouth. *And Mr. Dunstan will attest to it.*

Why, if one looked properly, this could be a godsend!

"Very well, Mr. Dunstan. Wait just a moment." She darted back toward the scene of the incident, stooping to retrieve her shawl. Lacey knew she'd need it to conceal her injuries—those would only distract from her triumphant portrayal as huntress.

Oh, well now. A wave of wooziness, punctuated with streaks of pain shooting from her shoulder, halted her when she straightened up. *I'll just take it more slowly then. No rush.* After all, she'd endured a difficult day—after yesterday, she really had been due for a pleasant one, but no matter—without the benefit of breakfast. Come to think of it, she'd been too overset to choke down any supper the night before either.

"What are you doing?" Dunstan's thunderous voice rumbled directly behind her. He'd followed when she left then.

"Fetching my shawl." Slowly, hoping he took her snail's pace for nonchalance, she folded it about her shoulders.

"You'd be plenty warm if you'd walked. By now you'd be snug in town in front of a fireplace with a doctor taking a look at that shoulder." The flurry of words seemed to exhaust his speaking abilities as he subsided into a fierce glower.

"Yes, let's go back. I'm certain the men will enjoy hearing your tale about how I shot and killed a rampaging wildcat."

He blinked at her smile, but for once Lacey doubted her beauty caused a man's bemusement. Her hair, straggling loose of its pins since her bonnet was knocked askew, tickled her neck. Smudges of dirt did little to enhance the once-cheery stripes of her shawl. By now Lacey knew her nose, too long exposed to sun and wind, matched the pink of her walking dress. Not her most attractive moment, to be certain. No, Mr. Dunstan's momentary confusion was caused by her sudden shift toward pleasantry.

All told, this day did little to bolster her womanly pride. *Luckily, I had womanly pride to spare,* Lacey soothed herself. *What I need is to maintain my position as acting owner of Hope Falls. And for that, I need the respect of men—not admiration.*

"I don't spin stories." His dismissal stung almost as much as her shoulder. Dunstan turned away again. "Now stay close."

He shifted the great cat as he spoke, making an awkward gesture with his arm as though to shoo his dog away. The dog obeyed.

Having been shooed away from his master, Decoy butted against her skirts once again, shoving his massive head beneath her arm. A gentle giant, the dog's motions didn't jostle her arm much to set it atop his skull—a convenient resting place.

If, of course, Lacey wanted to rest her arm atop the dog's head and follow his master at a docile pace. Which she did not.

"I'll thank you to put down my cougar first." She quelled a spurt of triumph as the man froze midstep with an odd sound.

"Your cougar?" Strangled, that's how the words sounded. As though squeezing through the tight vocal chords of an angry man.

"Yes." She brushed around him to stand directly in his path.

"*My* cougar. It attacked me, then I shot and killed it." Lacey made a show of tucking her gun into the hidden pocket in her skirts then holding out her arms. "Give it to me."

∞

"What?" Chase wanted to give her a thorough shaking and a one-way ticket back to civilization, where men had patience to deal with beautiful wantwits like the woman standing in front of him.

Of course, the men in civilization hadn't stopped her from leaving their midst to wreak havoc amidst the mountains. For all Chase knew, they packed her trunks and toasted a job well done.

"Give me my cougar," she repeated, bobbing her arms as though to emphasize the empty space in which he should deposit the sixty-pound cat currently slung across his own shoulders. Imperious as she sounded, the movement made her wince. "Now."

"Enough foolishness." Chase stepped around her and headed toward town, determined not to stop this time. Whether or not she followed, he would be in Hope Falls for supper. And a talk with Granger. If necessary, he'd send someone after the minx.

So long as it was someone else, it'd work out just fine.

"It's not foolishness!" Her cry gained volume as she took to her heels and whipped around him, trying to stop him. Instead she wound up skittering beside him, unable to match the length of his stride. "It's my cougar, and I want it!"

Spoiled society darling. He curled his lip at the assessment. "Is that how you grew up?" Chase couldn't help but ask. "Getting anything you wanted just because you whined?"

Her outraged gasp let him get in a few more steps before she launched a renewed verbal assault. "You arrogant cretin!" Her spluttered insult made him grin—making her angrier.

Cretin? She's spitting mad and that's the best she has?

"I didn't get everything I wanted when I was growing up!"

383

Her swiftest denial revealed what hit closest to home. If he hadn't already known it, little Miss Lyman just gave away how much her family indulged her. Still, she kept right on chattering. "Although I admit I was somewhat privileged and enjoyed many fine things others did not, those were gifts freely given."

"Why?" Let her reveal more about herself as her words measured the steps back to town. Maybe she'd let something slip.

"Because my parents loved me!" Her exclamation slammed into him with the force of a fallen tree. "They wanted to protect me and encourage my many fine qualities, so I could make my way in the world. Didn't yours do the same for you, Mr. Dunstan?"

No. Dad drowned his worry over the farm in the nearest tankard of ale, and Ma was too busy keeping away from his fists. Neither one concerned themselves much with me or Laura. We looked after ourselves. Anything we got was earned twice over.

"So you give insults but no answers?" Her observation stung. He rarely insulted anyone, but she'd brought out the worst in him. "Well, I can assure you, Mr. Dunstan. I *never* whined."

No need to respond to that. He snorted and kept walking.

"For one thing, *I* never stole from anyone to make myself look better." She gave a pointed glance toward the cougar. "Nor do I try to take credit for another person's accomplishment."

"Woman, I'm not going to claim the kill." Goaded beyond forbearance, he growled at her. "Tell your people whatever you like, but I'm not going to let a slip of a woman with an injured shoulder carry a carcass down a mountainside. Understood?"

The blindingly beatific smile she bestowed upon him told Chase he'd said the wrong thing—exactly what she wanted.

"Understood."

❦

"You want to run that by me again?" Jake Granger crossed his arms and rested one shoulder against the far back corner of the house. The telltale swish of skirts on the move and random cries of disbelief formed a background to feminine activity. What activity that may be, Jake couldn't say, but muffled thumps told of items pulled from shelves and deposited elsewhere.

Yep. They're upset all right. He eyed his longtime associate. Eyed the fallen cougar Dunstan started skinning. It didn't take a genius to figure out what had the women in a tizzy. What he needed to know was how much of it was his friend's fault—and if it meant the women wouldn't let him install Dunstan as acting authority in Hope Falls while he was gone.

The women got touchy about letting anyone take charge. If they took exception to the tracker squatting behind their house, methodically skinning a cougar, they'd kick up a mighty fuss. Jake needed to be prepared to soothe their ruffled feathers. But how to go about it depended on what Dunstan could tell him.

And Dunstan wasn't in a talking mood.

"Ask Miss Lyman," came the taciturn response to Jake's question of how the man came to be skinning a cougar.

Dunstan skinning a large predator wasn't something Jake would normally need to question—the man tracked and hunted better than anyone he'd ever met. But behind the women's house? Dressing any large animal counted as a messy, smelly process.

"I'm asking you." He didn't bother stating the obvious; only a madman would saunter into a house full of upset women.

"Granger,"—his friend's frustration seeped through the two syllables—"your two eyes can tell you I'm dressing a cougar. The rest is Miss Lyman's business. Take it up with her."

Dunstan met Lacey Lyman? Figured. Take the woman who'd have the most volatile reaction with his friend, and have them meet with no one to intervene. *It's a wonder only the cougar got shot.* Jake blinked and switched tactics. "How did you meet Lacey Lyman? I thought you went for a thought-walk in the woods."

Dunstan snorted and wiped his bloody blade on a piece of hide he'd retrieved from his rucksack. "Thought-walk?"

"Enough." Jake levered himself away from the wall, circled the other man, and lowered to look him in the eye. "I meant to introduce you to the girls tonight, easy and proper, so they'd accept you as my temporary replacement. Instead I turn around to find the women all aflutter, you skinning a cougar, and somehow Miss Lyman had a part in it. Looks like a royal mess I'll have to clean up before I leave. So what happened?"

NINE

Nothing happened I couldn't handle. Don't fret so." Lacey ignored the churning in her stomach and forced a smile.

Not one of the other three women offered one in return. Naomi sucked shallow breaths through drawn lips, apparently fighting horror over the idea her charge might be injured, and reached for the witch hazel. Evie's wide-eyed gaze flitted from Lacey's mussed hair to her rumpled skirts and blood-stained shawl in obvious disbelief before the kettle called her away.

"Don't you say a word until I get back, Lacey!" she shrieked as she bustled into the kitchen and began a series of thuds to indicate something delicious would soon emerge.

Cora tilted her head in silent question. Her mismatched eyes—one hazel, one blue—held the same concern and curiosity evinced by her companions. The suspicion glittering in those depths belonged only to Cora. When Lacey couldn't meet her gaze, Cora slid toward the window. She shifted curtains, peering out as though trying to see around to the back of the house.

The back of the house—where Lacey asked Mr. Dunstan to

take the cougar, thinking it would be out of sight of the workmen. Out of sight, away from prying questions she wasn't yet prepared to answer. Cora, her best friend and brother's fiancée—never mind what Braden said—knew her a little too well.

Luckily, she didn't have time to dwell on that before her cousin ushered her over to the nearest wingback chair. Naomi had Lacey's feet plumped upon a slightly rickety ottoman before she could protest. But when her cousin reached for her shawl, Lacey clamped a hand upon it and shook her head. *They can't see my shoulder. I don't even know how bad it is, but things always look worst before they're cleaned up. I don't want them alarmed.*

"If you don't let me see to it, the stains will set and you'll lose that shawl." Naomi's reminder would have done the trick any other time, but today Lacey shook her head again.

"It's of no importance." Lacey's response did little to assure them, most likely because they knew how very important the proper accessories were. Particularly soft, charming shawls woven of expensive kerseymere and dyed in one's favorite color.

Her cousin's eyes narrowed in suspicion—obviously caught from Cora, who'd come back over from the window to oversee things. "The last time you wore one of these shawls, a chipped teacup allowed the merest dribble of liquid to fall upon its corner. Then it was important enough for you to leap from the settee and disappear to your room for a quarter of an hour."

"You make it sound as though I ran off sulking," Lacey denied. "It needed to be tended immediately and done properly!"

She remembered the incident and had indeed taken the blue and primrose paisley printed shawl to her room for immediate treatment. A bit of blotting and a judicious sprinkling of talc—swiftly brushed away once it served its purpose—and the shawl looked good as new. A quarter of an hour was a small price to pay to save something of great beauty and artistry, after all.

"Precisely." Naomi reached for the shawl Lacey kept clutched about her shoulders. "And today is no different."

"Oh, but it is!" she cried, twisting slightly to avoid her cousin's grasp. The movement sent hot streaks licking from her shoulder down her arm. "Today we have urgent things to discuss!"

"You waited, didn't you?" Evie rushed in, bearing an overloaded tray. All Evie's trays came in loaded beyond good judgment. Nevertheless, they always left without so much as a crumb remaining. Just the sight of that tray set Lacey's stomach to rumbling, and she didn't even know what sat beneath the covers. But her friend kept talking as she set it down. "I want to hear absolutely everything about Mr. Dunstan and the cougar!"

"The cougar?" Naomi's echo came in a faint whisper.

"The *what*!" Cora's wasn't so much a question as a shriek loud enough to conceal the sounds of two men entering the house.

"Cougar." Mr. Dunstan's grunt confirmed Evie's statement and robbed Lacey of the chance to soften her story before getting to the parts that would make Naomi worry too much. The man obviously held a gift for intruding at the worst times.

"Oh Lacey." Her older cousin looked horror-struck.

"Now, Naomi." Lacey leaned forward, but fell back as her shoulder protested. "I'm here safe and sound. Don't fuss so."

"Who's this?" Cora's gaze darted from Lacey to Dunstan. "Where did he come from, and what part did he play in Lacey returning to the house more disheveled than we've ever seen?"

Lacey raised her good arm to check her hair, found things even worse than Cora let on, and went back to clutching her shawl. *I knew I looked a fright, but she need not have said so.*

"I don't know." Jake held up a hand in defense against Evie's raised brows. "I asked, but Dunstan said to ask Lacey."

Abruptly all five pairs of eyes turned to her. Four held unanswered questions. One held an unspoken accusation.

Obviously Dunstan realized she'd tricked him. Now he resented his promise to let her say whatever she wished about the dead cougar. She met his bad humor with a smirk. *Too late.*

"Oh, nothing much. A mountain lion with exceptional taste coveted my hat. The thing let loose an unearthly shriek and launched from the trees, but I shot him before he did any real damage." She gave a nonchalant shrug, ignoring any pain. A grimace would entirely undo her carefree facade. "Thankfully, my ensemble bore the brunt of the encounter. Mr. Dunstan happened by in time to hear the cat then helped me to my feet."

"Oh Lacey!" Her friends' exclamations held a gratifying mix of concern and admiration. None of them seemed frantic.

"Just yesterday you could have been killed out there! What were you doing alone in the forest?" The hard edge beneath Granger's question did little to endear him to her.

Oh, I'm glad I withheld my vote, and you don't yet have permission to wed Evie. If you hadn't lied about who you were and why you came here, yesterday wouldn't have happened! The gall of the man to imply that situation had been in any way her fault—or that she needed to be kept on some sort of tether!

"Walking." The distinctively low timbre of Dunstan's response pulled her from the quagmire of her musings. "That's what she told me when I asked. Miss Lyman was walking."

"I don't happen to enjoy running," she agreed. *Why did he interfere? And why did he have to let everyone know he interrogated me about why I was alone?* It seemed as though whatever she least wished to draw attention to, the men seemed equally determined to focus upon. "And after yesterday, which could not have been forseen by anyone in this room save one Mr. Creed-now-Granger, I felt the need to clear my thoughts."

Granger snorted the way a horse did before it bucked. "It's not safe for you to roam the mountainside alone. Any of you."

The other women shared glances. Naomi's considering look meant she leaned toward agreeing with the man. Cora's frown gave away little. Evie—well, Evie went ahead and spoke her mind.

"Seems to me Lacey did just fine this afternoon dealing with the *natural* predators of the area—though I sincerely hope none of us has need to repeat her success. Even if you're concerned, Jake, you don't have the right to tell Lacey whether she can or can't go for a stroll on her own property."

"Do you plan to publicly contradict me after we're wed?" Granger's scowl found a new target in his bride-to-be.

"Don't make this a choice between being a woman and a wife—I can't be one without the other." Doubt shadowed Evie's features. "I speak my mind, same as always. But this isn't public, Jake. This is you trying to issue orders to all the women in town and me saying that's neither fair nor appropriate. If I waited to tell you you're wrong in private, then it means everyone here would think I agreed with you."

"You should." Dunstan broke in for the second time.

Cora's question sounded more curious than outraged. "Because they'll be married, or because you think he's right?"

"Because Granger *is* right." The man excelled in short statements dropped into the conversation like blunt objects.

"He's wrong, and so are you." Lacey decided a reminder was in order. For both men. "You're new here and not staying long, but let me assure you, Mr. Dunstan, that the women of the town own—and run—Hope Falls. We make every decision, from whom we choose to marry all the way down to who's allowed to stay."

Silence reigned after her pronouncement. Granger didn't naysay her. Even if he wanted to, he couldn't. But the new man didn't respond either. After a too-long pause, he took action.

His jaw slid to the side before he emitted a whistle so high-pitched as to be almost inaudible. Instantly the enormous, shaggy frame of Decoy bounded through the entry hall. Which meant he leapt through the front door and sailed through the second door into the foyer in a single jump. He came to halt at his master's side and sat down.

His master, the far less tractable creature, flashed his own smile at Lacey. A challenge lurked behind that grin, and they both knew it had more to do with their interaction than with the moose-sized mutt now imitating a throw rug.

"What"—Cora goggled at Decoy—"is that supposed to be?"

"I think it's a dog," Naomi ventured. Her stiff posture indicated precisely what she thought about the presence of such a large, unkempt animal within the house. "A rather large one."

"Why is it inside the house?" Evie paused in the act of setting her heavy tray atop a side table. Decoy raised his head and gave a hopeful sniff in her direction, but didn't move.

"Miss Lyman assured me *he* is welcome in Hope Falls." Dunstan's emphasis of the word *he* reminded Lacey not only that she had, indeed, said this. It also told her he held a grudge. The man clearly hadn't appreciated her directive to leave Hope Falls and not look back. Now he'd found his revenge.

"Whatever was said, I'm certain you misunderstood. The. . . dog. . ."—Naomi's pause signaled doubts as to the animal's parentage—"may be welcome in town. But it is beyond expectation that he be allowed into the buildings. Surely you understand."

"Where I go, Decoy follows. Miss Lyman lauded Decoy for his loyalty before issuing his invitation to town." Dunstan didn't glance Naomi's way as he reached down to rub the dog's ears. "I don't believe honor is limited to men, but I believe only people who stand by their own word can expect the same of others."

He's threatening me! Lacey sucked in a breath. The man had some nerve. Unfortunately, he had enough brains to make it a problem. Dunstan backed her into a corner, and she'd have to capitulate. For now. *It won't be for long. I'll make sure he heads out for his new position before Granger leaves.*

"Unlike so many male creatures"—Lacey's grin was more a baring of her teeth, and she knew Dunstan recognized it—"Decoy is both useful and well behaved. The dog is most welcome."

"Lacey Lyman, what happened to you?" The question burst out before Evie could stop it, judging by her slightly sheepish expression. "You wouldn't get so much as a perfumed lapdog back in Charleston. Didn't you cite shedding as the reason animals— aside from cats proven to be good mousers—belonged outside only?"

"Now, Evie," Cora cautioned her sister, still eying Mr. Dunstan. "Every rule needs the exception to prove it."

"This man," Granger added, "manages to be the exception more often than not. You might not be thrilled about his dog, ladies, but I'm sure you'll welcome the newest addition to Hope Falls."

"Of course we welcome Mr. Dunstan. He already plans to enjoy our hospitality tonight before going on to start a new position." Lacey tried to smooth the conversation back on track. It looked as though Granger knew the man, but that curious coincidence needn't be explored now. When Granger was gone, so would be any pretext for Difficult Dunstan to remain.

"So you decided to sign on?" Granger clapped his friend on the back. "Glad to hear it, Dunstan. Ladies, you won't regret it. This man's the best hunter in the Rockies. He'll keep Evie's stewpan full and all four of you safe until I return."

TEN

"W hat?" Miss Lyman rose from her chair as though getting to her feet for battle. "He plans to stay the night, but *only* tonight."

"In town. I don't much care for bunkhouses." Chase felt the slow grin spreading across his face. "Your kind welcome of Decoy is what finally convinced me to take Granger's offer."

She didn't like that one bit. Miss Lyman's nostrils flared as she struggled to maintain her composure. *She allowed Decoy in the house thinking to keep me quiet about how dangerous the cougar attack was. Now she'll be stuck with that decision.*

"What offer?" The woman Chase judged to be eldest—more for the wisdom she'd evinced rather than the distinctive streak of white tracking through her hair—spoke from beside Miss Lyman's now-empty seat. Her attempt to tug the younger girl back into her chair failed when Miss Lyman pulled away to remain standing.

Bad idea. An eggshell boasted more color than she did at the moment. The stubborn woman refused to see the doctor until she spoke with her "business partners," so that shoulder still pained her. Added to a heated conversation, it was enough to leave Miss Lyman unsteady on her feet. She needed to sit down.

Not that she'd appreciate the observation. Chase heard enough to figure this was one woman—Granger's little lady made another, with the other two still undecided—who absolutely refused to follow male orders. They didn't look past their own importance to see sense, and while Chase found this a common failing in men, women worsened it tenfold. Men could be left to their own devices, but often wound up hurting innocent women. Which was why females needed to be looked after. At least a little bit.

Chase reached over to rub Decoy's head and gave a soft snap behind the dog's ear. When he sat at attention, Chase rolled his shoulders toward Miss Lyman, moving his hand in the gesture for "push." These almost imperceptible signals stood him in good stead many times over the years, and now would be no different. Decoy stood, ambled over to Miss Lyman, and all but tromped atop her boots in an effort to get close. In the coup de grâce, he leaned, resting his weight against her knees.

Like so many before her, Miss Lyman couldn't withstand the weight of Decoy's show of affection. This time the target wasn't knocked over, but forced to abruptly sit down. At Chase's short nod of approval, Decoy's tongue lolled out in happy satisfaction. The dog shifted to rest his head atop his victim's lap—effectively holding her in place for a while.

"Decoy!" Miss Lyman spluttered, unable to gain her footing but surprisingly unwilling to shove the dog away. Ultimately she recognized the inevitable and patted the top of his head. "What poor manners you have. Someone should teach you better."

She left no doubt just whose manners she felt were lacking.

"Maybe he wanted you to sit down," the eldest—Chase began to wonder when he'd have names to put to the women—suggested.

"Someone did." The other one whose name he didn't know—the sister to Granger's woman—assessed him with one coolly logical blue eye and one amused hazel one. She looked just long enough to make him wonder whether she'd noted his signals to Decoy before turning her attention back to Miss Lyman. "You'd gone pale as a new moon, and—Lacey! What have you been hiding?"

Her gasp barely preceded a storm of movement as she descended upon her now-seated friend and whisked away the concealing shawl. Decoy's antics had nudged it askew, so it came away easily. "Why didn't you go directly to the doctor?"

Now here's a woman a man could get along with. Chase shifted to the side to get a better view of Miss Lyman's now-exposed shoulder. The converging womenfolk managed to oust Decoy, who came slinking back to Chase's side. He caught another glimpse of pink fabric gaping open in jagged rips along one side, revealing a creamy shoulder smeared with darkened blood. At this distance he couldn't tell how deep the scratches were, only that Miss Lyman lost what little color she had left when her oldest friend brandished a bottle of witch hazel.

"Make your choice, Lacey. Either we go upstairs and you submit to my ministrations,"—a threatening wave of the bottle punctuated this—"or you let me take you to the doctor."

"Later. First we need settle the issue of Mr. Dunstan." She bobbed her head to glower at him through the crowd of women.

"Thanks for the thought, but I'll see myself settled, miss." He really shouldn't enjoy poking fun at her this much.

"He'll get on just fine," Granger hastened to assure them.

"That's not what she meant." Granger's woman tossed the comment over her shoulder. "But we'll see to it after we see to Lacey's shoulder. It needs cleaning to prevent infection."

"All this over a scratch!" Miss Lyman twisted away, only to

gasp when the motion pulled her wound. She closed her eyes.

The one with the witch hazel admonished, "Stop trying to make it sound like nothing. That wasn't a little kitten, Lacey."

"It wasn't full grown." Her defiant mumble made Chase fight a chuckle. At least she'd listened to his assessment earlier. "I'll go see the doctor as soon as we finish this discussion."

∽

"You'll have to trust us to finish it without you." Cora knew when her best friend had decided to dig in her heels. Worse, Lacey's pretty shoes left wicked marks behind any scuffle.

For whatever reason, Lacey decided she didn't like the enigmatic man quietly watching them. If Cora hadn't seen otherwise, she would have assumed it was the mammoth beast accompanying the fellow that put Lacey on guard. Instead her fastidious friend favored the beast and overlooked—no, openly set herself against—this most interesting male. *But why?*

She'd certainly never find the answer so long as Lacey stayed in the room, shooting daggers at the poor fellow. Besides, her friend had committed several sins against the agreement the four of them made before journeying to Hope Falls, and now she needed to pay the price. Lacey Lyman might own the bulk of the town, but that didn't mean she escaped its rules.

"It's not that I don't trust you, Cora!" Lacey sounded aggrieved. "But if I'm not present, it won't be a united decision, as all of our judgments are supposed to be."

"We already disagreed once today," Evie answered for them all, reminding Lacey that she'd voted against allowing Jake to be her husband. "In any case, you've already failed to uphold some of the decisions we all agreed to. Now you need medical attention, and you can't expect Hope Falls to grind to a halt."

"That's. . .that's not fair, Evie! You know I don't expect

everything in town to stop just because I see the doctor."

"But you did break agreements—first by not telling any of us where you were going, then again by not seeing the doctor straightaway." A familiar, helpless anger threatened to cut off her words, so Cora spoke more quickly. "Everyone gave me her word not to take any risks if one of us was sick or injured."

The single assurance I asked before I came here, the simplest way to safeguard us all, and Lacey didn't honor it. From the stricken expression on her friend's face, Lacey's knack for reliving conversations caught her now. *I followed Braden here after my fiancé broke his promise to me, instead going into the mines on a regular basis until they caved in atop his stubborn skull. Now his sister does the same sort of thing. It must end before another of us winds up bedridden and bitter.*

"Oh Cora." Lacey could see the tears Cora swiftly blinked back—her dearest friend always caught her distress before anyone else. Even her sister, Evie, couldn't match Lacey's perception when it came to these things. The vivid, guilty flush came in startling contrast to her previous pallor. "You're right, of course. I didn't think—I'll go see the doctor straightaway."

"Jake will see you safely there." Evie volunteered her fiancé, throwing him the don't-even-think-about-arguing glare for good measure. That glare never failed, so far as Cora knew. "Since he doesn't want any of us going anywhere alone, and it looks as though you could use the support of a strong arm."

None of the women missed the questioning look Jacob Granger aimed at the new man—Mr. Dunstan. Nor was there any mistaking the nature of the question behind it. Something along the lines of, *If I escort your main detractor to the doc, will you resent being abandoned to the mercy of the remaining three women?*

If she didn't find it amusing, Cora would think it insulting. Instead, she waited for Dunstan's response. If he indicated he wanted Granger to remain, the man didn't possess enough strength to stay in Hope Falls—much less look after it. Lacey seemed dead set against the idea, so he'd need considerable backbone to convince the rest of them otherwise.

Ah. There. Dunstan didn't nod or shake his head in overt answer to Granger's oh-so-obvious query. Nevertheless, Cora caught the slight angling of his jaw toward the door, a silent bid for Granger to take Lacey and take his leave.

The man didn't say much. It would be interesting to see how he fared in the ensuing conversation. *It'll take more than tilting his head and silently issuing orders to his dog before we decide Hope Falls needs him. Although,* she acknowledged, *a woman could glean a lot from the way he made Decoy nudge Lacey back into her seat. If his words speak half so well as his actions, I'll welcome him here. He'll do Lacey some good.*

These women were up to no good, but they weren't boring. Chase denied Granger's nonverbal offer to remain in his company. No offense to Granger, but it didn't look as though his friend were faring all that well for himself. Falling in love with the spunky cook probably had something to do with the veteran sawmill manager's sudden demotion to taking orders from women.

Chase would fare better without Granger trying to smooth his way. Rough edges kept a man sharp, and Chase learned early on to keep his instincts well honed. If that shaved off a few of the finer points, so be it. Best that the women understood from the start he wouldn't pander to their finer sensibilities.

"Thank you, Mr. Granger." The cook's sister turned her two-toned gaze toward the door as he escorted Miss Lyman outside. Whatever lay behind her reminder of the promise to safeguard one's health, it had proven effective in guilting her friend to the doctor. Guilt was one of those weapons women wielded well, and a man could do nothing but stand in awe of the results.

"After you see Lacey settled, I'm certain Mr. Dunstan would be pleased by your return." The woman spoke pleasantly, but anyone could hear the statement wasn't a request. "After the intensity of yesterday's events, I'd rather not see Braden overset again. We won't be delaying his recovery any further."

Granger frowned. "He'll not thank me for the omission, Miss Thompson. You know good and well the only thing to upset your fiancé more than a cougar attacking his sister is for him to be the last to know about it. Besides, he should meet Dunstan."

So Granger knows Lyman—at least, the man claiming to be Braden Lyman. Chase digested this, batting around the idea of allowing the meeting. *I'd find out if it's really Braden. If it isn't, I'll know what direction to take my investigation of the mine collapse.* That would save a great deal of time and wondering over the bedridden patient, as well as whether the pink fluff ball of the forest was Miss Lyman or an impostor.

But if the true Braden Lyman lies in the bed, he'll recognize me, and I'll be wedged into a too-tight corner. Because Chase had no way of knowing whether a Braden injured in the mine collapse could know of the shifty practices employed by his partners during his absence. If Braden were involved in skulduggery, the man would either protest Chase's presence outright or throw up obstacles to impede his search.

Too risky. I need more information. There might be a way to discover the identity of the man in that room before I face him. The only real decision to make was how to avoid the meeting without raising any suspicions, but he had an idea.

"No sense in meeting the man when I might not be staying." Chase shrugged and shot his friend a grin. "Looks like I still have to run the proverbial gauntlet before I'm found worthy."

"Hardly anything so barbaric as a gauntlet." The woman with the single white streak in her hair protested the comparison.

"Though we'll be sure to keep your suggestion in mind," Miss Lyman promised as Granger half escorted, half tugged her out the door. She knew she'd been temporarily outmaneuvered, but that last comment told Chase she wasn't declaring surrender.

ELEVEN

One skirmish at a time. He might not understand why women ran the town, but Chase understood he wouldn't be able to unearth the answers to his questions unless they tolerated his presence. Even with Miss Lyman out of the room, the remaining three women left him and Decoy seriously outnumbered.

The fistfight by the train offered better odds. He shook off the unwelcome thought and offered the ladies a rusty smile. He didn't interact much with ladies. The mountains provided the food, shelter, and living he needed. Decoy made a better companion than most men, unquestionably a more honest one.

Usually he let prospective employers approach him. Most boss types didn't like having to persuade a man to take a job; it took away too much control. But it worked well for Chase. He had no trouble walking away, and he liked folks to know it.

Not this time. If he was going to find answers for Laura, he'd be the one doing the convincing in this interview. Problem was, he didn't have the first idea how to reason with one woman, much less a pack of them. Particularly when they already had their hackles raised by Granger throwing his weight around.

"Ladies, looks like Granger neglected introductions." His opening gambit should appeal to their sense of propriety and make them think he shared it. "Chase Dunstan, at your service."

"Our service?" Granger's woman raised her brows. "Seems to me you and my fiancé hatched your own plans, Mr. Dunstan."

True. He held his peace on that one. Not only had he fallen into Granger's scheme, he held a few of his own, and none of those focused on serving these women. On the contrary, if he discovered any involvement with the cave-in or fraudulent claims filed under the Lyman name, the women wouldn't fare well at all.

"You'll have to excuse Evie, Mr. Dunstan," apologized the one Chase pegged as eldest. "A challenging day, preceded by several others, has put her in a somewhat adversarial mood."

An understatement. "If I understand correctly, she's agreed to wed Granger." Chase offered a plausible explanation for the woman's lapse. "That would be enough to throw anyone off."

"Under normal circumstances, my sister would follow the introductions *before* interrogation model of conversation. I'm Miss Cora Thompson, sister to Evelyn Thompson." The slightly built woman with mismatched eyes launched into a recitation. "The lady apologizing for my sister is Miss Naomi Higgins, cousin to Lacey Lyman. You've already made her acquaintance. Her brother, whose company you're spared, is Braden Lyman—my fiancé, nominal owner of Hope Falls and general curmudgeon."

The whirlwind recitation calmed long enough for her to take a breath. Chase couldn't have gotten a better setup if he asked, but he aimed for a casual tone. "Nominal owner of Hope Falls?"

"Until he recovers from the mine collapse, Lacey's been designated de facto executor of the Lyman estates." The one he now knew as Miss Higgins offered the implausible, but succinct, explanation with a wry smile. "The cause for the curmudgeonly behavior he's exhibited since we arrived in Hope Falls."

Not trusting himself to comment, Chase merely nodded. The entire situation was farcical, but so far every factor remained cohesive. From the ad, to Miss Lyman's remarks, to Granger's behavior, and even Kane's dubious report, every avenue available supported the women's claim that they ran Hope Falls.

Whether or not they had any right to do so remained in grave doubt until he resolved the matter of their Braden Lyman's true identity. But if this was a fraud, the women managed an unrivaled consistency and attention to detail.

"Let me make sure I have this all straight." He met Miss Higgins's gaze before beginning the recitation that would cement everyone's role in his mind. "Your cousin, Lacey, owns Hope Falls while her brother, your fiancé"—he gestured to Miss Cora Thompson—"recovers from a mining accident. Meanwhile, the four of you decided to turn the town into a sawmill and posted a highly unusual ad to make your plans a reality?"

At this point, he put his copy of the advertisement atop a centrally located tea table. The familiar bold print marched between him and the women in a brash request for God-fearing, single men with logging experience and a desire for marriage.

Here things got interesting. An unwilling smile played about the corners of the elder Miss Thompson's mouth. Miss Higgins issued a small, very regretful-sounding sigh. The younger Miss Thompson, supposed fiancée to Braden Lyman, didn't bother looking at the scrap of paper in the first place.

"Is this what brought you to Hope Falls, Mr. Dunstan?" Surprise crept in around the edges of her question.

The laugh escaped him before he could consider whether or not it might be considered insulting. "I'm no logger, ladies. You can rest easy on that. My business is to know the lay of the land." Here he reached out to tap the ad. "When this crossed my path, it seemed pretty clear you ladies aimed to change things."

"So you didn't follow the ad, and you didn't come here to find Jake?" Granger's woman—this business of two Miss Thompsons was just plain irritating—lost the vestiges of her smile.

"I didn't know Granger followed the ad here at all."

"He didn't." Her hands clenched into telltale fists. "His brother's murderer answered the ad. Jake came for Twyler."

Chase might not spend much time around women, but even he could see this struck a nerve. Hard to imagine he'd missed Jake trapping the killer and revealing his real identity—and purpose— by a mere day. He looked at it as a lot of fun missed, but obviously it hit a woman hard to hear her beau hadn't come to Hope Falls looking for love. He'd been looking for justice.

Easy to forget how much you have in common with a friend when you don't see the man in three years.

"Regardless, if we take you on, you won't be working for Mr. Granger." Miss Higgins didn't prance delicately around the issue. "How do you feel about answering to four women as your employers, carrying out their plans rather than those of your friend? We need to know your loyalty to Mr. Granger won't prove problematic should we enter into a good-faith arrangement."

Time to tread carefully. What sorts of plans does she anticipate Granger protesting? If they weren't what they appeared, they'd hidden a good deal from his friend. *And done so well Granger proposed to one of them.* Chase would have to walk a fine line between placating them and following his own plans.

"I answer to myself and don't take sides in matters between couples. Four women running a town deserve the respect of anyone within it, and employers have a right to expect the same. Seems only a fool would think otherwise." The women murmured favorably to this, so Chase cashed in on their approval before he lost it. He'd exchange that newfound goodwill for grudging tolerance, so long as it leveled the field. "But it's only fair to tell you I've never been one to report for orders."

"There's a difference between receiving orders and taking direction from one's employer, Mr. Dunstan." Braden's supposed fiancée pokered up in an instant. "By the same token, we can't accept a renegade who does as he pleases. We have rules in Hope Falls for a reason, and you'll not be exempt from them."

"Hold on now. I'm not going to be flouting the authority I'm here to uphold." He needed to nip that idea in the bud. "If you want a guard dog you can bring to heel, I can train you one. But if you want me making sure no one gets insolent while Granger's gone, I'll use your guidelines and my own methods."

"And if we dislike your methods?" Miss Thompson pressed.

"Like I said"—Chase shrugged to keep the tone nonchalant—"your guidelines. I'm happy to help ladies in need and put a friend's mind at ease, but I offer assistance. Not obedience."

"Obedience is required of children and expected of wives, Mr. Dunstan." Miss Higgins smoothed her skirts. "Biblical, wifely submission is far too often confused with obedience, but that is a conversation for another time. The pertinent matter is that all of us understand—and have rejected—the idea of owing obedience to a person with whom we wish to form a partnership."

Chase blinked. *What revolutionary ideas for gently bred females.* He drew a breath. *Of course, they may not be gently bred at all. Only time, and thorough investigation, will tell.*

"Then we understand each other. I'll maintain order in Hope Falls. Aside from that, I'll tackle your wildlife problem."

"Should you officially be hired, yes. There are other things we may yet require." The younger Miss Thompson still seemed hesitant. "To what wildlife problem do you refer? Lacey already killed the cougar that attacked her this afternoon."

"You're situated right on the water source hereabouts, so

the animals come to you." He wrestled with whether or not to add anything then decided to go ahead. "Same as you've already experienced on account of that ad—anything precious draws bad with the good. The volume of what you're dealing with should be cut down to something more manageable, just as a precaution."

Granger's woman gave a slow nod. "I won't argue against good sense, and we can certainly use the fresh meat in the kitchen. But, if you'd indulge my curiosity, Mr. Dunstan, I would ask how you came to know my husband-to-be?"

"Worked with him about three years ago, when his family started the RookRidge Mill. Granger put out word he wanted the best guide in the area to help scout his location." Chase shrugged. He'd never been one for false modesty. "Folks recommended he track me down and hire me on if he could."

A ghost of her former smile shadowed its way back. "Good way to catch his attention. Jake does like a challenge."

"If it's worth the reward." Granger ducked back in through the entry hall, making his way toward his woman and placing a propriety arm around her shoulders. "I like having the best."

"Is Mr. Dunstan really the best hunter and trapper you know? The best man to help keep Hope Falls under control until you can get back?" It looked like Miss Thompson planned to defer to Granger's judgment—maybe the compliment softened her up.

Miss Lyman, Chase couldn't help but notice, didn't follow him. *She must still be with the doctor.* Irritation lanced through him. *I should've made her stop as soon as we hit town.*

"Quit scowling, Dunstan." His friend read him too easily. "Miss Lyman got held up by Mrs. Nash asking whether or not she had a current Sears ordering catalog. She'll be fine once she stops being annoyed that she missed the entire conversation."

"That means she'll be back any moment." Miss Higgins straightened in her seat, sounding vaguely apologetic. "We'd best take a vote before she returns and wants to rehash everything we've discussed and argues against Mr. Dunstan. Surely you must have noticed she's taken you into dislike."

Some things didn't need a response. This was one of them.

"All right. I agree we hire on Mr. Dunstan. Although you should have discussed it with us before offering him the position, I could use the fresh meat for my kitchen. So long as he's also willing to teach us something of the animals on our land so we know how to trap them even after he's gone, I can see nothing but benefits to having a hunter around." Miss Thompson's yea earned her a grin and squeeze from Granger.

"Few ask how to identify and manage the wildlife on their land," Chase approved. "I'm happy to share my knowledge."

"I'll support her decision if you agree to keep a special eye on Lacey." Miss Higgins's brows slanted upward in obvious concern. "Evie and Cora are both spoken for, and I'm of an age to be more cautious, but Lacey is more vulnerable."

It took a deep, fortifying breath before Chase agreed.

"Without Lacey here, the decision must be unanimous—we decided early on there must be at least a strength of three." The younger Miss Thompson fixed her magnetic gaze on him. "But before I go against the wishes of my best friend and hire you on, Mr. Dunstan, I need your word not to meet with my fiancé."

Suspicion seized Chase. *The easiest way to conceal an impostor is to keep him isolated.* For now he avoided meeting with Lyman purely because he didn't know what to expect. As soon as he could anticipate the results of coming face-to-face with the man injured in the mine collapse, Chase wouldn't hesitate to confront him. *Any impostor will be ousted, but the real Braden Lyman would have much to answer for as well.*

If he'd survived the mine collapse to buy up the town, did Braden know how his former company treated the widows of its former employees? If not, would he have to be forced to make amends? Only a frank discussion would clear the issue, and Chase fully intended to have that conversation. Something of his reluctance must have shown on his face as the woman continued.

"Any little thing perceived as a threat to myself or his sister makes him so frustrated there's no dealing with him. I need your word that you'll focus on doing your job so Braden can focus on getting better. Any concerns will be brought to us, or Mr. Granger, before proceeding." She raised her chin, obviously determined to get her way or see him on his. "Are we agreed?"

TWELVE

N o, Mr. Lawson. I did not agree to the arrangement." Lacey gritted her teeth at the reminder of what transpired the evening before when her friends betrayed her trust and their own good sense. By the time the doctor finished with her, the girls finished making the monumental mistake of hiring Mr. Dunstan.

Looking back, Lacey clearly saw she'd been maneuvered away so she couldn't make them see reason. While she smiled sweetly over gritted teeth, allowing the doctor to bathe her tender shoulder in a stinging solution and cluck at her over the dangers of cougars, her friends were smiling at Mr. Dunstan.

Of course, Mr. Lawson held no share of the blame for any of it. The well-meaning engineer looked faintly bemused by the news they'd taken a mountain man into their employ. Of course, Mr. Lawson looked faintly bemused since they day he arrived in Hope Falls with his heavily *enceinte*, newly widowed sister in tow, which made it difficult to discern his thoughts.

"I wondered. Mr. Dunstan hardly seems the sort you'd enjoy having underfoot." Mr. Lawson took off his spectacles and gave her a penetrating look, making Lacey wonder whether perhaps only the spectacles made him seem perpetually absentminded.

The highly polished thin bands of gold encircling those lenses caught the light oddly, and the perfectly round shape evoked a stunned owl rather than a practical engineer. *A more oval shape would do better justice to his features,* she decided. Certainly the man who'd gallantly taken up residence in what used to be the downstairs study deserved to look his best.

Even if he had brought Mrs. Nash to the wilds of the mountains mere weeks before her child was due, and as her brother was the only appropriate choice to move into the women's house. Again, it wasn't Mr. Lawson's fault that they needed a live-in defender against any dishonorable men who might descend upon the house. *That business with Mr. Kane and his rabble caused quite a fuss, though Mr. Creed, er, Granger prevented them from so much as stepping foot inside the house.*

"Miss Lyman?" Mr. Lawson sounded concerned, making her realize she'd slipped off into her own musings for far too long.

She fought to regain her place in the conversation. "I beg your pardon. Recent distractions don't excuse my woolgathering."

"I say they do." He spoke with surprising force. "While I'm not one to argue semantics, the past weeks have offered more difficulties, challenges, and ordeals than mere distractions."

Odd. He seems precisely the sort of man to argue semantics. Lacey shook the thought, and his vehemence, away. "While one undergoes an event, it is as you say. But once something becomes part of the past, thinking of it becomes a mere distraction."

Unless, of course, one can still do something to alter the course of decisions made the previous evening. In that case, the thinking isn't a distraction; it's practical planning.

"In any case, I didn't intend to dredge up unpleasant memories by inquiring after Mr. Dunstan." Mr. Lawson wiped the lens one last time and carefully placed the spectacles back atop his nose. Almost instantly he acquired the familiar, puzzled look Lacey associated with him. "I should have known it would bring to mind your unfortunate attack. I do apologize."

"My attack?" *Planning doesn't constitute an attack, precisely. And I won't feel guilty about waging a campaign to oust Mr. Dunstan.* She squared her shoulders, but found her motion hampered by the mounds of bandages padding her left side.

It must have been apparent, as Mr. Lawson gave her a look brimful of empathy. "You poor, brave woman. I referred to the cougar, but with Twyler's abduction and the previous attempt to storm the house, you've undergone three in the past week!"

"Oh, never say so!" Lacey cried out, wishing to stopper his observation before it could leak out and befoul the ears of others. Dunstan needn't hear it, and Braden absolutely couldn't.

"Your sweet, gentle nature dislikes to dwell upon it." He blinked, looking, if earnest, still more owlish than before. "And I'll not discomfit you further. Miss Lyman, I hope you know you can rest easy and come to me with any concerns. If this Mr. Dunstan upsets you at all, I'll set him straight."

Words eluded Lacey as she stared at this would-be knight in shining spectacles. *How very kind and thoughtful he is.* "I'm certain Mr. Dunstan intends no harm. But thank you, Mr. Lawson."

He puffed up in response. "Whether he intends harm matters little if he achieves it. Your fine nature and fragile feelings have withstood great assaults lately. I'll do whatever possible to ensure nothing more threatens or even offends you. With Mr. Granger planning this short trip, it falls to me to safeguard the few delicate blossoms of womanhood adorning Hope Falls."

If you dip our dainty feet in wax and arrange us carefully in a sealed bell jar, we'll keep perfectly for a twelve-month. Lacey smiled at the thought of Mr. Lawson attempting to preserve her, Naomi,

Cora, and Evie in the manner of true blossoms. Just as swiftly, the ridiculous idea robbed her of all amusement. *Why must men continue to look at us as such weak articles, easily susceptible to corruption and useful only for decoration?*

"I prefer to think we're more than adornments."

"You are." The very edges of his ears, sticking out from under sandy hair pushed down by the handles of his spectacles, became tinged with a brilliant pink. "Much more, Miss Lyman." Ears still pink, he slapped on his hat and hastily took his leave.

"What did you say to Mr. Lawson to turn his ears such a vibrant shade?" Cora came down the stairs looking blithely innocent—the same look she'd worn when she'd first kissed Braden and wanted to tell Lacey she'd fallen in love with her brother.

Cora looking innocent meant Cora felt guilty, though only her best friend—or perhaps Cora's sister, Evie—could discern the signs. But Evie wasn't here to notice her sister's distress, and last night's betrayal was too fresh for Lacey to overlook. *After all, they all banded together to make things difficult for me.*

⌒

Go easy, Cora reminded herself. *Lacey's been through a lot the past couple of days. She wasn't thinking when she wandered off alone, put herself in danger, and got herself in a mess big enough to set back Braden's recovery and lose her control of Hope Falls.* Trouble was, the more she tried to remind herself why she needed to be gentle and careful with her best friend, the more worried she became about both of the Lymans.

But the Lymans were a stubborn set, difficult to manage when together and impossible to look after when they veered apart. *Which is why I needed Mr. Dunstan to stay on. Lacey won't like it, but his promise to look after her comforts us.*

"I'm not sure." Her best friend glanced toward the door

where Mr. Lawson had taken his leave. "He gave quite a pretty speech about the trials I've endured recently and how my delicate nature should not be called upon to withstand such aggravation. Unfortunately, I couldn't reassure him, since Mr. Dunstan is sure to bring me still more unwanted aggravation and trials."

"No more aggravation than you'll bring him." Cora moved forward to pluck her cloak from the peg beside the door. "Hopefully, we can all refrain from progressing to trials."

Lacey gave a dismissive wave and fetched her own cloak. "Perhaps there will be no provocation. Mr. Lawson seemed particularly concerned over Mr. Dunstan's presence nearby."

In the midst of opening the door, Cora snapped it shut. "Lacey Lyman, tell me you did not go to Mr. Lawson and make Mr. Dunstan out to be some sort of threatening wild man!"

"How could you imagine I would do such a thing?" Lacey opened the door and held it wide. "There is something untamed about Mr. Dunstan, but I spoke no word against him. Mr. Lawson came to me with his intentions to better 'safeguard the few delicate blossoms of womanhood adorning Hope Falls.'"

"For pity's sake!" Cora slanted an incredulous glance at her friend and went through the door into the unusually cold summer morning. She and Lacey were far behind Evie and Naomi, naturally early risers who somehow threw off warm, snuggly covers in favor of predawn darkness and cold stoves.

After the recent turmoil, it seemed as though the other two women decided Lacey needed some extra rest. Either that or their courage balked at rousing an already irate Lacey first thing in the morning. Since they'd all agreed not to go anywhere alone or leave anyone behind, her sister generously allowed Cora to sleep the extra measure and remain Lacey's companion.

Had I been consulted, I might well have chosen not to sleep late. Cora waited for Lacey to follow her outside, letting the brisk mountain air invigorate her for what was sure to be a trying conversation. Most likely several trying conversations.

"For pity's sake?" Lacey echoed Cora's outburst. "You showed no pity or forethought when you hired the man."

"I didn't refer to Mr. Dunstan, who's shown impressive integrity and will prove an asset to Hope Falls." She ignored her friend's strangled sound of disbelief. "Mr. Lawson's poetic expression of his regard for you is a bit overblown."

"Less an expression of personal regard and more of a concern for the welfare of us women." Lacey paused as though thinking over Cora's interpretation. "Despite his ears."

"Don't discount them." She tried and failed to stifle a giggle. "Perhaps his ears are the windows to Mr. Lawson's soul."

"How ridiculous you are. Everyone knows it's the eyes." Giggles softened Lacey's denial. "Though I did decide earlier his spectacles make for a splendidly tragic disguise of them."

"Only you would use a phrase like 'splendidly tragic,'" Cora accused. "Though it works. No matter how Mr. Granger assures us of Lawson's ingenuity in the field of engineering, his round lenses make him look perpetually perplexed."

"I wonder whether the glass within the frames is equally ill suited," Lacey mused. "Certainly such a problem would cloud his vision and explain why he thinks us such delicate blossoms."

A sweeping gesture indicated Lacey's cheery primrose dress and matching bonnet. "Ah, but you look the part and always have. For as long as I've known you, you've divided your time equally between dressing yourself like a china doll and bemoaning the way every man you meet persists in treating you like one."

"My wardrobe proclaims me a lady." Lacey shot her an indignant glower, and Cora knew her friend added that assessment to a remembered list of recent betrayals of her trust. But her best friend chose not to comment on the notion that Cora should show more support and less sarcasm. Instead she busied herself. Anyone who didn't know her would think it mere preening, but Cora knew Lacey used the time to compose her reply. Lacey might tend to speak before she thought, but she'd confided long ago that tending her ensemble offered enough distraction to keep her thoughts from flying free willy-nilly.

So neither woman spoke as Lacey stopped walking to tuck a single errant hair back into her coiffure and fluff the lace frilling her high collar. Then she rested a hand over her injured shoulder to make a solemn declaration. "Yet one must look beyond mere design. Much of the merit of any piece lies in the strength of the fabric from which it is cut. I am made of stronger stuff than most assume; they should look more closely."

Cora reached out to grasp her friend's hand. "How you relate anything and everything to one's clothing constantly surprises me. You're absolutely right." She could agree with that much and knew Lacey was sore in need of hearing she was right about something. Anything. "But that's not the way things work. People—men in particular—will judge by sight and behave accordingly. Some will manipulate, others destroy, and a very few will attempt to protect and preserve your beauty."

Lacey's laugh startled her, but boded well. "Protect and preserve. . ." She snickered as they reached Evie's kitchen. "Do you know, as he spoke I fought the strangest image of Mr. Lawson dipping my feet in a vat of wax and trying to seal me within a bell jar? All the better to keep me safe, you know."

"Then to be placed atop a nice pedestal?" Cora caught the giggles, too. "Because you're a blossom adorning Hope Falls?"

"I told Mr. Lawson I'm more than an adornment. Despite what he and Mr. Dunstan seem to believe." Giggles gone, a dangerous glint entered Lacey's eyes. The same glint Cora remembered from when her best friend hatched a plot to humiliate a foolish man who'd dared insult Cora at a dinner party, succeeding so well Mr. Dinper left town to visit relatives the next day. The *same* glint Lacey sported when she suggested moving to Hope Falls. In short, the glint warning they were all in for a lot of trouble.

"What's more, I intend to prove it."

THIRTEEN

How do you want to do this?" Jake tracked Dunstan where his friend camped out in the woods near town. The previous evening the women ate apart from the men, leaving Jake to explain about the incident with Twyler while they avoided any potential fray.

Jake didn't blame them. Even with the worst of the rabble forced onto a train out of town, every man left in Hope Falls nursed bruised knuckles and egos from the town-wide brawl the day before. If they caught sight of a woman, each and every one would start yammering, either bragging how they bested another man or bawling for sympathy over an underserved assault.

And they'd be barking up the wrong tree. None of the Hope Falls women had any patience for fools who began brawls, exacerbated one, or opened his fat mouth in a way sure to make his defeated opponent demand a rematch. Only the men who sustained their injuries trying to end the brouhaha would be welcomed warmly by the women. But Clump, Lawson, and Riordan wouldn't ask for accolades, even when they could use the aid.

Not even Lawson, the mild-tempered engineer, nor Clump, nor the behemoth Scots-Irish bear of a logger escaped without a bruised rib or two. The only three men unmarked by the town-wide scuffle were a bedridden Braden Lyman, his doctor, and the squeamish Mr. Draxley. This last reportedly took to his heels at the first sign of trouble and hid out in the telegraph office.

These men, along with the women who brought out the worst in them, all became Dunstan's motley mess the moment Jake left. *No wonder he's glaring at me fit to tear a strip from my hide.*

Jake held up his hands to both apologize and ward off that glower. "Dumb question. You don't *want* to deal with any of this at all. But you're going to, so I'd like to know your plan."

Dunstan grunted, yanking tent pegs from the ground in orderly succession. "Seeing as how you didn't tell your men why I'm here, I'll have to start there. Clump and Riordan already spread the word about yesterday's clash by the train tracks, so the others will circle with caution before challenging me."

"I forgot your tendency to predict human behavior as though you were still dealing with wildlife." Jake chuckled. "Even worse, you're right. Clump and Riordan's praise establishes you as someone not to be messed with, but it's Williams's silence that cements your reputation. I can't tell you how impressed everyone is that you managed to shut his yap for a while."

"Didn't hit him hard enough to break his jaw. Why'd he stop wagging it?" Dunstan plunged the pegs in a small canvas sack, folded his one-man tent down, and nestled both in his pack.

"For all his faults, and he boasts a slew of those, Williams isn't a liar. If he can't find a way to make the truth look good, he keeps it to himself." Jake riffled Decoy's ears. "But him gritting his teeth tells the story even better than Clump's recitations. The few comments Riordan's thrown out about how you handle yourself finish off any lingering doubts."

"Then I won't expect much trouble from the men. Safe to say Williams will wait awhile before he risks being beaten again."

"Never thought the men would be the ones to give you trouble." Jake grinned, but wiped the smile from his face before Dunstan turned that glower on him again. "What about the women?"

"I'll deal with the women same as I've always dealt with women." Dunstan shouldered his pack and started walking. At the movement, Decoy abandoned Jake to follow. "Make sure they're safe and otherwise keep as far out of their way as possible."

"Keep away from him, Lace." Evie bustled back from the storeroom with an apron full of strawberries. "He'll be busy keeping an eye on the men or out hunting in the forest, so your paths won't cross much unless you're determined to make trouble."

"*Me* make trouble?" Lacey saw red, and it wasn't just the strawberries tumbling onto one of the kitchen tables. *How typical that I'd be blamed for causing difficulties when they're thrust upon me!* "You know our paths already crossed once."

Fuming, she wrapped a towel around her right hand, opened the oven door, and slid forward one of the piping-hot bread pans. The enveloping, yeasty scent of fresh-baked bread beckoned her with a temporary distraction. Reaching forward, she gently flicked the top with her left middle finger, testing for the slightly hollow thump that told of finished loaves. Satisfaction blossomed, lending her a measure of composure and allowing her to form a logical response rather than an all-out attack.

"In any case, *I'm* not the one who hired on new help when it wasn't my place. Granger overstepped his bounds, Dunstan followed, and you did the same by supporting your fiancé's schemes rather than your business partner's wishes."

"Lacey! Your mother taught you better than to lash out in

anger, much less deliver such low blows." Naomi's disappointment twinged her conscience. "Cora and I agreed to hire on Dunstan."

"*I* didn't imply anyone would cause trouble." Lacey sniffed as she carried her loaves to the large worktable set along the wall next to the outside door. Here, where she baked bread at least twice a week, Lacey claimed a corner of Evie's kitchen. "If you see facts as insults, I suggest you look to your own consciences. For my part, I feel I'm the one struck down. When I left the room and could no longer speak for myself, rather than looking out for my interests—*our* interests—and giving me a voice in the proceedings, you deliberately undermined me."

You wanted me out of the way, so you could do what you wanted. Same as Papa and Braden. She drew a shaky breath, focusing intently on her small corner of the kitchen and excluding the rest of the room the same way they'd excluded her the night before. Let them talk among themselves now; she wasn't ready to listen to any excuses. Not when Evie started out by throwing down the gauntlet and accusing Lacey of stirring up trouble. The other women could look to themselves.

Lacey would look to her loaves. Only here, a safe distance away from the flurry of activity and pots bubbling atop the stove, did she turn loaves from their pans, tap their bottoms, and pronounce another batch ready to cool atop the windowsill. For a loaf to slice well, without the bread squishing down into sad smooshes, it needed cooling for two or three hours.

Bread is easy that way, Lacey acknowledged. *My temper heats, and I haven't finished cooling down by the next day!* But tempers weren't loaves of bread popped in the oven and baked. *It takes repeated tries before someone manages to fire my temper.*

She placed the two loaves on the sill, took a crock of butter, and regreased the pans before setting the next two loaves— already neatly rolled with ends folded beneath—inside. With their seam-sides down and tops bathed in a generous brushing of melted butter, this next batch would take about three quarters of an hour to complete a second rising.

Lacey peeked beneath the towels covering two waiting pans, judged these loaves roughly doubled in size, and lightly pressed the tip of her finger near the edge to see if an indentation remained. It did. Those towels went to cover the latest batch. These were off to the oven, and Lacey returned to her station before any of the other women caught her in their conversation.

Mr. Dunstan managed to ignite my temper in such a short time, she marveled. *Did he intend to, or did he blunder into it?* Maybe he got on her bad side purely by behaving like every other man who'd told her she couldn't possibly take care of herself.

Huffing at the insulting notion, she pulled her largest bowl across the table, whisked away its cover, and pressed in two fingers to the depth of her first joint. The dough did not spring back, having risen sufficiently for the next phase. This, though Lacey was loath to admit it, was her favorite part of baking bread. In fact, watching cook punch the dough down, turn it out upon a floured tabletop, and begin kneading the mixture so fascinated her as a child she begged to learn.

There'd been no time before, nor since, when she'd seen a woman permitted to punch anything, much less push and pull and test her strength against it. The power of imposing one's will on something else and forcing it into the form of one's choosing, Lacey knew well, was a privilege enjoyed only by men.

Entirely unfair! She cried against this injustice as she rolled up her sleeve and punched the dough, feeling it billow about her fist before deflating far lower. *I'm capable!* She turned the dough atop her floured table, sprinkled it with still more flour, and folded the whole of it toward herself.

There's no reason I can't learn new things. She pushed down with the heels of her hands, feeling the cool mass obey her motions as she folded it again. *Find new interests.* Lacey spun the lump a quarter turn before pulling it back. *And master them!*

She rhythmically worked the mound for a couple of moments before reaching for her knife. A swift, decisive stroke severed it in two. A few swift motions, and two smooth balls sat beneath their towel for a brief rest. Next she'd use a pin to flatten each ball then tightly roll them into the desired loaves.

"Are you even listening?" A voice almost directly beside her ear made Lacey jump. Naomi reared back, as startled as she. But her cousin recovered more quickly, disapproval tightening her features. "That's what I thought. You spoke your piece and didn't bother listening to anyone else's. For shame, Lacey."

"I don't have time for remonstrances." Lacey knew from practice she'd have just enough time to mix another batch of dough, perform the initial long kneading, and leave it for first rising before the pans in the oven were ready to come out. So she truly didn't have time to listen to Naomi's chiding, even if she'd tucked some spare patience away to call forth. Nor did she feel inclined to deal with the hot slide of shame loosening the anger at the back of her throat. *If I start talking, I don't know what I'll say. Apologizing isn't right because I won't entirely mean it, and I'm sure I'll just make things worse by trying to make it all right again. Why can't they let me be?*

"That's a nice trick." Cora slid into her path, forcing Lacey to step around her. "But we're not going to let you get away with it. You can't just opt out of a conversation."

"Why not?" She dodged Cora and kept on moving.

The first time she'd tried to make a dozen loaves in one morning, she'd run about breathless for hours, always a step behind. The next time she treated the entire production as a painstaking ballet of baking, allowing significant lengths of time between the starts and stops of each stage so she wouldn't miss a step. It worked, but it took an entire day.

So the third time, Lacey choreographed more carefully. If she staggered loaves in different stages of preparation throughout the kitchen, moving fluidly from one space to the next to keep each post ready, she finished the fastest. Today the practice would serve her well. Nothing and no one would keep her in that kitchen an instant longer than necessary!

No matter the other three joint owners of Hope Falls disagreed with her plans and tried to block her way. If cooking demanded their hands, they lobbed comments she couldn't ignore.

"Why not?" Evie put down her wooden spoon, an almost unprecedented occurrence when she stood beside the stove. "If common manners aren't enough reason, then because a woman who won't listen to others is a woman who no one will listen to!"

Lacey gave a humorless chuckle. "Now there's a moot point since we've already established that no one listens to me."

"Save the self-pity," Cora snapped. "Braden shows no sign of letting loose his hold on that monopoly, and I'd hate to think such self-indulgence represents a Lyman family trait."

"Just as I'd hate to think—" Lacey stopped short of firing back an unforgivable insult. Never mind her best friend accused her of being self-pitying and lumped her in with her sulking brother. Braden's pity party cast a cloud over all Hope Falls, raining with particular force on his former fiancée.

When Lacey herself wasn't bearing the brunt of her brother's poor temper, Cora stepped in to shoulder the burden. And since Braden tried to cast her aside, Cora didn't have to anymore. *What I bear out of obligation, she bears in love.*

Shame began its familiar hot prickle at the thought.

Cora's jaw jutted forward, eyes filled with suspicion. "You'd hate to think what, Lacey? Come on. We're *listening*." It was the emphasis on the last word to tip Lacey back to anger.

"Now you choose to listen?" She reached behind her waist and tugged at her apron strings. "Then hear this much, ladies. If you can choose to listen only when you want to, but deny me the same right"—the knot gave way and she whipped the apron off triumphantly, balling it up and tossing it atop her table—"then I can at least choose whether or not I wish to speak."

With that she left the ladies and the loaves to their own devices. Because, while Lacey didn't have anything to say to the women, she found she had a lot to say to someone else.

All she had to do now was find him.

And when she did, she'd make good and sure he listened.

Chase could hear her coming from a mile away—and so could any animal he might have hoped to bring to the dinner table. Not that it mattered. Once he identified one of the women blundering around the mountainside without the benefit of an escort—or basic common sense—he knew he'd be cutting his hunting short.

There go my plans to reassure the women they made the right decision. Without any game to prove his skill, Chase still relied on Granger's word to prove his worth. It didn't sit well.

Grudgingly, he engaged the safety on his shotgun and slid it through the leather straps across his back. He palmed his pistol and retraced a few steps before veering off to look over the edge of a bluff. A wise man never traveled through the wilderness unaware of his surroundings. Or unarmed against them.

Decoy trotted after, poking his nose over the rock facing and peering toward their stalker with misplaced enthusiasm. His panting shifted into the louder, more huffing version Chase knew signaled a particularly happy dog. Eyes widened, tongue lolling out, and tail wagging, Decoy clearly approved of the view below.

Most men would, Chase admitted as he watched the trim figure weaving through the trees. Clad in green, she blended more easily with her surroundings than she'd managed yesterday, but Lacey Lyman's ruffled skirts and overblown headgear still stuck out like a peacock among pigeons.

FOURTEEN

Pretty. . .but loud.

The excess fabric of her skirts rustled with every move she made, the heels—and Chase had no doubt they were higher than strictly necessary—of her boots rang at random intervals whenever her steps struck stone. But more than that. . .the daft woman was talking to herself. Chase couldn't quite make it out, but furious mutterings made their way up the mountainside.

He strained to hear, but the wind carried the words away, and eventually he gave it up as a bad job. Now the question was whether to start down, head her off, and traipse her back to town. . .or wait for her to find him. The obvious answer would be the former, as he might be able to return to his plans for the day afterward. But surprising her in the woods yesterday earned him nothing but enmity. Chase got the impression Miss Lyman had too much experience having her every move tracked by men.

The more intriguing option was to let her turn the tables and see how long it would take the intrepid Miss Lyman to find him. Because, oddly enough, in spite of his typical caution not to alter the landscape as he passed through, Miss Lyman seemed eerily good at tracing his path. Was it luck? Instinct?

Certainly it was worth waiting awhile to find out. Besides, the hike could siphon some of the wind from her sails before she caught hold of him. Chase may not know what the mutters said, but a man would have to be a fool not to know they meant the same thing as a snake's rattle. *Beware and back away.*

In this case, he'd settle for not getting close. Mind made up, Chase eased back and brushed aside some rocks and rubble before settling in. Dipping into his side pack, he drew out one of the biscuits Granger brought him that morning. Chase had already eaten a hearty helping of his own flapjacks by then, but biscuits traveled well, so he'd brought them along for lunch.

Still. . .Chase rarely ate food he hadn't cooked himself or at least seen prepared. He'd seen too many men retch their guts out after a poorly made meal not to take precautions. He split the bread open, noting its light, flaky texture with approval before lifting it to his nose and giving a cautious sniff.

Butter. He'd bet these smelled even better fresh from an oven. Chase peeled off a layer and looked at Decoy, who sat stiffly at attention, eyes fixed on the biscuit. The drool pooling between his paws showed his assessment of the biscuit. Chase tossed the piece, watching the dog catch and swallow the treat by thrusting his massive head forward. He didn't move another muscle. Or chew. But then, Decoy never chewed. He just gulped down whatever food came his way before turning plaintive brown eyes toward Chase as though to ask, "Where did it go?"

He grinned, shook his head, and sank his teeth into the biscuit. *Good as it looks.* Chase chewed a moment then conceded. "Better." He dug around in his pack, unearthed some cheese, and made a nice snack for himself as the muttering drew nearer. By the time he finished, he could make out the words.

"So very bright out here today. Should've brought my parasol." A scuffle that sounded as though she almost lost her footing. "Really must order more sensible footwear. Naomi was right, though only about the boots. Not about *that man*."

Chase held little doubt who "that man" might be, and his suspicions were confirmed when her short silence ended.

"And where *is* he?" Frustration made her huffy—or was it the climb? "Up ahead is all rock, and there'll be no boot prints."

Ah, she's worried. Chase put a hand on the ground, preparing to lever himself up. Now he knew how she followed him. There was no reason to wait longer and cause her distress. Who knew? Perhaps she'd even be glad to see him at this point.

"Wouldn't that be just like a man?" Her gripe froze him.

He'd gathered she didn't hold a high opinion of his gender, but that made no sense. *Wouldn't* what *be just like a man?*

"Lead you down the pretty path, show you just enough to get you interested and make you think you're really getting somewhere, and then cut you off with nothing to go on and no way to follow." Her footsteps halted on the other side of a large boulder, her voice taking on a deeper note as though mimicking someone from her past. "Oh no, Lacey, it's too dangerous. Run along back now, Lacey, you don't want to think for yourself or do anything interesting or try something new, do you?"

"Is that what you're doing?" Chase cut her off before she gained more steam with this speech. Interesting as it was, he knew she'd never forgive him if he heard more of the depth of what angered her about men. And since she stood a few steps away, he couldn't pretend not to hear, nor find a way to avoid her. The best he could do was break in before it got worse.

Though, from the expression on her face when she saw him turn the corner, he should have done a better job of it.

Things couldn't be worse! Lacey bit back a shriek of rage as Chase Dunstan loped around the boulder, clearly having heard her giving vent to her ire over being treated like a china doll.

There went all her plans to track him down unawares and explain to him, calmly and in a manner so utterly authoritative and superior he had no alternative but to accept her direction, the things she expected of him. Instead of looking impressed by his coolly collected employer, Chase Dunstan looked as though he was barely managing not to laugh at her foolish tirade.

Why must my mouth always ruin my best-laid plans? Lacey struggled not to turn around and march back down the mountainside, away from the site of her humiliation. Lymans didn't back down after all. *Oh yes. Because whenever I'm around people, I keep having to bite my tongue. So the moment I feel free to unleash my thoughts, they fly about and batter everything and everyone nearby.*

That's why I wait until I'm alone. But I'm never allowed to be alone anymore! Frustration mounting, Lacey eyed Chase Dunstan with growing dislike. *Not even when I think I'm by myself can I be safe with this man on the loose. Which is part of the reason I didn't want him here!*

And, most likely, part of the reason everyone else does. The sudden realization drained her. The anger, seething and swelling beneath her every step, carried her along this far. But sorrow made for a far weightier companion. Lacey acknowledged her friends might have a point in wanting to keep her more tempestuous side tucked away. It was safer for them. Maybe safer for her, too. *But it's boring. And constraining. How can Hope Falls become everything I came here to escape?*

She raised a hand to rub the bridge of her nose, hoping to ward off an impending headache. The resulting sting in her shoulder made her gasp, realizing she'd been far more active than the doctor authorized after her cougar run-in yesterday. Worse, her gasp made Dunstan's eyes narrow, bringing her an awareness that she hadn't responded to his question.

"What?" Lacey tried to sound unconcerned, but rather thought she might have sounded confused because Dunstan's expression softened slightly. There, in the way the lines of his jaw became less tense and his brows rose a fraction.

"I asked if that was what you were doing," he repeated, reaching for her elbow and leading her to sit upon the large boulder's smaller cousin nearby. "Trying something new, I mean. Most don't find solitary walks overly interesting, and it's obvious the women of Hope Falls already think for themselves."

"Oh?" Suspicion tinged the question, but his answering smile hid no barb. "Well. . ." She relaxed a bit but played for time as she answered. "If you were never allowed to do it, you might not think so little of going for a walk alone, you know."

"You mistake me." He answered after a lengthy pause, during which he seemed to be considering her limitations. He sank down, resting lightly upon his heels and drawing her arm forward to rest upon her knees, where it didn't pull against her bandages. "I spend a great deal of time walking alone. I enjoy it."

"Though I doubt I'll ever be allowed enough experience to form an opinion, I might share your affinity for the pastime. I envy you the freedom to explore it, Mr. Dunstan." She cocked her head to the side, stretching her neck. Honesty compelled her to add, "Though I doubt walking alone is what you meant earlier."

Again, the fleeting hint of a smile, gone before she could be sure. "I hoped talking to yourself ranked as a new activity."

"I'm afraid not," she confessed. "I find I'm good company for those times when I've something controversial or unpleasant to say and don't wish to burden others with the conversation. Or, conversely, they make it clear they don't wish to hear it."

"Airing your grievances, so to speak." He pushed back to his feet and offered her his hand, his expression inscrutable.

"Precisely." She took it, startled by the warmth of his strong grasp as he led her over the rocks and back to the earthen portion of the path she'd traversed on her way to him.

"If you've a grievance against me"—his grip tightened when she began to draw her hand back—"I would listen, Miss Lyman."

She'd tracked him down to give him a piece of her mind and demand his cooperation, but now that he asked for her thoughts, she found herself reluctant to share them. After all. . .

"It is not your fault you can enjoy more freedom in my town than I myself will be afforded. But it chafes, Mr. Dunstan. It rankles that you were hired—twice—without my approval and, indeed, once despite my express displeasure at the prospect."

She met his gaze unflinchingly, waiting for some response. He offered none, but did not break the eye contact. Nor did he release her hand from the reassuring warmth of his own. *We are stuck together, he and I,* she mused. *So long as he remains, and that is something I accept I have no say in, we must be allies. I don't know how much to trust him, but I know enough to be honest with the basics he must have surmised by now.*

So she plunged forward. "I do not know you, but you have seen me at my lowest point and that concerned me. My workers must not perceive me—nor any of us women—as weak. And recent events have greatly undermined us in that regard."

Here she stopped. She saw no need to share more about those recent events than he might already know. No doubt Granger shared whatever particulars he felt pertinent—and no doubt even that was more detail than Lacey cared for Mr. Dunstan to be told. For instance, he might already know about Twyler's abduction and her subsequent rescue, which was not something she wanted running through his mind whenever he looked at her.

It simply didn't put one in a flattering light. *Not,* she caught herself, *that I want Mr. Dunstan to flatter me.* But almost being crammed into the base of a dead tree hardly ranked as an identifier to inspire respect or establish her authority.

"I see." He gave a single nod and released her hand.

What he saw remained a mystery, but he looked far more businesslike. Never mind the sudden chill now that his hand didn't hold hers and he'd turned the intensity of his gaze away.

She pressed onward. "We're trying to accomplish something entirely new here. Not just the sawmill—there are other sawmills. But women as partners in business and managers of property, capable of more than adorning a man's life and home."

A long moment of silence stretched between them, pulling her nerves before he finally gave voice to his response.

"Capable is not the same thing as able. In business, there are allowances which must be made, and many will not be willing to concede them to women." He reached down to rub Decoy's ears. "It is both a surprise and mystery how women run a town at all."

"And no doubt it will be an even greater surprise and mystery to many when we turn it into the most successful sawmill in these parts, Mr. Dunstan." She squared her shoulders. "But make no mistake. We will succeed. Come what may, whatever price we must pay, Hope Falls will be the proof of what women can do."

He looked up so fast it seemed his neck might crack, and his eyes narrowed to dangerous slits. "With the help of men."

"Why not?" She barely kept herself from taking a step back, so intense had he become. "Women helped men for centuries."

"Be careful what deals you strike and where you find yourself compromising, Miss Lyman. Some decisions cost dear."

"I know, Mr. Dunstan." She drew a deep breath, pushing back thoughts of Braden's anger, of the unsuitable suitors swarming Hope Falls intending to court herself and Naomi, of the many mishaps they'd already encountered. *Surely things will improve?*

She steeled herself to finish. "No cost can be too great to gain one's dream and further one's freedom."

∞

"Don't even think about moving," Braden ordered. "It's my turn."

Cora blinked at him. "No, you just moved your knight, and I've still not gone. It simply takes me longer to strategize."

"Strategize?" He gave a snort loud enough to make an ox proud. "Is that what they call cheating these days? If so, I don't know why I'm surprised to find you excel at it."

Refusing to rise to his bait, Cora moved her rook and took one of his pawns, carefully lining it with two others along the left side of the board as her fiancé continued his diatribe.

"Though you sell yourself short. You, along with our sisters, are swift enough in bilking a man out of his property." To punctuate the statement he reached over and flicked the pawn, sending it tipping into its fellows and toppling all three.

"That was unnecessary, Braden Lyman." Cora righted the pawns and corrected her errant betrothed in one gesture. "Besides, I believe you'll find 'your property' "—she curled her fingers in the air as she spoke the words—"better cared for and much improved for our brief tenure as landholders."

"Tenure?" Another snort made Cora idly upgrade Braden to an ox with a cold. "Usurpation, you mean. And you sound like my mother or a bitter schoolmarm, calling me 'Braden Lyman.' "

"Your mother would be appalled by your lack of manners, and we'd both agree you could use some schooling to regain them." Her anger, always at a slow simmer these days, became hot enough to burn the back of her throat with words best left unspoken.

"Careful, Cora," he cautioned as he snagged one of her bishops. "Schoolmarms are usually bitter old maids. It's starting to look as though you fit the bill nicely enough."

That stung. Tears needled behind her nose, pricked beneath her lids, but she blinked them back and sought refuge in prayer.

Every time I see him, he reminds me he's tried to throw me over. Lord, how am I to continue to love him when he's not the Braden I knew? How do I go on when the promise I gave is now at odds with the hurt of my heart? I wait on You to bring about a change in him and to give me peace until that day.

Seeking the Lord gave her the strength to respond.

"We both know better. I won't release you from our engagement, Braden, so you might as well stop acting like a petulant child picking a fight." She shifted her queen. "Check."

"I'm not picking a fight." He stared at the board, avoiding her gaze. "I'm trying to avoid a lifelong battle." He moved his piece away from her queen, much as he had been distancing himself from her since the moment she arrived in Hope Falls.

"Men live with the decisions they've made." She waited until he had no choice but to look at her. "I'm one of the best decisions you can lay claim to, and I'm not going away." Cora sprang her trap, moving her own rook. "Checkmate."

FIFTEEN

Y ou should stop playing with her, Lyman," Jake observed. He strode into the room after Cora flounced out, having waited while the two exchanged chess pieces and verbal spars with increasing ferocity. "We all know she's going to win."

"I'm usually better," his friend grumped as he started setting the board. "Why don't you get over here and try me?"

"Because I wasn't talking about chess." Jake dropped into the chair Cora so recently left, but only after he turned it around so he could straddle it and rest his arms along the back.

Braden froze in the act of setting down a pawn then slowly pulled his hand back. "Don't know what you mean, Granger."

"I'd tell you not to act dumb with me, but given the way you've been treating your fiancée, I can't be sure it's an act." Jake watched irritation flash across the other man's face, swiftly replaced by consternation before his shoulders slumped.

"Whatever it is, Granger, it's not working." Lyman gave a gusty-guts sigh. "Not even a little bit. Doesn't matter how mean I manage to be to her, how well I ignore the way she looks and how good she smells, how often I tell her I don't want to marry her, Cora won't have any of it. Says I'm stuck."

If the man before him didn't look so miserable, Jake would've gone ahead and laughed. As it was, he fought for a straight face and asked, "I'm assuming you don't let slip any of that stuff about how pretty she looks or how good she smells?"

Lyman's head shot up. "Hey now! You're not supposed to be noticing things like that about my Cora. I thought you were good and wound up over Evie, or I would've warned you that I'm not going to tolerate you sniffing around Cora for half an instant."

At this, Jake let loose a guffaw. Shaking his head, he hooted, "And you sit here wondering why you haven't managed to convince her you don't want to marry her anymore?"

"Here now, I haven't done a thing to show any interest or soft feeling toward her." He had the honesty to look abashed. "In her presence, at least. That much I manage to do for her."

"For her?" Jake's laughter died. "I figured this foolishness had some twisted notion of nobility behind it."

"It's not foolish when my legs are what's twisted," Lyman shot back. "If you want to call it noble for a man to keep his word instead of be selfish, then I'll abide by the description."

"How do you figure that going back on your proposal—the promise to take a woman to wife and be true to her alone for a lifetime—is anything but the exact opposite of keeping your word?" Jake couldn't wrap his head around it, but figured this was where the "twisted" part would come into Lyman's actions.

A muscle worked in Lyman's jaw, ticking a long moment before he answered. "I promised I'd make sure she was taken care of for the rest of her life, that she wouldn't have to worry about the day-to-day for so long as we were together."

"Well, there's a problem for you." Jake tilted forward until he balanced on only two chair legs, leaning close to the bed. "It's easy to see how you backed yourself into a corner."

"Yeah. It's hard to admit you can't take care of your woman. Harder to let her go." A ghost of a smile passed over his face. "And hardest of all when Cora's so stubborn about it!"

"Maybe you should stop focusing on pushing Cora out of the corner you created and work on tearing it down instead." Jake thought about it for a minute. "In fact, I bet she could help."

Lyman goggled at him. "You haven't been listening at all!"

"No, my friend. You haven't been thinking." Jake allowed all four legs of the chair to crash back to the ground. "Your problem isn't that you're oh-so-noble about keeping your word. If you think about it, you made promises that cancelled each other out—either she could be your wife, which means your helpmeet through good and bad, or she could expect you to take care of her for the rest of her life. You set that up for failure, and now you're choosing to uphold the wrong promise."

"How dare you!" Lyman leaned as far forward as he could, upsetting the chessboard in the process but scarcely noticing.

"How dare I?" Jake got to his feet and headed for the door. "How dare you promise to love a woman, but abandon the effort and refuse to accept her love the moment you make a mistake."

"I'm doing what's best for her! She deserves better than to be tied to a crippled man for the rest of her life. Cora's too great a prize for a failure and a shell of a man like me, and eventually she'll realize it." He was yelling so hard, the veins in his neck stood out in sharp relief. "I'm doing her the favor of not having to fight her own conscience once that happens!"

"You mean you're making sure you never see it happen." Jake shook his head in disgust. "Your problem isn't being too noble for your own good, Lyman. It's pride."

"No cost can be too great," she'd declared in a quiet tone, equal parts pride and determination, trying to skewer him with those blue eyes as though he alone stood between her and success.

For all Chase knew, maybe he did. It all came down to what she'd done so far to get her way and whether or not his newly widowed sister paid any of the price for Lacey Lyman's ruthless streak. If Laura's husband had counted as part of that cost she spoke of so matter-of-factly, it had been too high for Chase. And that would mean he'd make sure these Lymans, whether they be impostors or schemers, paid in equal measure.

If she took part in masterminding the cave-in, Lacey Lyman would yearn for the day she grumbled over the strictures of Hope Falls. She'd enjoy far fewer freedoms and fashions behind bars.

"Then what troubles brought you out to the forest today?" Chase kept his tone light, giving away no hint of the suspicions edging his thoughts. His unwanted companion had already given away more than she imagined—no sense frightening her off now.

"You," she blurted out, brows winging inward in a sudden scowl; it appeared Miss Lyman remembered her dislike of him. Just as suddenly, she remembered her manners. One hand clapped over her mouth a moment too late to hold back her implication.

The woman spoke before she thought, but did she think more than she let on? Had she really cottoned on to the fact Chase Dunstan might mean deep trouble for Hope Falls, or did words spill from her lips faster than she could catch them? Chase figured on the latter, but couldn't count out the possibility he was making the critical error common to any man confronted with a beautiful woman. *Don't underestimate this one.*

He let the silence sit between them, comfortable for him, not so comfortable for her. Only when she looked ready to give in and mutter her apologies did Chase offer, "If I'm the worst of your troubles, things are beginning to improve for you."

Even if he sent her behind bars—and particularly since *if* remained the key condition for just about everything having to do with Hope Falls—Chase wasn't lying. The way he figured it, an attacking cougar counted as a worse threat than he managed. At the least, the cat presented a more immediate, lethal danger.

Or it had until they both shot it. *Which goes to show she may be every bit as dangerous, despite the frills and dimples.*

And Chase, with his own theories about why God gave various creatures certain attributes, didn't have much positive to say about such purely feminine lures as dimples. An honest, hardworking woman of character wouldn't need something designed to beguile. Nor would she stoop to using hers against men.

He'd noticed Miss Thompson—Granger's intended, not the one claiming to be Braden Lyman's fiancée—had a dimple as well. It begged the question how a man like him wound up in a town where roughly half the feminine population showed the trait. But the chef didn't wield hers the way Miss Lyman did as she flashed a saucy smile, deliberately deepening her dimples.

"You're an optimist, Mr. Dunstan. It seems we share something in common after all." She flattered him in a blatant attempt to give a sense they were allies. "I believe Mr. Granger told you enough for you to guess that yesterday, despite the cougar, provided a dramatic improvement from the day before it?"

If the woman had a parasol, she'd be twirling it. Chase took in her newly demure stance, gentle smile, and vulnerable gaze, assessing the picture she manufactured so easily. He may not be much for feminine wiles, but a man would have to be both made of stone and around pretty ladies a good sight more often than Chase before he'd stop himself from appreciating one so fine as Lacey Lyman. So Chase stood and looked his fill.

He considered the wide blue eyes with their lush fringe of lashes. *Probably flutters those at every man she meets.* Beneath the fussy bows of her hat brim, worn to draw attention, glimpses of blond ringlets glinted in midmorning sunlight as though enjoying their match. *Curling tongs and coloring? Surely that effect isn't achieved without some sort of womanly deception.*

If they stood inside, he'd judge the sweet rosiness of her cheeks and lips to be the work of pinching or cosmetics—he'd seen his sister smuggle rose stain into her room in days long gone by and best left forgotten—but after Miss Lyman's mountain climb Chase thought she might be flushed from exertion.

Certainly the fullness of those lips owed nothing to artifice, and a man would have to be blind not to notice. Especially with those dimples drawing his eyes back with every smile. And should a man strive to avoid the temptation of staring at those lips and dwelling on what thoughts they inspired? He found himself in still greater danger.

Because once a man managed to look past Miss Lyman's face, he discovered an even more spectacular figure. How much of her remarkable shape she owed to a constricting corset and perhaps even some strategically placed padding, a man could only discover one way. And once that thought crossed Chase's mind...

He walked away.

He'll come back. Lacey wiggled her shoulders to ease their tightness and shift her bandaging so it stopped rubbing. Certainly Mr. Dunstan would return in a moment or so. He must have heard something in the bushes and didn't want to startle it before getting close enough to evaluate the situation.

Which explained why he didn't utter so much as a word before striding away. *Hmmm...he's gone past those bushes now. Beyond that stand of birch. I can't think where he's off to.* Still, no need to worry about their abruptly ended conversation.

Although things seemed to be taking a turn for the better, and Lacey would prefer to finish charming Mr. Dunstan as soon as possible. When a lady conceded to alter her plans, the gentleman should remain present to enjoy her magnanimity. Otherwise she might recall her urge to berate him for his high-handed behavior and again decide to browbeat him into a model employee.

Of course, it became increasingly apparent Mr. Dunstan would never be a model employee. His headstrong, independent ways, coupled with uncanny intelligence, threatened those "troubles" Lacey accused him of in her earlier slip. Only his response, acknowledging her concern without embarrassing her further, prompted this sudden change in tactics.

Optimism and a sense of humor were qualities to be prized and boded well for a reasonable conversation. *Besides, men are more easily persuaded than ordered. At least*—Lacey peered off into the distance, where no sign remained of her errant employee—*they are so long as they remain in the conversation!*

The slight twinge of doubt swelled, but Lacey had the means to reassure herself: *Obviously he means to come back; he left his massive bear of a dog sitting on the toe of my boot!*

A shrill whistle, issued in three staccato bursts, pierced through the trees. Lacey jumped, her surprised shriek almost matching the same note. She did, however, succeed in dislodging Decoy from his perch atop her boot. The dog gave her a reproachful glance before heading off after Dunstan, in the same direction from which the whistle came. The whistle, she rapidly realized, he'd trained the dog to recognize and follow to him.

"He's *not* coming back," Lacey marveled. For an instant the chill of disappointment held her in its grip. She shivered, even that slight motion making the tears in her shoulder prickle. The discomfort jarred her from her brief bemusement and into action.

She took off back down the mountainside, rushing to keep Decoy in her sights. Following Dunstan this far proved she could track back to town, but if the obstinate hunter went in another direction she might not be so fortunate. The dog, blessed with four feet and a long, loping stride, trotted—she hadn't even known dogs could trot, but this neither walk-nor-run quickstep seemed just that—at a far faster pace than Lacey managed to muster.

Encumbered as she was with corset and her full skirts, keeping her guide in sight claimed every drop of her energy and focus. She halted abruptly after rounding a particularly large pine tree and finding both dog and man. *Waiting.*

She itched to give him a telling off, but on the balance decided she wouldn't accomplish much by wheezing at the man. Instead Lacey borrowed a page from his book and waited. For her breath. To lay down the law. For the chance and ability to tell him in no uncertain terms what she thought of his conduct thus far and what she had a right to expect from every employee.

No, not expect. Require. Her eyes narrowed as she watched him, insolently rising to his feet from where he'd been sitting on the ground, with his back propped against the tree, while she raced through the forest, answering his whistle. *With his dog.*

She gulped in another breath, as deep as her stays allowed, while the oblivious lout glanced at her and shrugged. Lacey watched, open-mouthed and with no nod to grace as she continued to struggle for breath, as the man grabbed a low-lying branch, swung his foot up onto another to ascend farther, and easily brought down a large pack. He nonchalantly shouldered it while she remained gasping like a landed fish. For all his expression could have been carved from stone, some indefinable aspect of his bearing told of deep amusement at her predicament.

No, not what I require, Lacey seethed. *What. I. Demand.*

SIXTEEN

She looked like she'd almost gotten her wind back. Chase judged it time to ease up on the ropes before she set sail on her rant.

"Water?" He gave his canteen an inviting shake. Chase emptied it himself on the way down in a bid to cool off then tracked off a ways specifically to replenish the supply. Freshly filled, the water within sloshed in an irresistible offering.

She gave the canteen a look of such pure longing Chase found his own throat working as though taking a swallow. Miss Lyman's thoughts played out across the canvas of her face. Desperation replaced desire as she remembered who offered her the canteen and what ground she might lose by accepting it. Square-jawed determination trumped both to emerge victorious.

"You. . ." She paused to lick her lips in a motion even Chase knew owed nothing to seduction and everything to do with thirst. Looking as parched as before, she tried again. "You think. . ."

Chase thought his gambit failed. He started to withdraw the canteen, only to watch a finely boned hand snatch the thing from his grasp with the deadly precision of a rattler strike. No words spoken. At that point he realized she'd stopped talking without finishing her thought. *First time for everything.*

If he'd thought of anything to say, scraped up any reason for leaving her talking to nothing but the air and herself, here lay the opportunity to start spinning the explanation so it sounded enough like an apology to mollify the woman. Now, while she tilted the canteen and glugged back half its contents in one go.

He didn't. The water would have to wash the awkwardness away without any help. From the looks of it, it might work.

"Good?" Relief rode in his chest when she nodded, took a deeply satisfied breath, and screwed the top in place before passing it back to him. "All right then. Back to Hope Falls."

"Hold it right there!" Water worked wonders. Her voice regained volume and took on a shrill quality Chase recognized easily; most mammals used warning cries to presage danger.

Since his boots remained right where he'd stood for the past five minutes, he didn't take that as an order. He did, however, see it as foolishness and saw no reason to keep the opinion to himself. "Regained your dulcet tones, have you?"

"What. . .ooh!" Something akin to an outraged squawk sounded. "How do you have the nerve to criticize my tone when *you* can't manage to use words at all, but resort to whistling as though expecting anything and everyone to come running like a dog?"

Chase bit back a smile. The woman made it too easy. With a little luck and some quick thinking, he could make it so she would avoid him like the plague for the rest of his stay in Hope Falls. He shrugged. "Always works with Decoy. Until you, can't say I knew it'd work on women. It's something to bear in mind."

Astonishment and, judging by the fire in her gaze, pure rage held her silent before she gathered herself to attack. "Now you listen, Mr. Dunstan. I don't know what passes for manners or even basic communication for a mountain man, but I'm beginning to believe you're unable carry on a civil conversation." The lone feather atop her bonnet quivered in indignation as she finished.

Close to pushing her over the edge now. All he needed to do was squint awhile and say, "Yep."

His answer deflated her some. She visibly grappled with trying to find some way to answer that before throwing him a look filled with disbelief and a tinge of defeat. "Yep?"

"Yep." He crossed his arms and bobbed his head. "You got it right." *Or at least closer than most, even if you don't know it.* "I'm a mountain man because I'm no good at civil conversation."

No need to split hairs about the difference between not being good at civil conversation and not being good at pretending to be civil to people who routinely acted like idiots.

She stared at him a long moment before her eyes widened. "You're bamming me!" Disbelief vanished beneath fury. "And it almost worked! You think I don't see what you're up to, Mr. Dunstan? You think I can't deduce you're treating me with such obvious disdain and mockery simply because I'm a woman?"

"*Bamming* you?" He raised a brow at her. "Can't say I have." Chase never heard the expression before. While he figured it meant joking, the phrase itself sounded questionable at best, and he wasn't above teasing her to regain the upper hand.

It didn't work.

"Yes, Mr. Dunstan, you most certainly have." She rounded on him. "Call it what you will—putting me on, pulling one's leg, playing me for a fool—it all amounts to the same thing. Callous disregard and flagrant insubordination will not be tolerated."

He expected her to go on like a spitting cat for a good while, getting out all her anger and denigrating his character until she got it out of her system and went more docile. Instead the woman confounded him midstream. With one pause, she transitioned from affronted female on the attack to a more hopeless, quiet sort of anger. Her voice lowered, and Chase got the sense the following words weren't just for his benefit. Chase might have believed the words weren't for his ears at all.

"I feared this when the prospect of hiring you first arose, and you wasted no time making a difficult position even worse." With that dismal statement, she brushed past him, apparently heading back to Hope Falls without any further argument.

A sharp tug in his midsection, long unfamiliar but recently reintroduced to him in association with his brother-in-law's death, caught Chase off guard. *What do I have to feel guilty for?* But no man battled his gut and won, and Chase knew he'd acted the part of a jerk too well for a lady to understand or forgive. No matter what his suspicions, until he turned up something concrete, he needed to tread softly. That meant treating her like he would any other beautiful lady who happened to be his new boss.

If he'd ever worked for a woman before, that is. And if he didn't usually avoid beautiful ladies as a matter of good sense. Chase rubbed the bridge of his nose and prayed for wisdom.

Lord, I have need of wisdom. Proverbs warns, "It is better to dwell in the wilderness, than with a contentious and an angry woman." And well You know my preference in the matter. But here am I, with a purpose and a need for patience. Guide me through this new wilderness of women, Father. It is strange. Amen.

Somewhat restored, but not without a sense of foreboding, he jogged after Miss Lyman, determined to keep her from Hope Falls until the two of them could reach some sort of understanding.

"You misunderstood me." His deep voice sounded right at her heels, the only warning of his presence before Mr. Dunstan fell into step at her side. The man moved with the sleek, silent grace of a hunter even when not tracking anything down.

Foolish, Lacey. He's tracking you *at the moment.* The realization shivered through her. Even with her gun, Lacey knew on the deepest level, with no argument, that nothing she did could match this man nor evade him. She sped up anyway.

After all, she'd spent most of her life recognizing her own limits then fighting against them anyway. *Hopeless doesn't mean helpless, and helpless doesn't mean hopeless,* she recited. Which quality she possessed changed by situation, but Lacey took comfort in knowing she always had one. She'd allow nothing less.

This morning the betrayal of her friends and the unchangeable fact she'd be stuck with Mr. Dunstan left her somewhat hopeless. Her refusal to be helpless spurred her to seek him out in an attempt to hash through their positions.

Now, given his behavior, it could not be clearer to Lacey she remained helpless to change him or his treatment of her. Worse, she'd be helpless to alter his impact on the other men if he remained. But now, armed with solid examples in his treatment of her, as well as his own admission of incivility, she had high hopes of convincing the other women to dismiss him.

No matter those fleeting moments in the woods, when she'd almost liked his humor. Priorities must be maintained. Examples must be set. Standards should never be lowered. And besides, "I understand you quite well, Mr. Dunstan."

Lacey refused to look at him, instead keeping her chin high and gaze fixed firmly forward as she plunged ahead. "You disdain to afford me the essential respect and courtesy due an employer then make light of it by claiming to be incapable of civil interaction."

"You're right that I didn't give you proper respect." The words came haltingly, grudgingly. Still, he said them. "But I wasn't making light about my lack of social graces, Miss Lyman."

Lacey fell over at that confession. More accurately, she'd hooked her boot in a protruding tree root and gone sprawling to the ground. *Which might be what one deserves, going about with one's nose in the air when a man makes an attempt to apologize.*

Nevertheless, it hardly made for a dignified position in which to accept that apology. If Lacey were inclined to accept the apology at all, when it sounded suspiciously more like an explanation than an apology. *Not an apology at all*, she decided as she rolled over. She sat for a moment and took stock as Dunstan hunkered down. Besides embarrassment at her clumsiness and the pain in her shoulder, mainly she felt. . .damp.

So she held out her hand in a silent request for his assistance to her feet, only to find it ignored. Rather than help her up, Dunstan wrapped his hand around her boot. She fancied she could feel the warmth of it clear through leather and stocking, a sensation so foreign she lost her breath.

Though, again, that might have been the fall. Whatever the cause for her lack of breath, she didn't immediately order him to remove that hand from her person. He gave a gentle squeeze. Lacey gasped and tried to yank her foot away, under the safety of her skirts, but he tightened his grip and made it impossible.

Unbelievably, he shot her a disgruntled glance from beneath lowered brows and issued the terse order that she, "Hold still."

"I will not!" She tugged her leg back, attempting to dislodge his clamp-like hold on her boot. For a long, ridiculous moment, she pedaled the air. Lacey pulled her foot back; he tugged it forward with surprising gentleness. "Unhand me!"

And then everything changed at once. The contrary man gave a deep, booming chuckle and did the last thing she expected. He complied with her request, letting go at the same moment she gave a final tug and effectively hurled herself flat on her back. Sharp pains shot up from her shoulder, stunning her.

She lay still for a moment to let the pain to both shoulder and pride subside, ignoring the damp seeping steadily into the green cambric of her dress. After all, a few more moments of indignity could do no more harm to the fabric. She'd tend it later with a solution of tepid water, glycerin, and vinegar to stave off general discoloration. Any persistent stains she'd treat with still more vinegar or, at worst, pure alcohol.

At least this dress stands a better chance than yesterday's pink, she consoled herself as Decoy sniffed about her bonnet in a show of canine concern. Green blended better with forest mishaps. *All to the good, as I seem doomed to plummet toward the ground whenever I'm in Mr. Dunstan's company.* Once might be an error, but twice bore the unmistakable markings of a pattern—a pattern Lacey was loath to sacrifice any more fabric toward.

"Miss?" His hesitant query made her aware she'd not spoken since her ignominious return to the ground. Also, he'd stopped chuckling and moved from her feet to the vicinity of her head.

Now that she gave the matter some attention, Lacey rather thought he'd stopped laughing the moment she'd winged backward. Dunstan even sounded. . .concerned. *As well he should be, dumping a lady on the ground after scandalously groping her ankle.*

Lacey gave an indignant sniff, but it didn't sound at all impressive from her current position. So she tried again, making her second attempt louder. *There. That's more impressive.*

"Don't cry." Dunstan certainly sounded impressed, if for the wrong reason. A bit aghast, too, as though crying females rarely crossed his path and he didn't know what to do with one.

Lacey gave another great sniff to cover up the urge to smile and again held out her hand in silent request to be helped up. This time he responded by helping her sit up.

Then she felt a rough square of fabric thrust into her hand. She rubbed the bandanna between her fingertips, testing its texture. Roughly woven for sturdy construction, made for long wear. Time and use softened the surprisingly clean blue square.

A mountain man's handkerchief. The gesture touched her more than she expected. Lacey slid it between her fingertips for a moment, considering why he'd decided to be kind. Wondering what changed since he'd laughed at her moments before. *He stopped laughing when I fell backward,* she thought again.

"Why were you laughing?" Lacey kept her gaze fixed on the soft blue square, bunching and unbunching it in her hands. She didn't know why, but that bandanna seemed the equivalent of a peace flag if she could just understand this one other thing.

"What?" Astonishment wrapped the word. "You're about to go weepy, not because you're hurt but because I laughed at you?"

His answer, or rather lack of it, made it clear she'd never understand him. *Foolish to think I might. Maybe he doesn't want me to?* Lacey folded the square and proffered it back to Dunstan. "Thank you. I almost never cry, so you keep it."

"It's clean." His lips compressed into a tight line.

"I know." Surprise made her add, "It was a very civilized thing to do, offer a lady in distress your handkerchief."

He looked at her a long moment before tucking the cloth into one of his pockets. "It's a bandanna. And I already told you, Miss Lyman. I'm many things, but I'm not civilized."

"Of course you aren't." It seemed Miss Lyman, in another of her quicksilver changes, decided to be agreeable. "The question then becomes, Mr. Dunstan, what are you? More specifically, why are you in Hope Falls? And why, if you cannot behave in civilized fashion yourself, have we hired you on to oversee the behavior of a town full of unruly lumbermen?"

For his part, Chase far preferred her when he caught her off guard and she was all flailing and ridiculous protestations. He hadn't admitted to it, but it was her melodramatic demand that he unhand her to give him one of the best laughs he'd enjoyed in several years. There'd been no artifice or scheming behind the overblown order—just female foolishness at its most endearing. Right until she fell over.

Then she'd hurt her shoulder. He felt guilt over mishandling his attempt to ensure she hadn't broken one of those tantalizingly trim ankles. Overtaxed, she looked ready to cry, and he handled that even worse and provoked her back to poking after his reasons and qualifications for coming to Hope Falls.

Having said her piece, she sat in the middle of dirt and dappled sunshine, blinking up at him as though she hadn't just tossed a series of shrewd questions designed to undo him. When angry, she'd been dangerous. When logical, she became deadly.

Her first question was easiest and most convenient to answer and gave him time to consider the other two. "I'm a hunter, guide, and best left on my own without interference."

A cursory examination told him he'd be a fool to tackle the second, so he moved on to the third. "Bullets know no manners. Brawls aren't stopped by polite requests. Lumbermen find their work an escape from the limitations of civilization. That goes without saying for most folks, but you're new to the sawmill business, so I'm laying it out as plain as possible." While he spoke he held out his hand and helped her back to her feet.

From the way she'd wriggled and kicked earlier, he figured she hadn't sprained or broken one of her delicate ankles. Despite a burgeoning tendency to lose her balance, Miss Lyman proved far sturdier than she looked. *More intelligent, too.*

Watching her, a man could be fooled into thinking her pretty little head held nothing but concern for her rumpled dress. Chase waited while she shook her skirts, smoothed them, then set about picking off bits of grass and pine needles. His amusement gave way to impatience when she began methodically removing her hatpins and tucking them into an unseen pocket before she took off her bonnet and looked about for a place on which to set it.

Finding none, she tied its ribbons and looped it about her arm before she set about tidying those lustrous golden curls. Patting her coiffure, she apparently considered the job satisfactory because she returned her attention to the bonnet. This time she cradled it in the crook of one arm and began fussing with the bows along its brim as though this were the most important thing in the world. The woman was *humming*.

SEVENTEEN

So practical to accomplish two things at once, Lacey marveled. First: her ensemble sorely needed tending before she ventured back to town, else others would notice her uncharacteristically shabby state and ask uncomfortable, nosy questions.

Second: as she'd once confided to Cora, tending to the tiny details of her appearance was one of the few ways she could avoid speaking too soon and allow time to gather her thoughts. Why this worked, Lacey didn't know. It wasn't, as Braden suggested, a by-product of vanity. So long as something kept her hands busy, be it making bread or learning to shoot or any old thing at all, she found it much easier to concentrate.

Thus, when Lacey stood up after hearing Mr. Dunstan's answers, she found both outfit and thoughts quite disordered. So she shook out her skirts and reordered her concerns; brushed off bits of grass and picked out some key issues; straightened her seams and realized she was ready to give her opinion.

But she rather fancied the idea of making him wait to hear it. Lacey hadn't forgotten the way Mr. Dunstan abruptly abandoned her atop the hillside. Nor, as she set her dress and mind to rights, had it escaped her notice that he'd yet to give any reason or even an apology for his behavior. Lacking manners might explain poor conversation; it didn't explain walking away from one entirely. *Turnabout,* she decided, *is fair play.*

She didn't walk away, as returning to Hope Falls just yet wouldn't suit her purposes. *It's time Mr. Dunstan learns that a woman doesn't need to leave to make a man follow her wishes.*

She relished every moment he stood there, waiting on her every tiny move the way Decoy waited on his. The biggest challenge, Lacey found, was keeping her smile from showing through. To prevent that from ruining her little lesson, she fussed more than necessary with her bonnet so she could keep more of her face hidden. Finally, just when it seemed as though he'd never break the silence and declare her the victor, he spoke.

"Miss Lyman?" The man sounded hesitant, but also curious. "Are you, by chance, trying to teach me better manners?"

Smile or no smile, the fleeting rigidity in her shoulders as she stifled a laugh probably gave her away. Still, Lacey played it out. "Why, Mr. Dunstan. Whatever gives you that idea?"

"Something in the way you withdrew midconversation and abandoned the topic at hand in favor of primping." The words came out flat, as though he'd stepped on them before speaking.

"If I *happened*"—she lingered on the word overlong before continuing—"to lose track of the conversation in such a way as to convey disinterest or even disregard, that would have been unforgivably *rude*. Particularly were the conversation a matter of business. In such a case, my partner would immediately deem me flighty and unworthy of continued association, don't you think?" She ended the lecture—which she'd planned so precisely—with a challenge so he couldn't wriggle out of responding.

"Maybe." The one-word answer wasn't the apologetic

revelation she hoped for. Worse, he'd gone steely-gazed again. "Maybe the person you're talking to would think your high opinion of yourself is undeserved, and you shouldn't try giving out lessons in manners until you've learned some virtue."

SMACK! The sound of her palm striking his cheek ripped through the forest before Lacey even decided to slap him. Iron bands closed around her wrist in an unbreakable grip, their pressure forcing her to turn or let her wrist be snapped in two.

"Down!" It sounded more like a bark than a word, given alongside a sinister growl, but Lacey rebelled at the order.

"No!" She flailed, jabbing back with her elbow and almost connecting with something. No. It was his hand, releasing her wrist but catching her elbow and pushing her away in a spin.

"Not you." His terse dismissal registered after she came to a stop and got her bearings. Dunstan crouched over Decoy, one hand behind the dog's neck, now murmuring low, soothing sounds.

When Lacey moved forward, Decoy tensed. So did Dunstan, changing his hold and saying, "No." Lacey froze at the scene, trying to fit the pieces together. A vague suspicion began to take form, solidifying when Dunstan extended a hand back to her.

"Come forward. Slowly now." He guided her to his right, away from Decoy's head. The dog's eyes followed her, but he didn't move as Lacey lowered to her knees. Dunstan kept his hand over hers, reaching forward to stroke the coarse but somehow soft brindled fur, still making those soothing sounds.

In time, Dunstan removed his hand from Decoy's neck, and slowly his tail began to wag. When he rolled onto his stomach, sphinx-like, Dunstan took his hand from hers and backed slightly away. He kept close, very close, as Lacey made friends again with the dog whose master she'd attacked and who'd tried to defend him in turn. Only after the fact did Lacey understand how Dunstan protected her from the loyalty of this massive beast.

Her shoulder ached more than it had when the doctor prodded it, but Lacey thought her heart bore the deeper bruise. *I don't want to be in his debt,* she protested. *Twice over!* But it went deeper than pride or who came out stronger from this interlude.

This even went deeper than worrying about what Chase Dunstan meant for Hope Falls. Deeper than not understanding why he walked away from talking to her or why a man who disliked her saved her from his dog. The thing that hurt was stranger, less important, and somehow more important than all of that.

How can he know me for less than two days, yet already see how far I fall short of being the woman my friends are?

∞

"It'll take a better man than me to get Twyler to justice in one piece," Jake admitted. Then added, "Aside from his leg, I mean."

"You shot him in the leg rather than shoot him in the back as he ran like a coward," Evie soothed. "We both know the choice not to kill him already makes you the better man, Cree—Jake."

Regret over how they'd met—that he'd needed to give her a false name, that the woman he loved still sometimes thought of him as Jake Creed rather than Jake Granger—stabbed him. He shoved it aside by taking her in his arms and stealing a kiss. Sure, kissing Evie didn't take away the mistakes from his past. But somehow bad memories didn't stand a chance against an armful of warm, soft woman with a warmer heart and the sweet smell of something delicious always lingering around her hair.

"Mmm... Jake...," she breathed, all thoughts of proper last names good and forgotten as they held each other. "Maybe it's not such a bad thing the doctor said he couldn't be moved for a while. This way you didn't have to leave right away." A satisfied smile played around the corners of her mouth, prompting him to kiss her once more.

"You know I'd like to stay," he agreed, ignoring the fact he'd been hunting Twyler to bring him home for half a year. Once an all-consuming quest for vengeance, now that he'd caught his brother's killer, it had transformed into a more tedious chore of tying up loose ends. "When this is over, I'll hurry back."

"I know, but I'm still not sorry you were delayed. If anyone deserves an infected gunshot wound, it's Twyler." Her vindictive announcement so beguiled him, he laughed.

"It's not the complication of his leg—worse comes to worse, Doc will amputate so Twyler can't escape clearing my brother's name and facing his own sentence." He peered at her in the dark of the storeroom cupboard, where they'd gone to sneak a few private moments. The others wouldn't oblige them much longer. "I'm anxious to finish it, put the old away and begin anew."

Light flooded the small room, ending their private conversation in an instant as Naomi Higgins peered around the doorway and cleared her throat. The oldest of the four marriageable women of Hope Falls, Jake got the impression Miss Higgins appointed herself something of the group's chaperone.

A thankless position, but one Jake appreciated. When it came to the other women. As far as he and Evie were concerned, they were engaged adults, and Miss Higgins's interruptions failed to amuse and succeeded in spoiling a fine interlude. He scowled.

"Don't you glower at me." She planted her hands on her hips, only to have the door start to swing shut. At that, she abandoned the schoolmarm pose in favor of propping the door. "Up until you two decided you liked cuddling more than arguing, nothing got Evie out of her kitchen before suppertime!"

"We're engaged, Naomi." Evie's exasperated remonstrance held more fondness than real irritation, but that was just one more thing to love about Evie. His woman loved other people.

"So are Cora and Braden, but back in Charleston we didn't let them traipse off alone for more than a quarter of an hour." Miss Lyman joined her cousin, effectively blocking the doorway.

"Of course, once Braden recovers his health and enough of his brains, we could change that policy. Your sister might well—"

Even before she finished, Jake knew Lacey Lyman won the war. The slightest mention of her little sister and the mother hen in Evie came out clucking. To be fair, he didn't like the idea of a healthier Braden spending unsupervised time with Cora either. The man might need another whack in the head first.

"Oh no!" Evie slipped from his arms and pushed through the chaperone barricade at the door. "As soon as Braden is able to get out of that bed unassisted, those two won't be left alone."

"Those two deal with different circumstances." Just because Cora shouldn't be alone with Braden didn't mean Jake would give up any and every opportunity to hold Evie. He was a red-blooded man, after all. And she was. . . He looked over at her. *Mine.*

"Only so long as Braden's incapacitated." Cora Thompson shrugged, seeming vaguely apologetic without giving an inch. How women managed that sort of thing, Jake would never know.

"If you envy his privileges"—Lacey Lyman gave him an appraising look that chilled him—"something could be arranged."

"Hush, Lacey." Evie didn't shout, but might as well have.

"It's all right, ladies." Jake walked across the kitchen and lowered himself to straddle one of the work stools. From this position, he made it clear he didn't intend to leave before supper, but he also lowered himself so he didn't tower over anyone. That was important for what he needed to say next.

Apologies weren't easy, but at certain important points in a man's life, they were inescapable. Much like chaperones.

Mrs. Nash was resting before the meal, and Mrs. McCreedy— always a discreet soul—had ventured off to go check on her and help her back to the diner. That left the four women of Hope

Falls—three who'd written the infamous ad to bring Twyler here, and one woman resolutely staying by the side of her querulous and now reluctant fiancé. In short, the four trusting women whose welfare he'd placed below his own personal vendetta.

"I owe all of you an apology." This statement had the instant effect of silencing the room; no mean feat even when one of the women was distant and huffy toward the others. It surprised him that, out of all the women, it was frilly little Lacey Lyman who seemed most furious and least inclined to forgive Jake's deception. *Then again, the victim of Twyler's final crime probably should be most difficult to placate.*

Hopefully, what Jake had to say would smooth the way for all of them—especially Dunstan, whom Jake suspected bore the brunt of Lacey's anger over how he'd mishandled things so far. Only later, when they seemed so put out, did he realize he shouldn't have hired Dunstan without consulting the women. He didn't regret the decision, but he didn't want them to either.

"There's a verse in Proverbs that keeps running through my mind." He started in full steam, intending to blast through this apology at top speed. " 'Bread of deceit is sweet to a man; but afterwards his mouth shall be filled with gravel.' "

"Since this is going to be an apology," Miss Lyman broke in, a reluctant smile twitching the corners of her mouth, "I'll just ignore the fact you've singled out the one item I bake."

Everyone else smiled wholeheartedly, whether amused by her comment or simply relieved at the indication she had a mind to listen. A little humor went far, as Jake had hoped when he chose the whimsically appropriate verse, though he hadn't known the particulars about who baked the bread. *I assumed Evie made it.*

"I arrived under false pretenses, using a made-up name and letting everyone believe I wanted to work in Hope Falls." His admission sobered everyone in a hurry. "I came here looking for my brother's killer and found myself a bride along the way. That's how I found the truth behind that verse—revenge seemed so sweet while I chased it, but the aftermath is bitter indeed.

"I tried to protect you, but chose to hide it. It leaves me sour to know my silence put you in danger." Here, he looked to Lacey. "Small deceptions have big consequences, no matter the intentions behind them. Please forgive my mistake and know I'll work hard to earn back the trust I failed to deserve."

Having spoken a lot longer than he'd thought he'd need to cover everything, Jake fell silent. And became distinctly uncomfortable as no one said anything. Four women, united by circumstance, but divided by emotion, stared back at him.

EIGHTEEN

Cora stopped gaping at her sister's fiancé before anyone else managed it. Naomi hadn't blinked in so long, she looked as though she'd forgotten how. Lacey seemed thunderstruck, unsure what to make of this and not certain she wanted to examine it.

If Cora knew her best friend, Lacey wanted to stay mad for a while longer, and Granger's humility pulled the rug from under her. Would Lacey forgive him or resent him even more for pressing her already overstressed emotions? Cora couldn't guess. Too much had gone wrong with her friend's grand plans, with no way for Lacey to express her frustration, for anyone to predict her reactions as of late. She was too hair-trigger.

Evie, predictably, looked at Granger as though he'd hung the moon, which seemed an almost equitable feat to what he'd just done. Silencing a room full of women wasn't easy, but, then again, men so rarely apologized for anything. . .and he'd *meant* it!

But how to acknowledge the extraordinary nature of what he'd done, when it was no less than he should have? No wonder they all sat there, dumbfounded and pleased, as things threatened to grow awkward. What could one say to the man?

Maybe I don't need to say anything to him! Instead of addressing Granger directly, she directed her comment to Evie.

"Do you think he might be able to teach Braden to do that?" She glanced at her sister's fiancé, offering a broad smile. "Because if he can show Braden how to admit when he's wrong. . ." Cora felt her own smile fade as the request freed her strictly pent-up thoughts about the Braden she'd found in Hope Falls.

Everything sprang forth, tumbling over each other in an unstoppable tide. Snatches of conversation, hurtful words Cora tried so hard to ignore, threatened to overwhelm her. To the fore rose the memory of the first time she saw Braden since mourning his death, discovering his survival, and leaving everything she knew to rush to his side. The first time in more than a year they'd laid eyes on each other, and her beloved shouted. . .

"Get out!" More and more agitated as she tried to console him, reassure him of her love and dedication, he ordered: "Just leave. . . . I don't want you here."

Things worsened until the only man she'd ever loved, who'd sworn he loved her, too, refused to even look at her. And suddenly it didn't matter so much that Braden survived the mine collapse after all. Cora was losing him all over again.

"She's not my fiancée."

"Some things can be shown, but not taught." Granger's voice pulled her from the bog of her thoughts, his gaze sad and kind. "A man has to admit to himself that he's wrong before he can do anything else about it. It takes time, patience, and prayer."

"I'm giving it all three." Cora sighed. Then, because everyone seemed to understand how much she'd been holding inside, she murmured, "But as time goes, so does my patience!"

⁓

If Cora's patience wore thin, Lacey imagined hers reached the breaking point last night. When everyone hired Dunstan against her wishes, she'd lost the last support shoring up her meager supply. Whatever patience Lacey possessed, it had been strained by cougars, kidnappings, and curmudgeonly brothers insisting she couldn't run Hope Falls.

It didn't help matters that the cougars and kidnappings made Braden's doubts seem somewhat realistic. Nor did an apology from the man responsible for provoking the criminal who kidnapped her do much good. All Granger's speech managed was to take away her righteous indignation, leaving behind all the worry and fear to churn her stomach into a mighty mess.

Worry and fear made short work of patience, after all. *Maybe that's why Mr. Dunstan claimed I lacked virtues? Then again, there are plenty of other virtues I lack. What did he mean?* Slapping him for his insult hadn't made her feel better. If anything, it added guilt to the unpleasant mix of her emotions since he'd protected her from Decoy's defense attempt.

So here she stood, plenty of guilt and worry and supposedly no virtues to soak any of it up. Lacey sighed at the hopelessness of it. Then she got to work on not being helpless against it. After all, just because Mr. Dunstan thought her incapable of loftier traits, that didn't make him right!

"Thank you, Mr. Granger." She tried to summon a smile, failed, and settled for a nod. "I, for one, appreciate how difficult it is to apologize for something. Especially"—now a rueful smile touched her lips—"when you were doing what you believed best. Intentions, we all hope, count for something."

I hope they do. She tucked a hand into her pocket and began worrying the fabric between her fingertips. *No matter how often*

*I hear about God's great mercy, I don't manage to convince myself it
really outweighs His sense of justice. If we "reap as we sow," then that
advertisement for husbands will see myself and Naomi saddled with
unacceptable mates for the rest of our lives. . .and it would be my fault!
My only hope is that God takes my good intentions into account when
He decides our futures.*

"Gracious of you, Miss Lyman." If he sounded surprised,
Lacey didn't blame him. Jacob Granger, intelligent enough to see
the error of his decisions, knew how much they'd cost her.

"Thank you, Lacey!" Evie enveloped her in a warm hug that
said what she couldn't in front of Granger. By accepting Evie's
fiancé's apology, Lacey began making amends for her outbursts.

In turn, her friend was willing to put aside the argument from
this morning. The breach between them began mending, and
the hug said it all. The tumult in Lacey's stomach calmed, their
unspoken reconciliation giving her some much-needed peace.

"We had good intentions when we agreed to hire Mr.
Dunstan," Naomi ventured then seemed to hold her breath.

"As had I when I didn't wish to." Lacey thought it would be
safe to speak her mind now. She'd had enough time to think and
let the hurt ebb so she wouldn't make things worse. "It wasn't
just the decision or even Mr. Dunstan himself that had me so
overset. If we don't stand strong together, Braden will have the
ammunition he needs to take back control of Hope Falls."

"We know. It shouldn't have happened that way." Cora shared
glances with the others. "But you were hurt and angry, and it looked
as though you and Mr. Dunstan got off on the wrong foot."

Naomi laid a reassuring hand on her shoulder. "Forgive us for
thinking that, after the past few days, your snap judgment might
not be the best basis for such an important decision."

"Dunstan doesn't spend much time around other people,
much less around women." Granger's observation reinforced what

his friend had told her. "Since I'll be taking Twyler back East, I jumped at the chance to have someone I trust watch over you. He's short on conversation, but long on loyalty and ability."

He's right about the short on conversation part. As for any abilities, I've only seen Dunstan display a knack for insults. Maybe he'll improve on further acquaintance. Or maybe I'll improve at avoiding the opportunity to further our acquaintance?

"What's done is done." Lacey didn't want to be angry anymore. Her temper wouldn't change their minds or make Dunstan leave. From here on out, she was stuck with their decision. . .and his presence. "I'll find a way to make it work." *Somehow.*

Chase couldn't believe it worked, but could only be grateful his hunch to visit that particular stretch of the river paid off.

Thank You, Lord! You provided me the means to prove my skill and at the same time a way to pacify whatever lumbermen go against the idea of me filling in for Granger. You are good!

Even when he was undeserving. Chase paused in the act of dressing his kills. Since Lacey Lyman thanked him for keeping Decoy in line, she'd not uttered a single word. Not while he walked her back to town. Not when he turned and went back into the forest to continue the hunting she'd interrupted.

Silence didn't sit well on her. Or maybe her silence after she slapped him—deservedly—didn't sit well with him. If he knew more about women, he'd be able to tell whether his actions with Decoy equaled an apology or some sort of truce. But he didn't. As far as he knew, she'd bypassed insulted and become wrathful.

The tricky thing, he mused as he tied his day's catch, *is that she didn't look angry. More. . .thoughtful. But what was she thinking about to make her abandon her plans to tell me off?* That's what made him uncomfortable. He'd set out to anger her, alienate her to the point she avoided him. *Did I succeed?*

He lifted his prize off the ground and headed back to town in evening's waning light. The closer Chase drew toward Hope Falls, the more restless he grew. Towns always made him restless, but this time felt different. And it was *her* fault.

Why couldn't she stalk off with her nose in the air again? That sort of thing a man could read clear as day. No questions, no qualms about whether or not he'd angered her properly. Instead the confounded woman turned around and *thanked* him for stopping his dog from mauling her when she had every right to defend her honor. Then she walked back to town with an air of...

Of what? The puzzle pricked his curiosity and his conscience until Chase finally admitted what Miss Lyman's mien reminded him of. She'd walked away with the dejection of an old moose, used to coming out on top, who'd finally lost the match to a younger bull. *She's just more...feminine about it.*

Which explained his unsettled gut. He'd meant to drive the woman away, not drive her into the ground. Chase groaned. Now that he knew what he'd done, he'd have to undo it. *Somehow.*

He didn't have time to figure out how before the forest's calm shattered. Chase kept walking, slowing his pace as he watched the Hope Falls workers. These were the men he'd been hired to keep in line. These were the men he'd need to impress tonight to build on his reputation as a force not to be crossed.

Everyone trickled toward town, sunset signaling suppertime for the lumbermen. Most boasted the woodsman's build: tall and muscular, their movements abrupt. By and large, axmen took their steps the same way they swung their axes, powerful and controlled. This helped balance out their top-heavy frames when going over uneven terrain. Chase could tell a lot about a man by the way he moved, and this sort of gait came from experience. Their jobs kept them in areas littered with debris, where a warning gave mere seconds to spring out of danger's path.

Lumberjacks couldn't afford long steps. But what their strides reserved in distance, they expended in sheer noise. The men descending on Hope Falls, with their heavy-bottomed boots and thudding steps, sounded like a herd of mountain goats. Or they would, if they stopped babbling for longer than a minute.

"Wonder what's for dinner tonight?" someone boomed.

"Doesn't matter," another grunted back. "It'll be good."

If the biscuits Chase sampled earlier were any indication, he agreed. When Granger promised him the best meals he'd ever eaten, Chase wrote it off as exaggeration. Now he started to allow a little anticipation. Lumber camps weren't known for their good company, comfortable beds, or easy lifestyle. What kept a man coming back was good pay and better food. When it came to his meals, an axman had high expectations and low tolerance for anything less than good food and lots of it.

All in all, Chase was glad to hear their appetites and their thoughts centered around supper. Their love for a special dish, particular to woodsmen, was key to his plan tonight.

"If the food didn't taste like it dropped from heaven's tables, I wouldn't stay on with no pay," someone muttered.

No pay? Chase angled closer to make out the rest of the conversation. The two hulking men paid no attention to him.

"It's always food with you," his friend dismissed. "Me? I'm working for a wife. There's only two left, so I have to choose which woman to cozy up to. Miss Lyman or Miss Higgins?"

At that point Chase drifted away. He'd already gotten everything of interest out of that conversation. And very interesting it was, too. Granger hadn't mentioned anything about the workings of the camp. Then again, there'd been no need. As far as everyone in Hope Falls was concerned, Chase didn't need to know that these three—four when one counted Braden Lyman's fiancée—women had hoodwinked these men into working for them in exchange for nothing more than their food and a fool's promise.

The whole thing reeked of fraud. Any idiot could see that these women wouldn't lower themselves to marry common lumbermen. Granger's fiancée, the only woman engaged thus far, nabbed herself a successful businessman with a fortune of his own. Bile burned the back of Chase's throat at the idea his friend was taken in, but he couldn't interfere there. *Granger's problem.*

Chase's responsibilities lay with his sister and the brother-in-law sent to his death by Lyman's Miracle Mining Company. As he walked up to the diner ahead of the rest of the throng, he knew he'd come one step closer to the truth behind this sawmill scheme. More would follow as he watched, waited, and went to the mine site for clues. He just had to win the men over first.

NINETEEN

Chase stepped inside, walked to the far wall, and stopped just short of the swinging doors to the kitchen. *Any minute now.*

"Hey!" An excited shout sounded. "Are those beaver?"

"Lemme see!" Someone farther away stirred the anticipation.

"Might be." Chase moved to face the men, effectively turning his prize to the wall. Out of sight or grabbing hands.

"Did you see them?" someone demanded of a companion.

"I saw summat brown and furry, but dunno what it were."

"Beaver." Reverence filled Clump's tone, and he stomped forward. "When you moved, I saw the tails swinging past." A roar of approval swallowed up the end of the German's pronouncement. It didn't matter. Everyone heard what Chase needed them to.

Now that their appetites had been whetted, he swung forward his day's work as mute testament to Clump's assertion. Things couldn't have played out any better. Chase had them right where he wanted them, pining for their beloved beaver-tail soup.

"What's going on out here?" Granger burst through the swinging doors, brows lowered in a stern expression. With all the ruckus, no way could he have missed Chase's victory. Swinging doors did little to block sound. No. Granger knew exactly what was going on and played into it like a master.

"New guy caught a coupla beaver!" A grubby thumb indicated Chase and punctuated the statement. "Good hunter after all!"

"Mighty hard hunting beaver these days," someone called from the back. "Not many left around these parts anymore."

"He's the best hunter, trapper, and guide I've ever met." Granger gave him a solemn look then swept a considering glance across the crowd. "Question is why any of you doubted it."

"We don't doubt it no more." The reassurance made Chase bite back a smile. When it came to men, stomachs held sway.

"Handy with his fists, too." Clump puffed up his chest. "Helped me, Riordan, and Granger get that bunch of galoots on the train yesterday morning. Ask Williams to tell you about it!"

Some laughs, some furious jabs as friends gave each other meaningful elbows between the ribs, and several smirks thrown Williams's way comprised the room's response. Whatever else Williams was, the man hadn't made himself popular.

"Fists, knife, guns. . .Dunstan here's master of them all." Granger clapped him on the shoulder. "That's why I asked him to keep an eye on things here while I take a trip to Maine."

Slowly the signs of jocularity vanished. General unease grew as Chase waited. Now was the critical moment. Either his claim to authority would go unchallenged or else—

Craig Williams lurched forward, face reddened with fury. His eyes narrowed to slits. "We don't need babysittin', Granger. None of us is going to start taking orders from a newcomer."

∽

Lacey glared at the women blocking her way. Had it been mere moments ago that she and Evie hugged, allies once more? Her

471

excellent memory must, for once, be wrong. No friend who was so recently regained would set herself against Lacey. *Again!*

But what other explanation was left for the sight before her? Cora and Evie planted themselves in front of the swinging doors, blocking her from following Granger into the hullabaloo beyond. Lacey attempted to push through, only to be rebuffed.

"What are you thinking?" she hissed, loath to miss anything going on in the next room. "We need to go out there!"

Granger's voice demanded an explanation for the noise, but Lacey lost the response as Naomi sidled up and began arguing. "Going out there is the very worst thing we could do right now. Somehow Granger has to make it clear that Mr. Dunstan is going to be taking his place. The other men will know that means he'll be taking charge of some things, and they won't like it."

"Who would?" Lacey shot back. "But it's *our* town. We're still the ones in charge, and we need to make our wishes known!"

"The men know Jake speaks for us." Evie seemed to realize she'd said the wrong thing as she hastily reprised, "That is to say, they know we speak through Jake. They respect that system."

"But he's telling them he won't be here," Lacey pointed out. "Him announcing that Mr. Dunstan will step in isn't the same as the four of us declaring that we wish it so."

"Exactly." Cora folded her arms. "Granger won the men's respect on his own. Otherwise he couldn't have kept order. Now Mr. Dunstan will have to do the same thing, or it won't work."

She makes sense, a small voice admitted. But Lacey was tired of hearing about how wrong she was about anything to do with Mr. Dunstan. The man hadn't bothered to earn *her* respect.

"We're the employers," she insisted. "We march into that dining room, explain that Mr. Dunstan will temporarily be filling in for Granger, and everyone else will fall in line."

"Right after you see mice turning cartwheels across my

kitchen," Evie added. "Face it, Lacey. You want to be seen as an employer, but we aren't paying them anything but their meals and the slim chance that you or Naomi will choose to marry them. They have their own sense of pride and will only take so much."

"So do I!" Lacey began pacing the kitchen, mind working furiously. Evie was right. The men weren't paid; they couldn't simply fire anyone insubordinate. If, en masse, they refused to accept Dunstan, the best she and the women could do was evict them from town. Which kept Lacey in the same place she'd been since Mr. Dunstan picked up that cougar. *Stuck on the sidelines.*

No longer arguing, they could all hear what was being said on the other side of the doors. It didn't sound promising.

"We don't need babysittin', Granger." A strident voice, familiar but not enough for Lacey to place him, broke through. "None of us is going to start taking orders from a newcomer."

The women shared worried looks, but none of them made a sound. Lacey couldn't speak for the others, but she held her breath to be sure she heard even the tiniest sound beyond. It didn't help. After a swell of agitated murmurs, no one spoke.

At least they aren't fighting. She tried to be optimistic. *Isn't that a good sign that Dunstan can take over peacefully?*

His voice, low and resonant, reached through the doors. "Granger didn't say I'd be giving orders." A pause as more low murmurs filled the room. The men sounded less agitated, but still undecided. At least that was the impression Lacey got.

"He didn't say you wouldn't," the belligerent man kept on. At that, the murmurs swelled to mutterings—a bad sign.

"Fact is, I shouldn't have to." This time Lacey realized a key difference between how Dunstan spoke compared to his detractor. The other man shouted to be heard; Dunstan spoke low and made the others work to listen. It made for a sort of effortless authority, forcing people to hang on his words.

I'm going to use that sometime, Lacey decided. *Against him!*

"I'm no mill worker or lumberjack to be telling anyone how to go on." Now the murmurs sounded approving, if louder.

The angry voice, which Lacey now suspected was Craig Williams, turned jeering. "If you know that, you know there's no reason to stay in Hope Falls. You're not needed or wanted."

"I want some beaver-tail soup!" Clump's distinctive, choppy pronunciation clued her in to the speaker's identity. From the round of swiftly stifled cheers, he'd also given them a hint as to what made the men so excited when they walked into the diner.

"Beaver-tail soup?" she mouthed, questioning whether she'd heard correctly. *Why would the men cheer for something like that? I'd be busy finding a way to politely avoid eating any!*

Cora and Naomi looked every bit as puzzled—and slightly repulsed—as she felt. Only Evie, with overemphatic nods and wide eyes, seemed to understand the sensational nature of beaver-tail soup. Her friend mouthed something back, but Lacey couldn't make it out. Neither did Naomi, nor Cora.

Finally, Evie leaned forward and hissed, "It's-a-delicacy!" making all the words run together in a single breath.

That, Lacey understood. Duck liver was a delicacy. Fish eggs were a delicacy. Some people considered *brains* to be a delicacy. As far as she was concerned, many a "delicacy" should never grace a plate. At least beaver-tail soup sounded edible. More than edible, if one went by the men's comments.

"We can all agree there's nothing finer than a bowl of beaver-tail soup after a long day," someone rhapsodized.

"Been pining for a taste for two years," another mourned.

Pining? Lacey stifled a giggle. She'd heard of pining for lost love, but she'd never imagined such a thing as a burly lumberjack pining for beaver-tail soup. But it sounded like several men agreed with that one—lots of yeahs all around.

Williams attempted to regain ground. "Wanting some soup isn't the same as needing the man butting into our business."

"He said he doesna plan to give orders, Williams." Riordan's brogue confirmed the identity of the rabble-rouser. "Don't mistake your personal grudge for business concerns."

An expectant hush fell over the room. Lacey could well imagine Williams's face just now. Red with humiliation, vein in his forehead pulsing with rage, teeth clenched as he fought for control of himself and the men he so badly wanted to lead.

At length he fired back his last, desperate shot. "If the bloody beaver are already dead, and he admits he's no lumberman with no plans to issue orders, what do we need him for?"

❦

"My cougar." Lacey Lyman sailed through the swinging doors the same way Chase imagined she would enter a grand ballroom.

Effective, he had to admit. Chase didn't doubt that she, along with her fellow females, waited behind those doors during the entire episode. How else could they know what was going on and precisely when to make their grand entrance?

Chase might have taken exception to the proof they doubted his ability to handle the situation. Instead, he acknowledged they listened and waited until only Williams remained squawking. With one birdbrain determined to ruffle feathers, Chase didn't mind letting the women swan in. After all, this was *their* town. Their show. He hoped it'd be an entertaining one.

"What?" Bemused by her beauty and confused by the cougar she mentioned, the men stood around like a bunch of imbeciles.

"My cougar." She stopped at his side, but her smile was for the crowd. "One showed the poor judgment to leap at me from a tree yesterday, so of course I had to shoot the poor thing."

Pandemonium. The woman's innocent comment elicited about

the same reaction as a skunk dropped in the middle of the room. No one wanted to go near the thing, but everyone wanted to talk about it. Questions flew from every corner, blanketing the room. And instead of looking mortified at the melodrama she'd caused, Lacey Lyman positively beamed. *Chaos must be her natural state.*

Abruptly, Chase wondered how any of the men got anything done with her around to distract them. Then it clicked in place. *She did it on purpose, all right. . .and made them forget Williams.* Sure enough, the rabble-rouser stood off to the side, now reduced to fuming in silence. No one paid him the slightest attention.

All that went to Miss Lyman, as she briefly and oh-so-bravely recounted the tale of her cougar attack. "And, to my surprise, there was Mr. Dunstan to help me to my feet!" She directed that dazzling bedimpled smile at him. "He made sure the kill was clean and kindly carried it back for me."

No mention that he, too, shot the cougar. No mention that she'd sustained wounds to her shoulder. Not so much as a word about her abandoned hat! If a man went by this version of the story, Lacey Lyman spotted the leaping predator, smoothly shot the beast, and nearly sidestepped the entire thing.

But I agreed to back her up when asked. Chase gritted his teeth at the realization he'd been drawn into one of her deceptions. *Worse, she uses the thing to validate my presence in Hope Falls, so even if I were the sort of man to go back on my word, I wouldn't be able to. She's devious.* He avoided the impact of her smile as she aimed it at him again. *And brilliant.*

"Isn't that so, Mr. Dunstan?" She, along with everyone in the diner—which was basically everyone in Hope Falls—waited.

Chase fought for the right balance between corroborating her account and maintaining his honesty. "All I can say, gentlemen, is that I'd watch myself around this woman. The little pistol she carries in her purse is more than decoration!"

A chorus of appreciative guffaws told him he'd hit the right note, though none of the men took his warning seriously. *Their mistake.* Chase hadn't come here to keep grown men from making fools of themselves. He'd come for answers. Tonight, however, all he'd get were questions. Of the stupid kind.

"How big was it? I mean from snout to tail, not tall. . . ."

"Didya get a yeller one, or was it one a them pumas?"

"Which one screamed louder, the cat or the girl?"

At this last, Miss Lyman stiffened. Some of her glow dimmed, and she fixed the unfortunate lack-brains with a haughty stare. "What, Mr. Gripley, makes you assume that I'd scream?"

"Because"—Mr. Gripley swallowed hard—"that's what women do, isn't it? Not all the time, but when they're attacked?"

"Miss Lyman didn't." Chase stepped in to save the man. "But she's an unusual woman, just as Hope Falls is an unusual town."

"See? Unusual can be good." Williams, not one to learn from past failures, shouldered his way forward again. "We like things the way they are, Dunstan. We don't need you changing things."

TWENTY

"Life brings change whether we wish it or not." Cora joined the conversation from where she hung back with Evie and Naomi. Lacey and Mr. Dunstan managed well so far, but who knew when that tentative truce might fail? "If the growing needs of Hope Falls conflict with your own, Mr. Williams, you have choices."

"Fewer now that Miss Thompson's off the market." His snarl inspired several men to start muttering. "And you were taken before anyone so much as stepped foot in this place. Seems the choices around here are getting pretty thin on the ground."

"Don't be sayin' things to upset the ladies!" Clump trundled forward, bullish expression on his face. "Yeah, Granger got Miss Thompson's hand—but it's a fool who talks like Miss Lyman and Miss Higgins are anything less than treasures."

"Thank you, Mr. Klumpf." Naomi's voice held more warmth than Cora had heard in days as she spoke to the short German.

"We came into this eyes open." Bear Riordan, so huge he didn't need to move forward to gain attention, joined in. "All o' us knew there were three ladies to be won, and no more."

"Williams is just sore that the cook picked Granger," someone yelled from the back. Chuckles rippled through the room.

"That's right." A high climber by the name of Bobsley, memorable for his slighter frame and crooked smile, wasn't smiling anymore. "Nothin' round here's changed 'cept you didn't win your woman. You made it awful clear which lady you wanted, Williams. Now you cain't have her, you plan to make trouble?"

"We don't allow rabble-rousers." Shorter than everyone but Clump, Lacey nevertheless managed to look down her nose at the entire room, ending with Williams. "From the moment you came to town, you aired suspicions that our ad was a hoax. We overlooked your poor manners and groundless accusations once, Mr. Williams. Don't imagine we'll be so tolerant now that you know better."

"Ah, and when I expressed those justifiable concerns, what did your men do?" Williams spoke more calmly. "I recall them throwing around words like *old, spotted, hideous,* and the like. But here I stand, bemoaning the fact one of the three ladies is taken, and I'm taken to task for being insulting?"

"It weren't so much what you said as the way it sounded." Clump flushed at the reminder of their unsuccessful attempt to keep Williams from staying in town, but didn't give up now.

"Combined with the things he's said before." Lacey rubbed her forehead with her right hand—the signal they'd agreed meant "wait and listen." She'd never used it before, which made the possibility of what she might say next slightly unnerving for Cora. Nevertheless, she and the other women dutifully waited.

Williams shifted. "Things said before can be taken different ways now. It's best to go by my meaning here and now since no one can remember the exact words on a later date."

And now Cora saw where Lacey had led him. No one she'd ever met, man or woman, had anywhere near the ability to recall conversations the way Lacey did. *She remembers things I said more than a decade ago. Williams goes back mere weeks in comparison.*

"I remember, Mr. Williams." Lacey's triumph made her glow.

"Whatever you think you remember," he hedged, "it's best to leave as bygones. Like you said, I've learned better now."

"Now, sir." Tall and balding beneath his ever-present top hat, the veteran known as Gent began what he did best. Namely, admonishing the younger hotheads for their behavior. "You took it upon yourself to throw our ill-judged phrases into the conversation. Don't cry 'bygones' when faced with your own!"

Guffaws and agreement sprinkled the crowd. If embarrassment over hasty words was universal, so was the desire to see Williams get his comeuppance.

" 'Some men know right away which women they're willing to court and which they won't' " Lacey recited. " 'I'm one of those kinds of men who knows his own mind and doesn't change it.' "

Surprise held the men in its spell. Several looked astonished, some stared at Lacey in awe of this new ability. Granger, who'd taken a dislike to Williams from the start, grinned. Williams, of course, looked poleaxed.

But the most interesting reaction, from Cora's point of view, came from Mr. Dunstan. When Lacey first claimed to be able to remember Williams's words, the men were expectant. They'd been in Hope Falls that day and had a rough idea what sort of comments Lacey might dredge up. Dunstan looked mildly amused.

His amusement faded as soon as he realized Lacey was, in fact, quoting a conversation from several weeks ago. Instead of astonishment, speculation glinted in his dark eyes as he watched her put Williams in his place. Mr. Dunstan didn't give Lacey the admiring gazes the other men did, but he stood transfixed anyway. For the first time, Cora found herself wondering what had gone on between the two of them when they met in the forest.

"The lassie remembers it true." Riordan clearly approved. "And we all ken which woman you chose to court, Williams."

Williams kept his jaw shut, but a muscle worked as someone jeered, "Doesn't that mean you should be moving on?"

"Or have you changed your mind after all?" Lacey didn't challenge him. Maybe she should have, but instead she asked the question that gave Williams the opportunity to stay on.

"As Miss Thompson said, life brought that change. I'm willing to adapt to it." A wolfish smile spread across his bearded face. "Seems to me, a woman who pays close attention to what I say is the woman I should have courted from the start!"

Chase tensed. *Williams shouldn't be allowed anywhere near her.* It didn't have anything to do with their differences in background either. Miss Lyman had bested the bully, but Williams wouldn't leave with his tail tucked between his legs.

No. The man wanted to win, he wanted a wife, and he wanted to make her pay for it. His predatory hunger as he eyed Miss Lyman was tinged with malice. *Like a cat tracking a mouse.*

Some of the other men seemed to pick up on the same thing. A low rumble of dissent grew to more audible grumbles. But, as Granger had filled him in, Williams was a bull-of-the-woods. Leader of at least one work crew with an established temper, he carried enough weight to quell any outright challenge.

Sheep. Dunstan shook his head, disgusted with the lot of them. *A man determined to win her wouldn't leave it to Miss Lyman to refuse Williams. He'd stake his claim now by objecting.*

Yet here stood more than a dozen burly men, doing nothing.

The problem didn't lie with Miss Lyman. These fools couldn't know whether she schemed her way into Hope Falls. All they saw was a wealthy, beautiful woman willing to work alongside them to make a go of this sawmill. They wanted her—Chase could all but sniff it in the air. But they were cowards.

Riordan stepped directly in front of Williams and shook his head. At about the same time, a fellow with round glasses pushed forward from way in the back. No lumberjack here. Everything from his slight build to his neatly pressed suit to the words he spoke set him apart from the men surrounding him.

"Now listen here, Williams. Miss Lyman ought to be a man's first choice." He cast a nervous glance toward Granger and swallowed. Hard. "If he's to enjoy courting her, I mean to say. Thinking she would accept the attentions of a man who pursues her only after he fails with another is preposterous."

This one wouldn't last a minute if Williams started swinging, but Williams didn't look inclined to hit him. And Chase knew it wasn't just because the smitten engineer ranked higher. It was because Williams plain out didn't need to bother.

The engineer's words didn't put the upstart in place; they sent a ripple of unease through the room. With Miss Thompson no longer available, every man who'd declared an interest in her found himself looking at the remaining women instead. They knew good and well that if Williams went, they could be next.

"Are you planning to kick Clump out along with me then?" Williams played on their discomfort. "For that matter, how many more of you will be gone when the next bride's off the table?"

"Don't be silly." Miss Lyman's laugh tinkled through the throng. If Chase hadn't been standing close enough to see how tense she'd become, he'd have believed her little act. The other men perked up for her decision. "We foresaw this little issue. That's why we asked you all to name two of us early on."

The crowd relaxed at her reminder. They were safe.

"Williams didn't." Granger spoke for the first time since he'd announced Chase's position. "Only man here who didn't."

Williams looked like he'd been kicked in the teeth, but recovered quickly. "That's because a man should only focus on one woman at a time—then, once she's won, for a lifetime."

Clever comeback. Chase appraised the manipulation and found another reason why the lumbermen might not have spoken up. Brawls would earn them the boot, but he doubted any of these men could match Williams for verbal sparring. *What a shame.*

"That's that then." Miss Higgins, her low voice carrying well enough for everyone to hear, put an end to the disagreements. "No one's leaving but Granger. Until his return, Mr. Dunstan will help keep the peace and fill the stewpan."

"Thanks to him, tomorrow night we'll serve beaver-tail soup." Miss Thompson—the cook—gestured to the tables lining the room, already outfitted with plates and the like. "Now, if you'll get seated, we'll start bringing out your supper."

"If I may ask before you leave?" The supercilious, reedy voice belonged to a thin man Chase hadn't seen before. Stooped as though trying to escape notice and far too pale to be a worker, he stuck out anyway. With sparse blond hair tufted around his forehead and glasses, slipping down his nose toward a twitching mustache, he gave off an air of a nervous rabbit.

"Yes, Mr. Draxley?" Miss Lyman didn't like the man.

Chase read it in the way her shoulders stiffened and her chin rose. She looked down at him with the appearance of polite interest, but Chase could tell she wasn't inclined to waste much time on Mr. Draxley. *How did he get on her bad side?*

"We're all wondering..." He went ahead and asked the question on everyone's minds. "What is on the menu this evening?"

In his interest over the answer, Chase stopped wondering what Draxley had done wrong. During the entire time they'd been preoccupied with Williams, delicious smells had filled the air.

"Fried chicken, baked potatoes, coleslaw, and buns."

"Fried chicken!" Men scrambled for seats as the women whisked into the kitchen. At Granger's nudge, Chase followed.

The second he hit those swinging doors, the smell made his mouth water. Things looked even better. Platters heaped high with golden-fried chicken waited on a table next to baskets overflowing with plump buns. Bowls held the potatoes and massive quantities of coleslaw, none of which would be wasted.

"Now that it's official." Granger took the beaver to the largest pantry Chase ever saw. "Welcome to Hope Falls."

∞

"Haven't you left yet?" Braden's truculent greeting warmed Lacey's heart the next morning. "With you not showing your face in three days, I'd started to hope you had a change of heart."

"In a short time, we've managed to hire on a crew of workers, chosen a mill site, and are pulling up the stumps to finish clearing it. By now I hoped you'd want this sawmill enough to stop asking us to leave." Lacey pulled up a seat beside the bed, refusing to let him disconcert her.

He harrumphed. "Between Evie's cooking for motivation and Granger's know-how to get things moving, you've gotten farther than I expected. I'd say you're lucky, but we both know better."

Not even five minutes, and he's angling to bring up that incident with Twyler. She gritted her teeth. Some small part of her had hoped her older brother, whom she used to look up to, would be supportive after her ordeal. Failing that, she'd try to avoid the worst of the conversation by skirting tricky topics. *I'd best pretend I don't know where he's heading with that.*

"It takes more than luck to start up a business. What you refer to is actually the result of research and planning." *My research into how to save Hope Falls from becoming a ghost town. My plan to advertise for husbands with sawmill experience.* Lacey wavered for a moment. *All right. That didn't go according to plan, exactly, but having the men reply to our ad in person brought us the workers we needed. If they'd responded by telegraph, as instructed, we'd have needed to hire some on.*

"You stole my property and dragged Cora and the others up here on the vague hope you could break into the lumber market." Braden no longer looked petulant. He was spitting mad. "Any success isn't yours. It's my land and Granger's effort!"

"The site for the mill and most of the lumber surrounding it are not your land!" Lacey burst out. "When word came of the collapse, we found our investment in Hope Falls next to worthless. I wondered about the lumber, did a great deal of reading, and asked some of Papa's contacts for their advice—same as you when you started to think about buying into the mine."

Braden opened his mouth, ready to refute what she said when he had no idea what things were like after news of his death. Lacey didn't let him get a word in; she kept going.

"Only when I was convinced of the project's potential did I move forward. I made the arrangements to purchase the other half of Miracle Mining and the surrounding land. Now when I've begun to prove my decision worthwhile, you call it luck? This took painstaking effort, thorough research, and personal investment."

And I did it all alone, thinking you were dead. Lacey felt a stinging in the back of her nose, the earliest warning of tears. She wiggled her nose and pushed the sentiment away.

"Ah, but that's just it." Braden leaned forward, eyes snapping. "It wasn't a personal investment at all. You used *my* inheritance to fund this project. And when you discovered you had no right, you contrived a way to keep control of *my* money."

TWENTY-ONE

There. He finally came out and said it. Lacey drew a shuddering breath. Oh, Braden had been griping about her use of the family funds since he learned she'd sold Lyman Place. Even worse, he'd been caterwauling about taking back control of their finances since the second he heard Lacey held the reigns.

But until now he hadn't tried to claim all of Hope Falls.

Lacey started smoothing her skirts and rearranging the way its folds draped around her chair. *It wasn't pessimistic to take those legal measures.* But that didn't make her feel any better about needing to implement safeguards against her own brother.

"You're wrong." She fought to keep her voice level. Whether she fought not to yell or not to cry, even Lacey couldn't say. "I used *our* inheritance. I know I invested the bulk of mine in the mercantile and its goods, but you sank your funds into your half of the mines." She held up a hand to keep him silent. "But aside from those, our father left us each certain assets. You were given the house, and I was given a dowry. That dowry became accessible four months ago. When I reached my eighteenth birthday, you no

486

longer held it in trust." *Not your money. Mine.*

Braden started, obviously unprepared for that reminder. Or perhaps he'd not realized she'd reached her majority in his absence. Either way, the news didn't sit well with him at all.

"You sold Lyman Place." The pain of that loss sat on his face for a fleeting moment, almost making her regret it. Then his jaw thrust forward. "As you said, that was mine and mine alone. Whatever the sale price, I'll expect every cent of it."

"I never touched it." Hurt beyond what she expected, Lacey stared at him. "Lyman Place was sold because we couldn't transport you there, and we thought you needed care." *We thought you needed us.* "Also, when the mines failed, your investors and creditors came crawling out of the woodwork. There weren't funds enough to maintain the house indefinitely."

"But somehow you scraped together the sum to buy land here." His sneer, Lacey knew, covered his shame and anger that his own grand venture failed. "I guess I should be grateful you took what was left and reinvested in Hope Falls. Seems I'll be a wealthy man when the doctor clears me and the attorneys give control of Lyman assets back to me. And they will, you know."

"In a manner of speaking." The moment she'd dreaded had finally come. "They'll return control of Braden Lyman's assets to you. These include the money earned from the sale of Lyman Place, one-half of the land formerly owned by Miracle Mining, and one-third of the property sustaining the new sawmill."

"Not so fast, little sister." Braden slapped the bed. "You're forgetting something. Since you're an unmarried woman, you can't own anything. I'll control all of your share. And since Evie and Naomi invested in my name, I'll control theirs, too. That means it all belongs to me after all."

Lacey sighed. "We were afraid you'd try something like that. It's why I consulted Mr. Rountree about this very topic." She saw her brother pale, as though he suspected. "My house, my mercantile, my half of the mines, and my third of the sawmill lands have been placed in a new trust in the guardianship of Mr. Rountree himself. Not you. My approval is required for any transactions until the time of my marriage, when management is transferred to my husband. The same has been done for Naomi and Evie's houses, Evie's diner, and their shares of the mill."

He was silent for a long time, wrestling with the news she'd given him. And, more importantly, wrestling with the question she'd left unanswered.

Finally, he lost the battle. His shoulders hunched forward, and Braden looked every bit as tired as Lacey felt. The lines around his eyes and the grooves bracketing his mouth deepened, and she decided to ask the doctor to give him something for pain when she left. He'd been overly agitated, moved around too much, and his shoulder and legs must be paining him even more than usual.

But it seemed something bothered him more because the brother she'd always admired finally asked a question Lacey wanted him to. "You didn't mention Cora. What about her?"

"My sister refused Lacey's generous offer." Evie stormed into Braden's room.

Jake watched her go and silently debated following her for a moment. Overhearing what sounded like the end of Lacey explaining how she'd divided her property from her brother's made for poor timing. He'd missed too much to know the particulars of the conversation. The main thing he'd caught was how badly Braden needed another man in the room, now that Evie'd joined in. *Actually, he needs to shelve his pride and come to his senses.* Barring that, the conversation promised to pit Braden's pride against Evie's protective instincts for her little sister.

With news of how much Twyler's leg had improved during the past two days and the doctor's estimation that he could be moved tomorrow, Jake didn't want anything to upset Evie. He wouldn't have much time with her before leaving, and Jake fully intended to enjoy every minute of it. *Right after this conversation.*

"What do you mean, she turned it down?" Braden's roar didn't ask a question so much as demand an answer. Immediately.

"Sounds pretty self-explanatory to me." Jake shot the other man a warning glance. They may be business associates and even friends, but he wouldn't allow Braden Lyman to shout at Evie.

"I offered Cora her pick of the houses in town and the same type of trust to protect it and her share of the sawmill." Miss Lyman's answer didn't soothe anyone's ruffled feathers.

In fact, it was the one time Jake had seen Evie and Braden in complete agreement. Well, *almost* complete agreement.

Braden blamed the women. "Why did you let her turn you down? Contact Mr. Rountree and have him draw it up immediately."

"Why did you put her in a position where Lacey even needed to make the offer?" Evie shot back. "Don't you yell at your sister for trying to soften the blows *you've* dealt mine!"

This comment struck home. Jake could see the muscles at Braden's temples throbbing when he shook his head. How much longer would it take for Braden to stop making his own injuries more important than the woman he loved? If he wanted to jilt Cora and really didn't want her anymore, the man wouldn't feel so guilty.

"It's not my place to make Cora's decisions for her," Lacey pointed out. "As a friend, I can offer my assistance. As the sister of the man who's trying so hard to jilt her, I can't offer much comfort. She sees accepting the trust as a betrayal."

Braden's misery was palpable. "A betrayal of what?"

"Of her faith that you'll recover, you dunderhead." Evie raked her fingers through her hair, unleashing a few glorious mahogany curls. "Cora believes you'll remember how much you love each other and start acting like an honorable man instead of a thwarted child." She left off talking and settled for glaring.

"You know how loyal she is," Lacey put in. She paused, her voice softening as though sharing a secret. "I think she refuses it because Cora equates that trust with giving up on you."

"She should!" Braden and Evie exclaimed in tandem then looked at each other in surprise. For a moment neither spoke.

"No she shouldn't." Jake decided he'd found the time to step into the argument—and hopefully settle it. "If she stops looking at it as a good-faith gesture, she'll let Lacey do it."

"I meant she should give up." Evie colored at how stark the words sounded, but quickly rallied. "She should know by now that he's not going to be the man who won her heart. Never again."

Jake winced at the way she'd said it. He, Evie, and Lacey knew she referred to Braden's surly demands and blunt treatment of Cora. But Jake knew Braden would think otherwise. Although his broken legs were mending, he'd never be the same carefree, able-bodied man who'd once joined his workers in the mines. As far as Braden's narrow vision could see, the best way to protect and provide for Cora was to make her free to marry someone else.

For his part, Jake had an inkling of why Braden thought that way. It wasn't exactly easy to fall in love with a woman as fiercely loving, loyal, and godly as the Thompson sisters. *Evie deserves better than me, too.* He looked at where she sat, hair tantalizingly mussed, frustration stamped on her beautiful, expressive face. *Difference between me and Braden is that I'll become that better man before I even think of letting her go.*

"Step back and tell me how it looks," Miss Lyman directed the bespectacled engineer. Perched atop a ladder, holding a sign advertising FRESH-GROUND COFFEE, she couldn't see that her eager helper was looking all right. But not at the sign.

"I'm not sure." Mr. Lawson hedged a series of instructions, watching her movements with unconcealed interest. "Try moving it a bit to the right. No, down a smidge. And to the left."

Chase strode through the wide-open door, silently making his way to the engineer's side. "Like what you see, Lawson?" He'd spoken low to make sure Miss Lyman didn't hear his warning.

"Oh!" The other man jumped a bit then began spluttering. His ears began to turn red. "Helping Miss Lyman get the sign straight, don't you know. She asked me for my expert opinion."

"I know exactly what you were doing," Chase told him. "Don't let me catch you doing anything like it again."

"What?" Up on the ladder, all trim ankles and round curves, Miss Lyman remained oblivious. Or maybe she didn't. A gently bred woman would know better than to shimmy up a ladder and show off her petticoats. "I didn't quite make that out, Mr. Lawson."

Maybe she wanted to catch Lawson's eye. The thought had merit. Out of all the men in town, the engineer boasted the most education, income, and fine manners. *Could she be that scheming?*

She leaned farther over and nudged up one corner, giving an improved view of her backside as she did so. "Good enough?"

"Excellent." Doubts driven away by the show she put on, Chase answered for the mortified engineer. "Come on down now."

She whipped around when he spoke, looking down at him in surprise. "Mr. Dunstan? I didn't know you'd joined us." She hurried down the ladder, bustled over, and looked upward.

For the first time since he'd walked into the tableau, Chase evaluated the sign. After Lawson's haphazard directions, the thing hung catawampus, as though tacked up by a drunk giant.

"That'll never do." Puzzlement colored her features as she turned to face them. She noticed the engineer's impressively red ears. "Don't worry, Mr. Lawson. We'll get it right next time."

While she consoled her embarrassed admirer, Chase mounted the ladder, untacked the drooping corner of the sign, and straightened the thing. Done in an instant, he hopped down.

"Much better!" She gave Chase a considering look. "But why did you pronounce its earlier placement as excellent?"

"Ladies shouldn't be climbing ladders." His reply made her smile vanish, and suddenly Chase remembered part of what he'd heard her muttering about in the forest. All that stuff about how limited women were and that she was capable of doing things men thought she couldn't. His words wouldn't be taken well.

"I assure you, Mr. Dunstan, I am fully able to climb my own ladder. You might take a page from Mr. Lawson, who encouraged me to ascend so he could gauge the angles of the sign from below. *He*"—her voice got very sniffy—"obviously thinks me capable."

He wanted an eyeful, and you gave it to him. But Lawson's guilty look confirmed Miss Lyman's explanation of how she came to be atop the ladder. She hadn't plotted the scenario after all—simply been naive enough to undertake it. Relief cooled his temper enough that he offered no argument, only a warning.

"Can and should are two different things, ma'am." He shot a dark look at Lawson, whom he'd have to watch more closely in the future. "Some dangers have nothing to do with your abilities."

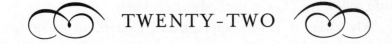

TWENTY-TWO

But I should have concerned myself more for your welfare than for pleasing you by getting the sign precisely aligned." Mr. Lawson resolutely ignored Chase's incredulity and addressed himself solely to Miss Lyman. "Ladders are perilous for ladies. Skirts, while fetching, aren't constructed for climbing." His voice grew fainter as he finished, most likely because he realized he'd said exactly the wrong thing to win Miss Lyman.

"Your concern is duly noted, Mr. Lawson." She smoothed the front of those very skirts as she spoke. As she did so, Chase realized the motion was becoming familiar. It didn't bode well for the engineer. "Though I am dismayed to realize I gave you far too much credit by believing you recognized my ability to perform the task at hand. My portion of which, I believe, I accomplished handily." She left unspoken the accusation that Mr. Lawson's direction as to the placement of the sign left something to be desired. Miss Lyman didn't need to say it.

"I say." Lawson's ears brightened as he began to try to dig his way out of the hole he'd jumped in. "Your work ethic is much to be admired, Miss Lyman. I merely meant that anyone would be hampered by this sort of attire." He made a flourishing gesture meant to indicate her well-tailored suit.

It made Chase take a harder look. Cut closer to the body without the fullness caused by bustles, these skirts looked less cumbersome than what she'd worn to go tromping through the forest. To be fair, the more billowy style would have made climbing a ladder difficult. But the lack of extra fabric made this outfit follow the lines of her body more closely.

"My attire is always appropriate." Everything about her bristled as she defended her clothing, of all things. "This walking suit, in particular, is designed to allow ease and economy of motion without the burden of excess fabric. It's a sensible choice for working in the store today with so much to be done!"

Chase frowned. *They're more sensible, but more revealing.* Little wonder Lawson grew fascinated with watching her bend and sway to shift the sign. Truth be told, Chase would have taken a moment to enjoy the view if Lawson hadn't ogled her first.

A woman shouldn't wear something so different as to make a man look at her all over again. Clothes were made for covering the body and protecting it from the elements, not attracting attention. But the fact was, Chase had been here for three days and not seen her wear the same thing twice. Three dresses, each in pretty colors with flounces or bows or lace to draw the eye.

Hadn't Granger mentioned something about her being more put out by her ruined dress than by the way her kidnapper marched her off at gunpoint and held a knife to her throat?

"You have a lot of dresses." The statement escaped before he thought it over. *At least I didn't come right out and say she had too many.* Chase waited for her to turn that glower on him.

"Precisely!" An enchanting smile lit the daft woman's face. "Something for every occasion and activity so I won't be 'hampered,' as Mr. Lawson so gracelessly described it."

"I meant no insult! Skirts allow less motion by their very design, requiring grace and discretion." The engineer protested vehemently, as though he held strong opinions on a topic requiring very little opinion or discussion. "You epitomize that grace, and each style you choose reflects your feminine beauty."

Chase looked around the jumbled mess of the store, wondering whether anything might serve as a gag before the man said anything else florid and foolish. *It's dung-brains like this that give women starched-up opinions of themselves.*

Spotting nothing offhand, he glanced at Miss Lyman. She'd yet to respond to Lawson's overblown compliments, so Chase figured she'd been stunned into silence. But those raised brows looked more disbelieving than flattered. *Good for her.*

"Thank you for coming to my aid, Mr. Lawson." It was unmistakably a dismissal, and the engineer took it as such.

"Call on me anytime, Miss Lyman. Particularly if you encounter any. . ."—he slid a sideways glance toward Chase, making the pause meaningful before he finished—"difficulty."

If I encounter any difficulty? Lacey bit the inside of her cheek to keep from laughing at Mr. Lawson's earnest offer. *I'm surrounded by men! They create difficulties on a daily basis.*

Not the least of which was their affinity for interrupting her ability to carry out her own business. Then, of course, they proceeded to dictate how and what she should be doing instead. Today was a perfect example. When Mr. Lawson wandered into the store, she'd seen fit to enlist his aid hanging the coffee sign.

Instead of climbing up the ladder and hoisting the heavy thing himself, as any gentleman would, he enthusiastically directed her to hold it aloft, so he could better judge its baseline. In the normal way of things, Lacey wouldn't mind a reason to climb a ladder. As a petite woman, she enjoyed the sense of height.

But after the past few days, her shoulder ached. Worse, Mr. Lawson turned out to be the most horrid sort of perfectionist. Why, she'd shifted and nudged and angled that sign six ways from Sunday trying to satisfy his sense of aesthetic. And in the end, she'd gratefully descended to find the thing slanted.

It did little to bolster her faith in the man's skills as an engineer. If he didn't come so highly recommended, with Granger having worked with him before to judge the results firsthand, Lacey would seriously consider looking elsewhere. For now she'd settle for seeing him leave the store—and her—in peace. Things lay hodgepodge in heaps and piles everywhere, and with the caliber of his assistance, the mess would double!

"I'll keep your offer in mind, Mr. Lawson." She tilted her head. Toward the door. Hopefully he'd take the hint.

"Anytime," he repeated before finally taking his leave.

Lacey started to breathe a sigh of relief when she noticed another interloper. This one stood amid a jumble of goods, intently sniffing a tin pail of None-Such Peanut Butter. She watched, thunderstruck, as Decoy decided he liked it enough to nose the thing over and start *licking the bottom of the bucket.*

"What," she gritted out, "is that dog doing in my store?"

"Where I go, he goes." Mr. Dunstan snapped his fingers, and the dog abandoned its exploration and trotted to his side. The man had the sheer nerve to look surprised at the question. "We already agreed. You called him well-behaved and welcome."

Before he started licking the canned goods. Lacey closed her eyes and fought for calm. "In the house, Mr. Dunstan. Your dog is welcome in the *house.* I've noticed you do not attempt to bring Decoy into the diner." *Evie would've thrown a conniption.*

The man looked supremely unconcerned. "He waits outside

for me. Decoy's well trained, but even I can't expect him to just drool when platters of fried chicken go by. I'm not cruel."

"Not cruel, but nigh unto impossible!" She pointed toward the upended tin of peanut butter. "I can't have him slobbering all over the foodstuffs every time you step through the door!"

He glanced at the peanut butter then took a long, considering look around the place. "Ordinarily, I'd tell you he won't. I trained him not to touch anything on shelves. Things on the ground or in junk piles constitute fair game."

"So it's *my* fault you can't control your horse of a dog, but choose to bring him into the store regardless?"

"Didn't say so." The dratted man looked like he was swallowing a smile. "I didn't expect someone so meticulous in other aspects would own a store that looks like someone picked it up, flipped it upside down, and gave it a good shaking."

Lacey decided to ignore the accuracy of his description. Agreeing would only encourage him, after all. What she needed was to get him out of the way and get things in order. Then the next time he brought Decoy on the premises and the dog so much as sniffed something he shouldn't, she'd throw them both out!

"For your information," she declared in tones that brooked no argument, "I've not yet opened for business. Today I opened the doors solely to capture some fresh air while I worked."

All the goods and displays she'd so carefully ordered should have been neatly stacked and sorted as per her explicit instructions. When she'd first arrived in Hope Falls and opened her mercantile, Lacey couldn't believe her eyes. Not only were none of the shelves up, but the main counters sat shoved against the walls. Reaching them required climbing over minor mountains of goods that had been removed from their packing boxes and crates only to be dumped unceremoniously across the floor.

No rhyme nor reason dictated the location of anything, dust

covered half of it, and the entire thing posed a Sisyphean task Lacey hadn't been able to make much time for. Too much happened all at once when they arrived in an abandoned town suddenly full of eager bachelors and a brother she no longer recognized.

"I can't believe you unpacked everything this way." Something akin to compassion softened his features, and once again Lacey was struck by how handsome Mr. Dunstan was. Or would be, if he trimmed his hair, became better acquainted with a razor, and stopped firing her temper every time they spoke.

"It doesn't matter," she sighed. "We take what's given and either triumph over it or let it defeat us. I don't intend to be defeated by something I can change, Mr. Dunstan."

He lapsed into that silent-but-looking-too-closely-for-comfort habit she'd noticed before. Rather than let his taciturn lack of response make her fidget, Lacey reached for the apron she'd removed before tackling the ladder. Its overlong ties could well have tripped her if they'd come undone.

As she tied it around her waist once more, she tried to stop herself from wondering what he was thinking. To distract herself, Lacey looked at the dog now lying placidly on a bare patch of floor. His brindled coat made it less obvious, but when she made a closer study, she could see areas of matted fur and the occasional burr clinging on. She wrinkled her nose. *He needs a bath. Maybe once the store is organized and Decoy's been properly cleaned, it won't be such a problem to let him inside.*

"Somehow"—Dunstan's voice snapped her attention back to the man—"I get the idea not much could defeat you."

But I will, if need be. Chase kept the last part to himself, curious to hear Miss Lyman's response to his statement.

She gave him a long, measured look. "Likewise."

No simpering, no effusive thanks, no coy denials for Miss Lyman. Her simple acceptance of the compliment, and matter-of-fact return of it, pleased him. He nodded in acknowledgment.

Then he rolled up his sleeves. Originally Chase wandered in hoping to find Granger and somehow work Braden Lyman into the conversation. Now he found himself reluctant to leave. Something in the way she'd declared her intention to triumph over the bad circumstances thrust upon her resonated with him. This sort of determination he not only understood, he approved.

She shouldn't be doing this alone. There were too many heavy items to be moved. Too many ways she could hurt herself, if she hadn't already overstressed that shoulder she kept ignoring. The place had too much. . .everything. And none of it where it belonged. As far as Chase could see, the wisest course of action would be to move everything out of the way, set up the shelves and displays, and sort all the goods onto them later.

"Essentially," she began hesitantly, as though unsure whether or not he intended to pitch in, "I planned to shift everything toward the front then set up the racks and counter."

"Smart thinking." Without another word, they set to work. Whatever sat in their path, they either scooted or carried out of it. Pails of Partridge's Pure Lard stacked alongside Velvetina Talcum Powder. Bottles of Liquid Doom insecticide loomed threateningly over Sawyer's Animal Crackers. Carter's Indelible Ink smugly sat atop Hansdown Hand Cleaner.

Irony earned a few smiles, but Chase took particular pleasure in tucking Shaker's Choice Garden Seed packets next to cans of Birdseye Sorghum. The Birdseye, a new product, came labeled with a single eye flanked by two swooping birds.

"Looks like they're going to peck it out." He expected the comment to elicit some sort of horrified reaction. Dainty ladies didn't think about such things. Nor were they acceptable topics for the sort of civil conversation she sounded so fond of.

Instead she laughed. "Do you know, the same thought crossed my mind! And somehow the eye follows you no matter where you move. It looks like it's watching everything."

"Let's test it." Chase climbed over mounds of rope, coffee, and tubes of Cow Clean to perch one of the Birdseye tins atop a tall shelf. After returning to the cleared area, he looked at the thing. It stared back from beneath a single, arched eyebrow.

"Eerie, isn't it?" Miss Lyman slid to the far left of the bare area. "I'd swear it's still looking at me even over here."

"Can't be." Chase went to the far right to test it. "It's watching this way. Only one eye, so it can only stare one way."

"Oh?" She scoffed. "Trade me then, and see for yourself."

He obliged, only to discover she'd been right.

"I like to think it has a blind spot somewhere." She sounded downright cheerful. "And when this whole place is cleaned up, I'll be able to walk far enough away to find it!"

"It's got the advantage." Chase went back to work.

"What advantage?" Miss Lyman tarried over by some canvas.

"It doesn't blink."

"I'll beat it anyway." She laughed as she said it. "You don't know me yet, Mr. Dunstan. But when you do, you'll learn there's no obstacle big enough when I set my mind on something."

Chase felt the day's lightheartedness drop right out from under him. *No obstacle big enough. . . What, exactly, did Miss Lacey Lyman set her mind to? What if Miracle Mining was an obstacle standing in the way of this grand sawmill idea of hers?*

He didn't have any answers. But he wouldn't let her charm him into forgetting that he'd come to Hope Falls for a reason.

I can't afford to let her become a blind spot.

TWENTY-THREE

Lacey took particular care preparing for dinner that night. The walking suit she'd worn earlier held more dust than fabric after hours spent shuffling items in the store. She'd taken it outside, flapping the skirts to release much of the debris, but henceforth the outfit would be worn strictly for work.

Tonight we're having a party! Lacey wore the anticipation around her like a bubble bearing her toward happiness. How long had it been since she went to a celebration of any kind? She couldn't even remember with any certainty except that it was before news of the mine collapse. When she'd been told her brother died alongside the majority of his best workers.

At first, mourning protected her from having to attend social gatherings and smile through the staggering loss. But even when they received news of her brother's miraculous survival, she'd not taken the time to celebrate properly. Her brother waited, alone and unable to move, thousands of miles away. Festivities would have to wait until after she'd seen to the seemingly endless preparations necessary to join him.

And of course, once they arrived in Hope Falls, the onslaught of suitors turned everything on its ear once more. Besides, no one felt like celebrating Braden's survival once they realized the Braden they knew had been replaced by this belligerent, selfish dictator. *We mourned his death, but who would rejoice about the hash he's making over his life now?*

Tonight they'd give Granger a cheery send-off and best wishes for his journey tomorrow. Lacey didn't envy the man—she'd heard enough of Twyler's ranting rambles to know she wouldn't care to spend days cooped up in a train car alongside him.

Beaver-tail soup took pride of place on the menu. Lacey had watched in the early hours of the morning, before daylight strengthened its hold on the town, as Evie began preparations. Those prized tails, thick flaps covered with protective cross-hatching, had begun to exude a sort of oil. This, Evie explained, made for part of its distinctively gamy flavor.

It didn't sound appetizing. It didn't look appetizing either. Not even after Evie plopped the things in her soup pots to eke out the most flavor. When she fished them back out to remove the underlying meat and bone, at least they weren't so slippery. *Ugh.* Lacey grimaced at the memory. *How that is supposed to make some mythically delicious meal is beyond me.*

For her part, she looked forward to a slice of one of the layered lemon cakes Evie spent most of the day baking. If she did say so herself, Lacey thought she'd done a superior job icing the treats with sweet-cream frosting. The dessert, if not the much-prized soup, would be both delicious and beautiful.

She tugged free another golden ringlet to better frame her face and decided she was ready. The maroon-striped sateen evening dress, though laughably simple when compared to ball gowns she wore back in Charleston, was ostentatious by Hope Falls standards. Lacey thought tonight deserved her fanciest dress.

Only her wedding garments, carefully tucked away, topped it.

The world seems brighter when one is well dressed. The thought, long familiar, seemed especially true tonight. How else to explain why her stomach finally ceased its anxious roiling? The constant worries accompanying her faded in the expectancy of a merry evening. *And Mr. Lawson will see that Mr. Dunstan is correct; I do have a dress appropriate for every occasion!*

Leaving her room, she went to check on Naomi. Her cousin and longtime companion had dressed for the occasion as well. "You look smashing! Blue always becomes you so well, Naomi."

Her cousin eyed Lacey's dress. "You quite put me in the shade, my dear." Naomi's smile made the compliment sincere.

"Stop putting yourself down," Lacey chided. Her cousin, while lovely with her single streak of shocking white cresting her midnight locks, never seemed to accept a compliment.

"I didn't." Naomi looked uncomfortable, as though uncertain how to say what she wished. "I've not seen you look so well since back in Charleston, Lacey. You must be very relieved to know that Granger removes Twyler from Hope Falls tomorrow."

"I'm certain we all will be glad to see the last of him." Her fingers skimmed over the healing cut at the base of her throat as she tried to change the topic. "It's always nice to find a reason to celebrate. Would you like to borrow my pearl hairpin? It matches your broach and would look wonderful, I'm sure."

"Not tonight." Her cousin rose from her dressing table to join Lacey at the door. "Evie and Cora are already decked out and waiting for us back in the kitchen." The women had changed in shifts, so as not to leave the food unattended.

The men of Hope Falls, while not thieves, would make short work of anything edible left unwatched and unlocked. With the promise of their beloved soup—no matter that Lacey couldn't understand the appeal—the temptation to sneak a sample would

prove too great. And having to exclude anyone over poor behavior
tonight would put a damper on the festivities for everybody.

They fetched Mrs. Nash, whose unborn child had grown so
greatly in the past few weeks she'd taken to napping most of the
day. The extra sleep appeared to be doing her some good since
she looked bright-eyed and rested as they headed to the kitchen.

When they drew close, they spotted a herd of hungry
lumberjacks milling outside the kitchen. Since the front door to
the diner remained locked until Evie declared things ready, they
crowded around the back door like a jumble of eager puppies.

"Can't I have a taste?" Bobsley wheedled loudly.

"Of course you can!" Lacey swept past them through the door.
"You and everyone else—as soon as it's set on the table."

Some groans, but no one contested the rules. Riordan, who'd
pushed back the group so the women could get through, pulled
off his hat. "You ladies look a sight for sore eyes, I'm thinkin'."

Belatedly, a few others whipped their hats off and began
a chorus of accolades. Lacey ignored the rest to smile at the
powerfully built Scots-Irishman. "Thank you, Mr. Riordan."

Chase saw the smile she aimed at Riordan and decided the man's
sheer size kept him on his feet. That smile aimed to single him
out, but even more to exclude the other men in the crowd.

*First she finds Lawson and invites him to help her in the store,
then she turns her attention to Riordan.* Either the woman was
fickle or playing a very deep game. If she didn't intend to marry
any of them, the easiest way to avoid it was to play them against
each other. Then, if a man became territorial about the others
sniffing around her, he'd be out of the running for good.

If he didn't need to find Granger, Chase would've turned back
and waited for the beckon of the dinner bell. As things stood,

his friend planned to leave in the morning—this time with the doctor's approval—and it would be Chase's last chance to slide some pointed questions his way. Granger knew more about this town and its strange occupants than he'd let on.

It didn't take much thinking to deduce that Granger sat in the kitchen, soaking in the smiles of his fiancée and the smells of her good cooking. Chase wouldn't mind stepping into that kitchen himself. Home-cooked meals and homey warmth eluded his campsite fires. Getting by on his own food for so long gave a man a healthy appreciation for Miss Thompson's domain.

What he did mind were all the people who felt the same way. The rough-edged passel of lumbermen pressing their noses to the door wouldn't take kindly to watching Chase walk on through. The front door stayed locked tight—he'd already tried coaxing it open, but the stubborn thing remained as obdurate as anyone connected to the Miracle Mining Company when asked a question.

Time ran out as he walked around the building in search of another entry point. Once dinner got underway, there'd be no getting Granger alone. No open windows allowed access, but he found a third door in the back of the place. *Maybe...*

Yep. This knob turned. He pushed it open and slid inside, closing it quietly behind him. It took a moment for him to be sure none of the other men had followed, but that allowed his eyes to adjust to the darkness of what seemed a very small room.

The pantry. He figured they'd put in the door for ease of loading goods after they arrived on the train. Not only did it make for a smart design, it turned out to be very useful. Reaching forward to keep from smacking into anything, Chase made his way to the second door and groped for the handle. *There.*

"'Scuse me," he said to anyone and everyone in the bustling work space. No sense frightening them with his sudden appearance. After the dark of the storeroom, the cheery brightness of the kitchen made him narrow his eyes so he could get his bearings.

"Mr. Dunstan?" An older woman Chase recognized by sight but not introduction tilted her head curiously. Not one of the four from the ad, Granger had said she came with her husband when he called McCreedy to round out his number of team bosses.

"Mrs. McCreedy," he acknowledged. Scanning around the room, he spotted an unfamiliar face. A heavily pregnant woman balanced herself on a stool near the swinging doors. Something about her seemed familiar, but it wasn't until her ears turned red under his scrutiny that he made the connection to the engineer.

"Mr. Dunstan." Miss Higgins glided over to perform introductions. "This is Mrs. Nash. Mr. Lawson's widowed sister."

No need to wonder why she added the part about her being a widow. These women already faced enough danger from men assuming they were less than ladies since they placed that ad. An unmarried mother-to-be in town would reflect poorly on them.

"A pleasure." He doffed his hat and offered a quick nod. Come to think of it, one of the women had mentioned that Mr. Lawson shared their house. Chase had just forgotten that the smitten engineer lived below stairs to better watch over his sister. Supposedly the arrangement helped protect the ladies.

But what of the man's obvious interest in Miss Lyman? It wouldn't be difficult to abuse his position in the household and take advantage of a sleeping woman. It hadn't happened yet, as evidenced by Miss Lyman requesting Lawson's help earlier, but it still could. *Are they all blind to how he looks at her?*

Abruptly he realized he'd missed Mrs. Nash's response. The woman looked at him expectantly. "Er—" He floundered a moment before coming up with, "It's good to see you up and about."

It worked. Women all around smiled at his thoughtful comment. Granger looked amused but held his tongue.

"Granger, I wondered if you'd give me a hand with Miss Lyman's cougar?" Filled in with sawdust and framed over the cat's own bleached skull, the cougar's head was ready to be hung. Chase could easily carry it alone, but hanging the thing made a good pretext to draw Granger aside for some questions.

"It's ready?" Miss Lyman plunked down a crock of butter and came scurrying over. "When you left the store to work on it, I hadn't imagined you'd finish everything so quickly!"

"Wanted it out of the way before Granger left." He shrugged. *She better not decide she wants to come with us.*

Her eyes sparkled. "I'll come along for the first peek!"

Chase bit back a groan. Didn't she have something better to do than ruin his final opportunity to question Granger? One look at her excited face told him the answer: *No such luck.*

"We'll be back in a moment," she called to the others.

"Everyone wait a minute." Miss Thompson looked suspicious. "If it's finished, where are you planning to hang that thing?"

"On the wall beside your 'Hats off to the Chef' sign." Miss Lyman's voice shrank to something almost apologetic.

"No." Done with the conversation, Miss Thompson returned her attention to the bubbling soup pots atop her stove.

The beginnings of a smile made Chase look down at his own hat. Suddenly he was glad he'd removed it before being told.

"Now, Evie, you know all the men are going to want to see it." Her sister's entreaty fell on deaf ears until she continued, "With proof of her shooting staring them in the face, maybe the men will think twice before crossing the line!"

They don't know I shot it, too. Chase held his peace. He'd bothered to dry the hide, scrape it clean, oil it to keep it supple, and mount it. What was the use if no one ever saw it? Besides, the other Miss Thompson made a good point. Lawson sure looked like a man to take a woman's skill with a gun seriously.

"Cora." The cook wavered but held her ground. "It's not as though they'll never see it if Lacey hangs the thing elsewhere."

"Out of sight, out of mind," Chase cautioned.

"Dunstan's right. Besides"—Granger looked fondly at his woman—"none of us wants every man in town trooping through your house. The diner and the bunkhouse are the only places the men spend any amount of time in. This will make the best impact."

"You know I can't hang my cougar in the *bunkhouse*." Miss Lyman sounded scandalized at the prospect. "Please, Evie?"

Miss Thompson's deep, put-upon sigh admitted defeat.

It was only later, as he carried the trophy back to the diner, that Chase realized what he'd witnessed. *The obstacles hadn't mattered a bit—Miss Lyman got her own way. Again.*

TWENTY-FOUR

Time plodded on for Cora. After the unveiling of the cougar and farewell dinner for Granger, the entire week might just as well have been one long, drawn-out day. The routine didn't vary: cooking for the workmen with perfunctory periods of supportively ignoring her own fiancé in awkward visits. Everything else went smoothly, so she counted her blessings. *I think we all expected some sort of trouble once Granger left.*

Oh, there'd been a dicey moment or two when he and Mr. Dunstan shepherded Twyler onto the train. Riordan and Williams flanked them, creating a sort of guard for the criminal on crutches. Clump scurried behind, but somehow Cora doubted the good-natured German would be much use if a fight broke out.

Several of the men had lined up, shouting threats and begging Granger to leave Twyler with them for a few minutes. Lacey's abduction was still a sore spot for both her admirers and the other men who'd missed a chance to prove their bravery to Naomi. Now they wanted an outlet for their frustration.

Granger and Dunstan didn't give it to them. Even in the days since the departure, no fights broke out among the men. As far as Cora could see, Dunstan managed most of it through eye contact. His icy stare quelled conflict, as though the men knew his vigilant watch was a warning. It impressed them all.

Except Braden, whose more subdued behavior lately couldn't be credited to a man he'd never met. *Lacey went to visit him, and he hasn't been the same since. I wonder if something she said got through to him? Or if he's just waiting for Granger?*

Evie's fiancé had been giving him daily updates and reports on their progress. Granger answered Braden's questions and ostensibly incorporated some of his ideas into the work routine. Cora didn't really know what all went on with the sawmill—but it occurred to her Braden would want to. Without Granger, he lost his information supply and link to the men. He grew listless.

"Do you think he's starting to come around?" She posed the question to Lacey as they headed for the kitchen one morning. "I mean, he's stopped bellowing all the time, and either I'm becoming accustomed to them, or he isn't putting his heart into his snarky comments." *Always assuming he still has a heart.*

"Well," Lacey's hesitation didn't exactly inspire confidence. "I believe he's giving up his plans to force us all from Hope Falls. You know he doesn't like to admit when he's wrong and turns sulky. If you want to call that coming around. . ."

"No, I don't." Cora rubbed the back of her neck where the tension built up. "I want him to be realizing how terribly he's repaid our concern for his well-being and hard work to make a success of this town. Sulking isn't the same as remorse."

"They both make people quiet," Lacey observed. "We don't have much choice but to give it time. He's already changing plans. Once he admits he's wrong, maybe the regret will come."

"I hope so." Cora's fervency startled Lacey, whose eyes widened. "Oh, it sounds awful to wish someone flooded with so much remorse he can't withstand it. But something has to break through this wall he's built around himself, and I think regret might be the only way. He hurts, you know." The tears welled up.

"Braden refuses the laudanum." Her friend frowned. "It seems to me the only sleep he gets is when we sneak the medicine so he can't turn it down. Then he's always so furious with us. Why? This stubbornness does him no favors. I keep trying to find the reason for his decisions, but I can't make sense of him."

Cora dabbed her eyes with a hankie. "More than anything, he needs rest. Otherwise, how can he heal? And if he's in pain all the time but never getting any sleep, is it any wonder his thoughts are so full of himself?" She'd puzzled over this so many times, trying to understand why he changed so drastically.

"Do you think that if he slept, he'd start thinking normally again?" Lacey paused with her hand on the handle of the kitchen door. "Would it improve his condition if we began administering more regular doses of the laudanum, do you think?"

"I don't know." Cora tucked her hankie away. "Let's not consider whether it will make him angry. He's angry no matter what we do, regardless. But if it might bring *my* Braden back, I'm willing to do just about anything to get the job done."

"Done!" Lacey nudged the last tin can in place and stood back to admire her sparkling, orderly shop. It had taken days of sorting, stacking, and scrubbing—and that was after she'd conscripted a few of the men to move the shelving one night—but the results made all the effort worth it. *It's what I pictured.*

The wooden counter ran along the far wall, its heavy iron coffee grinder easily visible the moment someone walked through the door. Underneath, it held bins filled with rice, flour, sugar, and cornmeal—all shown through little glass panels along the front.

Matching shelves stretched behind it from floor to ceiling, stacked with bolts of fabric and ordering catalogs down one half. The other held delicacies to tempt her customers. A wheel of cheese, a vat of the biggest pickles Lacey had ever seen, and clear jars containing taffy pulls and peppermint sticks beckoned the hungry. Here, too, were laid a massive quantity of paper bags in varied sizes, intended to contain the measured dry goods. A small door in the right corner led to the storeroom.

More shelves abutted the two longer walls, evenly spaced between the freshly washed windows. These held a variety of goods Lacey placed according to value and category—most expensive items resting at eye level. Everything from cleaning supplies to chewing tobacco waited for buyers to find them.

The larger items took more ingenuity to house, but Lacey thought she'd risen to the task. Saws and axes hung to the left of the door. Folded overalls, long underwear, bandannas, and balled socks nestled in wooden crates below the display of tools.

Along the right, she'd placed bins of apples and potatoes. Above these hung a selection of smoked ham and wrapped sides of bacon. A long, low shelf ran down the center of the store, creating two long aisles out of the single room. Here sat the pails of peanut butter, buckets of apple butter, and cans of condensed milk and honey. The Birdseye Sorghum looked up as though wary of anyone wanting baking soda or cream of tartar.

The potbellied stove sat at the midline of the room, back toward the counter. Off to its side, in the warmest spot, she'd set the enormous cracker barrel. A checkerboard leaned against it, ready to be laid down for a game any minute. Two chairs bracketed the barrel, inviting players to while away an hour.

Enough room remained to widen her selection of products once the mill was up and running. Lacey looked around the place and gave a sigh of satisfaction. *Someday families will live in Hope*

Falls. Our workers will bring their wives and children into my shop for aprons and pennywhistles. Someday. . .

The bell above the door clanged a welcome as Mr. Dunstan strolled in. Lacey's smile faltered when she caught sight of Decoy—fur looking decidedly grubbier than it had a week ago. Still, his stubborn owner might be her first real customer.

"What can I do for you, Mr. Dunstan?" Her smile returned as she saw the approval on his face as he surveyed the store.

"Nice." His comment, when it finally came, left something to be desired. The man looked every bit as impressed as he should be, considering how he'd seen the place at its worst.

Couldn't he say something about what an amazing difference she'd made? Or tell her how clean and organized everything was? Lacey would even settle for a simple heartfelt congratulations on her accomplishment. But no. The man came up with "nice."

Well, that doesn't make me *feel very nice.* There wasn't much to say, though Lacey wouldn't thank him for dredging up a single syllable to describe days of difficult, meticulous work.

"Mm." She made her acknowledgment shorter than his.

He didn't notice.

Dunstan stayed absorbed in perusing her shop. He circled the entire place and picked up and put down items from almost every shelf, all without saying another word. Finally, he lowered himself onto one of the checker chairs and placed his order.

"One pickle." He'd kept her waiting while he touched almost everything she sold, only to buy one lousy pickle?

Lacey yanked the glass lid from the huge vat, grabbed the long tongs lying beside it, and plunged them in to nab a pickle. Pickle chosen, she reached behind her counter and picked up the pail of None-Such Peanut Butter Decoy had desecrated on his earlier visit. Tongs held out far in front, far enough to keep brine away from her skirts, she marched to meet him.

"I'll put it on your tab," she sweetly told him. "Along with this!" She plunked the pail of peanut butter atop the other chair. Lacey intended to whisk back behind the counter and ignore him, but the man didn't take the pickle she offered.

So she stood there, uncertain, while he gave her one of those long, penetrating looks he used to keep the men in line. She turned, ready to go back behind the counter, return the pickle to its jar, and order Mr. Dunstan out of her store.

He reached up and snatched the pickle. Biting into it, his eyes closed in appreciation. After he swallowed, he mentioned, "I haven't had one of these in months. It's been too long."

Dunstan proceeded to finish it off before speaking again. "Pickles are tart and salty on their own, Miss Lyman. You don't need to go around with a sour look on your face to spice it up."

Shock held her speechless for a moment. "Out." She pointed toward the door, reduced to simply repeating, "Get out."

"I brought in an elk." He rose to his feet. "It needs dressing and butchering before it'll fit in the smokehouse." Apparently he expected praise for this because he paused.

If Lacey hadn't been so riled, she would've grunted, "Nice." But as things stood, she felt he didn't deserve even that much.

One hand reached down to rub the dog's ears. "Decoy here has a special fondness for elk. It would be helpful if someone watched him while I took care of things. He'll find a way out of the barn if I leave him alone with the smell of elk in the air."

"You aren't saying you want to leave him here!" Lacey was so aghast she forgot her anger. "In my nice, clean shop?"

"Told you before, Decoy's trained not to bother anything on shelves." A thoughtful look crossed Dunstan's face. "Or bins either. If he gets restless, you might have a care for those hams you have hanging in the window. They're low enough he wouldn't have any trouble reaching them if he wanted to."

"But," Lacey spoke in desperation, trying to avoid what Dunstan, at least, seemed to consider inevitable. "It's all put away perfectly. Didn't you notice how clean everything looks?"

"Yep." He headed for the door. "You got this place in order just in the nick of time. I'll be by later to pick him up."

"What am I supposed to do with him while you're gone?"

"He likes you." The door opened, its bell clanging an alarm. "You can manage him—you're a resourceful woman." With that, he abandoned Lacey to his dog, and the dog to Lacey.

Decoy sauntered over to his pail of peanut butter and gave a great, happy sniff. It fell to the floor and rolled away, the massive dog lumbering after it as though playing a new game.

"I suppose chairs weren't included with shelves and bins in your training." Lacey rubbed her forehead. By the end of the day, the smell coming off Decoy would fill the place. *Unless...*

She made a beeline for the hygiene shelf and pulled out a box of Snow Boy Washing Powder. A large tub sat in the back of the storeroom, waiting for the time when someone would need it. Well, that day came sooner than she expected. If Chase Dunstan thought he could leave a smelly moose of a mutt on her hands and ruin her store, he'd learn just how resourceful she could be!

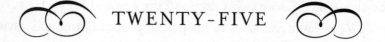

TWENTY-FIVE

"Miss Lyman?" Chase peered into the store an hour later. If he'd had any doubts, he wouldn't have left Decoy, but his trust lay more in the dog than the woman. So he'd come to check in.

She didn't call back an answer. Decoy didn't come bounding up as was his habit whenever they separated and Chase returned. Nothing stirred in the shop—except a few sudden misgivings.

He walked toward the back counter, thinking to check the storeroom. Along the way he surveyed the store for any damage. No signs of trouble. Not a single thing stood out of place in the newly pristine mercantile—Chase knew because he'd made a thorough study earlier. He rounded the potbellied stove and bypassed the cracker-barrel chairs. By now Decoy would have sensed him and come running, even from the back room.

A dull clang sounded as his boot hit something solid and metal. Decoy's peanut butter pail rolled a few forlorn inches. Chase doubled his pace to the storeroom door and yanked it open. Even in here, things were eerily tidy. No Miss Lyman. No Decoy.

Where did they go? Irritated, he turned on his heel and headed outside. Chase paused, unsure where to go. *Not to the diner. Miss Thompson wouldn't allow a dog within ten feet of her kitchen. But maybe she'll have an idea where Miss Lyman went?*

Too many tracks muddled the ground outside the door, imprints from people going in and out as they helped her get the store in order. Chase held slim hope of tracking them, so he headed for the diner. *She'd better not have gone out walking in the woods again,* he stewed. *I asked her to keep an eye on him in the store. What has that stubborn woman gotten into this time?*

"Hello?" He stuck his head through the kitchen door. Since the night Granger told everyone why he was here, Chase made the kitchen his base for Hope Falls. It harbored everything a man needed to keep tabs on: most of the women and all of the food.

"Hello!" The high, girlish greeting came from Mrs. Nash. She sat on a bench, shelling peas and trying to look past him. "Are they finished yet? I mean, did you see your surprise?"

"What surprise?" Those faint misgivings from back in the store grew to dread. "Surprise" was the name for unpleasant things people snuck up on you, suspecting you would object if asked about it beforehand. *Not good. Not good at all.*

"Well, if you have to be asking us, they haven't shown you yet." Mrs. McCreedy shook her head. "It's not for us to spoil."

"Oh, go on, Martha." Mrs. Nash finished shelling her peas. "He came back too soon, and he'll go poking around looking for who knows how long before he finds them or they find him. I'd say we might as well tell him he should go by the house first."

"Thank you." Chase started in that direction, only to duck back into the kitchen. "Do you know where they put Decoy?" The dog got underfoot in just about anything, his sheer size making it difficult to work around him. If they weren't careful, they'd trip over him or find their dainty toes bruised by his mammoth paws. Decoy hid a fondness for tromping on people's feet.

Whatever the women were up to, they'd most likely needed to shut the dog away from the action. And Decoy didn't like being cooped up for long. Disaster loomed large if they'd left him—

"Find the ladies." Mrs. McCreedy beat Mrs. Nash to the punch. "And you'll find your dog. We won't say anything more."

He looked to Mrs. Nash, but she smiled and pressed a hand over her lips, indicating they were sealed. Chase would get no information to prepare him for his "surprise." That left him with no choice but to head down to the ladies' house.

As he drew closer, snatches of laughter and muffled shrieks reached his ears. *Sounds like they're having fun.* Their merriment went a long way toward easing his tension. Such carefree sounds couldn't accompany anything too awful.

His knock on the door found no answer, but the noise was all coming from around back. Chase left the porch and crept around the house, the better to take stock of the situation.

No one would be catching *him* unawares. He'd turned the tables.

"I think we used too much." Someone sounded worried.

"It'll all wash out." Miss Lyman's giggles floated by. If a man could catch a sound and keep it for sad times, that would be it. She sounded positively gleeful. "Pass me the bucket?"

The sound of sloshing water as the bucket was emptied—not poured—made Chase thirsty. He took a sip from his canteen and wondered what they could be doing. He crept closer to find out.

"We're going to need a lot more than that!" This huskier voice belonged to Miss Higgins. Though she spoke least out of the four women, her throaty tones were easily identifiable.

A great deal of splashing drowned out anything else for a while. Then came a bark. It was the short, low blast of sound Decoy made when he played. The spasmodic thump of his tail sounded against something metal, underscoring more laughter.

Chase froze. Decoy loved the water. Any water. Whether it was a stream to wade through, a puddle to pounce on, or a deep pool for diving into, his dog enjoyed water to the fullest. Combine that knowledge to the sounds and comments bubbling behind the house, it added up to one mounting suspicion.

He poked his head around the corner of the house and confirmed it. *Those daft women are giving him a bath!*

"What do you think you're doing?" he demanded as he advanced on the tableau. Things were worse than he imagined.

Buckets of water trailed back toward the water pump, where Granger's cook stopped in the act of filling yet another. Miss Higgins clutched the end of a long rope knotted into a makeshift leash. The other Miss Thompson dropped the now-empty bucket she'd just poured over Decoy in an attempt to rinse him clean.

A failed attempt. There, behind the house, Miss Lyman crouched beside a tin hip bath, froth gloving her hands all the way up to her elbows. Cramped inside the bathtub sat a very happy, very wet, and very foamy dog. At least, it *used* to be a dog. Now it was a white, sudsy mess wriggling with delight.

"Giving Decoy a much-needed bath." Miss Lyman managed to sound nonchalant as she gestured to the frothy mountain rocking the tub from side to side. "What else would we be doing?"

"Anything!" Chase raked his hands through his own shaggy hair. "Cooking, puttering about your shop, wading through the calf-eyed glances of your moony men. Anything at all," he repeated, "except turn my dog into a walking mop!"

At this outburst, the women slowly began returning to their respective tasks. Miss Thompson fetched another full bucket from her sister at the pump, upending it over Decoy's back while Miss Lyman tried to work out the suds. She succeeded in raising more bubbles than had been washed away in the first place.

"He's not a mop, but I would've taken one to him if it would've helped clean him up." She sounded muffled as she scrubbed at the dog's fur. "He was absolutely filthy, you know."

Another bucket of water and more scrubbing unleashed another crop of bubbles. At this rate, they'd never get it finished.

"He's a *hunting dog*." Chase scowled at them all and picked up a bucket. "Or he used to be until you four decided to turn him into an overgrown, soap-strewn parody of a poodle."

Miss Lyman gave a half-strangled snort of laughter, so Chase figured he could be forgiven if half a bucket's water *accidentally* slopped over the tub and onto her skirts. Decoy wagged his tail even harder, delighted that Chase joined in.

"I've never seen a dog"—Miss Higgins shifted to the side to give him more room—"who looked less like a poodle."

With his silver-gray brindled coat further darkened from the water, even the soap continuously springing up couldn't hide his coloring. And nothing could cover his size. Still, whatever soap they'd used made a spectacular effort.

"Just how much soap did you pour in?" Chase asked after his fifth bucket of water made little headway against the froth.

The women darted sideways glances at each other, but no one saw fit to answer. Nor did they immediately respond to his query about what sort of substance they'd seen fit to use. As far as Chase knew, and after relocating most of the contents of Miss Lyman's store the other day, he had a fair notion no company manufactured dog wash. *Which should have tipped them off.*

It didn't smell like lye, which was harsh enough to irritate Decoy's skin after the bath ended. He would have asked again, to be sure, but found he didn't need to. He spotted Miss Lyman nudging something around the tub with the toe of her boot.

Chase grabbed it. He read the box then looked at the ground for the rest of its contents. With growing exasperation, he realized why he didn't see any granules or flakes—he didn't know which form Snow Boy came in—scattered across the grass.

"You used the whole box?" He shook the box in disbelief, confronting them with the evidence. "An entire *box* of soap?"

"He's large enough we thought it best to be sure." Miss Lyman carried on trying to rub the stuff from his fur. "With his thick coat to get through, we thought we'd need every bit."

Miss Higgins looked a bit embarrassed as she confessed to the obvious. "It seems we overestimated. Significantly."

He saw no need to comment on that bit of hindsight. Setting himself not to let his temper get the best of him, Chase kept bringing buckets. *I can't very well yell at all four of them.*

It took more buckets of water than Chase bothered to count, and far too much time, before they won the battle of the bubbles. Added with his attempts to hunt down his own dog, he'd lost half an hour or more of time he couldn't afford to see wasted.

He'd not managed to trap Granger in a productive conversation. In the week following his friend's departure, Chase set himself to poking around the unused parts of town. Hope Falls bristled with abandoned buildings. Most looked thrown together to meet the needs of a mining town rapidly outgrowing itself, some of such poor workmanship they needed leveling.

If he didn't need to bring back fresh meat on a regular basis, Chase would've gotten a lot further. Periodically doubling back to check on the women severely hampered his hunting, which in turn curtailed his nosing-around time.

The smallest structures most likely to hold tools and equipment he'd already searched. These were the places Chase figured a man in a hurry might hide unused blasting papers, fuse line, or anything else incriminating. They were common enough mining materials to be overlooked by the new residents.

But Chase knew for a fact that Braden Lyman refused to store explosives or any of their paraphernalia on site. Once they'd blasted the main tunnels into the side of the mountain, he'd shipped any remaining items back to the dealer. Lyman considered it an elementary safety precaution against blast-happy miners who might accidentally get people killed.

His common-sense approach was one of the reasons Chase agreed to work with Braden Lyman in the first place. Usually he steered clear of mining outfits. Whatever land they didn't strip bare, they blew up to get to the coal or silver ore. Miners were bad for the land and bad for business. Miracle Mining had been the best of the bunch. Their plans to build a town and capitalize on the railroad route offered assurance that they wouldn't carelessly destroy the surrounding countryside.

For this reason, Chase signed on to walk them over their land, explain its basic features and the way one area connected to the other, and suggest the best site for Hope Falls itself. They'd needed help determining a spot close enough to be productive, but far enough away so the town wouldn't be affected if and when they needed to blast their way farther in.

And Lyman's point-blank refusal to overuse blasting powder or even keep it on hand had been typical of the outfit. His partner protested, but Lyman maintained he could always order more if need be—their train access made short work of waiting.

Which was why Chase found it so hard to believe the story he'd heard about a blasting accident bringing down the mountain. Lyman hired surveyors to gauge the rock and engineers to design custom supports at intervals along every tunnel they made.

The man did everything right—so it shouldn't have gone wrong. If Miracle Mining had been a two-bit operation with shaky methods, Chase wouldn't have recommended Laura's husband for a job. He'd put his faith in Braden Lyman's company and lost his family. Now Chase needed to prove he hadn't misjudged the outfit. Then he could find justice for the men who'd died.

But instead of investigating, he had to deal with the daft woman who'd decided to give *his dog a bath*. His anger over her presumption, and the difficulty it would cause, paled in comparison to his rage over the time her foolishness cost him.

Chase controlled his temper by not talking. The rest of today and tomorrow morning would be given to butchering the elk, but its size bought him a day without needing to make a kill.

Tomorrow I hunt the real prey of Hope Falls. The thought calmed him. *But today I take Miss Lyman down a peg.*

TWENTY-SIX

O ops. Lacey didn't quite know how to regain control of the situation. Bathing Decoy had been a wonderful idea—thankfully, his enthusiasm for playing in the water kept him in place through the prolonged ordeal. *If only Dunstan didn't come looking for us.* Lacey caught the thought and sternly stopped it. The only things "if only" ever applied to were things that hadn't happened and most likely never would. *Useless things.*

But the man's timing proved *most* unfortunate. Lacey would not have chosen for him to ruin the surprise and certainly would rather have kept the mistake with the soap between just her and the girls. Mr. Dunstan looked as though he'd taken it well enough. He stood there, somehow taller than he'd seemed indoors, casting dark looks when the others didn't notice.

Dark looks, Lacey could handle. *Particularly when they're dark good looks.* This time she didn't even try to catch the wayward thought. She kept busy sneaking her own looks his way.

Since coming to Hope Falls, Lacey accepted that proprieties couldn't always be observed. She accepted minor lapses not only

524

for the sake of necessity, but also because it gave the women a bit more leeway than they could enjoy in an established town.

If she hadn't quite become accustomed to seeing men in their shirtsleeves, at least the experience wasn't new. Some of the workmen would either forgo or forget their waistcoats when they showed up for the midday meal. On long, hot days Lacey understood this to be common practice, and thus, unremarkable.

But there was nothing common about Chase Dunstan. Framed by the sunlight, he sported no jacket and no waistcoat—although Lacey had never seen him wear one. The tan trousers of hard-wearing canvas and his worn boots were familiar, if drenched.

The cambric shirt, striped by his suspenders, wasn't familiar in the least. He'd rolled up his sleeves. The futile attempt to remain dry exposed strong forearms sprinkled with dark hair. Decoy's exuberant splashing soaked into the once-white fabric up to Dunstan's shoulders. The fabric molded to those remarkably broad shoulders and an extremely solid chest. He'd left the top button undone, leaving his collar to gape open. Lacey was transfixed to discover a smattering of the same dark hair peeking just above the next button.

Who knew men had fur? And as far as she could see, he looked to be the same sun-kissed gold as his forearms. She tried to look away but found her thoughts running rampant. *Does Dunstan go without his shirt during those long walks in the woods?*

"You know better." His rumbling chastisement jerked her attention back to his face. Dunstan did not look amused.

Did he catch me ogling? The possibility mortified her. Lacey felt the telltale heat in her cheeks. *No! I can't blush! He'll see it as a sign of guilt.* Which, of course, it was.

"I'm sure I don't know what you mean." *I hope I don't.*

His scowl deepened, and he crossed his arms over his chest, mercifully blocking the distracting view. "Don't play games, Miss

Lyman. You had no right to try to change my dog."

"Excuse me?" It sounded like he was talking about the way she took initiative to clean his dog. Not. . .anything else.

"You shouldn't have taken him from the store at all." Dunstan rolled his shoulders, the movement shifting the collar of his shirt. A second button slipped its mooring, she noticed.

Lacey blinked. Now was not the time to notice such things. She blinked again. A lady *never* noticed such things! *Although,* a small, utterly inappropriate voice mused, *perhaps that's because ladies are never confronted with them in the first place?*

"I asked you to watch him in the store." Her lack of response drove him to expound, "You should have stayed there."

"It is not your place to tell me where I should or shouldn't go or when I might leave my own shop, Mr. Dunstan." Lacey refused to be distracted any longer by his state of dishabille. "You overstep your position to think otherwise."

A muscle worked in his jaw while he chewed that over. Clearly still angry, Dunstan couldn't refute plain facts.

"Furthermore"—she found her own temper fueled by his unreasonable one—"I very clearly protested you leaving Decoy in my barely finished, newly scrubbed store. You didn't listen."

He relaxed his stance a fraction. "When you asked what you should do with him, I took it you were accepting the task."

"You told me I would think of something," she riposted. "So I took the challenge and came up with a *resourceful* solution."

"Dumping an entire box of soap onto a dog doesn't qualify as being resourceful!" Clearly he remembered using the word, and Lacey's gibe hit its mark. "The kindest word is foolish."

"Mr. Dunstan!" Naomi's rebuke reminded Lacey that she and Dunstan weren't alone. Her cousin, Cora, and Evie stood around the yard, watching their every move and listening intently.

"The truth isn't always pleasant," he grumbled, looking

uncomfortable for the first time since Lacey met him.

"Everyone makes mistakes." Cora, who used the same sort of kind understanding in her continued visiting of Braden, came to Lacey's defense. "Besides, it turned out all right in the end."

Their championship of her acted like a balm to the still-remaining sore spot from when they'd hired Dunstan. Until that moment Lacey hadn't realized that she'd seen it as her friends taking his side, choosing him over her. *He's right—I am foolish.*

"It's not all right," he thundered. "Look at Decoy!"

At the sound of his name, the dog perked his ears. He left the tub, which he'd been sniffing as though curious where the water had gone, and gamboled to Dunstan's side. Just before he got there, the dog hunched lower to the ground and gave a massive shake that started at his shoulders and shivered down to his rump. Water flew everywhere. Then he plopped down at his master's side, panting happily as though pleased with his work.

Lacey looked at the dog, obviously none the worse for washing, then looked at Dunstan. She raised a quizzical brow.

"Useless!" the hunter declared. If he hadn't reached down to scratch behind Decoy's ears as he said it, Lacey would've felt sorry for the dog. "He can't go in the forest like this."

"What?" Evie scoffed at the ludicrous statement before anyone else could. "We didn't hurt him, Mr. Dunstan. It was your insistence that Decoy be allowed to follow you indoors that made this necessary. As you say, the truth isn't always pleasant." She paused as though trying to find a way around that then shrugged. "The dog stank. He's shedding from the heat. Something had to be done to make his presence indoors more acceptable."

Lacey could've cheered, but refrained. *Go Evie!*

Their opponent looked as though he'd dearly like to kick something. "He's a *working* dog. I don't bring him inside often."

"But when you did, you abandoned him to run loose in my

nice clean store." Lacey crossed her arms, mirroring his stance.

"You don't get it." He passed a hand over his face, rubbing his forehead. "When he smelled like a dog, it didn't alarm the animals. Now anything we track will bolt if it's downwind from us. Snow Boy Washing Powder might as well have been a warning cry."

"Then I suggest you attempt to remain upwind for the next few days." Lacey wouldn't give an inch. "It'll wear off."

He shook his head. "It doesn't work that way. Deer and mountain goats don't kindly turn around when the wind shifts. You just don't understand anything about hunting."

"And you don't understand anything about running a shop!"

"If this is what it takes, I wouldn't want to learn." Arms now resting at his sides, Dunstan revealed his drying shirt. Even the wet spots speckling its expanse no longer clung to him. "Cleaning a room is far easier than tracking an animal."

His dismissal of her hard work rankled. When he wasn't looking ruggedly handsome, Dunstan became irksome. He needed someone to push him off his high horse—and Lacey needed a project now that the store was ready but had no customers.

"We'll see about that, Mr. Dunstan." She gestured toward Decoy. "Having deprived you of your hunting companion, I'll join you tomorrow. Then you can show me just how difficult it is."

"No." He didn't waste any words refusing her company.

She'd suspected as much. What Lacey hadn't expected was how much she'd want to go tracking once the idea came to her.

"Hunting is your job. Knowing the ins and outs of Hope Falls is mine." She didn't come out and say she was the boss, but Lacey knew he caught the implication. "This is the perfect opportunity for me to learn more about my land."

"No." His return to monosyllabic responses goaded her.

"You agreed to teach us how to trap the wildlife hereabouts." Naomi's words made Dunstan go still.

"What?" Lacey slanted a curious glance toward her friends.

"It was one of the conditions of his employment," Evie filled her in. "He told us he'd be happy to teach us."

Oh, this is too perfect. Lacey beamed at this new development and made a mental note to ask Cora what other conditions Dunstan had agreed to in their meeting.

"Well, that settles it." She read the resignation on his features clear as day. "You'll start teaching me tomorrow."

And tomorrow would be a glorious day.

The next day dawned with one of those suddenly soggy quirks of mountain weather. Chase woke to the sound of rain beating on his tent. For a moment he lay there. With Decoy's shaggy—and admittedly better smelling—bulk warming the tent, he wasn't in any hurry to leave his bedroll and face the cold outside.

And that was before he remembered his plans for the day. Chase groaned at the thought of getting saddled with Miss Lyman on the day he'd earmarked for riffling through Hope Falls. *Of all days, it had to be this one.* Leading a pampered princess through overgrown brush already ranked as unappealing. Throw in a deluge of rain and the prospect went downright bleak.

Unless. . . *She won't want to go traipsing through mud and rain, getting cold and ruining one of those pretty dresses she's so fond of.* A smile crept across his face as Chase plotted.

All he had to do was show up ready to take her hunting. She'd refuse, and he'd be off the hook for good. Not even Miss Lyman could complain that he didn't fulfill his part of the bargain if she backed out. If she didn't follow through with their first set of plans, he wasn't obligated to make more.

And if she's stubborn enough to set out, I'll make Miss Lyman so miserable she'll head home early and not ask to go again. It wouldn't be difficult. Chase knew where the worst terrain lay, which low-lying areas turned to boggy muck from rainfall, where the river swelled to make crossing difficult. He made it a point to know and avoid those spots. If necessary, he'd direct the spoiled lady through every one of them.

It might even be fun. Starting to look forward to a day either free of Miss Lyman's interference or devoted to making her less demanding, Chase didn't mind leaving the warm tent. He got dressed, packed up, then booted a less-than-ecstatic Decoy out of the tent so he could take it down. Trying to keep a cook fire going in the midst of this weather was the act of a fool or a desperate man. And Chase had already learned that the breakfasts in Hope Falls were worth getting up for.

Dropping Decoy off at the cow barn, where the dog promptly curled up on a bed of warm, fragrant hay, posed no problems. He'd stay there until Chase came to fetch him, glad to be out of the rain. For a dog who loved water, Decoy sure didn't like rain. A shame, really, since Chase planned to bring him out in it for a spell. Some rain would help wash away the lingering detergent-like smell still clinging to the dog's fur.

Chase hit the door of the diner whistling. He stepped into the kitchen, found his prey, and gave a wolfish grin.

"Well, Miss Lyman, are you ready to start tracking?"

TWENTY-SEVEN

The man had to be joking. Lacey eyed him, wary of a trap. Dunstan knew full well that she—and he—couldn't leave the others alone with a group of lumbermen stuck inside all day. Not to mention that no one with an ounce of sense would go merrily marching through the wild in the midst of a downpour. *Did I actually hear him whistling before he opened the door?*

Something was wrong here, and it went beyond her usual suspicion of anyone who managed to be cheerful early in the morning. Dunstan didn't seem nearly so pleased with the prospect of taking her hunting yesterday. *So why is he raring to go now?*

There he stood, one eyebrow raised as in challenge, waiting for her to grab her cloak. Before breakfast. To go out in the rain. Surely he knew the weather would postpone their outing? Chase Dunstan was many things—aggravating, resourceful, blunt, and so on—but no one could confuse him for a fool. And only a fool would forgo one of Evie's breakfasts. What man chose to get drenched and sludge through mud over eating a good meal?

None. Not a single blessed one I've ever met, including Mr.

531

Dunstan. He's only inviting me because he's sure I'll refuse! Lacey's eyes narrowed as she tried to think of a way to refuse without falling into his snare. She'd trapped him into taking her. Now he was trapping her into letting him go.

And she had no intention of releasing him from his deal.

"Well?" He propped his hip against one of the kitchen stools, smirking at her. "Daylight, such as it is, is wasting."

"You cannot be serious, Mr. Dunstan." Naomi seemed to realize he meant it. "Your plans will have to wait; neither of you can go trudging through the forest on a day like today." Mercifully, she didn't mention the glaringly obvious fact that Lacey didn't *want* to go trudging through the forest.

A grin snuck across his face as though he'd expected their response. Even hoped for it, maybe. "Why not? Mud washes off."

But responsibilities don't. Lacey began to worry that she'd have to cancel after all. She held no doubts that Dunstan wouldn't allow her to reschedule either. *But I can't abandon them. How on earth can he even consider that I would?*

The answer stared her straight in the face. Lacey shook her head in disbelief that it'd taken so long to find the solution. She, after all, wasn't the only one with responsibilities!

"I take it that's a no?" He'd seen the motion and wrongly judged it as a sign of defeat. Victory showed in his smug smile.

"It's raining." She really shouldn't toy with answering, but he'd set her up to take a fall. Now she'd return the favor.

"I know. Why else would I tell you to bring your cloak?" He stretched out his long legs, making himself more comfortable. "It'll buy some time before you get too drenched. If you're worried about your dress, the cloak will catch the worst dirt."

Normally Lacey wouldn't take it askance that a man recognized her care in dressing. Even better if he avoided situations guaranteed to ruin whatever garments she wore. But Mr. Dunstan didn't say this out of courtesy or appreciation. Somehow, he made practical clothing concerns sound trite!

"Unless, of course, you take a tumble." Laughter crept around the edges of his nonchalance. "You do seem to make a habit of falling whenever you roam the mountainside."

"That is none of your concern!" Lacey couldn't contain her outrage. "And, for your information, a cougar knocking one off one's feet hardly constitutes a normal fall." Nor did jerking away from a man determined to examine her ankle, but she didn't want to mention it. The girls didn't know about that incident.

Nor did he apparently. He didn't pursue it further. Instead he again settled for trying to goad her into mucking around the mountainside. "It's my concern if you stumble while we're on a hunt. It might make us lose track of our prey."

At least he didn't pretend the protest stemmed from any genuine worry over her well-being. Lacey tried to bank her outrage. She failed. "Your devotion to your work is touching." She couldn't even try to make it sound like a compliment.

"Lacey. . ." Cora's call was a warning and a plea to control herself. Her best friend knew her temper too well.

"I do my best." At last Dunstan's grin disappeared.

"You'd do better to concentrate on the more important part of your post," Lacey informed him. "The rain means far more than mud. Slippery conditions keep the men from their work."

Recognition dawned on his features, but Lacey's righteous anger continued. "Do you consider it safe to leave Evie, Naomi, and Cora cooped up with a slew of bored men? Never forgetting the town-wide brawl that broke out during our last rainy day—"

"Enough!" The barked order interrupted her mid-tirade.

"It is not enough." She rounded on him. "The only reason you waltzed in here whistling is because, as you made so painfully clear, you expected me to forgo the excursion. And you didn't expect me to decline because I wouldn't dream of leaving my friends to entertain the men alone—you made it quite clear you believe my choices revolve around my own comfort."

"I did expect you to cry off in face of the weather," he conceded then fell silent. No apology followed the admission.

"We expected you to remain in town." Evie sounded disturbed to find this in doubt. "It seems our expectations of you are a good deal higher than your estimation of Lacey's priorities."

"I meant no insult." The statement bordered on apologetic.

"Yet you gave one. We all understood the implications of your plan." Only Naomi could make the remonstrance without making it an accusation. "I trust that will not be repeated."

"No, ma'am." He had the grace to look abashed before his gaze sought Lacey's. Speculation underscored his promise. "You can be sure I won't underestimate her in the future."

∞

I probably won't have to. In his experience, people who overestimated their own worth made mistakes accordingly. And Lacey Lyman, so indignant over an implied insult, showed that pride was her Achilles' heel. The whole scene would've amused Chase if that pesky twinge of guilt would go away.

It didn't.

Whether he wanted to admit it or not, he'd let his own ambitions and grudges block his better judgment. Chase could've kicked himself for overlooking the obvious need to stay in town. If he'd thought beyond his own irritation at being stuck with the woman, he'd have already been in the diner with the men. It was his job to make sure the men didn't get restless and stupid.

Instead, restlessness brought out his own stupidity. *I got so caught up in wanting to get the better of her that I gave in to the worst of myself.* It shouldn't take the likes of Lacey Lyman to remind him of his responsibilities. That rankled almost as much as overlooking them in the first place. Chase wasn't used to being wrong and found he didn't much like the feeling.

Nor did he like the increasing number of ways the woman defied his expectations. She penned the ludicrous ad responsible for bringing overeager, difficult bachelors swarming down on her and her friends. Then she turned around and tried to protect them from those very bachelors. Her clothes declared her shallow, fussy, and dainty. But she didn't turn a hair over shooting a pouncing cougar, taking on a mess to stagger stalwart men, or taking on the task of bathing his Irish wolfhound. A mass of contradictions, the only thing she kept consistent was her temper, and it, like the rest of her, was spectacular.

It'll be her undoing, Chase told himself as he left the kitchen to join the men in the diner. What remained to be seen was whether or not he wanted to hasten it along. For all his time in Hope Falls, he wasn't any closer to discovering the truth behind the collapse of Miracle Mining. Until he did, Chase needed to do a better job of getting on her good side.

He hadn't missed the undertones behind what Miss Higgins and Miss Thompson said in the kitchen: the women he'd won over were starting to wonder if they'd made the right decision in hiring him. Chase would have to walk a fine line from here on.

The boisterous din of more than a dozen men drowned out any chance of thinking. Chase surveyed them, watching for any sign of trouble, but they seemed in good spirits. Mrs. McCreedy circled the room with a fresh pot of coffee, refilling mugs. Mrs. Nash claimed the end of a bench near her brother, looking faintly green around the gills. Chase decided to join them.

At best, he might learn something from the two people who shared a house with the women running the town. At worst, he'd be in position to keep an eye on Lawson. After the stunt he'd pulled a week ago in the store, Chase made a point of watching the man. Lechery lurked beneath those fine manners, making Lawson next to Williams as most likely to cause trouble.

"Morning," he greeted Mrs. Nash and plunked down on the bench facing her and her brother. Lawson, he noted, didn't look pleased to see him. Chase's mood improved a notch. *Good.*

"Good morning." Mrs. Nash made a brave attempt at a smile. From the way she looked and what Chase gathered about females in the family way, her stomach troubled her. She sounded upbeat though. "Looks like we're all rained in today, doesn't it?"

"Looks like it," he agreed and ran out of conversation.

"Shame to lose a workday." Lawson filled the gap. "Though perhaps we'll think of something to make the day interesting." He faltered at Chase's scrutiny, evidently remembering the last time he'd been caught finding something "interesting."

"I offered to teach you how to knit," his sister teased.

Lawson understandably chose not to recognize the remark. Instead he turned his attention to the diner door, which swung open to admit a thin man along with a blast of cold air. The newcomer paused at the threshold, scanning the room before making his way over to their table. Lawson supplied the name Chase couldn't quite recall. "Good morning, Mr. Draxley."

"Morning, Lawson. Mrs. Nash." The blond-haired man gave her a nod and folded himself onto the bench, looking like he attempted to fold himself away from attention. Only then did he mutter, "Mr. Dunstan. Didn't know whether we'd see you today."

After the debacle in the kitchen, this rubbed a raw nerve. Chase shrugged rather than ask why the man thought he wouldn't show up on a day the women needed protection. More likely than not, the man referred to Chase's habit of bypassing the bunkhouse in favor of his tent, but assumptions were dangerous.

"I knew you'd be here," Mrs. Nash assured him. She lowered her voice and leaned forward to add, "After what happened the last time we were all rained in together, you'd need to be."

"I should hope you didn't find yourself in the middle of that brawl," Chase said to her, but looked at the brother who should have been doing a much better job of protecting her.

"Oh no," she hastily corrected. "I heard of it later. Just before it all broke out, I came down with the most dreadful headache. My brother had taken me back to the house to rest."

"Good." He turned to the men. "If either of you saw it firsthand, I'd be interested in hearing your account." *And learning whether Granger really got rid of the rabble-rousers.*

"Like Arla said, I'd escorted her back to the house." Lawson acted as though that explained everything. "I wouldn't leave her unattended and undefended with the men milling about."

So you left Miss Lyman and the others to fend for themselves? Chase swallowed the accusation and looked to Draxley for his answer instead. He doubted the skittish fellow could offer much insight; Draxley looked the sort to hop away at the first sign of trouble. In fact, he looked terrified to realize Chase was even asking for his recollections of the brawl.

"Can't say," he mumbled. His glasses slid down his nose, only to be pushed up again and repeat their descent. "Went back to the telegraph office after lunch finished, didn't I?"

"Telegraph office?" Chase's interest sharpened. Was it possible Draxley had been hired on as part of Miracle Mining's operation and stayed on? "How long have you manned the post?"

"Since they put the lines in," he confirmed. Inspired by his work, he went on. "Before that I headed an office in Richmond, you know. Different sort of setup, much more advanced, but the code coming in always stays the same."

"What prompted you to make the move?" Chase directed

the conversation back to Hope Falls. "Thirst for adventure?" It took some doing, but he got the question out without laughing. If anyone would steer far clear of adventure, it was this man.

"Favor to a friend. Lost him in the collapse, you know." He sighed, mustache twitching at a rapid pace as though attempting to brush away the unpleasant memory. "Everyone had such high hopes for the mines, but you see how that turned out. My old office already hired a replacement, so I couldn't go back to Richmond when things went south. Terrible tragedy. . ."

The way he put it made it sound as though the loss of his old post was the great tragedy, but Chase figured the man meant well. Poor fellow was one bundle of nerves. Obviously he regretted his choice to move to the Colorado Territory.

But Chase didn't regret it at all. He'd just found the only person in town who'd been there when the mine collapsed. "Sorry to hear that. What was it like when it went down? I wonder if the town felt the vibrations or if it's set too far back."

"Morbid thing to wonder." Lawson looked at him askance.

"No, no." Draxley waved Lawson's protest aside. "Curiosity is natural, after all. And when one survives something like that, it's good to get it out in the open." The man made it sound as though he'd been inside the mines and clawed his way out rather than tucked safely away in his telegraph office.

"You must have been terrified." Mrs. Nash played into Draxley's dramatics and gave a delicate shudder. "Did everything shake? Could you hear anything? I wouldn't sleep for days."

"I very nearly didn't." His chest puffed at her appreciation of his ordeal. Draxley leaned forward to confide, "The shaking wasn't the worst of it. The sound when it came down. . ." He trailed off as though unable to describe it. "BOOM!" He slapped his hands against the table to underscore the volume.

Mrs. Nash gave a small shriek of surprise, but quieted when

everyone in the room started to stare at their table. She gave a nervous laugh. "You certainly managed to give a sense of what it was like, Mr. Draxley. Just the rendition frightened me!"

Chase, unnerved for an entirely different reason, settled into his own thoughts. An avalanche would have gained noise as it gathered speed. A series of tunnels giving way would issue a rumbling sort of roar. What Draxley described more closely fit the sound of a large explosion—the sort of thing that had to be carefully planned out and set up in advance. If Braden Lyman and his partner decided to expand the mines, no workers would've been allowed in the tunnels until the dust cleared and the engineers shored up the passages with reinforced timbers.

Chase finally had more than vague suspicions to go on.

The collapse of Miracle Mining was no accident after all.

TWENTY-EIGHT

Cora watched as Chase Dunstan sat with his back to a corner, coolly surveying everything in the room. More often than not, his gaze returned to Lacey. *Something's going on there.*

But for the life of her, Cora couldn't figure out what it was. One day the two of them seemed to tolerate each other fairly well—Dunstan going so far as to help Lacey clear out the shop for reorganizing. The next, he became disproportionately angered over something like giving Decoy a bath—which had been an excellent idea, even if the execution of it had a few hiccups.

The way they bickered gave away their heightened sensitivity over the other's words. Sparks flew between the two, but they didn't ignite anything but arguments. This morning, for the first time, Cora wondered if a sort of instinctual wisdom made Lacey protest hiring the man. *Maybe it was a mistake.*

Then again, who knew the hunter's favorite target would be Lacey's temper? Besides, the man unquestionably succeeded in keeping the peace amid their shrinking population.

She'd looked around the dining room after they'd finished a

breakfast of Cornish cheese bread and bacon noting with some surprise how swiftly their numbers had dwindled. Originally two-dozen strong, only about fourteen men still remained.

Smooth-talking Robert Kane and the three men he'd led in a failed nighttime raid on the women's house took out four workers with one stroke. The town brawl prompted Granger, Riordan, Clump, and Williams to force another four overly temperamental failures onto the train. With Granger escorting Twyler back to Maine to face justice, they'd lost a solid ten fellows.

If she didn't let herself get worked up over all the unpleasantness preceding their departures, Cora could appreciate how much calmer things were around town. In startling contrast to a few weeks prior, this rainy-day diner congregation showed little inclination to cause a ruckus. They did, however, look bored—and when bored men tried to find a way to pass the time, Cora noticed they usually found trouble instead.

They needed some form of entertainment before they drove someone to distraction—or worse, brawling. And the only thing Cora could think of was the same thing that failed so spectacularly the last time around. Would this time be any better? *Do I dare suggest we attempt a cribbage tournament?*

After all, they had more than enough boards to play, and Lacey had gone through numerous trunks and boxes to unearth the pegs she'd packed. . .just in case. Between the four of them, Cora had no doubt that she, her sister, Naomi, or Lacey managed to haul almost everything along with them to Hope Falls.

Why let it all go to waste? It had been ages since she'd played any card games, save the whist Braden sullenly cheated at. Besides, Cora knew Mrs. Nash, for one, could use a break in the monotony of days spent resting for the sake of the baby.

"I have a proposition," she announced to the room at large. "Why don't the men go back to the bunkhouse and fetch their cribbage boards? It seems a good day to get around to that tournament." *At least, enough time's gone by to try again.*

"Cribbage never did appeal to me," Draxley declined. Then again, the telegraph operator hadn't taken the initiative to get involved in anything since the women arrived in Hope Falls. Why should they expect a game or two of cribbage to be any different?

"Those who don't wish to play can watch those who do," Naomi declared. "For more fun, we'll set it up in the style of a tournament. A little competition adds spice to the game."

"What does the winner get?" Williams, as always, made the question into a demand. His gaze slid to Lacey. "I can't think of a better reward than a walk with the lady of our choice."

"I'll play for a prize like that!" Chester Fillmore, a faded-looking fellow who blended in with the background whenever he wasn't working, sent a shy grin Naomi's direction.

"Four ladies. That means there should be four winners, ja?" stated Clump.

"Two winners," Evie corrected. "It would disrespect our fiancés if Cora or I agreed to go strolling with another man."

"I propose a change to the reward." Lacey, Cora noticed immediately, was looking at everyone except Mr. Dunstan. "Let there be four winners, and let all of us go for a little picnic on the next Sunday when the weather is fine. Mr. Dunstan will arrange the location and hunt for a suitable main dish."

Mr. Dunstan looked anything but pleased with the suggestion, but held his tongue. Maybe the man knew better than to argue after the debacle earlier this morning. Maybe he realized that keeping an eye on the four of them when they weren't in town, and possibly exposed to greater danger that way, counted as part of his position. And maybe. . .just maybe. . .he felt a twinge of compunction over the way he'd treated Lacey earlier.

TALL, DARK, AND DETERMINED

Cora couldn't be sure of his reason for keeping quiet, but she knew Lacey volunteered his help as a form of revenge. Her best friend was as hurt as she was angry by Dunstan's low opinion, and that sort of thing always made Lacey lash out.

It must be a Lyman trait, she decided. Braden did the same. *I wonder whether he'll be unhappy letting another man accompany me on a picnic?* Jealousy, although not ideal, meant a man cared. Trust could follow love, if the feelings remained.

A sigh escaped her. *How low I've sunk if I'm hoping he's jealous!* There had been a time once when Braden wouldn't leave her side long enough to become jealous. Before Hope Falls.

"Sounds like a splendid idea," Cora seconded Lacey's plan. Whether or not the ploy worked would be telling. If Braden rose to the bait, it would be a good indication that he merely hid the feelings she kept hoping to rekindle with her visits to him. Otherwise, he no longer cared. His reaction would tell her if she should continue hoping. . .or if all hope was lost.

❧

Lacey hoped her burst of inspiration would unsettle Chase Dunstan—and remind him of his place. *Not out of snobbery,* she reassured herself. *But because he deserves to feel as unsettled as he makes me. The man may not follow convention, but that doesn't mean he can do as he pleases and insult whomever he wishes!*

The cribbage reward clipped his wings, since usually Dunstan came and went as he pleased. But the contrary man gave no outward sign of displeasure at the imposition. He fought dirty to find a way out of taking her along on a hunt, but maintained total equanimity when faced with shepherding eight people on a picnic. A chill spread through Lacey's midsection.

He didn't protest because I curtailed his freedom, she suddenly realized. *The picnic doesn't bother him. Most likely, he wouldn't have* argued if Cora or Naomi wanted to learn how to track animals. *No. He's doesn't want to be saddled with* me.

An odd numbness gripped Lacey as the men around her enthusiastically agreed to the competition, rising to their feet to go fetch the cribbage boards they'd made weeks before.

Draxley, the avowed cribbage critic, looked like he was weighing whether or not to throw his hat in the ring. Strangely enough, his question wasn't about food—the only thing he'd showed interest in for the entire time Lacey knew him. "Where is this picnic going to be? Any sort of spot in mind, Dunstan?"

"Doesn't matter where we go, so long as the women are with us." Williams already took for granted that he'd win a place.

"What sort of food will there be?" Clump worried. "Will there still be lunch for those of us who don't get a spot?"

"No one misses a meal!" Evie sounded scandalized. To her, the very idea she'd let someone go hungry was deeply offensive. "I believe Lacey meant that Mr. Dunstan would be going out of his way to catch a special treat for the picnic goers."

"Already have something in mind. As for the place"—he wore an odd look of determination as he decided—"toward the south, just past the mines, there's plenty of spaces already cleared. It'll be far enough away from town so the party stays private."

"Braden won't like that." Cora's mutter didn't sound like a protest. In fact, her best friend looked pleased at the idea of irritating her fiancé. "He won't like that one little bit."

"Here, now!" Draxley's high, reedy voice reached the breaking point. "Those mines aren't safe! Even if there wasn't any danger, it'd be a dismal place to try and enjoy yourself. It reeks of morbidity to picnic in the shadow of such a tragedy."

"I think it speaks of honoring life," Cora argued. "The lives that were lost and the way life should move along for those who remain. Laughter leaches away sorrow, and we've allowed the sorrow to take hold for long enough, Mr. Draxley."

Lacey could only guess what that speech cost her friend, but Cora's face absolutely shone with the power of what she'd said. *She's ready to move past the tragedy,* Lacey realized. *Braden's the only one determined to wallow in it—and he drags Cora down along with him. Little wonder she's eager to tell my brother that we aren't making the mountainside a macabre memorial!*

"Mr. Dunstan has greater understanding of the land and how it lays than any of us," she chimed in. "Whether you agree with his choice or not, I have every confidence we'll be safe. It's not as though he plans to take us on a tour of the ruins."

Surprise and speculation stamped Dunstan's face before he schooled his expression into impassivity. Lacey abruptly became aware that she'd never complimented his abilities before. Declaring her faith in his judgment made a considerable leap from arguing with him over his faulty ideas about her character.

Well, Mr. Dunstan. There are some things we can agree on and others you'll have to learn. Perhaps I shouldn't hope to aggravate you—I should hope you'll get to know us well enough to become more agreeable! She smiled as the men brought their games and cards to the tables, their chatter humming through the room.

"Think he can rustle up some more beaver tails?" Someone spawned an avalanche of fond remembrances over the soup.

"Naw. They's too rare nowadays." Regret coated every word as the man slapped his cribbage board down atop the table.

"Do you suppose we get to choose which woman we want to take there?" Bobsley shot an assessing glance Naomi's way.

"Dunno, since two of 'em aren't up for grabs anyway." One of the buckers from Williams's crew gave an unconcerned shrug. "So long as you get to go along, you've got a chance to cozy up to whichever one you like." Bobsley's sharp elbows jabbed the man into realizing Lacey could hear every word. He quieted.

Lacey drew her packet of cribbage pegs from the pocket of her apron—she'd tucked them inside on the way to the kitchen that morning when the skies made it clear they'd be spending the day indoors. It never hurt to be prepared—or to save herself from getting soaked to the skin in a dash back to the house.

"All right. Now, everyone who doesn't wish to play can take a seat at that table." She pointed toward the front of the room, away from the kitchen. "Then head to the left if you know how to play, or go to the right if you need a demonstration first."

Thankfully, more men headed to the left. Lacey didn't have the patience of a good teacher, but she would've stepped in if more competitors didn't know the complex game. Her cousin, with unshakable composure and a fondness for giving lessons, made an excellent teacher. Lacey gladly left the beginner table and all the explanations of values, rules, and terms to Naomi.

Among the rest, she was surprised to see Mr. Draxley. "I was under the impression you didn't enjoy cribbage," she couldn't resist remarking. After all, the man made his opinion known to all of them, and to top it off he'd criticized the picnic site. *What made him decide to join the competition?*

"I'm curious to see what our new hunter brings to the table." He didn't look particularly excited. "Besides, I rarely take a day away from my desk. It'll break the monotony a bit."

Lacey didn't question him further, instead divvying up the remaining men into pairs. "We'll do this properly. Each pair will draw to see who deals, and the cards will be dealt and pegs in place for every table before anyone starts playing." Hopefully that would regulate the timing of the games and give Dunstan the opportunity to make sure no one tried to cheat.

With the exception of Naomi's table of learners, who'd already gotten underway in a team-style match, they readied themselves swiftly. When Lacey judged everyone prepared, she nodded to

Evie, who stood beside the dinner bell. Her friend rang it with an impressively loud, resounding *clang*.

On cue, Lacey called out, "Let the games begin!"

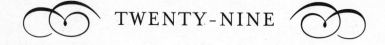 TWENTY-NINE

I'm being watched. Chase felt her eyes on him, sensed the impatience with which she waited for him to finish his outstanding breakfast of eggs in overcoats. He'd never seen the like of the dish and refused to rush through it.

Miss Lyman could cool her heels while he enjoyed this admirable creation. After the stunt she'd pulled last week, foisting a picnic on him with the cribbage winners, Chase didn't feel particularly inclined to accommodate her.

Maybe if Williams hadn't managed to snag a spot, he wouldn't mind so much. But the man had joined Riordan, Clump, and—surprisingly—Draxley in victory. Clump and Riordan were good sorts to have around. Draxley might prove useful if Chase could pump him for more information about Hope Falls when it was owned by Miracle Mining.

Williams ruined what could have been an enjoyable afternoon. Now, instead of questioning Draxley or even relaxing, Chase would have to keep a hawk eye on the rabble-rouser. The man made no bones about the fact he was angling for Miss Lyman,

548

and he'd already started making noise about wanting to go for a little walk after the meal ended. *Not going to happen.*

Today they'd be hunting partridge for the special main dish Miss Lyman recklessly promised. Food was a form of art Chase really appreciated, and he intended to savor this example. Besides, he deserved to linger over breakfast before facing the next few days. Chase picked up another one of the eggs in overcoats and surveyed it closely before sinking his teeth in.

As near as he could figure, they'd baked potatoes, cut off the tops, and scooped out the insides. They mashed the potatoes real nice and creamy and added bits of ham to the mix. That alone would've made for good eating, but the estimable Miss Thompson didn't stop there. She'd gotten *creative* and plunked a boiled egg between layers of the ham mash and baked cheese.

Chase had no idea the egg lurked inside until he bit into the thing. Then the name made sense. *Eggs in overcoats, indeed.* He put away four of them before so much as reaching for the coffee. Since then, he'd polished off three slices of buttered toast and was now reaching for his fifth overcoated egg. Miss Lyman, he'd been instantly aware, started watching him while he enjoyed the third egg-and-potato surprise. Now the heat of her impatience could've kept a cabin warm on a winter day.

"If you're quite finished, Mr. Dunstan?" Apparently reaching her breaking point, she stood before him. Her graceful fingers played with a small watch dangling from a thin chain.

Actually, he had been. While she kept silent, he figured he'd kept her waiting long enough to get the message across. But she'd shot herself in the foot by coming over here. *Now I have to show her we're on my timetable—not hers. When we hit the forest, it's my way of doing things, and she either learns to live with that and follow my directions or gets left behind.*

Chase reached for a sixth egg in an overcoat, his gaze never leaving hers as he bit into it. *Too good. . .but too much*. He put down the food and reached for more coffee, slugging back an entire mug before he bothered to answer. "Ready when you are."

Her scowl got the better of her before she calmed. "I'll just fetch my cloak." She slowly picked it up from where she'd laid it on the bench, a silent testament to her long wait. They were the only two people left in the dining room now.

Chase pushed away from the table, walked over to the peg by the door holding his hat, and grabbed it. Hat in hand, he gave her a long, assessing look. Two things struck him about the dress she'd chosen. First, it was green, so the woman had some sense that they'd need to sneak up on their prey. Second, it was the *same* green dress she'd worn the last time she followed him into the forest. *Must be her stalking dress*.

"What do you plan to go after today?" She sounded eager.

"Partridge. Since you volunteered me to provide something out of the ordinary for the picnic, we have two days to take down nine birds." One for every member of the party.

"Eleven," Miss Lyman corrected. "Mrs. Nash decided she'd like to attend if at all possible. Her brother will be coming along to offer his arm and support, so she doesn't fall."

Despite his low expectations, Chase knew the picnic just got worse. Lawson wrangled his way in, even though he lost his first round at the cribbage tournament. *Selfish fool probably talked his sister into feeling like she was missing out*.

"Mrs. Nash shouldn't be trekking around the forest with the doctor back in town." The woman looked ready to go into labor at any moment, and Chase didn't want the risk of it on his watch.

"Do you think we should invite him as well?" Miss Lyman fastened her cloak. "That's a splendid idea. Not only for Mrs. Nash, but for his own sake. The poor man stays cooped up in that house with Braden all the time. Clump even takes him his meals.

Of course, he'll bring the number up to an even dozen."

"Ambitious, but not impossible." Chase reeled at how much the woman talked—and what she'd revealed. Why did she feel sorry because a man spent so much time with her brother? Did they arrange for the doctor to remain inside so he wouldn't talk to anyone? He'd bring down another bird for the chance to find out.

"Gun?" He didn't see a purse dangling from her wrist, and her cloak didn't have pockets. Remembering the day they'd met, Chase didn't think for an instant that she'd left it behind.

"Here." She reached into a pocket cleverly tucked into the billow of her skirts and presented the mother-of-pearl inlaid pistol. Someone taught her elemental gun safety. It rested on her palm, barrel facing away from her, away from him, and away from the kitchen where her friends were still chattering.

No more than five inches long, it nevertheless boasted six cylinders. Impressive, but not nearly enough for hunting.

"You're going to need more bullets." Chase knew he couldn't predict the day's events, but he planned on bagging several birds. In spite of her luck with the cougar, he didn't hold much confidence in her marksmanship abilities with that tiny thing.

"Check." She checked the safety before sliding the gun into her right pocket then drew an entire box of bullets from her left. "If you're satisfied, I'll just get my bag and we'll go."

Nothing snobby about that. She wasn't challenging whether or not her equipment met his criteria, but genuinely asking. For the first time since he'd known he'd be stuck with her for an entire day, Chase found hope it wouldn't be unbearable.

"Bag?" A quick look around the diner turned up nothing.

"I left it in the kitchen, since I noticed you didn't mention our expedition to the other men." She hesitated, and Chase knew she was pushing back the thought that she was going alone into the forest, entirely unchaperoned, with an unmarried man. "It might've raised some uncomfortable questions."

I have a few myself. Chase nodded and waited as she slipped through the swinging doors and disappeared into the kitchen. *Like why she's not more concerned about propriety. Or why she's so determined to go hunting if it's not out of spite?*

Because his first idea was that her decision to tag along had been simply to aggravate him. She'd accomplished that well enough last week, when she'd handed him his head over how little he knew what motivated her. But the woman had a point.

What do I really know about the woman claiming to be Lacey Lyman? Once you got past her distractingly good looks, something more complex peeked through. *Brave*—she conquered the cougar without any hysterics. *Loyal*—she stayed in town to protect her friends. *Fiery*—not many could hold their own against her. *Ruthless*—no price too great, no obstacle she wouldn't overcome to get what she wanted. *The last one's the kicker.*

It would be dangerous to get in the way of anyone with that sort of relentless determination—even worse to cross her. Because in spite of the intriguing traits, Miss Lyman didn't seem nearly as concerned with moral questions as she was with getting her own way. Chase didn't know if she was a believer or if she only put her faith in herself. In a lot of ways, she carried herself like a Christian, but the underlying motivation always seemed to come back to her plans for Hope Falls.

Did she hatch those plans back when the town housed a mine?

"Ready!" Excitement flushed her cheeks, as though she really looked forward to the grueling day ahead. Slung over her right shoulder, strap crossing her body, a leather game bag bumped against her hip. A *very full* leather game bag—which couldn't possibly be holding any game *before* the hunt.

"What all did you squirrel away in that thing?" Chase eyed it dubiously. They were in for a long trek, and she shouldn't be carrying any more weight than was necessary. Besides, she already packed her pistol and her bullets in her skirt pockets. What more did a fine lady think she'd need to go tracking?

"My canteen—I don't want too many things swinging around while I'm walking, so I put it inside." She started ticking things off. "My pocket-knife, for field dressing. Some good strong twine to use for carrying small game, a few handkerchiefs because it's going to be dirty work. . ." The woman sounded like she'd swallowed a manual for beginners. Otherwise, how would a fine lady like Lacey Lyman know anything about field dressing?

She'd trailed off as though she couldn't remember everything she'd crammed into the pack. This was proven when she sidled close to a table and plopped the bag atop it. Then the intrepid and overly prepared Miss Lyman began rummaging through, continuing her list as she rediscovered her necessities.

"A fan to use when I'm overexerted." She shot a quelling glance his way when he snorted at that find. "A fresh jar of feverfew infusion, so I can reapply it if the insects become troublesome later in the day. Oh, and lunch of course!"

For a moment Chase sat on the proverbial fence, trying to decide whether to laugh at her long laundry list or ask what she'd packed for their midday meal. It seemed a safe bet that anything from Miss Thompson's kitchen would prove better fare than the jerky and biscuits he kept handy while working.

It was a toss-up, but Chase figured he'd find out about the food later in the day. "Put your knife in the pocket with your bullets, put your canteen around your neck, and give the bag here. Anything you carry gets heavier as the day wears on; you can't tote that much." But he could see his way clear to toting lunch around, once he'd gotten rid of everything else. Except the twine—that might come in handy but would tangle in a pocket.

"Why, thank you, Mr. Dunstan." She slid the strap over her

head and held it out. "That's very kind and thoughtful—what, precisely, do you think you're doing!" She ended on a squawk.

"Lightening the load." He tilted the bag to one side, so things shifted. Chase reached in, pulled out an ivory fan, and tossed it on a nearby table. A garden of embroidered handkerchiefs bloomed in the emptied space. He chucked those, too. *What sort of nonsense is this?* A glass jar held some slightly cloudy liquid. Chase held it up for her inspection.

"The feverfew infusion," she informed him, her arms crossed over her chest as though to hold back a flood of angry words.

"Don't need that either." He placed it next to the hankies. "We'll stop by your shop and grab you a few bandannas, and that'll do. Everything else can stay here till we get back."

"Very well, Mr. Dunstan." She sounded as tightly wound as she looked. "If you insist on leaving the handkerchiefs and my fan, I'll not quibble. But the feverfew comes with me."

CD

"Won't do a lick of good." He slipped her bag over his head.

"Oh, it most absolutely does!" Lacey fought the urge to pick up her fan and throw it at his obstinate skull. Her temper hadn't won her any favors, so she decided to appeal to his sense of competition. "In fact, I can prove it. Let me bring the infusion and use it, and as the day progresses we'll see who suffers more bites and stings. If I'm correct, I can bring whatever I like on our next outing together. If you win, I'll bring only what you approve on our future excursions."

"Future excursions?" Genuine surprise colored the question.

"Of course." She held out the jar. "I'm a quick learner, Mr. Dunstan, but I don't think either of us believes I'll catch on to more than the rudiments the first time around."

He looked at the jar as though it might bite him. Then

he looked at her, and Lacey knew with absolute certainty that Chase Dunstan never considered she might want more than one lesson. By taking the jar, whether he won or lost the game, he'd be agreeing to continue her education with additional trips.

"Or you could simply admit you're wrong, and we'll leave it at that." Lacey knew she was goading him, but the stakes now went beyond keeping her insect repellent. It was about safeguarding her only opportunity to get outside the shop or the diner and actually learn something about all this land.

"I'm not wrong." He swiped the jar from her hand, looking repulsed at both the idea she'd be right and the knowledge that he'd just agreed to take her on future lessons. "Let's go."

When he turned to lead the way, Lacey grinned. No matter what Chase Dunstan thought, she knew this was going to be fun.

THIRTY

Four hours later, Lacey was ready to admit that she might have been mistaken. While time seemed to trudge by more slowly than they did—Dunstan set a grueling pace and expected her to maintain it—an entire morning with nothing to show for it could put a damper on anyone's spirits. *Especially when the man who's supposed to be teaching you about the forest and how to track animals only opens his mouth to tell you to be quiet.*

Well, Lacey had stayed quiet long enough! "Mr. Dunstan?"

"Sssh," he hissed, not even looking over his shoulder. The man kept walking as though he knew exactly where he was going. Maybe he did, but he hadn't bothered to tell Lacey about it.

She put the tips of her fingers in her mouth and produced a gratifyingly shrill whistle. For the first time in hours, her guide stopped to look at her. Decoy came bounding back to sit atop her foot, and Lacey remembered the last time she'd been in the woods with his master. Then it had been Dunstan to whistle.

"What do you think you're doing?" He spoke so low it became a rumble of words more than actual speech. "I told you—"

"To be quiet," Lacey whispered back. "Yes, I know. It's the only thing you've said all morning! After following nothing but you and your dog around for the past four hours, it's safe to say I've learned nothing at all about how to track an animal!"

"You should have." He approached her. "Learning to be quiet is the first lesson, and it's one you're far from mastering."

"I haven't spoken a word in over two hours!" she protested. Forest scenery may be beautiful, but it didn't exactly hold her attention when there wasn't anything in particular to see. A little conversation—even instructions on the sort of thing she should be noticing—would've made things a lot more interesting.

"Talking"—he returned to a more normal tone of voice—"is the most obvious part of silence. The way you walk comes next. Every move should make as little noise as possible." Dunstan's glance swept down her skirts toward her boots. "First off, you need sensible heels to minimize the sound of your steps."

"I'll order some," she told him. "There's nothing I can do about my footwear for today. I hoped to learn something more..." *Interesting!* She paused and finished, "Immediately applicable."

"Fine," he ground out. "The most important tool a hunter uses is patience. Move slowly and surely, take time to notice the signs around you. Know that you might fail to best the beast you track, but don't abandon your task unless necessary. The largest portion of hunting lies in waiting, Miss Lyman."

I waited a couple hours to hear you tell me that? Lacey kept the thought to herself. Provoking him wouldn't make Mr. Dunstan become a better teacher. Maybe questions would.

"Is there a way to muffle my footsteps? Wrap my heels with cotton or some such?" She tried to think of a way and failed.

Dunstan looked at her a long time, as though measuring whether or not she truly wanted to learn. Heartbeats passed before he decided to speak. "Don't assume the problem lies with the shoes, though in your case they need to be changed. Start with controlling the way you walk. Step on soft ground wherever possible—not mud, but solid earth. Do a better job of avoiding rocks and twigs, which do nothing but broadcast your presence. If you need to push aside a low-lying branch, don't shove it back to rebound and smack against the tree. Dry grasses rustle when your skirts brush by; the same for low bushes."

That makes sense—but it's a lot to remember when I typically set one foot in front of the other without thinking. I'd try going on tiptoe, but we're walking too fast and far!

"All right. You said we're hunting partridge. What signs have we been following for so long?" She peered at the ground, already knowing she wouldn't spot any tracks. Not surprising, since birds flew more often than hopped up a mountain. What did Chase Dunstan know that he hadn't bothered to share with her?

"We aren't. I know a spot where they've roosted for years."

"You've been shushing me all day for *nothing*?" Lacey sucked in a sharp breath as disappointment stabbed her. *Are there any lengths he won't go to in order to avoid talking with me?*

He shrugged at her outrage. "You still needed to practice being quiet, and there won't be time once things get underway."

"I can hold my tongue!" *When I have to. If I bite it, at least.* For now, Lacey didn't feel inclined to prove it.

"No way of knowing that." He arched a brow. "Last time I saw you walking in the forest, you didn't stop talking even when you thought there'd be no one around to join the conversation."

She felt the blush coming but couldn't stop it. "This is an entirely different situation!" *I know you can hear me, so I'd be more careful with what I said, for one thing.* "You're supposed to be teaching me, showing me things I didn't know."

"Told you to get different shoes and stop tromping around without looking where you're stepping." Somehow his summary of the advice sounded far worse than when he'd first mentioned it.

"You could've done that much sooner," she argued. "If you mentioned the finer points earlier, I might've been practicing something *useful* all the way up here! Now I have a late start."

"Do your best. This is poor terrain for stealth. Your shoes will ring against the rocks." As he mentioned it, Lacey realized they stood at the mouth of a canyon. Rocky outcrops shadowed patches of the healthy stream winding its way down the mountain.

"I thought birds liked trees." Lacey eyed the beautiful landscape and realized they'd be leaving the forest behind.

He smiled, and it transformed his face. No longer stern, disapproving, or smug as he'd looked in turn throughout the morning, it gave Lacey a sense that he'd been a mischievous boy. "Partridges aren't good fliers unless they're heading downhill."

"Heading downhill?" Lacey pictured a bird hopping atop the rock faces, only to trip on a rock and drop down into the stream because it didn't fly well. "You mean falling?" *Do birds fall?*

"Nah." Dunstan looked like he was thinking of a way to explain it better. "More the equivalent of a running start. They run pell-mell up a cliff or mountain or what have you—and these birds run faster than you or I could ever manage—then jump over the edge. Quick way to hit the air and drop out of range. They land just fine when they get to the bottom. You'll see."

The birds in her imagination began to look like plump chickens trundling as fast as their legs could carry them. Trouble was, chickens didn't move very quickly. Lacey tilted her head and looked at Dunstan. *Was he trying to trick her?*

"I'm going to be outrun by a bird who can't fly well but hurtles itself over mountainsides?" She wanted to be sure.

"Don't be silly." He took a swig from his canteen. "You're not going to chase them. It's better strategy to have Decoy flush 'em out. Easier to shoot them when they hit the air."

"What do they look like?" They couldn't be small like sparrows or huge like turkeys if one could feed a man.

"Bit longer than a foot. Brown and white with black markings. Red legs longer than a chicken's but shorter than a snipe. Close to quail-sized but look more like pheasants."

This amalgam of comparisons made Lacey envision a long-legged chicken with the head of a pheasant. Either Dunstan's descriptions needed work, or her imagination was rusty. *We'll see when we get there. . .but I think it's the description.*

"This partridge sounds like a very strange bird."

"It is. Harder to hunt than most, so it'll be enough of a treat for your picnic." He swirled the top back on his canteen.

Lacey's stomach grumbled at his mention of the picnic. She'd been too excited to eat much that morning, and all the exertion left her famished. The sun shone straight overhead, and she didn't need her watch to tell her they'd hit midday. "Should we enjoy our lunch before heading farther?" The rocks ahead wouldn't provide shade, and a short rest sounded heavenly.

"There's a little pool a few hundred yards ahead." Dunstan started walking again, but Lacey took his words to mean they'd be stopping soon. Men didn't usually argue against lunch.

She followed after him, noting they were still moving upward. It seemed to Lacey they'd gone uphill all morning, and her legs protested the hard work. When she slowed, Dunstan moved out of sight around a thick copse of trees. The soft gurgle of gently running water enticed her to follow a bit farther.

When she turned the trees, Lacey smiled in delight. An exclamation tickled her lips, but she remembered to whisper.

"How beautiful!"

"Beautiful" didn't do the view justice. Chase brought her as a reward—he hadn't expected her not to say anything for more than two hours, but she'd surprised him again. She deserved a short rest in one of his favorite shady spots. It'd been a while since he'd come here, and Miss Lyman's wonder made him look anew.

Half forest, half grotto, the forest came right up against the back of the rock face overlooking the river. A small overrun, too small to count as a waterfall, trickled down the rock into a small pool beneath. By late August the offshoot would dry up, but for now the gentle burbling of water over rock played like soft music. Trees, long sustained by the pool's spring-and-summer appearance, dappled the sunshine with cool shade.

Its beauty gladdened the eye, and Miss Lyman made a fitting addition to its charms. She sank to the ground without another word, obviously enchanted with the place. After a few moments of silence, she scooted forward to dip her hand in the water.

"Ooh!" A breath of an exclamation told Dunstan the water remained every bit as cold as he remembered. She hastily drew her hand back and shook free several drops of sparkling water.

Decoy showed no such compunction. Hunkering on the bank, he bent his head and began lapping water with great enthusiasm and much slopping of water on his paws. When he quenched his thirst, the dog moseyed on over beside Chase and collapsed with all the grace of a train car. After bolting down the eight strips of jerky Chase laid out for him, the dog stretched into a nice nap.

For his part, Chase wouldn't have minded doing the same. This little nook, tucked into a rocky crag, made good cover. Nothing—and no one—could creep up from behind or either side. Unfortunately, his pretty little concomitant precluded napping.

Not because Miss Lyman wouldn't appreciate the rest— Chase read fatigue in the way she didn't just lean against the rock behind her. The woman practically sank into the boulder, letting it prop her up while her eyes drifted shut for a moment then snapped back open. Ladies didn't routinely go for half-day treks up mountains, so it didn't surprise him if she looked tuckered.

What did still surprise him was how good she looked, even when worn to the bone. Lacey Lyman might be tired, but restless energy still coated her from head to toe. She looked happy. *The woman,* Chase decided, *is a bona fide, beribboned adventuress.*

"Would you be so kind as to pass me a clanger?"

"A what?" Chase searched his memory and couldn't remember her mentioning anything by that name when detailing the contents of her pack. Which, by default, meant she referred to lunch.

"Have you never tried one?" Her blue eyes grew brilliant. "Then you're in for a treat. Evie made a small batch before we left Charleston, and we tried them on the train. She's always trying new recipes and thought this one would sell well in her diner. It's portable enough for passengers to pick up when the train begins to bring more people through Hope Falls." All those words, and she still didn't manage to answer his question.

Chase opened the bag and drew out something wrapped in a clean kitchen towel. He tossed her the first one and kept the second for himself. When he unwrapped his bundle to find two apples and a nice wedge of cheese, disappointment descended.

Did she really say this *is one of her favorite meals?*

"Why would you call this a clanger?" Chase tried not to sound accusing. It sounded so promising before he saw it.

"Bedfordshire clangers," she supplied. "I think part of the reason I like them so much—besides the delicious way they taste and how there's dessert included—is because the story goes that milliners invented them. They made an easy, hearty lunch to leave for their husbands before they went off to work. It shows how women can be good wives and still do something more."

"You call apples and cheese a hearty lunch?" *She must count the apples as the "dessert."* He stopped polishing the first apple with his shirttail to cast her a doubtful look. Then he froze.

"Apples and cheese?" She paused in the act of raising a large golden-brown, delicious-looking pastry to her lips.

"What is that?" Chase's mouth watered, and he began to hope. "Is *that* a clanger?" He didn't wait for her answer, but dove into the bag for the last towel-wrapped bundle loitering in its depths. Pulling aside the fabric, he uncovered a second pastry.

"I didn't realize Evie added anything else." Miss Lyman shrugged and took a dainty bite of her own clanger. "Mmmm. . . ."

Mmmm was right. Chase chomped in, savoring the combination of crust with pork-and-peas filling. *That's more like it!*

"Oops, that's dessert." As he watched, Miss Lyman turned her pastry around before taking a second, much larger bite.

Now curious, Chase upended his clanger. Careful to keep his hand over the hole he'd made in the first side, he tried the second. Same buttery crust with sweet spiced apples this time.

Suddenly, he knew why Miss Lyman called it one of her favorites. The combination of sweet and savory made for a rib-sticking meal to satisfy any preference. And all in one easy-to-carry package.

"This is genius," he informed her between mouthfuls.

"Isn't it?" She beamed at him. "There's a sort of dividing wall of more pastry in between the two fillings. That way you can eat the meat side in one sitting and come back for the sweet side later. If you want to, I mean." Her eyebrows rose as he finished making short work of his succulent lunch.

Cool shade, good food, and a pretty woman to share it with. Chase leaned back, replete. He couldn't ask for anything more.

For now.

THIRTY-ONE

Since they'd stopped in the gorgeous hidden haven, Dunstan's mood improved. After lunch he became downright talkative. "See that?" Dunstan pointed to the edge of the small pool. "Funny little bird's called a dipper. Watch him and you'll see why."

Lacey squinted and didn't see anything at first. Then something moved on the rocks dotting the bank. "Oh, I see!" A little bird—small enough to rest in her cupped hands, perched atop a rock not much bigger. Beneath a head of brown feathers, it looked as though it wore a white cravat tucked beneath a red waistcoat. She didn't know much about birds, but his legs looked surprisingly long and spindly to support the rest of him.

As they watched, the bird stepped from its dry rock onto one partially covered with gently running water. Then it waded to an entirely submerged perch, hiding its legs and looking like a tiny, narrow-billed duck floating atop the water. Wading forward, it dipped its head into the pool and kept walking.

"Can he breathe?" she whispered. Lacey didn't really know why she was whispering, since she and Dunstan had been talking normally all through lunch. The little bird with its head beneath the water certainly wouldn't hear her and be spooked.

"They can hold their breath for a surprisingly long time," he told her as their feathered friend came up for air. "It's the only bird I know of who truly swims—flies underwater, really."

"Penguins do," Lacey recalled from her wildlife reading. "They don't really have feathers the same way others do though. But it's not really fair to say it swims better than a duck."

"Wait." With that enigmatic reply, Dunstan said no more. Then again, he didn't have to. Almost immediately the dipper dove underwater. His entire body plunged beneath the surface.

Transfixed, Lacey stared at the place where he'd disappeared. *Birds can't swim. He'll bob back up in an instant.* Only it seemed to be taking him rather a long time. Far longer than he should be able to remain underwater. *Maybe he drowned.* Sadness crept upon her at the idea they'd lost the brave fellow.

"There." Dunstan's voice called her to attention.

Lacey peered at the spot, anxious to still not see him. Her gaze scanned the bank, but still she found no sign of the bird. "I think you must have wished you saw him," she mourned.

"No." Dunstan leaned forward and tugged on her bonnet ribbons, turning her head to the far side of the pool. *"There."*

The little dipper splashed his way to the opposite bank—not such a great distance to Lacey, but impossibly far for him to have traversed below the surface. He held something triumphantly aloft in his beak. Happiness flooded her to see his victory.

"He made it!" Wonder filled her. "Dippers really do swim!"

"Yep." Dunstan rose to his feet and plunked his hat back on his head. "They go to the bottom, hunting for insects. Diving is more what they do than dipping. I'd have named it fisherbird."

"Because he fishes for his food," Lacey agreed. "Fisherbird makes a far better name. It describes how special his is."

"If you didn't pay close attention, you'd miss it." Dunstan's words somehow seemed to hold more meaning than the conversation warranted, but Lacey couldn't grasp why. "It's your next lesson. Don't look around for what you expect to see, or things pass you by. Always look to see what's really there."

Lacey couldn't answer at first, so electric was the force of his gaze. She'd had many men stare at her, but this was the first time one looked at her as though trying to plumb the depths of who she was. It was tempting to write it off as him trying to impress the lesson on her, but the fine hairs on the back of her neck prickled. He didn't force that intensity.

As quickly as the moment came, it ended. He turned to pick up the now almost-empty leather bag. Which reminded her. . .

"Wait a moment while I use some of the feverfew infusion," she half-asked, half-told him. When she took the jar from his outstretched hand, their fingers brushed. She pulled away, but chills traveled down her spine at even the brief contact.

She studiously ignored him as she set the jar atop the boulder where she'd been resting and began to untie her bonnet and roll up her sleeves. After unsealing the jar, she poured some of the cloudy liquid into her cupped palm. Lacey couldn't have looked at him now, even if she wanted to. The simple act of rubbing the solution onto her skin now seemed terribly intimate.

To avoid more discomfort, she turned her back and made swift work of the job. Only after she retied the bonnet ribbons beneath her chin, rolled down her sleeves, and smoothed the fabric, did Lacey feel composed enough to face Dunstan again.

He looked at her, expression now inscrutable, and held out his hand in an unspoken demand for the almost-empty jar. Once she'd passed it to him—careful not to touch him—he thrust it back into the bag. Without a word, he started walking.

But he didn't head toward the mouth of the canyon, as she'd

expected. Instead he skirted around the pool and began ascending a low incline up to the rocky overhang. Decoy followed him closer than a shadow, but Lacey found herself hesitating.

Walking or even hiking through the forest was one thing; scrambling up a series of large rocks was entirely different. *My feet hurt. My legs ache. I'll snag my skirts on those jagged edges. . . .* The litany ran through her mind. But swiftly on its heels came thoughts about how Dunstan didn't have to share the beautiful oasis with her—he could have kept walking. He didn't have to be congenial over lunch. In fact, Lacey expected him to remain taciturn. Instead he spoke pleasantly and decided to tell her about the dipper so she could watch it dive and rise.

Without making the decision to, Lacey began picking her way up the rocky slope, following the trail left by Dunstan and Decoy. *After all,* she reasoned, *who knows what I might miss if I look for what I expect? I expect the climb to be difficult, but what will I see when we reach the top? What more will I see of Chase Dunstan if I stop assuming he'll always behave rudely?*

She didn't know, but she'd never forgive herself if she quit trying to find out. Lacey kept her eyes on her feet and her focus on Dunstan as the incline sharpened, loath to look down. Who knew? The climb might take her farther than she expected.

◌∞◌

She'd come a lot farther than he expected, Chase grudgingly recognized. Maybe she and the other women had been right in saying he underestimated her. *Dangerous habit, Dunstan.*

Yesterday he'd gotten to thinking Lacey Lyman might be every bit as innocent—and intriguingly intrepid—as she appeared. A woman who couldn't hold her tongue couldn't have much guile, after all. But today she'd destroyed that theory by keeping quiet for hours on end—though she hadn't been happy about it.

Well, I'm not too happy about it myself. Chase slowed his pace slightly, so he didn't get too much of a lead. He'd teased her before about her proclivity for tripping, but the smaller rocks this way shifted underfoot and made the going slippery.

Her shoulder healed well enough. Now that she'd gotten back into fighting shape, Chase didn't plan on watching her hobble about with a sprained ankle. *Predators go after the injured.* The rule of the wild applied all too well to men on the prowl. And Miss Lyman already had far too many men prowling after her.

Besides, he added, *I don't want to have to carry her back!* If he'd gone alone, Chase would've reached the summit of the rocky overhang hours ago. Then again, if he'd gone alone, he wouldn't have gotten to eat one of those tasty clangers. On the balance, having her shadow him almost seemed worthwhile.

"All right?" He waited for her to catch up a little ways from the top. When she nodded, Chase didn't know if she was determined to stay quiet or if she'd become too out of breath. He gestured to her canteen then took a drink from his own.

"Here's the way it'll work." He kept his tone low more from habit than necessity. "The roosts are farther to the west, tucked in a niche a couple yards beneath the overhang."

"Underneath the—" Those blue eyes widened. "From what I saw, it's a steep drop after that overhang. You don't mean we're going to try to weasel our way into some crevices down there?" Despite her anxiety, she managed to keep her voice fairly quiet.

"Not in the plans," he assured her. "When we get close, I'll signal like this." Chase made a fist and moved it sideways, as though pulling rope in a game of one-handed tug-of-war. "Then you'll know it's time to be absolutely silent. If the partridge hear us coming, they'll panic and flush before we're ready."

"How will we flush them?" Her brow wrinkled in confusion.

"Decoy. Those dinner-plate paws of his give him sure footing, and he's better able to navigate the decline than we are. He'll nose down there then look up and wait for my signal once he's beneath the roost. Decoy coming at them will make the entire covey rush right out into the air. That's our chance."

"Does he bring them back afterward?" She cast an admiring glance at the dog and reached over to scratch behind his ears.

"When they fall on parts of the decline he can reach. Often the birds flush and get heights of about fifty feet. If we're lucky, we'll drop a few right up here." With that settled, he started moving again. At the rate she traveled, they'd need a good bit of time to make it back to town. Longer than it took to get here, even. They'd be tired and hopefully weighted down with all the partridge they'd bagged. Chase snorted.

All right, all the partridge *he'd* bag. The little pearly pistol she packed wouldn't hit anything, but Chase didn't have time to teach her how to use a shotgun before they set out. He might've if it weren't for the picnic looming the day after tomorrow. *Maybe I'll show her the next time we go.*

The idea crept into his thoughts and hit him unawares. Before they'd headed out, Chase would've laid odds that Lacey Lyman would find hunting a miserable pastime and never ask for another lesson. Since then, she'd proven surprisingly adaptable. It looked more and more likely that she'd want to learn more.

Then the time for thinking was over. They crested the ridge and crept several hundred yards westward before Decoy began wriggling his back end and sniffing toward the edge of the cliff. Birding behavior, as far as Chase ever heard, was only ever ascribed to retrievers or pointers. But hounds were good hunters, and few people ever came across an Irish wolfhound. Decoy might well be the only one trained in bird hunting.

Chase made the gesture, moved toward the edge of the overhang, and lowered himself onto his stomach. Peering down, he spotted piles of droppings and an occasional feather. *Promising.* He started to slide back so he could gesture to Miss Lyman, but found her already at his side, shimmying down to lie on her own stomach and peek over the side for herself. *Good enough.*

He made the motion for Decoy to scent and hold the birds, and off the dog loped, picking his way carefully down the steep decline. Time stretched while he lay beside Miss Lyman, waiting, but snapped into high gear the moment he saw Decoy stiffen, locked up and staring fixedly at a point Chase couldn't see. After holding still for a moment, he tilted his head back, searching for Chase's signal. Chase got to his knees, still looking over the edge, and gave the silent command for Decoy to flush them.

In a heartbeat about thirty startled partridges burst from the shelf in the rock. Some sprang high, most dropped low in effective, gravity-assisted escapes. Chase focused on the ones to go up and started shooting, dimly aware that Miss Lyman had risen to her feet and was doing the same with her handgun.

After the long walk, difficult climb, and restless wait, the whole thing finished in five minutes. One bird lay at their feet. Chase immediately spotted two more on nearby outcroppings as Decoy made his way back with a fourth between his jaws. He dropped it at Chase's feet. Tail wagging and tongue lolling out to the side, he enjoyed some well-deserved praise and scratching behind his ear. On Chase's signal, he headed back down for more.

Only then did Chase turn his attention to Miss Lyman. There she stood, silhouetted in the afternoon sunlight, a smile on her face and a partridge dangling from her right hand. There was a fierceness in her victory, and it made her even more beautiful.

"My first bird!" She thrust it toward him, and it dangled close enough to hit him if he didn't take it. "Look at it!"

Chase looked. Sure enough, the bird Decoy had brought up bore a wound too small for his shotgun to inflict. *Well, I'll be... She hit something after all. And it's the right thing.*

He gave a solemn nod of acknowledgment and handed the bird back. Decoy maneuvered between the two of them to drop another kill at his feet. More praise, and he sent the dog off again. Belatedly, he realized he'd given the dog more encouragement than the woman.

"Most men I know don't bag a partridge like this one the first time they try." Any man would be proud at the compliment

Miss Lyman's brow furrowed. "So. . .you didn't think I'd be able to do it? Then why did you bother bringing me along?"

Chase knew he'd been run to ground, and he couldn't think of a way to escape telling her the truth. There wasn't even a way to make it sound better, so he told her plain and simple: "You didn't leave me any choice."

THIRTY-TWO

Ask a foolish question. . . Lacey berated herself for forgetting, even for a moment, that Chase Dunstan didn't want to be saddled with her. Whether he went hunting or stayed closer to Hope Falls, the man couldn't be more eager to see the back of her.

"Turns out you're better company than I expected," he offered. Dunstan didn't give false compliments. In fact, he didn't give compliments at all, so she could trust he meant it.

Silly though it was, his words gave her something to grab hold of and pull herself from the sadness threatening to swamp her.

"It's easier to exceed expectations when they're set low." She sent him a small smile to show she wasn't haranguing him. Then she went about picking up another one of the partridges and stuffing it into her now-empty game bag. Lacey let him carry their lunch on the way up; she didn't plan to make him carry the fixings for the picnic all the way back without help.

"Up here it's easier to remember God has higher expectations for all of us." Dunstan adjusted his hat brim to better take in the vast panorama laid before them. "The lower you go, the less you expect to see people trying to match them."

"But the more chances you have to meet someone who's living that way," Lacey encouraged. "It's incredibly beautiful up here, but I'd imagine it becomes lonely with no one to talk with."

"Not all of us are as fond of talking as you." His murmur held no rancor as he made the observation. "Sometimes words can't do justice to what's displayed all around us in nature."

Curiosity battled with Lacey's newfound ability to keep silent. The curiosity won. "What do you see, Mr. Dunstan?"

"Power and majesty. A humbling, constant reminder of the verse in Deuteronomy." Dunstan left off appreciating the view to stare at her with unnerving directness. He quoted, " 'He is the Rock, his work is perfect: for all his ways are judgment: a God of truth and without iniquity, just and right is he.' "

It felt to Lacey as though the air itself grew thinner. The breaths she drew did little to fill her lungs as she contemplated the meaning behind the verse. *All his ways are judgment.* The phrase seemed to resound, caught in the rock around her and hammering into her heart. *And how far will I fall short of His perfect judgment on the day I stand before Him? Will He look at my selfishness? My thirst to prove myself? The way I led my closest friends to an abandoned town, only to fill it with unscrupulous men posing as suitors? Or will He go straight to the worst of it? So many ways I've failed. . . .*

"Striking, isn't it?" His eyes hadn't left her face.

"Unsettling," she admitted. "Since my mother's death I've devoted less and less time to the study of scripture." *Since Braden's death, I avoid it altogether.* But she couldn't very well admit that to a man who'd recited a verse from memory.

"I've always liked to read how God is my Rock. His constancy is a comfort when the world and people around us change." His intensity grew. "He's the one thing that will never fail."

Lacey was eager to end this conversation. "Somehow, I find little solace in the constancy of His judgment when I'm one of those who fails far too frequently." *There. I admitted it. Let that be one less black mark against my character.*

Dunstan looked flabbergasted. "We all fail. It doesn't say our work is blameless; we celebrate the perfection in His."

"And He judges us for falling short," Lacey finished. As far as she was concerned, this conversation had finished, too. She turned to start walking back down the rocky incline they'd climbed up. If Dunstan planned to sermonize, she wouldn't wait for his help going back home. Lacey longed for solid ground and trees— staying up here in the wide open left her feeling exposed.

"He's merciful if we confess our faults." Dunstan's words made her freeze, as though stuck to the stone beneath her. "Just where did you fall so far short you're afraid to trust Him?"

He can't know. Panic clawed its way up her throat as Lacey started walking again. Faster. "That is none of your concern."

∞

It concerns me very much. A woman so afraid of righteous judgment is guilty of something. Chase broke into long strides, determined to begin his descent before the foolish woman started down ahead of him. If she took a fall, he'd be there to break it.

"I can respect that." *Until I find more information.* For now he'd change the subject and try to sneak back around to the things he needed to know. "A woman who bags a partridge first time out deserves that much consideration. I don't know of a man who could bring one down with anything less than a shotgun."

"Men get more opportunities to practice," she retorted. "It doesn't mean they possess greater skill, Mr. Dunstan."

"True." *Occasionally.* "Even with practice and skill, there are times when no amount of preparation changes the outcome."

"If the bird gets away, you try again." She didn't acknowledge any deeper meaning behind his statement, and Chase wondered whether it was because she didn't notice or was avoiding it. "I find success is often measured in steps. Today, for instance, we bagged five birds. This success will lead to more when tomorrow we collect another seven for an even dozen."

We? Chase had no intention of taking her with him tomorrow. Nothing could be left to chance when one day remained. *This isn't the time to mention it,* he decided. *Besides, she'll awake in the morning with more aches than she anticipates.* He'd had full-grown, burly men who'd opted out of a second day of trekking with him after the first tested their strength. Granted, he'd not led her through terribly difficult terrain, but the vast majority had been uphill. That was unavoidable.

Instead of acknowledging her intent to join him the next day, Chase focused on the numbers she listed. "Seven at least."

"At least?" The swift patter of sliding rocks tattled that she'd halted. "They're large enough that we won't need more than one per person. Evie will be bringing some accompaniments, too."

Chase didn't stop walking and was gratified to hear her footsteps resume. It was time to spring his trap. "It occurred to me that since we can't bring Mr. Lyman to the picnic, we could at least bring a part of the picnic to your brother."

A faster skittering of rocks, a heavy footfall told him Miss Lyman slipped a bit at the mere mention of her brother. Turning to face her, he saw her arms extended in the act of adjusting her balance. She hastily put her arms at her sides, but her mouth held a pinched look telling of her displeasure.

"We're not all going to picnic in Braden's sickroom." This wasn't a protest with room to negotiate. It was a flat denial. She still didn't want Chase to meet her brother—perhaps didn't want anyone to meet him. Her reticence raised his suspicions.

"Of course not." His agreement immediately relaxed her, some of the tension leaving her shoulders. "I highly doubt we'd all fit, and that many people would be tiring. My idea was more that we could bring him a partridge after we returned to town."

"How thoughtful." Her lips pursed in that pinched look again. "I'm certain Cora would be delighted to do that."

Did he imagine the slight emphasis on her friend's name? Perhaps. . .but Chase knew he'd pricked a nerve at the thought he might want to venture into her brother's presence. *Good. When people are flustered, they're more likely to make mistakes.*

"You wouldn't want to take it to him yourself?" he pushed. "I've noticed that his fiancée spends far more time with your brother than you typically manage, since you have the store."

"To be frank"—she started walking, leaving him the choice to either get moving or collide with her—"you're not in town for the greater part of the day, Mr. Dunstan, and you are not privy to what I do with my time, nor whom I visit."

Chase resumed walking rather than let her run him down, but was aggrieved that he could no longer read her expressions. "My mistake. I'd simply thought you kept so busy you might welcome the chance to brighten your brother's day. The picnic is something everyone involved is looking forward to, and it might soften the sting if he takes exception to our chosen location."

"How very diplomatic of you." She sounded as though she gritted her teeth. "I'm surprised by how talkative you are, Mr. Dunstan. It makes for quite a contrast to earlier in the day."

Irritating, isn't it, when someone utterly ignores the fact that you might not be enjoying their company and conversation? Chase kept the jab to himself—provoking her further wouldn't get him any new information. He'd already discovered what he needed to know. *She's determined to hide her brother. But why do I get the sense Miss Lyman herself would rather avoid him?*

Put together with her earlier comments about falling short and facing judgment, Chase could easily believe Lacey Lyman's strong sense of guilt stemmed from something to do with her supposed brother. *Maybe Braden wasn't supposed to be in the mines that day.* His mind raced at the implications of that. Unmarried, she'd need a man to maintain ownership of the land for any considerable length of time. *Maybe her Braden did die, as was first reported, but she needed him as the figurehead.*

It all came back to his suspicion that the hidden invalid in Hope Falls wasn't the real Braden Lyman. *She might have found a survivor and cooped him up in a room to pose as her brother.* It wouldn't work for long though. Eventually the man would either recover or pass away, and she'd be in the same position.

Unless she found a husband. It felt as though all the air in the mountains had suddenly been sucked away. Chase couldn't seem to breathe properly. In the past few weeks, he'd decided the woman had no real intention of marrying any of the men. But what if he'd read the situation wrong? Her friend Miss Thompson snagged Granger right off the bat—maybe they were serious.

> *Wanted:*
> *3 men, ages 24–35.*
> *Must be God-fearing, healthy, hardworking single men*
> *with minimum of 3 years logging experience.*
> *Object: Marriage and joint ownership of sawmill.*

The words swam in his memory, the outrageous ad that sparked his suspicions to the point he'd sent Kane to Hope Falls. Back then Chase disregarded the post as a distraction to cover up the sabotaged mine. He still thought the whole plot interwove somehow with the destroyed mine, but now Chase wondered if the ad wasn't genuine. Miss Lyman couldn't hold the land indefinitely. She needed a man to keep her claim legal—and a husband with sawmill experience would be doubly useful.

What was it she'd said when they first discussed her plans for Hope Falls? *"No cost can be too great to gain one's dream."* Back then he'd suspected it referred to the lives lost in the cave-in. But maybe Miss Lyman referred to the price *she'd* pay to keep her goals aloft. The notion wasn't reassuring. If the woman was ruthless enough to marry for money—and force her closest friends to do the same—she'd be unscrupulous in other ways.

The picture became clear. *Too bad I don't like what I see.*

THIRTY-THREE

"What are you looking at?" Cora walked into the parlor to find Lacey tightly curled into a wingback chair, catalog balanced on her knees and pen in hand as she perused the page.

Her friend looked up, nibbling on her lower lip. "Shoes." The single word explained her intense focus.

"Are you finally going to purchase some sensible boots?" Naomi came in from the opposite entrance and settled herself on the settee. "You won't be sorry once you feel the difference."

"After today, I can no longer ignore the fact that my Louis XV turned heels simply aren't practical for long-distance walks in the woods." Lacey wiggled the toes peeking out under the edge of her skirts. "I don't believe I've ever ached more than I do now," she confessed as she pulled her foot back to hide her shocking dishabille. Mr. Lawson had gone to the McCreedys' house to confer with the senior bull-of-the-woods over beginning the flume, but they couldn't be sure when he'd return to the house.

"You seemed so excited earlier." Cora remembered it well because when she'd seen Lacey burst into the kitchen, flushed

579

with victory over her successful partridge hunt, she'd had to tamp down a spurt of jealousy. *She'd* spent the day with Braden.

"Excitement wears away more quickly than soreness." Naomi angled behind Lacey's chair to get a better look at the page. "Bloomingdales, then? Montgomery Ward has some good options."

"I already looked in that one." Lacey gestured to a stack of catalogs on a nearby table. "To make a good comparison, you know. But I've always felt Bloomingdales carries the best footwear options when one can't have her boots custom-made."

Although perfectly pleased with her own boots, Cora moved to stand at Lacey's other side and get a better look at the catalog. "Have you seen any that will suit your needs?"

"Those look practical." Naomi pointed to a picture of a low-heeled lace-up model with short ankle rises. "Comfortable."

Cora didn't understand how Naomi could think Lacey would ever wear low-fashion, sturdy lace-ups. She smiled at her friend's stricken glance as Lacey tried to come up with a way to refuse the dowdy boots without offending Naomi. Their friend, of course, wore sensible, low-heeled, long-wearing lace-ups.

"I simply can't see Lacey in Old Ladies' Shoes." Cora came to her rescue by reading the name above the picture itself.

"How can you call them that?" Naomi bristled visibly.

"She didn't." Lacey ran a fingertip beneath the print. "They're actually listed that way in the catalog itself!"

"They're shown under the Ladies Common Sense Boots column." Naomi squinted at the print atop the page—print referring to the picture just below it, rather than the next image of her favored Old Ladies' Shoes. "You see?" She ran her finger down and hitched on the protested title. "Oh dear."

Lacey giggled as Naomi snatched her hand back as if burned. "It's an easy mistake to make," she consoled her cousin.

"Those Common Sense Boots are much better," Cora commented. This model showed a modest blocked heel and side-fasten buttons.

"Oh, those aren't bad at all, Lacey!" Naomi transferred her attention immediately. "And the name promises what you need."

"It's between those or the ones pictured here." Lacey pointed to the bottom of the page. "Look at the name: Waukenphast. When you say it, it sounds like 'walking fast.' "

Cora evaluated this other pair of side-buttoned boots. Another stacked heel, but this one straighter than that of the Common Sense version. "Oh, look at the description! 'The most comfortable shoes manufactured.' " She read it aloud for Naomi.

"Yes." Lacey sounded decisive. "These are the ones for me. I'm also going to try one of these." Her voice lowered, and she darted glances about to make sure Mr. Lawson hadn't returned.

"What are you three up to?" Evie strolled over. Heeding Cora's warning of a finger over her lips, Evie didn't say a word. She simply watched as Lacey flipped through the pages and came to rest in the section entitled Corset Department.

Lacey pointed to the Pivot Corset and began to read in a very hushed voice. " 'Has an expanding hip and bust, yielding to every movement of the wearer, constantly making an easy and elegant fit. . .which preserves the perfect contour of the figure.' "

No wonder her friend first looked about to make sure no man burst into the room! Evie looked at the picture, which didn't seem much different from any of the other corsets on the page. "What a find! It would be so much easier to walk and sit and cook and do just about anything if we weren't encased like sausages, unable to bend. I believe I'll place an order, too."

In fact, all four of them did. Lacey, who boasted the neatest penmanship, wrote up the order but left room along the bottom. "Thumb through and make sure there's nothing more you'd like.

By now we've hit the maximum for freight charges anyway."

Maybe I'll find something to shake Braden from his doldrums. As they each sat down with a different catalog, Cora took the Bloomingdale's Brothers when Lacey finished with it. Turning pages, she came across a sketch of a woman lying in a hammock strung between two shady trees. *He might be able to use a hammock soon. Once we're able to move him from the bed, it would be good to go outside. The fresh air might work wonders for his disposition.* She turned down the corner of the page.

Nothing more caught her eye until she turned to the section of advertisements taking up the last several pages. Everything from electric curlers to pocket watches to dumbwaiters and dress shields jumbled together with no rhyme nor reason. Cora began reading, stopping when she spotted a box with no pictures.

SCIENCE OF A NEW LIFE TO ALL WHO ARE MARRIED, proclaimed the ad in bold capitals. Slightly smaller beneath it added OR ARE CONTEMPLATING MARRIAGE and went on to declare the book recommended by both medical and religious critics and worth its weight in gold. In miniscule print, they ran the table of contents along the bottom, just above its ordering information. Cora pulled the page close to her nose. Some of the print smudged, and she could only make out some of the chapter headings.

Chapter I—Marriage and Its Advantages
Chapter II—Age at Which to Marry
Chapter IV—Love Analyzed

Several of the middling titles were hopelessly obscured, prompting Cora to give up and skip ahead to the last two.

Chapter XXVII—Subjects of Which More Might Be Said
Chapter XXVIII—A Happy Married Life—How Secured

Sorely tempted by the final chapter, Cora considered whether or not the book itself, containing more than four hundred pages and one hundred illustrations, would be worth three whole dollars.

Then she caught sight of the offer running just beneath the title.

Any person desiring to know more about the book before purchasing it may send to us for our sixteen-page descriptive circular, giving full and complete table of contents. It will be sent free to any address. J. S. Ogilvie & Co. Publishers.

Thoughtfully, Cora took up Lacey's abandoned pen and began jotting down the address. If the description pleased her, she'd buy the book and read the first and final chapters. A mischievous smile spread across her face as she decided. *After I'm finished, I'll make it a special gift to my fiancé.*

∞

The woman had a gift for giving him trouble. Chase could think of no other way to describe it when Lacey Lyman insisted on coming to the picnic site to help prepare the main course.

"The entire thing was my idea, and I'm responsible for making sure things go as smoothly as possible," she argued.

She'd been put out by his refusal to bring her along to finish hunting partridges. He'd cited her shoes—and noted her wince as though reminded of aching feet—to justify his decision. All in all, she'd acquiesced easily. So easily, Chase suspected more than her feet ached. But a lady wouldn't tell him what men would admit to—no mentioning of anything half so scandalous as sore limbs—so it remained pure speculation on his part.

At least, it had been pure speculation until she'd insisted on carrying the cleaned, beheaded, and stuffed partridges to the site with him. Then Chase could trust his observations on the subject. He kept a close eye on her as they walked to the mines.

The mines where he'd hoped to explore a bit while the partridge cooked. The mines he'd come to Hope Falls to examine, but been unable to due to inclement weather and interfering females. The mines he wouldn't be able to examine even today.

No changing it though. So he contented himself with watching Lacey Lyman slowly make her way toward the picnic area. She'd never be anything but graceful—so long as she wasn't falling, at least—but there was a stiffness about her movements that hadn't been there two days before. *Headstrong woman.*

"Watch your step." They'd reached an area still raw from the collapse, with some spots of earth strangely pitted and others unexpectedly pushing up. Chase had seen this sort of upheaval in areas where there'd been large quakes, but while disturbing, at least those sights had been natural. This wasn't.

The sadness of the place seemed to catch hold of her, too. She didn't speak again until they'd gone through the trees and into the meadow he'd earmarked as their location. *Is her silence out of respect, guilt, or both?* Chase couldn't very well ask.

"You already laid the fire?" She looked at the place where he'd readied six smaller pit fires the evening before. From this angle, it wasn't surprising she'd thought it one large setup.

"Yep." Chase had, in fact, lit fires there the night before to help fill the pits with ash. The trenches, now partially filled with ash and debris, he'd topped with small tinder and again overlaid with larger branches. They need only be lit. He set down the two bags of prepared partridges he carried and set to it. The fires needed to burn long enough and hot enough for the ashes to cook the birds once they were made ready.

"What's that?" Miss Lyman set down her own bag, looking intently at the small silver box he pulled from his pocket.

"Man who gave it to me called it a 'chucknuck'." Chase held it up for her inspection then thumbed the steel band running around the box to open it. Inside lay a small store of dried moss to be used as punk and a trusty, battered piece of flint.

"I've never seen one of these before," she marveled.

"Never seen another one," he agreed. Removing some moss and placing a bit on the tinder of each prepared fire pit, he circled back. Chase knew she watched every move as he hunkered down and struck his flint against the steel to light the moss. The tinder around and beneath it smoked almost instantly.

"You don't like matches?" She sounded curious, not mocking.

"Get 'em wet and they're ruined," Chase told her. "Makes them pretty useless when you live in the open and need a fire whether it rains, snows, or sleets. This serves me better."

"How do you light a fire in the rain? Won't it extinguish?"

"If a fire's well-laid and started, it pretty well takes a torrential downpour to put it out." He finished lighting the final fire and stood next to her. "Take a good piece of bark and lay it down so your logs aren't resting on the wet ground. Split your wood to get to the dry middle, and keep it dry under a blanket until you're ready to lay and light the fire. Once it's lit, keep it covered from whichever direction the rain's driving until the flames leap and the logs are ablaze."

She watched as he grabbed one of the buckets of clay he'd hauled over yesterday. "I'd like to try it sometime, I think."

"It's not fun when it's necessary," he warned. Chase fell silent as he dumped out the contents of the first bucket and pressed it down to make a semi-flat surface on the ground. Then he took another bucket, emptied it atop the first, and grabbed his canteen. He sprinkled the riverbed clay with water until it became soft and pliable then added more until it gained the consistency of mud. *Now we'll see how delicate she really is.*

 THIRTY-FOUR

It looks like he's making mud pies. Lacey watched, fascinated, as his strong hands kneaded the reddish-brown clay. She could have been suspicious about what he planned to do with that clay, since he'd been so reluctant to let her come along and help.

Instead, after his explanation of the chucknuck and concise directions on how to lay a fire in the rain, she adopted a wait-and-see approach. *Come to think of it, it's almost the same thing he advised after he showed me the dipper bird.*

"Bring out two of the birds." His blunt instruction sent her diving into a bag as he dumped more mud next to the lump he'd worked water through. "Keep one and give me the other."

Lacey sat, cross-legged, holding a stuffed bird. "Are we plucking the feathers now?" She still couldn't reconcile the fact that they'd cleaned, beheaded, and stuffed the partridge with their feathers still attached. How would they cook?

"We aren't plucking them, exactly." Dunstan grabbed a lump of runny clay and held it over his bird. Then he started *spreading the muddy mixture on top of its feathers!*

"What"—she struggled to mask her horror—"are you doing?"

"Prepping the partridge." He made it sound like the most natural thing in the world. "You're falling behind, Miss Lyman."

Suddenly she realized that he intended for her to do the same thing to the bird in her hands. Lacey eyed the sludge with revulsion. "You want me to slop mud on this bird, too?"

"All of them." He plopped another handful down and smoothed it over the feathers like a plaster. "And it's clay, not mud."

"But. . .why?" Lacey had to know. "What's the difference?"

"Mud dries, crumbles, and leaves dirt everywhere." By now he'd coated his entire partridge with enough of the clay to turn the bird brown. "Clay dries, hardens, and cracks when broken. By coating the feathers with moist clay and covering that again with a firmer, drier layer, it forms a sort of individual oven."

Even as he told her this, he grabbed a handful of the clay he hadn't put water into. This he molded and patted on top of the entire thing until the bird resembled a misshapen mud ball. Dunstan held it up for her to see. "When the fire pits are filled, I'll stir the new ash with the old to make sure it's hot even from the bottom. We put the birds inside and cover them."

"I can see how that might work with cooking them." Lacey tried and failed to find a diplomatic way of voicing her doubts. "But then we're left with hard balls of clay over befeathered birds. How is that going to make an easy-to-eat picnic?"

"After they cook for an hour or so, you fish them out and hit 'em with a thick branch." He set the prepared bird aside and reached for another. "When the clay comes off, the feathers come with it, so you're left with a ready-to-eat partridge."

"Well." Lacey blinked at the bird in her hands and thought of all the time she'd spent plucking chickens for Evie to fry for a dozen lumberjacks' dinner. "Isn't that convenient?"

She set the bird aside, pushed up her sleeves, and retrieved it.

Steeling herself, Lacey plunged her hand into the sticky clay and slapped it over partridge feathers, smoothing it over the same way she'd seen Dunstan do it. By the time she moved on to the more dry substance, she caught him staring.

"Is it wrong?" The bird looked properly muddy to her.

"Nope." He shrugged and grabbed another partridge. "I wasn't sure you'd believe me enough to get your hands dirty."

"Mud and clay wash off." Lacey proudly added her first partridge to his growing pile. "By now you've earned my trust." She selected another one and looked up to see him staring again. Surprise shone in his gaze, and she wondered why he would be so shocked to hear that she trusted him. Lacey stared back at him.

"Is your trust usually earned so easily?" He sat unnaturally still. "Do you change your mind that quickly?"

Regret pulled at her. "You know I didn't want to hire you on, and I won't pretend otherwise. And I resented your implication that I was self-centered and weak-willed on the day of the cribbage tournament." She sighed and kept going when it looked like he might speak. "But you weren't trying to insult me, and I can't fault you for an honest opinion. Even a wrong one."

"There's a vast difference between not holding an opinion against me and deciding I'm trustworthy." He sounded curious. "I've been here for three weeks. What changed your mind in that time?"

"Your temper is as quick to fire as mine." Lacey studiously avoided his gaze and kept working, finding she enjoyed the feeling of the cool clay squelching through her fingertips. "But there's an honesty in that. And although we've angered each other, you've tried to protect me from cougars and the men. You even became a really good teacher once we got past the silence."

He'd fallen silent again, and now he was the one focusing too intently on the partridge. It was the first time she'd seen him uncomfortable like this. *It's good to know he can be thrown off balance like anyone else. I'd been starting to wonder.*

"Besides"—she strove to lighten the mood—"you've told me other improbable things, like the dipper bird who swims and the partridge who falls more than flies, and they turned out to be true. I can't imagine, after all the trouble we went through to get these birds for the picnic, you'd be wrong about this."

"I'm not wrong about the clay." *But am I wrong about you?* Chase withdrew from the conversation by getting up and stirring the fire-pit ashes with a long branch he'd saved for that purpose. There she sat, blithely believing his word over her own experience, telling him he'd earned her trust with his *honesty.*

I've been careful not to lie to any of them, he acknowledged. *But holding back the true reason I came to Hope Falls means I've not been honest.* Not that he had a choice. A twinge of regret hit him as he surveyed a gleefully clay-smeared Lacey Lyman, who seemed to be enjoying herself now that she'd overcome her doubts. Tempting to trust her in return, but the woman boasted too much charm and hid far too many secrets.

Every bit of information he'd uncovered pointed to Lacey Lyman as the mastermind behind the mine collapse. But that didn't mean Chase couldn't hope his suspicions were wrong.

That he even entertained the thought proved she was dangerous.

And intuitive enough not to engage him in conversation while his well-founded suspicions raged against his foolish hopes. They didn't speak even as he pushed the ashes aside and allowed her to drop two clay-covered partridges into each pit. In silence he prodded ashes over the birds to cook all through.

"Hello!" The rest of their party, toting an assortment of

canteens, boxes, and baskets cleared the woods and moved into the meadow. They obviously had no trouble following the rope markers he looped around easily spotted branches along the way.

Immediately Williams broke away from the pack and hastened to Miss Lyman's side. He glared at Chase in accusation even as he hovered at her side. "Are you hurt? Did you fall on the way?"

"What makes you—oh!" She looked down at her hands, streaked with red-brown clay. "No, I'm fine. It's from our cooking."

"Here." He offered her a bandanna and his canteen to wash up. If anything, he looked disappointed at the news that she hadn't fallen. Or maybe Williams took exception to her use of "our," allying herself with Chase. Either way, the man's hackles rose high enough he could've jousted with porcupine quills.

For some reason this cheered Chase considerably. Instead of examining it too closely though, he turned to the rest. Lawson, the only man not carrying a parcel, supported his ungainly sister and trailed behind the rest. The glower he aimed at Williams should've left a hole in the back of his shirt.

It was the first time Chase would've sided with Williams in a fight. Williams might be a bully, but he'd won his way to the picnic fair and square. Lawson egged his sister into a clearly ill-advised trip just to sneak his way in. He not only lacked the honor to play by the rules and accept his defeat, but he also was willing to put Mrs. Nash's health in danger to get near Lacey.

Miss Lyman. Chase shook his head to clear the unwanted familiarity. Obviously, keeping company around riffraff like this made it easier to forget his own boundaries with her.

Aside from Williams stalking after Lacey Lyman's every move and Lawson resentfully tracking his rival's progress, everyone seemed in high spirits. When they began unpacking Miss Thompson's additions to the celebration, Chase understood why.

One box cradled plates, mugs, and cutlery. Out of another came jars of water and cool, sweetened tea. An entire basket overflowed with dozens of cornbread squares. Another basket boasted crocks of butter and jars of jam. Two dutch ovens, immediately tucked in the fire pits to stay warm, held fried parsnip balls. And the last basket, well bundled and tucked in the coolest shade well away from the fires, guarded a custard.

"It all looks wonderful!" Mrs. Nash exclaimed from where she'd been seated in the thick of things by her brother. The brother, of course, joined Williams in hovering by Miss Lyman.

"Quite a sight," agreed Draxley as he sank down next to her. His mustache twitched even more speedily than usual as he tried to situate himself atop the log without falling back.

"An unparalleled view." Lawson offered her a slight bow.

The sycophant bows to her in the middle of the mountains. At a picnic. While she wears a smudge of clay on one cheek.

Actually, Chase liked that smudge. She looked even better slightly mussed. But the bowing. . . Chase held back a snort.

Williams showed no such compunction. He lumbered forward, inserting himself between the other two. "Don't grovel, Lawson."

"Back up a wee bit and let Miss Lyman breathe, Williams." Riordan sauntered over. His sheer size, along with his status in town, worked in his favor. The massive Irishman loomed over the shorter, balding man for mere minutes before Williams conceded.

"Where's your food, Dunstan?" Clump peered around as though expecting it to magically appear on the ground before him.

"Almost ready." Chase crouched between the first two fire pits, using a well-curved branch to push the clay pods out of the heat. "I'll pass it out when everything else is served."

Grumbles of disbelief and curiosity followed him as he freed the partridges and corralled them in one area. Soon that spot was littered with thirteen clay pods—but Chase counted only eleven people present at the picnic. They were one short.

One of the birds was earmarked for the supposed Braden Lyman, but where was his doctor? Chase wouldn't be able to gather any information from a man who didn't bother to show up. "Where's the doctor?" he asked of Miss Thompson while she finished dotting butter and dishing up the fried parsnip balls.

"He doesn't enjoy the outdoors," the younger Miss Thompson answered. "We asked him to come, but he chose to stay behind."

No checking the mines, no interrogating the doctor. . . The afternoon was swiftly looking to be a great waste of time. The only man who might make the day worthwhile sat next to Mrs. Nash, looking supremely uncomfortable and unforthcoming.

"A shame. I'd think that a doctor would be more in favor of exercise." Inspiration struck. "Maybe we can all go for a walk after lunch, explore the area closer to the mines. It makes for interesting hiking, now that the ground has settled again."

"Absolutely not!" The forceful protest came from Draxley, who looked as surprised at himself as everyone else was. Mustache twitching and glasses slipping, he stuttered, "I mean, that is to say, it's dangerous that way. Dips and ridges and who knows what all. Mrs. Nash shouldn't take such risks." He gave her a look both anxious and adoring. "We must stay safe."

"Makes no never mind to me." Clump sat down like a bag of bricks between Miss Thompson and Miss Higgins. "We can walk around it, over it, or in the other direction. So long as we talk about it after we eat all this good-smelling food!"

And that quickly, Chase lost the chance to do any investigating. He couldn't slip away and leave Miss Lyman the veritable prize in a tug-of-war between Lawson and Williams. But why didn't she protest poking around the collapsed mines? Did she simply not get a chance when Draxley voiced his anxiety?

Now that the partridges had cooled, Chase vented his

frustration on the first one. He brought the heavy branch down with precise force, watching with satisfaction as the clay cracked open to reveal a feather-lined cook pod. The tasty white meat of the bird lay pristine and steaming atop its broken bed.

He pulled away the top half and handed the first bird, still dished in the other half of the pod, to Miss Thompson. Usually she cooked and served everyone else, so Chase thought it a fitting tribute to the chef of eggs in overcoats and clangers.

"I've never seen the like!" she exclaimed then promptly began firing a barrage of questions at him about how he did it.

"Ask Miss Lyman—she helped hunt the birds and then cook them." Chase gave her the opportunity to extract herself from the competitive conversation of the men bracketing her, and Miss Lyman hopped up in an instant to join her friend.

She cast him a grateful look, which Chase couldn't stop thinking about. *If I'm right and she wants a husband so desperately, why would she jump at the chance to avoid suitors?*

It made no sense. *But then again. . .* Chase eyed the woman as she pointedly ignored the men trying to win her attention. *Nothing about her makes much sense.*

THIRTY-FIVE

It's almost over. After three weeks of travel and an expedited hearing, Jake couldn't wait to go back to Hope Falls.

He stood beside his mother and father, watching as the officials took Twyler back to the jail. After everything it had taken to get to this point, Jake expected to feel more of a sense of triumph. His brother's murderer didn't escape justice. Edward would no longer be remembered as a gambling cheat, and his parents had begun to openly mourn for their firstborn.

"Justice is finally served." His father sounded satisfied.

Finally? It still angered Jake to think that they'd ignored the notice of Edward's death, refusing to announce his passing so long as the story reflected poorly on the family. They'd gone on as though he'd never died—as though he'd never lived. *There should be some sort of punishment for parents who view their children as extensions of their reputation and nothing more.*

But the Grangers did everything in their power to suppress any mention of scandalous events, trying to hide Edward's "dishonorable death" after being told he'd pulled a gun over a card game. Jake's father went so far as to pay Twyler hush money in an attempt to keep the story from spreading.

I could have tracked him down sooner if he'd not had the money and head start to run. Jake still hadn't spoken to his father about this, too conflicted to broach the subject. If he'd found Twyler early on, he wouldn't have found his Evie. Besides, his father finally put good use to his riches by greasing the wheels and pushing the trial through the system. It landed before the judge far sooner than Jake ever would have expected.

"He won't hurt anyone again," Jake agreed. In fact, after hearing about the murder and the kidnapping afterward, the judge—whom Jake made sure his father didn't go anywhere near—didn't hesitate in his ruling. Twyler's established history of continuing crime made him an ongoing threat, and placing him in a prison wouldn't provide adequate protection to society.

When the prison wagon drove out of sight, Jake turned to his parents. "It's finished now. Everyone knows Edward was a good man." *Instead of thinking he'd run off with some of Father's money to fund a new life out West, as you let them believe.* He didn't speak the accusation—the time for blame had ended. The way his parents handled things would always spark some anger, but forgiveness wasn't a feeling. *It's a choice.*

"I don't know if I can watch," his mother fretted as they headed back home. "There's no time to consider it either."

"We're going." His newly vengeful father didn't share her reservations. "The wretch killed our Edward. We'll see this through until Twyler no longer twitches on the end of his rope."

"But to go into the prison. . ." His mother grew pale. "Even staying in the portion with no prisoners. . .it's so tawdry!"

"They don't do public hangings anymore," Jake reminded her. "It's a good thing. The sight of them didn't instill fear, it drove people into a frenzy and inspired even more violence."

"Hanging in the prison yard sends a message to the criminals held there without exposing the sight to more delicate sensibilities." His father opened the door. "I know it will be difficult tomorrow morning, my dear, but we must go."

"I'm going tonight." Jake made the decision that moment.

"It's not until the morning." They looked confused.

"I mean I'm going back to Hope Falls," he clarified. He'd hunted Twyler down—literally shot the man to bring him back. "There's nothing left for me to stay for now that it's over."

"You'd dishonor your brother's memory by not attending?" His father drew himself to his full height. "Unthinkable!"

"I honored Edward by believing him to be the brother I'd always known and tracking down the man who murdered him." Jake kept his voice level, stating facts rather than throwing the comparison in his parents' faces. "My part is complete."

"What do you mean, you're going?" His mother clutched the door frame, eyes darting down the streets as though gauging how much the neighbors might hear. "With this finished, you'll be able to step in and help your father with Granger Mills."

"No, Mom." He'd told her before. "I'm going back to Hope Falls to build a sawmill—with the woman I'm going to marry."

"Whether you like it or not, you have an obligation to this family." His father wasn't asking him to stay out of affection or gratitude—in his mind it was about the family name. "I founded Granger Mills, and a Granger will run it after me."

"My obligations are to God and my wife, and I've kept her waiting long enough. If you're set on keeping the company name for another generation, I suggest you track down cousin Billy." Jake started down the porch steps. "I've got other plans."

"You planned that picnic," Braden accused. It might have fazed Lacey if he hadn't been caterwauling about the same thing for the past two weeks. "But you sit there and act like it's fine?"

"Absolutely." She cocked her head to the side and surveyed the color in her brother's cheeks. He looked angry, yes, but on the balance he was more animated and healthy-looking in these past weeks since the picnic than he had been since they arrived. Even better, the picnic didn't stick in his craw purely because of the location. He objected to Cora going—and Lacey had a fantastic, sneaking suspicion it had something to do with her being surrounded by the eager bachelors of Hope Falls.

He still loves her. Until relief overwhelmed her, Lacey hadn't realized that she'd begun to doubt Braden's affection for her best friend. *Why does he keep pushing her away? Why does he keep pushing all of us away? And how can I get him to remember the brother he used to be? The man I saw him grow into?*

"Now you have the nerve to look upset?" He snorted.

"You'll find I have every bit as much nerve as I did when I was six and you dared me to climb the Wilson's oak tree." The memory of her doting brother from back then made her smile.

"And every bit as gullible and foolhardy," he grumbled. "If you'll recall, you fell out of that tree, sprained your arm, and got me stuck polishing all the silver in the house."

"Backing down from a challenge isn't the Lyman way," she reminded. "You knew that when you decided to test my courage. Now that we're older, you try my patience instead."

"You beat my patience into the ground the day you dragged Cora to Hope Falls," he snarled. "Then I thought things couldn't be worse, but somehow you keep proving me wrong. Advertising for husbands, scurrilous mongrels trying to sneak into the house in the middle of the night, murderers carrying you off into the forest, cougar attacks. . .every time I think you've outdone yourself, you demonstrate an even more heinous lapse in judgment than the one before. It's nothing less than a miracle Cora and the others have survived your scrapes so far."

Now that's simply unfair. Lacey brushed his list away. *The only thing in that whole litany that can be attributed to my poor judgment is the ad itself. Everything else would have happened in spite of me, or to spite me. But maybe it means something good that he worries so much. I worry, too.*

"Our survival isn't the miraculous one, Braden." Her voice softened as she looked at the familiar face, once filled with confidence and happiness, now etched with misery. "It seems you overlook the fact *you've* been given another chance in your haste to make sure no one else makes good use of theirs."

"It's not the chances you're given which disturb me. It's the chances you take." He turned it back on her. "Of all the opportunities and places in the world, you bring yourself and the others squarely in the middle of danger and death."

Lacey thought for a moment, but was unable to be sure of his meaning. There was nothing for it but to ask. "Do you mean Hope Falls itself, or are you referring to the picnic again?"

"Both! But most recently it is your cheery visit to the site of my ruination which grates against my thoughts." His brows drew together, compounding his scowl into something epic.

"Pishposh. The land remains. We remain, and most of all we remain thankful that you were brought out of those tunnels alive. Even now your body heals." *But your thoughts and mind remain in the dark, and we don't know how to pull you out.*

She stared at her brother, willing him to hear the truth behind the words she now whispered. "The cave-in didn't defeat you then; don't let it defeat you months later."

"You don't know what you're talking about." His throat worked, telling her that her brother wasn't just angry. For as long as she could remember, he'd done that. She privately thought he was trying to swallow away anything upsetting.

She'd tried it once. It didn't work. *Maybe that's what's wrong. He can't move past the bad things by wishing them away.*

"Then tell me." Lacey laid her hand over his.

He looked at her hand, looked up, and looked right past her. Braden yanked away from her grasp. He turned to face the window. "Leave, Lacey." His voice sounded hoarse. "Just...leave."

"Come on." Cora spoke from the doorway, and Lacey suddenly understood why Braden pulled away instead of answering her.

She wanted to reach out and grab the moment again, but knew it wasn't possible. Lacey stood, reluctant to leave but knowing she wouldn't be able to get anything more from her brother. Drained of his anger, there seemed to be nothing holding him up.

Maybe this will let him think clearly and come to his senses. I should have reached out to him sooner and not let his snapping keep me away. Regret swam in her stomach as she followed Cora out of Braden's room and out of the doctor's house. Lacey tucked her hands in her pockets and rubbed the fabric between her fingertips, but the gesture didn't soothe.

"All I've done since I got here is argue with him," she told Cora. "We fight about everything and anything, but I haven't asked him to tell me about the collapse until now."

"It's not your fault." Cora sat down on the bench running along the front of Lacey's store and dabbed her eyes with a handkerchief. "None of us expected to find him this way."

"But I haven't done anything to help." Lacey sank down beside her. "Spending all my time and focus on preparing for the sawmill doesn't do my brother any good. If anything, the progress we've made seems to aggravate Braden even more."

"Everything aggravates him, and nothing pleases him." Tears slid down her best friend's face. "I kept thinking we'd see an improvement, but time goes by and he stays the same. Lacey, he says he doesn't want me anymore. . . . You've heard it, you've seen the way he acts. I'm starting to believe he's lost our love."

Dread overtook Lacey's feelings of regret. Cora had been so strong, always standing by Braden and refusing to give up. Her friend's constancy was Braden's last hope. *But no one can go on being rejected forever. Cora needs assurance, too.*

"Don't think that." Lacey wrapped one arm around Cora's shoulders. "He slipped today that he was angry you went to the picnic. When we talked about money, he asked about what I'd done to see you settled. Whatever he tells us, Braden always comes back to what's most important to him—and that's you."

"You're wrong, Lacey." Cora drew a deep breath. "He pouts about the picnic, yes. But when he asked about provisions for me it's because he hopes I'll no longer hold him to our engagement. He doesn't love. All this Braden cares about is himself. As soon as he's able, he'll leave Hope Falls, and us, far behind."

THIRTY-SIX

Chase's search remained at a standstill. Despite his well-laid plans, he'd made no progress in the two weeks following the picnic. *And it's all Lacey Lyman's fault.* He'd been avoiding the woman and the confusion she caused, but she still threw a spoke in the works. At least, her overeager suitors managed it on her behalf.

It started at dinner, the same night as the picnic. Lawson's round glasses looked nowhere but Miss Lyman, Williams, and then Chase. After the incident with the ladder and the way Miss Lyman's attention was monopolized by the burly lumberjack during the picnic, Lawson's courtship of Miss Lyman hadn't been progressing nearly as well as the man so obviously hoped.

The light reflecting off the engineer's owlish lenses made it impossible to tell what the man was thinking, but Chase suspected Lawson was calculating his chances with Miss Lyman. No surprise if he considered both Williams and Chase a threat.

But Chase couldn't prepare for the way Lawson went about minimizing that threat. When the man left his sister to join their table, he'd not suspected a scheme. The conversation turned to the progress being made on the sawmill. With the site cleared, first by cutting down the trees then by removing their stumps, the men could move on to the next important project.

"We need to map the route of the flume before we go about deciding the orientation of the sawmill itself," the slighter man mused. "I need input from one of the team leads as to the feasibility of the proposed route. If the trees or the landscape present too much trouble, I'll need to adjust the schematics."

It didn't mean much to Chase until the engineer turned to Williams and requested his assistance. His apparent eagerness to work alongside his rival set off alarm bells—but too late. The moment Williams agreed, Lawson roped Chase into the project by claiming he could make use of a guide's "geologic understanding of the region and familiarity with the landscape hereabouts." The women bought the twaddle hook, line, and sinker.

It couldn't have been clearer that he'd planned to make sure Williams and Chase didn't have the opportunity to get near Miss Lyman while he wasn't in town. And within five minutes, he succeeded in trapping both of them. Chase played peacekeeper for tense, tedious days as Williams gave orders and thinly veiled threats and Lawson made detailed riverbank sketches.

This afternoon marked the first opportunity he'd found to head out to the mines and poke around—but first he had to circle back and check on the women. Since the picnic, Williams doubled his efforts, edging out any other man who got near Miss Lyman.

Williams hadn't forgotten the evening he'd been humiliated by Miss Lyman's ability to recall his empty boasts. That the entire thing centered around his failure to win the cook provided a further blow to his ego—something bullies didn't take well. As time went by and he made no progress with his attempts to woo Miss Lyman—who'd given him no encouragement that Chase could discern—Williams might well try to take matters in another direction and force her to accept his proposal.

It wouldn't be difficult. Chase disliked admitting it, but Williams had the kind of sly cunning to recognize the way to make Miss Lyman bend to his demands. *If he threatens one of the others, she'll sacrifice her own happiness to protect them.* But the wily lumberjack would know he couldn't accomplish that while the ladies were surrounded by his fellow workers. He wasn't the type to push ahead when he knew he'd be outnumbered.

There was no telling whether Williams had hatched the plan Chase feared, but he'd seen the man studying a train schedule last night outside the bunkhouse. Which made it look like Williams planned to take a page from Twyler's manual and kidnap her while the other men were busy. If Williams timed it right, he could whisk the woman out of her shop, onto the train, and be halfway to Durango before anyone was the wiser. Once the two of them were wed, he'd return to Hope Falls to show off his new trophy.

Not going to happen. As this was the first day he hadn't been able to keep an eye on Williams while they worked, Chase made it a point to coincide his trips back to Hope Falls with the incoming train schedule. Just as a precaution.

So Chase doubled back to town, four braces of rabbits slung over his shoulder—enough for him to give to Miss Thompson and end the men's grumbling that they wanted fresh meat. Enough, he thought, to earn him a free afternoon. *If I don't find evidence very soon, I'll have to face the so-called Braden Lyman without it. The man might break down when faced with an accusation.*

Chase tucked the rabbits into one of the two smokehouses to bring out later when he returned to town that night. No one needed to know he'd finished his hunt in the morning, and this way he wouldn't get roped into helping with something else.

He checked the kitchen first, seeing most of the women inside.

"I'm becoming accustomed to you checking in on us, Mr. Dunstan." Miss Higgins slid a plate of cookies toward him. "It makes me glad to know you're diligent in seeing to our safety."

"So long as there's not trouble, I'm satisfied." Chase crunched into a crisp oatmeal cookie. "And I enjoy the perks."

They laughed at his appreciation for their culinary skills.

"Are Miss Lyman and Miss Thompson at the store?" It wasn't uncommon for her to be in the shop. Situated right between the diner and the doctor's house, they seemed to think she'd be safe working there alone so long as she kept the doors wide open. That way they could all see and hear if anything went wrong.

"Oh, Lacey went to visit her brother a good while ago." Mrs. Nash poured herself a tall glass of milk. "Cora followed after her, but she hasn't been gone very long yet."

So she's visiting her brother today. . . . Interesting. Chase wondered whether she'd made a practice of dropping by more regularly after their little talk. *Is she going to keep up appearances, or is she conferring with a coconspirator?*

He didn't know what to make of the fact the younger Miss Thompson visited the invalid often. In the long month since he'd met these four women, Chase had come to believe they were exactly who they said they were. Why not? Their identities didn't make them innocent. Miss Lyman could have schemed to take over Hope Falls more easily than a stranger, in any case.

But he leaned toward thinking she hadn't meant for her brother to be involved in the mine collapse. It was even possible she'd planned for the mine to be empty, but something went awry. *Despicable, but far more understandable.*

What he didn't understand was how the other women got roped into it. Chase might believe they had no idea the collapse was a crime, not a tragedy, and that they needed to marry to keep the town together. But this wasn't the case with the younger Miss

Thompson. As Braden's fiancée, she'd know instantly that the man in Hope Falls was an impostor. The others might be fooled by keeping the invalid in isolation, but Miss Thompson visited him.

Which made her just as involved as Lacey Lyman.

They were both at the doctor's house, visiting the supposed Braden, right now. Chase thanked the ladies and headed toward the general store. If he snuck around it and kept low, he might be able to go undetected until he reached the doctor's house.

But as he edged around the back of the store, he heard voices. Annoyance flooded him as he realized he'd missed the chance to eavesdrop on their visit with the impostor. Chase stood, fighting his frustration, until he heard snatches of the ladies' conversation. They were talking about Braden Lyman.

"All this Braden cares about is himself. As soon as he's able, he'll leave Hope Falls. . . ." Miss Thompson warned.

This *Braden? So he is an impostor!* Pulse pounding, Chase edged around the back of the building. He crept along the side, ducking windows, until he stood as close as possible without alerting them to his presence. Then he waited. And listened.

"You're wrong." Lacey couldn't temper the vehemence of the denial. "Deep down, he's glad we've done so much to save Hope Falls. Besides, you know Braden would never abandon us."

"The Braden I *used* to know would never abandon us. But he wouldn't have been so hateful either." Cora choked back a sob. "When I first saw him, I knew it would take time to adjust, but time won't be enough for either of us. He's too different."

Lacey fought to restore Cora's hope. "His temper will cool as he heals and accepts his new role in Hope Falls."

"Even if he accepts his place, I don't know if my place is at his side. He's still ordering us to leave his room!" All the pent-up hurt of the past few months came out. "How can I marry this hate-filled stranger who's taken the place of *my* Braden?"

"Cora, you don't have to marry any man you don't want to. Remember, that was one of the most important things we said when we wrote the ad, and it doesn't change for you." Lacey's heart sank, but she had to look after Cora. Her friend had gone through so much; it was amazing how long she'd persevered before the pressure and the loss went too deep. "I know you never expected anything like this. When we heard of Braden's death—"

"You decided to cover it up." Dunstan rounded the building, anger in the line of his jaw and the tone of his voice. "Did your brother mean so little to you, Miss Lyman, that you deemed him replaceable? I doubt he'd agree, 'cause I sure don't."

Lacey blinked, thrown off by his sudden appearance and senseless accusations. She glanced over, but Cora looked every bit as confused as she felt. "What are you talking about?" *And why are you so angry?* "Braden wasn't—isn't—replaceable at all."

If he were, we would've done it the same week we arrived, rather than be stuck with a foul-tempered fool who's abused Cora.

"Don't play the innocent with me, Miss Lyman. I heard everything you two said about your brother. I know what you've done, and now I want you to know you won't get away with it."

"Get away with what?" Cora couldn't make sense of it either, which relieved Lacey in some small measure.

At least I'm not the only one with no idea what he means. Why would the man even care that she'd told Cora no one would want her to marry Braden if she couldn't reconcile herself to it? None of them would be forced into marrying the wrong man.

"There you sit, talking about your brother's death in broad daylight," he thundered, "while the impostor you found is trapped at the doctor's, waiting for the day he can escape. Have you no shame for what you've done? No regret whatsoever?"

"Impostor?" An inkling began to dawn as Lacey realized Dunstan had heard them talking about the "different" Braden. "You've misunderstood, Mr. Dunstan. Braden is much altered after his ordeal in the mines, but that doesn't make him an impostor!" Though the word seemed to sum up how Lacey felt about the angry man who stared at her through her brother's eyes.

He took all three of the stairs leading to the porch in one stride. "The game is up, Miss Lyman. Stop this pretense."

"This is no game!" Anger began to simmer beneath her confusion as he loomed over them, rebuking her for something she hadn't done. "My brother survived the mine collapse, but even if he hadn't, why on earth would we bother creating a fake Braden?"

"To keep your claim on Hope Falls until the three of you could rustle up husbands to do it for you." He growled more than spoke. "That's what the ad was all about, wasn't it?"

She gaped at him. "We need husbands to guard our property— particularly because our country doesn't permit unmarried women to own any themselves—but that has little to do with Braden."

"It has everything to do with your brother. His name is on the deeds, isn't it? So you call him the 'nominal owner.'"

Lacey felt all the blood leave her face as she realized the full extent of what Chase Dunstan accused. "You believe that because my brother is the only one of us able to legally own or hold property, I covered up his death and am imprisoning an impostor until such a time as our husbands secure the claims?"

"Finally, you admit it." Grim satisfaction etched deep lines on either side of his mouth. "I didn't want to believe it, but you're so ruthless you believe 'no cost is too great.'"

"You've got it all wrong." Cora found her tongue. "How you can believe such terrible things? Why you would even bother to invent such a convoluted plot in your own mind is beyond me."

Lacey looked at Chase Dunstan, sorrow burrowing into her heart. "You use my words, but everyone understands some things cost too dear." *Like putting your trust in the wrong man.*

"Yes." Rage burned in his dark eyes. "Some things do. I'm sure your brother would tell you that if he were still alive."

"He is still alive!" Exasperation grew to fury. *How dare he think such things about me after the time we've spent together?* "How dare you accuse me of such vile schemes! Cora, my friends, and the doctor himself will all attest to Braden's survival."

"All with a vested interest in Hope Falls, needing to perpetrate fraud and deception." He waved away her witnesses. "I don't know whether you've threatened the doctor or paid him off, but it's obvious the man is under your thumb as well."

"Then you've made horrible, baseless accusations and left no way to prove how wrong you are." Cora stood beside Lacey. "You've cast aspersions on us all with no cause and no proof."

"The proof sits in the doctor's house, trapped by his health and your plots." Dunstan shook his head. "Who do you think acted as your brother's guide through these mountains, Miss Lyman? The Braden Lyman I knew was a good man and deserves to have his memory honored by the women he loved in life."

"The Braden Lyman you—" Lacey became speechless for a moment as she realized what he meant. "You knew my brother?"

"Oh yes." He curled his hand beneath her elbow and tugged her toward the stairs. "I knew the real Braden Lyman. Now it's time for you to take me to meet the man you've kept hidden."

"Oh," Lacey seethed, jerking her elbow away from him. "We'd be glad to take you to him. This way, Mr. Dunstan."

THIRTY-SEVEN

Chase stared. Braden Lyman—the real Braden Lyman—stared back.

How can this be? All his certainties came crashing down.

"Dunstan?" The pale man on the bed asked. "I didn't know you'd come back." His head fell back against his pillow, his eyes rimmed with dark circles. "Don't know why you'd want to."

This last was said in a resentful mutter that sounded nothing like the Braden Lyman Chase once knew and respected. Still, Chase couldn't answer. The shock of seeing Braden sent his mind reeling. The man before him obviously wasn't faking any injuries to deflect suspicion that he'd been involved in the collapse. *He didn't know what would happen. Maybe he still doesn't know what happened.* This gave him pause. *I still don't know what happened. What am I supposed to say to the man?*

"Well?" Lacey Lyman stood on the opposite side of the bed, arms crossed and glaring daggers at him. Suddenly Chase wasn't concerned so much with what he'd say to Braden.

What am I going to say to Lacey? Guilt and shame flooded him for his incorrect conclusions about her brother. *But someone still sabotaged the mines. I can't discount her as a suspect.*

"No one should see me like this!" Suddenly irate, Braden sat back up. Obviously the man took Chase's silence as shock over Braden's appearance. "Why did you bring him here?"

It began to dawn on Chase why Lacey and Miss Thompson spoke of this different man as replacing the Braden they knew. What had Lacey said when he began accusing her? *Braden is much altered after his ordeal in the mines. . . . You misunderstand. . . .*

"We brought him here to prove that you're you," Lacey informed her brother. "Your friend decided I'd gone to extreme lengths to conceal your death, and you were an impostor."

"I was wrong." The admission sounded hoarse even to Chase. Still, he couldn't bring himself to apologize around his thoughts. *Something is still wrong here. Too much doesn't fit.*

"I'll say." Miss Thompson's glower seared through him.

"What?" Braden tried to push himself into a more upright position. "What's all this about an impostor, Dunstan?"

"We knew you wouldn't want visitors." His fiancée referred to his anger mere moments before. "So we didn't bring Mr. Dunstan to meet you when Granger recommended we hire him."

"But I know him!" Braden looked incredulous. "Why didn't you tell them we'd worked together and ask to see me?"

"Because he'd already decided we'd hidden a fake Braden," Lacey hazarded a guess. "He wanted proof of our perfidy before he deigned to accuse us openly and come confront you."

"Where did you get such a fool notion?" Braden demanded.

"The ad." Chase could tell them that much before he finished putting all the pieces together. "The women were too desperate to find husbands. There had to be a reason."

"The reason is they don't have the sense God gave a gnat."

"Braden." His fiancée's tone was both warning and censure.

"Not from what I've seen." Chase couldn't let the insult pass when he'd provided the instigation. "These women keep tight control over the town and are more capable than most men." The women looked startled by his sudden defense, but it was true.

"Are you comparing their sawmill to my mine?" Braden started on a low whisper, but got louder with every word. "Are you saying that, because the sawmill looks to be viable, these women are more capable than I was at running Hope Falls?"

"Stop seeing insults where there are none," his sister snapped at him. "We're too busy with ones that actually exist!"

"Is that why you wanted us gone?" His fiancée moved closer to the bed. "Not because you were afraid we'd be in danger, but because our sawmill might succeed where your mine failed?"

"The mine didn't fail!" He slumped and whispered, "I did."

"No you didn't." All three of them spoke the words at once, trying to wipe away the defeat lining Braden's face. A second of surprise, and then everyone looked at Chase.

"What do you mean, Dunstan?" Braden looked so tired. "I lost three-quarters of my men in that collapse and didn't even manage to die with them. I failed on every possible level."

The women gaped at him, apparently horrified by the revelation that Braden held himself responsible for the cave-in. Dunstan wasn't surprised to hear it at all. Every good leader took on responsibility for both his men and their mission.

"Isn't that why you've come here? For restitution?"

"What?" Lacey resumed glaring at him. "Why would he want restitution? We paid all the investors what they owed, Braden."

"My brother-in-law died in the collapse," Chase volunteered. "My sister, Laura, was left destitute. She didn't just lose the man she loved. She lost her home, too." *Or she would have, if I hadn't stepped in and made things right.*

"So that's why you've come to Hope Falls, full of suspicion?

You're looking for *revenge?*" Lacey looked at him as though he were a snake about to strike her down.

"No." He met her gaze, willing her to be as innocent as she looked now. "I came to Hope Falls looking for justice."

"Get out." She flung her arm toward the door. "The train just pulled up, Mr. Dunstan. Get on it and don't come back."

"Ever again," Miss Thompson added for good measure.

"We'll see that your sister is handsomely compensated." Braden sank back wearily. "I promise you that, Dunstan."

"I can take care of Laura," he told them. "I didn't come here for money or for revenge. I came to find the truth."

"Well, now you know it. Braden really did survive, we put out the ads to help hold the large size of the claim and get the sawmill underway, and there are no plots or impostors. *Now go.*" Lacey looked furious, but her voice cracked on the last words.

"I can't." Chase drew a deep breath and laid his cards on the table. "Not until I find out who sabotaged the mines."

∞

The man has a bad habit of leveling me with shocking comments, Lacey decided. After this one, she could only gape at him. *Is it possible he's unbalanced?* No, that would be an easy explanation.

"What?" Unbelievably, Braden perked up. "What did you say?"

"I know how seriously you took safety," Dunstan clarified. "Surveyors, architects, extensive support systems. . . It made me wonder how Miracle Mining, of all the outfits, caved in."

"Didn't make sense to me either." Her brother leaned forward eagerly at the idea the collapse hadn't been his fault. "Do you have any proof, Dunstan? Anything concrete to go on?"

"Just Draxley's recollections," he admitted. "To hear him tell it, it sounds like an explosion started everything."

"That's what you're going on?" Lacey heard herself screech,

winced, and modulated her tone. "The impression of a cowardly little twitch when he wanted to look good in front of Arla?"

"He didn't say it sounded like an explosion," the hunter admitted. "And I don't doubt Draxley exaggerated for his audience. But he didn't describe rumbling or shaking. The first and most important recollection he had was of a great boom."

"So the telegraph operator says 'boom,' and you suspect sabotage?" Cora sounded as incredulous as Lacey. "The same way you saw our ad and decided we'd manufactured a fake Braden?"

Put that way, Dunstan's speculation looked as ludicrous as Lacey believed it to be. "We can only be thankful you haven't sought to use your investigative skills in law enforcement."

"He's right." Braden sounded full of wonder. "I hadn't thought about it.... It didn't seem important which aspect of my operation caused the collapse, since any of it was my fault. I signed off on the route, the tunnels, the supports—all of it."

"Anyone can make a mistake," Cora was quick to assure him. It looked as though Braden's newfound liveliness gave her hope.

"Oh, I made a mistake all right." Braden's expression turned grim. "By avoiding the memories. If I hadn't fought so hard not to relive it, I would've remembered the blast."

Lacey gasped. "You don't mean to say he's *right*?" For a moment she didn't know which to hope for. That Dunstan was proven a raving lunatic, seeing conspiracies everywhere—or that Dunstan's instincts were right, even if his theories were wrong. Because if he was right, then the cave-in wasn't Braden's fault, and her brother would really have a reason to start recovering.

"I know the sound of a blast when I hear it," he confirmed. "But I didn't realize it at the time. The world collapsed around me, everything buckling, the air impossibly thick with dust, and rocks crushing everything in their path. Then, when everything settled, men screaming in the dark. . . I couldn't think about it then, and I didn't want to think about any of it afterward."

Men screaming in the dark? For the first time, Lacey began to get a sense of the horror Braden endured. *All this time I've been impatient for him to move past it. How do you move past something like that? Even worse if you think it's your fault?*

"Will you keep searching, Dunstan?" Her brother looked to her accuser. "Can you find the proof we need to catch a killer?"

"He's been here for weeks on end." Cora seemed hesitant to voice her doubts, but pressed forward nevertheless. "If he's not found anything by now, I fear you'll have to look to your own memory for comfort, Braden. But now you know. *It wasn't your fault.* And I hope you know that we never thought it was."

"I've managed to search the town fairly well," Dunstan intervened. "But with everything else, I've yet to inspect the area around the mines, nor what's left of the tunnels."

" 'Everything else' meaning the job we hired you to do"— Lacey tried to vent some of her smoldering rage—"completely unaware that you were trying to prove your foul suspicions."

He didn't have the grace to look shamefaced as he nodded.

"So will you do it?" Braden's eyes lit with hope.

"I planned to try this afternoon," Dunstan admitted. "It's why Decoy's in the barn with a beef bone. I misinterpreted some things and have lost some time, but there's still daylight enough to get the job started as soon as I grab my supplies."

"You're going into the mines?" Cora looked aghast.

"No." Lacey didn't give him a chance to answer. "*We* are."

"Oh no you're not!" Her brother lapsed back into the scowling, yelling oaf they'd been stuck with for months. "I forbid you to step foot inside or even anywhere near my mines."

Lacey gave him a sweet smile. "I won't. We can just consider anywhere I happen to step foot a part of my half. I own equal shares of those mines, and it's my decision to make."

"You're not equipped to go down there," Dunstan refused.

"Of course I am." Lacey's smile grew even wider as she hitched her skirts to her ankle. "You see, I have new shoes."

THIRTY-EIGHT

G o back inside." Once Chase managed to pull his jaw from the ground, he started issuing orders like a stern papa. "Right now. Before any of the men see you wearing that getup." *The woman has a bad habit of wearing outrageous, impractical outfits that look far too good on her. She's going to start a riot.*

"I'm not listening to you." Lacey Lyman stuck her nose in the air and walked on, her hips swaying hypnotically beneath the buff-colored, fitted *pants* she'd donned for the trip ahead. She showed enough sense to reach for her cloak and swing it on, concealing the all-too-revealing clothing. "They won't see a thing, and it's not sensible to try dragging a crinoline and skirts through a half-blocked mine. This is the safe choice."

"Only if none of the men catch sight of you." Chase didn't mince words. "If they do, I won't be able to fend them off."

"Careful, Dunstan." She pinned the cloak in place and gave him a tight smile. "You wouldn't want to give me a compliment."

"It wasn't a compliment," he growled, shouldering his pack and heading out. "It was a warning. With a getup like that, you may well survive the mines only to be attacked here in town."

"After your baseless accusation, I've already been attacked here in town." The look she shot him could've frozen stew.

Each carrying a bag supplied with candles, torch material, some food, and a canteen, they cleared town and hit the woods. "I admitted I was wrong," Chase pointed out. "And I'm letting you come with me to search the mines." *What more does she want?*

"Admitting you're wrong is not the equivalent of apologizing for your spurious accusations," she sniffed.

"Would an apology take it all away? Make it better?" If she said it would, Chase would apologize here and now.

"No. It would indicate that you regret maligning my character." She gave a small, sad sigh. "And that you truly know you're wrong and maybe even that you're glad of it."

"I regret maligning your character," he offered. *Until I find the evidence and know for sure that you're not insisting on coming along to hide proof of your guilt, I can't say more.*

Lacey didn't accept his apology, maintaining stony silence until they reached the mouth of the mines. There she drew off her cloak and stuffed it into the bag then addressed him.

"Despite what you believe, Mr. Dunstan, I am neither a fool nor a criminal." Her lips compressed into a thin line, giving something for him to train his eyes on so they didn't wander down to her legs. "It's painfully clear to me, if no one else, your suspicions about Braden hint at much darker assumptions."

Chase looked at her for a long moment before nodding. "You're the person who stood to gain the most and who's gone to such extremes to ensure the sawmill gets off the ground." Even as he said it, something inside him withered at the words. All his instincts clamored that he'd gotten it wrong.

Some things cloud a man's instincts, he reminded himself. *Beautiful women top that list—particularly ones in pants.*

"That's what I thought." She pulled the strap of her bag tighter and lit her candle. "So here we are to find evidence to exonerate me of your speculation and Braden from his own guilt."

"I hope so." Chase lit his own candle. "You have no idea how much I've wanted to be wrong about all of this."

"Let's go then." Her expression softened infinitesimally. "I trusted you when you didn't truly deserve it. You don't trust me when I do. It's time for those two wrongs to come right."

Chase ventured toward the gaping maw in the mountainside first, holding his candle aloft to catch sight of the tunnels within. The left branch lay blocked by boulders, but the straight path had been cleared by the rescue party long ago.

He started in with a heightened awareness of the woman following at his heels. They picked their way over and around various rocks and clumps of earth strewn throughout the path. The farther they went, the darker it became. The air grew damp and heavy, smelling of dust and metal. Various offshoots branched away from the main canal, but Chase ignored them.

Once they'd gone through the mother tunnel, they'd go back and thread guide rope before exploring the rats' maze. Or what was left of it. Entire passageways were obscured by stone, remnants of splintered supports the only evidence that there'd once been paths. The ceiling bowed in places, cracked in others, and the deeper they went, the worse conditions became.

At length they reached a cavernous room—the main worksite of the mine. The hairs on the back of Chase's neck stood on end as they made their way around the perimeter of what space remained. Pockets of the room remained open, but here the destruction was most evident—an entire wall had buckled, making the roof slant down at a sharp angle to meet the ground.

"We can't go any farther, but this was once the hub of operations." Chase spoke for the first time since they'd left sunlight. "Used to be many more tunnels leading away from here, going deeper into the mountain where the silver ore waits."

"All gone." Her voice was somber as she peered into corners and nooks. "The supports I can see make me think the room collapsed in the very middle." She held her candle high, pointing to the ceiling, where the roof supports of the column-like supports branched toward the middle, making a half circle.

Chase bent down to where the floor met the ceiling, looking for any open spaces or seams to peek through. He came up empty. "Whatever happened in here, it was thorough."

"Wait!" she called. "Here's another passage. Much smaller."

At her words, dread pooled in Chase's stomach. *Danger.*

"No, Lacey!" He rolled away from the sloping roof and jumped to his feet, catching her arm before she continued farther. Chills coursed down his arms, a warning that had never been wrong before. "We're leaving."

He pulled her back the way they'd come, but she fought him. "Look! There! What is that?" She crouched down, poking a thin wire running along the ground. "Why isn't it covered in dirt?"

Fear curdled in Chase's gut as he grabbed her. He didn't bother trying to be gentle as he jerked her to her feet and headed back down the passage. "We have to get out of here."

"When we found something?" she cried. "What's wrong?"

"It's a fuse line, Lacey!" He broke into a run, half dragging her behind him. *"Run!"* Chase felt the moment she obeyed, her weight no longer pulling him backward. It seemed like years before he saw the faint glow of sunshine at the mouth of the tunnel, and he put on an extra burst of speed.

"Stop." A figure moved forward, blocking the light as he raised a pistol, grip firm as Chase and Lacey skidded to a halt.

"Mr. Draxley?" Lacey tried to push past Chase, but he held her behind him, out of aim of the gun she hadn't yet seen. "What are you doing? Why are you here?"

"Finishing what I started." Mustache twitching as much as ever, Draxley gave no other sign of nervousness. "Pity you two didn't wait another day—it would've all been hidden by then. Now you'll be part of the next tragic accident of Hope Falls."

"Why?" Chase couldn't move for his gun, couldn't launch himself at Draxley and protect Lacey at the same time. All he could do was keep the man talking as long as possible.

"Because you started poking your nose where it didn't belong," the telegraph operator snapped. "And because you"—he pointed the gun higher to indicate Lacey—"meddled where women don't belong at all. Hope Falls was supposed to be ours, you interfering witch. But you stepped in and ruined everything!"

"The other bid," Lacey gasped. "You're the buyer who made that abysmal offer for our half of the mine you destroyed?" She sounded both horrified and outraged at Draxley's daring.

"Start walking." Draxley waggled the gun. "I don't want to have to shoot you and drag your bodies far enough back they won't be found. You'll go there yourselves." He moved forward, forcing them back. "It would be most fitting to take you to the chamber where your brother was trapped, but I'm afraid that's too easy to get out of. Now drop your candles and go left. I don't want you able to light them later."

They didn't have a choice. Darkness surrounded them on all sides, save the flame of Draxley's candle and its pinpoint reflection on his glasses. "Now right." He barked directions until they'd wound themselves deep into the maze.

"Why?" Chase heard the sorrow in Lacey's voice as she asked. "What made you kill all those men? There's silver in other places where you might strike a claim. Why do this?"

"Didn't your brother tell you?" Surprise halted Draxley's progress, and they all came to a standstill. "This mountain, about to be so tragically wasted, holds more than silver."

"Your friend," Chase guessed. "The one who brought you here to man the telegraphs—it was Lyman's partner, wasn't it? Owen."

"A sentimental fool!" Draxley spat on the ground. "He knew the plan, but ran back when he realized Lyman was inside. Had some fool notion he could outrun the fuse and save his friend."

"But not the others?" Rage laced her words. "Not the men he hired on and brought here, in the bowels of the earth?"

"They might have guessed about the gold—we couldn't have them flapping their gums. I told Owen it'd be the same problem with your brother, but he had the fool idea Lyman would give up mining after the cave-in." Draxley shook his head. "As though any man would leave gold in the ground he owned. The investor we had lined up didn't want to leave Lyman as a loose end."

"What investor?" Lacey asked sharply. "If Owen didn't plan it and you were helping Owen, who put you up to this?"

"I'm not going to tell you." Smugness settled on Draxley's pallid features. "You won't have the mystery neatly solved. You'll go to your deaths with questions—not at peace."

"The fuse wasn't lit when Owen went in, was it?" Certainty settled over Chase. "You pushed down the detonator after."

"Doesn't matter," Draxley sneered. "You know, I could give you quick deaths. But you've cost me the mine and everything I worked so hard for, so I'm going to leave you to its mercy. You don't know the way—but I've haunted this place for weeks trying to find a way back in to the mother lode. Good-bye."

With that, he pinched the wick of his candle and plunged them into pitch-black darkness, his footsteps sounding the path of his retreat.

Chase wrapped his hand around Lacey's and, for the second time that day, dragged her through the tunnels. All his time as a tracker and hunter rose to the fore in those desperate moments as they fought to find a way out. Listening for footsteps and following his gut, he wound back the way they'd come—the air grew less stale.

"I see it!" Lacey gasped for breath as they caught a glimpse of light once more.

They sped for it, only to be thrown to the ground as the first blast echoed through the tunnels. Chase rolled atop her, sandwiching her between his body and the wall as daylight disappeared.

THIRTY-NINE

Jake felt the mountain lurch moments before the last train of the day pulled into Hope Falls. The car tilted on the tracks, but didn't tip over. His mouth went dry. *Evie!*

The moment they pulled to a stop, he vaulted over the edge of the iron guard, over the pull-down steps, and hit the ground running. He didn't stop until he reached the door of the diner. When he saw her, unharmed, Jake could breathe again.

"You're all right?" He wrapped his arms around her before she could even turn around. "No one's hurt?"

"Jake!" She shifted in his arms, gorgeous amber eyes bright with tears. "I'm so glad you're back!"

"Don't cry, sweetie." He thumbed a tear away from her cheek. "It's all going to be fine." *I'll make sure of it.*

"No it won't." Cora entered the kitchen, a bulging rucksack over her shoulder and a shovel in her hand. Miss Higgins followed close at her heels, similarly equipped.

"Lacey and Dunstan went to explore the mines." Evie's tears ran afresh. "Jake—they might still be inside the tunnels!"

No. He struggled to hide his horror as he extricated himself from her arms and swiped the shovel from her sister. "I'll send Lawson to get word to the men to come help. The sooner we get through, the sooner we'll find them."

Please, God, let them still be alive.

∞

Lacey couldn't breathe, and for once it wasn't because of her corset. Grit filled her mouth, and a heavy weight pressed her into the ground. *Chase.* She tried to call his name, but managed nothing more than a dry wheeze. She took a breath and tried again.

"Chase?" When he didn't answer, the sour taste of panic filled the back of her throat. Lacey squeezed her hands under her and pushed upward, trying to jostle him. "Chase!"

He groaned and stirred, but then went still.

"Come on, Chase." Heart beating fast enough to race a train, Lacey pushed up again.

"Don't move," croaked a voice next to her ear. "Can't. . . breathe. . ."

She could have cried for joy at hearing him speak. *He's alive! Thank You, Lord. Please help him. . . . Help me help him. We have to get up and find a way out.*

"We're pinned." Still raspy, he sounded stronger as he shifted his weight. "The support's bowed over us."

"You can't move?" Panic began its slow creep again.

"A little." He strained, and Lacey felt some of the pressure ease off her. "Scoot to the right, Lacey."

Wiggling and sliding, ignoring sharp jabs from pieces of rock, Lacey moved over. Her bag halted her progress, making her stop everything to slip the strap over her head and push it away. Then she began to move again. It went slowly, agonizingly slowly, as Chase couldn't hold himself up indefinitely. Finally, she slid free and dragged air into her starved lungs. Dimly, she realized Chase was doing the same thing—he'd been compressed beneath the weight of the bowing beam. She crawled beside him.

"Can you move now?" Lacey pressed her hands against the wooden support, feeling the tension, knowing it wouldn't hold.

She heard the slide of rocks and a grunted breath as he tried to move and failed. "My coat's caught at the side and the bottom of my sleeve." He didn't say he couldn't take it off.

But he didn't have to. Lacey groped around for the bag she'd pushed aside, found it, and felt around the interior with trembling fingers. It seemed as though years went by before her hand closed around the slick wax of a candle, and she found the pocket holding her matches. It took five tries before she lit one properly then managed to light her candle.

The soft glow looked abnormally bright in the blackness, but Lacey held it forward to better see Chase. Sure enough, his jacket was pinched between the leaning wall and the floor, which pushed higher than the area mere feet away. From the looks of it, the beam must have pressed down on his back and ribs.

But he didn't complain.

"I can cut it away," she told him. "If you hold this." She pressed the candle into his outstretched hand, letting her fingers linger atop his. "It'll only be a moment."

"Thank you." A cough punctuated the words, and Lacey realized he'd probably breathed in far more dust than she had.

"Here." She took back the candle and pressed her uncapped canteen into his hand. "Take a drink before I get started."

It took some shifting, but he rolled slightly, tilting his head to drink. "Aaah. That's better." The difference in his voice astonished and pleased her as she withdrew her folding knife from the pocket of her pack and knelt over him.

"Hold still," she cautioned unnecessarily. The moment she

drew close, he'd stiffened as though bracing himself. Lacey reached out and felt the fabric, tugging slightly to get a sense of its weave and strength. Thick and somewhat stiff, it refused to pull free. Lacey lifted it as far from Chase as she could before puncturing the cloth then sawing to start a rip line. Soon the rip was long enough for her to grab both sides and tear the fabric down to the bottom seam. This she cut.

Slicing down the length of the sleeve made for trickier work, but she'd gotten a feel for the fabric by now. Chase held still as a stone until she finished. Taking back the candle, she scrambled backward, so he could move away from the wall.

He moved to the side before pushing himself into a sitting position, rolling his shoulders and pressing one hand against his ribs. "Thank you." Chase took the candle and held it aloft.

For the first time, Lacey saw their surroundings. Beyond the buckling wall, they had mere yards before the tunnel collapsed in a mammoth tangle of dirt and stone. She moved toward it and began pulling at the smaller rocks, pushing them away.

Please, God, she prayed. *I know I'm not worthy of Your grace, but we need help.*

Beside her Chase began working on larger rocks. Between the two of them, they cleared a good-sized heap off to one side before the sheer size and weight of the remaining rock defeated them. Lacey sank down, panting slightly from the work.

"They know we're in here." Again pressing his hand against his ribs, Chase settled beside her. "There's air coming in—I feel the draft on the right side of the pile. We'll be all right until they find us."

"Yes." Lacey stared at the small stub of candle they'd sandwiched between some rocks. "Do you have any of your candles?"

"No." He looked at her for a moment, dark eyes missing nothing. Then he slid his arm around her shoulders and tugged her closer. "But I'm here."

Somehow the warmth of his arm around her shoulders, the feel of his strength along her side, kept the fear at bay as her candle guttered. Now there was nothing but darkness. . .and Chase.

"Lacey?" His voice rumbled, low and reassuring.

"Yes, Chase?" She noticed they'd slipped into using first names, but liked it. *Besides,* she reasoned, *when you're wearing britches and sitting on the floor of a caved-in mine, the proprieties went out the window a long time before.*

"I was wrong, and I owe you an apology." Of all the things he might've said, he chose to remind her of their differences?

She brushed it aside. "You can apologize once we're out of this place." *For now I don't want anything to divide us.*

"Lacey?" He shifted closer. "What is it that makes you think God won't forgive you?"

"Does it matter?" Any other time she would have pulled away.

"Very much." Certainty underscored his words like bedrock. "Because I can't understand what a woman like you could have done to make her unworthy of God's mercy."

She thought about that for a long time and decided it was a compliment. *So now that he thinks the best of me, I'm supposed to tell him the worst?* Lacey sighed at the irony of it.

"I resented my brother." The words dropped like fellows of the stones around them. "When he came to Hope Falls, leaving me behind because women of quality weren't welcome in a mining town, I resented him. His freedom made me jealous. I could buy the mercantile and take part in Braden's plans, but I couldn't make my own. In his last letter, he told me to stop asking when I could come join him—he'd send for me when he wished, and until then I should keep myself busy. He suggested shopping. I wrote back that if the mines made it so Hope Falls would never be readied for us, I might begin to hope they failed. The next day we heard of the cave-in."

She heard him suck in a sharp breath and knew he was starting to understand. "It was a coincidence, Lacey."

"I know. But I still thought it, and then I heard he was dead. Gone forever, and the last words I'd written him were in anger. It was the second time I cried in the last ten years."

"When was the first?" His hand cupped her shoulder, rubbing up and down in a soothing motion.

"The day my father died. Before that," she rushed on even though he hadn't asked, "was the day my mother passed away. We were told she wouldn't make it, and I cried for a week straight until we lost her. Crying doesn't make a difference—it just keeps you from appreciating what you have while it's here."

"And it lets out some of your emotion, lessens how easily something can provoke your temper." He gave her shoulder a squeeze. "You couldn't have saved your parents or spared your brother, Lacey. As for envying Braden for his opportunities—it's understandable. It's human." Chase squeezed again. "It's *forgivable*, so long as you regret it and do better."

"That's what I thought, too." The hot prickling of tears warned Lacey to stop talking, but she couldn't keep it in anymore. "But then I found out Braden lived. I was so relieved, so happy.... I sold our family home and convinced the women to come here and find husbands to help protect us. What they really needed protection from was my planning." She gave a dry laugh.

"They're adults, Lacey. You were trying to take the burden off your brother and provide for your friends." He paused. "However misguided your attempt became."

"But..." Lacey gave a hard swallow and plunged into the worst of it. "When we arrived and Braden began raging and yelling and trying to kick us out, throwing my failures in my face every day...I began to think we would have done better without him, that if the brother I knew and admired couldn't have come back from the mines, I didn't want what was left over." The tears won, sliding down her cheeks and dripping off the tip of her nose. "How could I resent him all over again? It's a fatal flaw. I've tried to suppress it, tried to ignore it, tried to confess it and start again. But it didn't work, Chase."

"Repenting doesn't mean you never make the mistake again," he told her. "It means you fight your hardest not to. From the sounds of it, you've been fighting yourself and your brother for so long, you don't know the difference anymore."

"Maybe not." Lacey sniffed back more tears. "So long as I'm fighting all the time, I'm not at peace. I'm not gentle or patient or long-suffering like Cora. You were right when you said I lacked virtue, Chase. You knew it on the second day you met me! No matter how much I try, I'm not a good-enough Christian. I don't think I ever will be."

"Stop trying to be a good-enough Christian," Chase advised. "You're a believer in Christ, so focus on Him instead of on all the things you think you need to change about yourself. Maybe then you'll realize how brave and clever and caring He made you to be."

Lacey's breath hitched at the sweetness of the words and the conviction behind them. *If only he really believed that.* "You thought I was a murderer."

"I said I was wrong." He slid his hand down her arm. "Didn't you wonder why I didn't apologize, Lacey?"

"Men don't give apologies." She shrugged.

"They do when they mean them," he corrected. "You see, Lacey, there's a world of difference between being wrong"—his fingers twined with hers as he finished—"and being sorry about it."

FORTY

Chase sat in the dark, at least one rib broken, and smiled like a fool. The woman nestled against his side wasn't talking anymore, but she'd heard him—*and she's still holding my hand*.

"Chase?" She sounded hesitant, but he loved hearing her say his name.

"Yes, Lacey?" He liked the newfound freedom to say hers, too.

"Why don't you like people?" The question made his ribs hurt, as though she'd given him a hit to the midsection.

After everything they'd made it through today, she wanted to talk about how different they were? Chase drew in as deep a breath as he could without it hurting and squeezed her hand.

She squeezed back, and suddenly it didn't seem like a bad thing that she'd asked. Lacey snuggled closer, waiting.

"It's not that I don't like people." He eased into it. "It's more that I don't like very *many* people."

"Oh." She shifted a bit then settled. "Do you mean you don't like to have very many people around you at once or that there aren't many people you like in general?"

"Both, probably. Lots of people cause lots of problems."

"But you like Granger," she mused. "And my brother, when he was himself. And I think, maybe, after today. . .you might like me, too?"

"Sometimes we fight hardest against the things we want most." Chase found it hard to explain, even to himself. "I've never fought harder than when I met you, Lacey."

She went so still, he could barely hear her breathe. *She understands. I'm bad with words and worse with women, Lord, but here sits one who understands.* Something light fluttered in the vicinity of his heart, and Chase recognized it as hope.

"Why do you think you're unable to have a civil conversation when you can say sweet things like that?" She sounded perplexed and slightly put out, like she'd been fooled.

"Because being civil usually means two people who don't like each other pretend that they get along," he explained. "I don't like pretense, and I don't go in for games. It's better to say what you think and mean it."

Another, longer silence. For the first time, Chase began to understand why it worked so well on other people when he did it to them. He made it a rule not to break silence—but rules were meant to be broken. "What do you think?"

"I think that's surprisingly civilized." She surprised him. "And I'm thinking that this means you were sincere about what you said. . .about fighting hardest for what you want most."

"I meant it." He turned his torso to face her, even though he couldn't see her. Chase heard her breathe faster.

"Then tell me, Chase Dunstan. What is it, exactly, that you want?"

From beyond the wall of rock came the sound of scraping and chiseling and many men working hard to break through. *We're saved.* But for some reason, Chase wasn't as happy as he should have been.

"Lacey!" a woman shrieked from the other side, the cry mercifully muffled in their chamber. "Dunstan! Are you there?"

Lacey pulled her hand from his, and pain blossomed in his rib cage. Then she cupped her hands over his ears and screeched back, "Yes, Evie! We're in here!"

A flurry of shouts on the other side, and the sounds of work doubled. Chase wanted to ignore it for the short time they'd have left, but first he had to do some yelling of his own. He reached over, felt the softness of her hair, and clamped his hands over her ears to holler at the men.

"Don't let Draxley leave town! Some of you hunt him down if you have to!" He moved his hands to Lacey's shoulders, keeping his fingers in the silkiness of her loosened tresses.

"He won't go anywhere." Granger's grim promise came through loud and clear. "Draxley's just outside the mines, head crushed by a boulder from up the ridge."

Chase heard Lacey gasp just before she buried her face against his chest. He looped his arms around her and held her close. "It means he won't hurt anyone else, sweetheart."

"I know." She pushed away from him slightly, and Chase resisted the urge to pull her back. "Chase? Did you mean to call me sweetheart?" Lacey sounded almost shy.

She never sounded shy before. Chase started grinning. "Yep." He went ahead and pulled her close again. "Are you ready to hear what it is that I want most?"

He felt her nod even though she didn't say anything.

"Right now I want to kiss you." Chase waited for her answer, but he couldn't even hear her breathing anymore. Just as he started getting concerned, she took a great, gulping breath.

"And later?" came the shaky query. "What do you want later?"

Before he answered, Chase moved his hand to cup the side of her face. "When we get out of here, I want you to forget about your ad and say you'll be my wife."

He lowered his lips to hers before she could make a decision, hoping the kiss would convey the tenderness and longing he couldn't find the words for. She matched him, soft and sweet and passionate as she curled her hand around the nape of his neck.

When he pulled back, Chase tilted to rest his forehead against hers. "Do you know what it is that you want, Lacey?"

She nodded. "Right now I want you to kiss me again."

Chase's breath hitched, but he needed more. "And later?" He echoed her question. "Do you know what you want later?"

She threaded her fingers through his hair and ignored the calls of their rescuers as they began to break through the barrier. "I want to marry you, too." Enough light seeped through for him to see her smile as she moved closer to whisper, "And you know how I am when I set my mind on something. . . ."

STRONG AND STUBBORN

DEDICATION

First and foremost, this is dedicated to the Lord.
Without His strength, no story would fill these pages.
It's a simple truth but sometimes not simple at all to
live with. When I alone try to wrestle the words
into submission, they fight back!

Second, this novel is dedicated to my amazing husband,
who encouraged me when I faltered, prayed with me when I struggled,
and celebrated each chapter. I am so incredibly blessed to have found my
partner in life, and I thank God for you every day.

Finally, this story is for the readers, without whom books
would not be published. Use your power wisely, well, and often!

CHARACTER LIST

Hope Falls Heroines:

Naomi Higgins: Cousin to Lacey and Braden Lyman. Ex-fiancée of Harry Blinman.

Coraline "Cora" Thompson: Ex-fiancée of Braden Lyman. Sister of Evie Thompson. Best friend of Lacey Lyman.

Lacey Lyman: Cousin to Naomi Higgins. Fiancée of Chase Dunstan. Sister of Braden Lyman. Originator of Husbands for Hire advertisement and idea to turn the town into a sawmill.

Evelyn "Evie" Thompson: Fiancée of Jake Granger. Sister of Cora. Owner of Hope Falls Café.

Miscellaneous Ladies:

Charlotte Blinman: Estranged sister of Naomi Higgins. Wife of Harry Blinman.

Althea Bainbridge: Mother of Leticia Bainbridge. Mother-in-law of Mike Strode. Grandmother of Luke Strode.

Leticia Bainbridge-Strode: Deceased wife of Mike Strode. Mother of Luke Strode. Daughter of Althea Bainbridge.

Arla Nash: Widowed sister of Mr. Lawson, the sawmill engineer.

Dorothy Nash: Newborn daughter of Arla Nash.

Martha McCreedy: Wife of sawmill worker. Friend to Arla Nash. Helper in Evie's kitchen.

Hope Falls Heroes:

Michael Strode: Widower. Carpenter. Father of Luke Strode.

Luke Strode: Mike's son—though not biologically. Ten years old. Target of kidnap attempts by his maternal grandparents, the Bainbridges.

Braden Lyman: Brother of Lacey Lyman. Original owner of Hope Falls mine, caught and injured in the initial mine collapse. Ex-fiancé of Cora Thompson.

Chase Dunstan: Fiancé of Lacey Lyman. Hunter, tracker, wilderness guide. Originally helped Braden Lyman survey Hope Falls area. Came back to investigate suspicious mine collapse.

Decoy: Chase's silver-gray Irish wolfhound. Almost four feet tall and six feet long.

Jacob Granger: Fiancé to Evie Thompson. Family owns successful chain of sawmills. Originally came to Hope Falls under alias of Jake Creed to find his brother's murderer.

HOPE FALLS LOGGERS:

Volker "Clump" Klumpf: Good-natured German farmer turned logger, distinctive for heavy boots.

Rory "Bear" Riordan: Gentle giant of a Scots-Irish logger.

Gent: Oldest logger in Hope Falls with a penchant for top hats.

Bobsley: Youngest worker in Hope Falls.

Craig Williams: Arrogant logger who's tried to court every single woman.

Mr. Lawson: Mild-mannered engineer. Brother to Arla Nash and uncle to Dorothy.

HOPE FALLS MINE INVESTORS:

Mr. Draxley: Telegraph operator. Involved in mine sabotage, although not the mastermind. Attempted murderer of Lacey Lyman and Chase Dunstan.

Mr. Owens: Business partner of Braden Lyman and original owner of Hope Falls mine. Initially survived the collapse but died of injuries later. Discovered to have been part of mine sabotage.

Harold "Harry" Blinman: Ex-suitor of Naomi Higgins. Husband to her sister, Charlotte. Original investor in Hope Falls mine.

"Cautious" Clyde Corning: Original investor in Hope Falls mine. Interested in Cora.

PROLOGUE

Baltimore, Maryland, 1881

*I*t *should have been me.*

Guilt crept around the edges of the thought, but Naomi Higgins brushed it away with the first of her tears—the first of an inevitable deluge. She'd held them at bay for far too long, and when the ever-present pinch behind her nose blossomed to a sharp tingling pain, Naomi sought solace in her favorite refuge. The books surrounding her showed more spine than she, who had abandoned her only sister's wedding reception.

It *should* have been Naomi, not Charlotte, who celebrated. It almost had been. After all, Harold Blinman became familiar with the Higgins household when he began courting *Naomi* a scant year before.

He'd wooed her just long enough to steal a place in Naomi's heart. Her advanced age of more than twenty-one years, though well beyond most ladies' first courtship, offered no protection against a handsome smile, a hand at the small of her back, and a whirlwind of dances.

Her advanced age did, however, offer Harry a reason to transfer his affections to her nineteen-year-old sister. The two looked astoundingly alike—so alike, in fact, that polite society recognized the switch slowly—fashionable hats and bonnets hiding their one clear difference. Charlotte dressed to impress and generally succeeded. She'd flounced home from her beloved French boarding school, only to flounce right back out the door with her sister's beau.

With their mother's blessing.

In fact, Charlotte's "success" led to endless edicts that Naomi abandon her love of books and take up her sister's ruthless study of fashion plates and scandal sheets. Delilah Higgins had long denounced her eldest daughter as "overly bookish," which somehow made her far too "adversarial and masculine" to attract a decent match. When Harry chose Charlotte, he as good as announced to the entire world that he felt the same way.

"Naomi Glorianna Higgins!" Her mother's hiss snaked through the room. "Whatever are you about, closeting yourself in here? Hasn't your reputation as a bluestocking cost you enough?"

Her tears halted as suddenly as if her mother stoppered their source. Showing emotion, Naomi learned long ago, issued an invitation for condescension, correction, or outright criticism. Speaking one's mind brought a more vehement version of the same.

For once, Naomi didn't care.

"If Harry spurned me for my intelligent conversation, my only loss is a miserable marriage." *Though that miserable marriage would have given me a honeymoon in Paris and moved me out of this household*, Naomi silently added. Saying anything more would prove disastrous—she'd never been a good liar.

Harry's defection still hurt. She'd believed he wanted her, been lured into wanting him, only to be told in no uncertain terms she wasn't woman enough to keep him. And while she didn't want a thing to do with the Harold Blinman who'd stood today in front of everyone and declared he would love her sister until death, a corner of Naomi's heart grieved for the Harry she'd thought cared for her.

"Harold." Her mother cracked the word like a whip, satisfaction in her smile. "Although he is now a bona fide member of the family, and thus you may claim the familiarity of his given name, you will never again use his pet name. Do I make myself clear?"

"As you please, Mother." Naomi shrugged, trying to dislodge her dismay at the way a single word betrayed her.

"Do not shrug. It's vulgar." Delilah Higgins made a moue of disapproval. "And you've ruined our hard work styling your hair!"

Glad for an excuse to turn from her mother, Naomi moved toward the massive mirror above the fireplace. She peered at the image of a tall woman, shown to advantage in an utterly inappropriate shade of crimson—her sister insisted that her maid of honor be clad in the Blinman colors in homage of her new husband—her hair loosely gathered into an intricate series of knots. The coiffure, meant to be sophisticated but not overwrought, was achieved by dint of dozens of hairpins *still* stabbing into her scalp.

But aside from a sadness lurking in her eyes, Naomi saw nothing amiss. In fact, the jewel tone suited her far better than the pastels typically deemed appropriate for any unmarried miss. *So I wear spinsterhood well.* The notion garnered a rueful grin.

"It seems secure and unfrizzled, Mother." Naomi kept her puzzlement out of her voice—uncertainty signaled vulnerability.

"Are you so secure in your resemblance to me that you presume others will discount your disfigurement? Your father wore his oddity well, but you're a woman. That coloring will mar your crowning glory until old age wipes clean any vanity."

"All and sundry know of it." Naomi couldn't fathom why her family persisted in fussing over her hair on today, of all days. The shock of white brightening black began just at her hairline and swept down to her waist. Eight hundred seventy-three strands of pure white amid the darkness—eight hundred seventy-three reminders of the first husband her mother hated too much to forget.

Naomi counted them at age nine as she plucked out each and every one in a desperate attempt to please her mother. Instead she'd been confined to the house for almost a year until the bald spot grew in sufficiently. No concoction brewed by the apothecary, beauty shops, or French maids could darken them beyond dull gray, and she'd long since given up trying to change herself.

"Yes, everyone has seen it, but out of sight, less in mind." Her mother pulled, twisted, and fluffed the hair to cover the telltale white then viciously stabbed more hairpins to keep the locks in place. "Now that Charlotte is wearing the Blinman ring, none shall mistake the two of you. It's to your advantage now to look your best, and all of Baltimore has turned out here tonight."

I know. Naomi closed her eyes against a sharp pain in her skull. Whether it sprang from her situation or her mother's hairdressing, she didn't ponder. *All the pitying glances and inane comments made me slip away in the first place.*

"There. Now you're presentable. Back to the party, young lady."

Naomi knew she should. Knew that walking out the door and joining the celebration with a smile on her face and a sparkle in her eye would help quell the gleeful gossips. But she hesitated. *Why run the gamut when I lost the race long before?*

Unexpectedly, her reluctance didn't wring a reprimand from her mother. Instead Delilah Higgins gave her eldest daughter a considering look, then crossed the room. Pulling on the axis of the massive standing globe, she revealed a set of cut crystal decanters and tumblers. Without a word, she poured a splash of dark amber liquid into a tumbler and handed the strong spirits to Naomi.

"I realize it's too much to ask that you be happy for your sister's marriage—try instead to be happy in spite of it. At the very least, paste a more convincing smile on your face. You look well enough tonight, otherwise." Her mother swept toward the doors. "Charlotte wouldn't fly against convention, but for once your stubbornness can serve you well. If you can forget yourself long enough to enjoy tonight, you'll out circle the buzzards yet."

Naomi gaped at the doors long after they shut. Only the sound of the fire collapsing into the grate startled her. She swirled the mysterious brew in her tumbler, wondering at its strength. Her mother—and society at large—never allowed her more than a glass of watered-down wine with dinner or a weak Madeira punch.

Forget yourself. . . . Her mother's advice was tempting. What would it be like to forget the troubles of Naomi Higgins, if only for an evening? What would it be like not to think about the mother who despised the living reminder of her first husband? Not to ruin a conversation by mentioning a fact or opinion about philosophy, history, or even politics? Forgetting that everyone knew the man she'd chosen had chosen her sister instead?

Yes, Naomi thought as she raised the glass to her lips and gulped its contents. She gasped for a few heartbeats, unable to breathe. The liquid seemed to burn a fiery path of determination straight through her. *It would be quite nice to forget.*

ONE

Boston, Massachusetts, June 21, 1887

How quickly you seem to forget, Michael." Althea Bainbridge raised one finely arched gray brow. "I, on the other hand, am blessed with a superior memory." Her tone indicated all too clearly that she believed herself blessed with superiority in every way.

"I remember." Mike saw no sense in wasting words on deaf ears. He could tell his mother-in-law just how exceptionally he remembered the deal they'd struck ten years ago. A single decade, after all, wasn't enough to fade the most important day of his life.

Or the worst.

"Then you know I'm right." Somehow the woman gave the impression of leaning back in satisfaction; something Mike knew couldn't be possible. Althea Bainbridge corseted the bend from her spine and the compromise from her conversation.

"No." As a matter of fact, the woman couldn't be more wrong.

"No?" Mr. Bainbridge, whose sole function as far as Mike could see was to fund Mrs. Bainbridge's ambitions, made a good parrot. But then again, the man had a lot of practice. Surely his only path to peace lay in agreeing with whatever his shrew of a wife demanded.

"Humbug." His mother-in-law looked as though she smelled something foul. "Despite the impression you give so readily, Michael, I know you are no fool. You've proven your good sense before. Dredge it back up from the mire you've made of things, and make the right decision."

Not for the first time, Mike wondered what the indomitable Althea Bainbridge would do if he upended her bone china teapot atop that ridiculous—and obviously ridiculously expensive—wig of hers. But he'd forgo outright fighting with the Bainbridges, for Luke's sake.

"I already have."

"Excellent." His mother-in-law looked at him expectantly. When he failed to react, her magnanimous mood vanished. "What are you waiting for? Go fetch the boy and bring him here at once! We've already outfitted the nursery and schoolroom. His new governess and tutors await, and I'll not allow my grandson's fine intellect to be wasted a moment longer. As it stands, it will take years to fix the damage you've undoubtedly done."

"I said I made the *right* decision. I won't leave my son."

"He ain't yours." Bainbridge looked pleased with that brilliant observation until his wife took him to task for letting his "unfortunate" background seep through the veneer of sophistication.

"Not, dear. Lucas *is not* Michael's son."

"'Xactly right, my dove." The man beamed, typically unperturbed by the fact they were discussing his only daughter's disgrace.

"Luke." It came out louder than he intended, but Mike didn't mind. "His name is Luke, not Lucas. I wrote it on the birth certificate myself." He'd had to literally yank the paper from his mother-in-law's grasping hands in order to name his son for his grandfather. Mike had been pulling Luke out of her clutches ever since, and today would be the last time. He'd made sure of that.

"I remember that." His mother-in-law lost her icy composure for long enough to glower at him. "But you will note that I am being gracious enough to overlook your audacity and rectify the error."

"*Gracious* is the last word I'd use for you." He allowed some of his rage to show. "Our agreement gave both your daughter and her unborn child the protection of my name. My name, *my son.*"

"Give over, Michael. Lucas bears your name but not your

blood. Everyone here knows precisely why you married Leticia, and, more importantly, why our darling lowered herself enough to wed you. Your mother's familial connections combined with your father's unfortunate tendencies toward trade made you a beautifully unknown and marginally acceptable mate in the eyes of society. The marriage maintained Leticia's good reputation, but your usefulness to the family has reached its end."

She "lowered" herself to wed me because first she laid down for another man. Mike bit back the caustic words, knowing better than to let the past leach into the present. He'd known the situation when he married Leticia Bainbridge—though he hadn't anticipated the extent of his in-laws' constant interference in his household.

Leticia gained a new last name, quickly enough to squeak past too much gossip when her son emerged eight months after their nuptials. Michael gained money enough to buy whatever care could soften his mother's worsening case of consumption. Mama still passed on, but Michael's marriage bought her a measure of peace. She never knew the bitter truth behind his marriage, praise God.

"You're still wrong." Michael shook his head. "Leticia's life has ended, but Luke and I continue on. And we'll stay together."

"Sentimentality doesn't suit you. Think, man. Here Lucas will have every luxury, the best of educations, and more opportunities than you could possibly imagine. If you won't give us our grandson to ease our hearts or your burdens, bring him for his own good."

"He's already lost his mother." Though Leticia rarely saw the boy. "It's best for him to keep as much of the familiar as possible." Having spoken his piece, Mike headed for the door.

"We'll pay you!" Althea Bainbridge's reserve cracked, desperation making her voice shrill. "Whatever you like, however much. You'll take the money—I know you will. *You have to.*" She drew a loud, calming breath, oblivious to the fists now clenched at her son-in-law's sides. "You were bought once before after all."

"Yes, I was bought once." Mike didn't bother turning around. "But Luke never will be. My son is worth more than that."

"Of course. Lucas is worth anything." She spoke softly, consideringly. "There is no sacrifice too great for his sake."

Michael decided to ignore the vague threat and continued toward the door. A jarring crash against the far wall stopped him in his tracks. He stared at the shattered remains of Althea Bainbridge's fine Sevres teapot as a cup spiraled across the room to join it, sloshing tea across the Aubusson rug before it, too, smashed to pieces.

"Such a display of temper!" His mother-in-law calmly pitched the cream pot next. Then she surveyed the destruction and gave a smug smile. "I can't imagine what the servants will make of it. But perhaps over the next few days reports will arise as to your unstable and volatile nature, Michael." She tsked.

Her husband spoke up. "It's only a matter of time before someone in power sees to it that Lucas is removed from your care for his own safety. Our friend Judge Roderick will make sure of it."

"You've gone mad." But whether or not she'd lost a few of her marbles, Althea Bainbridge made her point. She had the connections—and the sick determination—to have Luke taken away from him.

"Well, I bore a fondness for that tea set." A hint of regret clouded her features before her lips thinned with heartless determination. "But, as I said, there's no sacrifice too great for my grandson."

"I will never allow him to be taken from me."

"We shall see. Since we both agree Lucas is worth more than your miserable life, you can't imagine what I'm willing to do for him." Something reptilian flickered in her gaze as she glanced at the shattered china. "Then again, perhaps you can. I was fond of my tea set. It served a purpose. But you? You're no more than a problem—and I have ways of making those disappear."

This brought things to a new level. Mike could push aside the prospect of a ruined reputation or vague threat—Althea Bainbridge just threatened to have him killed. The idea of being hunted didn't make him fear for himself, but the danger to Luke sent a chill up his spine.

No matter how much I have to give up, how far I have to go, the Bainbridges will never take my son. I won't let him out of my sight.

∞

San Juan Mountains of the Colorado Territory, July 3, 1887

"Have you seen Lacey?" Naomi couldn't suppress her nervousness over the way her cousin kept flitting away from their company in favor of trailing behind Hope Falls's new hunter. The girl didn't understand that a good reputation was as fragile as spun sugar— and as easily shattered.

"The mercantile with Arla." Evie Thompson's mention of the sawmill engineer's widowed sister made Naomi relax. "She's drawing up lists of things to order. I don't know who's more anxious for the baby to be born—Lacey or its mother. Lacey keeps saying she needs to know whether it will be a boy or a girl."

"You know how Lacey loves to shop. Hope Falls may have reduced her options to catalogues, but she'll find what she needs." And a half-dozen fripperies besides, if Naomi knew the young woman she'd helped raise for the past five years. "Is Cora with them? She and Arla seem to have struck up a friendship."

"Not that I know of." A frown crinkled Evie's brow at the mention of her sister. "It seems unlikely she'd go pay Braden a visit, considering the way he's been acting, but I'm guessing you already checked the house."

"No sign of her there. Would you like to go check the doctor's?" At her friend's nod, Naomi hovered by the door as Evie draped the stained apron over a stool, plopped a lid atop a simmering pot, and banked the fire in her prized cookstove. The two women fell into step as they journeyed toward the doctor's quarters.

"Between you and me,"—Evie's words dropped heavily, as though weighted with regret and resignation—"I think Cora's had enough."

Naomi sighed. "Between you and me, it's a testament to how

648

well you raised your sister that she's stayed by Braden's side this long. Her devotion and commitment are stronger than he deserves."

"Heaven knows I didn't encourage her to withstand Braden's foul moods." A note of regret crawled beneath Evie's strong words—true words. "I didn't want her subjected to that kind of heartache. But I underestimated how deeply she loves him, and now I know I should have encouraged her loyalty and bolstered her spirits."

Naomi instantly understood Evie's change of heart. Now that Jake Granger came along and earned her love, Evie held a new appreciation for the bond between a woman and her chosen mate. Naomi could only pray that appreciation never became pain or bitterness.

"Your own loyalty made you protective," Naomi soothed. "In fact, I think knowing you would support her decision if she left Braden helped Cora to keep fighting for him." They came to a stop.

"Naomi,"—her friend shook her head—"you have a way of making something preposterous sound wise. I feel like if I turn it around enough times in my mind, I'll find the sense in what you say."

"Think about it, Evie." Naomi moved toward the benches lining the front of the mercantile and sat down. Despite niggling worries over Cora, she felt the other two of their foursome were safe enough together. Right now Evie needed some assurance.

Out of them all, Evie Thompson worked the hardest from sunup to sundown. She gave the most to make their fledgling town run and asked the least in return. Between cooking for two dozen lumbermen, falling in love with a man whose secret nearly destroyed them all, and trying to care for her sister, Evie handled more than her fair share of troubles. By all rights, she deserved a rest!

"Better yet, let me walk you through my reasoning so you can see the way I do." Naomi paused a moment to collect her thoughts. The extraordinary events since the mine collapse left a lot of ground to cover. How best to address the treacherous without losing sight of the triumphs? She silently prayed for the words.

"You financially supported Cora when your father died." Naomi began with the facts. "You emotionally supported her when she fell in love with Braden—or, rather, the man Braden used to be."

Here she paused as they both remembered that man. Braden, the handsome cousin Naomi never met until her family cast her out. Braden, whose immediate pretense that Naomi *honored* the Lyman family by becoming his sister's companion almost convinced Naomi herself that she hadn't been exiled in disgrace. How she missed *that* Braden!

"Yes." Evie broke into Naomi's recollections. "I stood by her side when she accepted Braden's proposal—but when I learned of his plans to start a mining interest, I should have told her to wait."

"Ah, but the Hope Falls mine seemed a perfect investment. All the geographical surveys, the rich geological samples, the location near the railroad. . . Braden gathered plenty of investors who saw the value of this place." Naomi looked around the now-empty town. "When he put up his inheritance and accepted your and Lacey's investments for a diner and mercantile, Braden had every reason to expect Hope Falls would be a success—and the perfect place to raise a family."

Evie gave a mirthless laugh. "Yes, it seemed perfect. We should have known nothing is. We should have realized—"

"That the mine would collapse?" Naomi's voice sharpened as she interrupted. "None of us could have imagined such a thing! You knew Braden would bring Cora here, so you bought in. I knew Lacey would follow her brother—and any opportunity for adventure—so I made the same commitment. Where love leads, each of us chose to follow."

"Of course you're right." Evie jumped off the bench to pace before it. "At least the first time. Investing in Hope Falls, the mine made sense. But surely we should have learned from that first disaster? After hearing Braden died in the collapse, we vowed to have nothing more to do with this place. Instead we jumped back in and compounded our mistakes! How could we be so *foolish*, Naomi?"

Talking this out wasn't helping much. Naomi wondered what on earth she could say to reassure Evie now. Because the truth was...

"I have no idea." Her own admission caught her by surprise. But she couldn't escape the fact that their mad scheme to save Hope Falls was foolish in the extreme. Except... "Except that when we learned Braden actually survived the mine collapse, nothing could have stopped Lacey and Cora from coming here. And neither of us could let them gallivant across the country without us. It wasn't safe."

"No, it wasn't safe for the two of them. But joining them didn't give much protection from the real danger here," Evie cried. "I followed Cora to her fiancé, only to watch my sister's heart break."

"You're wrong." Hearing voices inside the mercantile, Naomi realized that Lacey and Arla had left the supply room and might be within earshot. She rose to her feet. *The worst of it is that we brought most of the danger upon ourselves with that ludicrous ad!* But now wasn't the time to say so. There never would be a time to say so, now that the ad brought Jake Granger into Evie's life. And, unless Naomi was much mistaken, the same ad brought Lacey's match to Hope Falls. The sparks flying between her cousin and the town's new hunter had less to do with disagreements than a powerful attraction.

"How?" Evie's desperation held a hint of hope. "How am I wrong?"

"Let's head back to the café." Naomi tilted her head toward the store, where Cora's voice joined Arla's and Lacey's. She saw recognition flutter across Evie's face as they moved away.

When they'd reached the halfway point, Evie resumed the conversation. "I sheltered Cora too much, but I hated to see her hurting. Braden's enmity—so soon after her grief at news of his death—is too harsh a blow for my sister's tender heart."

"Cora's heart isn't broken. It may be badly bruised, but it's not broken." Naomi stepped off the raised wooden platform surrounding the store. "If your sister's heart had broken, she wouldn't persist in visiting Braden and weathering his storms."

Evie walked a few steps more before giving a grudging nod. "I still think I should have encouraged my sister not to give up. No matter how terrible Braden's become, he's still the man she loves."

"And I still think the opposite. Consider this," Naomi propositioned. "If Cora dragged you out of Charleston, uprooting both your lives and dragging you to the wilderness, how do you think she felt when Braden took away the reason you both traveled here?"

"Furious with his wretched, ungrateful hide. What else?"

"No, that's how *we* felt, Evie. Not how Cora sees things. Turn it around. What if it were *your* fiancé, and *you*'d asked Cora to give up everything so *you* could be with a man who no longer wanted you?"

"Guilty." Evie's eyes widened with equal parts of understanding and horror. "Oh, Naomi! Cora shouldn't feel as though she's to blame for the challenges we've faced. Hope Falls was—and still is—beyond what any of us imagined. She couldn't have changed any of it."

"To an extent, I think both she and Lacey do blame themselves." It had been Lacey, after all, who convinced them to write that accursed ad. But now wasn't the time to dwell on *that* mistake.

"How awful. What can we do to show them otherwise?"

"You already have." Naomi reached out to pat Evie's shoulder as they returned to her kitchen door. "That Hope Falls brought you a fiancé of your own goes a long way toward alleviating Cora's worry, I'm sure. But I think the fact that you never make your sister feel as though she had to stay with Braden helped. Cora knew she wasn't trapped by your expectations because she knew you cared more about her happiness than you cared whether you'd left Charleston for nothing."

Evie gave her a long look as though weighing the words. Finally her dimple surfaced. "I knew you'd turn out to be right."

"Of course!" Naomi opened the doctor's door. "Sometimes the best way to support someone is to let them make their own choices."

TWO

It's the right choice, Mike reminded himself with every mile he put between Luke and his grasping grandparents. There was no contest between losing a house and losing his son.

"Come back here." Mike wrapped a hand around his son's wrist and tugged it away from the open window and safely back inside the train car. This made the first of a days-long journey, and he knew from experience that he had to lay down the law at the start if he had any hope of keeping his ten-year-old's high spirits in check.

"I like the wind." Color rode high on the boy's cheeks as he beamed with excitement. "It makes it feel like we're going fast!"

"Fast is good." *The faster the better.* Mike wouldn't rest easy until thousands of miles separated his son from his in-laws' grasp.

His hand crept to his coat pocket, where a slip of paper linked this madcap flight to the possibility of a future free of the Bainbridges' threats. Softened from much handling, the telegram's short message offered opportunity, if not promises.

HOPE FALLS, COLORADO. *Stop.*
BETWEEN DURANGO AND SILVERTON. *Stop.*
NEW SAWMILL GOING UP. *Stop.*
MIGHT HAVE USE FOR CARPENTER. *Stop.*
ASK FOR ENGINEER LAWSON. *Stop.*
GIVE MY NAME AS REFERENCE. *Stop.*
SOUNDS LIKE A STRANGE PLACE. *Stop.*
GOOD LUCK AND GODSPEED. *End.*

Mike didn't bother to take it out of his pocket, just fingered the edges to make sure it remained in place. These days a man's word—especially a stranger's word—wasn't trusted. He needed the telegram itself as a makeshift letter of introduction and proof of reference.

For that matter, he needed the telegram for his own peace of mind. The way Mike saw it, even if this Lawson fellow didn't need a carpenter or joiner—or simply didn't need one yet, as engineers often lavished time upon blueprints and schematics before getting down to the real business of construction—he might find other work.

True, he'd only ever swung an ax to break up or square off logs already cut down. But from what Mike heard, a strong back and a way with wood were traits that served a lumberman well. So long as he could make arrangements for Luke to remain out of the way, Mike was more than willing to try his hand felling trees.

"It doesn't feel like we're going so fast now." Luke flattened both palms against the lower half of the window, which didn't open, squinting as though trying to make things blur by more quickly.

"We're going just as fast as we were with your hand out the window," Mike told him. "But this way a tree branch won't hit you."

Luke frowned in concentration. "If we're going as fast as the wind outside, then why does it feel so different?"

"How does it feel different, aside from being warmer?" Mike stretched his legs out, glad no one occupied the seats ahead.

"I don't know, 'xactly." Small fingers tapped on the armrest. "But the wind feels like adventure, and the train feels like. . ."

Mike suppressed a smile as his son reached for an explanation.

"Sitting!" Frustration seeped into the proclamation. "Like we aren't really doing anything much different than taking tea at home. If it wasn't for the noise, I'd hardly know we'd left!"

"Except the chairs at home are more comfortable," Mike teased. "And even if your hand isn't out the window, you can still see things whisk past. Before the trip is over, you'll see a lot of places and people you never would have if we were still home."

And hopefully none of the people we left behind, Mike prayed as

Luke settled into watching the world go by, his nose now pressed against the glass. And when he wasn't sleeping, Luke's nose pressed against the windowpanes of several other trains as the days and miles rolled past. By the time they reached Dallas, Mike fancied that the tip of his son's nose looked flatter than before the trip.

"Why do I have to stay behind?" A note of fear quivered beneath the question. "I thought we were leaving so Grandma couldn't take me away. I thought you said we were staying together and going on an adventure!"

"We are." Mike squatted back on his heels to be at eye level, searching for the words to explain his reasons for leaving. "But every adventure has different stages. For just a little while, until the next part of our lives begins, you need to stay with your aunt."

"But our adventure is supposed to be for both of us." Luke rubbed his eyes, though Mike couldn't tell whether he wanted to keep from crying or to work out grit from the train ride. "Together!"

He reached out to hold one of his son's achingly small hands. To tell the truth, those hands—and the rest of Luke—had grown by leaps and bounds lately. All too soon his son would leave childhood behind. But for now there was enough of the little boy about him to need his daddy—and Mike was glad of it.

"Yep. That's why we left Baltimore. This is all about making sure our adventures are always together. You know that." He gave Luke's hand a comforting squeeze, pleased when Luke squeezed back a little harder. Mike topped that, and they engaged in a short battle before Luke couldn't summon any extra strength and conceded defeat by trying to pull away. So Mike held on tighter and didn't let him.

His son tried to scowl, but his smile crept in around the edges. Luke didn't say anything about it, but Mike knew that their playful tussle assured the boy more than any words he could string together. Come what may, Luke knew that his dad was strong enough to get the job done and not let go of him in the meantime.

"As soon as I have everything settled and made sure I've found the right place, I'll come back and fetch you." He stood up, knees tingling. "If all goes well, I'll be back before you miss me."

Any possible response would sound childish, so Luke settled on a snort. It both dismissed the notion that he'd miss his father and dismissed the idea that he wouldn't. Then he spoke up.

"I don't much like waiting." Luke jammed his hat down and muttered, "So make sure the first place is the right place, all right?"

"I'll do my best." Mike couldn't get his son's parting request out of his mind for the rest of his journey.

No matter how he tried to tell himself that Hope Falls would be the answer to those prayers, doubts lashed him at every turn. *What if the Bainbridges were already having him followed?* He shook away the grim idea. Mike had purchased three different sets of train tickets in case someone tried to track them. He'd even boarded the first train, only to step off the back end and track around to their real ride. He'd closely watched everyone who boarded or left the train but saw nothing suspicious so far—which meant they'd gotten out of Baltimore free and clear.

But can we stay that way? That was an entirely different question. Someone might be waiting to snatch Luke away at the next train station. Or some dodgy back-alley tracker might sniff them out after they reached Hope Falls. He had no way to know for sure.

Of course, Mike had done his best to find a location few people ever heard of so no one could deduce where they'd go. From what he'd gathered, Hope Falls had been a mine of some sort before being turned into a sawmill. No one with a smattering of logic would think that Michael Strode—carpenter, joiner, and cabinetmaker— would take off for a silver mine. Particularly not one so far away.

Yes, the location seemed perfect. So why did that one line in his telegram keep streaming through his thoughts? What on earth could his old friend mean by "*Sounds like a strange place. Good luck.*"?

Because, despite Mike's determination to build a new life and a safe home for Luke, he couldn't stop wondering. . .shouldn't all the bad luck have run out for a town that suffered a mine collapse? And, perhaps more importantly, just how strange could Hope Falls be?

STRONG AND STUBBORN

Hope Falls, July 5, 1887

Strange how much effort it takes to accomplish so little. Braden Lyman gritted his teeth and leaned back to ease the strain on his knee. During the past week, the doctor had determined his kneecap well enough healed to be taken from traction. Then had begun the agonizing— and agonizingly slow—process of "training" his leg to bend again. Thus far, through a makeshift system of pulleys, bandages, and bars, the doctor had managed to manipulate his damaged leg to a far-from-impressive one-hundred-forty-degree angle. No more.

Yes, it meant a forty-degree improvement from lying flat, as he had for more than two months—but it remained a solid fifty degrees away from him being able to bend his knee as though sitting properly in a chair.

Which meant fifty degrees away from him getting out of this blasted bed and into the wheeled chair ready and waiting for him.

If he'd made enough improvement, Braden would be in that wheelchair *right now.* He would've rolled himself straight out the door, across the meadow, and up to the opening of the mine he'd hewn into the mountain. The very mine that collapsed on him three months ago, killing several of his men and leaving Braden badly concussed with a dislocated shoulder and shattered kneecap.

The mine, where his little sister was determined to uncover evidence that the collapse had been a cleverly engineered catastrophe—not a result of poor planning or careless construction, as he'd believed. Braden's fists clamped around twisted bedsheets, the twin bullets of hope and helplessness piercing him anew.

Braden sucked in a deep breath and tried—as he had been for the past hour or so—not to stare at his fiancée while she quietly sat beside him and read. If he allowed himself more than a glance, he wouldn't be able to tear his gaze from the red shimmers in her ginger hair, the pale perfection of creamy skin touched with saucy freckles. If he looked once, she'd catch him staring at her, greedy for the comforting presence of the woman he no longer deserved.

She shouldn't be here. Fury, sharp and vicious as barbed wire, squeezed his chest. *I can't provide for her from this sickroom. I can't protect her. I can't even make her go back home, where it's safe.* His rage coiled more tightly, crushing any last hopes.

"Why are you still here?" He lashed out against the woman whose presence reminded him of the man he'd been—and what he'd lost.

"Because, for the first time since I arrived in Hope Falls, you haven't ordered me out of your room." Cora didn't look up, merely ran a delicate finger along the seam of pages. "I suppose I took it as an encouraging sign." She paused. The page turned.

Her calm disinterest needled him. "Didn't I order you out of my room this very morning? Have I not said from the very beginning that you females should never have come to Hope Falls with your far-fetched schemes? At every turn I've said I don't want you, don't need you to do anything but leave here and behave like the ladies you've shown you aren't. Don't accuse me of inconsistency, woman!" The moment he spoke the words, Braden wished he'd choked on them.

Of course Cora could accuse him of inconsistency—he'd once pledged to love and protect her until his dying day. But Braden could no longer protect her. He could only love her enough to give her up. But the contrary woman made even that impossible. His glorious Cora wouldn't see reason, defied him at every turn, and obstinately refused to return to the safety and security of home.

"If I were to bother accusing you, Braden, inconsistency would hardly be the worst of the charges." She raised her head, pinning him with the mismatched gaze Braden swore saw straight through him. One hazel eye, one blue. . .both shimmering with unshed tears.

His throat closed. For every time he'd sworn he didn't love her anymore, didn't want her, would order her from his sight and his town, Cora had looked steadily at him and refused. For the first time, she allowed him to glimpse the grief in her remarkable gaze.

I'm sorry. He swallowed another of the thousand apologies he owed her and crossed his arms so he wouldn't reach out to hold her close and assure her how incredible a woman she was. *You deserve better. If the only way I can make you see that is to hurt you, I know it will still be best in the long run. You'll thank me someday.* And when that day came, he'd still be cursing himself.

THREE

Cora Thompson blinked back tears, knowing they wouldn't vanish. Tears lurked all too close to the surface these days, and every time she pushed away the sorrow, it returned more quickly than before.

At this rate she'd be watery-eyed in another ten seconds.

Braden knows it, too. Cora swallowed her hurt, refusing to cede her fiancé the victory. Instead she gave him the full force of her fury. "But since 'inconsistent' is the sin you want to address first, how about we discuss it. How dare you berate us—daily—for two solid months over putting ourselves in danger and then put up only a token protest when Lacey tromps off to the mines?"

"None of you listen to me anyway," he pointed out. "What you call a 'token protest' was a reiteration of what I've been saying—as you admit—for the past two months. None of you women should be here at all. At this point, does anything make much difference?"

"It should. Your vague, insulting objections to our presence hold no water when your only reason is our gender. When it comes to a mine that already caved in on top of you, I would have thought you could offer better guidance. Lacey's life is at stake!"

"The mine construction stayed sound, and they shored it up farther to pull me out. It's safe enough if Dunstan keeps to the main way and doesn't stay long. But you don't have to believe me. If it makes things easier, believe that I don't care about my sister, too. Accuse me of whatever you like." A sneer distorted his once-handsome face. "In the end, your words mean nothing to me."

Cora drew a shuddering breath, refusing to let him see how deeply that struck her. When hope waned and even her love itself began to falter, she'd found pride to be her saving grace. Ironic, when one considered how pride numbered among the seven deadly sins.

But, if she was honest with herself—and Cora always tried to be honest with herself, even if the thoughts were too outrageous to share with anyone else—she'd imagined that she'd lovingly support Braden and see him through his time of pain and suffering. Cora had thought of helping mend broken bones or closing wounds.

Instead, every moment she spent with the man she loved fractured her own heart a tiny bit more, prying open the scars she'd thought healed over with the miraculous news of Braden's survival. As his body began to heal, their relationship wasted away.

"Who are you trying to convince of that, Braden?" She concentrated so hard on keeping her voice steady, she almost missed the flicker of emotion in his eyes. It caught her off guard, since she'd begun to believe his pretense that he no longer felt anything.

"I don't have to convince anyone of anything." Again something shadowed his gaze. On him it looked like misery, but to Cora it looked as though hope wasn't completely lost after all!

"Yes you do because I don't believe this farce you've become. And until you can convince me, I won't release you from this engagement." She crossed her arms over her chest. "So now what do you have to say?"

Maybe we've finally come to the point where Braden can no longer cocoon himself in his own misery and anger. It's smothered him for long enough—he has to begin breaking free of the past.

Slowly expectation leaked from the air, leaving it brittle with unanswered anticipation. Silence crept in, softly at first, gaining ground, growing heavier with each passing moment.

Cora found herself holding her breath in spite of herself—but as a crumbling defense against the renewed onslaught of unshed tears. *Sometimes,* she realized as Braden turned his head to the wall, *the worst possible answer is no answer at all.*

I've lost him.

"So Lacey's disappeared again," Naomi murmured when she and Evie walked into Braden's sickroom a few days after their talk. Even stranger, the room held about enough tension to crack the walls.

Obviously Braden had said or done something upsetting. But right now she didn't have the patience for the troubles of Cora's engagement. Instead Naomi's worry had clicked up another notch.

"Where's Lacey?" It sounded more like a demand than a question, but Naomi knew her sharpness would be forgiven. After all, the young cousin she'd watched over for the past five years had a vexing habit of disregarding danger and disappearing into the forest surrounding Hope Falls. In the past month alone, the stubborn girl had been abducted at gunpoint *and* attacked by a cougar.

The mere fact that a cougar attack ranked as a *lesser* concern meant Lacey shouldn't be allowed in the forest alone. Ever. Naomi's stomach churned at the newfound proof that Lacey had wandered again.

"My peahen of a sister went off with Dunstan." Braden roused himself to glower at them as though it were all their faults.

Maybe it is my fault, Naomi conceded. After all, she'd been the one to help raise Lacey when the girl needed a mother. Worse, she'd gone along with the harebrained plan to save Hope Falls. *If I'd tried harder, maybe I could've talked sense into the others and saved us all.* Even as she wondered, Naomi knew better.

Lacey was a force of nature, going where she wanted and getting there in whatever manner she pleased. One could either go along with her or be swept to the side, and Naomi would always choose to stay with her cousin. *For all the good it seemed to do either of us.*

"Oh good." Evie sounded relieved. "She's not alone then."

"We have bigger concerns than that." Cora glowered at Braden.

Naomi believed she understood the larger issue. "She's without a chaperone." The attraction between Lacey and the hunter rapidly grew too obvious for things to continue this way. "This isn't the first time she's gallivanted off alone with Dunstan. I know we asked him to keep an eye on her, but it shouldn't be so blatant!"

Evie looked troubled. "Perhaps we need to ask our new hunter to stop taking Lacey on his expeditions. Our reputation as ladies is one of our safeguards out here. If the men begin thinking we're less than paragons of virtue, we'll have a situation on our hands."

Guilt fisted at the back of her throat, cutting off Naomi's ability to agree. *Paragons of virtue.* A laughable thought.

Braden snorted. "As though they believe that anyway, after the stunts you four pulled. The lumbermen are playing along in hopes of striking it rich, but deep down all of them see the four of you as the strange hussies who set out to hire their own husbands."

"Three," Naomi hissed at her cousin, a part of her longing to brain him with the bedpan. "Three of us set out to hire our husbands. One of us gave up everything to be at her fiancé's side."

"And who asked *any* of you to come here, hauling enough luggage to sink an ocean liner and attracting enough trouble to keep a dozen writers' pens scratching? There can be no peace with you here."

"Peace is what you had before, Braden?" Cora's tone went silky. "I would call it shame and the waste of a town."

Naomi gaped for a moment, struck by Cora's uncharacteristic attack. Evie, she couldn't help but notice, failed to hide a grin. Perhaps it was time for Cora to stop standing by Braden's ill humors and begin challenging them instead. Braden himself looked flabbergasted by the change—and well he should be. For the past seven weeks since their arrival in Hope Falls, his fiancée crossed him only in her refusal to dissolve their engagement.

Grin out in full force, Evie apparently decided to leave the estranged lovebirds to sort things out.

"Well, since Lacey's accounted for, I believe I'll go back to making supper. I wouldn't want to disappoint the men. And who knows? Maybe Jake will come back this afternoon." With that, Evie slipped from the room. They heard her footsteps speed to a near run as she made her way down the hall and through the doctor's front door.

"But Lacey needs—" Cora spoke too late to reach her sister.

"Granger won't be back yet," Braden predicted then muttered, "I wish he was. Then he could go help Dunstan in the mines and send Lacey back to keep company with the rest of you women. You're less in the way when the four of you stay huddled together somewhere."

As used to as she'd become to ignoring Braden's mutters, it took Naomi a moment to sift through his sulk and pinpoint what made her so uneasy. Surely no one was wandering around the collapsed mines?

"Dunstan isn't out hunting?" A lump blocked her throat.

"Oh, he's hunting all right." Grim satisfaction showed in Braden's first smile in months. "But this time, it's for proof."

"Where?" Naomi was desperate for answers. "Proof of *what?*"

From the way Cora eyed the pitcher beside Braden's bed, she was barely managing to restrain herself from dumping its contents atop her self-involved fiancé. "They went to the mines."

Naomi knew a vague pride that her knees didn't buckle. All of a sudden she understood Cora's newfound hostility. She felt a large dose of it herself and felt only marginally better as Cora ceded to temptation and upended the pitcher atop Braden's head.

"You let Lacey go into the mines?" Naomi seethed. "Your sister, who can't so much as go for a brief stroll without some disaster?"

"Yes." Braden raked a hand through his sopping hair, flinging drops of water around the room. "My sister, who *you* couldn't stop from selling our family home and planting herself in the middle of the wilderness without protection and no plan of how to handle things."

"We had a plan," she snapped back, stung by the bald accusation that she'd failed in her responsibility to watch over Lacey. Besides, Lacey *had* thought up a way to join her gravely injured brother and reenergize the town that almost stole his life. And although the idea proved incredibly foolish, quite probably dangerous, and definitely impractical, there had been a plan.

Which didn't make Naomi feel one whit better about having

gone along with it. Nor did it alleviate her worries about Lacey now. Nothing would make her breathe easy until she saw her cousin safe and sound—and far away from collapsed mine tunnels.

"Which entrance did they take?" She began rolling up her sleeves—as though that might save the soft gray serge of her day dress from the dirt of the mines. "Eastern or southern facing?"

"How should I know?" He made an abrupt gesture drawing notice to his leg. "I'm stuck in here while they go search for proof that Dunstan's hunch is right. If I could be with him, Lacey wouldn't."

Naomi paused in the act of tightening the new Common Sense bootlaces she'd ordered from Montgomery Ward. Now that she'd had a moment to catch her breath and think about it, she couldn't deny how strange it was for Lacey to go into the bowels of a mountain.

Yes, her cousin dearly loved adventure. Yes, Lacey seemed to find particular delight in discomfiting Chase Dunstan, the new Hope Falls hunter. But at Lacey's core was a creature born of sunlight and sparkle who vigorously guarded the beautiful things with which she surrounded herself. Lacey wouldn't sacrifice one of her gorgeous gowns to dankness and dust without good reason.

"What hunch?" Naomi finished with her laces and leveled her stare at her still-soaked cousin. "Why would either of them go?"

"I hired Dunstan as our territory guide when I first came to set up the mine. After the collapse, he thought I was dead. Since my partner sold his shares so swiftly, the sudden news that I lived after all roused his suspicions." Braden shifted, betraying an uncharacteristic eagerness. "When he caught wind of my sister's featherbrained ad, he assumed it was either code or a scam and decided to look into the real reason behind the mine's collapse."

Naomi blinked, sorting through Braden's answer and finding more surprises than she liked. Questions sprang up where before there had been blind acceptance—the sort of blind acceptance she thought she'd left behind on the day of her sister's wedding. Her head pounded.

"It seems Jake Granger wasn't the only man to come to Hope

Falls hiding his identity." Cora brought up one of the more troubling points. The women had forgiven Granger's deception—though just barely—because the man had been hunting a murderer. Though even that good reason might not have been enough, had Evie not fallen in love with the rugged lumberman and supported him after.

"Nah." Obviously seeing that the women were taking exception to these circumstances, Braden rushed to defend Dunstan. "Chase Dunstan really is his name. He's one of the most capable men I've ever met, and possibly the only one I think could hold his own against my sister. Since he's the best guide and hunter in these mountains, he's the best choice to keep an eye on Lacey—even if you couldn't have known that when you hired him. Just because you didn't look into the man's background doesn't mean he hid who he is."

"He hid his connection to Hope Falls," Cora contested. "Dunstan deliberately left out his reason for coming back then went out of his way to avoid you because you knew his connection to the mines."

"You deliberately chose to keep me in the dark—don't blame Dunstan for your duplicity. What were you thinking, hiring on another man—particularly one as potentially dangerous as a hunter/tracker—behind my back? You're lucky it was Dunstan!"

"Granger vouched for him." Naomi decided to cut off the brewing argument. They could snipe at each other after she fetched Lacey from the mines and wrested her cousin's promise never to go back. "You can quibble all you like—it doesn't change the fact he misled us. And while he's proven his ability to look after himself and Lacey in the forest, a mine that's already collapsed once is drastically different! Its construction is compromised."

"No! The problem wasn't in the construction." Braden punched the mattress with his fist. "If the mine was sabotaged, the design and supports of the tunnels were just as safe as I intended."

"Originally." Cora rubbed her temples. "But you know that your original design was ruined—even though they cleared debris and shored up the main tunnels to get you out, it left the entire network weakened, strewn with shifting rubble. Who knows what Lacey might disturb, bringing the whole thing down again?"

"You're right." From a man who'd spent the past two months telling them they were wrong about anything and everything, the admission offered little comfort. "We'll need to shore up the supports and send in a team for safety's sake. I shouldn't have let them go. Lacey was being stubborn and Dunstan goes his own way, but I encouraged them." He looked as though he was about to be sick.

Cora looked as though she might want to reassure her newly humbled fiancé, but Naomi yanked her friend out the door. When Cora would have run straight back to Evie's kitchen, Naomi veered them toward Lacey's mercantile. In a matter of minutes, she and Cora looped lengths of oiled rope over their shoulders and around their waists and grabbed rucksacks and shovels. If they had to brave the tunnels to fetch Lacey, they'd go in prepared. They headed for the door, only to freeze in place as the earth let loose a booming roar.

FOUR

T he train had already begun slowing for the upcoming stop, so for a moment Michael thought something had gone horribly wrong with the engine. A muted boom sounded before the train car shuddered, nearly tilting off the tracks as it came to a whining, skidding halt.

As it stood, Michael had a hard time distinguishing when the train itself stopped moving—because the earth itself hadn't stopped. The ground beneath the tracks shook; a mountain in the distance roiled enough to look like a mythical dragon sprung to life, stone suddenly struggling to draw breath. Rumbling, roaring, the quake sent dust swirling into the air and obscuring parts of the horizon.

Before the sound and motion ceased, one of the few passengers in the train car bolted to his feet, sprang through the door, and burst from the vehicle in an impressive leap. The man hit the ground running and kept going, headed for the nearest building.

Slinging his rucksack over one shoulder and grabbing his tool case, Michael disembarked. His first real glance of Hope Falls showed a bewildering contradiction. Chaos reigned supreme—the mountain he'd glimpsed before seemed to be sagging in on itself. The dust started settling but still caked several buildings with a tangible coating of catastrophe. But where were all the people? For such a sizeable outpost, there was hardly a soul to be seen.

Michael absorbed the details, sifting through possibilities and explanations. *I thought the mine already collapsed?* Which would account for the almost-abandoned air of Hope Falls. *Maybe the tunnels remained unstable, and the same mines caved in farther?*

That seemed the only way to explain the booming rumble that shook the mountainside. As far as where he could find the townsfolk, Mike could only pray that they hadn't been so foolish as to be poking around the old mine site and set off the earlier ruckus.

For now he headed in the direction mapped out by the other fellow. If he found no one and nothing else, at least he wouldn't be the sole inhabitant of the town. And for a town supposedly raising a sawmill, there definitely weren't enough people to get the job done. *Perhaps Hope Falls abandoned the sawmill idea?*

Acid clawed at the back of his throat at the very thought. Surely the Lord wouldn't have brought him all this way for nothing? Mike shook his head and kept walking, now hearing excited voices.

"It's all going to be fine." Deep tones rumbled reassurance.

"Lacey and Dunstan went to explore the mines!" came a sob in return.

"We're going after them." The beguiling, husky tone sent a shiver down Mike's spine.

He paused, now understanding the true nature of the crisis. The mine had, indeed, suffered another cave-in. Worse, it sounded as though this woman's friends might well have been caught in it.

"I'll send Lawson to get word to the men to come help." The unknown man, still trying to assure the women, began making plans. "The sooner we get through, the sooner we'll find them."

Lawson? Mike didn't have to check the well-worn copy of his friend's telegram to know that this was the name of the engineer. In spite of the tragedy he'd walked into, Mike acknowledged a surge of relief. *If the engineer is here, and there are 'men' to fetch, it looks as though the Hope Falls sawmill does exist after all.*

He set down his carpenter's chest and rounded the corner of the building, determined to give whatever assistance he could. In that moment he got his first glance at the occupants of Hope Falls.

Three women clustered around a doorway—and the man from

the train. Little wonder the fellow leaped from the car as though fearing for his life. By the way the plump, pretty gal in his arms stared up at him, the man had an awful lot to lose. Beside them hovered a wisp of a girl whose face bore some resemblance to the other. But the third woman caught Mike's attention and held it.

Her sensible gray dress used no ploys to play up feminine curves, but to Mike's eyes that enhanced the woman even more. Her skin was as pale and fine as smooth-sanded birch and all the more striking given her hair. That single streak of white racing through the dark tresses showed her singularity. Mike instantly knew she belonged to the incredible voice he'd heard before.

And in the same instant he knew a fierce joy that she wasn't the one cradled so protectively in the other man's arms. At some point, after he'd helped find her friends, he'd ask around to see whether the striking beauty was spoken for. But for now he needed to offer assistance and not a distraction from the task at hand.

"Came in on the train." He gave a nod of acknowledgment to the other man and received one in return. "What can I do to help?"

"My cousin looks to be trapped in the cave-in." The beauty studied him, seeming to measure his strength. "If you're willing, we'd be grateful for your help—though it may prove dangerous."

"I'm willing." Mike knew he'd be willing to do more for this woman than to dig out a collapsed mine tunnel but knew better than to say so. A few times in his life he'd summed up people within moments of their meeting. Without fail, he'd found his initial judgment eerily accurate. At least this time it was favorable.

"In that case,"—the slender girl took a loop of rope from her waist and handed him a rucksack—"I'll go fetch Mr. Lawson. You and Granger will make more headway than I could manage in his place." With that she trotted off, leaving Mike to follow "Granger" as he led them out of town and toward the ominously sagging mountainside.

Under normal circumstances, Naomi would be hesitant to accept a handsome stranger into their midst without thorough questioning.

Of course, she thought, suppressing a mild twinge of panic, it had been so long since she'd found herself in "normal" circumstances that catastrophes seemed more the usual way of things.

So here she stood, blatantly eyeing a strange man—who happened to be more than average in the looks department—and deciding that he looked fit enough to heft large boulders. *Splendidly fit.*

Naomi squashed the thought, accepted the stranger's offer of help, and set about agreeing with Cora. As much as she loved her friends, Evie or Cora should go fetch Lawson. Granger and the stranger—she fought back an absurd giggle at the phrase, knowing hysteria could manifest in inappropriate levity—were the only two here whose physical strength could start moving the mountainside.

There was no question of Naomi fetching Mr. Lawson herself. She hadn't already headed for the mines because she stood precious little chance of accomplishing anything alone. Her running ahead would only pull attention away from the task at hand, and everyone needed to focus on finding Lacey.

Alive, Naomi prayed. *Please, Lord, let Lacey still be alive.*

"Are you the kind of folks who'd want to pray before we head out?" Quiet words, spoken low but clear. The stranger knew how to command attention without distracting from the current crisis.

Of course, the others just stared at the man without answering. Naomi couldn't tell whether they were surprised and touched by the offer or abashed no one had suggested praying before now. It didn't much matter. At this point Naomi could only be grateful.

"Yes, Mr. . . ." She trailed off at the sudden realization none of them knew his name. A forgivable oversight, given the circumstances . . .but awkward nevertheless. "Thank you for offering."

"Strode." The stranger shifted his weight from one booted foot to the other. "Michael Strode, and I'd be honored to pray with you."

Naomi registered the newcomer's surprise as she reached out and twined hands with Cora. Cora linked with Evie, who held on to Jake Granger, who shrugged and held out his hand to Mr. Strode at the same moment Naomi reached out to close the circle. The stranger hesitated a heartbeat before joining them. His hand surrounded hers, as warm and strong and comforting as the words he began to speak.

His prayer washed over them all, a plea for the lives of those in the mines, an offering of thanks for the Lord's provision, a request for the strength to face what was to come. But most of all, the low words became a reminder that they weren't alone.

If asked, Naomi wouldn't be able to repeat a single sentence of it. She didn't need to. It was enough to take part in the asking and offering of comfort and protection. Somehow, prayer blunted the thin edge of panic and steadied the flickering flame of Naomi's hope.

"Thank you, Mr. Strode." She remembered herself just in time and restrained from the impulse to give his hand a grateful squeeze.

"You're welcome, miss." A brief smile graced his black-stubbled jaw before he turned his attention to Granger. "I see shovels already, but do you have any lamp helmets? Pickaxes?"

"This way." Naomi headed off and didn't look back to see whether or not they followed her to the mercantile. If they didn't, she'd just grab what they needed and hoof it up the hill behind them. So long as she hurried, they wouldn't lose any more time, and she wouldn't feel the gnawing sense that time was running out.

The tinkle of Lacey's customer bell when Naomi opened the mercantile door sounded more like an abbreviated lament than a cheerful welcome. Even so, she couldn't help but be grateful Lacey had recently come into the shop and set everything to rights.

When she considered the condition in which they'd found this store—boxes and crates stacked higgledy-piggledy, coated with a thick layer of grit and no clue as to their contents—Naomi breathed a prayer of thanks. If Lacey hadn't whirled into the shop and set everything to rights, they wouldn't have a prayer of finding things.

As things stood, Naomi veered left as soon as she entered the door, heading for the wall of tools. She reached for a pickax, only to have a strong arm reach farther, faster, and snatch it from her grasp. An unfamiliar prickle of awareness told her it was the stranger, but Naomi didn't tilt her head back to make sure.

With the men grabbing the pickaxes, she ducked away and made a beeline for the back counter. Behind the rear counter, she slid through the door to the storeroom. Tucked in here, she knew, Lacey stashed anything and everything originally intended to help outfit the Hope Falls mines. With the mines closed and the town now slated to become a lumber mill, the mercantile wouldn't see much business for the strange paraphernalia used solely by miners.

When she didn't immediately spot what she needed, Naomi began eyeing the crates and boxes stacked in the farthest corner. Knowing Lacey's penchant for order, she would have placed heavy items at the bottom to support the lighter or more fragile goods. In a matter of seconds, Naomi had pried open two boxes.

One held what looked to be small machine parts, and she set it aside. The second held small bottles of Sunshine Lamp Oil, which she kept close at hand. The next crate, with SUNSHINE LAMPS thoughtfully stamped along the wooden slats, defeated her. She set it aside as requiring a crowbar and reached for the next box. The sound of the crate being moved farther away made her jump.

A startled glance showed the stranger, Michael Something-or-other, scooting the crate for another few inches of clearance. Without a word, the man hunkered down and began working at the tacks with the tines of a hammer. Naomi watched for a moment before realizing that, at this pace, he'd not only have the lamps out of the crate by the time she unearthed the helmets, he'd have them filled with the Sunshine Oil she'd found mere moments ago.

With renewed vigor, she shoved open the box before her, relieved to see what looked like overgrown brown raisins. Once picked up and shaken out, the wrinkled leather took the form of stiff, close-fitting skull caps with a narrow pocket sewn to double thickness along the front seam. Naomi's triumph at finding the helmets darkened to dismay. Yes, this was what she was looking for—she remembered from almost a year ago, when Braden demonstrated how the lamp's long metal prongs tucked into the narrow openings.

But while these caps would hold the teapot-shaped lamps

emerging from the now-opened crate, they would only provide light. With such flimsy head-coverings, was it any wonder so many of Braden's miners had perished in the first collapse? The contraptions offered absolutely no protection from falling rocks.

And Lacey doesn't even have one of these. A small round stain darkened the leather between her fingertips, and Naomi realized she was crying. She gulped in a shuddering breath and rose to her feet.

Feelings interfere with getting things done, and emotions cloud judgment, she reminded herself. Today she could afford neither.

FIVE

Mike heard the other man—Granger—and woman rummaging about in the front of the store. When he'd seen the husky-voiced beauty slip around the back counter and through a door, his feet followed before he made the decision to go after her. Propriety, he knew, would have stopped him before he went through the door.

Mike smiled at the thought and kept right on walking. After all, he'd left propriety—along with the other inconveniences in his life—a few thousand miles behind him. *Why not enjoy the freedom?*

Besides, it seemed to Mike that while the other man bore the trademark signs of a leader, the quietly determined woman looked like she knew where she was going. Mike decided he liked her initiative—and her productivity. In the mere moments it took for him to catch up with her in the storeroom, she'd already begun sorting through a heap of boxes and crates in the far corner. As he watched, she shook her head and nudged a box to the side—out of her way—and kept on.

Mike grabbed a hammer from a nearby shelf and squatted down to lend a hand with the crate she'd just abandoned. Its tacked-down top would have taken too much time away from finishing her hunt. He pulled the thing closer, making the move louder than necessary in case she didn't already know he'd come into the room behind her.

She hadn't. A small jump tattled that he'd startled her, even before her wide-eyed glance confirmed it. *Green.* Mike hadn't realized until then that he'd wanted to know the color of her eyes. Such an unimportant detail in the midst of a mission, but in that moment it hit him hard. He'd never thought about it before, but it seemed he must've thought of green as a cool color. How else to explain his surprise at the warmth of this woman's gaze?

She'd turned back around and resumed working while he sat there like a fool, pondering the color of her eyes. So Mike made up for it by working his fastest. He didn't look up at her again until he'd opened the crate and unwrapped all of the teapot-shaped Sunshine Oil Lamps, which were to be fitted into leather mining caps.

A quick peek showed her still facing forward. Doubt speared him—what if they were unable to find the caps after all? They would have wasted all this time fumbling in a storeroom when they could have been helping scout out the mines or unblock passages!

If they were on a wild goose chase, he'd need to redirect their efforts to where they could do the most good. Mike craned his neck, trying to look over her shoulder without attracting her notice. The stack of goods seemed to have diminished somewhat, and he noticed the first box he'd seen at her side happened to be the oil for the lamps he'd finished unearthing. . .two parts of a three-piece puzzle.

And there, almost blocked by her bent form, stood the missing item. Creased and pressed into a box for who knows how long, the leather looked more like bark than hoods. Even so, their very necessity made them beautiful. Mike reached for one, only to pull back when he saw she already held a cap. *Then why had she stopped?*

As he watched, a drop of darkness wet the leather in her hands. Understanding dawned. Her sudden stillness meant she was crying. Or, he realized when her shoulders stiffened with resolve and she returned the cap to the box, she was trying not to.

Something clenched behind his rib cage, powerful enough to make him pause. *She shouldn't have to cry,* his instincts clamored. *And she shouldn't have to stop or hide her tears if she wants to cry.* Mike cupped his hand beneath her elbow and raised her to her feet.

"Let's go tear that mountain apart." Without waiting for her response, he dumped the oil lamps back in the crate, slammed the now-loosened lid back on it, and plunked the box of oil on top. Mike reached for the box of leather hoods, only to come up empty.

The woman—it began bothering him that he had no name for her, but right now it felt too awkward to ask—finished slipping the last cap into a large canvas bag, which she then slung over her shoulder. With coils of rope looped over her other shoulder and around her waist, she looked like a prim adventuress.

And if such a thing hadn't existed before now, in Mike's humble opinion, it was a terrible oversight. Since it wasn't his place to say so—*yet*, a small, determined part of his mind insisted—he snagged the pickax he'd grabbed earlier, hefted the stack of lamps and oil, and followed her surprisingly swift march out the door.

Outside, they found not only Granger and the lady Michael already thought of as Granger's woman, but also the girl who must be related to her. As they drew closer, the girl spoke.

"Mr. Lawson is off to the areas where the men are working today." She sounded winded. "They'll meet up with us at the mines."

"You're not going to check on Braden?" Granger's girl looked surprised, and Mike found himself wondering who Braden was.

"No. He shouldn't have let Lacey go into the mines." The girl held up her hands as though to stave off any disagreements. "I know he couldn't actually stop her, but he didn't even argue with her the way he's been arguing with us about anything and everything else."

"All right." The beauty at Mike's side handed the girl a shovel and turned away, squinting toward the sunken-in mountain.

"Do we know which entrance they took?" Granger looked the same way. "To my recollection, there are two, but I don't even know which one was the most cleared out from the first rescue."

"Southern," chorused the three women in response, and Mike wondered why the women would know that when the man didn't.

"Do you hear something?" The dark-haired beauty inclined her head to the side, as though listening for a faraway sound.

Everyone waited, almost holding their breath, as though whatever she heard might make the difference between finding their friends alive or facing failure. After a moment she shook her head.

"I must have imagined it, but for a moment I thought I heard Decoy."

"Decoy?" This time Mike couldn't reign in his curiosity. He powered on with the rest of them as they headed toward the mines, but his own mind raced far ahead—or behind. Everyone here knew far more than he did, and he didn't like bringing up the rear.

"Mr. Dunstan's dog," the young one answered. "And since Mr. Dunstan is the one who took our friend Lacey to the mines, it was probably just wishful thinking on Naomi's part. Because if Decoy's nearby, then they probably are, too. . . ." Her explanation faded away at the sound of frantic barking, coming from not too far ahead.

When a massive creature came tearing around the bend, Mike was glad he'd asked; if he hadn't been told that Decoy was nothing more than someone's pet dog, he might well have reached for his pistol. The beast was, quite simply, the largest animal he'd seen off a farm or outside of the circus. And it wasn't in a good mood.

The thing had to stand about four feet tall—at least that was Mike's best guess, since what he now identified as a brindled Irish wolfhound came to a stop several yards ahead. Agitated, the dog bounced about, prancing almost in place and shaking its huge head from side to side. The dog's message couldn't be clearer: *Hurry up!*

"He's alone." One of the women gave voice to the chilling truth no one really wanted to acknowledge. If their friends weren't with the dog, then their fears proved correct: the mines had taken them.

∞

"We haven't lost them yet." Naomi urged everyone on, frustrated beyond reason by the way they'd all stopped to stare at Decoy. "The dog isn't the specter of death. If anything, he's telling us that Dunstan and Lacey are still alive. He's not crouched down, slinking around and whimpering. He's telling us to get a move on!"

At that, the others perked up visibly. They surged forward, filled with a renewed hope Naomi prayed wasn't false. As they drew closer to Decoy, the dog let loose an anxious howl and turned tail. He bounded up the mountainside a short ways then stopped and resumed what Naomi would call pacing if the beast were human.

As though reading her thoughts, Decoy raced back toward them, gave a sort of urgent growl, and darted back up the mountain. Again, he stopped to perform what Naomi decided to call the "I'm waiting for you to catch up, you slowpokes" dance. Somehow the dog's confident insistence that they follow him seemed comforting.

The troupe of them dutifully carried on their part in this dance, following the dog's lead up toward the mines. When Decoy began doing his impatient prance near the eastern entrance, Granger gave a grunt of. . .of what, Naomi couldn't be sure. In truth, she didn't decipher grunts very well, but it sounded like a good one.

Then again, maybe she was grasping at straws—anything to keep hold of the idea that they could still save Lacey when things looked increasingly bad. The closer they drew to the mountain, the more damage they could see. Boulders from much higher up had toppled from their lofty perches, knocking loose chunks of earth and smaller stones as they tumbled down the hillside. They left furrows in the dirt behind where they skidded to a halt. Dust hung heavy in the air, and Naomi reached for one of the bandanas she'd stuck in her apron pocket. Tying it around the lower half of her face made her feel oddly like a bandit, but maybe that was only fair. After all, she was trying to take something precious from this mountain.

She heard another grunt, this one conveying irritation. When she looked back at the newly sealed entrance to the mines, Naomi realized why Granger sounded so dissatisfied. Decoy had sidled to the left and back, almost out of sight. The dog was leading them to the other mine entrance—which was that much farther to go and that much more time they lost. Naomi stifled her own annoyed grunt, reminding herself to be thankful that the dog was pointing the way.

"Better to go the long way to the right place than start digging in the wrong one." She said it to raise her spirits as much as everyone else's. She fell, as she so often did, into prayer.

Thank You, Lord, she praised, *that Dunstan trained him so well.* Her silent conversation with her creator continued, falling into the rhythm of her steps. The prayer might not be formal, but it was heartfelt. *If he were a typical dog, we wouldn't trust Decoy's guidance today. You use all things to further Your plans, and I only ask that You find as much use for me today as You have for that dog.*

She drew as deep a breath as she could manage through the thick covering of her folded bandana and stepped aside when she couldn't fight the need to cough. The new man hesitated until she stepped back toward the main path, but Naomi was pleased to see the others pushing forward as swiftly as possible. She hurried to catch up, skirting around a giant boulder and almost tripping in the process.

After finding her balance, Naomi looked down to see what had caught her. It hadn't seemed as solid as stone, but nothing grew roots this far up the rocky terrain. Maybe it was a rucksack or Lacey's cloak and they shouldn't be following Decoy to the other entrance after all. A thick layer of dust coated everything, but a closer look erased any doubts. Naomi swallowed a scream and backed away, bile clawing at the back of her throat and stealing her voice and leaving her alone with her gruesome discovery.

Pinned beneath the biggest boulder she'd ever seen, obscured by the debris of a mountain's convulsions, protruded a pair of legs.

SIX

Mike noticed the way Naomi—as the youngest girl had called her—withdrew into herself as they walked along. Before she'd been determined, anxious, and practical by turns. Now *preoccupied* seemed the best word to describe her trek. With her face half hidden beneath the bandana she used as a mask, Mike couldn't tell whether Naomi strengthened her resolve or sank deeper into her worries.

When a short fit of coughing stopped her progress, she'd still thought to move aside. Obviously she wasn't about to slow things down. After he passed her, Mike hesitated, waiting for her to come back on the path. When she moved, he continued on around a turn. He wanted to wait for her but didn't want to make her uncomfortable. A few steps later Mike realized she still hadn't followed.

So he went back for her. Awkward or not, he needed to make sure she was all right. Mike went back around the bend, gaining speed when he spotted her. Half bent over beside a large boulder, with her breath coming in short, uneven gasps, she was in trouble.

Mike's first thought, looking into her wide, frightened eyes, was that she was choking. It sounded like she was still drawing air, so something must've stuck in her throat. . . . There was only one thing to do. He slapped his hand against her upper back, hard enough to dislodge whatever was blocking her airway. The thump of the blow made him wince—nothing but this could have made him strike a woman.

Mike peered at her. The woman remained doubled over, but the

681

strange little gasps stopped. Fear gripped him—had he shifted the obstacle and made the situation *worse*? She wasn't speaking. . . .

He grabbed her shoulder and pulled her upright, yanking the bandana down. She gave a strangled-sounding hiss and jerked away, eyes narrowed. Yep, the lady looked angry, but since she was breathing again, Mike didn't care. He wanted to hug the woman.

"What are you *doing*?" Her indignation effectively doused his triumph. "Do you usually swing first and ask questions later?"

"You weren't choking." Now he sounded as foolish as he felt.

"No." The outrage vanished in a blink, replaced by tears as she looked back toward the massive boulder. "I just couldn't. . ." She swallowed visibly, struggling to explain and finally giving up. She gestured toward the base of the huge rock. "Over there."

Fighting back a terrible suspicion over what would so upset this woman, Mike moved over to look. What he saw made his own lungs stop working for a minute. Beneath the stone stretched the bottom half of a man's torso and his legs. A closer look revealed a hand covered in dirt, outstretched in a silent plea for help.

No blood caked the ground, but Mike knew the man's head had been crushed instantly. Without knowing what else to do, Mike gathered a grief-stricken Naomi in his arms, shielding her from the horrific sight. She buried her face in his shoulder and sobbed, unable to keep a brave face in the sight of a man's destruction.

Mike sent up wordless prayers, half-formed hopes for the man's soul and supplication that the other missing person—the woman—hadn't met the same fate. He'd gotten the impression that it was the missing girl whom Naomi held close to her heart. But a look around the area revealed nothing to suggest a woman had died there.

Reluctantly Mike eased Naomi from his arms. They needed to fetch the others and form a new plan. He cleared his throat to say as much but found it unnecessary when the others came storming into view. From their fast pace and the looks on their faces, concern for Naomi had won out over irritation at the delay—but barely. And as they saw her standing there, evidently unharmed, they slowed.

"He's dead." Naomi's announcement brought them to a stop.

Granger's woman started shaking her head. "We don't know that, Naomi. Now's not the time to become hysterical and lose faith—we might still find both of them safe and sound and waiting for us."

"She said *he*, not *they*." Mike gestured toward the crushing boulder and defended Naomi as best he could. "She's far from hysterical—though she has every right after what she found."

By the time he finished his sentence, Granger reached the boulder—and its victim. Other than an audible swallow, he kept calm and collected. "Ladies, hold off. There's no sign of Lacey, and no one should see this unless there's a darn good reason."

It looked like the young one wouldn't follow his instruction, but Granger's woman caught her arm and held her back. After some furious whispering, the young one decided to hold her piece. But Mike was inclined to attribute her change of heart to Naomi, who'd started up the trail to wait with the women. When she reached the others, they engulfed her in embraces and reassurances, all the while casting fearful looks toward the boulder below.

Now that Naomi was in good hands and out of harm's way, Mike returned his attention to Granger. The other man bent down for a closer look at the corpse. A puzzled frown creased his face, letting Mike know something was wrong beyond the obvious. But what?

"Let's hear it." Mike hunkered down and waited. Whatever Granger was thinking, it looked like he'd need a sounding board.

"Dunstan—the man who went to explore the mines—is a hunter. A mountain guide." Granger gestured toward the corpse's boots. Even coated in dirt and rocks, they had a stacked heel and rigid stiffness. "I've never known him to wear anything but leather boots worn so soft even a deer couldn't hear him move through the forest."

Mike swiftly realized what Granger was trying to say. "You're thinking this isn't our guy." He waited for a curt nod of agreement before taking it to the next logical step. "Do you know him?"

"Hard to say." A moment later Granger quit musing. He narrowed his eyes and considered a small lump in the dirt around the vicinity where the man's head should be. "What's that?"

It turned out to be part of a pair of spectacles, broken at the nose and the lens shattered within a thin gold rim. Granger palmed the piece, gave those boots a considering glance, and shook his head. Whatever he was puzzling over, it must not add up.

"You know him." Mike didn't press, but spectacles weren't a common item in a mining camp. Or a sawmill for that matter.

Granger nodded. "Only two men in town wear glasses, and Cora just sent one of them off to fetch the axmen." He used the spectacles to gesture toward the corpse. "That leaves the telegraph operator, Draxley. But for the life of me, I can't figure out why a man scared of his own shadow would be strolling around up here."

Mike saw that the wolfhound had tracked them and was now circling around the women, whining loudly and butting his head against their skirts in an attempt to herd them back to the mines. For all that the others trusted the dog, and it seemed well trained and admirably determined to rescue its owner, Mike didn't like the situation. He straightened up and started toward the women.

"Maybe Dunstan and the missing girl have the answer."

When the men finally joined them, none of the women could find words to ask about the body below. Naomi knew because she tried and failed to form a question. Part of her didn't want to know any details beyond the horrible sight already emblazoned on her mind. But the larger part needed to know something—anything—about what was going on. Maybe there was some clue to help find Lacey.

"Well?" For the first time, Naomi understood the appeal of one-word sentences. They moved fast and left no room for anxieties.

"It's Draxley." Granger didn't mince words, just pulled out the broken spectacles as evidence. "Or a stranger new to town."

Naomi sagged in relief—if she hadn't been holding on to Cora and Evie, she might have humiliated herself by sliding straight down to the ground. But shame swiftly chased away any relief. *A man is dead*, Naomi chastised herself, noticing that the other women looked as guilty as she felt. They, too, must have welcomed the news that the crushed corpse wasn't Dunstan, who should be protecting Lacey.

"Lawson's fine, so I think it must be Draxley." Cora came to her senses first. "No one new's come to town since Dunstan." She slid a glance toward Mr. Strode, the newcomer, and faltered. "Until today. But no other glasses."

Decoy butted his head against Naomi's skirts and issued a pleading whine. The gesture inspired Naomi's gratitude. Once they'd established it was (most likely) Draxley beneath the boulder, her thoughts turned right back to Dunstan and Lacey. But she couldn't see any graceful way to pull attention away from a dead man.

So when the dog prodded them back toward the caves, Naomi tugged her bandana back over her nose and mouth and made haste up the mountainside. Peripherally, she was aware when Cora spoke briefly with Evie and turned back toward town, but she didn't catch the reasoning behind it. Nor could she work up any curiosity.

As the entrance to the mine came into sight—or rather, what had been an entrance less than half an hour ago—fear spiked higher than ever. Dust hung heavy in the air, but even if it were clear as a mountain stream, Naomi would have had difficulty drawing breath. Where there used to be a tunnel, a heap of stone and earth cascaded from higher up the mountain all the way to the ground. The debris mounded high enough Naomi couldn't tell whether it had merely sealed off the mine or if the mine utterly caved in upon itself.

The sides of his chest heaving like bellows, Decoy leaped atop a medium-sized boulder and began frantically clawing into the gravel and dirt sealing it in place. Naomi rushed up beside him, scuffing her leather gloves as she grabbed smaller stones and heaved them out of the way. She heard Evie come alongside, helping with a too-heavy stone, while the men set to work on the other side of Decoy.

"Lacey!" Her shriek bounced around mountain rock, shrill echoes obliterating any chance of hearing a response from within. Naomi bit her lip and dug in with even more fury than before. Where were the men? If anyone should be coming to help rescue Lacey, it was all the lumberjacks she'd brought here by writing that blasted ad.

It felt as though hours passed before a dull thudding preceded the woodsmen. Using chisels and ax handles, pickaxes and shovels, they attacked the shifting mass of rubble with a vengeance. More than once Naomi fought silly little battles with men trying to dislodge her from her post. Her sharp elbows rewarded a few who reached for her arms. One unfortunate soul who misguidedly tried to grab her waist discovered just how sturdy her boots were. And, as occupied as she was, Naomi found herself slightly disgruntled that no one tried to move Evie or even Decoy from their stations.

Although, she conceded, *every man here knows they'll lose whatever hand they put on Jake Granger's fiancée, so Evie won't be bothered. As for Decoy. . .* Naomi wouldn't try her hand at ousting the wolfhound from his digging site. The dog dug like a. . .well, a beast.

In some distant, practical portion of her mind, Naomi knew the burly lumberjacks only wanted to help Lacey and Dunstan. Even worse, she acknowledged that their methodical use of strength and leverage would move things along faster than her frantic scurries.

But ceding her spot would feel like giving up on Lacey, and Naomi knew she'd cling to these stones like a barnacle until they found her cousin. Besides, the rhythm of scraping and digging, pushing and pulling, shoving and dislodging small pieces of the mountainside was the only thing drowning out her frantic worries.

Time scraped by, measured in fistfuls and shovels of dirt and a steadily growing pile of stones and boulders pushed away from the entrance of the mine. Eventually the thick grit of dirt and stone dust became a natural part of breathing. Naomi kept scrabbling at the stone separating her from her cousin, eyeing the progress they made. At what point should she shout again? Had they made enough headway for Lacey and Dunstan to hear voices through the blockage?

How could she keep on if she called and Lacey didn't answer?

"Lacey!" Apparently having waged the same battle with herself,

STRONG AND STUBBORN

Evie called out before Naomi could bring herself to try again. At the sound of her voice, everything ground to a halt, waiting for a response as she called again. "Dunstan! Are you in there?"

SEVEN

"Somebody tell me what the hell is happening!" Braden's yells welcomed Cora to Hope Falls long before she reached the buildings.

"Stop swearing, you miserable, self-centered fool!" Cora knew she shouted at Braden to siphon away some of her frustration and worry, but the man deserved it. "You've been a wretch for weeks on end, and I won't listen for another minute. Right now we need to help Lacey and Dunstan, so your tantrums will have to wait!"

"Where's my sister?" he roared back, face shockingly pale beneath his dark hair. Braden leaned forward as though trying to escape the bed, and Cora noticed that his knee was bent farther than he'd managed even with the doctor that morning. "Where's Lacey?"

Oh, so now you care about your sister? Where was this concern when you let her go to the mines? Cora bit her tongue hard to hold it back. Blaming Braden for not being able to stop Lacey was like blaming a farmer for not stopping a tornado as it ripped through his cornfields—ineffective at best and downright dangerous at worst.

"We don't know." The words tasted every bit as bitter as those she'd just swallowed. Her best friend was either dead or trapped in a collapsed mine—just like Braden had been a few months before.

"Don't tell me what you don't know." Oddly enough, his snarling comforted Cora. So long as Braden kept on snapping and shouting at her, things seemed almost normal. "Tell me what you *do* know!"

"I know you need to stop cursing, shouting, sulking, and demanding, Braden Lyman." Cora matched his glower. "If you're going to help Lacey, I need you calm enough to think properly."

"Is she in the mines?" Fear made his pupils so large his eyes looked black. His hand groped for hers for the first time in months. "Tell me my sister isn't in the mines, Cora. Tell me she's okay."

"I—" Cora gave a hard swallow, but the tears won this time. She gulped out the words anyway. "I can't tell you that. No one's seen Lacey or Dunstan since they left for the mines, and we all know that means she's in some kind of trouble." Otherwise Lacey would be rushing like a whirlwind trying to make sure everyone was all right.

Braden closed his eyes, so still it looked as though he wasn't even breathing. When he opened them, Cora could see he'd banked his fear with determination. "Do we know which entrance they used?"

"Eastern." Cora pushed pencil and paper into his hands, giving him not only a purpose but something tangible to hold on to while he faced his own memories of the mine collapse. "I assume they thought they might find more evidence on the side not facing town."

"That's the side where I—" His throat worked for a moment before he changed the wording and finished, "—they pulled me out of."

"I know." Cora tapped the paper to keep his attention away from whatever horrors lurked in his memory. "Can you draw the tunnels? Do you remember at all which ones were cleared after the collapse and which were left alone? Once we get past the blockage at the entrance, we'll probably need to go farther inside to find them."

"God help me." Braden's eyes shut, and Cora knew he wasn't swearing this time but genuinely asking for help. "I don't know which branches they would have cleared out before they reached me. I know what they absolutely would have needed to clear to get there, but the rest. . . I just don't know." His knuckles went white. "If I could be there—I could tell you. I'd know just by looking."

"Your memory can go where you can't," Cora urged. "Braden, you can still be our guide. Think. When they emptied the tunnels needed to reach you, they shored up the supports, didn't they? So the strongest places are the only ones Lacey and Dunstan found access to—and the only places we should look. You can help us find them!"

Cora held her breath as Braden's pencil crawled across the page, first hesitantly then with more confidence. A web of lines spidered away from a single entry point. When Braden's hand stopped moving, Cora leaned close to peer at his makeshift map.

Her heart sank at the number of tunnels winding away from the entrance, deep into the mountain. *It's more of a maze than a mine.*

"Impossible." Braden's mutter echoed her fears, making Cora raise her eyes to meet his. But he wasn't looking at her. He tapped the pencil against the page before crossing through lines with dark Xs. "Lacey and Dunstan couldn't have gone this way."

He only meant one tunnel. Relief had Cora sagging into a chair beside the bed as Braden considered his sketch. *It's not impossible!*

"We started to close off this tunnel a week before the collapse. Found a footwall, decided it was safer to make a transverse passage to the highwall and pull it out from above. Less falling debris that way." He muttered obscure technicalities to himself, crossing out various branches. "Down here, groundwater kept rising. We made it a sump, to funnel drips from other areas." He cocked his head to the side and marked out another passage. "We had to abandon this adit when we hit a deep fissure—highly unstable. After the collapse, I wondered if we should have stopped sooner."

The admission caught Cora's attention, but Braden fell silent. Cora watched him studying the drawing but wondered what else he was sorting through in his mind. *How terrible for him, to shoulder responsibility for the tragedy. And now, when he begins to hope it wasn't his fault, he'll feel responsible for Lacey's fate.*

"Here." He thrust the paper toward her. "It's all I can do."

"Thank you. We won't be going in blindly—and with as much as you've crossed out, we won't waste time." Cora gave him an encouraging smile, not daring to reach for his hand a second time.

"Go on then." His irritable dismissal had her speeding to the door so fast she almost didn't hear the rest. "But come back."

She clutched the paper to her chest, refusing to turn around and invite the tears again. "You already know I will. I always do."

$$\infty$$

"Lacey!" Granger's woman called a stop to everyone's hard work.

Michael halted his pickax and held his breath, praying they would hear someone answer her. He knew it wasn't likely—every single man, woman, and even dog working against this wall of stone knew they fought fate. There were simply too many unknowns.

Were the people they sought—Lacey and Dunstan—even alive? If they lived, were they awake and in condition to respond? And if they were so fortunate, how far back were they?

Even given the perfect combination of circumstances, there was every chance the pair was much deeper in the twists and turns of the mines. There was no telling how many mounds of collapsed mountain they may have to get through before nearing the couple. Worse, there was no telling whether they had enough time to save them. Air might run out. A critical support might buckle.

Despite Mike's fervent prayers otherwise, the expedition was practically drowning in doubts. He imagined he could smell the sour scent of despair mixed amid the dust. They needed a reason to keep hoping—they needed a sign that God was working alongside them.

"Lacey!" The two women yelled in tandem, forcing their voices through the cracks. But nothing came back. Not so much as a moan.

"Oh God." Naomi sagged against the boulder, where she'd been working alongside the hunter's dog. She tugged the bandana—now encrusted with dirt—away from her face, and Mike could see her lips moving in soundless prayer. Dust caked her face, save where tears cut clear paths down her cheeks. Her eyes closed in supplication.

"Dunstan!" Granger's woman kept on screeching. "Are you there?" When she stopped, it seemed as though the mountain swallowed all sound. Despite the impossible odds, everyone still hoped to hear—

"Esh!" came a muffled female cry. "Eve wherin ear!"

"Yes!" Naomi clutched at the other woman. "Evie, they're in there!" The two wrapped each other in a dancing, circling hug.

"Donut drag he live on." The man's deeper tones came in echoes, difficult to decipher. "Sum of ewe want him down if you ax to."

Granger frowned, repeating the sounds in a furious whisper before his brow eased. "Don't let Draxley leave town." The rest of it seemed a greater challenge. "Hunt him down if we have to?"

Mike gave a quick nod. Once sounded out, without the distance and the interference, the words made perfect sense. Except for the fact they had no idea why Dunstan would want to hunt Draxley down.

"He won't go anywhere." Granger took care to speak slow and loud—apparently not caring that everyone could hear. "Draxley's just outside the mines, head crushed by a boulder from up the ridge."

Shaken from their hushed expectation, the men began murmuring to one another. Mike picked up on their shock—but he noticed no one seemed broken up over the loss of the town telegraph operator. Added to Dunstan's directive that they hunt him down if necessary, Mike pieced together an unflattering portrait of the man—as well as a few suspicions. A telegraph operator had no business lurking around the mines—on the very day Dunstan and Lacey decided to investigate. So what were the chances that this second cave-in was a coincidence?

Mike shook his head and kept his musings to himself. Who wanted to hear half-fledged theories from someone new in town? Nobody. If he turned out to be wrong, he looked insolent and self-aggrandizing. And if he turned out to be right. . .well, in that case, Hope Falls had enough to worry about without adding in a know-it-all.

The strike of a shovel against a nearby rock demanded his attention. Everyone else was looking at Granger, waiting to be sure the conversation with their trapped townsmen had ended. Everyone, that is, except Naomi. It seemed as though Granger's pronouncement shook loose her fears. The people trapped inside the mountain could still be crushed. She gripped the shovel handle with gloves torn enough to show the blood beneath, working feverishly to break through the wall still separating her from her unfortunate friends.

Mike knew he should do the same, should attack the rocky barrier with equal enthusiasm and twice her strength. His hands tightened around the pickax he'd been using to dislodge larger rocks and lever them away. Beneath his leather work gloves, he felt the ridges of the handle where the new tool had yet to be worn smooth by hours of friction. Calloused as his own hands were, the rougher surface hadn't registered until he spotted Naomi's gloves.

And now that he'd seen, Mike couldn't convince himself to turn away and get back to work. There was no way of knowing whether Naomi herself realized the damage—the woman was obviously caught up in the rescue and not giving a thought to taking care of herself. Before they heard the answering call, how long had it been since she'd paused for a breath? When was the last time she drank from her canteen? Mike didn't know, but he knew it had been too long.

Why hasn't anyone else noticed? Someone needs to look after the woman. Common sense warred with a surge of protectiveness, cautioning that it wasn't Mike's place to step forward. *She only turned to you earlier out of shock and grief.* To take care of her now would signal an undue interest and arouse suspicion.

He couldn't afford to start off on the wrong foot with the residents of Hope Falls. It would jeopardize his chances of bringing Luke to the isolated safety of the town. And as much as it went against the grain to leave a woman hurting, Mike couldn't risk it.

Lord, You've answered many prayers from these parts today, and I'm going to add one more to them. If You can give me an opportunity, any window to stop Naomi from shredding her hands without sacrificing my son's future, I'll gladly make use of it.

As he had many times before, Mike lamented that prayers weren't often answered immediately. He'd never manage to figure out the whys and whens of God's work, but he knew God heard him. Sometimes that had to be enough while a body waited for a clearer response.

With a sigh, Mike turned his attention back to the challenge he could handle. Women, with all of their complications, were beyond Mike, but some of his frustration eased with the work at hand. He wedged his pickax beneath the next stone and prized it loose. Too large to roll aside without endangering another worker, the rock had to be hefted over to the makeshift pile of larger rubble.

Setting his load down, Mike glimpsed a figure making its way toward the work crew. He squinted and realized it was the third woman he'd met—the one related to Granger's woman. He'd noted when she left, but now Mike had a moment to wonder where she'd gone. The girl clipped along at a rushed pace, clutching something in her hands. Whatever she carried, she obviously thought it important.

Too bad I'm not settled enough to be more involved. A powerful curious streak coursed through him, and Mike knew he wouldn't be able to satisfy many of his questions that day. The girl's message would be for a select few. Most likely Granger and the women.

Ah! That wasn't just a girl rushing up the hill—it was the opportunity he needed to get the shovel out of Naomi's hands!

Mike moved quickly, heading over to let Granger know of the girl's impending arrival. When the other man and his woman stepped away from their work and went to meet the newcomer, Mike sped over to where Naomi chipped away at the packed earth wedging several rocks in place. So intently did she work, she didn't hear him clear his throat. She didn't so much as slow down her furious pace.

"Miss?" Mike raised his voice but didn't yell at her—the last thing he wanted to do was try to grab her by the arm or waist. He'd watched from the corner of his eye when the lumberjacks joined in. The small skirmishes as Naomi protected her place made him smile at the time. But now he knew she wasn't going to take it kindly when he interrupted her work. So he called a couple more times.

The woman wasn't going to make it easy on him; she kept right on working. When it was clear she couldn't hear him, Mike knew he'd run out of options. He was going to have to take away her shovel.

EIGHT

She's alive! Lacey's alive! Naomi rammed the metal lip of her spade into the densely packed dirt cementing a slew of rocks in place. *It didn't even sound like she's hurt!* Again and again she thrust the shovel against the barrier, grinning as the debris began to loosen.

Of course, they'd barely managed to decipher Lacey and Dunstan's words at all, much less pick up on any tones of distress. If Naomi stopped to think about it, the fact Lacey didn't attempt to carry on a longer conversation could be seen as troubling. The Lacey Lyman that Naomi knew and that helped Mother would be shouting through the barrier, demanding details about Draxley's death. But for right now, Naomi refused to stop working long enough to think about it.

She took up the rhythm of striking and pulling back, chipping away at the chaos before her. The incredible noise enveloping the mountainside didn't distract her. Every sound of tool against earth or stone sang the praises alive in her heart. *Thank You, Lord.* Her shovel thunked against packed dirt. *They're alive.* A scraping clang as she hit stone. *Thank You, Jesus!* A dull thud then skittering pebbles as she pulled back. *They're right on the other side.*

On that happy thought, something ruined her rhythm. Or rather, *someone.* Naomi glowered at the huge hand that snagged on the handle of her spade. Unwilling to waste time arguing, she tightened her grip and tried to dislodge the disturbance by shoving.

The spade didn't budge. Naomi found herself having to take

a huge step forward to keep her balance, stubbing her toes in the process. Gritting her teeth against the sudden streaking pain, she readjusted her hold, keeping one hand above the interloper's and putting the other below it. Then she tried again. She pushed. She tugged. She even tried to wiggle the thing loose, but no luck.

"Let go," she ordered. Didn't the man know he was *in her way?* Finally acknowledging that the man couldn't be sidestepped, Naomi decided to look trouble in the eye. She needed to tilt her head back to manage it. *When did trouble get so good-looking?* The inane thought made her scowl fiercely as she tried to intimidate the new man in town. And repress a sudden memory of crying on his shoulder.

"Sorry." He loosened his grip but tightened it again when she would have snatched her shovel away. "I tried calling, but you didn't hear me. I thought you'd want to know your friend came back." A strong jaw tilted over to where Cora joined Evie and Granger.

"Oh!" Naomi would have dropped her spade if the man hadn't continued holding it. "I wouldn't have noticed. Thank you!" She reached down to grab her skirts, raising them enough so the fabric wouldn't hamper her steps while she raced over to her friends.

"Wait." His other hand shot out and circled her wrist, startling Naomi with the sudden warmth and familiarity of the motion. His daring left her breathless, unable to do more than stare at the sight of his broad, dusty fingers clamped around her small wrist. As she watched, he gently turned her palm upward, placing a clean band-ana in her grasp before releasing her completely.

Only then did Naomi realize she'd worn her leather riding gloves—the thickest pair she owned—clean through. The tatters rubbed against his bandana while tiny pinpricks of red appeared on the green field of fabric, slowly blossoming into a field of crimson.

As the stain seeped into the fabric, its meaning sank in. Suddenly she identified the pulsing in her palms as the throb of pain. It sharpened when she clenched her fingers over the bandana, trying to hide the damage she'd done without even noticing it.

"Here." He produced a black bandana from his back pocket,

unfolded a knife, and sliced it neatly into two bandages.

Naomi watched, thunderstruck, as he draped the pieces atop the crook of her elbow and pointed her toward the women to have her hands bandaged. She stammered her thanks and left before she could waste more time making an even bigger fool of herself.

By the time she reached the Thompsons, Granger left to get back to work. Naomi drew a deep breath to clear her head and pasted a smile on her face when the other women noticed her. She didn't want them to worry, but Naomi couldn't very well bandage her own hands.

Cora's smile far outshone Naomi's weak attempt, clearly rejoicing in the news that Lacey and Dunstan were alive and in reach. Her friend's delight rekindled Naomi's own thankfulness. Compared to the miracle of today, what did it matter she'd waged an absurd war, wiggling her shovel at the new man in town? What did it matter that she'd ruined her gloves and blistered her palms? Gloves could be replaced, blisters healed, and embarrassments faded.

So Naomi hugged Cora and Evie and listened as Cora waved a hastily sketched map and explained what she'd been doing. Apparently, Braden dug deep in his memory and rendered the layout of the mine, indicating which passages Lacey and Dunstan might access.

"If they weren't right on the other side of the landslide, this would have been our best hope of finding them." Cora carefully folded the paper and slid it into an apron pocket. "I'm glad we don't need it, but I'm just as glad Braden made this."

Naomi nodded. "It couldn't have been easy for him to face his memories. Not just of his own time trapped in the mine but all the dreams and hard work he put into planning and building this place."

They all stood in silence for a moment, considering how selfless Braden had been. Naomi was sure she wasn't the only one hoping this was a sign that the curmudgeon who'd taken over her cousin would be departing soon. She'd missed the old Braden.

"Granger said it will be a couple more hours before the men get through," Evie ventured. "We're torn between staying up here and helping or going back to town. The men will be ravenous after this kind of work, and the least they deserve is to have supper."

"I want to stay," Naomi blurted out without even thinking. "When Lacey comes out of that dark, forsaken place, she'll need us. I can't go back and wait in the café for everyone to come down for dinner!" Frankly she couldn't believe Evie suggested it at all.

"No, no, no." Evie shook her head. "I left stew on the stove, and we already have bread and rolls. I was thinking of slicing up some ham for sandwiches then bundling it all up and carrying it back. It won't take very long, and we'll get everything taken care of."

"I think we'll be more in the way than helping if we try to go near the rocks," Cora confessed. "I don't want to slow them down because I'm too stubborn to admit that I'm not equipped for this."

Her friend's wisdom speared Naomi, making her feel her heartbeat in her injured hands. *I would be slowing the men down, trying to work like this. And if Lacey needs help once she comes out, I won't be of any use if I keep abusing my hands.*

That thought clinched things. Naomi nodded and held up her hands. "It's not as though I'll be of much use here anyway. I need to get these taken care of so I can help with other things."

Her friends' clucks of dismay vied with the clamor of men tearing apart the mountainside, both ringing in Naomi's ears as they made their way back to town. She enjoyed a brief interlude of quiet while the doctor inspected and cleaned her hands, the other women watching and waiting for his pronouncement. Naomi bore no illusions—she knew her friends expected her to make light of any ailment. They'd known each other too long and too well to pretend otherwise, though at one time none of them would have stayed alone with a male doctor—back when they'd thought more of guarding their reputations than rebuilding a ghost town or saving a friend in need.

At this point none of the Hope Falls women would meet the standards of polite society. Their unconventional choices, along with their story-spawning residence alongside two dozen lonely bachelors, managed to tarnish their once-sterling reputations.

Lacey, in particular, had shown a disturbing talent and enthusiasm for ruining herself. If word ever reached Charleston that her cousin had gone on long escapades in the woods with a hunter and finally been trapped alone in a dark mine for hours on end with that same hunter, Lacey Lyman's name wouldn't be worth a plug nickel.

Which isn't fair! Lacey deserves to be treated as the lady she is. No matter that she thought up the ad, Lacey's innocent. Naomi flinched as the doctor dug his tweezers into her flesh, picking out bits of stone. *If any of us should be ostracized*—she flinched again as shards of buried memories pierced through her—*it should be me.*

Not Lacey! Braden clenched his teeth against the urge to start shouting. If he started railing against God, he didn't know whether he'd be able to stop. *Not my sister! You already did this to me*, he raged in silence, as though even whispering the accusation might bring down whatever remained of the mountainside he'd once claimed.

His eyes burned from staring down the small wooden cross nailed on the opposite wall. Braden blinked, but his eyes still felt dry, swollen, and sore. He knew it was because he didn't close them often or long enough, but to do so meant succumbing to darkness.

Groaning, he closed his lids, pressing his palms against them as though to blot away his accursed memories. It didn't work. The nightmare that used to plague him only when the doctor forced morphine down his gullet had grown stronger over time. His breaths came short and shallow as the darkness pressed in on him, around him, surely seeping into his very soul through every breath. If he stayed this way much longer, he'd start to see them again.

He waited anyway. His eyes needed the rest, but Braden deserved what came with it. It began slowly. . .it always started slowly. Braden knew the collapse happened in a deafening, blinding rush of sound and suffocation so fast he barely knew what happened. But memories spooled more slowly, giving the destruction its due.

His partner Owens's angry words were drowned out by an incredible roar as the mountainside tore apart. Wooden supports buckled, stones tumbled, dirt rained until it gave way to clouds of dust coating Braden's face, mouth, throat—and his very soul.

Cave-in.

While it lasted, he prayed for it to end, but in the silence he heard the screams, shouts, and cries of injured men the next tunnel over. Oh Lord—what have I led them to? *It wasn't until he heard a moan but couldn't move toward the sound that Braden realized his legs were pinned beneath something—his hands told him it was a wooden support burdened by rock and earth.*

I can't feel my legs. *It didn't seem to matter. He lay, time measured by ragged breaths and unrelenting thirst. His men grew quiet. Braden strained to hear them, but silence steadily won until he prayed for even the screams and sobs from before.*

He opened his eyes to the harsh sound of his own breath, safe and sound in the doctor's home. The sunlight streaming through the window did nothing to reassure Braden that the nightmare had ended. How could it, when the same tragedy had just played out all over again?

Not Lacey, Lord. His chest hitched in a dry sob. *Don't let her suffer in the darkness.* He knew he was a beggar with precious little to barter, but Braden shed his pride. *Please, God. Don't take my sister for my mistakes. Take anything else. . .stop the healing so I never walk again, but let Lacey live a long and happy life.*

"Braden?" Cora's soft question jolted him from his pathetic attempt to strike a bargain with God. Concern creased her brow, making Braden notice the fine lines he knew were his fault.

"Where's Lacey?" He peered past Cora, hoping against hope.

"We haven't broken through the barricade at the mine's entrance yet." Cora crossed the room to fold his hand in hers. "But we're close—and we spoke with Lacey and Dunstan. They're right on the other side, so we won't have to go searching once we break through!"

Her touch, her words, offered a warm comfort Braden wished he could sink into and soak in forever. *Lacey's been found, and soon she'll be freed.* He could have cried out with the relief of it. But there was still so much he didn't know. Were Lacey and Dunstan going to be all right once pulled out of the mine? Were they hurt? There would be no way of knowing their condition until then.

"We didn't stop working long enough to talk much, but I'm told they sounded in good spirits." Cora squeezed his hand, making Braden realize how pathetic he looked if she thought he needed assurance.

"What took you so long?" he snapped, swallowing his fear and guilt. They weren't for her to see. His pain wasn't hers to pity. Braden could keep that burden at least from her slim shoulders.

"Naomi wore through her gloves and blistered her hands bloody from trying to dig through the landslide." She didn't say anything more, but the unspoken accusation stung him. *Because Naomi is doing your work—we all are and have been since we came to salvage Hope Falls from the mess you made of the town—and our lives.*

"Fool." He snorted back a bellow of rage that he couldn't be out there, tearing his own hands to bring down the mountain. What was a woman doing up there, taking on a man's work? That was the problem with all four of them—they didn't know their place, so the women found themselves in a heap of trouble Braden couldn't prevent. "After today you girls should learn to stop sticking your noses into men's business and just stay where you're wanted."

Cora didn't speak for a moment, instead staring at their joined hands. Slowly, as though handling a snake that might lash out at any sudden movement, she withdrew from the contact. She drew a deep, shuddering breath, squared her shoulders, and headed for the door.

"I have more questions," Braden shouted. "Where are you going?"

She paused but didn't turn back to him. "Where I'm wanted."

"Wait!" Braden called out and reached for the woman he'd always loved, but it was too late. She was too far gone, and so was he.

NINE

There wasn't a man on the mountainside who didn't sense the women's return long before they rounded the bend. Never mind the distance. Never mind the noise. Never mind the dirt and debris weighing the air.

Stew. Mike's stomach rumbled after the aroma winding its way up the mountain. The few cold biscuits he'd eaten early in the morning didn't even make a decent memory now. The men around him paused in appreciation of the heavenly scent then attacked the earthen barrier with more vigor than they'd displayed in the past hour.

Mike followed suit, loathe to appear idle when the women appeared. The work distracted his grumbling stomach—or, at the very least, disguised it. Once he smelled supper, nothing could actually stop his stomach from sulking. Loudly. Not even the last of the warm water sloshing in the bottom of his canteen muffled it.

He put his back into the work and tried to keep his mind off his stomach by keeping one eye on the road. The rhythm of his pickax became a series of countdowns awaiting the women. *Three. . . Two. . . One. . .* Nothing. *Three. . . Two. . . One. . .* Still no sign of them, but Mike's nose stubbornly insisted that supper stayed nearby.

Suddenly his gut clenched—and it had nothing to do with an empty stomach. Images of a faceless man crushed by a massive boulder flashed across his mind. If their excavation caused more damage, the men wouldn't have heard the rumble of rocks cascading down the side of the mountain. Given enough speed, it wouldn't take a large one to hurt somebody standing below. *What if the women were hurt?*

Mike almost dropped his pickax at the thought but caught himself and the tool before anyone noticed. Leaving the implement leaning against one of the multitude of rocks lying around, Mike scrambled down from his perch. He noticed some of the men watching him, saw the scowls darkening their faces, and knew the axmen assumed he was trying to get a jump on the supper line. Earning the enmity of the men he hoped to work alongside wouldn't serve his son well. Mike glanced around for an acceptable reason to leave.

A pile of canteens caught his eye. Earlier the women had filled the extras and left them for the men. By now Mike suspected the men had drunk every drop. Digging was dry, dusty work. He snagged one, forcing himself to look disappointed when he discovered the thing was bone dry. Shrugging, he looped a dozen of the things over his shoulder. Fetching water—especially enough so that other men could partake—made an excellent pretext for heading down the mountain. He rounded the bend in record time, only to pull up short.

There was no sign of the women, save that same tantalizing aroma. For a moment Mike wondered whether hunger muddled his mind, that he smelled supper when there was in fact no supper to be found. To his right stood the outcropping where Naomi found the body. Mike had heard Granger instruct a team of men on how to retrieve the body and had seen the men return, so it was safe to surmise the stones no longer hid the corpse. Nor did it seem as though any dangerous pieces had shifted. In fact, now that he could take time to think it through, Mike figured that any trouble would've raised the type of caterwauling and carrying-on sure to bring the men running.

Then again, Mike had thought it safe to assume that the death site would be the last place any woman would think to set up supper.

So with no sign of trouble and no sight of the women up ahead, Mike stopped in the middle of the road, stymied. The copse of trees to his left should preclude that area—who would want to dodge trees and underbrush while carrying cookery? But as he stood staring, he glimpsed a flash of blue skirts swishing between the trees.

Relief had him heading toward the trees without a minute's thought. Sure enough, he spotted all three women almost right away. The trees didn't signal the start of forestland, as Mike assumed. Instead they shaded a wide clearing. *The women probably chose it because they knew the sight of food might make the men stampede.*

It sure smelled good enough to stampede for. Now that Mike knew the womenfolk were fine, he should head back. The canteens wouldn't fill themselves, and his fellow workers might note his long absence. But Mike found himself loitering near the trees, mouth watering as he watched the women set up no fewer than three stewpots atop makeshift fires. A large stump held baskets of some kind of bread with stacks of tins waiting to be filled and served to the men.

At that thought, Mike managed to pull himself away from the welcoming sight and hurry off to what he'd nicknamed Canteen Stream. Water flowed clear and strong into the empty containers. Mike filled his own canteen and emptied it in long gulps until the cool water washed away the layer of dust coating his lips and throat. Mike would take the honest freshness of sawdust over mountain dirt any day of the week; at least sawdust smelled good.

Though the water helped, persistent thoughts of dinner got him to thinking about how bad he must look if his face matched his hands. The idea of Naomi handing him a plate made Mike plunge his hands back in the water for a good scrub. For good measure, he splashed his face free of dust and the grime made where sweat met dirt. Mike remembered too late that he'd given away his clean bandanas, leaving him less grubby but sopping wet instead.

Oh well. At least he wouldn't show up filthy to his first dinner in Hope Falls. Besides, he might have time to bake dry before being called in for supper. *Unless. . .* Mike frowned. Any work dust he gathered in the meantime would probably make him a muddy mess.

"Here." A soft, feminine voice made him spin around. There stood Miss Higgins, holding out a fresh bandana in a now properly bandaged hand. "With my thanks for your thoughtful loan earlier."

Unsure how to thank someone who was thanking him, Mike nodded and accepted the gift, swiftly mopping up before shoving the bandana into his back pocket. His search for something to say ended when he spotted the buckets. One rested on the ground beside her, where she'd obviously laid it down so she could dig out the bandana. A second swung from the cradle of her other freshly bandaged palm.

He shrugged his canteens so they clanked against his back and grabbed the bucket at her side. When she made no motion to give him the second, he reached out and offered, "Let me help with that."

"Oh no." She gave a shy smile. "You're already toting all those canteens. Besides, I came down here to get water for you—well, all of the men—to wash up for supper. It's little enough to thank you for the hard work you're putting in to save my cousin."

"Believe me, miss,"—Mike grinned—"if the rest of the men are anything like me, they'll be glad enough to see dinner that they might miss the washtub altogether in their rush to appreciate *your* work."

"*My* work?" Naomi discovered that once she started smiling, it was hard to stop. Maybe it was relief over knowing how close they were to saving Lacey. After so much worry, she might have gone a little giddy to know her cousin would be home soon. But honesty forced her to admit—if only to herself—that the day would have held far fewer smiles without the man standing in front of her. *Mr. Strode.*

There was something endearing about him. Despite his size, strength, and calm capability, Naomi found his good-natured awkwardness most appealing. The way he'd smacked her back, mistaking panic for choking. The mulish glint in his gaze when he grabbed her shovel. The sheepish look on his face when she caught him shaking like a dog because he'd forgotten he had no clean bandanas left. For a man named Strode, he managed to stay a little out of step.

Naomi understood. No matter how hard she tried to keep ahead of Lacey, she usually got caught in the wake of her cousin's search for adventure. Today's disaster proved more the exception than the rule.

"Your cooking." Mr. Strode patted his stomach as though in anticipation. "There's no thank-you like a home-cooked meal."

"If I didn't already know that you're newly arrived, that comment would give you away." She felt the bucket slip along the soft surface of her bandages and tightened her grip. "Everyone in Hope Falls knows that Evie deserves the credit for our cooking."

"True. The mountainside hadn't finished shaking when my train pulled in." Something akin to concern flashed across his face too fast for Naomi to gauge it better. "In all the commotion, I clear forgot about my hopes for lunch—so you can probably see why I'm happy to give credit to anyone who stepped foot inside a kitchen."

Hopes for lunch. . . Naomi frowned at the implication behind that phrase. *Had he planned to get back on the train after he ate but stayed and helped out of nothing more than Christian kindness?*

"If needed, we'll replace your train ticket." She couldn't dredge up a smile at the thought of him going. For a town with more males than females, Hope Falls was short on hardworking gentlemen. It would be a shame to see such a helpful one ride off so soon.

"Ah. That won't be necessary since I planned to stop in Hope Falls." His shirtfront gave a faint crinkle when he patted the pocket. "This is a letter of recommendation to give to Mr. Lawson."

"Lawson?" Naomi hid her grin at his response by sidling closer to the stream. "Are you another sawmill engineer looking for work?"

"Not quite." Mr. Strode stepped forward alongside her, his big boots making it more of a shuffle. Before she could dip the bucket into the water, the warmth of his large hand brushed against hers, slipping the handle away from Naomi's suddenly nerveless fingers.

Blaming her clumsiness on her bandages, she waited until he filled both buckets with water before reaching to reclaim one.

"I've got them." He hefted both of the large buckets easily.

"But you shouldn't," she protested. "I'm supposed to be—"

"Resting your hands so they heal?" He raised his eyebrows. "Because I'm fair certain the doctor didn't list hauling heavy water buckets around the mountainside as a recommended activity."

"He didn't give a list of recommended activities," she shot back. "Only to change the bandages daily and keep them dry." Naomi knew she'd lost as soon as she said it. If Mr. Strode's brows were high before, by now they rose practically up to his hairline.

"My mistake." To her astonishment, he set the first bucket down. "Here I thought the weight and friction might aggravate your wound, but I should have been concerned with the water itself."

"I'm not likely to spill upward." She moved for the bucket, only to pull up short when his arm slid behind her back. Distracted by his proximity, at first she didn't notice that he'd removed his collection of canteens and looped them over her shoulder instead.

"Just in case." His voice went low as a whisper, catching her as surely as his brown gaze. The moment passed as quickly as it came. Mr. Strode retrieved the bucket and gestured for her to lead on.

Naomi shifted the canteens—which were heavier than they looked—to shake off her bemusement. It had been ages since a man looked at her with admiration and far longer since one left her so unsettled.

As she led the way back to their makeshift supper station, Naomi had plenty of time to think about how foolish she'd made herself. Yes, it had been an emotional day, and it wasn't surprising that the newcomer who'd been so much a part of it would unsettle her. But that was all. Lacey would come out of the mines, and life would return to some semblance of normality again. *Besides*, she reminded herself, *I'm much too old for a handsome man to turn my head.*

All the same, she caught herself looking back more than once.

TEN

Naomi ignored the speculative glances Evie and Cora cast her direction when she returned with Mr. Strode at her heels. What she couldn't ignore quite so easily were their loud remonstrances.

"I couldn't believe it when I saw you'd slipped away with those water buckets!" Evie shook a wooden spoon to illustrate her ire, making Naomi swallow what would have been an inappropriate chuckle.

From the corner of her eye, she saw Mr. Strode marshal his features into a mask of polite concern. *He's having just as much trouble as I am, trying to keep from laughing at the spoon of wrath.*

"You know I would've seen to it." Cora's softer chastisement didn't strike Naomi as so humorous. "Think of how upset Lacey will be when she sees the way you've injured yourself trying to help her. Take better care of yourself for her sake, if not your own healing!"

"You're right," she conceded more humbly. "I don't know where my good sense has gone today. Without Mr. Strode's help"—she gestured for him to move forward, thinking that "help" seemed like a weak description for his determined assistance throughout the day—"I wouldn't have noticed that I'd hurt myself in the first place."

"Mr. Strode, is it?" Cora gave an unladylike grunt as she hauled the heavy metal washbasin farther away from the foodstuffs. "It's rare that a man becomes a blessing to an entire town, but you've managed it in a matter of hours. We owe you our thanks."

The man made a noncommittal sound as he emptied the buckets into the washbasin. "Kind words, but the blessing will be when we work through the barrier and get your people home safe and sound. Then we ought to be giving all our thanks to God for His mercy."

"You're right." Naomi felt like she could snuggle under the weight of his words, burrowing into their comfort like a blanket. "We have much to be thankful for." *And I've been busy worrying about all of it for the past three months instead of enjoying it!*

"This is a mighty big basin and could use more filling." Mr. Strode kept hold of the now-empty buckets. "I'll be right back." With that, he left the three of them to finish setting up dinner.

And, apparently, to gossip. The minute he passed through the trees on the edge of the field, Cora and Evie began interrogating.

"Did he follow you to the stream?" True to form, Evie sounded like a concerned mother hen looking after a wayward chick.

"No, I stumbled into him while he was filling canteens."

"Still,"—Cora managed to look both solemn and pleased at once—"it seems the new arrival has taken special notice of you, Naomi."

She huffed away the idea at once, seeing where her friends were heading. "The poor man's been thrown alongside me since the moment he stepped off the train. He's done more for Lacey than anyone else, but no one would speculate he's taken some sort of interest in her."

"That's ridiculous. He hasn't even *seen* Lacey," Evie countered.

"But if he had even glimpsed her, we'd all be thinking he was working so hard because he's sweet on Lacey." The truth of that statement tasted sour to Naomi, but she knew better than anyone how a young girl could turn a man's head—especially a beauty like Lacey.

"She does have a way of catching attention," Cora agreed.

Even when she's not present. Naomi smiled at the realization. Her younger cousin's zeal for life transformed those around her, and Naomi knew God had made the exile to Lyman Place her saving grace. Newly grieving her father, a younger Lacey needed love, guidance, and stability just as much as Naomi needed a reason to rejoin the world. They found it in each other, and neither one would have changed it.

Though, if possible, I would've changed a lot of things since.

Naomi shook the maudlin thoughts away. Regrets didn't change the past—but they had a sneaky way of staining the future if they weren't caught and corralled early on. The trick was to focus on what was possible today and how today could make tomorrow better.

So she put all her energy into making supper run smoothly, knowing that well-fed men could break down the wall more quickly to get Lacey back. Besides, work helped her keep her mind from worrying. It distracted her from the way the shadows stretched on the ground as the sun slowly sank behind the mountains.

Indeed, the light had grown thin and pale by the time Mr. Lawson came running through the trees, arms flailing like a rag doll's. "We broke through!" He gasped for air. "They're saved!"

Time itself seemed to speed up at his words—Naomi certainly did. She hiked up her skirts and raced across the clearing, through the trees, and up the mountain path almost before she blinked.

Panting, she skidded to a halt just in time to see Lacey wriggling through an opening in the stone wall, her hands clasped in Granger's as he steadied her progress. No one made a sound, afraid to distract them. Maybe afraid that one of the now precariously stacked stones might shift if they dared breathe too heavily. Then Lacey was out of the mine, and Naomi was running once more.

∞

As soon as the lady—for the life of him, Mike couldn't remember her identity beyond the fact she was Naomi's cousin—emerged from the mines, pandemonium broke loose all around her. If he was honest, Mike would ascribe some of the chaos to the woman's garb.

On the one hand, a man could admire her practicality in wearing britches. On the other hand, a man couldn't help but admire the fine figure she presented in those same britches. From the furious whispers flying around, the workmen focused on the latter.

Mike stepped back, farther away from the hub of activity, trying to give everyone as much space as possible. Even so, he caught an elbow to the gut for his trouble. From what he could make out, the perpetrator was a terrified lumberman trying to scramble away from the wolfhound. Once Mike got his wind back, he forgave the fellow. After all, it was taking the efforts of a behemoth to hold Decoy back while they maneuvered his master up out of the mine.

Amid the high-pitched cries of the women, the loud cheering of the workmen, and the hoarse barks of the wolfhound, Granger called out. No one seemed to hear him—even Mike, who'd seen the man's mouth move from his detached viewpoint, couldn't make out the words. The man beside Granger tried waving and adding his own shouts, but the chaos around the rescue site swallowed the sound.

The lady who'd already been pulled out tried to get everyone to calm down and listen but was ignored in the clamor. When she tried to scramble back up to help the rescuers, the other women pulled her away. Their efforts added more deafening noise but not much else.

Mike pushed through the crowd—which managed to be very dense for fewer than two dozen people—and climbed up to where Granger had the man from the mine half in and half out of the opening. The thick layer of dirt caking the man's skin and clothes couldn't hide his grimace of pain or the way he gritted his teeth against it.

"What do you need?" Mike surveyed the situation, noted the way the man was lying on his side, obviously keeping weight off his left arm and rib cage, and deduced that the poor fellow had broken something. His shoulder. . .a rib. . .maybe even his collarbone.

"Shoulder's dislocated, and he has at least one cracked rib." Granger's detail of the man's injuries explained why they weren't simply pulling him free by his arms or even bracing beneath his underarms. "We'll need to construct a rigging to pull him out."

"Right—are you wearing a belt?" Mike directed the question to the injured man, trying but failing to remember his name.

"Yep." He drew a deep breath. "Can't stand suspenders."

"They would've come in handy." The shorter man beside Granger, who happened to be wearing suspenders, spoke with a German accent.

Mike decided to forgo pointing out that a pair of button suspenders wouldn't hold a sturdy man's weight without the buttons popping loose. Instead he focused on finding a workable solution.

"Here." Mike slid his own sturdy leather belt from its loops, and he saw Granger do the same. "If we loop them around his belt, one on either side, we should be able to pull him through with the least amount of strain on his injuries." He paused, unwilling to be less than honest. "It's still going to hurt like the devil."

"It'll hurt worse once Dunstan's out and I pop his shoulder back," came Granger's grim prediction. "I wish we could do it without the ladies present, but there's no prying them away now."

"Bite on this." Mike slid his knife off his belt, stuck the blade in his boot, and offered the thick leather sheath to Dunstan. In a matter of moments, they'd rigged their belts and began pulling.

Dunstan grunted and bit down on the leather sheath but otherwise issued no sound of protest. Sweat beaded on his brow, but he held firm until they'd pulled him completely free of the mine. Then he spat out the sheath and lay there, panting until his breaths grew more normal. When he finally nodded, they helped him to his feet and removed their makeshift rigging from around his waist.

The stocky fellow picked up Mike's knife sheath and tried to return it to him, but Mike pushed it back to Dunstan. Resignation was written in every dust-creased line of his face as he turned his back to the crowd below and accepted the sheath once again. To his credit, he didn't give more than a low groan as Granger jerked his shoulder back into place. He didn't manage to bite through the leather but left such deep impressions Mike wouldn't use it again.

Nor did he care. They'd managed to get both victims free of the mine without causing more damage or further upsetting the women.

"Draxley." Dunstan ground out the dead man's name as he cautiously picked his way down the slow grade of the rocky incline.

"Dead." Granger spoke with finality, sending the other man a look that cautioned against going into further detail. But this response seemed to satisfy the other man, who gave a short nod.

Leaving Mike to wonder again just how Draxley—supposedly the town telegraph operator—came to be by the mines during the collapse. And, more importantly, why the man they'd just pulled from that mine seemed reassured by that fact. The mystery awoke Mike's curiosity.

Once they reached the ground, Mike hung back. It wasn't his place to come between the townspeople and thrust himself in the midst of their joyful reunion. For all that had happened since the train pulled to a stop, he remained an outsider to Hope Falls. But being an outsider was a good reason to observe very carefully.

He watched as the rescued woman barely restrained from flinging herself into Dunstan's arms, not bothering to hide tears of relief that they'd both made it out safely. Mike saw the way Dunstan moved as close to her as possible, angling his body to keep the rest of the men distanced from her while he wrapped her in the warmth—and, it had to be said, concealment—of a cloak. Anyone with eyes could see that those two were as much a couple as Granger and his woman.

More interesting was the way Dunstan's dog, Decoy, reared up on his hind legs as though to give his master a canine hug but immediately dropped back to all fours when Dunstan snapped his fingers. The wolfhound, impressively trained, pressed against the man's uninjured side and stayed there during the walk to town.

Unsurprisingly, Mike found the most interesting member of the scene to be the woman who'd caught his eye from the very beginning. Naomi—Miss Higgins, he tried to remind himself—kept to her cousin's side. Eyes shining with love and gratitude, she positively beamed.

And Mike wasn't the only one to notice. All the way back to town, the lumbermen all stared at the trio. Understandably, their gazes went to the couple they'd worked so hard to free. But just as often the men stared at Naomi. Their expressions ranged from considering to downright greedy, and while Mike couldn't blame them—he caught himself staring the same way—he didn't like it one bit.

He wanted to shield her from prying eyes, and he wanted to know what she and her friends were doing in a town full of rough axmen. No other women showed up to help with supper, and it was clear as could be that no man laid claim to Naomi or the younger girl with mismatched eyes. But even without any obvious protector lurking nearby, the men deferred to them with more respect than could be explained by their gender or even the fine food they served.

Now that the immediate danger had passed and the crisis averted, questions crowded Mike's thoughts. And underscoring every query was that unexplained line from his telegram about Hope Falls. *"Sounds like a strange place,"* his friend warned. *"Good luck."*

As Mike stepped back into the small town, unsure where he should go or whether he could even count on being allowed to stay, Hope Falls seemed far stranger than he could have imagined.

∞

Cora slowed her steps when they reached town and the doctor's house moved into view. Since she'd left Braden earlier, she'd managed to submerge her thoughts of him beneath all of the evening's activity. But now they'd gotten through the rushed shifts of feeding the men and finishing the rescue. Now the sun, which stayed in the sky so late during these long summer days, had finally set. And now, as the day's excitement faded, darkness crept across her thoughts.

I left him. I left Braden. Cora drew in a deep breath and held it, trying to stop what was promising to become an unending mantra. It didn't work. The refrain stuck stubbornly in her mind and heart. Even as every step drew her closer to returning, her thoughts wouldn't budge from the prospect of leaving. After all, she'd already done it once. *How much harder would it be to keep it up?*

She didn't know whether her obsessive ruminations were meant to encourage her decision or scold her against it. Did her feet drag because she dreaded the idea of apologizing or because she didn't want to have to walk away again? Did it even matter which one?

Ultimately, it came down to the same issue. Spending time with her fiancé had become a pain rather than a pleasure, and time wasn't making any improvements. Neither was patience, nor, it seemed, prayer. Yet sometimes no response was, in and of itself, an answer.

It was time to let Braden go. The doctor seemed pleased with his physical progress, confiding his belief that Braden would be rolling about in a wheeled chair before the week ended. Then the fresh air and stimulation of movement should encourage recovery. Such freedom meant that Braden wouldn't need to rely on her help.

She'd done her duty, stayed by his side for as long as he truly needed her. Now that he wouldn't, Cora owed it to the independent man her fiancé had been—and was trying to become again—to step back. *But I never thought that stepping back would mean walking away.*

Lost in her musings, Cora didn't realize everyone else had stopped until she practically ran right into her sister. Evie merely reached out a steadying hand and gave an encouraging smile. Her sister probably thought Cora worried about Braden's reaction to seeing Lacey. She didn't know Cora had effectively ended things.

Or that Cora had only barely accepted that she'd ended them.

But now wasn't the time to think about these things. No matter she was seeing Braden for the first time since she'd done what he'd been demanding for three months and left him alone. Right now the denizens of Hope Falls had more pressing matters to resolve.

Cora normally would have gone in ahead of everyone to absorb the worst of Braden's anxieties and give him a chance to collect himself before facing everyone. Tonight she stayed to the back.

She watched while Granger directed Riordan and Clump—his almost comically mismatched pair of right-hand men—to take the men back to the bunkhouse and settle everything in for the night. Cora waited when Naomi steadied Lacey's elbow and drew her toward the doorsteps, distracting her while Granger moved to support Dunstan's climb up the stairs.

Dunstan took shallow breaths for the majority of the walk, and it hadn't escaped Cora's notice that the men used far more time and careful effort to pull him free than they'd used for Lacey. Dunstan tried to mask his pain, but stairs would most likely jar whatever injuries he'd sustained. *That's why Naomi guided Lacey ahead.*

They all tried so hard not to upset each other, and the funny part was that they were going in to see the one man who would try to upset everybody in the room! Cora shook her head at the irony of it.

That's when she noticed the new man. He was hanging back, too, shifting in the uneasy way of a man who doesn't know what to do. With a start, Cora realized that he probably didn't know what to do. In all the hullabaloo of the day, the new arrival hadn't been officially interviewed, accepted into town, or given any welcome.

Mr. Strode saw a town in trouble and pitched in without complaint. Normally Granger—or if Granger happened to be out of town, Dunstan—would have gotten to know the new arrival and found a place for him. But with Dunstan out of commission and Granger overseeing the fallout, their new guest was left out in the cold.

"Come on in." Cora gestured toward the door, eliciting a pair of surprised glances from first Mr. Strode and then Granger.

Understanding dawned on Granger's face then warred with an obvious reluctance to invite a stranger to what would certainly be a very specific and private discussion about Hope Falls business. His hesitation reminded Cora that Granger only returned to town that same afternoon and doubtless would have had a lot to talk over with Braden and Dunstan even if the mine hadn't gone and collapsed.

Which also meant that Granger didn't know Dunstan came to town to investigate the first cave-in or that both he and Braden now believed the mine was sabotaged. And wasn't it strange the way the second cave-in happened on the same day they went to investigate?

Oh yes. Tonight's conversation should be very interesting. *And won't it bunch Braden's britches to have a stranger stroll into the middle of everything?* That alone was worth inviting Mr. Strode!

"Er—yes." Granger had reached the forgone conclusion that they couldn't very well ignore the man after all he'd done today. He even showed the grace to look somewhat abashed at the oversight.

For her part, Cora tried to ignore her sister's questioning glance. Evie could wonder why she'd invited Mr. Strode, but in the end she probably wouldn't ask. Somebody had to see to the man. Besides, there were far more interesting questions to ask tonight.

ELEVEN

"Where's Dunstan?" Braden craned his neck, trying to peer around the people who'd crowded into his room. He saw his sister, looking a complete mess but otherwise safe and sound, edging toward the door. "Lacey! Come and let me see you. Where are you sneaking off to?"

"To check on Dunstan," his sister called back. "I know he'll be fine, but he's not the sort to take kindly to doctoring."

"What does Dunstan need doctoring for? What happened to him?" Braden locked eyes with Granger, who he hadn't even been told had returned to town. How long had he been back in Hope Falls?

"A mine caved in on him." Cora gave the obvious answer with no further explanation. Obviously she was still upset with him.

"I know that!" He waited for Granger to fill him in, chafing anew at the fact he hadn't been at the scene in person, helping.

Granger seemed to sympathize with his frustration. "Doc's binding his ribs. Dunstan got pinned under a beam in the collapse."

Braden swallowed against a sudden onslaught of memories. He'd been struck by a falling beam in the first cave-in, and the mere mention of the same thing befalling another man made him taste bile.

But cracked ribs would heal. It could have been so much worse.

"You look all right, sis." He desperately tried to be positive.

"Out of all the opportunities to give me a compliment, only you would choose the night when I'm covered in grime." Lacey quirked a small smile at him. The smile grew when he opened his arms in invitation, and she bustled across the room for a long overdue hug.

Thank God, you're all right. He gave her a last squeeze. Now that he had her back, he realized how much he would have missed Lacey if he lost her and how disappointed he would have been if she'd obeyed him and left Hope Falls as soon as she'd arrived.

He suddenly realized he couldn't remember the last time he'd seen his sister's smile. *How much of that can be laid at my door?* Guilt snagged away his satisfaction in knowing she and Dunstan would be all right. *They shouldn't have been endangered to begin with.*

Thankfully, Dunstan's entrance pushed away Braden's gloomy musings. The hunter shouldered his way toward the bed—an impressive feat for a man with a couple cracked ribs and a dislocated shoulder.

"Do you want the good news to start, or do you want to get the bad news out of the way first?" Dunstan's attempt to lighten the mood failed when Braden saw the way Lacey sidled up to him and put her hand on his arm. Even worse, Dunstan folded his hand over hers!

"Depends." He fought to keep his voice level. "Is the bad news that you've fallen for my little sister? Because I have to warn you, Dunstan, that might be the biggest catastrophe of the day."

Lacey's blue eyes widened then narrowed. "Don't make any assumptions," she hissed. "It's not yet midnight, and who knows what might befall a beloved brother with a mouth two sizes too big!"

"That's my sister, always ready with a retort." Braden tried to return her scowl but felt the edges of his mouth quirk upward. He was gratified to see her fighting the same losing battle until they stood there, grinning at each other. "Some things never change."

"And others do." Dunstan looked at Lacey when he said it, but Braden felt the impact of those words in the pit of his stomach.

"What did you find?" Now that there'd been a second cave-in, Braden didn't know what to think. His hopes from the morning seemed no more than a faint memory, the shining idea that one of Braden's own mistakes hadn't taken the lives of several men. The hope, odd as it may seem, that an unknown party deliberately sabotaged his mine.

But even if Dunstan managed to find evidence of tampering amid the original destruction, it would be long gone by now. Worse, if their suspicions were confirmed, it would bring today's cave-in under question. Secondary landslides, smaller collapses caused by the destabilization of an original cave-in, were common enough to be expected. But what were the chances that the second incident would take place only when Dunstan began investigating?

Coincidences like that, in Braden's experience, were no coincidences at all. So, did the saboteur remain in Hope Falls? Everything rested on the answer Dunstan wasn't giving him. The longer the hunter remained silent, the more frustrated Braden became. He looked around the room, searching for an explanation among the friends gathered around him. He found a surprise.

"Who's he?" Braden pointed at a stranger leaning against the wall, almost hidden in the corner farthest from the bed.

"Mr. Strode." Naomi gave the man's elbow a light touch, nudging him forward. No one else seemed to find it strange that she'd shown such familiarity, but it didn't sit well with Braden. Naomi was the oldest and, if such a thing could exist amid a group of women, the voice of reason and sensibility. If Naomi slowly abandoned the edicts of propriety, what would happen to the rest of the girls?

The thin threads binding them all to polite society frayed the instant the ladies placed that benighted ad in the paper. Their arrival in Hope Falls and subsequent antics further unraveled the order of things. Wasn't it evident in Lacey's headstrong adventures? Even more so in Cora's sudden denouncement of him?

Braden eyed the newcomer with suspicion, wary of both the man's calm confidence and his sudden appearance on a day already filled with chaos. His timing was enough to make Braden wonder. *Why did he come today? Can this be the saboteur they were looking for?*

Cora paid to that notion immediately. "I know what you're thinking, Braden, but he arrived on the same train as Granger."

STRONG AND STUBBORN

Why is Cora supporting the stranger? Robbed of a reason for his mounting animosity, Braden still couldn't welcome the man. For one thing, the man had an unpleasant effect on the town's women. Braden supposed the fellow was attractive enough, but that didn't help matters. A sudden thought grabbed hold with a vengeance. *Is Strode the reason Cora walked away? She thinks she found a better option?*

"What are you doing here?" Braden didn't try to sound friendly. He wasn't inclined to waste time making nice to some Lothario.

"The young miss asked me in." The fellow gestured toward Cora, and Braden immediately lost track of anything he said afterward.

"Why?" He gritted the question at the man but kept his gaze on his errant fiancée. What was she thinking, inviting a stranger to take part in an important meeting? Braden might not like having a town council made up mostly of women, but he accepted that they'd all earned their places. The stranger had no place among them.

Mike hadn't felt so conspicuously out of place since his wedding. He hoped this town suited him better than the arrangement with his late wife. Just like then, the commitment would change his life. And, just like then, he had someone counting on him to see it through.

Why am I here? Against all odds, Mike found humor in the question. He didn't know many people who hadn't asked that question, along with a plethora of others related to it. *Why am I here? What is God's purpose for my life? Am I doing the right thing?*

Too bad the answers were harder to come by—especially when an entire room filled with people was waiting for his response! But Mike knew one thing for sure: he didn't intend to begin his stay in Hope Falls as a target for anyone's bad temper. A man started the way he wanted to finish, and Luke needed him to start strong.

"If you're asking why she invited me,"—Mike kept any hint of emotion from the words—"I couldn't tell you. Every time I try to figure out a woman's reasoning or speak for her, I get it wrong."

Granger let loose a guffaw, Dunstan gave a chuckle, and even the grump in the bed seemed to soften. The women seemed surprised, pleased, and amused by turns. It couldn't have turned out better.

Encouraged by the response, Mike ventured further. "Now, I haven't caught everyone's names, but I don't think I'd be far off the mark in thinking you're the ones running Hope Falls?"

He addressed the room at large, not wanting to alienate the women. Mike sensed they held more power than women usually managed, but he'd steer clear of making assumptions until he knew more. As things stood, his lack of knowledge about Hope Falls put him at a severe disadvantage. He hadn't had the time to research the town before taking off and had relied on talking with Mr. Lawson first.

"You're correct." The rescued lady kindly took it upon herself to make introductions. "I'm Lacey Lyman. This is my brother, Braden." She indicated the invalid. "Together we own the bulk of Hope Falls, including the town, the mine, and the surrounding forestland."

"Granger's asked to purchase shares in our sawmill venture, and we're allowing that because his expertise is invaluable." Braden Lyman took over. "Otherwise, the women own the remaining shares."

"I'm Evelyn Thompson, and I run the café. For now we can call it the diner." Granger's arm around the amber-eyed woman provided the rest of her identification. "This is my sister, Cora Thompson,"— she indicated the girl Mike already pegged as a relation—"and on your other side is Naomi Higgins, Lacey and Braden's cousin."

"Chase Dunstan"—Granger looked like he wanted to clap the man on the shoulder, but thought better of it at the last moment— "hired on as our hunter. He knows these mountains better than anyone."

"And you are?" Not surprisingly, the pointed query came from Braden. The man looked like he was itching to get rid of Mike.

"Michael Strode. I was referred to Mr. Lawson in hopes your new sawmill could use a woodworker for carpentry, joinery, and so on." Mike ignored the sea of names, faces, and details pushing for places in his memory, instead concentrating on the task at hand. "If Hope Falls isn't at that stage yet, I can swing an ax and work a saw."

"We aren't at that stage yet," Braden Lyman said flatly. "And as far as I know, we aren't looking to hire any woodsmen."

The words slammed into Mike with the force of a sledgehammer, knocking the air from his lungs in a sudden rush. He'd been so focused on getting to Hope Falls, he'd not let himself consider where he'd take Luke if things didn't pan out like he hoped.

"Aren't we? We lost a hefty percentage of our workers when we kicked out the brawlers." The younger Miss Thompson looked toward Lacey Lyman, who stayed snuggled up against the hunter. "And Granger's and Dunstan's increased involvement changes things."

Mike knew he'd missed something, but for the life of him he couldn't figure out what the girl was talking about. If he hadn't seen the way everyone responded to Granger's command throughout the day, he would assume that the workmen didn't like Granger and Dunstan. But that wasn't so, which left Mike wondering why everyone looked like somebody snuck up behind and goosed them. Miss Higgins, in particular, looked pale and delicate as fresh-hewn birch.

Whatever hid beneath Miss Thompson's speech, it gave him one last chance to make his home in Hope Falls. Why, then, did it make Miss Higgins look like she was being frog-marched toward a noose?

TWELVE

Naomi made a strangled sound. Then she had to cover it by clearing her throat. Hopefully everyone would chalk it up to the amount of dust she'd swallowed during the course of a long, trying day.

But they knew better. Cora's comment forced them to examine the implications of Lacey's newfound fondness for Dunstan, and there was only one conclusion for everyone to reach. The same conclusion that made Naomi's mouth turn dry and her fiercely stinging hands go numb.

Wanted: 3 men. Thinking about the words they'd once written so boldly now made Naomi feel violently ill. *Object: Marriage.*

It didn't matter that Cora's commitment to Braden was weakening—Naomi knew she wasn't the only one to notice that Evie introduced her only as her sister and not Braden's fiancée. With Evie promised to Granger and Lacey now all but announcing her engagement to Dunstan, two of the three women were already brides-to-be. Now for them to make good on their promise to the workmen of Hope Falls, Naomi had to shed her spinster status and select a husband. Her time was up, and all at once everyone in the room realized it.

Everyone, with the exception of Mr. Strode, who was trying and failing to hide his puzzlement. Apparently the newest addition to Hope Falls would be the only man who hadn't been lured by their ad. A strange mix of gratitude and disappointment swirled together at the realization that Mr. Strode hadn't come seeking a bride.

Naomi wouldn't allow herself to wonder what he'd think once he learned about the advertisement. *It shouldn't matter one whit what he thinks*, she told herself. But somehow it did anyway. Just like it mattered whether or not he was able to stay in Hope Falls.

She cleared her throat again, this time because she had some difficulty getting her words out. "Yes, things are changing in Hope Falls. I like to think they're changing for the better. The men we lost are men we'd escort from the grounds if they ever returned."

Vehement nods met this proclamation as the women gave their full support. Granger did the same, his opinion chiming in to the tune of ominously cracked knuckles. Obviously Evie's fiancé hadn't forgotten the time he stopped four men determined to break into the women's house in the dead of night. Naomi hadn't forgotten either.

"I can't speak to what progress has been made in my absence," Granger admitted. "But I can say that hiring more men will be very difficult. Warm weather makes the sap run too freely—most loggers stop working altogether in the summer, wary of the difficulties."

If Mr. Strode found the prospect intimidating, he didn't show it. To the contrary, there seemed to be a glimmer in his eye, as though he welcomed the challenge. Or perhaps he merely welcomed the opportunity, since Braden so quickly tried to turn him away.

"They've mapped the route for the main leg of the flume and managed to clear most of it." Dunstan's assessment surprised Naomi, mostly because she hadn't thought the hunter was keeping track of matters related directly to logging and establishing the sawmill.

Keeping Hope Falls in fresh meat and keeping Lacey out of trouble was more than enough work to keep him busy, but Dunstan continued. "They've also cleared and leveled the sawmill site. Soon we'll be ready to order ready-cut lumber and begin construction."

"I hadn't realized we'd come so far." Braden sounded surprised but not entirely pleased, and Naomi guessed at its cause. How frustrating he must find it, not being able to oversee his town.

"Evie's cooking makes the men able and willing to work hard." Granger's boast wasn't far off the mark. If it weren't for Evie's cooking, they would have lost the remainder of the men in a blink.

"Miss Higgins mentioned that credit for the cooking goes to you," Mr. Strode addressed Evie. "Now, I know hunger seasons any dish, but your stew can settle a man's stomach and soothe his soul."

"She's spoken for." Granger good-naturedly tightened his hold on a blushing Evie. "But for as long as you stay on, you'll be able to fill up on her cooking for breakfast, dinner, and supper."

"Wait a minute," Braden protested. "Who says he's staying?"

"I do." Naomi surprised herself by speaking up first. "Mr. Strode barely stepped off the train before he started hauling equipment up the mountain and breaking down the barricade. We didn't have the chance to welcome him, but his actions surely make him a member of Hope Falls."

"I agree." Lacey slapped her britches to emphasize her point, raising a visible cloud of dust. "Any man who helped haul Dunstan out of that mine is welcome to stay on. That's all there is to it."

"I couldn't argue with that even if I wanted to." Dunstan gave an uncharacteristic grin. "But, for the record, I vote he stays."

"Especially since he and Naomi found poor Mr. Draxley." Cora's contribution shaded things a little, but Naomi forgave her.

"Poor Mr. Draxley, my eye!" Lacey looked mad enough to spit, mad enough that she didn't notice Dunstan and even Braden trying to get her to hold her tongue. "The weasel just about killed us!"

"What?" Mike's confused question got swallowed whole in the pandemonium following Miss Lyman's denouncement.

Her brother sat bolt upright in bed, demanding details in a voice better suited to commanding new troops. Dunstan, whom Mike had seen try to hush his woman, sighed at his failure. The ladies shrieked and gasped, save Miss Lyman, who seemed pleased by the uproar. Granger got over his surprise fastest of all and seemed to be mulling over the startling revelation.

Which made the carpenter in Mike start fitting pieces together for himself. He hadn't bothered to ask why Dunstan and Lacey went into the mine in the first place—it wasn't his place. Furthermore, by the looks of them, he hadn't been able to discount the possibility that the couple had sneaked off for a private interlude. Once he'd understood that this wasn't the first collapse, he'd entertained the idea that the couple had somehow brought on the second cave-in by being too loud or knocking into a precarious support. What he hadn't questioned was whether it was an accident.

This missing clue shifted the entire picture. From Miss Lyman's statement, Mike understood that the destruction was intentional— and possibly intended to kill the people trapped inside the mine. This created new questions about what the couple had been searching for, but Mike put that aside to examine later. For now he was fiddling with bits of information about the late and unlamented Mr. Draxley. Now he knew why the telegraph operator left his post to poke around the mines. Now he understood that the type of man capable of such deception wouldn't be the sort to inspire goodwill in everyday life—hence the lack of grief at the news of Draxley's death.

"So did Draxley cause the first cave-in, too?" Mike realized he'd spoken aloud when every head in the room whipped toward him.

Silence reigned for several heartbeats as the denizens of Hope Falls regarded him. Surprise, suspicion, even admiration played across their features as they considered his question. And, if Mike didn't miss his guess, considered his sudden involvement. It didn't take much brainpower to know that Dunstan and Lyman hadn't planned on making this part of the conversation public. But it was too late.

Even Miss Lyman held her tongue, now aware of her mistake.

Dunstan, in particular, stared at him with unnerving intensity, grappling with the problem he posed. All the same, it was the hunter who spoke first. "You don't miss much, do you, Mr. Strode?"

"Not if I can help it." Mike walked a fine line. "Woodworking takes attention to detail and an eye for piecing parts together. I take note when something doesn't fit or goes against the grain."

"In Hope Falls,"—Miss Higgins sounded a warning—"people

and projects are never predictable."

"Yep." Dunstan raised his brows. "You'll fit in just fine."

With that acceptance, Mike relaxed. Everyone understood without saying the acceptance was conditional upon his performance. So Mike didn't mention Luke. First he'd prove himself. Then when they valued him and his work, he'd be able to bring his son home. Thankfully, the people seemed smart enough. It shouldn't take them long to notice how hard he worked and the quality of his results.

"I want to know how you got the idea Draxley caused the first cave-in." Respect mingled with suspicion in Lyman's request.

"Others mentioned this was the second cave-in and that it was strange to find Draxley so far from his telegraph station." Mike paused then decided to speak plainly. "Judging by the reactions, he won't be much mourned. Miss Lyman indicated that Draxley intentionally caused the cave-in today."

He waited for Dunstan and the lady to confirm this. After they nodded, he continued. "So either Draxley set out to kill the two of you, or he had another purpose. The only reason I could devise for creating a second cave-in was to destroy evidence that might remain from the initial collapse."

"I didn't connect it so quickly, and I've been involved for months." The cook blinked at him.

"No matter how damning it seems, any proof that the original cave-in was caused by sabotage has been thoroughly eradicated by now." Lyman leaned back again. "It's all conjecture at this point."

"Not quite." His sister edged over and perched along her brother's bedside. "Although it isn't proof you can hold in your hands and show to the world, Braden, we know for certain. Draxley confessed that he'd brought down the mine back in the spring."

"How did you coax that from him?" Lyman looked desperate to believe her but didn't dare.

The depth of the man's emotion confirmed Mike's suspicions. Braden Lyman lay in this bed because he'd been trapped in the first cave-in. No one said so—even if it weren't common knowledge, it wasn't the sort of thing loved ones gossiped about—but it made sense. It made even more sense when Mike considered that Braden Lyman owned most of Hope Falls. The mines predated the sawmill venture by at least a year—it stood to reason that Braden Lyman began them. And the man who oversaw the mines would, by default, shoulder any responsibility for unstable design implementation.

It explained why a man would be so eager to hear that his property had been sabotaged. Why else would Braden Lyman seem filled with hope instead of rage that another man ruined his life?

It's easier than thinking he ruined his own life. Mike breathed deep. He and Braden Lyman shared more in common than he'd thought.

THIRTEEN

N o, you're wrong." The muffled moan emerged from beneath a heap of bedclothes, followed by the glare of a bleary-eyed Lacey Lyman. Hair mussed and pout in place, she looked much the way she had five years before when Naomi first met her cousin. "It's not morning already!"

"For all the hundreds of times you've attempted to argue the sun away, I've yet to see you succeed." Naomi tapped her small pendant watch before dropping the chain back inside her bodice. "It's already half past four, Lacey. Bread doesn't bake itself."

"To hear you tell it, anyone would think the sun was shining and I'm a slugabed." Lacey pushed herself up and stretched. "But how can I argue the sun away when it hasn't even shown itself?"

"Piffle." Naomi loved the whimsical word but rarely employed it. When something was overused, it became underappreciated, after all. "After all the trouble the men went through to dig you from the mines, you need to dish out a few smiles with their breakfasts."

"Don't you think my smiles would be more genuine if I could sleep in for another half hour or so?" Lacey never could resist getting the last word, even though she'd already gotten out of bed.

"You're difficult to drag from bed, but that doesn't mean you need to sleep in. Besides, you're the woman of the hour. Enjoy it."

"Ah. . ." Lacey looked over her shoulder as Naomi tackled the tangled ties of her cousin's corset. "But *I'm* not the woman of the hour, am I? Everyone will have guessed how things stand between me and Dunstan, even before we make an official announcement."

Suddenly Naomi wanted to crawl beneath the covers and not come out. "That doesn't make me anything more than I was yesterday."

"The only single woman amid a dozen or so bachelors?" Lacey tackled the wayward wisps of her blond hair, utterly oblivious. The girl was prophesying doom but viewed it as a dream come true.

"Now, Lacey, don't go putting it like that." Naomi sat down on the bed hard enough to make the ropes creak. "You know as well as I do that a good portion of those men didn't list me as one of their choices. It's not as though I'll be surrounded by the entire dozen!"

In the early days, when bachelors descended on Hope Falls en masse, they'd asked each man to list which two of the three ladies they'd like to court. Unfortunately, they'd never worked out what to do with the men left over after the first two women made their choices. That left Naomi with a handful of men who'd listed her name—and an even larger handful who'd wooed but not won their women.

"That's true." Evie and Cora trooped into the room with Naomi's favorite part of the morning—hot chocolate and sweet buns.

"What are we going to do with the men who chose me and Lacey?" Evie settled herself beside Naomi on the bed, concern creasing her temple. "Now that they've lost their chance at winning a bride, we can't expect them to stay on for nothing more than room and board."

"Even if we scraped up the wherewithal to pay the. . .erm, if I call them losers, you'll all know that I don't mean it negatively. If we pay them fair wages, we couldn't expect Naomi's suitors to go on as before." Lacey cautiously lowered herself to perch atop a rounded trunk.

"I say, Lacey." Cora sounded somewhat awed. "However did you manage to bend so much without losing your balance? That's amazing."

For a brief moment, Naomi remembered the two times Cora had fallen from her chair. The first time she'd been informed of Braden's death. The second, she'd been told he was still alive. Both times, after she came around again, Cora's corset made her employ some vaguely turtlish movements to get up off the ground.

"It's that new Pivot Corset I ordered!" Lacey practically jumped to her feet then resumed her seat with impressive ease. "It expands to let one bend. I can't tell you how grateful I was to be wearing it yesterday. A traditional corset would have made breathing impossible, and I hate to think about the cost if I'd fainted."

Everyone took a restorative sip of chocolate at the thought. Naomi engaged in a silent argument with herself, trying to decide whether to draw out Lacey for a more detailed account of her experiences or if her cousin and friends needed a moment of levity. She looked around, seeing that ultimate social signal that someone needed to steer the conversation: the sweet buns sat untouched.

"Marvel though the Pivot Corset may be,"—Naomi allowed a wry note to enter her tone—"it wasn't the new garment that caught everyone's attention when you reappeared. You ordered something else from the Montgomery Ward catalog without telling us, didn't you?"

Lacey stuffed an overlarge bite of bun into her mouth, chewing slowly to delay her answer. Evie and Cora began nibbling during the wait. Naomi smiled and enjoyed a bite of her own pastry. She'd made the right choice. The conversation now offered both amusement and instruction, holding Lacey accountable for those appalling trousers.

"Well." Even if her cousin typically arose in an amiable mood, her tone would have been overly bright. "I could've sworn I'd pointed them out to everyone since the name is so clever. And yes, I wore my new Waulkenphast half boots yesterday. Although they are plain, I can't complain about comfort. They're entirely practical." She shifted her skirts and flexed her foot, displaying the boots.

"While an admirable attempt to *sidestep* the issue. . ." The rest of Cora's comment was lost amid a round of good-natured groans.

"I hadn't realized it, but it's been a long while since any of us punned." Evie grinned at the revival of their old game. "Lacey took last honors. After Granger caught him, she told Twyler that my chances of hitting him brought new meaning to the term *long shot*."

"That wasn't so long ago—just over a month." Naomi briefly relived that awful day. Granger revealed that he'd come to Hope Falls tracking his brother's killer. Spooked by Granger's pursuit, the murderer panicked, kidnapped Lacey, and forced a showdown. Justice had been served, but Naomi couldn't help but worry. "Please tell me you won't make a monthly habit of terrifying us, Lacey!"

"I don't plan to." Lacey sniffed. "Listening to you, anyone would think I asked Twyler to abduct me or begged Draxley to light that fuse. It's not as though I routinely endanger my own life!"

"Of course." Evie took a dainty sip of cocoa. "It must have been another woman who donned britches and raced off to investigate a sabotaged mine. What were we thinking to make such a mistake?"

"Touché." Lacey shook her head. "Though exploring the mines was more of a calculated risk. They'd been stable for months and in all likelihood would have remained so if it weren't for Draxley."

"For a moment, we'll ignore the myriad of perils presented by any mine, much less a system of tunnels already compromised by a cave-in." Naomi paused, allowing everyone to imagine those unnamed perils. "Tight trousers are no calculated risk, Lacey. Our comportment as ladies is one of our few protections against lascivious advances.

"It was bad enough when you insisted on accompanying Dunstan on his hunting trips, but at least the workmen didn't notice your absence. Now it escaped no one's attention that you slipped off, indecently clothed, to spend time with Dunstan in a secluded space."

"I'm sorry it seems so unsavory." Lacey sounded duly contrite. "But I couldn't let Dunstan go alone, and if there was any chance to bring back proof, I couldn't let Braden down. Showing him that the cave-in wasn't his fault is the only way to bring my brother back, and in spite of all that happened, I can't say I regret going."

Naomi knew she'd already given one lecture but couldn't stop herself. "Frankly, Lacey, it's fortunate that you and Mr. Dunstan stopped fighting long enough to acknowledge your attraction to each other. If he hadn't offered the protection of an engagement, you would have opened yourself to dishonorable advances. At the very least, you would have ruined your chance of marrying a good man."

She stopped there, unable to speak past the lump in her throat. Dimly, she heard Lacey apologize for endangering them all, but Naomi didn't believe her cousin truly understood her precarious position. Lacey's life wasn't in danger any longer, but her way of life was. A fallen woman had no hope of happiness. And the worst part of it was, Naomi couldn't tell her cousin the true reason behind her concerns.

I don't want you to go through the same heartbreak I did. Part of Naomi longed to give Lacey the truth. *That kind of sorrow, the constant shame and uncertainty, is no way to wake up every morning.*

Mike woke up groggy and disoriented, the noise of the bunkhouse reassuringly unfamiliar. The splash of the washbasin and irregular thunk of men shoving boots on their feet almost varnished over a few last stubborn, spluttering snores. It was about as far away as a man could get from waking alone in an overly elaborate Baltimore bedroom.

Galvanized by the realization he was one of the last to rise, Mike lurched from his bed and just about clocked himself on the upper bunk. In truth, the loggers' bunks were little more than two wooden shelves, built wide and well supported at frequent intervals, running along three of the four walls. The pallets were rendered comfortable by exhaustion rather than padding, but Mike didn't mind.

He'd worked hard enough yesterday to fall asleep on the bare ground, and he fully intended to work that hard all day, for six days a week, until he'd secured a home for himself and Luke. With only two exceptions, his bunkhouse mates stood tall and broad as the trees they felled, testimony to a logger's strength and endurance.

Their swift exit from the bunkhouse gave another testimony— that Mike needed to hurry if he wanted to enjoy some breakfast! Mouth watering at the thought, Mike made short of his morning wash. He threw on his clothes, strapped on his teeth-marked knife sheath, and wondered whether he could make it through the day without shaving.

Stubble pricked the palm of his hand when he felt his jaw, making Mike grab his straight razor and soap. He'd seen a cloudy mirror hanging above the washbasin, but another man was using it. Oblivious to the dark streaks running from his obviously blackened hair, the man methodically finished shaving and rinsed his razor.

"All finished." When he turned around, Mike could see that the man was a good bit older than the others he'd seen. The man eyed Mike's bar of soap before producing a small brush. "Would you like to borrow this? I always need one to make a good enough lather."

"Thanks." Mike accepted the offer and quickly filled his face with thick suds. After rinsing and drying the brush, he returned it.

"Anything to welcome the new man in town." He returned the brush to his shaving kit. "You can call me Gent, by the way."

"Mike Strode." Making quick, short strokes of the razor, Mike couldn't shake the man's hand. "Any reason why they call you Gent?"

"Old-fashioned wisdom." His new friend donned a top hat, carefully tilting it at a jaunty angle that hid his bald spot. "A fondness for good manners, and of course, my sense of style."

What did a man say to a logger sporting a top hat? Nonplussed, Mike splashed away the soap residue while he thought it over.

"I can see I surprised you." Gent spared him having to answer. "Good of you not to look concerned, since I'm entirely sane. Besides, you'll soon see that an acceptance of the unusual is a valuable trait for someone choosing to set up in Hope Falls."

"You're comfortable in your skin, that's all." Despite his oddity— or perhaps because of it—Mike warmed to the man. He offered a grin. "Seems to me we ought to worry about the people who aren't."

FOURTEEN

Try as he might, Braden couldn't make himself comfortable. He couldn't ignore the persistent throbbing of his injured knee, which he'd pushed hard this morning. At least he could bend it farther than yesterday. He kept imagining that if he just tried hard enough, he could push past some crucial point of pain and he'd be beyond it.

So far Braden hadn't passed that point. *Maybe tomorrow.* Or the next day. He was determined to be able to bend his knee ninety degrees before the week's end. At that point the doctor promised Braden would be permitted to use a wheeled chair. For now, the doctor refused to bring the contraption into the room. The man claimed it was unhealthy to fixate beyond the current goal, but Braden harbored his own suspicions. Most likely the good doctor kept the chair out of his reach because he knew Braden would seize the thing, muscle his way into the seat, and wheel himself away if given the slightest chance. Or, at the very least, he'd try.

"Leave it to you to enlist the services of a retired army surgeon," Dunstan griped by way of greeting. "The man is small, but I'd wager Doc gets his way more often than you or I manage."

"If I kept a tally, I'm afraid he'd have a hundred to one ratio against me." Braden tried to keep the bitterness from his tone. Doc, after all, was the one who'd signed over the management of Lyman Estates to Lacey. Even after Braden recovered from his concussion, Doc refused to rescind the orders. Apparently he'd seen too many men make uncharacteristically poor decisions after suffering trauma.

"That's why it's best not to keep score." Dunstan moved more slowly than usual, cautiously lowering himself into the chair. Although his friend didn't complain, Braden recognized the signs of suffering. "Besides, we have more important matters to discuss."

"Draxley." It was a name, a question, and a curse in one.

"Last night I didn't go into detail. It didn't seem prudent."

"I wish Lacey shared some of your prudence." Braden sighed. But what was said couldn't be undone, and the newest addition to Hope Falls knew more than he should. And what the man didn't know, he showed an uncanny ability to deduce. "What else did you discover?"

"As we suspected, the original cave-in was caused by carefully placed explosives, rigged together and detonated in one fell swoop." Dunstan shifted in his chair and wordlessly accepted the pillow Braden passed his way. Once he'd wedged the brace against the chair back, Dunstan seemed more at ease. "Much the same way Draxley set his charges yesterday. Lacey discovered the fuse while we poked around, but it was too late. Draxley engineered things so that we'd be trapped in the bowels of the mountain long after he ran out."

Braden's rage at Dunstan's revelation squeezed his chest and cut off his breath. He couldn't begin to calm himself until black spots swam across his vision. He'd known last night of Draxley's duplicity, had surmised that the greedy telegraph operator intentionally made the mines collapse atop Lacey and Dunstan. But something about the way the hunter spoke about being trapped in the bowels of the mine triggered memories of other men who'd suffered the same fate—but weren't fortunate enough to tell their story.

"But before he left us like rats to scramble through his own maze, Draxley grew chatty. His partner disappointed him on the day of the cave-in by racing back into the mines." Dunstan paused as though unsure whether to divulge more. "Trying to save you, Braden."

The tight, squeezing sensation abruptly ended, leaving his skin and skull feeling oddly swollen. Refusing to become light-headed, Braden grappled with the implications of Draxley's confession. Very few men knew of the massive gold vein they'd unearthed in the midst of the Hope Falls silver mine—and only one of them came rushing in, gasping with panic, moments before the world turned upside down.

"Why are you here?" Owens had shouted. "You shouldn't be here!"

"My partner." Braden sagged against the headboard, staggered at the depth of the betrayal. "I don't want to believe it of Owens, but it makes a horrible sort of sense. He'd known me for years. Knew me well enough to guess that I wouldn't be able to reopen the mines if I thought I'd made a fatal mistake and gotten all of our workers killed. I would've given him my share to try and make amends."

"Honor isn't something to regret, Lyman." Dunstan's words did little to comfort Braden as he added, "Integrity itself isn't a flaw, but the predictability of an honorable man can be exploited."

"If you're trying to cheer me up, you'd do better to call Doc back in here." Braden gave a slight stretch and ended the experiment with a hiss. "Telling a man he's easy to exploit is bad for morale."

"If you want to look at it that way, it's disheartening."

"How else am I to look at it?" Braden seethed. Even when he'd been whole, he'd been unable to protect those who depended on him.

"I read some redemption in the loyalty you inspire. It's convoluted, but Owens forfeited his own life trying to save yours."

"The death of a trusted friend—however unworthy—is cold comfort." Braden choked on an impossible mix of grief and loathing. Owens survived the collapse and Doc sent him home to recuperate—but he never made it. A damaged blood vessel burst in his brain before they took him off the train.

"Maybe you should be looking to strengthen your resolve." Dunstan's brows lowered. "Because Draxley and your partner weren't the only ones responsible for the collapse. They answered to someone else, someone powerful enough to put the plan in motion."

"Who?" Fists clenched, Braden had to remind himself that he couldn't leap from bed, find the fellow, and throttle the dastard.

"Beyond implying that the man was a Hope Falls investor, it's the one thing Draxley wouldn't tell us." Far from looking defeated,

Dunstan grinned. "So how about you and I exploit that reputation of yours one last time and lure the mastermind back to Hope Falls?"

"If you've got a plan," Braden promised, "I'm listening."

"This can't go on much longer." Lacey flounced in with a frown.

Naomi's heart sank. She'd reached the same conclusion even before breakfast, but hadn't come to terms with it. Unfortunately, she didn't have time to dither. Perhaps if Lacey and Dunstan's courtship had been more measured and conventional, she would have found a solution before they announced their engagement. Then again, Naomi should have known better. Lacey bucked convention at every turn, and Dunstan could hardly be termed traditional.

"We're going to have to do something." Lacey plopped down on one of the kitchen stools. "This has to be settled today!"

"Jake took care of it yesterday." Evie's calm pronouncement shook Naomi. "So we wouldn't be obligated to make arrangements."

"How did he take care of it?" Naomi thought back over breakfast but couldn't remember anything out of the ordinary. Shouldn't there have been some sort of upset? Even if Granger managed to make most of the men happy, there would still be a few grumblers. And what if they needed to overturn Granger's high-handed arrangements because they didn't have adequate funds? "He didn't get our approval or even discuss how much we should pay!"

Lacey looked equally unsettled. "I know he's your fiancé and he has more experience than all of us put together, but Granger is not the owner of Hope Falls. He can't take over our accounts."

"What on earth are the two of you going on about?" Cora didn't seem to share their sense of outrage. "I, for one, am grateful to Granger!"

"Changing our arrangement with the men," Naomi burst out. "I know now that Evie and Lacey are taken, we'll need to address the issue, but I'm not ready to abide by whatever Granger set in place."

Heart pounding, Naomi nevertheless noticed that no one blinked.

Wide-eyed, they stared as though she'd sprouted a second head.

"Hold up," Evie raised her hands. "We're talking at cross purposes here. Jake hasn't changed our agreement with the men!"

"Is that what you thought, Lacey?" Cora looked confused.

"I was talking about the larder," Lacey ventured. "The last two supply orders haven't arrived, and we're running out of foodstuffs. But Granger isn't in the position to authorize the use of funds."

"He didn't do that either." Evie settled herself on a stool. Now that she no longer needed to defend her man, she looked at ease. "Though Lacey's right about how badly the pantry needs restocking."

"Then what did Granger take care of?" Naomi felt like a fool.

"He had the men move Draxley and cover him with stones. He called it a cairn." Cora grimaced. "To keep scavengers away."

"I knew that, and I am grateful to Granger." Naomi stifled a shudder. "Draxley deserved his fate, but we couldn't leave him."

"Let's not think about it any longer. Naomi looks ill." Lacey took her arm. "We'll go try our hand at sending telegrams."

"Wait." Naomi pulled her arm free. "Foolish as I sounded earlier, we still have a problem looming. We can't expect the men to continue working without pay—and we need to decide their wages."

"I say that any man who wants to court Naomi should stay on as agreed," Lacey sniffed. "Because she's worth as much as Evie or I."

"But we can't very well expect to ask my. . .um. . ."—Naomi needed to swallow before she could say the next word—"suitors to work without wages alongside men who are paid for the same day's efforts."

"Agreed." Evie looked thoughtful. "The trouble lies with those men who elected myself and Lacey. We can't expect their free labor when they've no chance at winning one of the Hope Falls brides."

"What if they still had a chance?" Cora lifted her chin. "I mean to say, what if Naomi wasn't the last Hope Falls bride?"

Evie slapped the countertop loud enough to make them wince. "Absolutely not. Cora, whether you leave Braden or not is your own decision, but we all agreed you aren't ready to wed someone else."

"Naomi isn't ready to marry one of these loggers, but we all expect her to choose one of them in the near future." Cora's lower lip began to tremble. "Why should the burden rest on her alone?"

"It doesn't!" Naomi hurried to assure her friends that she was willing to do the last thing she wanted. "Evie and Lacey are holding up their part of the bargain—they chose men who came to Hope Falls and helped set up the sawmill. It's only fair that I do the same."

Except it isn't fair, is it? Naomi's conscience sounded as dejected as she felt. *Whatever man you marry won't know he's taking on damaged goods, not a virtuous woman. How can that be fair?*

"No it's not." Cora frowned. "I know you, Naomi. You'll rush your decision to end the tension among the men and because you don't want to make Evie and Lacey wait to marry the men they chose."

"Yes." Naomi seized on the opportunity. "It would make things less rushed if Evie and Lacey went ahead with their weddings."

Silence blossomed as the prospective brides thought it over. Anyone could see that they didn't relish the idea of waiting, but it didn't take long before both of them were shaking their heads.

"No. We've already found out the hard way that it's not safe. Even with four of us living together, we had to bring in Mr. Lawson." Evie's logic couldn't be assailed. If it weren't for Granger's fists, the men would have broken in under cover of darkness to "claim their brides" and take away their choices.

The reminder sent a chill up Naomi's spine. Afterward, Mr. Lawson and his widowed sister moved in with the women. The engineer made his bed in the downstairs study. Even then, his presence wouldn't be acceptable if Arla weren't so heavily pregnant.

"Besides, we all planned to marry on the same day," came Lacey's more sentimental logic. "I want us all to stand together as united as when we came to Hope Falls. The joy of the day can't be complete unless we've all found the husbands of our hearts."

"Then I might as well go up alongside Naomi." Cora's quiet resolve ruined the romance. "Because unless he can convince me otherwise, and I don't think he can, I won't be marrying Braden."

FIFTEEN

C an't say that I blame you." Granger's voice made Cora jump. "Sorry, I didn't mean to startle you. Just popped in to ask if anyone needed to add their telegrams to the ones Braden gave me."

"As a matter of fact, we haven't received the last two supply shipments we ordered." Lacey expertly smoothed things over, sparing Cora from having to reply to Granger's comment about Braden.

The thing of it was, Cora wanted to reply. "You don't?"

"Nope." Granger didn't miss a beat. "In fact, I'm glad to hear it. Braden's a friend, but he needs to break through that crusty cocoon he's built up around himself and come out a better man."

"You think that's possible?" Cora caught her breath. She might not be willing to marry Braden as things stood, but she couldn't help but hope that would change. And even if he couldn't change her mind, her feminine heart still wanted him to want her enough to try!

"All things are possible through Christ." Granger angled over to Evie. "It's a matter of whether or not Braden's going to lean on God's strength or his own as he recovers and gains independence."

Lacey frowned. "We Lymans have always had trouble with that. Braden's gone sour *because* he's lost his independence."

"Helplessness is a harsh torment for any man," Granger agreed.

"There's more to it than that." Cora didn't want to defend Braden, but there was more to his transformation than thwarted independence. "Pain doesn't improve anyone's disposition." *And the festering pain of his guilt makes things ten times worse!*

She bore no illusions. Braden probably wouldn't be improving at all if it weren't for the absolution of Dunstan's discovery. Her love certainly hadn't been enough to pull him from his despair. If anything, Cora wondered whether her steadfast support hadn't enabled Braden to wallow in his own misery. She could only keep praying.

"It doesn't mean you have to marry him," Evie argued fiercely. "And it certainly doesn't mean you have to marry anyone else!"

"What?" Granger, normally so stoic, looked shocked. "Who?"

"I don't know." Cora flapped her hands as if she could shoo away the question. "Naomi shouldn't be the last Hope Falls bride when there's another one of us who isn't engaged to be married."

That set off another round of vehement protests from the women. Interestingly enough, Granger didn't look nearly as appalled as he had when Evie first mentioned the possibility. He looked as though he were considering the option and finding it had merit.

"Why not?" He broke through the arguments being volleyed about the kitchen. Granger even ignored Evie, who looked as though she'd dearly love to apply a cast-iron skillet to her fiancé's thick skull.

Cora knew that look as well as she knew her sister, and it couldn't help but make her smile to see it directed at someone else. Of course, it didn't hurt that Granger was taking up Cora's cause.

"She doesn't have to marry anyone," he clarified. "But why not let Cora decide whether or not to allow a man to try and win her heart? The men will all know she's fresh from a broken engagement, and we can make sure they won't expect any speedy decisions."

"I don't think distracting her from Braden is the answer." Now that the tides had turned, Naomi looked deeply concerned. "A hurt heart seeks comfort, and affection can be mistaken for love."

"I'll be careful, Naomi." Cora couldn't help but give her friend a warm hug. "My friends will always be my greatest comfort and trusted advisors. Remember, we set up safeguards. At least two of you have to support my choice before I can marry anyone."

"Including Braden?" Evie had a shrewd look, and Cora realized that her sister didn't trust her not to fall back in love with him.

"Are you joking?" Lacey was fervent. "*Especially* Braden!"

"It's a wise woman who knows when to walk away," Granger encouraged. "And a wiser one still who knows she's worth the chase."

What if Braden doesn't come for me? Cora ruthlessly squashed her first thought. She deserved a man who valued her—a man who looked at her the way Granger looked at her sister. And besides. . .

"Braden's spent a lot of time trying to chase me away." Cora gave a tiny grin. "Now we'll see if he's man enough to catch me."

"A man's only a man when he works hard for those he loves." Dad's advice cut through Mike's growing fatigue as steadily as his saw bit through felled trees. Back and forth, give and take, progress made and measured in mere inches. But every inch brought Mike closer to the time he and Luke could call Hope Falls home. Together.

As an admitted "sapling"—the logging equivalent of a greenhorn—he'd been paired with Gent as a "bucker." Bucking consisted of stripping the branches from felled trees then using a two-man whipsaw to cut the massive pines down to more manageable sizes. It made for less dangerous work than wielding an ax and less skilled labor than making precise undercuts and swift, even back-cuts to determine which directions the trees would fall. But what bucking lacked in those areas, it more than made up for in the monotonous, muscle-straining push and pull pattern of the crosscut saw.

As Gent put it, "One of the best things about working as bucker is that it means keeping well clear of the fallers so you don't get hit by mistake. The team foreman, and for us it's Bear, doesn't tend to bother so much with buckers either. We're pretty much left on our own, so long as we get the job finished in good time."

Come noon, Mike noticed a drawback to the bucker's isolated position. By the time he and Gent heard their team's echoing calls to come 'n' grub, the other men were already cracking open the lunch pails. Thankfully, their team leader held out their fair share.

"Here now." The massive redhead passed them a pail kept cool beneath shady underbrush. In spite of Gent's observation that buckers were left to their own devices, Bear Riordan didn't stint when it came to checking on the "sapling" throughout the morning. The giant gave Mike a nod of approval and added, "You've earned it."

"Feels like your arms are going to fall off, don't it?" The youngest member of their crew looked like a stiff breeze could blow him over, so Mike figured that he was commiserating, not teasing.

All the same, Mike wasn't about to complain. No one liked a whiner. "What kind of workman would I be if my own arms detached?"

"That would, I believe, depend on if you can reattach them." It was easy to recognize the short, stocky German with a fondness for suspenders. His ready grin rendered him instantly likeable.

"I wouldn't want to find out." Mike brushed away the idea that he might have to. From the ache across his back, he'd be stiff as untreated oak when he tried to roll out of bed tomorrow morning.

"*Ja*, neither would I." Even without the accent, the amiable man would have been recognizable. The unexpectedly thick soles of his boots made for an unforgettable clomping sound when the man walked, reminding everyone of his nickname with every step he took.

Easy to see how Volker Klumpf earned the nickname Clump. Just as it took no time at all to realize why the impressively burly Rory Riordan went by Bear. With Gent rounding out the crew, Mike began to suspect that loggers hid a fondness for creative nicknames.

"Ah!" Bear sounded absolutely delighted as he pulled something from one of the pails. "Slap me if they didn't make Scotch eggs!"

"This is from an egg?" Clump squinted at one of the large brown balls. "Looks more like fried chicken. What kind of egg is this?"

Trying not to be conspicuous about it, Mike surveyed one of the round objects presented as lunch. It didn't look like anything he'd ever eaten before, and he wondered whether that was a good thing. Mike downed half his canteen, waiting for Bear Riordan's summation.

"Mam used to make these," the large man rhapsodized, emptying the contents of his pail onto a clean bandana. He then upended the pail and transferred the bandana atop it as a sort of makeshift table. He flicked out a blade and set to slicing one of his Scotch eggs. "First, she'd boil and peel the eggs. Then she'd wet her hands and mold seasoned ground pork sausage all 'round each one."

He split the thing neatly in two, revealing the boiled egg in the center. "From there, she dipped the sausage-covered egg in beaten egg, rolled it in bread crumbs, and fried it in hot oil."

By then, Mike caught up with the foreman. He'd laid open one of his own eggs and had it halfway to his mouth before realizing he hadn't prayed. It took a fair bit of will to set down his lunch and give thanks, but at least he was sincere. From the inroads made in the food, it looked like Scotch eggs tasted as good as they sounded.

And better than they look. Mike made short work of the first and reached for a second. Crispy fried sausage with a spicy kick, cooled down by the chewy egg, lent the portable meal an array of texture and taste. The butter-baked biscuits made a welcome addition. They gave the food it's due, making their way through the first two-thirds before slowing enough to allow for some conversation.

"I don't know much about logging," Mike hedged, "but it was my understanding that the teams were much larger—say twenty-five men?"

"That's the way of it." Bear sounded grave. "But Hope Falls doesn't have so many men at the moment. Besides, men disperse even when working in a team. It's not safe to set two teams of fallers working close, nor should the buckers stay nearby. The work's dangerous enough without trying to clump men together. If the foreman can see his whole crew, then one tree can crush them."

"For now," Clump joined in, "it doesn't matter whether the units are small. We're mostly clearing a path for the flume. Once that's up and running, work will really begin. Granger can gauge the labor and determine whether to keep smaller teams or change over."

Mike rolled his neck and stretched, his muscles protesting the idea that this wasn't the "real" work. "Thanks for letting me know."

"I say it depends on the donkeys." Bobsley, the youngster, grew animated. "The more donkeys, the farther apart you can set up."

"The farther apart you *have* to set up," Bear corrected. "I doona trust the newfangled machinery. Steam engines are fine for ships and trains, but for hauling logs? Bah. One cable snaps, it cuts down two trees and three men before coming to a halt."

"Sounds like a different sort of donkey than gets hitched to a wagon." Despite Bear's obvious dislike of the machines, Mike couldn't help but be curious. "If Granger's bringing in steam engines to move the logs, why are we bothering to build a flume?"

"That's the trick of it. The Colorado River runs through these mountains—Lawson's building the mill atop a strong-running off-shoot to power the wheel—but it winds. Donkeys could haul sectioned logs straight to the river, but they'd float right past the offshoot." Bobsley filled in the gaps. "If the donkeys haul the logs to the right place upstream, a good flume can rush them straight to the mill."

"Provided we have the manpower to set things up." Gent made his first contribution to the conversation. "Given recent events, the ladies will have to make some changes to keep things progressing."

"That's not for us to speculate on." Bear quickly cut things short, leaving Mike completely in the dark. "Until things change or you decide to pack up and leave, we've an agreement to keep."

As Mike followed Gent back to the Douglas fir they'd been breaking into thirty-two-foot segments, he tried to make sense of the cryptic conversation. *What did Gent mean, the ladies would have to make some changes? Why would any of the men suddenly pack up and leave?* And, perhaps most mysterious, *What kind of agreement?*

SIXTEEN

W e're going to have to offer wages to all the men." Naomi broached the topic again once she, Lacey, and Granger were en route to the telegraph office. "Especially now that Cora's set on joining me."

"You know how much I hate to say you're right." Lacey sighed. "So I'm not going to say it. We're just going to have to figure out what makes a fair wage and how meals and lodging factor in."

"I can help you there." Granger reached the telegraph office first and held the door open for them. "Though it varies by outfit."

"Any guidance would be helpful—" Naomi walked into Lacey, who came to an abrupt stop at the threshold. When she recovered, she saw why.

"What on earth happened here?" Lacey edged over to allow Naomi and Granger entrance. "This could be an entirely different office."

Naomi knew what she meant. The haphazard stacks of paper, crumpled missives, and skewed stacks bore no resemblance to the office she'd seen as recently as last week. Draxley had kept the place so obsessively tidy even she'd wanted to mess it up a little.

"He must have panicked after the picnic." Lacey shook her head.

"What picnic?" Granger obviously couldn't make the connection. He'd been all the way in Baltimore, taking Twyler to trial.

"We had a picnic a little while back in the same clearing where we served supper last night," Naomi explained. "Draxley became very agitated when someone suggested we take a stroll around the mines."

748

"Something triggered this." Granger bent down and began retrieving fallen missives, plunking them atop the desk. "I remember every time I came to his office, he'd neaten his papers into perfect piles, made everything parallel. I'd put the pencil down sideways, just to see how long it took him to straighten it."

"Not long." It sounded as though Lacey spoke from experience. For a while, there was nothing but the sound of papers sliding and shuffling together as they made a collective sweep around the room.

"Little wonder our supplies never arrived." Naomi smoothed out a badly crushed order spilled from the overturned wastebasket. "It looks as though he threw them away as soon as you left the room."

"When's the last time you received an incoming telegram?" Flipping through a stack of paper filled with barely decipherable scratches, Granger looked troubled. He tapped a page. "There are several messages here in the hastily penciled translations of incoming telegrams. I'm not seeing any of the official ink copies."

"The lazy, scheming reprobate!" Lacey huffed. "You'd think he could have at least done his job properly before trying to kill us!"

Naomi giggled before she could even think to stop the sound. And once she started, she couldn't stop. By the time she caught her breath, the other two were chuckling. "Only you, Lacey," she gasped, "could work up such indignation over a murderer's filing skills."

"*Lack* of filing skills," Lacey justified. "In all fairness, I would have granted him much more leeway about the state of his office if he hadn't done all of those other nasty, terrible things."

"I think we can all agree that Draxley exceeded his allotment of terrible deeds." Naomi managed to keep a straight face this time.

They got back to work, creating various piles of paperwork. As the sorting continued, it quickly became evident that Draxley had been negligent long before the picnic. He'd just hidden it better.

While the stack of penciled translations grew high, there were precious few official ink telegrams. Several outgoing messages were found balled up beside the wastebasket, making it doubtful that Draxley ever sent them. Even worse was the expanding pile—it became too large for a simple stack—of undistributed post office mail.

"He abandoned his post long before that picnic." By the time they'd gotten everything sorted, Granger was downright irate. "I'll start resending the messages and orders we found in the trash."

"You know Morse code?" Lacey's brows rose, and Naomi shared her surprise.

"Yep. I've set up several logging outfits. Finding a telegraph operator isn't as easy as you'd think, so if I needed to get messages out I had to learn. It was easier than learning how to wait on someone else." He grinned at their chuckles.

"Why don't you give me the pencil copies?" Naomi offered. "I can probably make out the messages. It can't be any worse than trying to decipher Braden's letters." She smiled at the memory.

"I'll organize the post then." Lacey lowered herself to the ground with an ease that reminded Naomi to order a Pivot Corset.

For the next hour the tapping and mechanical clicks of the telegraph were the only sounds in the room. Finally, Granger pushed away from the desk and stretched. "That's the last of them."

"I'm just about finished here, too." Naomi blinked and rubbed her eyes.

"I hope you didn't tire your eyes already." Lacey wore a satisfied grin as she pushed a large pile—by far the majority of the post— across the floor. "By the looks of them, these belong to you."

For a moment, Naomi couldn't imagine who might have sent her so many letters. It wasn't until she plucked one from the pile that she realized what had happened. Across the envelope, the smudged lines were addressed, appallingly enough, "*To My Future Bride(s).*"

"Oh!" She dropped it as though its author might emerge from the envelope then used her foot to push the pile back toward her cousin. "Stop looking so pleased, Lacey. Those do not belong to me."

"I doubt Dunstan wrote this." Lacey plucked the offending letter from the pile and waved it in the air. "So it's not mine."

By then Granger had ambled over to see what was going on.

With a shrug, he plunged his hand into the heap and brought up another letter. "This one's to 'The Three Fair Maidens of Hope Falls.'"

Naomi couldn't even blame him for snickering when he reached the "Fair Maidens" bit. The whole thing was absolutely ridiculous.

"The sad thing is this was the kind of response we'd hoped for—oh, don't look so quizzical, Granger. I don't mean the overblown forms of address. I mean that we'd anticipated going through letters and selecting a few men to come visit Hope Falls in person."

"Our welcome committee disabused us of that notion." Lacey was obviously remembering the day they'd arrived in Hope Falls, believing that the men gathered around the train were recent hires. "I don't know why we never thought to check the post—we should have realized there might be some men who replied as requested."

"I know why." Naomi set aside several other obvious ad responses. "We haven't had time to think beyond the basics." *And even then we haven't managed to handle things very well.*

Naomi flipped through a few more. "We should burn them."

"No!" Lacey grabbed them back and cradled the replies to her chest, looking for all the world like a mother protecting her child. "How could you even suggest letting all of these go to waste?"

"Yeah." Granger flipped another find toward Naomi. "Think of all the fun you'll have opening these. Hours of entertainment."

A snort escaped her as Naomi glimpsed the writing on the letter Granger selected. "'To the Lovelorn Logging Ladies.'" She snickered.

"We're also known as the 'Sawmill Sweethearts.'" Lacey set this gem to the side but wrinkled her nose at the next one she picked up. "'Wilderness Women'? Why does that make it sound as though we parade about in grubby buckskins, brandishing firearms at hapless men?"

"I'm sure they didn't mean it like that," Granger soothed. "Though this one probably did." He tore up the envelope but not before Naomi was able to decipher the words *Shameless Hussies*.

The indictment wandered through Naomi's memory, a painful echo.

"You're going to Charleston, where my brother needs a woman to guide his daughter. You're not fit for the position, but it's your last chance to make something of yourself. If you can't find some fool to marry you and cannot control yourself in any other way, simply stick your nose back in a book. It's better to be known as the bluestocking you were than the shameless hussy you've become."

"Naomi?" Lacey's call, accompanied by a nudge against her boot, recalled her to the present. "Whatever is going through your mind?"

"Oh. . ." She searched for an acceptable answer. "Only how unlikely it is that I can find a good husband by reading these." *Or at all.*

"Pish." Lacey brushed away her protest. "That's no reason to look so glum. You can't read a man by looking at his envelope."

"There's some wisdom to brighten your day." Granger stood up, holding out a letter Naomi didn't have the heart to take. "This one's different. Looks like a lady wrote it, and it has your name."

Naomi fought to keep her hand from trembling as she accepted the envelope. In return for the scores of letters she'd sent to her family during the past five years, she'd received one response. A terse telegram from her sister advised that their mother's funeral had been the day before and Naomi should cease writing home.

She peered at the envelope as though it could somehow prepare her for its contents. Who would bother writing to her from across the country? And more importantly. . . *What can they possibly want?*

"Supper's ready and waiting," Miss Lyman assured a hungry crowd.

"Then what's it waitin' on?" someone grumbled, loud enough to be heard but not so loud Miss Lyman couldn't graciously ignore it.

"An announcement." Dunstan's growl warned away more grumbling. When the men stopped shifting on the benches, he relaxed. "I'm pleased to tell you that Miss Lyman has agreed to be my wife."

For a moment the men all looked at each other. It wasn't as though they hadn't seen the writing on the wall, but they still seemed at a loss how to handle the proclamation. From where Mike sat, the problem had nothing to do with whether the men respected or even liked Dunstan. This wasn't even about the supper holdup.

The problem stood beside Dunstan. Covered in dust and sporting britches, Miss Lyman turned heads. Dressed up in pink frills, she shimmered like an oasis. And now Dunstan had made her unreachable. Little wonder the room full of lonely lumbermen wasn't cheering.

From the growing displeasure on the ladies' faces, supper might never come out of the kitchen. So Mike did what any exhausted man with an empty stomach and a waiting bunk would do. He started clapping. Not loudly, just prompting the other fellows to join him. Granger helped ease the tension by offering hearty congratulations.

"Course *he*'d be happy for them," muttered one of Mike's tablemates. "Granger already got himself the cook, didn't he?"

"Now Dunstan's gone and nabbed the dazzler," another lamented. "That means I'm out. First frost, I'm heading for another outfit."

"Leave sooner," Bobsley urged. "Less competition for me!"

"Didn't you hear me?" The man who'd spoken of leaving peered sadly into his empty coffee mug. "I'm out. No more chances. Only reason I'm sticking around at all is for the food. That's worth staying for, so long as there aren't paying jobs someplace else."

Mike blinked at that last bit. "You aren't getting paid?"

There had been too much going on last night to broach the subject of wages—considering the mine contretemps, Mike figured he was lucky to have gotten a bunk to sleep in and an offer of employment at all. He hadn't pushed about further details because it would've done him more harm than good—and he hadn't cared. Mike didn't lack funds. The Bainbridges gave him and Leticia a house as a wedding present, and he'd recognized a good profit even on a quick sale.

All the same, this lack of logging wages was a revelation. Maybe the employees of Hope Falls expected to receive a lump sum once the mill was up and running? That might explain Gent's earlier comment about changing the agreement.

This could be the advantage Mike needed. *I'll gladly work without wages until the mill's set up—if they let me bring Luke.* Mind galloping along, he almost missed what came next.

"In light of these changing circumstances,"—Miss Lyman could be awfully loud for such a delicate-looking thing—"we understand that some changes are in order. Tonight we modify our arrangement."

The resulting swell of sound swallowed anything more the women might have said. Mike recognized that the women had foreseen this problem. In a bit of brilliant strategizing, the elder Miss Thompson used the one weapon guaranteed to inspire fear, reverence, and awe.

She rang the dinner bell.

SEVENTEEN

Conversation ceased so abruptly it might have been cleavered. Speakers stopped midsentence. Every man perked his ears and sniffed the air as though he hadn't already noticed the aromas wafting from the kitchen. It went so still, Mike fancied he could hear the rumbling of a dozen stomachs. *Or maybe mine is just that loud.*

"Now that we have your attention,"—Miss Thompson lowered her dinner bell to continue—"we'll explain the terms of our new offer."

Mike couldn't help wondering about the terms of the old offer—particularly since so many men had taken them up on it, and now he wouldn't get the chance to find out if he would have done the same.

"As you know, Mr. Granger is an authority on the lumber business, having left Granger Mills to join us in Hope Falls."

Mike puzzled over the ladies' pointed mention of Granger's pedigree. Perhaps they wanted a subtle reminder that they knew the business and wouldn't be taken advantage of. More likely, the mention of Granger's connections was a warning not to cause trouble.

Granger himself took over at this point. "Beyond industry standards, Hope Falls has high expectations and plans to pay well for its workers to meet them. We're offering each man a working wage of thirty dollars a month, less fifteen dollars room and board."

Aside from a few hushed whispers, men just nodded. New as he was to this side of the industry, even Mike understood this to be an excellent offer—practically engineers' wages. He'd known factory men paying fifteen dollars a month for a bunk and mediocre meals. For Miss Thompson's fare, they would have gladly shelled out more.

"Sleep on it. I'll be asking for your decision come morning." Granger most likely didn't want to hold up supper any longer.

"Is the girl still up for grabs?" one logger wanted to know. "Or is she hands-off for anyone who signs on and works for pay?"

Mike felt a surge of sympathy for the young Miss Thompson. Obviously the girl in question, she betrayed her discomfort by beginning to fidget. The fellow who asked if she was "up for grabs" needed a knock upside the head and a lesson in how to treat a lady.

"None of us was ever 'up for grabs.'" The girl's sister came to her rescue. "And to answer your question, nothing has changed save the addition of your wages. If you wish to woo a woman, you may still try, provided you remember to keep your hands to yourself."

"Y'all got no entertainment hereabouts." Someone's holler set off a fresh round of speculation. "When you gonna put up a saloon?"

Mike craned his neck for a clearer view of the idiot. Men like that needed watching. Sometimes they just needed to be steered in the right direction. Meanwhile, they needed to be steered clear of the women. Mike would start with the latter and pray for the former.

"Never." Naom—*Miss Higgins*, Mike caught himself—bristled like a stepped-on porcupine, every inch rigid with warning. She looked as though she knew precisely what "entertainment" was. Or, at the very least, she was thinking of the sort of saloon that served more than whiskey and cards. In short, exactly the sort of saloon most loggers wanted.

"Your wages are your own." She softened her approach slightly. "But no part of Hope Falls will become a venue for hard drinking, gambling, or anything else you wouldn't want to tell your mamas."

"While the ladies head back in the kitchen to bring out supper,"—Dunstan waited while the women dutifully filed out, staring down the audience and bearing a striking resemblance to the snarling cougar someone had suspended on the wall behind him—"I'll remind you that Hope Falls is a decent town, run by ladies. You will address them as such, or you'll be escorted aboard the next train."

"Ladies," snorted the man who said he'd stay for the food.

"*Ladies*," Mike growled back, ready to stick him on a train.

"What would you know about it?" his companion jeered. "You're what, a day old? Fresh off the train and thinking you know anybody?"

"I know you're not staying long." Mike pushed back his mug in case he needed to move quickly. "And I know a lady when I see one."

"What tipped you off to how proper they are? The britches?" He gave a knowing smirk. "Not that any of us are complaining about that privileged sight. No, it's the starched-up, skunk-haired one—"

Mike choked off the flow of bile by grabbing the man's grubby shirtfront and twisting. It tightened around the neck and gave Mike a good enough grip to haul the arrogant cuss off the bench. He got halfway through the diner before the other men realized what was going on. He almost made it to the door before they hit their feet.

A shadow slipped past him just before the room grew too small for Mike to move any farther. Surrounded by a dozen suddenly silent loggers, Mike didn't know if they were interfering on behalf of the wriggling idiot in his grasp or if they wanted to watch a fight.

The door creaked open, making heads swivel. There stood Granger, ushering them outside. In a whisper obviously not meant to carry back to the kitchen, he ordered: "Not in Evie's diner."

With that, the seas parted to let Mike haul his opponent into the evening light. Until he felt the cool breeze on his face, Mike didn't realize how hot his blood boiled. The men, now less quiet, filed out behind him and formed a much larger circle. An arena.

Mike abruptly realized he hadn't thought beyond evicting the foulmouthed fool from the diner, where the aspersions he cast on the ladies wouldn't do any further damage. He didn't plan on a fistfight and wouldn't engage in one to satisfy a blood-thirsty mob—unless of course the aforementioned fool forced him into it.

"What do you do with men who belong on the next train?" He addressed Granger, wondering whether the obvious leader of the

Hope Falls loggers had already needed to deal with this type of thing. Mike also noticed Dunstan picked up on the fracas and joined them.

"Depends." Granger planted his feet in the dirt, a little wider than his shoulders, and issued his first order. "Let him down now."

Mike's sudden release made the man stumble, even though he'd only been high enough to keep from bracing his heels. As soon as the man steadied himself, he swung a clumsy punch at Mike's midriff. Mike sidestepped him, wrapped his arm around the man's wrist, and flipped him on the ground. A wave of quickly hushed cheers followed.

"Never can trust a man who leads with a blind punch." With that, Bear Riordan established himself as Mike's supporter and ally.

"What about a man who grabs another by the collar at the supper table?" The whine came after Mike's opponent regained his feet.

"Depends," Granger repeated. He paused for a long moment as though thinking. "I didn't peg our new woodworker as a man with a temper. What did you say to make him decide you needed to leave town?"

"Told him he was too new to know anything about Hope Falls." His sullen response sparked Mike's anger anew, but that was mild compared to the outraged indignation of Volker Klumpf.

"Ja!" The German stomped forward in a succession of aggravated clomps. "Only after Strode said he knew our women were ladies!"

"You were saying the women weren't ladies?" Even in the dark, Granger's expression made the object of his inquisition gulp.

"I never said that. We all know better than to say that."

"His meaning was clear." Mike negated the coward's hasty disavowal. Repeating the comment about Miss Lyman's britches would be disrespectful, but he needed to make sure everyone understood the gravity of the situation. "He also insulted Miss Higgins's character and appearance and made suggestive remarks about Miss Lyman."

"Ja, that he did," Clump avowed with much vehement nodding.

"Oh, come on." Giving up his pretense of innocence, the man launched a counterattack. "We all know that proper women don't advertise to hire husbands, and real ladies wouldn't be here."

STRONG AND STUBBORN

Advertise to hire husbands? The ridiculous accusation hung in the air, waiting to be refuted. But no one corrected the man. Mike couldn't make a lick of sense out of the comment, but it dawned on him that none of the other men looked confused or even surprised.

"You're lucky Mr. Strode showed such restraint." Dunstan must have understood Mike's message. Decoy, picking up on his master's mood, bared his teeth at the object of Dunstan's displeasure.

"That settles things." Granger shared a glance with Bear Riordan, and the massive Irishman broke from the surrounding circle.

"To the privy then?" Bear waited for Granger's nod. Then he simply lowered his head, jammed his shoulder into the condemned man, shouldered him like a sack of potatoes, and strode into the night.

"Outhouse?" Mike grinned at the Hope Falls's detention cell.

With the excitement ended, dinner beckoned everyone back into the diner. His grumbling gut urged him to follow the crowd and find a seat, but his curiosity got the better of him. He waited until only Granger and Dunstan remained outside then asked what was on his mind. "Advertise to hire husbands? What was he talking about?"

"He doesn't know?" Dunstan asked Granger, sounding surprised.

"Tomorrow morning." Granger looked Mike over as though trying to discern something. "After breakfast. We have things to discuss."

"Mrs. Smythe spotted my dollhouse just before we left for Hope Falls. I had it brought down to the parlor for crating, and she caught sight of it." Lacey tilted her head. "Why do you ask?"

"She's commissioned me to make one for her." Naomi rubbed her temples. "I've never spoken with Mrs. Smythe about it. I didn't know she'd ever seen the Lyman Place miniature! But in the pile of mail today I found this. It's the 'second installment' payment because I didn't send back the first."

"Why didn't you tell me earlier this afternoon?" Lacey huffed as she scanned the missive. "And where's the first part then if this is the second?"

"I checked every piece of post—twice. It's not there. It's not as though a letter requesting a custom dollhouse would be difficult to find amid the ad responses." Naomi crumpled the remaining letter and fumed. "Draxley didn't just stop sending telegrams and distributing messages—he must have opened any that looked thick enough to have money enclosed. It's a wonder he didn't get his hands on the second letter and steal it, too!"

"Bad business all around." Evie scooted toward the head of her bed in order to make room for Lacey. With Mr. Lawson already ensconced in the study for the night, they couldn't converse freely in the adjoining parlor. Somehow Evie and Cora managed to find two small beds—practically hammocks topped with mattresses—in one of the abandoned houses of Hope Falls, so everyone crammed into their room.

"If Draxley did take Mrs. Smythe's first letter and steal the funds she enclosed, how will we be able to fill the order?" Cora eased herself beside Naomi, causing the bed to shift softly. "I mean, I know the second letter contains more money, but is it enough to even purchase the necessary supplies? What about the specialty pieces?"

"Mrs. Smythe paid well." *Very well.* Part of the reason Naomi hadn't been able to confide in Lacey that afternoon was her shock. Aside from the dawning horror of the situation, she simply hadn't been able to register such a large sum. Of course, she only received half of it, which created the current problem. "With God's help, a little ingenuity, and some hard work, I believe I could fully furnish a six-room dollhouse without overextending the amount."

"Then the timing is the only problem?" Lacey brightened. "Why don't you just have those specialty German pieces delivered directly to Mrs. Smythe since the passage to America already takes so long?"

"Because that's only part of the problem." Naomi smoothed the letter again. "I can't furnish a house that hasn't been built. With the advance funds she enclosed in the first letter, I would have been able to commission a master craftsman to devote his entire attention to this as a special order. Even then I would have needed to be working based on its dimensions until it arrived here."

"And now you don't have the money to commission the house." Evie considered for a moment. "What if we raised the money?"

"It's too late." Naomi pushed against the floor, making the bed sway. "The project would have been incredibly ambitious to begin with, and I've already lost two months! There's no time to find a craftsman, work out the project details, and pray he gets them right and ships it to me on time! Nor can I try to find a house that's already constructed—Mrs. Smythe has some specific requests here."

"What if you took away the distance?" Cora put down her foot and stopped the swaying. "What if you could speak to the craftsman, monitor the construction, and not waste time waiting for the shipping?"

"I suppose it might be possible." Too anxious to sit still, Naomi hopped up and began pacing the narrow space between the beds. "But even so, I couldn't pay a reasonable fee! This is highly skilled labor—artistry, really. Anything I could scrape together would be laughable at best, insulting at worst."

"But the Hope Falls sawmill can. As of tonight, all of the workers are paid by the company." Lacey beamed at Cora, who beamed back as though they shared a secret. "Including our new carpenter."

Mr. Strode. Naomi sank back onto the bed, overwhelmed at the prospect. "We hired him as a carpenter and joiner to help construct the mill. What makes you think he'd want to build a dollhouse?"

"What makes you think he wouldn't?" Evie grimaced. "Especially since the alternative is going to the woods and cutting down trees."

"That's more masculine." Naomi didn't even know why she was arguing. "The men accept that because he's working for the mill."

"The men will accept the way we decide to do things." Cora set her jaw, reminding everyone of her newfound determination to put Braden in his place. "Every man does the work he's contracted for."

"What about the work I'm responsible for?" Naomi needed to be fair. "Evie needs help with the cooking, and laundry doesn't wash itself."

"Remember, we've lost a good dozen—well, a bad dozen—men. We all know we can thank Mr. Strode for the removal of the latest bad egg." Evie grinned. "That means less work. So long as Lacey bakes the bread and we get a jump on things in the morning, I'll manage."

Cora set her bed swinging again, as though the motion helped sort her thoughts. "We never decided what I'd do once Braden no longer needed a nursemaid. I'll take over the laundry for a while. I don't mind washing our clothes, so long as the men continue to see to their own. Arla's been kind enough to take on their mending."

"Unless we're pushing you to take on a task you don't want." Lacey peered at her. "You seemed so happy while you transformed my old dollhouse, I just assumed you'd enjoy a fresh challenge."

"Yours was a labor of love," Naomi tried to explain. "And I loved working on it. But it was a hobby, tiny projects spaced out over years. This is entirely different, and I'm not at all certain I can finish in time. I'm hesitant to inflict such a close-looming deadline on anyone else—especially a man who's already working."

"Mr. Strode is waiting until Hope Falls is ready for a carpenter. Meanwhile, he's been hired on prospectus, and we're paying him a retainer for the time when he's needed." Lacey shrugged, oblivious to the way everyone was staring at her after all that business jargon. "What he does until that time is negotiable."

"What if Mr. Strode doesn't want to negotiate about this?" Naomi knew she was looking a gift horse in the mouth, but somehow she sensed a cavity looming ahead, waiting to swallow her hopes.

"Ask," Evie ordered. "You might be surprised by his reaction."

"All right." Naomi accepted that she wouldn't get much sleep that night thinking about this. "What's the worst that can happen?"

EIGHTEEN

Braden kept the smile glued to his face until the doctor departed, still marveling over the "incredible progress" his patient had made. Only when he was certain he was alone did Braden turn his head into one of his plethora of pillows and give the hoarse shout he'd been choking back for the past half hour. Even that small movement screamed through his knee, intensifying the already bone-deep ache.

"Breakfast!" If the smell of food weren't enough to turn his roiling stomach, the cheery voice of his erstwhile fiancée managed.

She exhibited the uncanny ability to show up whenever Braden felt his worst. It wasn't enough for Cora to see him trussed up like a Christmas goose, trapped in a doctor's bed. No, the contrary woman flitted into his room every time Braden was least able to be civil.

"Take it away," he groaned, not bothering to lift his head.

She plunked the tray on his side table with a jangle of abused dishes and cutlery. "You don't have to tell me to leave anymore, Braden. I already agreed to find my place in the world without you."

Still not daring to look up from his pillow, Braden blindly groped the air, searching for her. He found some sort of fabric and grabbed hold of it, keeping her at his side. Clinging in spite of a sudden onslaught of slaps and scolds, Braden focused on controlling his body. He focused on taking shallow, measured breaths until his stomach retreated to its customary position beneath his ribs. *Finally.* Braden looked up. He'd caught Cora by the apron strings.

The irony wasn't lost on Braden. Leading strings, they were

called, because mothers the world over bid their children hold on tight in crowded places. A boy began the transition to manhood only after Mother had "cut the leading strings." Independence meant not being tied down. But here Braden was, a grown man of twenty-six, clutching a woman's apron strings as though they were a lifeline.

Because they were. Those strings were his final, tenuous connection to Cora. If he let her storm from his room for the second time in as many days, he deserved to lose her. If he was honest, Braden would admit he already deserved to lose her. But he'd also admit he was a greedy bounder who wanted far more than he deserved.

So he held on, not letting go until Cora stopped twisting, turning, and generally flailing about like a fish caught on a hook. Her contortions traveled along the apron strings, through his clenched fist, and reverberated to his knee. By the time she stilled, Braden felt like the landed fish—green about the gills.

From Cora's expression once she got a good look at him, he probably looked as good as he felt. Without a word, she dipped a clean handkerchief in the washbasin, wrung it out, and draped it across his forehead. Then she set herself in the seat beside him.

"I came across the doctor in the hall, mumbling about your most excellent progress this morning." She didn't bother beating about the bush. "You're pushing yourself too far, too fast, Braden."

Yes—but still not far enough. Yesterday Granger sent the telegrams to set Dunstan's plan in motion. They'd dangled the bait; now it was only a matter of time before their prey came skulking into their trap. *I have to be out of this bed before they arrive.*

But first he needed to apologize to Cora and make things right.

"I didn't want *you* to go." He gritted his teeth, repositioning a few pillows to brace his back before gesturing toward the covered breakfast tray she'd brought. "My stomach couldn't take the smell."

"Is it still bothering you?" Cora shot the tray an apprehensive look, as though it might jump up and bite one of them at any moment.

"No, it's passed." He struggled to find the words then gave up and offered a simple confession. "I don't know how to apologize."

"Well, you never did, and I won't expect you to start over a bout of queasiness." Cora subtly nudged the tray farther from him. "It was my own fault for assuming you meant to expel both of us."

He'd managed to make a hash of that to make Cora begin offering apologies. Braden took a deep breath and tried again. "No, I don't blame you for making that assumption. I've tried to evict you often enough. I've been a first-rate cad since the day you arrived here."

"Worse than a cad." Her gaze became a green-and-blue battering ram. "A demanding, order-spewing bully entirely without feeling."

Her assessment stunned him. When the sense of shock began to recede, Braden recognized the familiar tingle of pricked pride. "However irritable I may have been, I am not without feelings."

Cora began hazarding guesses. "Entitlement? Anger? Jealousy? I'm curious, Braden, just what types of feelings you believe you've shown during the past two months. The only emotion I've seen that even remotely recalled the man I loved was your fear for Lacey two days ago. Even then, your self-indulgent petulance overshadowed all else."

"A man feels far more than he shows." Braden pushed aside his mounting indignation and tried to explain what he could. Even if she hadn't called him self-indulgent, he wouldn't discuss the shame, guilt, and despair he'd been battling. "You can't deny that I've been protective of you women and determined to get back on my feet."

"When your protective instincts devolve to the point where you threaten to call law enforcement and evict us from our own property—simply because it's legally held under your name—it's no longer admirable." She crossed her arms, closing herself off. "As for your will to recover, I wonder at the source behind your motivation."

"What do you mean?" Braden would've paced the room if he could. "Right now I can't protect any of you women. I can't do my part to start the sawmill. I'm all but useless as long as I lie here." It killed him to say it out loud, but how could she fail to understand?

"So you want to force everyone to do things your way. If Hope Falls remained a failure, no more than a ghost town, would your will be so strong?" She rose from her chair, looming over him like an avenging angel. "Would you push yourself half so hard if you weren't fighting to wrest control of Lyman Estates back from Lacey?"

Unwilling to lie, unable to explain his other reason for pushing so hard, Braden condensed his protests. "That's not fair."

"Tell me about it," Cora countered as she gathered up the tray and swept from the room. "But that, Braden, was *the wrong answer*."

$$\infty$$

"I have to make it right." Miss Higgins looked at him, green eyes alive with anxious hope. "Are you willing to help me, Mr. Strode?"

Mike didn't even have to think about it. For all he knew, he *couldn't* think. Not when she made him feel like the answer to all her problems. How could a man turn down Miss Higgins? "Absolutely."

She blinked, probably taken aback by the speed of his answer, then gave a low, husky laugh that sent tingles down his spine. "I suppose this means the others were right. They said it wouldn't hurt to ask you, but I never imagined you'd make it quite so easy."

"It's work." Mike shrugged it off, but something stuck in his craw. If it was just work, why did it bother him that the women encouraged her to ask? She made it sound as if the others knew he'd be easy to convince. Did he seem so susceptible to feminine wiles?

"You're frowning." She now wore the same expression. "Why?"

"I don't just agree to anything a pretty woman asks." Mike wouldn't go forward with her thinking he could be manipulated.

Once a woman glommed on to that notion, it was practically impossible to convince her otherwise. Hadn't it taken years of refusing to play her games before Leticia tired of trying? His late wife and her mother seemed to think they'd purchased him outright when he owed—and gave—nothing more than the protection of his name and his best efforts to fulfill the sacred vows they'd made.

He wouldn't let another woman think him so gullible a mark. Not even if she stood there, lovely and lush as the forests around them. Belatedly, he realized that he'd let her know he found her pretty.

But she'd already suspected as much—or at least her friends did. Or maybe they hadn't. *If not*, Mike winced, *they certainly will now.*

"It's simply a business proposition." The sparkle in her eyes seemed to say she liked being told she was pretty—even if in such a roundabout way. Her pleasure at the backhanded compliment made Mike relax a little. "Whatever your reasons, I'm grateful you agreed."

"I do have reasons!" Opportunity stared him straight in the face, and Mike had been too busy ogling her to notice until now. Here was his chance to secure a home for Luke. "One reason, really."

"Oh?" She pulled back, looking suddenly wary. "What's that?"

"My son." Praying that she'd understand, that his instincts about Miss Higgins were correct, Mike pressed on. "Luke. He's ten, and I came here hoping to find a good town where I could raise him." Suspicion softened then sharpened. "Is he with your wife?"

"No." Mike drew a breath. "Luke's in Texas with my sister, waiting for me to fetch him. My wife passed on a few months ago."

"Oh." A kaleidoscope of emotions rippled across her face, leaving behind any trace of the wariness. "I'm sorry for your loss."

"Thank you." He couldn't tell her not to worry, that he'd lost more on the day he married Leticia than on the day he buried her. "I was hoping I could work hard enough to make it worth you letting me bring Luke home with me—whenever you all think the time's right."

She probably didn't realize she was doing it, and probably no one else would have noticed, but Mike was looking hard enough to see her nibble on the inside of her lower lip while she thought it over.

"The thing is. . ." The silence—and the nibbling—unmanned him. The thought that he'd blown his chance made him begin babbling. "Luke's already started learning carpentry. I haven't had a chance to show him much in the way of joinery, but he has the makings of a fine apprentice. I understood there wasn't a place for him while I was working with the lumbermen, but I figured it'd be easier to keep an eye on him once construction began. He'd even come in handy."

"All right." Her cool words cut across his frenzied speech.

For a second all he could do was stare at her. "All right?"

"Yes, Mr. Strode. You've agreed to help me with a very difficult and detailed project, sure to consume all of your time for weeks to come. In return for your assistance, your skill, and the heartwarming love you exhibit for your son, you may bring Luke to Hope Falls." She paused for a moment. "I'll have to discuss timing with the others, but it won't be long before you'll need to make a trip for supplies. I would hope you could pick him up then."

Mike wanted to kiss her, but all he could do was nod. "If you're willing to let him watch and try his hand at some of the more minor detailing, it would even be a good chance for him to learn."

"Not to sound desperate, but I'm happy for any help I can get." She smiled and extended one delicate hand. "Do we have a deal?"

He wrapped his entire hand around her soft one. "Deal."

NINETEEN

Y ou're not keeping up your end of our agreement," Cora chided, steering the ponderously pregnant Arla back to the bentwood chair they'd brought outside for her to use. "You need to take it easy."

"Seems as though I've done nothing in days." Arla Nash grudgingly allowed herself to be settled into the seat, legs up on a stool.

Cora scoffed. "You're working twenty-four hours a day!"

"Nonsense." Arla picked up her needle and began stabbing stitches into another of a dishearteningly long parade of holey socks. "You'd feel the same way, sitting around day in and day out. I'm not accomplishing a blessed thing, resting on my laurels!"

"Do you think setting hens don't accomplish anything?" Cora intentionally chose Arla's favorite animals in the modest Hope Falls menagerie. "Because you're doing the same thing—the human way."

"I'm incubating?" Her friend put down the sock and laughed until her shoulders shook. "That's one way of looking at it. But I must say that this isn't turning out at all the way I envisioned."

"Although we're happy to have you, you know we weren't informed of your situation when we hired your brother." Cora hadn't quite managed to forgive Mr. Lawson for packing his newly widowed, heavily pregnant sister out to the wilderness for the sake of a mere job.

"It was an unpleasant shock when my brother told me we needed to move. I did think he could have left me back in the city to mind the house, but he refused to leave me alone." Arla sighed. "I dared ask him whether he might forgo this particular opportunity and await the next, but he's anxious to secure a future for the baby. I'm afraid Mr. Nash didn't leave us much after the estate settled."

"I understand." Some of Cora's resentment toward the engineer ebbed away. "We went through the same thing when Papa died. Evie had to sell the house after the money ran out. Then she worked her fingers to the bone setting up her diner and keeping us going."

"We are blessed in our siblings." Arla stroked her stomach fondly, her voice catching slightly. "I always hoped to have at least two children, so neither one would ever have to be alone."

"You never know." Cora finished pinning the last of the freshly washed garments across the clothesline and steeled herself to start another batch. It never ceased to amaze her how much filth their skirts collected out here—and that wasn't even counting Lacey's mining getup. "There might still be another man for you."

Even as she spoke the words to Arla, Cora wondered if they'd prove true for herself. Having found the right man and lost him, was it possible to love another in the same way? Or was a second love doomed to play second fiddle to a memory, always second best?

"I hope so," Arla murmured. "Even if it seems disloyal to Mr. Nash's memory, no woman wants to be alone for a lifetime."

"No." Cora agreed, plunging her paddle into the steaming vat of wash water. Her hair frizzled instantly. "We all hope to find love."

"Since everyone needs love"—Arla started sticking her needle into the fabric again—"you'd think it would be easy to find."

"You'd think so," Cora agreed, watching her clean, soapy water turn gray, then brown, then blackish. It had been the same with Braden. They'd been so clearly, purely in love. But time changed things, tragedies muddied the waters, and it took a long time for the filth to fall away. If you were patient, things settled. If you kept agitating the water, things never cleared up, never improved.

If someone asked about Braden, Cora wouldn't be able to say whether she was letting things settle or trying to stir things up. Maybe, just maybe, it was better to let Braden decide for himself.

Decision to help Miss Higgins made, the deal to bring Luke home to Hope Falls in place, and the troublesome fool still locked away in the privy, Mike sat down feeling better than he had in months. It didn't hurt that the table all but vanished beneath a bountiful breakfast.

The fare wasn't fancy or unexpected like those Scotch eggs. Still, Mike never met a man who'd turn down hot coffee with a heaping helping of fluffy flapjacks smothered with butter and syrup. Even the cougar he'd noticed before looked less like he was snarling down at the diners and more like he might be licking his chops.

Riordan and Clump made for good company at the table. They knew that the time for talking was after a man filled his stomach. They ate in companionable silence until they'd done justice to the food. For the first time, Mike didn't pepper them with questions; he was saving those for his meeting with Granger later that morning.

Mike was also loathe to lose the newfound camaraderie of his logging team. These men moved from working at his side to backing him last night. Mike had no doubts they would've fought alongside him if needed, the sort of friendship usually forged by years. How could he explain that he wouldn't be working with them much longer?

"I'm going to borrow Mike for a bit." Granger clapped a hand on his shoulder and addressed Bear. "He'll join you at the worksite."

With that, Mike didn't need to explain anything. Bear nodded, got up, and made his way out the door. Clump followed, one of the last of the men trickling into the bright sunlight of a workday. In almost no time at all, Mike and Granger sat alone in the diner.

"There've been a few changes since I arranged this meeting. You've already spoken with Miss Higgins, so you know the bind she's in." Granger poured a cup of coffee and eyed Mike through the steam. "And since I've spoken with Miss Higgins, I know about your son."

It seemed to Mike that the room shifted. Everything around him came into sharper focus. In his conversation with Miss Higgins, he'd revealed his vulnerability because requesting her assistance in return for his own made for an even trade. Now Mike needed Granger's agreement to finalize the bargain—a different dynamic.

Alert but not allowing himself to be anxious, Mike waited. He waited while Granger took a few slugs of coffee. He waited and fought off thoughts about what the man before him might want. He waited until Granger realized he'd go right on waiting for however long it took for the other man to explain what he wanted.

"Dunstan does the same thing." Granger scratched his jaw. "Waits out a conversation so the other man spills his guts."

Mike raised a brow and drank more coffee to hide his grin. He could be compared to far worse than a man like Dunstan. The hunter didn't seem to speak much, but he commanded respect when he did.

"Most men would've told me about their boy, I expect. Tried to convince me what a good lad he is and how he wouldn't cause any trouble." Granger tilted his head. "Why aren't you convincing me?"

"I don't like it when people go on and on about their progeny, so I try not to inflict my parental pride on others." Mike saw the smile but couldn't relax yet. "Ask questions. I'll answer them."

"Why didn't you mention the boy when you first got here?"

"When would I have worked it into the conversation?" Mike shook his head. "From where I stand, Hope Falls sets a fast pace."

"From where I stand, you don't have trouble keeping up. When you aren't already a step or two behind, that is." Granger pulled a folded newspaper from his pocket and laid it on the table. "You're the only man in town who hasn't read this—one of very few who didn't find their way to Hope Falls because of it." He pushed the paper to the middle of the table, but kept it anchored beneath his hand.

"I was warned this is a strange place, but I'm not sure I follow what you mean." Mike had never held a more convoluted conversation in his life. They were no longer talking about him helping Miss Higgins or determining whether or not Luke was welcome. Mike's fingers itched to snatch the paper and make sense of things.

"This paper holds an unexpected answer to some of your

questions about the way we do things," Granger advised. "But since it didn't bring you all the way out here, I want to know what did."

In spite of the gallons of coffee Mike downed that morning, his mouth went dry. He'd told Granger to ask his questions, and now he was honor bound to answer. A couple of dry swallows bought him time.

"You read the telegram." He croaked out the most honest answer he could give. "I needed work, and I was told I'd find it here."

"A man with your skill set can, if you'll forgive the pun, make a place for himself just about anywhere." Granger flattened his palm against the paper and leaned forward. "It makes me wonder why you'd decide to raise a child near the dangers of a new sawmill."

"Boys can find danger wherever they're raised," Mike hedged. "Hope Falls seems as good a place as any—and better than most."

"I'm not saying it's not a good place to find yourself—but I'd be a fool if I didn't know it's a better place to *lose* yourself." The steely glint in his gaze belied his wordplay. "So why are you here?"

"For Luke." That gallon of coffee sloshed bitterly in Mike's stomach. He'd prepared to answer a few questions, but he hadn't reckoned on Granger's astute appraisal of his situation. He made his message clear: either trot out an explanation or ride out of town.

"Most would say I married above myself." Mike forbore to mention that he didn't agree with the general consensus about his bride. "Leticia was an only child. Now that she passed on, my in-laws demanded they be allowed to raise their only grandson."

"And you won't fork him over." It wasn't a question, though Granger looked curious. "I can understand that. What I don't understand is why your in-laws thought they could force the issue."

Again, Granger didn't ask. Mike still answered. "They can't."

"They shouldn't," he corrected. "But I've more than my fair share of experience with wealthy flea-brains who think money gets them whatever they want." Granger paused. "It usually does."

"I know." Mike sucked in a breath. "You're right about the reason I chose to come here. I'm doing my best to get us lost."

"Don't let anybody else find out." Granger took his hand away from the paper. "Go ahead and read it. You'll find it interesting, but I don't think it'll make you change your mind about staying."

"It won't." His relief was so intense, he didn't grab the paper. Mike realized his mistake when Granger picked it up again.

"Probably shouldn't say this. . ." The other man tapped the paper against his palm as though deciding whether or not to pass it over. In the end, he shoved it toward Mike. "But I'm saying it anyway. Don't let this change your mind about Miss Higgins either."

"What?" Mike turned around so fast he worked out a kink in his neck that'd been pestering him since yesterday. It was just in time to see Granger slap his hat on his head and walk through the door.

"What does this have to do with Miss Higgins?" Knowing there was no one to hear him ask, he muttered the question and started scanning the newsprint. The first page ran an article about trains, but a quick read turned up nothing out of the ordinary. On the other side, columns of classifieds paraded up and down, jostling against each other all the way across the page. Mike turned back to the first page to make sure he hadn't missed anything important. *Nope.*

A prickle of unease raised the hairs on the back of his neck. Mike carefully turned the thin paper over again, looking closer at the jumble of advertisements. A single ad took up more space than any three, demanding attention from the bottom third of the page.

Wanted:
3 men, ages 24–35.
Must be God-fearing, healthy, hardworking single men
with minimum of 3 years logging experience.
Object: Marriage and joint ownership of sawmill.
Reply to the Hope Falls, Colorado, postmaster by May 17.

Mike read the thing through three times before laying it back atop the table. Only then did he realize he'd been gripping the news sheet hard enough to poke his thumb clear through the page. He propped his feet against the bench across from him and leaned his head against the wall, trying to take in the irony of his situation.

Trying to outrun a past where he'd married for money, Mike stumbled upon the only town in all of history where the women were trying to hire husbands. It was his own mistake, multiplied by three and magnified by the men who came to "apply" for the position. All his questions, the unexplained oddities of Hope Falls, and the bits and pieces he'd seen firsthand joined together with what he'd read.

Now he understood why the men answered to the women. It explained why men worked for room and board to start. It even made sense that they began to offer wages when, as one man put it, there was only one more "girl up for grabs." The odds of winning a wife had changed. After all, Granger claimed Miss Thompson, and then Miss Lyman chose Dunstan, leaving only the youngest of the three without a fiancé. The poor girl was about to be deluged with would-be suitors.

The only thing the ad didn't explain was why Granger thought it would change Mike's opinion of Miss Higgins. Did he think Mike would think less of her for not joining the other three in a husband hunt?

Mike snorted. If anything, it reassured him that the woman he'd agreed to spend months working alongside wasn't a mercenary female desperate to nab a husband. It probably took great strength of character to withstand her friends' pleas and refuse to join them in this farcical scheme. How could this advertisement make him think less of Miss Naomi Higgins? *If anything*, Mike decided as he shoved the distasteful thing deep in his pocket, *I admire her more than ever.*

TWENTY

He thinks I'm pretty. No matter how Naomi tried to push the inane thought aside, it kept bubbling to the surface of her thoughts. All day yesterday, like a tune she couldn't get out of her mind, the phrase hummed in her head. *Mr. Strode thinks I'm pretty. Me. . .pretty!*

It was distracting. It made her smile. It would have been downright mortifying if anyone suspected her of such foolishness. Of course, no one caught on. Naomi was far too sensible for such girlish foibles. At least that's what she sternly reminded herself when she woke up with the chipper refrain ringing in her ears.

Unfortunately, Naomi found her own reprimands surprisingly ineffective. It was, to say the least, disconcerting to be ignored by one's own self. Though it did explain why Lacey found it so easy to disregard Naomi's sage advice—there were things a woman's heart found far more interesting than plain, old-fashioned common sense!

And Mr. Michael Strode is one of them. Little wonder she'd found the notion of working with him so unsettling; those qualms were the last vestiges of her instinct for self-preservation. They must have been the last. They'd gone quiet since the moment Mr. Strode told her, in a roundabout way, that he found her attractive.

Naomi knew how dangerous this was. She knew she shouldn't entertain the hope, not even for the briefest moment, that Mr. Strode might be interested in a more permanent sort of partnership. Because even if he indicated interest, Naomi couldn't allow things to progress beyond mutual regard. Newly widowed, Mr. Strode was trying to build a new life for himself and his son. *Far too fine a man*, Naomi lectured herself, *to overlook my checkered past.*

By the time she'd gotten through breakfast, she'd worked very hard to talk sense into herself. It didn't take Naomi long to figure out that she'd fixated on the carpenter as an appealing alternative to her real suitors. With that sobering realization, she managed to replace the happy little "he thinks I'm pretty" hum with a "he deserves better" refrain. It sounded as sprightly as a dirge.

"Granger tells me you're ready to get started." A deep voice broke through the plodding rhythm of her new favorite dirge.

"If there's nothing to interfere." Naomi made it a point to sound brisk and businesslike, but couldn't help returning his smile.

"It's all been arranged on this end," he assured her. "I didn't bring my toolbox, but I can fetch it in a jiffy if it's needed."

Naomi gave a rueful shake of her head. "I'm afraid things aren't nearly so neatly arranged on my end. The furthest I've planned is to set up a work space. Beyond that, I'll need to do some digging to find my own materials so we can create a scale for the project."

"We get a workshop?" Mr. Strode's eyes sparkled like a child's who spied a bulging Christmas stocking with his name. "Lead on."

"First, you'll need to lower your expectations." She couldn't help but laugh, picturing his reaction to what lay ahead. With that, she took him to the short row of houses behind the diner, pausing at the threshold of the second building. "This is where we'll work."

The door swung open to reveal a modest-sized room adorned with a block table, two chairs, and a questionable-looking old pipe stove. The dirt floor had been hard packed by the miners who'd lived there and would be fairly easy to sweep clean. Three windows, covered with cloth to keep out the elements, let in plenty of light.

"Strong light," Mr. Strode approved, making a quick circuit around the space. "We'll need another two tables—work space for each of us and a display station for completed or in-progress pieces. If none are available, I can put a pair together this afternoon."

"That won't be necessary." Naomi felt her shoulders relax and realized she'd been anxious for his approval. "Tables I can provide, but we're going to have to sort through some things before we clear them off. Things have been so busy since we got here. Anything we didn't immediately need got shoved into storage."

"It doesn't take long to clear a table," he assured her in the confident voice of a man who hasn't seen the task ahead of him. After Naomi opened the house next door, he revised his opinion.

A low whistle escaped Mr. Strode. "I believe I spoke too soon."

"How could you know?" Naomi asked, torn between amusement and resignation as they stood on the threshold. Boxes and bags, crates and trunks, luggage of all sizes crowded from floor to rafters, with a few pieces of furniture thrown in to keep things interesting. "Clearing off a table is one thing, but I didn't know how to explain that we'd have to clear out a house to get to the tables first."

"I see." Mr. Strode looked up, looked down, ducked his head through the door, and swiftly pulled it back. "Not to criticize the plan, but it would be less hassle for me to build the tables."

Naomi shuffled closer to the door and glanced at the chaos within. Like the sun, it was best seen in glimpses. Otherwise its full power made a person close their eyes and turn away. Even in small doses, it was overwhelming to take in the sheer mass within.

"It's worse than I remembered," she admitted. For a fleeting moment, she wondered whether Lacey had managed to organize the colossal mess of the mercantile by ferrying merchandise here. But another quick glimpse revealed nothing from the storeroom. "When we were packing back in Charleston, everything seemed important. If you left something behind, it might take weeks to order a replacement."

"So instead you borrowed a page from Noah and brought two?"

"No." The giggle escaped before Naomi could even try to stop it, but it erased Mr. Strode's dawning chagrin at his outspokenness. "Between the four of us, we probably brought along a few spares."

"When you put it that way,"—he braved the threshold and squeezed inside—"it doesn't seem so bad, for four women."

"Er. . ." Naomi wondered if discretion wasn't the best course of action but decided in favor of full disclosure—some of her things might have been misplaced, and she didn't want to go through explanations. "All things being equal, how about two out of four?"

He eyed her incredulously. "You mean to say there's *more?*"

"The next house." Naomi gestured to the right, where an almost identical structure stood. Doors shut, it looked unprepossessing.

"The whole house? Another like this?" He sounded faintly awed, but Naomi found it encouraging that he didn't just sound faint. The prospect of going through everything made her think longingly of a nap. How must he feel, faced with the task of hauling it all out?

"We made some attempt to categorize things," she soothed. "So we won't tackle the second house. My supplies should all be here."

"So we're going in after more than just the tables." Mr. Strode squared his shoulders and eyed the Herculean challenge ahead. "I'll haul out whatever you want, so long as you don't expect me to open things up. It wouldn't be right to go through ladies' luggage."

"That's fine, since I'm not even sure what I'll find!"

Five hours and countless boxes later, Mike began to suspect this was retribution for his thoughts on how building a dollhouse would be easier on his back. At the start, he figured it looked like there were more things crammed inside than there really were because the eye couldn't focus on individual pieces. He'd been wrong.

The farther he burrowed into Miss Higgins's storage, the more he marveled at how much a one-room structure could hold. He'd practically built a fort out of the pieces she immediately rejected—and not the size fort he'd hammered together for Luke back home. The saving grace of that pile was Miss Higgins's offhand remark that she needn't look through them—they all belonged to Miss Lyman.

If Mike had to slap a ratio on it, he'd say that two-thirds of the contents of the house went to the fort. In comparison, the heaps surrounding Miss Higgins seemed downright reasonable—especially since they owed most of their bulk to two tables and a small shelf.

"Why don't I tote these over to the workshop and out of your way?" Mike gestured toward the shelf and one of the tables. The other table made itself useful as a type of sorting station.

"Yes, let's do that." She snapped shut the satchel she'd been looking through and added it to the heap nearest Miss Lyman's fort. "If you'll take the table, I'll get the shelf—it's not heavy."

"Spruce is surprisingly light," Mike agreed. In general, he wouldn't want a woman lifting any furniture, but he was learning that the women of Hope Falls were a determined and capable breed. He'd save his protests in case she tried to move something heavy.

"Is that why?" She slid her hands beneath a shelf and lifted without much effort. "It's surprisingly sturdy without being dense."

"Yep." He shouldered the door open and set down the table, unable to hold the door open for her if she went through first. "You'll find a lot of crates, ladders, and ship masts made from it."

"I never knew." She tucked the shelf into a corner and smoothed her apron. "As part owner in a prospective sawmill, I suppose I'll need to brush up on the types of wood and what they're used for."

"Start with the softwoods," he suggested. "Pine, spruce, fir, and even cedar grow hereabouts, and that's what you'll be milling."

It was a novel experience, talking business with a woman. Or rather, talking business with an *interested* woman. Mike thought of all the times he'd tried to share something of his craft with Leticia. She waved him away, refusing to hear about "trade." Wasn't it enough that she allowed Luke to come home covered in sawdust?

"They're called softwood?" Miss Higgins's astonished query amused him. "All things considered, isn't that a bit of a misnomer?"

He shrugged. "It's a classification based on the tree itself. Evergreens are generally less dense than trees that shed their leaves. They grow faster, so the layers aren't as compacted."

"How fascinating." Eyes alight with interest, *she* was fascinating. "If you don't mind, I'd like to learn more as we work."

"It would be my pleasure." Mike couldn't remember a time when he meant it more. "I'm not the sort who requires silence to work."

"But you do require sustenance." Miss Higgins squinted at the sky when they exited the building. "It looks about time for lunch."

"I'll never turn down a good meal." Mike happily followed her to the diner, where a medley of smells made his mouth water.

"Oh!" Miss Higgins held up a finger and backed toward the door. "I'll be right back. I forgot something!" With that, she was gone.

"Strode." Until Dunstan's greeting, Mike didn't notice him. Like any good hunter, he had a way of blending into the shadows.

"Dunstan." Mike joined him, taking a seat nearest the swinging kitchen doors. He avoided the man's injured side, where Decoy hunched beneath the table. "How goes it?"

"I'm trussed tighter than a turkey," he grunted. They lapsed into companionable silence for a moment before Dunstan added, "Don't remember if I thanked you for helping haul me out of the mine."

"Don't mention it." Mike watched as the other man dug around in his pocket and pulled out a new knife sheath of tooled leather. Mike accepted the gift with a nod of recognition but no words. Neither one of them wanted to talk about what happened to his old one.

Miss Higgins bustled back in, clutching a grubby lump of cloth trailing a mangled set of ribbons. She paused for a moment to look around the room, apparently satisfied to see no one but the men. Then her eyes widened—she'd caught sight of the massive wolfhound curled up under the table.

"Does Evie know he's here?" Her murmur scarcely made it across the room.

"Yep. Miss Thompson says he's earned a place—just not at mealtimes." Dunstan reached down to scratch between Decoy's ears. "And not in the kitchen. The other women are in there now."

Mike thought he heard her mumble "excellent" beneath her breath as she crossed the room and came to a halt in front of the mounted cougar. He watched as she gave the cat a considering glance, set down her bedraggled bundle, and began tugging at one of the benches. Before Mike could offer to help, she'd worked the bench closer to the wall and climbed up. She looked quite pleased with herself until she realized she couldn't reach the thing she'd set on the table.

❧

"It's the hat." Dunstan sounded as though he was trying to hold back his laughter—probably because it made his ribs hurt.

"Yes it is." Naomi held a finger to her lips, signaling him to hush. She wanted to get things in place before Lacey decided to investigate. Unfortunately she'd hit a snag; now that she could reach the cougar, Naomi couldn't stretch far enough to get the hat!

"It's a hat?" Mr. Strode sounded as though he had doubts about that, but Naomi forgave him since he was kind enough to pass it up. He'd see that it was a hat as soon as she got the thing situated.

Only now that she had her hat in hand, so to speak, she couldn't decide quite how to place it. Too far back and it wouldn't make enough of an impact, but the ears presented another problem entirely. No matter how she tried, Naomi couldn't further squish the already-squashed accessory to fit between the cougar's ears. Nor would it balance atop the furry tufts. The more Naomi failed, the more she imagined the great cat was laughing at her paltry efforts.

Until she pulled a packet of hairpins from her apron pocket. Jabbing hairpins into place, Naomi discovered, was far easier when the subject of the primping couldn't feel anything. In almost no time at all, she'd anchored the hat at a jaunty angle, with one ear artistically uncovered. As a finishing touch, she tied a large bow beneath its hairy chin. Then she hopped down to survey the results.

"Please forgive my earlier skepticism," Mr. Strode apologized. "I failed to consider your superior knowledge of feminine frippery."

"Obviously." Naomi swallowed a snigger at the sight. Lacey's prized pink hat, now squashed and stained almost beyond recognition, listed drunkenly atop the snarling beast. Tattered ribbons dangled limply over one eye to tangle in its whiskers. It was perfect—especially since the cougar faced across from the Hats Off to the Chef sign

Evie carted clear from Charleston.

"I suspect there's a good reason Dunstan's got the giggles?"

"Sure is." Dunstan stopped chuckling. "But I don't giggle."

"Who has the giggles?" Lacey popped through the swinging kitchen doors, caught sight of the newly adorned cougar, and froze. Slowly, as if seeking something lost, she smoothed back her hair. "My hat. . ." She turned to Dunstan to demand, "You went back for it?"

"Later that night." Suddenly the hunter looked uncomfortable. "You tried so hard to retrieve it, and then you said that thing about how a gentleman would pick it up. . .so I went and picked it up."

"Why didn't you tell me?" Lacey's mushy, in-love-with-a-man-who-saved-my-hat expression changed. "Why didn't you give it back?"

"I couldn't very well waltz up to you and present the thing on a silver platter, so I shoved it in one of those rooms you had filled with stuff." Defensive and sheepish, Dunstan glowered. "You were bound and determined to run me out of Hope Falls. Remember?"

"What's all the commotion in here?" Evie and Cora joined them. Cora gasped. "What on earth have you done to that poor cougar?"

"Don't look at me." Lacey held her hands up. "I just shot it."

"I found the hat when Mr. Strode and I started sorting through luggage, trying to unearth my supplies." Naomi tried not to look too pleased with herself. "I wanted to display it in honor of your engagement and decided the cougar deserved to be part of it."

"Why?" Mr. Strode's baffled query reminded her that he didn't know the story behind the cougar or its significance to Lacey.

"I met Lacey when she decided to go for a walk in the woods. Alone." Dunstan threw his fiancée a pointed glance. "Granger warned me that the women needed looking after, but I didn't expect to find a cougar stalking her. It must've been the fluttering ribbons."

"Which is why I think the hat belongs right where I put it," Naomi finished. Then she thought better of it. "If Lacey agrees."

"Well. . ." Lacey's smile flickered, and she admitted, "I certainly won't ever be able to wear it again. But it was my favorite hat. I hate to see it looking so sad and frumpy—cougar notwithstanding."

"Try to stop thinking of it as a ruined hat," Evie suggested. "Instead, why don't you see it as a one-of-a-kind souvenir?"

"Of what?" Lacey's brow furrowed. "A souvenir of what?"

"Of one of the best days of your life." Naomi tried to keep the wistfulness from her tone. "The day you finally met your match."

TWENTY-ONE

Is this the one you've been looking for?" Mike asked after he'd brought Miss Higgins back into the storage area. To the very back, a three-foot-square crate crouched atop a lacquered cabinet.

"What do you mean, what I've been looking for?" She moved to his side, the better to see around him. "I've been looking for a lot of things today, and I've found very nearly all of—oh!" Whatever else she'd meant to say was lost in a soft exhalation of happiness.

Mike tried not to think about how much he liked hearing her go all breathy. "There's something you've been waiting for. All day yesterday and all day today you've looked up every time I've stepped through the door. You check what I'm carrying, sometimes shake your head, and almost always go right back to whatever you're sorting."

He didn't add that he liked the way she looked up, eyes alight with expectation, every time he passed through the door. He didn't tell her that what kept him hauling things out of this one-room house was the chance that any item might be the thing she hoped for. He wanted to see her face when he carried it to her. But since that mysterious item happened to be huge, heavy, and stamped on every side with the word FRAGILE, Mike settled for that sweet little sigh.

"It's the dollhouse!" She turned to him, eyes shining. "The replica of Lyman Place that I restored and furnished for Lacey."

"The one that impressed the lady so much she hired you to make another one?" Curiosity getting the better of him, Mike started looking around for the crowbar he'd barely used this whole time.

"One and the same," she confirmed. "I'll go get Granger so the two of you can transfer it to the workshop. We'll open it there."

With a swish of her skirts, she all but ran from the room, barely giving Mike enough time to dig up his missing crowbar before she returned with Granger in tow. And Miss Lyman, and the two Miss Thompsons, and a woman who looked ready to give birth any moment. Mike couldn't recall having ever seen her before, and he was pretty sure there could only be one woman in Hope Falls expecting a child.

Actually, until two minutes ago, he'd been fairly sure there were no women in Hope Falls who were expecting a child. So maybe, Mike decided, he needed to stop making assumptions and get to his side of the crate. Granger already stationed himself on the far end.

Once in position, Mike waited until Miss Higgins herded the rest of the women outside and out of the way. Then he and Granger lifted the crate—which wasn't as heavy as Mike first thought, but unwieldy enough to require two men—and half shuffled, half walked it over to the workshop next door. They hadn't set it down before Miss Higgins bustled in, brandishing his crowbar and directing them to set the crate atop a console table she'd tucked into the far corner.

"Thank you." Mike snagged the crowbar when she turned to speak with one of the women currently congregating near the entrance.

In a few minutes, he removed the top panel and pried off the front piece to reveal. . .cotton batting. With him supporting the house from the bottom, Granger eased what remained of the crate to the floor. Mike offered Miss Higgins his knife when she drew close, rewarded for his efforts when her fingers brushed against his.

After a few slight tugs to pull the packing away, she began slicing open the cotton, letting it fall like snow and drape around the house. When she stood back, she revealed an astonishing replica of a Georgian brick home, complete with two faux marble pillars bracing the architrave above the door. From dormer window to gable to mullioned windows, they'd executed every detail impeccably.

"Oh." Miss Lyman's hand went to her throat. "Do you know I'd forgotten how beautiful Lyman Place is? How many memories it held. . ."

"Memories can be kept forever, but you can only live in one place at a time." Miss Thompson gave her a quick hug. "Better to choose the people we love than hold on to a place we once lived."

"You're so blessed you could bring Lyman Place with you!" The younger Miss Thompson brought the focus back to the dollhouse.

"Yes." Miss Lyman straightened her shoulders and moved toward the table. She touched the side of the structure, and with a little pressure, it turned on the table. "My home away from home. I'm so glad I didn't let you talk me out of bringing this, Naomi!"

"What?" Mike tore his gaze away from the model, which he surmised revolved on a sort of broad turntable, to stare at Miss Higgins. The lovingly crafted details evident on the exterior of the house would surely pale in comparison to the loving attention she'd lavished on the rooms within. The idea that someone would willingly abandon such a masterwork, an unquestionable labor of love, boggled his mind. He had to know. . . . "Why would you ever leave this behind?"

"How quickly you forget the mountain you moved to reach this crate! With so much to oversee already, I didn't want Lacey to bring along something so large and difficult simply to spare my feelings."

Her feelings were reason enough, but Mike didn't care what motivated Miss Lyman to bring the thing. He was just glad that she had. At that point, the women clustered around the table, pulling tiny wooden boxes lined with more cotton out of every single room. Within the boxes, Mike saw, lay the furniture and frilly bits females used to cover perfectly good hardwood floors, mantels, and walls. Feminine exclamations of delight accompanied the excavation of each room's box, driving Mike back to the storage next door.

On his way he noticed that Granger was nowhere in sight. No fool, the head of the logging operation skedaddled once he finished the heavy lifting. That left Mike with nothing but time on his hands and little left to go through. Most of the room had been emptied—he'd carted Miss Lyman's possessions to a separate building and carefully kept everything Miss Higgins already went through off to one side. By now there wasn't much left, aside from the lacquered cabinet that he'd found supporting the dollhouse.

It sat on squat little cabriole legs, oddly fashioned of mahogany inlaid with blond oak—an uncommon combination, since blond oak didn't echo the rich red tone of the mahogany. Then, too, the broad oval shape of the piece was perplexing. Square, rectangular, or even circular tables and cabinets were all common enough, but doors to fit an oval piece were difficult to execute evenly.

Upon closer examination, he saw that the design worked onto the top surface was a fancifully elaborate letter *N*. *For Naomi*. Mike traced it with his fingertips, more intrigued than ever now that he knew it didn't belong to Miss Lyman. Custom pieces like this became costly, and he wondered whether she'd commissioned the unique design or if someone special presented it to her as a gift.

Tiny golden hinges, expertly recessed along the back, tattled that the top lid lifted. Mike stopped tracing the letter, dropping his hands to run beneath the edge. There he found a tiny button. He pressed it before he could talk sense into himself, hearing the slight click of a released clasp before the lid angled upward.

A recessed shelf occupied the middle of the piece, but the design of the doors caught his attention. They were oval because they'd been designed to loosely bracket a chest of drawers. When he opened the doors, small spikes with slight bends at the tips thrust from each side. Tightly wound spools of sturdy thread and colorful embroidery floss, neatly ordered by shade, stood at attention beside more incongruous windings of wire, fishing line, and even twine.

Having identified the piece as a sewing cabinet, Mike wasn't surprised to see a small pair of silver scissors, a magnifying glass, and a matching slender tube for needles. Nor did the various yarn hooks and such give him pause. But there, neatly laid along the side, sat something very familiar—a combination tool set.

Mike knew what he'd find if he opened the case: a small-grade chisel, gouge, screwdriver, tack puller, gimlet, scratch awl, and brad awls in four different sizes—all hand-forged steel and all interchangeable for use with the included hardwood handle. Impressed with the quality and sure that the size would suit a young boy, he'd ordered one for Luke from the Montgomery Ward catalog a year ago.

Mike quietly closed the doors and lid of Naomi's workbox. His discoveries eradicated any doubts that this dollhouse was a whim, the sort of poorly planned project sure to end in disaster. Miss Higgins knew full well the complexities ahead, and she'd undertaken the challenge with the confidence of an experienced craftsman.

Craftswoman, Mike corrected. *One I'll enjoy working alongside.*

∞

"Do you think he'll like it?" Naomi scrutinized the parlor, reaching in to nudge one of the mantel candlesticks a smidge farther inward. "I know men don't usually think much of dolls and dollhouses, but we're going to be putting in long hours working on the next one."

While she didn't expect Mr. Strode to share her enthusiasm for all things miniscule and perfectly ordered, Naomi did hope he would find the work interesting. Nothing put a damper on her enjoyment more quickly than someone who didn't savor the process of creating the pieces or worked as though rushing through an unpleasant task.

"What's not to like?" Cora looked up from where she sat on the floor, cross-legged, the box for the ballroom half unpacked amid the cushion of her carefully smoothed skirts. "It's amazing!"

"I wish I had these full-sized!" Arla exclaimed. At some point, Granger had brought in a small rocking chair for Arla to sit comfortably amid them. She'd pulled it up to a table and was gingerly unwrapping the pieces that belonged to the nursery. Arla held up a wicker bassinet tiny enough to rock in the center of her open palm. "However did you make this, Naomi? It must have taken you days!"

Naomi laughed and admitted, "I cheated. It's a regular cradle made out of sandalwood with braided broom straws glued on top and painted. To tell the truth, it went quickly once I learned the straw bent more easily if I soaked it overnight in a bucket of water."

"Clever." Evie turned the house slightly so she could place the baking table in the center of the kitchen, offset so it didn't block the stove and scrub sink already situated against the back wall. She let out a little squeak of pleasure as she unwrapped the next bundle. Tiny rounds of cheese, braided loaves of bread, and a cone of sugar—complete with tiny wire tongs—spilled into her hand.

"You thought of everything!" From Evie, this was the highest compliment any kitchen could receive. "When you've finished your work for Mrs. Smythe, I might have to beg you to make me one of these model kitchens. I'd keep it on my shelves for inspiration!"

"I'd be honored." The thought that another project might follow this gave Naomi a surge of energy. There was something galvanizing about the idea that she could keep doing what she loved.

"We're the ones who should be honored." Lacey lifted the lid to the small hope chest she'd slipped against the end of a canopy bed. She smiled, tugging out a set of tiny washcloths for the washstand. "Isn't it awful, the way we become used to the blessings we're given and stop seeing them? Honestly, Naomi, it's as though years of familiarity blinded me to how special you made this Lyman Place."

"Working on this was a gift to myself as much as a present for you," Naomi confided. "I would have gone mad if I didn't find a way to keep myself busy!" Indeed, losing herself in a thousand tiny details kept her from losing herself in a quagmire of self-loathing and sorrow. When she felt powerless to fix the mistakes she'd made, Naomi found comfort in the tiny world she kept in perfect order.

# TWENTY-TWO

oday Braden would regain control of where he went and how he chose to spend his days. Just as soon as Doc stopped dilly-farting around.

"You want to run and get a protractor, Doc?" Braden asked after the doctor checked and rechecked his progress. He'd flexed his leg and brought it back one time too many, and Braden knew he couldn't conceal his discomfort for another round. *Time to move things along.*

Three months after the first mine collapse, and more than a week since the second, Braden finally reached the doctor-required forty-five-degree angle. He'd earned the right to get out of bed and into his wheeled chair—and the sooner, the better. He needed to gain proficiency in using the device. By the time the targets of his trap wandered into Hope Falls, Braden wanted to wheel like the wind.

"Congratulations, Mr. Lyman." Doc adjusted his spectacles and consulted his chart once again. "You have regained enough range of motion to progress to the wheeled chair. We'll attempt it tomorrow."

"Today." Braden couldn't wait another minute, much less a day.

"Tomorrow, Mr. Lyman." Doc eyed him with obvious disapproval.

"Listen." Braden grabbed the edge of his bed to keep from throwing the medical chart out the window. "We made a deal. You said I could get out of this bed once I bent my knee forty-five degrees."

"It would be best to be certain you can do so consistently. One more day gives me the assurance that you haven't overexerted your knee this morning in a misguided attempt to reach your goal." He tapped the chart. "Another day's rest won't do you any harm."

"Yes it will." Braden clamped his hand on the chart, trapping Doc's pencil and demanding his attention. "I've rested for more than three months. That's more than a hundred days of sitting in the same bed, staring at the same three walls, and slowly going stir-crazy. I met your criteria; I've earned the chance to leave this room. *Now.*"

Doc cleared his throat and tugged at his precious chart. When he realized Braden had no intention of letting go, he sighed. "Your determination is evident. I'll bring in the wheeled chair then."

The man staggered back when Braden released the chart then scurried from the room. Whether or not he'd return remained to be seen, but Braden's fears faded when he heard rolling wheels nearby.

Doc parked the contraption and poked his head through the door.

"Just a moment—the first attempt is always tricky. I'll need to find someone who can assist you while I hold the chair in place." He vanished almost before he finished, before Braden could protest.

He stared at the wicker chair, outfitted with wheels and a foot-rest, and groaned in frustration. So close. . .and he couldn't do a thing about it unless he wanted Doc to find him facedown on the floor. Braden considered trying anyway but decided that the foolishness of the maneuver might make Doc rescind his approval.

"Good morning." The new carpenter strolled into the room.

"Where's Granger?" Braden demanded. He would have settled for Dunstan if he hadn't been nursing his cracked ribs, but Braden recoiled at the idea of this stranger seeing him at his weakest. This was supposed to be a moment of triumph, not more humiliation!

"He just finished with the Bible reading, and now he's praying with a few of the men," the unsuitable replacement explained. "If you prefer, I'll go back and let him know you're waiting on him."

It's Sunday? Braden hadn't realized it, but that made today an even better choice. *The workers won't be going into the forest. I'll be able to spend the day with the whole town, same as any other man.*

"I can assure you,"—Doc took advantage of the short pause,

obviously still peeved over Braden's abuse of his medical chart—"that Mr. Lyman won't wish to wait a second longer than he has to."

"If it's all the same to you, Doc, I'd rather hear Mr. Lyman's decisions from Mr. Lyman himself." The carpenter crossed his arms—arms that were strong enough to get the job done. "He may not be back on his feet yet, but it's my understanding he still runs this town."

Good man, that new carpenter I hired. Doc looks like he swallowed a bullfrog. He couldn't resist rubbing salt in the wound.

"Doc's right—no sense in waiting." Braden scooted his rear as close to the edge of the bed as possible without falling off then angled slightly so he could slide into the chair. "Mr. . . ."

"Strode." The carpenter crossed the room and stood beside the bed.

"Right. Mr. Strode here can help as well as anyone." Braden gave a tight smile to the carpenter and a scowl to Doc, who hadn't taken the hint. "If you'll just move the chair into position?"

Begrudging but blessedly silent, Doc decided to cooperate. He maneuvered it through the doorway without any difficulty, passing the first hurdle. If the contraption hadn't fit, Braden didn't know whether his newfound approval of the carpenter would extend that far. Having a man help brace him as Braden slid into a chair was one thing; having a man carry him to it was a beast of another color.

Doc nudged the chair right up alongside the bed and employed the locking mechanism to keep the wheels from rolling, but the next step proved more difficult. When facing him, the footrest's extended "comfort design" proved too extended for Braden to reach the seat.

With the chair sideways, he could place his legs in the vehicle, but the armrests stopped him from sliding into the chair. Braden could grasp the far armrest, but the angle was too awkward to provide any stability. In the end, Braden had no choice but to allow Mr. Strode to help lift him into the chair while Doc held it steady—locking wheels or no, the thing could still tip over.

By the time they'd finished, Braden was breathing hard. He was unaccustomed to the exertion—his upper body weak from lack of use. The pain streaking from his overworked knee didn't help matters. Inspecting his new conveyance helped mask his weakness. Braden kept his head bent, peering at the footrest, the wheels, and even the braking mechanism until he could look the other men in the face.

"It's more comfortable than I expected." Braden found he particularly liked the way the back of the chair rose so high. When he wasn't in motion, he'd be able to lean back and relax. Outside.

"Press here to unlock the brake," Doc instructed. "But before you do, put your hands on the outer rim of the wheel and tell me whether it will be awkward for you to push forward. We can always add pillows to your seat and raise you an inch or two higher."

"Let's see." Braden loosely grasped the outer rim, sliding his hands forward and deciding that freedom felt like cool metal—a sharp contrast to overly warm cotton sheets. He pulled his arms back, placed his hands, and tried again. "I'm not scrunching up to grab the wheels, and it's not a reach either, so it fits right."

"Good." Doc demonstrated again how to set the brake, had Braden release it, reengage the mechanism, and release it again before he proclaimed himself satisfied. "Now, a few things before you begin."

"A few things?" Braden all but gaped at the man in disbelief. "Maybe you haven't noticed, Doc, but I've gone through a few things to put me in that bed, then a few more to work my way back out of it. A few more and I doubt I'll ever make it through the door!"

He let his exasperation show but kept things light. No way he'd let his deepest fears spring to life in front of an audience. They did enough damage where they were, whispering in the dark. *You'll never be whole. . .never be the man you were. . .never walk again. . .*

"Your impatience fails to impress me." Doc sounded full of bravado, but he made sure to keep the chart far from Braden's reach.

"Over three months since I've been out of this room. That's plenty patient." Braden gripped the wheels and pulled back, trying to gain room enough to angle past the doctor. One good shove and—

Nothing.

While he'd been plotting, Doc nudged a wooden wedge beneath the nearest wheel, effectively ending any forward motion. Nor could Braden reverse enough to maneuver around the blockage— his back was pressed against the bed. Even if his arms reached far enough to remove the object, he'd most likely tip himself over and wind up on the ground, helpless as a turtle turned on its shell.

"In light of your earlier. . ."—Doc took a moment to choose a descriptor—"*vehemence*, I suspected the doorstop might be needed."

Wings effectively clipped, Braden gritted his teeth and waited. He noticed that the carpenter had the good sense to make himself scarce. Braden wished he could do the same thing but would have to settle for not being further humiliated in front of an audience.

"As you've already begun to discover, you will need to rebuild your strength. This is the case not only for your legs but for your core, your back, and your arms." Doc gave him the hairy eye until Braden nodded. Then he kept going. "The effort required to maintain an upright position will be greater than you anticipate. The muscle and movement needed to propel the device will further fatigue you."

"I'm overwhelmed by all this encouragement," Braden quipped.

"You will rebuild your strength, but gradually. Thus, your initial forays will be brief." Doc held up a hand, forestalling protests. "This may be extended if you allow someone to assist you."

"You mean let someone push me like a babe in a pram?" Braden couldn't hide his contempt. *First the apron strings, now this.*

"Your choice, Mr. Lyman." Doc removed the doorstop. "Mr. Strode thought of laying planks of wood over the doorsteps so you can come and go more freely. I will check on you in two hours."

Braden didn't ask any more questions. He pushed himself straight through the door and took some time in the hallway to gauge how best to move. Swift, short pushes gave more speed but took more energy. Longer, smoother motions allowed for more control with less effort. Stopping was a matter of catching the wheels and pulling back, and this, too, was more effective with longer pushes.

When Braden was satisfied he wouldn't make a fool of himself with the town watching, he rolled onto the porch. There he stopped, wanting to imprint the moment in his memory. The sun hung low enough for its rays to reach down and warm the porch. Braden tilted his head into a welcoming breeze. It brushed across his face, cool as a mountain stream, crisp as pine needles, and whispering of freedom.

TWENTY-THREE

Trapped. No two ways about it. Nor three, or four, or five. Five men surrounded her when Naomi tried to sneak off to the workshop after breakfast. Five men who all wanted the pleasure of taking her for a walk. Five very determined men, none of whom would give way to the next, and none of whom broke ranks to let her escape—er, pass by.

Honestly, the one man Naomi wanted to speak with was just about the only man who didn't insist on the pleasure of her company. It was enough to make a woman disgruntled—especially since she knew, in all fairness, that this was a mess of her own making. This wasn't the first time Naomi had cause to regret placing the infamous ad, and she harbored an unpleasant suspicion it wouldn't be the last.

"Good weather for walking." Clump had headed her off at the door. If he weren't such a sweet, earnest fellow, Naomi might have blamed him for her current predicament. After all, he'd stood in the doorway—*still* stood in the doorway—effectively ending her exit.

"I'd be pleased to act as your escort." Gent seized Clump's opening to insert himself into the conversation. Unfortunately Gent's exuberance for good manners got the best of them all. His flourishing bow caught the attention of every man in Hope Falls.

So three more had decided to swoop in, cutting off Naomi's alternate route. Until that point, she'd been steadily edging back along the wall, hoping to sidle straight back to the kitchen. None of the men would dare follow her there. Evie laid down the law as soon as they arrived: any trespassers forfeited their next meal.

"I was askin' her!" Clump's indignation was almost comical.

"Brevity is the soul of wit." Gent wasn't apologetic.

The youngest lumberman, Bobsley, tossed Naomi a grin. "Looks like you'll have your choice of company this morning, Miss Higgins."

"Some choices are better than others," interjected Craig Williams, a loudmouthed team leader who'd arrogantly tried to claim Evie from his first day in town. Evie's acceptance of Granger didn't humble the man; he merely turned his unwelcome attentions on Lacey.

"And why are you thinkin' you're one of her choices, Williams?" Bear Riordan raised one impressively furry red eyebrow, and Naomi wondered if he hadn't joined them to keep an eye on the adversarial Williams. Despite his intimidating size—or perhaps because of it— Bear's well-intentioned interference helped keep things peaceful.

"Yeah!" Bobsley, whose slight build was an asset to high climbing but didn't lend itself well to confrontation, allied himself with Bear. "You used up your chances on the other two!"

Privately, Naomi agreed. Each man chose two of the three, with the understanding that the woman he didn't name wouldn't accept his suit. Early on, when some of the men tried courting all three ladies at once, this cut down some confusion. The idea also took into account this sort of situation, so the last unengaged woman wasn't hounded by every man in town. *So why do I still feel hounded?*

"Those were the old rules." Williams smoothed his thinning hair over his bald spot with a sickly smile. "Things are different, but they specifically said we can take pay and still court the lady."

"It was understood that the courting would be done by those of us who listed Miss Higgins as a desired bride," Gent corrected.

A desired bride. Naomi felt the soft heat of a rising blush, enchanted by the description in spite of herself. Amid all the pressure of choosing a groom and praying he would accept her past indiscretion in return for the position and property she offered, Naomi never noticed that some of these men might find her desirable.

"You were clear as water that you chose Miss Thompson." Clump readily sided with Gent against this new opponent. "She didn't want you, and neither did Miss Lyman. Don't horn in on Miss Higgins!"

"Why shouldn't I? She and I got a lot in common." Smile long gone, Williams plowed ahead. "Like you said, we're both leftovers."

Naomi gasped, her brief hope for becoming a "desired bride" crushed by Williams's more accurate assessment. *He's right. Harry threw me over for Charlotte, and I'm last choice in Hope Falls.*

"Walk away, Williams," Bear growled, his face darkening. "Plenty men asked to court Miss Higgins in the beginning. She deserves to be courted by men who recognize her value—not insulted."

"It's no insult when a man offers a woman the protection of his name." Williams wouldn't back down. "My courting is a compliment!"

"A compliment that's become cliché." Naomi lifted her chin. "One you'll no doubt extend to the next unwed woman you find. I happen to prefer men who are more selective with their attentions."

Williams's eyes became beady slits. "You're making a mistake."

"No she ain't." Bobsley sounded as certain as Naomi felt, beaming as Williams, unable to salvage his pride, stomped away.

"Now that he's gone, would you like to take that walk?" Clump slid a glance toward Gent and immediately clarified, "With me?"

Naomi looked for an excuse but saw only three hopeful faces and Riordan's more impassive expression. Again she wondered whether he'd come to her defense as part of his position, or if he was one of the men who'd, as he put it "chosen" her. She'd have to ask Lacey, whose memory about which man chose whom was more reliable.

"I think the forest is large enough for all of us," she announced. Naomi owed them a chance, and she owed it to herself to learn enough to make an informed decision when the time came. At least this way she wouldn't need to go on more than one walk!

If the men looked less than enthusiastic at the prospect of a group outing, so be it. No matter what she decided, several of them would have been disappointed. Besides, this way she could rotate the conversation if things lagged or became otherwise uncomfortable.

No one said much as they left town, crossing the railroad tracks and heading into the forest. Naomi couldn't tell if they were sulking over the situation or waiting for the scenery to give them something to say. She refused to consider whether they were waiting for her to come up with a topic of conversation. They'd asked for her company—it wasn't her responsibility to keep them entertained!

The forest rose up around them, majestic pines and stately spruces pointing straight to heaven. Dappled sunlight streamed through the canopy of branches, highlighting some areas and leaving others mysteriously shadowed. Here the fresh mountain was more strongly scented with pine, with moss lending a musky note not found in town. Dry pine needles snapped underfoot with each step, a crisp counterpoint to the cheerful bird calls from high above them.

"It's lovely." Despite her decision that the men should lead the conversation, Naomi spoke first. Since arriving, she hadn't had much opportunity to leave town. If not for the pure air she breathed, she might almost convince herself that the surrounding scenery was no more real than a well-executed oil painting.

But it was real—a tangible display of God's grandeur, set down to nourish the body and inspire the soul. For the first time, she understood what lured Lacey to her solitary walks and later why her cousin insisted on accompanying Dunstan on his forest treks.

When Naomi spotted a white-and-brown-speckled feather resting atop some bushes nearby, she stopped and picked it up. Stroking her thumb upward, it felt so soft. Running downward, it resisted. *Just like Lacey—always reaching high and not stopping to look down.* The thought made her smile, and she tucked the feather into her pocket.

"You like feathers, Miss Higgins?" Bobsley squinted around, moved to the left, and gave a short hop. In a moment, he returned with a longer feather, white in the center and dove-gray at the tip.

"I was thinking of Miss Lyman," she explained as she accepted the gift. "She's sad to see her favorite old hat looking so. . ."

"Scraggly?" Riordan supplied the word Naomi couldn't find.

"Exactly," Naomi agreed. "I was thinking to spruce it up a bit, tack on a few feathers and whatnot to hide the worst spots."

From that point on, the men made a game of spying fallen feathers and fetching them for her. It nicely broke up the silence while leaving everyone free to enjoy the beauty around them.

"Will it all be destroyed?" Naomi stopped beside one of the trees, peering up at a knothole. Above a tiny black nose, reflective eyes peered back at her—most likely wondering what she wanted.

"Not here." Gent stepped forward to assure her. "I won't tell you it hasn't happened in other places, because they logged the forests right out of most New England. But it won't happen here."

"Why not?" With a twitch of its nose, her friend disappeared, and Naomi returned to the well-worn path. She hadn't given it much thought before, but wasn't this the reason Lacey's idea would work—they'd ruined most of the forestland back East? "Isn't that what logging does? Chops down all of the trees to mill the lumber?"

"Ja, this is done in some places still." Clump looked aggrieved, mirroring Naomi's newfound concern. "But, too, this depends on who owns the land and also who they hire for the working of it."

"Oh." In spite of the odd way Clump phrased things—Naomi suspected the German language put words in different order than English—she understood his meaning. "So how can Hope Falls cut enough logs for a sawmill without taking down all of the trees?"

"We're lucky to have Granger on board. Granger Mills was one of the first to head West for fresh timber sources and one of the first to stop strip-logging the sites." Bobsley's disembodied voice reached Naomi from where he traveled behind her, Gent, and Clump.

"Sometimes it's good to thin the forest." Gent gestured toward a thick stand of trees, dense branches casting shadows. "If no light comes through, the smaller trees die and nothing new can grow."

"But don't the old ones keep growing, things still the same if it's left alone?" Naomi persisted in spite of their explanations.

"Overgrown areas hide dead trees, withered brush, and dry, broken branches. Loggers avoid them or clear out the kindling before starting work." For the first time, Bobsley sounded serious. "One spark to those places and an entire mountainside goes up in flames."

"Granger's way, we clear out areas we need for construction then cull through the timber." Riordan veered around Gent and stopped a few steps ahead, patting a tree. "What do you see, lass?"

"Um. . ." *A tree?* Suddenly, Naomi wished she'd asked Michael how to identify the different kinds of wood while they were still trees. "It's not as thick or tall as some, and the branches start low?"

"Verra good." Riordan was pleased—his accent was coming out. "It's young, green, and supple. The saplings and the smaller trees make for more work with less profit. In old days, we'd take them anyway. Here and now, they stay behind to continue the forest."

Naomi broke out in a grin. "I'm so glad to hear that!"

"We are the kind you said to Williams that you wanted." Clump hooked his thumbs through his suspenders, rocking back on his heels.

She blinked, trying to understand but coming up with nothing.

"For beautiful trees and also with beautiful women," Clump explained. "We pay attention and make good choices for the future."

"Selective," Naomi murmured, fighting another blush as the men around her nodded. She'd gotten so caught up in her concern for the land, she'd forgotten the reason she'd ventured outside to enjoy it.

Lord, Naomi prayed in silence as the group headed back to town, *I know I don't deserve this embarrassment of riches, but You've put it before me anyway. They're good, kind men who've all chosen me. So why is it that I can't bring myself to choose one of them?*

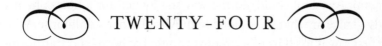

TWENTY-FOUR

"W here's Miss Higgins?" By the time Mike returned, she'd vanished. To his way of thinking, he'd gotten the bad end of the deal if his brief absence meant he'd traded her company for that of Braden Lyman. The other man seemed more agreeable than Mike remembered from his first night in Hope Falls, but he was still no Naomi.

"She went for a walk with—" Granger's woman didn't finish her thought, instead shielding her eyes and squinting out toward the forest. "There she is. Looks like they'll be back in a few minutes."

"They?" Mike mimicked her motion, putting his hand against his forehead to block the morning glare. It didn't take long to spot the three, four, no. . .make that five figures walking through the trees. And only one wore skirts. *Why is Naomi walking with four men?*

For a moment he wondered whether Miss Thompson mistook her own sister for Naomi, but Mike knew which woman was picking her way down the mountainside. It wouldn't grumble his guts any to see men circling around the younger Miss Thompson like hounds after a hare.

Mike didn't want to think about why he reacted so strongly seeing Naomi surrounded by would-be swains. Nor did he want to think about why he'd been so disappointed in the first place when he'd returned and found her gone. No matter how she monopolized his thoughts lately, Mike had nothing to offer a woman like Miss Higgins. Even if she and Luke got along well—which was a big assumption, given Luke's experiences—Mike hadn't established himself in Hope Falls. He couldn't give her a home so long as he slept in the bunkhouse.

And if any woman deserved a home to make her own, it was Naomi. Any fool could see the way she longed for a house; he need only glance at what she'd done with Miss Lyman's dollhouse. When he first saw it in all its glory, rooms emptied of boxes and transformed with treasures, he'd been staggered. Naomi filled every corner and crevice, left her stamp on each nook and cranny until the model home overflowed with tangible proof of skilled hands and a giving heart.

For the first time, Mike wished that Naomi's looks didn't mirror her spirit. Her trim figure and pretty smile attracted too much attention in a town full of bachelors. If anything, he should be surprised that he hadn't seen men trying to court her before today. Of course, this was the first day the men hadn't been excavating a fallen mine or spending ten to eleven hours in the forest, so perhaps Mike had missed the subtler signs of wooing.

"I've seen soaked cats wearing less peeved expressions." Braden wheeled up beside him as smoothly as though he'd been doing it for days. "And it doesn't take a detective to see where you're looking."

"It surprised me to see the men swarming like that." Mike admitted part of the truth. "Up till now, I thought the ladies had a better handle on that sort of thing—making sure they didn't let one get outnumbered if the others could step in and even things out."

"They probably used to." Braden rubbed at a crick in his neck. "But with Evie and Lacey off the market, there are too many determined bachelors with high expectations from that consarned ad and no one else left to draw their attention away from Naomi."

Mike frowned at that interpretation. Why wasn't the youngest girl stepping in? Unless. . .the prospect of angering the town chef could easily turn a hungry man's mind from one woman to another less thorny option. "Is Miss Thompson overly protective of her sister?"

"You mean Cora or Evie? Eh, doesn't matter. You'll get the same answer either way. They're protective of each other. Cora couldn't stand the idea of coming here and leaving Evie alone, and Evie couldn't let her little sister come to the wilds of Colorado Territory without her. And all that hullabaloo when we were already engaged, if you'll believe it." Braden shook his head at the memory.

"Engaged?" Mike repeated dumbly, too astonished by his mistake to say more. He thought back to his first night in Hope Falls, thinking of when Granger's woman made introductions. She'd called the other Miss Thompson her sister—no one made any mention of her engagement to Braden Lyman. Nor had anyone brought it up since.

"You didn't know." It wasn't a question. Braden peered up at him, the corners of his mouth flat and tight. "You should have known Cora was taken, even if nobody told you who claimed her. Didn't you wonder why the ad only asked for three husbands?"

"The ad didn't bring me here." Mike tried not to snap at the man who was still his boss. "I caught wind of it after I got to town."

"And you made the wrong assumption about which women wrote it." Braden scowled and decided, "You look like you swallowed a slug."

Mike didn't comment, though the description wasn't far from the truth—the realization that Naomi was the last woman from the ad definitely left a lump in his throat and a bad taste in his mouth. Mere minutes before, he'd been grappling with his inability to offer this woman the stability of a home and marriage. Now he learned that if he had tried, he'd be nothing more than a hired husband. *Again.*

Lord, it looks like You've saved me from repeating my biggest mistake. Mike tried to drum up some gratitude for the intervention but came up empty. *I can't say I'm happy about the situation, but since I was reminding myself I couldn't marry her anyway, it's not as if I lost a chance I was willing to take. Help me, Lord, as I work alongside this woman. In spite of what I've learned, there's still a lot to admire about Naomi Higgins. Enough that I think I'm going to need Your help to remember the way things really stand.*

"So," Braden prodded. "What made you think it was *Cora*, anyway?"

"Think *what* was Cora?" Cora froze about four feet behind Braden. Flabbergasted to see him out and about, she'd hurried to greet him without paying any attention to the conversation going on. All she heard was his question to Mr. Strode—and though the words might be innocuous, she didn't care for his dismissive tone. Not one bit.

Even from behind she could tell she'd taken him by surprise—his shoulders stiffened that much. She could have made things easier for him by walking around his chair so they could speak face-to-face. But Cora was finished making things easy for her former fiancé.

So she waited for him to turn around, and while she waited, she became more and more irked. There he sat, in the wheeled wicker chair she'd brought all the way from Charleston. Without being asked. Without having him even bother to roll up and thank her.

Instead, like the fool she thought she wasn't, she'd rushed over to share the joy of his achievement, only to hear him speaking her name in the same tone usually reserved for creepy-crawly things. It was one thing for the man to denounce her in private, worse when he did so before their tight-laced group. But publicly? The closer Braden got to getting back on his feet, the lower the man sank.

"Cora!" Braden started to reach for her hand, but Cora crossed her arms. His smile hadn't fooled her; the man wasn't happy.

"Yes, Cora. The same Cora you were discussing?" She slid a glance toward Mr. Strode, noticing the man looked to be suffering from a stomach ailment of some sort. When neither of the men responded, she prompted, "You thought I was what?"

"One of the women who wrote the ad." With that simple statement and a glance toward the group of men bidding for Naomi's attention, Mr. Strode's sour expression made much more sense. The man wasn't ill; he was disappointed!

So our new carpenter isn't as indifferent to Naomi as he'd like to be. It took a lot of willpower for Cora to keep from smiling. She, Evie, and even optimistic Lacey all worried about their friend. It would be just like Naomi to tire of all the fuss and choose the first man she deemed marginally acceptable. Then they'd have a terrible time convincing her that an "acceptable" man was insufficient. Naomi simply didn't see herself as extraordinary.

But Mr. Strode obviously did, and that was a more important development, even, than Braden finally getting into his wheeled chair and out of that dismal room. Braden, of course, wouldn't agree with that assessment, but then Braden hadn't been agreeable in a long time. At least Cora now understood why he'd been so sour about it.

He wasn't disgusted with her. Far from it. He didn't like the idea that another man thought she was available. Even when that other man was obviously smitten with Naomi! Cora felt as happy and relieved as when they'd finally pulled Lacey from the mines.

"As it just so happens, I did help write that ad." Cora let loose the smile she'd been holding back. It felt wonderful.

"Not as one of the would-be brides, Cora. Somehow the new man in town got the idea that you were the last bride, and I wanted to know why he didn't realize it was Naomi."

"The night everyone was offered wages, the men talked about the last girl up for grabs. It seemed to me that between yourself and Miss Higgins, you were the girl. Then your sister started warning the men to keep their hands to themselves, and it seemed like she was protecting you." Mr. Strode grimaced. "I didn't know you were engaged."

"I'm not." Cora knew her comment would confuse Mr. Strode a bit, but more importantly, it would clear things up for Braden.

"Don't go mixing up the truth with trouble." Her former fiancé looked mad enough to spit. "He thought you were one of the women advertising for a husband, and I told him you were already engaged."

"True. When we posted the ad, I was engaged." She shrugged. "Hope Falls has a funny way of turning things on their heads."

"I'm getting that impression." Mr. Strode looked from Braden to her then back again, no longer confused. "It sounds like the two of you have some things to talk through, and it sounds like they're private. So I'll just leave you to it." With that, the carpenter extracted himself from their convoluted conversation. He also, Cora couldn't help but notice, headed straight for Naomi.

"What do you think you're playing at?" Braden demanded, looking positively outraged. "Telling him you're not engaged. If he repeats that around town, all the men will think you are up for grabs!"

"It's the truth." Cora sighed. "I signed Lacey's paperwork, Braden. My dowry has been returned, along with my own portion of Hope Falls. As of now, the engagement is officially dissolved."

"No it isn't!" Braden pounded his fist on the arm of his chair, making the wicker creak. "You can't end it just because things aren't going your way, Cora. We made a commitment."

Cora's jaw dropped at the vehemence of his hypocrisy. Was this the same man who'd ordered her to leave his side, leave town entirely? Was this the Braden Lyman who'd looked her in the eye and told her he didn't want her anymore? She'd had to hold his use of her dowry over his head to make him accept that he couldn't back out of their engagement. So how could this be the same Braden who'd begged her to sign Lacey's paperwork so they'd both be free?

It can't be. The man sitting before her bore more of a resemblance to the Braden she'd loved than the Braden she'd battled in Hope Falls. Staggered by the realization, Cora decided to leave him in the company of his own hypocrisy while she sorted through her conflicting emotions. She needed to decide where to go from here.

The bottom floor is where the kitchen, dining room, and parlor belong." Naomi bent over the sketches scattered across the tabletop. "Since we're making this home with six rooms rather than eight, we'll need to move the study upstairs with the bedroom and nursery."

"Do you have any preference as to which room is the starting point?" Michael seemed more businesslike than Naomi remembered from the first few days. But then again, he'd been moving crates and setting up the work space. Now that the room was ready, it was understandable that he wanted to get the project fully under way.

At least that's the explanation Naomi hoped explained his sudden lack of warmth. It wasn't as though he was rude or dismissive—merely detached. As though he'd withdrawn in some way from their burgeoning partnership. Whatever the reason for his altered demeanor, Naomi hoped his enthusiasm would return. Soon.

"It needs to be one of the side rooms on the ground floor," she mused. "So either the parlor or the kitchen would be a good choice."

"What if the location of the room didn't matter?" He looked up from the prints. "Wouldn't it be easier for you to develop a room if it wasn't already locked in place? I mean to say, would it help you work if I could build the rooms first and connect them later?"

"That would make it much easier to work on the ceilings, wall coverings, and flooring." She caught herself nibbling on the corner of her lip and immediately stopped. "But I would imagine that would interfere with your work on the exterior. Doors, windows, shingles, the scalloped siding would all wait for the house to be together."

"True. . . ." He looked to be off in his own thoughts, but this was the sort of distance Naomi didn't mind. Anyone could see he was turning around options in his head, trying to find a solution to the problem. Michael left the drawing board, so to speak, moving to stand in front of Lyman Place. He moved from side to side, turned the model to view it from different angles, bent lower to run his forefinger along the edges of floors and ceilings. Then he returned, picked up a pencil, and began drawing. Quick, slashing lines across the blank page formed the now-familiar outline of their design.

Except this was shaping up to be anything but familiar. As she watched, he outlined the house, using it as a frame and running two lines across it—one beneath the eaves and another about halfway down the walls so the whole sketch looked rather like a bookshelf. When Naomi began to ask a question, he held up his left hand, forefinger extended in the age-old request that she wait a moment.

So Naomi waited. And wondered. And watched.

She watched as he added two lines, dividing the house with one-third to the right and two-thirds of the space to the left, and understood that he was leaving room for the hallway and staircase on each level. Again, she wanted to ask why he felt the need to draw again what they'd already decided, but then Michael's pencil veered to the margin of the paper, abandoning the skeletal structure. In quick succession, he drew six cubes floating around the house. He lifted his tilted head and erased the top line from each cube.

"Movable rooms." Naomi's mind raced with the possibilities of this innovation. It was an entirely new dimension for those who loved dollhouses, allowing them to arrange not only the furnishings and décor of the home but the floor plan of the house as well. "It's genius!"

"Just practical," Michael demurred but seemed pleased with her reaction. "You were right before, when you said that working on the rooms would stop progress on the exterior. This way you'll be able to work more comfortably without losing time elsewhere."

"This way I can even work on multiple rooms. I won't need to wait for paint to dry or glue to set!" Naomi was almost giddy. "It will be so much easier than hunching down, straining my neck to see what I'm doing. This makes all the difference."

He made all the difference, but Naomi couldn't tell him that. It sounded too intimate. *That's because it is too intimate, you ninny!* Her common sense was putting in almost as many hours on this project as Naomi, constantly delivering stern reminders and scolds. *You can't tell a man that you wake up looking forward to spending the day with him. Michael isn't one of the men who's courting you, and you already decided that you couldn't marry him even if asked. You should not enjoy his company this much. Compose yourself!*

At this rate, *Compose yourself!* was vying with *He deserves better!* as Naomi's mantra. It seemed a pity that she didn't like either one. But a more encouraging, uplifting sort of motto would be of no use in restraining her fascination with the man beside her. She hadn't known Michael Strode for long, but his strength of character set him apart from most of the men she'd spent time with.

He made no secret of his love for the Lord. In fact, her first memory of Michael was his offer to pray. Then he'd proceeded to help pull apart half a mountainside without even knowing whether he'd be allowed to stay. That spoke of a servant's heart.

Then there were the things she learned as they worked. Michael treated her like an equal, never resenting having to work with a woman. His determination to provide for his young son merited respect, as did his formidable intellect. Naomi found herself transfixed by his unique ability to puzzle through problems.

How could she compose herself when he stood so close, smelling of soap and pine, his sleeve brushing against hers? Or when his eyes lit with enthusiasm for a fresh idea? Naomi sighed and accepted her weakness. When it came to Michael, common sense went out the door.

Mike wondered if Naomi realized how long she'd been thinking without saying anything. He wanted to know what, exactly, she'd been thinking about for such a broad range of expressions to cross her face. And most of all, he wondered why on earth Naomi Higgins would need to hire a husband. With or without part ownership in a new sawmill, the woman was a prize. So how come some man hadn't swept her off her feet long before she resorted to such extreme measures?

"Is there a reason behind your decision to not enclose the rooms?" She'd apparently decided to rejoin the conversation. "I would think ceilings stabilize the unit, so won't the room be more easily damaged if it's moved around without the covering?"

"Yes." Mike tapped the drawing on the table. "But I was thinking about how much simpler it would be for you to work with the rooms open so you could reach in from above as well as from the side. Also, it makes for less work if we address the ceilings all at once, doing the painting and so forth along the undersides of the support shelves before I insert them into the frame."

"Clear advantages." She paused, clearly torn between the function of the design while they were working as opposed to the function once they'd finished.

"I also considered that the lack of a roof would make people more cautious when handling the rooms. They should always be supported from the bottom, but a closed box might encourage rougher handling." Mike wanted her to decide in favor of what made her work easier, but he wanted her to feel good about the decision.

"I agree." Until her smile returned, Mike hadn't realized he'd missed it. "The increased difficulty in this approach falls to you—there's no margin for error when each portable unit must be precisely the same dimension as the next."

"Not a problem," he assured her. "I'm known for precision."

"Oh?" Her green eyes lit with curiosity, and Mike knew he'd made a mistake. Naomi seemed to have been waiting for an opportunity to ask about his past. "How did you gain such a reputation?"

"Mark the line and measure twice; a single cut should then suffice." He smiled as he recited the rhyme. His father drilled it into his head from the time he'd been old enough to hold a hammer.

"Sound advice in a clever phrase." Naomi smiled, but she wasn't finished questioning him. "Where did you learn it?"

"My father made sure I learned that lesson long before he let me put it to use." Mike didn't mind telling her that much. Trades were often handed from father to son through generations. "I did the same with Luke when he started to show an interest in the workshop."

"You had a workshop?" She seized the word like a dog on a bone.

"Yep." How was he going to change the topic now? If he didn't derail the conversation soon, she'd keep digging for information he needed to stay buried. No matter how he racked his brain, Mike could think of only one answer a woman wouldn't question further. "I closed it down after my wife died. Luke took it pretty hard."

This, at least, was true. Although he'd manfully refused to indulge in tears when he heard of his mother's death, Luke shed a few when they visited the workshop for the final time. Mike understood— Leticia didn't involve herself in Luke's upbringing, preferring to leave the difficult task of parenting to a coterie of nursemaids, nannies, and tutors. Although not altogether indifferent, she'd been absent more often than not. Far more often.

But the workshop. . .that had been a constant in his son's life long before Luke spoke. Mike started sneaking his son into his sanctuary while the nursemaid napped and continued the visits more openly after Luke could walk. In the workshop, he'd read fables to his son, and when Luke began to write, they'd traced letters then words in layers of sawdust. While Mike worked, Luke kept himself busy, happily playing with the trains, spinning tops, and building blocks Mike gave him—toys Mike fashioned in the early days of his marriage, when he still hoped to build a real family.

Naomi seemed subdued. "You must have loved her very much. It would have been hard to stay in a place that held so many memories."

"It was hard to leave," he admitted. When he'd locked the door for the final time, Mike almost cried along with his son. Leaving behind the workshop meant leaving the place where they'd both been happiest, without knowing when or where they'd find a new sanctuary. Mike could only thank God that he'd found Hope Falls and pray for patience until he could bring Luke home to build new memories.

"It's never easy to leave what we know." A hint of hardness crept into the set of her jaw but quickly vanished as she whispered, "But sometimes it's the only choice you have left."

Mike gladly took the chance to turn the conversation around. If things went well, he might be able to answer the questions plaguing him about that ad. "It couldn't have been easy for you either."

"No, it wa—" She stopped, the unnatural pause and her widened eyes telling that she'd been about to agree with him but didn't want him to know it. Naomi cleared her throat. "It was much easier than you might think—certainly easier than staying behind."

"Why?" Mike knew better than to pry, but his inability to solve the puzzle that was Naomi Higgins goaded his conversation.

Naomi looked astonished at his brazen question but still deigned to answer him. "You might not understand, Michael. You left your home because a family member died. I left because we found out that Braden survived the cave-in. Lacey and Cora were going to find him whether Evie and I came with them or not."

The sadness behind her words tore at him, and Mike could have kicked himself for being an insensitive boor. Apologizing was the only thing to do. "I'm sorry. I didn't realize the Lymans were your only family. Did you lose your parents at a very young age?"

"My father died two days before I was born. They say I share his coloring." Absently, she reached up and traced the streak of white brightening her hair. "My mother passed away two years ago."

"My condolences for your loss." Mike was glad to know he hadn't trampled over a fresh tragedy, but he also knew that the loss of a beloved mother never lost its sting. "My mother traded this world for heaven shortly after Luke was born. At the time, I thought she'd held on so long just to see her grandson. It gave me comfort to know I'd been able to give her that final joy." More than any medicine paid for by the Bainbridge largess, Mike believed that his mother's delight in seeing her grandson gave peace to her final months.

For that, and for Luke himself, he couldn't bring himself to regret the bargain he'd struck. But he knew all to well that was an undeserved blessing. Mike ached at the thought Naomi might make the same mistake he had. Would a decade with her hired husband leave her with all the regrets and none of the satisfaction a marriage should hold? She deserved more—why could she not see it? Did she feel that her lack of family left her so alone, she had no choice but to marry the first man who'd be an asset to Hope Falls?

"A child is a joy unlike any other, and even better since no two are alike." She smiled, but her eyes swam with sorrow. "Your wife must have grieved to be unable to give Luke a brother or sister."

"Luke is enough." Mike heard his own fierceness and softened his tone. "God saw fit to bless me with one wonderful son, and I never wanted him or his mother to think he wasn't enough."

Not having any more children was one of the few things he and Leticia had actually seen eye to eye on. Despite Mike's dogged determination to honor their wedding vows, Leticia returned to her faithless ways almost as soon as she'd healed from giving birth.

Mike married her knowing it meant accepting another man's child as his son, but he'd felt no bitterness about it. The deed was done before he'd ever met the woman. Somehow he knew he wouldn't be able to accept the same situation with the same equanimity after they'd wed. Perhaps it wasn't logical or fair, but he was honest about it. For her part, Leticia refused to endure the pain again or ruin her figure.

"Of course! I didn't mean to imply that your son was in any way lacking. My thoughts were more that siblings add a new dimension to a child's life. . . ." Naomi trailed off, lost in consternation.

"I didn't take offense." He saw she didn't believe him and searched for a way to smooth things over. "Do you have a sibling?"

"A sister." If she'd seemed sorrowful at the mention of her mother's passing, now Naomi looked lost in the Bog of Despair from

Pilgrim's Progress. Blinking rapidly, she croaked out, "Married."

She seemed so distraught at the thought of her sister's marriage, Mike wondered at the cause. Perhaps she disapproved of her brother-in-law and felt concern for her sibling. Or maybe theirs was a happy marriage, and Naomi battled envy. Either way, the comparison between her sister and herself could only cause pain.

He hated to see her suffer, but more than that, Mike hated his own inability to do anything about it.

TWENTY-SIX

W hat are we supposed to do?" Cora hissed at Braden, trying to keep her voice low enough that the stranger loitering in the hallway wouldn't hear. "And who, exactly, is this Mr. Clyde Corning? You didn't discuss inviting him, and now all of a sudden *he's here!*"

This last statement smacked of the obvious, but Cora wanted to get the true urgency of the situation through Braden's thick skull. Because the man looked completely unperturbed by the fact that they had no accommodations for the "honored" guest he'd sprung on them.

"Corning's a potential investor, and I didn't know he was coming." He sounded less unconcerned than tired, and suddenly it occurred to Cora that Braden might have already worn himself out.

He'd made a habit of finding the most difficult inclines to practice rolling himself up and down several times. But this didn't satisfy Braden, who seemed bound and determined to build up his strength. The few times he'd tipped over had been due to trying to control his descent down an incline while going *backward*.

As if that weren't enough, Braden didn't even get into the chair until Doc put him through so-called physiotherapy every morning. Even the doctor himself admitted that it was a new field of medicine—pioneered by Swedish gymnasts of all things! Even though the techniques were finding widespread use for rehabilitating wounded soldiers, the process remained both inexact and exhausting.

Now that she took the time to look, she saw the telltale tightening of the corners of his mouth—the ones that said he was in pain but determined not to let her know. His color, while much improved from a week's worth of outdoor sessions, looked pale. Cora chastised herself for not noticing sooner. After all, she knew that he'd already gone through his personal gauntlet by late afternoon.

Keeping track of his schedule helped her know how to evade him. Otherwise she never would have managed to avoid him for an entire week while she floundered from one sort of feeling to another. Cornering Cora seemed to be Braden's only goal—aside from his almost maniacal determination to regain his strength. It didn't matter how many times people told him he didn't need to rush, he—

He knew better. The realization whisked away Cora's guilt over misinterpreting Braden's fatigue as disinterest. *Braden hasn't been pushing himself so hard simply to recover—he's been getting ready!*

"Oh, you knew he was coming." Cora jabbed a finger at him, stopping just shy of his nose and making his eyes cross for a second. "Mr. Corning says you invited him, and you've been working yourself into a lather readying yourself!"

"Erm." Braden uncrossed his eyes and slid his gaze over her shoulder, toward the closed door. "He didn't respond to the invitation. I didn't know if anyone was coming, much less when."

"What do you mean, 'anyone'?" Suspicious, Cora peered at him, but Braden kept his gaze firmly fixed on some spot behind her. He only refused to meet her gaze when he had something to hide. "Just how many people did you invite without consulting everyone else?"

Briefly Braden's temper flared to life, giving him the energy to push himself into a sitting position. "Now isn't the time to discuss it, Cora! Right now you need to escort Mr. Corning in here and go find Dunstan and Granger so they can join us. While the men talk, you women can bustle around and get something ready for him."

"While *the men* talk?" She gritted her teeth to keep from shrieking at the obstinate fool. "You don't run Hope Falls, Braden. *We women* do. Dunstan and Granger answer to Lacey and Evie, and we will not be treated as housekeepers while you hold court in here!"

"Stop making things so difficult!" he snapped at her.

Cora arched a brow and left the room—closing the door behind her so Braden couldn't hear what she said to Mr. Corning. As far as she was concerned, he deserved to be shut out of things for a while.

"Mr. Corning." She nudged the corners of her lips into what she hoped passed for a gracious smile. "I've informed Mr. Lyman of your arrival, and he is anxious to greet you. He'll need a few moments, so I'll escort you to the house where you can freshen up a bit."

Within five minutes she'd directed the doctor to ready Braden's chair, stopped by the mercantile with Mr. Corning to pick up Lacey and ask Dunstan to find Mr. Granger, and shooed their unexpected guest into the kitchen to wash up. As expected, Dunstan found Granger in the kitchen, which made Evie go fetch Naomi, so Cora had just long enough to apprise everyone gathered in the parlor of the situation. It didn't take long since she knew precious little. She finished before Mr. Corning emerged from the kitchen.

By the time Braden rolled in, it was good he brought his own seat. Disgruntled women monopolized the parlor—and the conversation.

Braden could hardly get a word in edgewise. He sat there fuming while the women sent him scowls and cozied up to Corning. Corning!

Of all the strategic invitations he'd sent, no one showed the good grace to respond. But Clyde Corning, who Braden only included because it might raise the saboteur's suspicions if only some of the previous investors were invited, landed right on his doorstep.

"Cautious Clyde," as he'd been nicknamed in college, made a tidy living on the stock market by selecting only the safest shares. Corning's reputation for careful investing convinced others to back Miracle Mining when geological surveys and Braden's own powers of persuasion failed. Every businessman in Charleston knew there was no better bet than a venture already backed by Cautious Clyde Corning.

A more methodical man couldn't be found. He shied away from

all but the slightest risks. So what in blue blazes brought him across the country without so much as a question asked or research piled into every nook and cranny of his meticulous, massive desk?

Dunstan kept looking from Corning to Braden, as though trying to decide what made this man a suspect. Judging by Granger's furrowed brow, his attempts to solve the same puzzle were failing. The only signal Braden could give was a short shake of his head. It wasn't as though he could outright announce that Corning didn't count as a suspect and Braden never expected him to show up.

"A pleasure to meet each of you." Corning awkwardly addressed the female population in the room and rubbed his chin. "I apologize that I didn't have the time to shave and present myself properly."

"We don't rest on formality," came Naomi's understatement.

"Do you know, Mr. Corning, that I believe a beard would look well on you?" Trust Lacey to try and hide the man's weak chin. His sister waged a constant war to help people look their best. So far Naomi was the only person who'd held out against Lacey's guidance.

Cautious Clyde went ruddy at the comment, thoughtfully fingering the sparse stubble along his jaw. "I've considered it."

Braden held back a snort. The man had probably been considering the change for years, judging it too drastic to attempt.

"What do you think, Miss Thompson?" Corning shifted slightly to better face Cora, who occupied the seat beside him on the settee.

Wait. Braden's eyes narrowed. *Why is he sitting beside her? He doesn't need to be that close. And why ask Cora's opinion, as though it matters more than Lacey's or any other woman's in the room?*

"I'd say now is a good time to test it out, while you're away from home." Cora's smile held a shade too much warmth for a new acquaintance. "If you dislike it, shave before you return. If you do like it, you can surprise everyone with it when you get back."

"Well reasoned." Corning's smile matched hers. "I'll do it!"

"I'm surprised to see you." Braden managed to break into the conversation while everyone was busy agreeing with Cora's summation. "If we'd known of your imminent arrival, we would have prepared something for you." *Like some skillfully designed questions to ascertain why you ventured so far from your well-ordered life.*

Because the more Braden thought about it, the more suspicious Corning's sudden adventure seemed. As far as he knew, the man rarely left town and never journeyed beyond state borders. *Until now.*

"Did you not see my telegram?" Corning's brows tented upward.

"We lost our telegraph operator a couple weeks ago." Dunstan stepped in to smooth things over—and closely eye Corning's reaction to this vague revelation about Draxley. Would Corning take the bait?

"Sorry to hear that." Corning looked genuinely disturbed as he looked around the room. "I never intended to inconvenience you. I should have waited until I received confirmation from you, Braden."

"It's fine," Braden lied, still digesting the fact Corning hadn't asked after Draxley. Of course, an innocent man wouldn't know the telegraph operator's name, much less inquire further. But a canny saboteur would know better than to display interest as well. Who knew whether or not Corning actually sent a telegram? *Maybe he wanted to swoop into Hope Falls and catch us completely off guard.*

If so, the tactic worked far better than Braden cared to admit. He'd pushed himself hard throughout the morning and early afternoon, and by suppertime he'd tired himself sufficiently to be grateful for the bed that had been his prison for so many months before. Right now his wits weren't nearly as sharp as he needed them to be.

"Even so," Braden prodded a bit further, "I must say I'm surprised that you took me up on the invitation. I expected a few to come, but it didn't strike me as something you'd be interested in."

"My interests might be more varied than you think." Was it Braden's imagination, or did Corning slide a glance at Cora before continuing? "A few of the men who'd asked for my input regarding the Hope Falls mine came asking me about this new sawmill you proposed."

"Oh, did they?" Lacey sounded sweet as syrup while she glared daggers at Braden. "Perhaps you should tell us who *we* invited."

"Businessmen." Braden gave an indolent shrug, as though the

telegrams weren't highly specific. "No one you'd know, really."

His sister gritted her teeth. "I didn't think Hope Falls was ready to begin inviting businessmen and seeking new investors."

"We needed to." Granger threw the weight of his experience behind Braden's decision, knowing that the women would assume he meant the sawmill needed start-up capital. As things stood, they wouldn't have been able to begin paying wages if Granger himself hadn't bought into the business. They'd all agreed that the women didn't need to know the reason behind this particular group of investors—if they knew, the girls would give the game away.

Evie gave her future husband a meaningful look and observed—in a thoroughly pleasant voice, "So you knew about this decision."

"The sawmill benefits from investors." Braden somehow summoned the energy to give a credible performance. "It seemed only right that the men who speculated in the mine should be presented with the opportunity to recoup their losses. So we contacted them first."

"Indeed." Corning gave a repugnant little snuffle, digging around in his waistcoat for a handkerchief. "Should the mill be as promising as described, the mine investors should be among the first to benefit. It's why they came for my opinion and why I came here. Given the last fiasco, I need to review things firsthand, you see."

Fiasco? The word hung in the air like a foul stench, reminding Braden that his business venture had failed so spectacularly it jeopardized even the reputation of Cautious Clyde. He tried to swallow his rage, knowing that the time would come when the safety of his mines would be vindicated and the saboteur exposed. But that day loomed long into the future, and for now Braden found it incredibly difficult to drum up the appropriate response for Clyde.

"I owe you my thanks." He almost choked on the words, the truth of them weighted like bricks. "After the failure of the mines, you would have been within your rights to denounce Hope Falls entirely."

"No, I won't denounce you." A martial glint appeared in Corning's gaze. "The mines did not fail. You promised silver, and the mine produced silver until the unfortunate, *unforeseeable* collapse."

Dunstan and Granger's eyes widened at the stress Corning placed on the word *unforeseeable*, and Braden knew they wondered the same thing he did. Was Corning consoling a friend or trying to emphasize the "accidental" nature of the collapse for another, darker reason?

Perhaps I was too hasty in writing off Corning as a suspect. Braden leaned back. Clearly the man merited a close watch.

TWENTY-SEVEN

I t's time!" Arla's voice wafted downstairs on a gasp of breath.

Naomi jumped up from the armed chair she'd just claimed, thinking to settle in and get as comfortable as possible for what was sure to be another long, awkward argument with Braden Lyman. They'd scrubbed a mining cabin and scrounged up a bed for Mr. Corning while the men ate supper. Afterward, Cora caught Braden by the back of his chair, refusing to let him return to the doctor's house until the owners of Hope Falls conducted an urgent meeting.

A meeting that wasn't nearly as urgent as Arla's cry.

"Fetch the doctor," Naomi shouted over her shoulder at the men, who'd clustered together like schoolboys awaiting punishment. "Evie, you'd best get some water boiling! Lacey, bring the cloths we washed and set aside. Cora, fetch Mrs. McCreedy—Arla will want her."

And even if Arla didn't particularly want the company of the sole married woman in town, Naomi needed her calming influence. Martha McCreedy could stare down a roomful of loggers, keep up with Evie in the kitchen, and calm a heated conversation with a grace born through years of experience. Naomi could only hope the older woman would be able to help usher a babe into the world as easily.

"Oooooh," Arla panted from the bed, where she huddled on her side with her arms around her stomach. She rolled over when Naomi nudged her shoulder, staring with wide, slightly unfocused eyes.

"It's all right." Naomi reached up and pulled off the frilly nightcap

Arla favored, already damp around the rim. It wasn't warm in the room, so the layer of perspiration dotting her forehead meant Arla had been struggling for some time before she called for help.

Naomi kept her expression schooled in an encouraging smile, refusing to frown at a woman in labor. "When did the pains start?"

"What kind of pains?" Arla shifted around, obviously unable to get comfortable. "The dull, achy ones started, but I drowsed through them. My back always hurts these days, and I didn't realize that these were—" She broke off, breath stolen by another contraction.

Too close. Naomi's mind raced as she remembered everything she'd read on childbirth. She and Lacey had dug through their extensive collections of books once Arla arrived in town, determined to read up on the subject and prepare themselves for the ordeal ahead. From what she could recall, the pains shouldn't be coming this close together until the baby was practically ready to slide out!

Naomi reached for Arla's hand, trying not to wince at the force of the woman's grip. She eased back the sheet, unsurprised to find blood staining Arla's nightgown and the bed beneath her legs. *It's normal.* She reminded herself that this had been expected, but somehow the knowledge hadn't prepared her for the horror of reality.

"Don't fret." Martha McCreedy swept into the room, closely followed by Lacey with her arms full and Cora, who wedged herself between Naomi and the wall to bathe Arla's face with a damp towel.

"Her contractions are coming close," Naomi told them as they eyed the bloodied bed in horror. "Every few minutes already."

Mrs. McCreedy clucked her tongue. "Arla, my dear, you've tricked us into leaving you alone while you did all the work." She rolled up her sleeves and moved to the edge of the bed. There she softly nudged Arla's knees until her legs were tented then rolled back the nightgown and started tucking towels all over the bed.

Naomi edged to the far corner beside Lacey, trying to give Arla more room to breathe. "How can I help, Martha? What do you need?"

"To have this room cleared." Doc burst into view, looking in disapproval at the cramped quarters. "Everyone can leave, now."

"Noooo!" Arla's refusal ended in a scream as she gripped Cora's hand and shook her head. After the pain subsided, she panted out, "Cora. . .Martha. . .stay." She leaned back against the pillows, drained.

"That's it, dear." Mrs. McCreedy scooted over to give Doc his rightful place. She gestured for Lacey and Naomi to leave. "Save your strength for the next one. We'll tell you when to bear down."

Not wanting to abandon Arla, but not wanting to get in the way, Naomi skirted around the washstand and out the door. Lacey followed her, and they both stood in the hallway, not certain what to do.

"We might as well see if Evie needs help," Lacey suggested. They trooped down the stairs, spurred by another one of Arla's heart-rending shrieks. As they made their way to the kitchen, they passed a panicked Mr. Lawson. Or rather, they tried to pass him.

"My sister. . .is she all right?" He blinked behind his spectacles, looking like an incredibly worried owl. When Arla screamed again, he held his breath until she stopped, letting it loose in a long, shaky exhalation. "Does everything seem normal?"

"It shouldn't be long." Naomi gave him an encouraging nod, hoping he didn't notice the way she avoided answering whether things seemed normal. She didn't know much about the normal way of things, but she did know things were progressing at an unusually rapid pace.

"Come and have a seat, Lawson." The familiar bass of Michael's voice washed over her. "Let the ladies get on with their work."

"Right." Lawson scurried away as though he'd been endangering his sister by blocking their way. "Thank you for coming, Strode."

His heartfelt gratitude rang in Naomi's ears as she entered the kitchen. Wasn't it just like Michael to stand by a friend under circumstances when other men fled the scene? She noticed that Dunstan, Granger, and Braden cleared out quick as could be, not stopping to think that poor Mr. Lawson would be on pins and needles.

They all were. Naomi, Lacey, and Evie found themselves pacing the perimeter of the kitchen, loathe to let the men see their anxiety. Aside from bringing water and fresh towels and carrying soiled ones away—carefully concealed from the men, of course—the three of them didn't have much to do except wait. And worry.

So Naomi did what she always did when fear nipped at her heels. She prayed. This time she prayed while she paced, sending an unceasing flow of thoughts and requests with each and every step.

Lord, thank You for speeding this delivery. I know most women labor much longer, and in Your wisdom You spared Arla that trial. Maybe it was to spare all of our nerves because You knew what a state we'd be in. Whatever the reason, I'm grateful. Please let Cora and Martha and Doc be the comfort and assistance she needs. Please let her be all right. Please let the babe be healthy. Please, Lord. . . .

She prayed and paced until Cora burst through the room, grinning from ear to ear and announcing, "It's a girl. A teeny, tiny, perfect little shriveled raisin of a beautiful baby girl!"

Then she went back to the parlor to tell Mr. Lawson how beautifully his sister handled the delivery, that Arla was already holding her new daughter, and that Doc would be down to answer questions shortly. And then there was only one thing left to say.

The women gathered in the kitchen, clasping hands to form the prayer ring, and thanked God for the tiny miracle snoozing upstairs.

Another hour's sleep would have been nice, after turning in late last night, but Mike rolled out of his bunk at the same time as the other men. There'd been a few grumbles about his change in status when the men realized he spent all day with Naomi—practically alone. He didn't plan to give them more ammunition by sleeping in.

The others probably didn't know Lawson had dropped by the workshop to get Mike's opinion on plans for the sawmill. They didn't know that when Dunstan came rushing in with news of Arla, Lawson had asked Mike to go with him. It made sense—of the men Lawson spent any real time with, Mike was the only father in the bunch.

And while Lawson was the uncle, he'd be the man raising the babe along with his sister. Mike understood full well how nerve-racking it could be to wait out the delivery of a child. He fought against his own helplessness, knowing he couldn't soothe the pain or make sure things would turn out right. The sound of a new mother's anguished cries made any man's blood run cold.

He hadn't been thrilled to go with Lawson, but he accepted that the man needed company. Mike didn't regret going—how could he? The babe and mother were doing well, and Lawson didn't break down. What were a few missed hours of sleep compared to those blessings?

Besides, he knew full well that the women found their beds much later and awakened a solid hour earlier than he did. That thought galvanized him as he splashed frigid water on his face and rubbed the bleariness from his eyes. He left the bunkhouse, further invigorated by the chill morning air and the enticing scent of coffee. Mike breathed deep. *And bacon.* He picked up his pace.

He wasn't surprised to find the dining room almost empty, but it did prompt him to bolt down a meal that deserved more appreciation. Then again, all of Miss Thompson's meals deserved appreciation, so Mike determined to give extra attention to the next one. Or two. Or. . .

"Good morning!" Shadows smudged the delicate skin beneath her eyes, but Naomi's smile said she didn't mind the missed sleep.

"Good morning." He hid his surprise to find her already in the workshop. Mike expected her to be doing what all women did, hovering around the newborn and rushing about with tiny clothes and whatnot.

Of course, Naomi never fulfilled his expectations; she exceeded them. With plenty of other women to fuss and coddle the infant and mother, Naomi didn't shirk her responsibilities. She went to work. Her very presence in the workshop told him everything was fine.

Still, Mike knew he should ask. "How are the mother and babe?"

She positively beamed. "Quite well. Doc said Arla's labor was the easiest kind, very short, so she'll have a quick recovery. Granger is showing Mr. Corning around, which is fitting since Mr. Corning is concerned with the business side of the enterprise, so Granger is the best man to explain what we've accomplished and how we plan to proceed—they'll meet with Mr. Lawson a bit later. At any rate, it frees any of us from having to play hostess today.

"Cora and Martha are taking turns, switching between helping Evie with supper and staying with Arla. Doc will check in soon, and Lacey dragged Dunstan to her mercantile to dig up baby supplies. I expect she'll inundate Arla with piles of catalogues tonight."

"I never saw Mrs. McCreedy before last night," Mike admitted.

"The men don't see her much," Naomi assured him. "She keeps to the kitchen or watches over Arla. Martha makes a point of taking supper home so she and Mr. McCreedy can enjoy each other's company."

"That explains it." Mike began laying out the pieces he'd work on that afternoon. So far he'd spent the bulk of his time planing shingles down to extreme thinness. Now he had a stack of wood sheets, each meticulously shaved to a quarter-inch thickness. These would make the removable rooms. The stack of larger boards he'd left at a third of an inch to create the exterior and house supports.

"I think it's wonderful"—the wistful note in Naomi's voice grabbed his attention—"that they set aside time to be together."

"Spouses should make time for each other." Mike wished he could flatten the worries buzzing around her thoughts like little gnats. Of course she worried about what her own marriage might entail. The bond between a man and woman happily growing old together wasn't likely to develop with a spouse chosen without love. Mike should know—he'd failed with Leticia. Instead of stopping her worries, he should add to them—warn her away from such a disastrous decision.

But I can't tell her that I married for money. Women made this arrangement every day, but for a man to admit he'd sold himself the same way. . .it made him less of a man. Weak. *No one can ever know.*

"Did you?" She looked at him expectantly, with a trace of defiance for having dared ask such a personal, prying question.

"Did I make time for my wife?" Mike had no easy answer for that. In the beginning, he'd catered to Leticia's every demand, believing her temper would even out after Luke's birth. The physicians who knew no more of Leticia's character than Mike assured him that women were notoriously emotional when expecting.

After Luke's birth, Mike brought the babe to visit Leticia every day, even though she refused to nurse the child herself. When Leticia regained her strength, she ended the visits entirely. Dinners were eaten in silence across a long table.

His attempts to interest her in the workshop were met with open disdain. Invitations to take their son for a walk earned him a frosty glare while she informed him that nannies pushed prams—did she *look* like a servant? As time passed, Mike slowly stopped making overtures to his wife. They lived as strangers in the same house.

"I should have tried harder." The admission tasted sour. He'd been the only one trying, but Mike took Leticia as his bride. As the head of the household, the marriage rested on his decisions. There was no excuse good enough for giving up on his wife. *None.*

Sensing that she'd pushed too far, Naomi settled herself in her chair and devoted her attention to the list she'd begun yesterday.

Mike thought she'd ended the conversation until he heard her whisper, hesitant and husky, "All any of us can do is try."

TWENTY-EIGHT

I t's not enough." Naomi pushed her chair back from the table an hour after the awkward end to her and Michael's conversation. Up until today, she'd been setting up the work area and poring over catalogues to place orders with German manufacturers for things she couldn't possibly make herself. Now that she'd inventoried her supplies, she realized how much she still needed to move forward.

"What isn't?" Michael stopped sawing and walked over to eye her list. A frown puckered his forehead as he read over her supplies.

"These." She circled the lower portion of her list and began reading aloud. "Tin ceiling panels, pressed cork sheets, model ship masts, wall-covering samples, linoleum, one-inch diameter wooden dowels—the manufacturers won't ship small orders. Except the wall-covering samples—I don't think those will be shipped at all."

"The ceiling panels, linoleum, and wall coverings make sense." Michael paused before asking. "Cork? Model ship masts? Dowels?"

"Cork is wonderful!" She got up and rooted around Lacey's dollhouse, bringing back a handful of items. "It's thin enough to cut, more pliable than wood, inexpensive, and it takes paint well."

She set down one of the beds and tugged off its coverlet to expose the cork nestled within the bed frame. "It's perfect for mattresses or padding-covered furniture. If you slice a bottle stopper, with a little paint it makes an excellent rind for cheese."

Naomi smiled at his thunderstruck expression as her "cheese" spilled onto the table—some already with wedges cut out. She added her pièce de résistance—a "copper" bathtub. "The flexibility allows me to cut the pieces, glue them together, and paint it easily."

"Cork it is." He picked up the tub and turned it around. "I'd only ever seen it used as insulation for walls or even flooring."

Naomi set down one of the flights of stairs and pointed to the railing. "Here are the ship masts. They're already the right size, shaped nicely, and take almost no effort to trim. I also use them for furniture." She indicted the posts on the disassembled bed.

"That'll save a lot of time carving." Michael seemed impressed.

"Oh, you wouldn't believe how much I rely on toothpicks and pieces made for ships in a bottle." Naomi laughed. "And fan blades."

Admiration shown in his gaze. "Clever—very clever. I wouldn't have any idea where to find a supplier for fan blades though."

"I found a fan maker who was closing her shop, and I bought all of the pieces she had on hand. Strips of sandalwood and balsa mostly. I use them for everything from fireplace grates to furniture. But thank heavens there are still plenty of those—I doubt we'd find an accommodating fan maker out here in the territories!"

"I can't wait to hear how you plan to use the wooden dowels."

Naomi didn't keep him in suspense. "Scalloped siding. If you cut the dowel into thin, angled rounds then layer them so the thicker bottom part overlaps the thinner upper portion, it looks like siding. If Lyman Place hadn't been brick, I would've tried it."

Michael rubbed his jaw, as he frequently did while thinking. "That's going to save me a considerable amount of time, and the results will be much more uniform than hand carving each shingle."

"Oh, I'm sure your shingles would have been wonderful." Naomi couldn't remember when she'd enjoyed a conversation more. Here she stood, discussing her techniques with a man who appreciated her method and made her feel almost as innovative as he was himself.

"There are dowels at the mercantile. I remember seeing some the first day I arrived." He looked uncomfortable, and for the first time Naomi wondered why Michael, of all people, had followed her back into the storeroom that day. Why not stay in the main area of the mercantile, grabbing spades and pickaxes with the others?

She slowly put a line through the dowels, crossing it off her list if not her thoughts. "That helps. The other thing we'll need is glass cut to fit the windows, but I don't know the measurements."

Michael grabbed a piece of paper and a pencil to start making notes of his own. "I'll write them out and take them to a glassmaker when I go to fetch the other supplies. The ship masts will be the most difficult to come by, but maybe we can place a large order since we'll use a lot on things like staircases and porch rails?"

"True." Naomi put a careful little question mark beside the item, trying to hide her smile at the way Michael listened to and was already finding ways to tailor the materials for new purposes.

"When do you need these things?" He tapped his pencil on the top of her list. "How long before the lack starts to slow you down?"

"Soon. The linoleum and wall coverings are the foundation for most of the rooms. So you should go next week." Naomi nibbled the inside of her lip, not wanting him to see her distress at the idea of him leaving. She couldn't show how much she'd miss their daily conversations and the simple pleasure of working with a partner.

"It's fortunate," she began brightly. Too brightly—Naomi realized she'd overdone and modulated her tone before continuing. "Lacey and Braden were determined that Hope Falls be a place where workers could bring their families. The little houses are so useful—if one doesn't think about the people who left them behind."

"And why." He sat with her in a moment of silence, acknowledging the losses incurred by the mine collapse. Families torn apart. "But they came in handy when Corning showed up."

"And for storage," she teased, knowing it would make him smile. "But I was thinking more along the lines of setting up a house so when you go for supplies, you can bring Luke home with you."

"You mean. . ." His face lit up as though all his Christmases came at once. "I can bring him back with me next week? To a house?"

"Well, we aren't going to put him in the bunkhouse." Naomi tried to look stern but couldn't manage in the face of his joy. "A one-room cabin is the least we can do. Aside from Arla's little Dorothy, he'll be the only child in Hope Falls. Our first family." She tried not to think about how it wasn't actually hers at all.

$$\infty$$

She's not mine, Mike reminded himself, watching Naomi return from another nature walk, surrounded by lovesick swain. *Don't interfere.*

Not that she asked him to. Actually, by the looks of it, she didn't seem to mind being swarmed every time she stepped foot outside their workshop. But try as he might to convince himself otherwise, Mike minded. He wanted to swat the suitors away from her.

It was maddening, seeing her smile at all of them and no one in particular. He'd come to loathe seeing what new addition perched atop the cougar's hat in the dining room—one of the men actually added a small bird's nest, ostensibly to go with the abundance of feathers fluffing up all over the raggedy thing. Each one of those multihued plumes reminded Mike that other men gave her gifts.

Gifts she accepted, doling out smiles in reward for shameless scavenging. Mike wouldn't be surprised to find out the men were trapping birds, just to pluck a few feathers and bring them to her. And there was nothing he could do to stop it. Nothing he could say to make her see reason. No way to reclaim her attention when they moved beyond the cozy confines of their work space and half a dozen men clamored to speak with her, sit beside her, gape at her....

No. Naomi chose to put herself through this. Even worse, Naomi was going to have to choose one of the men, all now tripping over themselves to snag her smiles. Had they no pride? If Mike could join them, would he? Didn't she know she deserved better than this travesty of a courtship, where half their enjoyment came from the competition?

In two days Mike wouldn't be around to keep an eye on her and make sure none of those men stepped over the line. He wouldn't know how she handled things or how the lumbermen stepped up their attentions. The longer this went on, the more intense it became. And with Mike not present in the workshop, she'd be alone. *Unprotected.*

By the time she emerged from the diner, having shed her coat of companions, Mike worked himself into a thoroughly foul mood. When Naomi settled herself beside him to watch Braden engaging in a cutthroat game of horseshoes, he couldn't keep it all bottled up.

"How did you ditch them?" He slid the diner a sideways glance.

"Don't let anyone else hear you say that." She hushed him, but her grin went a ways toward soothing his pique. "Evie made a batch of shortbread, and she was kind enough to bring out a full plate."

"Good timing." Some of the tension eased from his shoulders. "Good to know someone's keeping an eye on how things are going."

"Oh?" Her green eyes snapped with suspicion. "How's that?"

"You shouldn't be dangled in front of the men like a piece of meat before wolves." Mike jabbed a finger toward the diner. "At least someone's keeping tabs on where you are and with whom."

"And if that 'someone' is supposed to be Evie,"—she pinned him with her gaze—"why did you decide to take on the task yourself?" *Oops.* Mike swallowed, unable to refute the accusation but not willing to own up to it—or open the door for more questions. So he borrowed Luke's method of evading the question. He snorted. Loudly.

"Don't be so dismissive." She folded her arms over her chest. "It's clear that you've been keeping tabs on me, so why deny it?"

Technically he hadn't denied it, but Mike deduced she wouldn't take kindly to the observation. It would help him think better if she didn't look so pretty, with anger making her cheeks all pink. He realized he'd waited too long to talk when she started squinting.

"It doesn't matter." He waved it away and looked fixedly at the game of horseshoes, where Braden was gleefully trouncing Corning.

"Then why did you bother bringing it up in the first place?" Exasperated, she wouldn't stop pestering him. "If it didn't matter?"

"I don't understand why you did it." He shrugged as though her answer wouldn't make much difference. "That's all there is to it."

"We go for walks because the forest is beautiful, and I can spend time with all of them at once, without obviously favoring anyone."

She sounded calmer now. "It keeps from causing trouble."

"No." Mike turned to face her again, wanting to see her face, needing to know what she might refuse to tell him. "I meant I don't understand what possessed you to put out that advertisement."

For the first time, he understood what people meant by the expression "her face fell." It was as though everything happy and bright about Naomi just crumpled until she wouldn't look at him. She looked like she might cry, and that was enough to make him want to pull her into his arms and start apologizing until he fixed it.

Only he couldn't. Mike couldn't hold her. He couldn't fix it.

TWENTY-NINE

What a mess. Naomi stared down at her hands, neatly folded in her lap, and wished she could go back to the day Lacey talked them all into that awful ad so she could talk sense into everybody.

"It was a mistake." She hated how pathetic she sounded. She hated how pathetic she *felt*. And, truth be told, Naomi wasn't too fond of the tell-me-something-I-didn't-know look Michael gave her.

"When the mine went bust, we lost all of the money we invested in Hope Falls. Not just Braden and Lacey, but Cora and Evie and me, too. We'd all gone in together to buy shares. Lacey and Evie invested in the mercantile and café—so they stood to lose the most."

"That explains why you decided to start a sawmill." Michael didn't say it, but Naomi heard the unspoken part of the statement: *but it doesn't explain why you put out an ad to hire your husbands!*

"It's like dominoes." She knew it was cliché, but she couldn't really think of another way to explain how everything came crashing down, piece by piece. "The mine failed. The town went bust. We lost our investment, but Lacey saw a way to turn things around. Problem was, none of us knew the first thing about sawmilling, aside from what Lacey researched. And it wasn't as though we thought we could traipse into the forest, swing an ax, and fell trees ourselves."

"Right." He looked aghast at the suggestion, but beneath that she saw a glimmer of recognition. "The four of you needed help."

Naomi tried to speed things up. "But even if we had the funds to hire men, we wouldn't know who to trust. When Lacey first suggested it, we thought Braden was dead. We had no other brothers or fathers or cousins to come with us. We'd have to go alone."

"Too dangerous." If she'd thought he looked horrified by the idea of them chopping trees, it was nothing compared to the expression on his face as he considered the alternative. "You couldn't surround yourselves with strange men without protection."

Naomi nodded vigorously, glad to see that he understood their reasoning. "Exactly. But when Lacey suggested that husbands could solve our problems, we balked. Every one of us refused to listen. We decided we'd rather take the financial loss than strike out with such a far-fetched scheme. Saving Hope Falls wasn't a good enough reason to endanger ourselves and do something so outrageous."

"And then you learned Braden hadn't died." Michael demonstrated that spectacular ability to piece things together. "You said Miss Lyman and the younger Miss Thompson were coming with or without you. So they came for Braden, and you and the older Miss Thompson came to make sure they didn't get themselves killed along the way."

"That's a rather blunt way of putting it." Naomi considered it for a moment before confessing, "Very blunt—but dead right." A smile played about the corners of her mouth at the pun.

"Which brought you right back to where you started—heading for an isolated place where none of you had the strength or know-how to save the town." Understanding was dawning, but Michael didn't look happy about it. Which was just fine with Naomi, since she wasn't very happy about the situation either. "Without male protection."

"Precisely." Naomi sighed. "At this point, we were also concerned that Braden's injuries might clear the way for unscrupulous men to encroach on the property. We couldn't defend the land, we couldn't protect each other indefinitely, and we couldn't trust any men who'd be willing to follow us to an isolated area."

By now Michael was raking his fingers through his hair in obvious agitation. "Did it occur to you to just wait until Braden recovered? Until either he came home or he could look after you?"

"It occurred to us. But we'd been mourning for my cousin for

weeks already. It was only natural that his sister and fiancée would
rush to his side when we heard he'd been pulled from the mine." She
sniffed at the memory of those intense days. "At the time, there was
still some question as to whether or not he'd survive. You know about
his knee, but the more dangerous injury was a severe concussion that
left him unconscious for two days after he was rescued."

She fell silent, having explained all she could. Michael stayed
quiet, too, and Naomi knew he was turning the problem around in
his mind, trying to puzzle out a solution that was already too late.
Anything more she could add ventured into very personal territory,
and Naomi wasn't about to reveal the other salient points Lacey made
while convincing all of them to take such drastic action.

How could a woman explain the impact of Lacey's argument that
hiring a husband wasn't merely a mercenary flouting of convention,
it was a chance for them to decide what they really wanted from a
spouse? A unique opportunity to select a life partner who could fill
those needs. Instead of waiting for a man to offer a ring entwined
with a lifetime of *his* expectations, they would choose for themselves.
And instead of feeling privileged to have been chosen, they would
feel valued by the men who'd proven themselves worthy.

The idea awakened a dormant hope Naomi had long since left
for dead. A man responding to the ad wouldn't expect an overly
traditional bride. A man willing to view marriage as a partnership
might value her for the prospects she brought to the table. In short,
she might find a man willing to overlook her lack of virtue and
even—here's where the temptation became overwhelming—feel
as though he wasn't making an unspeakable compromise in wedding her.

How could she explain any of that to the man sitting beside
her? She couldn't even explain it to her closest friends. And the way
things turned out, Naomi couldn't justify it to herself. She'd done an
excellent job of backing herself into a corner, and her only possible
escape would be on the arm of a man she didn't really want.

Wrong man. No matter how kind and attentive Mr. Corning was, Cora found herself thinking the same thing every time she saw the admiration in his gaze. *Why isn't Braden looking at me like that?*

This made it difficult to keep up her end of the conversation. At a certain point, Cora realized that it didn't make much difference to Mr. Corning. So long as she contributed the occasional smile, a few nods, and the odd "mm-hmm" or "oh?", Mr. Corning kept things going. Either the man loved the sound of his own voice or else he didn't get much opportunity to speak without interruption.

Her only consolation was the dark looks Braden kept casting poor Mr. Corning whenever he looked the other direction. Of course, Cora couldn't be sure that Braden wasn't just taking exception to having another man take his place pontificating. But somehow she thought his irritation had more to do with the attention Mr. Corning was giving her. That thought alone kept her smiling and nodding.

She'd enjoyed a brief respite during supper, but when everyone bundled in their coats and gathered around a large fire, he glommed on to her again, and Cora couldn't help thinking that after all his practice, she thought Braden could wheel to her side a bit faster!

Gradually she realized that Mr. Corning wasn't yammering on any longer. He was, in fact, looking at her with that very specific combination of expectation of a response and concern that she wasn't giving him that response. But no matter how hard she racked her brain, Cora realized she'd lost the gist of the conversation entirely. She didn't know whether to agree or disagree, and the time clearly passed for a politely vague murmur to suffice. *Oopsie.*

"I'm afraid I just realized I forgot something," she hedged, casting about for an appropriate excuse. She caught sight of Evie bustling back from the kitchen storeroom with a bag of what looked like. . . "Marshmallows! I'm supposed to help Evie pass them out so everyone can toast a few over this lovely fire. You might want to find a long twig or a thin branch or something of the sort."

With that, she hopped up and hurried to meet her sister. As usual, she didn't need to fill Evie in on why she'd rushed over.

"Quite chatty, that Mr. Corning." Evie shook half of the marshmallows into Cora's waiting apron. "You'd think Braden would be so kind as to absorb some of his guest's fondness for conversation."

"You'd think so, wouldn't you? But apparently we'd both be wrong. Thank you for the distraction." Cora tilted her apron so the fluffy little treats lumped together more or less in the middle.

Evie looked from her half-empty bag to the fire, where the men were already holding out stripped branches in obvious readiness. "Well, these won't hold him off for long, I'm afraid. They don't take long to chew. . .but fires are good for more than roasting marsh-mallows. What if I get everyone to ask you to tell a story?"

"All right." Cora began thinking of stories, weighing options and discarding several that wouldn't hold the attention of a bunch of lumberjacks. She smiled at her sister. "My voice is well rested."

They laughed together as they rejoined the group and enjoyed their marshmallow-influenced popularity. In a few moments, the treats were passed out, and the men were briefly silent as each tried to toast their treat the perfect golden brown. The odd failure, blackened like a lump of coal, induced much teasing. One fellow seemed to get it just right, only to have the gooey morsel slide down the branch and plop, hissing, atop the licking flames.

As promised, Evie took advantage of the quiet. "I always think that a good fire with good friends needs only a good story to make it perfect. Cora, why don't you see if you can tell us a tale?"

A chorus of agreement went up around the circle, including Mr. Corning. Now that she was the focus of so much avid attention, Cora found herself grateful that Naomi hadn't allowed her to announce her newfound availability. She couldn't imagine how Naomi dealt with this type of attention so often—it was absolutely unnerving. Cora looked around the circle, her gaze snagging on Braden. He nodded, and suddenly she knew exactly which story she wanted to tell. It was a legend he needed to hear—and a lesson she needed him to heed.

"All right," she announced to the waiting group. "In honor of the fine men seeking to woo my good friend, Miss Higgins, I will tell the "Legend of the Loathly Lady." Listen well, because the moral of the tale reveals the answer to an almost unanswerable question.""

"She's anything but loathly," Mr. Strode objected, giving Cora a look that told her Naomi might have one more suitor than she knew.

"Listen to the story before you judge it." Naomi, who'd taught it to Cora in the first place, smiled in anticipation. "Go on now."

THIRTY

I t's one of my favorites," Naomi whispered as the story began.

So Michael listened and found himself caught up in the story woven around the campfire. He noticed that the other men, some of whom politely feigned interest at first, perked up when they realized this "lady" story revolved around Arthurian legend.

Swiftly, Miss Thompson set the scene. King Arthur, separated from his loyal knights during a hunt, is drawn deep into the forest. The king slays his deer but finds himself at the mercy of an enraged dark knight. Unarmed and alone, Arthur faces certain death by the hand of this opponent, but the dark knight offers him a deal: Return in a year, unarmed and alone, and if Arthur can answer the knight's question he may go unharmed. If he does not give the right answer, he will lose his head and Camelot will be undone. Arthur, of course, agrees to find the answer to the question.

"And what do you suppose was the knight's question?" she asked the crowd. "Something so difficult that the king's failure was certain?" After a moment, the men began to bandy suggestions around the fire.

"Why bad things happen to good people?" Clump guessed, only to be outvoted on the grounds that a *dark* knight wanted to leave the ways of evil a mystery so people could stay weak and afraid.

"Oh, I know!" Bobsley slapped his knee. "If a tree falls in—" He didn't even finish the old saw before groans drowned him out.

Naomi quirked a brow, daring Mike to make his own guess.

But Mike couldn't. Not when the only unanswerable questions

bumping around in his brain concerned the woman sitting beside him. He gave a prayer of thanks when Miss Thompson took up the story again.

"The knight's challenge to King Arthur was to discover. . ." She paused, making everyone lean forward. "What do women want the most?"

Groans and guffaws went up, the men shaking their heads.

"An impossible question indeed." Mike kept a straight face.

"I bet you could find the answer, the way you puzzle things through." Naomi gave him a small smile. "Think about it awhile."

"It's not so obvious for us men," he told her, biting back the first answer: *love*. A part of him still believed everyone wanted to be loved, but hadn't Leticia proven him wrong? What about Naomi, whose plans for the future centered around a business arrangement? No, Mike knew better than to say love was most important to her.

"Security!" Gent announced from across the way. "Women want to be looked after and to know that they and their children are safe."

"Nah, she's right. There is no good answer. Women can't pick one thing when they want so many," grumbled someone in the shadows.

"Don't be sore because you aren't one of them, Williams!" For a moment, it looked as though a scuffle might break out, but Miss Thompson picked up the story and averted the blossoming problem.

"Disheartened but bound by his word, Arthur returned to Camelot. There, his nephew, Sir Gawain, notices the king's melancholy and pries the reason from him. For the next year, both Arthur and Sir Gawain ask thousands of women for the solution to the riddle. But every woman gave a different answer from the last." At this statement, the men starting laughing, and Mike joined them.

Mike shared his answer with Naomi. "Maybe the answer is that every woman wants something different because no two women are the same. Maybe they want their uniqueness appreciated."

She tilted her head and gave him a searching look. "Clever, but I think it depends on how the man shows her his appreciation."

"Something special, just for her." Mike decided to ask his own impossible question. "How would *you* want to be appreciated?"

"Say!" a man shouted. Braden recognized the high climber but couldn't remember the name of the man talking through Cora's story. "There's a better question. What does Miss Higgins want? That's what we need to know!"

If it wasn't for the fact Braden had just been wondering the same thing about Cora, he wouldn't have any patience for the interruption. As things stood, he wondered if this question might open an opportunity to wrangle an answer to his own version. As it stood, he wasn't doing a good job figuring out what Cora wanted, much less how to convince her to let him be the man offering it!

Naomi froze, eyes wide as a startled deer, and Braden felt a little sorry for his cousin. She hated being the center of attention and usually exhibited a distinct talent for fading into the woodwork. If Braden hadn't seen it for himself, he wouldn't believe any woman could render herself almost invisible while staying in plain sight. But Naomi could go quiet, tuck herself in a corner, and watch as most of the people in the room forgot she was still there.

But that wasn't possible anymore. She—along with the rest of the women—thrust herself into the limelight when they posted that ad. *Wait.* The ad! Why were the men asking what Naomi wanted when she'd been kind enough to spell it out for them in the clearest possible terms? Even better, Cora swore she'd helped write the thing. So didn't that mean she wanted the same things on the list?

What had they required, aside from logging or sawmill experience to help get the business off the ground? He racked his brain, trying to remember the exact words. *God-fearing* was the first one. *Hardworking* was another. They'd wisely added *single* because, even though that should be obvious, some unscrupulous fellows might try to trick them. With that in mind, Braden made a split-second decision to surreptitiously have the men looked into. Just to make sure none of them had a surprise bride tucked away in another state. But hadn't the ladies listed something else? One last criteria?

"Right now,"—Naomi all but shouted to catch everyone's attention—"I most want for everyone to let Cora finish the story." The announcement left the men no choice but to quiet back down.

Then Cora was talking, and Braden forgot everything except how her hair glowed in the light of the fire and her eyes shone with mirth while she spoke and her words flowed around him with reassurance and familiarity, weaving a spell through the story. Of course, magic didn't exist anywhere other than legend. No. Such wishful thinking was just a way to spring life lessons on unwary listeners.

"Despairing, with only a day remaining,"—she looked directly at him, and Braden knew King Arthur wasn't the only one whose time ran short—"the king returned to the depths of the forest, hoping to reason with the dark knight. Instead he came upon a hideous hag tucked atop a snow-white mare. Oddly formed of sparse hair, shriveled skin, and yellowed nails, the Loathly Lady looked down upon the good king and bared her blackened teeth in a sad smile.

"She told Arthur she was the sister of the dark knight, and she would tell him what women wanted if he granted her one small request: that she be allowed to wed Sir Gawain. Horrified by the idea of handing over one of his bravest, most handsome knights to this foul creature, Arthur refused her request and left the forest."

"Ah, big mistake," someone hooted. "Rather die than let a friend get shackled to a hag? People marry for worse reasons." Eventually he realized the silence around him turned ominous and probably recalled that most of the men around him were trying to marry a woman who'd advertised for a business partner as a husband. He tried again. "Erm. That is to say, I didn't mean, you know. . ."

"Quit yer jawin' and let her finish the story," someone yelled, making the fool gratefully shut his mouth and stop his retractions.

"And again, Sir Gawain recognized his uncle's sadness and wrangled the truth from Arthur. When he heard of the Loathly Lady's request, Gawain agreed immediately. They wed the very next day, the court full of whispers and regret for the fate of this good knight."

"Well?" Bear Riordan prompted when Cora's pause lasted long enough to show that she wanted someone to ask. "Did she keep her promise? Did she tell Arthur what women want most and save him?"

"Yes. After the ceremony, she revealed to Arthur and Gawain that the thing women most want is sovereignty." Cora stared pointedly at Braden. "The ability to make their own decisions."

Dimly, Braden knew that the men were full of comments. Some agreeing, some contesting an answer obviously supported by the women around them. It might be a story, but Braden reeled at the truth. *Independence? The thing women most want is the same thing I do?*

Even more surprising was the fact that it surprised him. It made perfect sense! Hadn't his sister, his fiancée, his fiancée's sister, and even his mild-mannered cousin been arguing with him for months about their ability to make their own decisions? And he'd ignored them, making demands and handing down orders as though he had the right to personally control every one of their lives.

But it was for their own good! They put themselves in danger with terrible decisions! He protested against the guilt rising in him, but it did no good because, as Cora doubtless intended to show him, *those decisions were* theirs *to make after* my *choices blew up.*

There was an unfamiliar sensation prickling in his stomach and clogging his chest, and Braden suspected it had something to do with the sudden realization that he was a first-class idiot. *I never was before. How did everything change so much? How did I change so much?*

The cave-in. It only took one catastrophe in his well-ordered life to destroy his equilibrium—and not just because it knocked him off his feet either. One crisis took away his choices, and instead of accepting it and moving on, he tried to steal everybody else's.

No wonder Cora avoids me. He swallowed, mouth dry and tasting like the ashes of the fire. *How can I win back my lovely lady now?*

"The story isn't over, gentlemen." Naomi tried to hush them.

"What about Gawain?" By the looks of it, Strode hit on the

right answer again, naming the one element of the legend that didn't resolve happily. He received approving nods from the women, but, more importantly, his reminder that a knight remained in peril made the men quiet down in respect for the fate of the brave Sir Gawain.

"Very good, Mr. Strode." Cora made a point of acknowledging the carpenter, but Braden didn't feel any stab of envy—it was far too obvious that Strode had his eye on Naomi. "That night when Sir Gawain went to his bride, he could not find the Loathly Lady."

"Lucky man." The mutterer got a quick elbow in the ribs.

"Instead a beautiful maiden waited in her place. As it happened, her brother cursed her with hideous looks when she refused to marry as he demanded. The spell could only be broken if she married a handsome knight. Their marriage lifted part of the curse."

"Did you say 'part' of the curse?" Dunstan looked up from scratching behind Decoy's ears until the massive dog nosed his arm.

"Yes, only part." Cora's eyes gleamed, and Braden knew the last part of the story would be the most interesting. "The lady regained her beauty for half of the day but would remain loathly for an equal share. She explained that Sir Gawain could have a beautiful wife at night, in private, or he could have a beautiful wife by day, in public. But his decision could not be undone or changed later."

Corning shook his head. "There's a catch to every contract."

"What a catch." Gent twirled his beloved top hat on the tip of his finger. "To trade the respect of your peers for the bride of your dreams or maintain one's stature and live with a monster."

"It takes a strong man to choose his bride for her own sake and not for what other people will think." Naomi's cheeks glowed, and she'd half risen from her seat in a rare display of irritation.

"So tell us," Braden intervened. "What did Gawain choose?"

"He chose to listen." Cora spread her arms and looked around the circle. "Gawain remembered the answer to the impossible question and honored his bride with the thing women want most. He told the lovely maiden he couldn't make the decision for her."

The answer was so obvious it could have smacked him in the

head, and Braden still hadn't recognized it until Cora finished. His only consolation lay in the fact that the other men hadn't realized it either. Maybe that's why only a legendary knight figured it out.

"The Lovely Lady smiled and told him that, in return for listening to her answer and giving her a choice, the spell was entirely broken. Lovely she would remain for all the hours of the day and night, and none would ever see the Loathly Lady again."

THIRTY-ONE

It can't be her. Naomi staggered, guilt pressing her lungs toward her spine and shame making her want to hide. She watched in disbelief as a very elegant lady daintily disembarked down the train's folding steps. Naomi watched a very familiar face turn toward her, and suddenly it was too late to pretend this wasn't happening. Too late to seek sanctuary in the workshop and pray that the visitors were just passing through and might miss her entirely.

An enigmatic smile tilted the corners of her lips as Charlotte spotted her sister for the first time in five years. That smile pounded in Naomi's heart with the force of a battering ram. *She hates me. I know she does. But she's smiling. Maybe there's a small chance we can rebuild a relationship, that blood is thicker than betrayal and the years have softened Charlotte toward forgiveness.*

She needed to move, but that terrible mix of fear and hope kept her rooted in place in the shadow of the diner. Because her sister hadn't come alone. No. There, smoothly taking Charlotte's arm and oblivious to Naomi, stood the man who'd torn them apart. *Harry.*

Oh no. Her chest pinched, making it difficult to breathe. Five years had passed, but her first glimpse of them brought her right back to the most horrifying moment of her life. The terrible truth Naomi privately mourned and desperately kept hidden from everyone. *Lord . . . Oh Lord. . .why have You brought this upon me?* Naomi desperately sought reassurance. *Why now, when I'm so close to choosing a husband? I know things aren't going as well as I'd hoped, and I spend far too much time thinking about Michael, but still—* A sudden thought grabbed hold of her with iron claws. *Is this why You brought them? Not to restore the last member of my family but only to remind me of the heartache of choosing a man who isn't meant for me?*

She thought she might be sick, right there in front of her estranged sister and the man who'd ruined her life. *How uncivilized.* Then there was no time left to be sick because now Harry caught sight of her and began steering Charlotte over. Naomi could only watch as the Blinmans descended on her like some dark dream.

Perhaps they're going to denounce me. What am I going to do?

Smile. Or at least, Naomi tried to smile. She nudged her mouth into some semblance of a welcome. Then she took a step forward as though on her way to give the congenial greeting propriety demanded. A single step toward doom. It was all her wobbly knees could manage.

"Mimi!" Charlotte launched herself into a crushing embrace.

What on earth is going on? Naomi's mind whirled. Why was the sister who'd shunned her for half a decade now enacting this overblown reunion? Why did this embrace not feel forced and grasping, when Naomi longed for the day Charlotte would accept her?

Mimi. Naomi's nose wrinkled. She'd forgotten the way Charlotte always insisted on using the pet name Naomi disliked most but still threw herself into a tizzy if anyone dared to call her Lottie. *Funny, the things you forget,* she mused. *Almost as strange as the way one's brain stops working properly just when one needs it most.*

"How *have* you been?" Charlotte disentangled herself at last, still smiling. "It's been positively *ages* since I've seen you."

Wait. What? Why did that make it sound as though Naomi abandoned her? Her precarious smile slipped, and Naomi tried to tack it back on, too saddened by the realization that her hopes were for naught. Not that she blamed Charlotte for forbidding so much as letters—her sister had every right to cut Naomi from her life after what happened—but why enact such a grand performance here and now?

Unless. . .unless she kept her promise and never told Harry what happened. The fine hairs on the nape of her neck prickled. *Unless she somehow hid the fact that we haven't so much as written each other, and Charlotte is trying to make sure he never knows about it.*

"Since the wedding." How had she failed to notice how nasally Harry's voice sounded? "Yes, that's it. Such a long time since you left to help your cousins, and now we find you all the way out here!" Astonishment underscored this last, bringing the dawning realization that Harry—and perhaps Charlotte, too—hadn't known Naomi was here.

What a muddle. But at least she could take comfort in the knowledge that they hadn't tracked her down intending to ruin her. Charlotte's affection might be staged, but that was preferable to hostility. Her presence threatened more than Naomi now. If Charlotte started stripping away Naomi's veneer of respectability, Lacey, Cora, and Evie's reputations became vulnerable by association.

"What brings you to Hope Falls?" she blurted out once she could finally speak. It sounded too harsh. Unwelcoming. Accusing, even. Naomi dredged up some enthusiasm. "Such a surprise to see you both!"

"Naomi?" Lacey detached from Evie's side, where they'd both been gawking at the spectacle, and fluttered over to join them. She looked from Charlotte to Naomi, recognition flaring in her blue eyes. "I didn't realize we were expecting guests this afternoon."

"We weren't." Naomi knew she sounded less than gracious, but she refused to be blamed for another unannounced arrival. "I mean, I wasn't. And I don't think they expected to find me here either."

"Oh no." Harry patted Charlotte's hand. "We knew. It's the reason my wife insisted on coming along, wanting to see Naomi."

"You knew?" Naomi's heart, which only just resumed regular beats, plummeted. The sensation was so physically uncomfortable, she rather suspected that her next step would end with a sickly *squish*.

"How intriguing." Lacey tilted her head as though puzzled. "Surely you're Cousin Charlotte? The resemblance to Naomi is absolutely uncanny. But didn't you send notice of your arrival?"

"Wanted it to be a surprise," Harry chortled. "Charlotte ran across your brother's invitation, and when I told her I wanted to see this sawmill venture for myself, she refused to stay behind."

"I wouldn't hear of it." Charlotte tittered like a parakeet.

"Oh, I'll just bet you wouldn't." Lacey's sickly sweet tone didn't fool Naomi, who remembered her cousin's outrage when she'd learned that Harry had originally courted Naomi then switched.

No, Lacey. Naomi gave her cousin a pleading look and a swift shake of her head. *Don't antagonize Charlotte or rile her temper!*

"So many adventures to be had in such a wild place as this!" Charlotte tightened her grip on Harry's arm and gave Naomi a pointed look. "Why should I let my husband and my sister have all the fun?"

She might as well have kicked Naomi in the stomach. The air whooshed from her lungs, and she had to take a step back to keep from keeling over. And Charlotte knew it, too. Her sister's grin became positively feline, and Naomi suddenly knew, without a doubt, that her sister was toying with her. Even worse, she *enjoyed* it.

As the danger grew clearer, Naomi's guilt faded beneath panic. She'd probably been waiting for this chance since Naomi ruined her wedding. With Mama gone, Charlotte could finally take her revenge.

<hr>

"Vengeance belongs to the Lord, but He encourages us to seek justice," Granger reminded Braden when he spotted the new arrivals.

Since Granger came back from his trip to Baltimore, having seen his brother's murderer tried, found guilty, and slated for execution, Granger had mellowed. Or maybe that was Evie's influence. Either way, Braden didn't appreciate his friend's well-meaning reminder that *finding* the saboteur didn't end things, because Braden couldn't mete out the murderer's punishment.

For some unfathomable reason, letting the court decide to hang the criminal counted as justice. To Braden's way of thinking, justice should be more along the lines of breaking a few bones before leaving him enclosed in a cold, pitch-black cave to die slowly—the same sentence his greed handed down to Braden's miners.

Luckily, Braden could shove that aside for further contemplation *after* he caught the criminal. More urgent matters demanded his immediate attention—for instance, the newly arrived suspect who'd just strolled past Braden's window. "Harry Blinman?"

"Say again?" Dunstan craned his neck to look around the paper he'd been perusing. Half curled beneath his master's chair, Decoy raised his head from his paws and cocked his ears. "Harry who?"

"Forget Harry Whoever-he-is." Granger crossed over to the window for a better look at a mysterious woman in violet. "Who's *that*?" From his tone of voice, Granger was more wary than impressed.

Braden let out an exasperated snort. "If you stop blocking the window so I can get a better look, I might be able to tell you."

By now Dunstan took the opposite side, bracketing the window and making it even more difficult to see anything. If Granger sounded wary, Dunstan sounded downright suspicious. "Fancy dame."

"Dame?" Braden snickered. "Never thought I'd hear that word coming from you to describe a lady. She must be Blinman's wife, though why any man would bring his wife here, I can't even imagine."

"I don't use it to describe ladies." Dunstan abandoned the window and returned to his paper. "And the one all decked out in purple might look like Miss Higgins, but she's a rotten egg."

"Looks like Naomi?" Braden took another look. Without Dunstan blocking part of the window, he caught the resemblance he'd missed. He fell back with a groan. "Lacey's going to have my head. How could I forget that Blinman married Naomi's sister? That's Cousin Charlotte—and I've never met her, but Dunstan just might be right."

"How did you know?" Granger squinted over to where the purple lady stood, watching porters remove her luggage from the train. "That she's a rotten egg, I mean. You can hardly see her face."

"Way she carries herself." Dunstan strolled back to his spot, careful not to block the view this time. "See how it's not just good posture?

Her chin's forward, nose up, eyes narrowed. She holds her arms stiff and straight when she directs the porters—keeping as much distance as possible. Very hoity-toity. Thinks too much of herself, too little of others, with just enough charm to hide it from the 'important' people." He nodded as Harry Blinman reached his wife's side. The woman visibly softened. "See? She rounds her shoulders toward him, making him feel bigger and stronger—building him up. For him, she's all big eyes and pretty smiles. Pure manipulation. That woman's a cobra disguised as a kitten, coiled and ready to strike."

"I don't know how you do that." Braden stared, seeing everything Dunstan described and agreeing with his assessment. "If someone asked, I'd say she was just directing the workers and then welcoming her husband to her side. Never would have noticed."

"The shift is too big." Granger rubbed the back of his neck. "She's the kind to ruffle feathers, and Evie's too much a mother hen to let it happen. If I were you, Braden, I'd make the most of my time with Blinman because, like as not, it's going to be cut short."

"I would say Harold Blinman is the last man I would've expected to have drop in, but Corning takes that honor. Remind me to thank Lawson for fielding all his questions about the mill design—and for taking him off our hands for a few hours." Braden rubbed his temple. "An entire week, and I've found nothing to indicate his involvement in the mine collapse. The most suspicious thing about the man is the sheer fact that he toddled out from behind his desk and came here."

"I've got nothing to add to that." Granger cracked his jaw. "For as many questions as he asks, they're all about the sawmill plans, logging, or supply routes. Thing is, he might be avoiding the topic of the mines because he thinks I won't know anything. We made it pretty clear I came on board to run the sawmill, not before."

"We also made it clear that I helped survey the property, recommended the geologists, and helped start the mines." Dunstan put down the paper. "But he hasn't said a word to me either. He's either very optimistic about the new venture and reluctant to bring up past failures, or Corning is trying hard to seem disinterested."

"We can't condemn a man for his lack of conversation." Braden swung his feet over the side of the bed, ready to get into his chair and greet his guests. "Maybe we can do better with Blinman. Even if he plays close to the vest, maybe his wife will let something slip."

Dunstan grinned. "Either way, I won't worry about Evie's ruffled feathers. Lacey's more than a match for any snooty miss."

"I'm not worried about either of them," Braden admitted. "It's Naomi. I can't remember hearing her mention her sister—not one single time in the five years she's lived with us. Naomi isn't a part of her sister's life, and there's got to be a good reason."

THIRTY-TWO

"You stole my wedding night." Charlotte turned on Naomi a moment after Harry closed the door. Just long enough so he wouldn't hear.

At least Naomi hoped he hadn't heard. She hoped no one heard, that no one would *ever* hear. Because if she couldn't make it untrue, at the very least she needed to keep it her and Charlotte's secret. The thing of it was, Charlotte didn't seem very inclined to keep it a secret anymore. That fear, more than the old guilt and shame, is what kept Naomi silent beneath her sister's scathing scrutiny.

"You slept with my *husband*," Charlotte hissed, almost exactly the same way she had on that awful morning five years before. She seemed to think the word *husband* held particular pain for Naomi, and once upon a time she'd been right. Today she probably noticed that it lacked the same impact, so she tried again. "*My* husband."

And even though Naomi knew this was all her fault, knew the shame of her sin and the aching regret for the destruction it caused... she surprised herself. How often had she dreamed of a reunion with her sister? So many times imagining that she'd be overcome with guilt again, offering profuse apologies that just might be accepted this time...but anger steadily overpowered regret.

Lord, what right have I to be angry? After what I've done, I don't deserve to grieve the loss of my innocence or still ache over the reminder that Harry betrayed me with my own sister. Not when I betrayed us all ten times worse. I know I'm in the wrong. I know it.

But still a tiny, stubborn kernel of her heart raged at Charlotte's callous egotism. That she'd intentionally stolen the man Naomi once loved, just to get pretty dresses and a more respected name in society. She hated the way Charlotte saw Harry as nothing more than a belonging to dangle in front of Naomi's nose, the trophy that forever proclaimed her ability to upstage her older sister.

Because in Charlotte's mind, Naomi hadn't betrayed a sacred moral vow or even their bond as sisters. No. For Charlotte, the cardinal trespass had been Naomi's assumption of her position—for daring to touch what *belonged* to her. Harry was just a possession.

"Is that why you came?" Naomi folded her hands in front of her then decided that made her look too much like a penitent child. She wouldn't grovel for a forgiveness her sister would never offer. Not anymore at least. Charlotte didn't know it—and Naomi knew her sister well enough to accept that it wouldn't make a difference even if she did—but ruining Naomi meant ruining Lacey, Cora, and Evie. Their connection to a fallen woman, coupled with their unconventional choices, made all three sitting targets for slander.

Naomi could no longer wallow in a bog of despair, refusing to defend herself against a crime she'd never intended to commit. Now was the time to challenge Charlotte—let her know Naomi had grown too strong to be destroyed by catty comments, snide reminders, or even outright threats. Now wasn't the time for self-flagellation—now was the time to protect Hope Falls and throw her sister off-balance.

"You tagged along to keep an eye on Harry?" She used his nickname to goad Charlotte. Sure enough, her sister's eyes narrowed, but Naomi continued. "To keep an eye on me? Make sure I didn't catch your husband's eye and tempt him into an illicit affair?"

"Don't make me laugh." Charlotte jerked at a knot in her hat ribbons, freed herself, then flung the overblown creation atop the bed. "You possess the charm and grace of a moldering turnip. Do you think I don't know the measures you've resorted to, trying to snare a husband? Everyone knows you couldn't catch a man of your own."

Naomi sucked in a breath. Charlotte wouldn't *inadvertently* destroy the other women of the town by destroying Naomi. No. Her sister *knew* about the infamous advertisement. She knew the depth of the destruction she'd cause if she alienated the only men who might overlook Naomi's past in favor of the future they could create. As much as Naomi hated to admit it, her sister was right. *I can't catch a man.* But lagging behind the bitter reminder came indignation. *Who's Charlotte to say anything, after she stole Harry from me?*

"I might not have caught a husband," Naomi's fingernails dug into her palms, "but at least I can say I didn't steal one either."

"No, you didn't." Charlotte skimmed her hand along the footboard, examined her fingertips, and rubbed them together as though trying to remove nonexistent dust. "But not for lack of trying. How very lowering it must be, to have failed like that. Tell me. What is it like, trying so hard for so little recognition?"

Naomi bit her lip, the taunt jabbing a tiny, tender spot of what used to be her pride. The fact that Harry never realized he'd bedded the wrong sister still hurt. Naomi might not remember that night, but she'd been a novice when it came to hard liquor. Naomi hadn't known better than to follow two fingers of aged whiskey with a few glasses of wine and several champagne toasts. Naomi hadn't known she'd become such an embarrassment that her sister had to drag her from the ballroom and back to the family wing. Most of all, she never would have imagined that she'd wake up in the wrong bed. If Naomi had known any of that, she would've taken the tumbler from her mother's hand and smashed it against the wall!

"Speechless, are you?" Charlotte sank down onto the mattress. "Well, I can't blame you for feeling mortified. If you can't be successful in stealing a man, you should at *least* be memorable."

And that was the crux of the matter. If Harry knew what he'd done, Naomi wouldn't have been able to leave quietly. But a small part of her hadn't forgiven him for not remembering the night he took what only belonged to her husband. Harry had no excuse. He drank with his friends. Often. He knew better than to overindulge and should have abstained on the eve of his wedding, if for no other reason than to respect his new bride. Instead he'd gotten caught up in revelry, taken too many celebratory sips, and lost his head.

Charlotte flapped her hand. "Now go away. You've made me tired, and I need rest because, unlike you, *I* always make an impression!"

Naomi left without another word, too needled to trust herself to speak, too confused by the sudden storm of emotions. She'd tried so hard not to think about Harry, and now the maelstrom hit. She found herself thinking she could almost—*almost*—have understood if he'd only realized his mistake when it was too late to undo the damage. After all, hadn't Jacob done the same with Leah and Rachel? But Harry didn't realize he'd made any mistake. He'd stumbled back to his own chambers, never noticing he'd bedded the wrong sister.

And while his ignorance saved her reputation from certain destruction…it rankled. An insult upon injury. The man who'd taken her virginity *didn't even recognize her*. Harry took her pride when he chose Charlotte, then he stole Naomi's innocence. How could it not hurt? Despite their history, Harry never bothered to notice the real Naomi. Not the woman she was, and not the woman she wasn't.

∞

Was she the woman for him? The question flitted around Mike's mind, swooping in and mixing with his excitement over fetching Luke. *Is Naomi Higgins the woman I should marry? The right mother for Luke?*

Decency dictated that he mourn his wife for at least a year, but widowers with children were often given greater latitude—especially out West, where a man worked sunup to sundown and nannies were all but a foreign phrase. Even if some sticklers balked at a short mourning, no one here knew how long he'd been a widower.

Nor did they know Mike hadn't really lost a wife—how could he lose what he never really had? A wife was supposed to be a helpmeet, a mother to their children, faithful to her husband. Leticia, God rest her soul, fulfilled none of these, and although Mike regretted the way she lived her life and mourned his inability to reach her, he didn't grieve for her as a husband for his mate.

Still, he never imagined he'd be contemplating marriage to another woman so soon. If things were different, he'd have time to court Naomi properly. Time to introduce her to Luke and cultivate the respect and affection sure to blossom between them. Mike didn't doubt Naomi would love Luke—but his son would be more reticent. A new town, a new home, and a new workshop were a lot of big changes to take in all at once. It might already be too much, too soon.

But if he waited to woo Naomi, he would be too late. Even now, during the few days he'd spend away from Hope Falls, the loggers were closing in. *By the time I get back*, he couldn't help the bitter thought, *they'll have constructed an entire tree around that cougar.*

For now he could only keep doing what he'd been doing—praying. Mike prayed for wisdom, he prayed for guidance, and most of all he prayed that the woman he wanted just might happen to want him back and that it was God's plan to bring them together in time to swipe her from the lumberjacks. If not, surely He would have brought Mike to Hope Falls after she was safely married? Or at least not let Mike's thoughts continually drift toward her changeable green eyes.

Mike rubbed his hand along his jaw, resisting the urge to scratch the itchy growth. He'd intentionally gone without shaving for two days before leaving Hope Falls, and after four days his full-fledged beard provided something of a disguise. He prayed it wouldn't be necessary, that the threat of the Bainbridges' selfishness no longer chased his son, but Mike came prepared.

He rested in the assurance that his sister never sent their coded warning. Given the telegram situation in Hope Falls, he might have missed such a message. But Paula knew to send a written letter—addressed to the fictitious Miss Nouveau—as an additional precaution. If they'd been tracked down, there was every chance that her messages might be monitored. Mike had been surreptitiously riffling through the post ever since Granger and the women had cleaned out Draxley's office. No telegram, no letter, no trouble.

And no taking chances with his son's future at stake. As the train eased into the station, all steam and straining steel, Mike tugged his hat brim a shade lower. He grabbed the burlap sack he was using in lieu of a satchel—the better to look like a random deliveryman, if necessary—and moved in an ambling shuffle completely at odds with the urgent need to reach his son. *I was gone too long.*

He felt it with a bone-deep conviction, even though Mike never expected to be back so soon. He'd even warned Luke that it might take the rest of the summer to find a new home for the two of them. Mike realized he'd started to speed up, spurred by the thought of surprising his son. He slowed by degrees, no sudden stops or any abrupt shift in stride. Nothing to draw the attention of passersby.

The nonchalant pace took an agonizingly long time to traverse the few short blocks to his sister's house. As Mike turned the corner, he very obviously checked the street sign and squinted at the structures as though not entirely sure where he was headed. By the time he shuffled up the steps and knocked on the door, Mike felt he'd given a credible performance. It was all he could do to keep his head down so he could hide his grin. *Luke will be so happy.*

The door cracked open. Paula looked out, pale and suspicious, before she ushered him inside. She sagged against the closed door as though to brace against intruders. Her eyes, wide and troubled, made Mike's heart pound long before she confessed, "Luke's not here."

THIRTY-THREE

The sack slipped from his fingers, meeting the rough planks of the raised wood floor with an audible thunk. "What? Where is he?"

"Safe." Paula pushed away from the door. "For now at least."

"Where?" Mike repeated, tensing to bolt out the door and take off running as soon as his sister told him where to find his son.

She laid a restraining hand on his arm. "Mrs. Roberts has him, but you can't go haring after him. If you do, you might as well carry a banner proclaiming, 'Follow me, he's right this way!'"

"Yeah." Mike closed his eyes, forcing his fists to unclench, his shoulders to relax, his breathing to slow. When he had himself under better control, he followed Paula to the table and drained a glass of water. "When did they come for him? How did you know?"

"God watches over His own." Paula refilled his glass and slid it across the table. "I kept in mind what you said about not leaving Luke alone but not taking him around more than necessary—that he might be recognized. So when I needed to go to market last week, I took him over to my friend's place. It does him good to romp around with the other boys a bit. Then he's just one more child in a group—easy to overlook by someone snooping around, peering past fences."

"Are they?" Mike scraped his chair back from the table and flattened himself along the wall, peering through a crack in the curtains. "Looking over fences? Skulking around, asking questions?"

"I'm afraid so. There were two of them waiting for me when

I came back with my groceries, wanting to know if you'd been in contact, if I'd seen my nephew, if I planned to see him soon." Paula smoothed back a strand of hair. "Thank the Lord I thought to put the pot roast in the icebox before I fetched Luke from Mrs. Roberts. If I hadn't stopped by home, those men could have followed me straight to him!"

"Thank God, indeed." But Mike's gratitude couldn't mask his own lack of foresight. No matter his intent, he'd left Luke behind, left him vulnerable to the hired men sniffing around Paula's place. As the picture became clearer, he turned to face his sister again.

"A week, you said?" He waited for her nod. "Why didn't you send the letter and the telegram? I would've boarded the next train!"

"We've been under surveillance since the day they came." Paula started wringing her hands but stopped when she realized it. "Two of them I know by sight. One short, stocky, all in gray with a squashed-in nose. Sits on the bench on the far side of the street for hours. Doesn't move, doesn't blink. He's more rock than man."

"I didn't see him." Mike headed for the other window to check.

"You wouldn't. We can't see the bench from here. Besides, it might be the other one. Tall and gangly, wears all brown, likes to stand in the grouping of trees on the other end. Sometimes they're both out there at once, so we couldn't get by on either side without them seeing. They follow me to market. They follow my husband to work. Our telegraph operator told me they threatened him if he didn't write down a copy of anything I sent or received, and I just know they'd steal the mail from the drop. As long as I didn't send word, they had no reason to stay. I kept hoping they'd leave."

"Well, now we'll be hoping they stay." Mike put his arms around his sister, trying to absorb the tension he'd put her through. "How do you check on him? How does Mrs. Roberts know what's going on?"

Paula's shoulders squared and she stepped back, smiling for the first time since he'd walked through the door. "Our neighbor—she's gotten on in years and her son's away on business, so I do the shopping for her as well. She uses the oldest Roberts boy to do other errands and send messages. So that's how I warned them, and that's how I hear about Luke and know he's still safe."

"That's brilliant." Mike knew she needed to hear how well she'd done, needed to know that her worry and caution had been worth it. "There's no other person in the world I would have trusted to take care of him, and no one could have protected him better. Thank you."

"Don't be silly." She dabbed her eyes and blotted her nose with a hanky and stuffed it back into her apron. "After all the ways you've helped me? I'd do anything for Luke. Ask and it's done."

In spite of himself and the situation, Mike felt the beginnings of a grin. "I can't tell you how glad I am to hear you say that. Now tell me, have you ever gotten a book of wall-covering samples?"

"What are you talking about?" Cora tucked an errant strand of hair behind her ear and tried to concentrate on Martha McCreedy's explanation. She wasn't managing very well, unable to make out most of the words beneath her own panicked chorus of, *No, it can't be.*

Because if Martha was right, there was nothing they could do. And after they worked so hard to see Arla and baby Dorothy through the birth, Cora's mind refused to accept that. Arla would be fine simply because she had to be fine. Or because too many people had died on—or in—this mountain during the past year. Or because Mr. Lawson certainly wasn't up to the challenge of raising his niece. But whatever the reason God chose as the most compelling, Cora couldn't see beyond her blind need for things to be all right.

"No," she interrupted Martha, only to realize that the older woman hadn't been speaking for a while. "You're wrong. When I checked on her this morning, Arla was fine. A little tired, but that's to be expected. She's very excited about our plans to make a nursery, and when she's not with Dorothy or napping, she's knitting. The most dangerous thing in Arla's life is those knitting needles."

Martha's eyes brimmed with compassion and resignation. "I'm

sorry, dear. But you're going to have to face the truth and send away for a nursemaid. There won't be much time to find a good one."

"I'm getting Doc." Cora abandoned the half-finished ironing but found her exit cut short when Martha grabbed hold of her elbow.

"He's already with her." Martha didn't let go immediately. "And you can't go storming in there, demanding to hear pretty lies. Soon enough Arla will know deep down that it's too late, and if you don't start making preparations, she'll be fretting over Dorothy's future instead of enjoying what time she has left. Don't make it worse by pretending things are all right; make it better by promising a mother you'll make sure her daughter is cared for."

Cora jerked her arm away and glared. "Hope is not a pretense. Giving up doesn't give God room to work and show us His will."

"*His* will, Cora. Not yours. Not mine." Martha took a deep breath. "Hope as hard as you can and pray harder still, but prepare yourself for the worst. Send for a nursemaid. If Dorothy needs her, she'll be ready. If she doesn't, I'll happily send the woman home."

"She seemed fine this morning." Cora sniffed, trying to ease the prickles of fear and sorrow. "She's seemed fine since Dorothy was born. How did I miss this? Could we have done something sooner?"

"Childbed fever comes on like this." Martha patted her hand.

"I thought it presented by the third day. We're past that."

"It can come on as late as ten days after the birth," Doc's rough voice interjected. He hunched his way forward, burdened by bad news. "If it were just the stiffness in her joints and the headache, I would be suspicious. But she's cold and clammy to the touch, didn't want me to move any of the blankets she's heaped atop herself to try and keep warm. The cold fit confirms puerperal fever, I'm afraid."

"Some women pull through, don't they?" Cora heard the shrill of her own demand and tried to soften it. "Arla might not die?"

"Few women live once they've contracted it. It's an infection of the blood itself, not something to be isolated for treatment." He set down his bag and rummaged through, pulling out various bottles. "Next will come the fever—the heat is terrible, so put her in a cool bath until it subsides. She'll have a powerful thirst, so let her drink her fill until her stomach starts to pain her. Then she won't want to eat, and she must if she's to continue feeding the babe."

He pointed to a small brown bottle, giving directions on dosage and timing to lessen nausea. Then he gave other instructions for a green-bottled syrup to help her sleep. "For now, make her as comfortable as possible. I'm sure Mrs. McCreedy's already spoken with you about seeking out a nursemaid. I'll come back later."

Cora made it to the nearest chair and plunked herself down. *Not Arla*, she began to importune. *I know I've used up more than my fair share of prayers lately, begging for Braden's recovery and asking for good men for Evie and my friends, but Arla. . . Oh Lord, why would You take Arla so soon after giving her the joy of a daughter? When Dorothy will already never know her father, why imperil her mother? I don't understand. How could it be Your will to orphan an infant?* Cora swallowed against the tears. *Everyone needs to be loved.*

∞

"I don't like her." Lacey plopped onto the settee, not bothering to modulate her tones. "Charlotte may be your sister, Naomi, but I refuse to claim such a condescending cow as any relative of mine!"

"You will *not* antagonize my sister." Naomi fixed her cousin with an icy glare. Lacey may be adept at social sparring, but there was nothing Charlotte loved so well as sharpening her claws on another woman. And this time she'd dipped the points in venom.

"Listen." Lacey leaned forward, dropping her voice so Cora and Mrs. McCreedy wouldn't hear her all the way up the stairs. "I'll admit, I held a bias against Charlotte even before I met her. You've never complained or spoken ill of her, but I've not forgotten Mr. Blinman courted you first, and she intentionally cozened him into marrying her instead. I can't imagine you've forgotten either."

"No." Naomi tried for a wry smile and felt it fall flat. "Some things a woman never forgets." *Even if she can't remember it all.*

"She wears your face but hasn't your heart. I can't understand how two sisters so close in age can be so far apart in character."

"Different fathers, different upbringings. I went to boarding school here in the States, but Charlotte's father insisted she be educated at an exclusive finishing school in France. Mother fought against it, but in the end familial tradition held sway." Naomi shrugged as though she could nudge away the painful memories.

She didn't tell Lacey that she and Charlotte had been close when they were little or how badly she missed her sister when she went to school. She and Charlotte begged and pleaded when they'd learned they were to be separated so often, but their tears changed nothing. Two decades and one debacle later, Naomi knew tears still changed nothing. Whatever connection she and Charlotte once shared had been severed long ago. A quick, clean end might not have done so much damage. But it had taken years of distance and difference to unravel their bond, leaving Naomi with frayed feelings worn raw with regret.

Lacey harrumphed her back to the present. "Well, the French ruined her, I say. I could just throttle Braden for bringing her here." Her face screwed up as she recited in a low voice, " 'No one you would know.' Ugh. Trust a man to forget the important things."

"Braden might not consider it important when so much time has passed and Hope Falls is in need of investors. He meant no harm."

"I suppose." Lacey fell silent as Cora bustled down the stairs, waiting to drag her into the conversation. "Cora! You'll never guess what's happened. Braden's invitations brought two more arrivals!"

Cora joined them, eyes downcast and nose reddened as though from sobbing. Or perhaps from trying not to sob. Sometimes it was difficult to tell. "There'll be one more new person soon enough."

"What's wrong?" Naomi guided Cora to a chair when it looked as though she might simply sink to the floor. "Who else is coming?"

"A nursemaid." Red-rimmed eyes rose to meet their scrutiny. Her voice lowered to an almost inaudible mutter. "Arla's taken ill."

"I'll get Doc!" Lacey practically leaped from the settee.

"He knows." Cora's pronouncement had them all sit back down.

Tears slipped down her cheeks as she told them, "Childbed fever."

"No." Naomi's jaw dropped, and she struggled to compose herself. Childbed fever took almost every mother it chose. So few women survived, the diagnosis might as well be a death sentence.

"But..." Lacey's protest sounded feeble. "The birth went so well."

"There's still hope we might contain the fever and bring it down." Despite the words, Cora looked as worn as their hopes.

You work miracles where You wish, Lord. I pray You see fit to bestow one on Arla and let her live to be a mother to Dorothy. She adores that baby girl, and I know she'd never make her daughter feel unwanted or flawed just because Dorothy's father has passed away. Naomi's heart clenched at the thought and the memories behind it.

Lacey rallied before any of them. "What can we do to help?"

"Keep her cool and comfortable, lots of water. I've contacted an agency, and they're sending a nursemaid for Dorothy. She'll arrive tomorrow. Doc put in an order for ice. Arla gets agitated when he comes in—when anyone but Martha or I go into the room actually." Cora frowned. "Mr. Lawson isn't handling things well. As soon as he heard, he rushed up to see her. Then he left—and hasn't come back."

"Perhaps it's best that he grieves now so he can be strong if he needs to handle the worst," Naomi ventured, although privately she couldn't imagine leaving her sister's side if Charlotte were the one suffering. Time took away precious things, leaving family with nothing to hold on to. How could anyone let go a moment early?

THIRTY-FOUR

Mike struggled to hold on to his patience, anxious to hold Luke and see that he was fine. Unfortunately, patience was one of those virtues he found easier to cultivate than to exercise. Generally he felt patience was a good thing. He worked to have stores of it so he could wait through difficult days, months, years. . .an entire marriage. But longsuffering was a completely different sort of patience than the kind that kept a man from stomping around, being short with shopkeepers, and generally buzzing around like a demented bee.

He wrestled with his agitation with each step, each word, each stop he made to gather Naomi's dollhouse supplies. Mike and Paula hatched the plan together. She'd go about her daily business, stop for the wallpaper samples, and drop them off at her elderly friend's house with instructions for Mrs. Roberts. When the Bainbridges' henchmen had gone for the night, she would place one of the white patterned squares in the front window to signal the all clear. If the wallpaper remained in the morning, Mike would grab Luke and hop on the first train out of Dallas. It didn't matter which direction the train headed—he could always double back after they were safe.

Meanwhile, Mike would gather everything on Naomi's list. He forced himself to move slowly, unhurriedly, like a man going about his normal daily business. If anyone followed him—and he caught sight of The Stone several times during the course of the afternoon— they'd find nothing suspicious in his activities. Thankfully, it kept him busy. If he'd had nothing to do, Mike would've gone mad.

Actually, that part remained in question. He'd taken a bed at a lodging house, careful to make sure that the room he shared with four other men had a back window. While they slept, he'd slip out and return to Paula's street under cover of darkness. Mike would conceal himself well, wait for daylight to dawn, and watch for the wallpaper. If one of the lackeys appeared, he'd wait them out.

He lay awake the entire night, going over possible scenarios and praying that Luke was fine and they'd escape without leaving any trail behind. Other than Paula, Mike had no family. He'd left his friends behind when he skipped town. After this, the Bainbridges would have no leads left to track. They'd have to accept defeat.

The thick, almost smothering darkness of night began to thin. Mike sat up, his legs on the side of the bed, his hand fisted around the burlap sack. He waited, watching black soften to charcoal, charcoal seep to gray. Mike edged to the window, thankful that none of his roommates protested leaving it open on a warm summer night.

He lowered the bag, swung his leg over the sill, and slid down. Staying in shadows marginally darker than the rest of the world, he pulled his hat from the sack and tugged it low over his brow then moved into the night. Mike hid himself in a cluster of trees as morning dawned, illuminating the streets with watery light. He smiled to see the white square in the window, glowing with promise.

Somewhere inside that house, Luke slept. He'd always been a sound sleeper—his head hit the pillow and he slept like a log. That was good—he needed Luke well rested and in good spirits for the journey home. *Home.* Strange how quickly home became a workshop in Hope Falls and the woman who ran it. Mike hoped his son would see the town—and Naomi—as he did.

They'd specifically instructed Mrs. Roberts not to tell him about the plan ahead of time. Exceptional as Luke was, ten-year-old boys weren't known for their prowess at intrigue. They couldn't hide all their excitement, and if one of the Bainbridges' men caught a glimpse of Luke peering through the window in anxious anticipation, things would get very ugly, very fast. To make sure that didn't happen, Mike planned to wait it out, take things nice and slow.

Or agonizingly slow, as the case may be. Mike couldn't remember the last time dawn's soft light spilled forth so gradually. The sun decided on a leisurely morning, but Mike couldn't afford that luxury. He shifted his weight from one foot to the other and back again, peering around the tree trunks in every direction to make sure no one arrived. To make sure no one was watching him in return.

Finally, the day began. Women bustled about, lighting cook fires and sending spools of smoke into the crisp morning air. The piping voices of young children joined the background. Smells of bacon, coffee, and biscuits ventured from open windows to scent the air and tempt slugabeds to the breakfast table. And still no sign of the men who'd been lurking in the lane for more than a week. Even better, Mike didn't see anyone else set up watch on the street.

As casually as he could, Mike swung his now-heavy sack over his shoulder and ambled across the way and down toward the Roberts' house. After a nonchalant glance around to make sure no one looked interested in his destination, he nipped behind the house itself. A tap on the frame of an open window. A few endless moments while his heart slammed against his ribs. And then a small boy was shoved through the opening, hair ruffling as he descended, a book of wallpaper samples clutched against his chest. Mike caught him and slapped a hand over Luke's spreading grin before he could shout a greeting.

The last traces of bleariness vanished. Luke's eyes widened as Mike raised a single finger to his lips, warning to keep quiet. He pulled back his hand and caught Luke again, this time when his son flung himself into his arms. This time Mike picked Luke up and didn't let go until they were tucked away on a departing train.

"Where are we going, Dad?" Luke burst out as soon as Mike told him it was safe to speak. "This time we stay together, right?"

"We're sticking together, and we're going home." Mike wrapped an arm around Luke's shoulders. "There's someone I want you to meet."

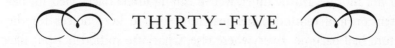

THIRTY-FIVE

N aomi!" Her sister's trill pierced through the workshop window, which Naomi left uncovered even in the drizzling rain. Overcast though the day might be, some natural light still shone through.

For a brief, cowardly moment, Naomi considered ducking beneath said window in hopes that Charlotte would peek in, see an empty room, and keep walking. But Arla's rapid decline had strengthened Naomi's resolve to make the most of her time with Charlotte. Perhaps they'd never be reconciled—Naomi knew she didn't deserve forgiveness even if her sister were the sort to extend it—but perhaps they could blanket the past in a newfound peace. *I have to at least try!*

So she stood up, brushed her hands against each other to dislodge some sawdust, and waved through the window. "In here!"

Astonished by a deluge of icy drops, Naomi hastily pulled her arm back inside. She'd been focusing so intently, she'd not registered that the morning drizzle became a downpour. Now that she noticed, Naomi realized the biting chill seeped into the workshop, too. As her sister flung the door open, Naomi headed for the modest cookstove. She added logs until the fire blazed hot and bright.

"So this is where you escaped to!" Charlotte swept over to warm her hands by the fire, gaze raking the room in abject disapproval.

"The workshop isn't an escape." Naomi recognized the lie as it dropped from her lips. Even without Michael's conversation and smiles, the workshop remained her refuge. Primarily, it was a place to work—but in her work, Naomi found an escape. Focusing on minute details distracted her from the many hurts haunting Hope Falls.

At the house, Arla moaned in pain and baby Dorothy wailed for her mother. In the diner, well-meaning lumberjacks vied for her attention and reminded her just how limited her choices for the future had become. Everywhere else, Charlotte sniffed her out like a hound chasing a hare. And the daily train stops heightened hopes she shouldn't have but never brought Michael home with Luke.

None of that followed her into the workshop. . .until today.

"Well, it's not *my* idea of an escape," Charlotte conceded in a tone that implied she held higher standards than her sister. "But it is out of the rain and away from the diner where that Evie woman acts like she owns everything and won't answer questions. Would you believe she told me to make myself useful or make myself scarce?"

Naomi smothered a chuckle by pretending to clear her throat. "Yes, well, Evie does own the diner and doesn't answer to anyone over how she runs it. I know it seems strange the way we do things, but in Evie's kitchen, if you're not helping you're in the way—and, yes, she'll tell you so. The men aren't allowed inside at all." She tacked on this last in an attempt to soothe Charlotte's indignation.

"She did seem to have her hands full." Charlotte unbent a little. "I vow, Naomi, you could *hear* the men sniffing on the other side of those batwing doors! They all tromped in once the rain started coming down in sheets. Something about dangerous conditions—sticky summer sap and slippery rain making things too difficult."

"Oh, I didn't realize." Naomi closed her eyes, knowing she needed to go join Evie in the kitchen or at least help Lacey come up with a way to occupy the displaced workers. As she knew from previous experience, rainy days made the men ornery, and the last thing they needed was for a fight to break out in the diner. Again.

But she had so much to do. *I'm already short on time, and somehow everything takes longer when Michael isn't here with me.*

"I assumed not." Charlotte gave another sniff as she looked around again. "So this is where you spend your time, cobbling together tiny knickknacks? When Mother shipped you off to Charleston, I never imagined you'd resort to taking up a *trade*." She managed to make honest work sound like the lowest sort of crime.

"How fortunate," Naomi murmured, giving her sister a faint smile, "that my choices are not limited by your imagination."

Charlotte tittered as though amused, but her eyes narrowed. "Yes. Your unconventional choices have brought you unexpected options. However will you decide among your throng of suitors?"

Her shoulders slumped forward, but Naomi recognized the sign of defeat and pulled them back before her sister could comment. Now was not the time to indulge in morose feelings and show weakness. Now was the time to show her sister that she'd moved on. That she'd rather be sitting in a sawdust-strewn workshop in the middle of a mountain storm than pouring tea as Mrs. Harold Blinman.

"I don't know how I'll choose." She screwed the silver-plated cap and brush onto the cut-crystal paste pot Lacey gave her instead of admitting that the only man Naomi might consider didn't see her as anything more than a fellow worker and friend. *How can a woman choose a husband when the man she wants doesn't offer for her?*

Not that she could have chosen Michael. Choosing him would mean telling him about her past, and then he wouldn't want her anyway. When he remarried, Michael would choose an upstanding woman to be the mother of his children. Naomi picked up the tiny crib she'd been gluing, inspecting the rails while she thought. *Michael is too good a father to give Luke anything less than a good mother—a shining example of what a wife and woman should be. Not me.*

With a sharp crack, four of the crib rails splintered away from their frame, broken by Naomi's clenched fist. She carefully set the piece down, knowing better than to further reveal her inner tumult. She shrugged at Charlotte and announced, "Not sturdy enough. I'll drill deeper impressions with my awl before gluing the rails. Everything that goes into the dollhouse has to be strong enough to withstand being grabbed by children and shoved about the room."

"If only there were so easy a test to eliminate unsuitable husbands." Speculation lit Charlotte's avid gaze. "Although, I must say, you've done an admirable job of making sure they're all impressively strong. Perhaps you need to see how they temper all that raw physical power before you make your final choice?"

"Perhaps." Naomi didn't see any harm in agreeing with her sister when Charlotte accepted the crushed crib as Naomi's barometer of her own work. Besides, anything that bought her more time before she was trapped into accepting one of the men couldn't be so bad.

⁕

"Worse, much worse." Doc shook his head as he whispered his assessment of Arla's condition. "Her pulse is over one hundred thirty beats per minute, and the white coating of the tongue is darkening. You'd best say your good-byes while she's awake."

Cora gave a mute nod, unable to muster any further response. She drew a bolstering breath as the doctor took his leave. For two days she and Martha had watched over Arla, bathing her with cool cloths, giving her water, coaxing broth down her throat. Almost insensible with the fever, Arla no longer protested when Lacey and Naomi took turns through the night so Cora could close her eyes.

"We failed." She looked at Martha now, stricken afresh by their inability to avert the tragedy. "What can we do for her now?"

"The same as we have been. Pray, keep her as clean and comfortable as possible. But for now, I need to find Mr. Lawson and tell him he won't get another chance to say good-bye to his sister." Martha's lips tightened in disapproval, adding a few more lines to those already creasing her cheeks. "Doc will have given Arla something, so bring her Dorothy. Let her hold her daughter one last time so the happy memory can ease her heart on the way to heaven."

Blinking back the tears she'd seen mirrored in Martha's eyes, Cora grasped the banister and pulled herself onto the first stair. Every step seemed so much harder than before, weighted with sorrow unalloyed by hope. They'd fought for Arla's life and lost. Cora might have been better able to accept the failure if it didn't wear the face of her friend and shape the fate of her beloved baby girl.

She pushed open the door to see her friend propped up against a multitude of pillows, draining yet another glass of water. Arla's hand shook as she replaced the empty cup, knocking it against the side of the table and then the top before managing to set it down. After being insensible with fever throughout the night, an ice bath that morning had revived her to an almost miraculous degree. For a moment, Cora thought perhaps Doc read things wrong, that they'd lessened the fever boiling Arla's blood enough to give her a chance.

"Will you bring me my Dorothy?" Face flushed and eyes bright, she looked like a happy young mother as she asked for her daughter. But the flush warned of fever regaining its stronghold, and Arla's bright gaze looked wide and glassy rather than joyous and alert. One hand pressed against her swollen abdomen as though holding back pain, and her breaths sounded sharp and shallow between each of her words.

"Of course." Cora crossed the room, lifted Dorothy from the bassinet Lacey ordered weeks in advance, and straightened the tiny white cap frilling across her forehead. She cuddled the tiny bundle close, drawing comfort from her sweet warmth as she returned to the bedside. A few rearranged pillows helped provide the support Arla couldn't manage so Cora could tuck the baby into her mother's arms.

"Precious." Arla snuggled close to her daughter, rewarded with a gummy little yawn as Dorothy snuggled back. "Such a blessing."

"Yes she is." Looking at the baby, Cora couldn't help but share her mother's smile. There, in Arla's arms, lay a blessing to believe in. The miracle of life lessened the disappointment of death, if only just enough to help a grieving heart hold faith.

Arla's shoulders sagged, and Cora hastily slid another pillow beneath her friend's forearm to keep the baby supported. She wouldn't take Dorothy away unless Arla asked her to. That tiny daughter wouldn't know many moments in her mother's arms, so each second became something to cherish, blanketing a soon-to-be-orphaned child in the knowledge and depth of her mother's love. When Dorothy grew, she'd hear the words, be told by friends and family how Arla adored her—but this moment, this half-formed memory, could be hidden in her heart forever, an underlying certainty every child needed.

"Thank you." Arla's whisper drew Cora's gaze from Dorothy. Her friend's flush had deepened even in that short a time. "For helping me. For helping bring my daughter into this world so I could hold her even a few times." Tears rendered them both silent for a while.

"I wish I'd been able to help more," Cora finally burst out.

"Will you?" More than tears and fever brightened Arla's gaze. The hand not supporting Dorothy reached out, fingers curling in Cora's sleeve. "Will you help my daughter? See that she's fed?"

"I already took care of it." She patted her friend's hand then enclosed it with her own. "The nursemaid came this morning, Arla."

She blinked, her gaze unfocused for a moment. "Good." Arla blinked a few more times, obviously fighting against the medicine. She grimaced, knees drawing toward her stomach as if to ward off a sudden wave of pain. Arla curled herself around Dorothy until the spasm stopped. Then she cupped her daughter's cheek, pressed a final kiss to her forehead, and lifted Dorothy. "Will you take her, Cora?"

"Of course!" Cora gently accepted the fidgeting baby and unwound the top blanket. Even such a short time with her mother made Dorothy overly warm, and fussing gave her a moment to collect herself. She shifted in her seat so Arla could look at her daughter as she drifted off into peaceful rest. "See? She'll be just fine."

"Thank you. My brother can't take her." Arla's hand clutched hers again as she fought to finish before sleep claimed her. "But I can rest, knowing you have Dorothy. I trust you, Cora. Like. . .a sister."

Cora suddenly realized what her friend meant. "Wait, Arla!"

But her friend's grip already went slack, Arla's eyes drifting shut as she whispered, "Trust you. . .with Dorothy. Take care of her. . . ."

THIRTY-SIX

I've taken care of everything!" Charlotte sashayed into Naomi's workshop the next afternoon, eyes alight with triumph and mischief.

Too tired after helping look after Arla through the night and distracted by the knowledge that their efforts weren't succeeding, Naomi didn't understand what her sister meant. At least not until Charlotte moved aside and began ushering lumbermen into the room.

Rory Riordan edged in first, instantly making the room feel half its size. Gent trundled after him, unwrapping a sodden scarf and flinging water droplets on everyone nearby. Bobsley bounded in next and rabbited over to the stove, looking very pleased with himself. And, though she couldn't spot him at first, Naomi heard Clump's distinctive, heavy tread bringing up the rear. He shouldered himself between Gent and Riordan, beaming with open enthusiasm.

"Never enjoyed the rain so much as today," he announced loudly.

"We should have asked about your work before." Riordan sounded partly apologetic, partly interested, and entirely uncomfortable—as any very large man would feel if surrounded by delicate miniatures.

"You did ask!" Naomi found her voice, if not her wits. "We've spoken of it during several of our walks together, remember?"

"Yeah." Bobsley sauntered over to the table displaying the replica of Lyman Place. "But picturing things ain't half so good as seeing them. That's why we hopped on your sister's invitation to pay you a visit and maybe lend a hand so long as this rain keeps up."

"Lend a hand?" Naomi repeated faintly, shooting her sister a look she couldn't even name. Part glower, part disbelief, part plea to fix this awful mess. Needless to say, Charlotte disregarded it.

"Absolutely!" Her sister glided to a stool in the far corner and waved one leather-gloved hand to indicate the worktables. "Just yesterday we discussed how you already know they're strong but wanted to see how they balanced that considerable strength with the other, finer qualities a woman might hope to find in a husband."

"Such wisdom alongside such beauty." Gent swept his ever-present top hat from his head, dousing everyone anew with dislodged rainwater. Incidentally, the gesture also revealed sooty black smudges and streams where the water passed through his dyed hair.

Riordan moved away, found himself too close to Charlotte, and shifted back as though he'd been poked with a knitting needle. Clump shot Gent an unacknowledged glare and made a fuss over brushing water from his beloved suspenders. Bobsley missed the entire thing, his nose mere millimeters from the mullioned windows of the Lyman Place model as he squinted, trying to view the rooms beyond them.

"This is no wisdom of mine," Naomi refuted, hard pressed not to giggle at her gaggle of suitors. Really, it wasn't funny. Lack of sleep and a myriad of emotions were just converging and making her somewhat silly. Though in all honesty, the men's antics didn't help.

She suddenly wondered what Michael would say if he saw their workshop invaded by her earnest, bumbling beaus—and her smile faded. Michael wasn't here, and she didn't know when he'd make it back. And even if Michael were here, he wouldn't be actively seeking her company; he merely accepted her presence as a business necessity.

Then, too, if Michael were here, there would be no interruption. After all, the men respected another man's work—they just didn't consider extending the same courtesy to a woman's work. Naomi remembered how these men tried to take away her tools and bodily lift her from working through the landslide to free Lacey. Their strength lay in their muscles, perhaps, too, in their protectiveness and obvious willingness to help in any little way.

But they were weak when it came to understanding how to approach her, how to respect the woman they strove to win as their life's partner. The thought was downright depressing. One man worked alongside her but didn't seek her hand. Four other men vied for her hand, but her only options would never want to work alongside her. *Charlotte is right. . . . I need to learn more about them and let them learn more about me. Maybe something can come of this after all!*

"Wisdom, whim, or what-have-you, I'm glad." Clump crossed the room, barely needing to stoop beside Bobsley for the same view.

"Well." Charlotte regained everyone's attention, gave a dainty sneeze, and said, "I do believe it's an excellent idea for your beaus to prove that they have the patience, creativity, and gentle touch needed to bring my sister's dreams to life. First, in building your dollhouse and later, so you can build your lives together."

If Naomi saw her sister smirk at that last, maudlin sentiment, none of the men caught on. Whatever game Charlotte played to amuse herself, it seemed to their advantage to follow along. Trouble was, Naomi didn't understand where Charlotte's enmity had gone. Why was Charlotte working so hard to help orchestrate Naomi's wedding? The only explanation she could think of made Naomi cringe. *Does she think I'm still in love with Harry and might try to win him back? After all that happened, he's the last man in the world I'd want . . . But maybe Charlotte's trying to protect us all from my past mistake.*

She tried to give her sister a reassuring smile as Charlotte slipped from the workroom, lamenting that sawdust made her sneeze. Whatever her reasons, Naomi appreciated that her sister was trying to make her choice easier. Amid so many disappointments, this unexpected alliance—however oddly motivated—warmed Naomi's heart.

Perhaps God did bring her sister to Hope Falls to remind her not to lose her head over the wrong man—but maybe He'd also brought the chance to heal old wounds. His blessings changed things.

Naomi didn't have to force her smile as she approached Bobsley and Clump, still trying to peer through tiny windows. She gestured for Riordan and Gent to join them then placed her hand on the house.

"Let's see what happens when we turn things around."

◯◯

No going back. Braden watched as everyone piled small stones atop Mrs. Nash's grave. Prayers had been lifted, hymns sung, memories shared, and tears spilled over the now-covered ground. Funny how he'd never noticed that people buried these things alongside their loved ones, as though cold earth could actually absorb hot grief.

Her passing had been unexpected, swift, and awful for those who'd grown to know the woman and helped care for her through the birth of her daughter and later the futile fight against her fever. Lawson refused to speak, as though his mouth were a Pandora's box of pain that he couldn't allow to be unleashed in public.

Cora cuddled the baby close, tears slipping down her cheeks in a nonstop stream that told of a deep friendship Braden's fiancée had established with the now-dead mother. She looked in sore need of comforting, and Braden promised himself he'd go to her. *After.*

For now he waited as everyone filed away from the grave site, waving Granger away when it looked as though his friend might try to wheel him off. People probably thought the long, difficult rise up the uneven path wore him out, but he was staying because he chose to. Because the weight of his own guilt, shame, and grief pressed hard against his chest, demanding release before he could leave.

I should have come sooner. When he was finally alone, Braden pulled out a bandana and quietly—because sound carried through these mountains, even if no one could see him—shed his own tears. He wept for each wooden cross marking the ridge, for each man who'd died in the mines he'd cut deep into the neighboring mountain. His chest heaved with sorrow at the knowledge that several of the plots held nothing more than names, their owners never found. *Lost forever.*

Why, God? Why let this happen? Why let them die? Braden's heart cried its own lament. *Why didn't You let me die with them and save another in my place? They didn't deserve their fates, and I didn't deserve Your grace, even if I didn't cause the collapse.*

When the tears slowed, Braden looked over the ridge. Below, a sparkling stream wound through the lush forest. In a land of such abundance, the loss of life seemed senseless and wasteful. He rolled over the uneven dirt, brushing his fingers over every wooden cross and praying for the souls they represented. He knew each name, could envision each face, and for the first time since the tragedy, this didn't haunt him. Finally, Braden saw the blessing in his knowledge.

If I hadn't insisted on personally hiring every worker, meeting every man, who would mourn them this way? Braden came to the end of the row, his tears slowing to a stop as resolve replaced sorrow. *More important, who would hold their murderer accountable?*

∽

"Her?" Nose flat against the window, Luke jabbed his stubby little finger against the glass each time he caught sight of a woman. "No, she's too blond, and you said Miss Higgins has black hair, so maybe . . . Her? Or maybe that one—no, that one's got to be too old. How 'bout her—no, she has a baby already so she must be a Missus not a Miss."

So far he'd pointed at Miss Lyman, the elusive Mrs. McCreedy, and the younger Miss Thompson who happened to be holding Mrs. Nash's newborn. Mike didn't spot Mrs. Nash herself and assumed she must still be recuperating—or maybe just taking a little afternoon rest.

"No, none of those." He pried his son away from the window and smoothed down the bangs tufting up at all angles. "Now calm down. You'll see the workshop and meet Miss Higgins in just a little bit, and it's nothing to get overexcited about in the meantime. Got it?"

"Why not?" Luke blinked, tilted his head to the side, and stated, "You are, and I know why. It's 'cuz you like Miss Higgins."

"Well," Mike hedged, wondering how on earth his ten-year-old boy figured that one out so quickly. "I know you'll like her, too."

Luke's grin grew wider. "Just not in the same way you do, Dad."

This needed to be nipped in the bud before his son mentioned this to someone else—especially if that someone else turned out to be Naomi. He had enough obstacles without his son adding to them. Mike crossed his arms. "What makes you think something like that?"

"Aw, come on! I'm not some little kid anymore." His son raked a hand through his hair, sending shocks springing up at random intervals across his head. "You catch yourself, but you almost say her first name—right? It starts with an *N*. And when you talk about her, you smile with your eyes the way you used to. It's *obvious!*"

Mike held up his hand to stop his son's litany. Luke's voice had risen with every reason, and the now-stopped train couldn't mask it. Besides, the obvious thing was that Luke was right—he wasn't a little kid. After dealing with the death of his mother, losing his home to grasping grandparents, and evading dangerous thugs, Luke started the transition from boy to young man. *And an observant one.*

"What's obvious to you might not be so easily seen by others." *I hope.* Mike smoothed Luke's hair again. "So keep it down."

"Then you admit it?" He clamped a hand atop his head as though trying to plaster his hair in place. "That I'm right this time?"

"I'll tell you this." Mike leaned down as he whispered, waiting for Luke to shuffle a step closer. Then he added, "I admit nothing!"

"Aw, Dad. It's not something to be embarrassed about." Luke gave him a good-natured cuff on the arm. "You found a woman *with her own workshop*. I'd be more worried if you *didn't* like her!"

And with that bit of irrefutable logic, his ten-year-old son turned Mike's difficult decision into a forgone conclusion. Luke, who'd never met Naomi, held no doubts about how special she was. So why should he, who'd spent so many hours enjoying her company, waste another minute trying to argue away his deepening attraction?

"Got your rucksack?" Mike asked, shouldering his bulging bag.

"Yep." Luke narrowly missed slugging him in the head as he

swung the sack over his shoulder and darted out into the aisle. He didn't slow his pace until he'd gotten through the car, down the steps, and off the train altogether. Then he stopped to gawk at the town around them, effectively boxing his father on the steel steps.

"Scoot over, son." Mike resisted the urge to nudge the back of his son's knees with the tip of his boot. The gesture might lessen Luke's newfound dignity as he greeted Hope Falls for the first time. Mike scanned the group, his gaze hitching on Naomi's smile and staying there. In that moment, it felt like he'd come home again.

"What"—Luke's tone mixed trepidation and wonder—"is *that*?"

So much for dignity. Mike grinned as his son inched to the side and gaped at the group of people now crowding around the engine. Or, more specifically, at the massive, brindled wolfhound circling them.

"Dunstan!" He called the hunter over, knowing Decoy would follow his master. Meanwhile, Mike clapped a hand on Luke's shoulder so he'd know not to be frightened of the approaching beast. "I need to make introductions, but your dog's stealing my son's attention."

"Decoy, right?" Far from being frightened, Luke moved forward. He glanced at Dunstan. "Dad said a big dog helped save some people trapped in a mine, but I didn't realize he meant one *this* big!"

"He comes in handy." Dunstan's reply might have sounded cool, but the corners of his mouth quirked as though holding back a smile. He snapped his fingers, made a motion, and the wolfhound promptly lowered his hindquarters and sat. The movement didn't make him any smaller, but the show of obedience reassured Luke—and Mike, if the truth be told. Somehow he'd forgotten just how large Decoy was.

"Can I pet him?" Luke's hand twitched, belying the effort it took to ask permission instead of reach for the gray-black fur.

"Let him sniff the back of your hand first," Dunstan instructed. "Dogs are like horses that way—like to get a sense of you before they let you touch them. It's kind of like a handshake."

"Yeah?" Luke beamed as Decoy gave his hand a thorough snuffle.

"Now you can pet him. See how his ears went back? That means he's relaxed. Just remember, if they went flat against his skull, that means to get back." Dunstan kept up a steady stream of instruction, though it was easy to see Decoy loved being scratched behind the ears. No one could see the way his tongue lolled out as anything but bliss.

"Well, now that Decoy's approved of you, you're officially welcome in Hope Falls." Miss Lyman stood on Dunstan's other side. "I'm Miss Lyman—the other person stuck in the mines until Decoy led my friends and your dad to come dig us out of there. It seems your father has a knack for showing up in the middle of difficult days."

THIRTY-SEVEN

*M*ichael has a knack for showing up when he's needed. Naomi drank in the sight of him, from the unruly hair she wanted to run her fingers through to the smile lines drawing attention to his deep brown eyes and the broad shoulders she'd cried on the first day they met. Had it really been just under a month since he came to Hope Falls? It felt as if she'd known him a lifetime and missed him for half that.

"And who, pray tell, is *that?*" Charlotte twirled her parasol, gaze fixed on Michael as though committing his features to memory.

"Mr. Strode." Naomi's hackles went up at her sister's appreciative murmur and discreet ogling. Discreet ogling still counted as ogling. Charlotte had no business going goggly-eyed over the way Michael stood there, silhouetted by the late afternoon sun.

"Your carpenter?" Charlotte practically purred. "Now I begin to see the appeal of staying shut up in that sawdust-strewn room."

"The Hope Falls carpenter," Naomi corrected, unwilling to let Charlotte see that she hated making the distinction. *Not mine.*

"My, my. How very precise you're being." Her sister gave her a knowing glance. "It looks as though Lacey is finished explaining about Mrs. Nash, and the boy's wandering off to walk with that massive mutt. Isn't it the perfect time for you to introduce us?"

"Of course—why don't you get Harold while I fetch Mr. Strode?" Naomi knew full well that Charlotte hadn't included her husband in that "us," but she seized the opportunity to give her sister a subtle reminder. The fact that it also allowed her to approach Michael alone, if only for a scant moment, added another reward.

"Welcome back." She swept toward him, moving as quickly as possible to greet him before her sister intruded. Naomi wanted to give him a hug or at least clasp hands, but couldn't. She knew better than to single Michael out with such attention in front of her suitors, to say nothing of giving Charlotte such ammunition.

"Thank you. I should have realized the whole town didn't turn up to greet us." He kept the words light, but his gaze held hers, strong and steady. "It's never easy saying good-bye to a friend, and I know you'd become fond of Mrs. Nash. I'm sorry for your loss."

"Loss is never easy." Charlotte swept into the conversation, positioning herself as close to Michael as possible. "Of course, the arrival of an old friend and the promise of new acquaintances means life continues. The reminder makes any loss somewhat more bearable."

Michael looked poleaxed, but Naomi couldn't tell whether he was overwhelmed by her sister's charms or caught off guard by her boldness in inserting herself into their private conversation. Additionally, it looked as though Charlotte's ambiguous statement had perplexed even Michael's ability to puzzle things together.

At best, Charlotte was saying that Michael and Luke would ease the grief Hope Falls felt at losing Arla. Possibly she meant that she herself along with Michael might provide the distraction and entertainment needed to lighten the dreary day. But the worst interpretation of all seemed most likely: Charlotte had insinuated that she—who'd never exchanged so much as a word with the deceased—needed comfort and expected to find it in Michael, her new friend.

Not that Naomi could call attention to the inappropriateness of Charlotte's conversation. Her sister would claim the best of intentions, casting Naomi as petty and petulant. *Am I being petty? Is it really Charlotte's words that I find objectionable, or am I looking for offense because she barged in to Michael's homecoming?*

"I didn't realize your sister planned to visit." Michael's comment was part question, part answer. At least it explained why he'd looked vaguely confused and definitely at a loss. Michael hadn't been trying to puzzle through Charlotte's meaning at all—he'd been busy looking for her connection to Naomi. And he'd found it.

"Nor did I, but she and her husband arrived the day after you left. Apparently Mr. Blinman was one of the previous investors Braden decided to invite." Naomi noticed Charlotte hadn't bothered to fetch Harold for introductions. "Mrs. Charlotte Blinman decided to join him on the journey. As you guessed, she is my sister."

"*Younger* sister, though I'm certain you would have guessed that, too." She peeped from beneath her fanned lashes, pretending shyness but obviously expecting his swift and admiring agreement.

Naomi fought a sudden urge to step on her sister's toes. Wasn't it enough that Harry chose Charlotte for her youth and supposedly better ability to bear little Blinmans? Did Charlotte have to trot out their age difference to make her seem spinsterish to Michael?

"No, ma'am." Michael either didn't notice or pretended not to notice the astonishment then fury flashing across Charlotte's face before she composed herself—most likely to avoid getting wrinkles. "I can't say I would've guessed that, seeing as how a smart man doesn't go around speculating on the age of ladies he's just met."

But a smart man does *soften the blow of calling an obviously vain woman "ma'am."* Naomi struggled against giving in to giggles—not because of Charlotte's indignation, but because Michael hadn't played her sister's game. He'd deliberately refused to flatter Charlotte at Naomi's expense and almost complimented her instead!

Charlotte's simper held a slight edge. "An excellent policy."

"We do look very much alike." Naomi intentionally sounded apologetic. Hopefully it would appease her sister while letting Michael know she regretted putting him in such a difficult spot.

"Could almost be twins." Michael must have caught another flicker of Charlotte's irritation because his jaw set and his eyes sparked with mischief. "Same height, similar features and coloring. When you're wearing bonnets or hats, a man would be hard pressed to tell you apart at first glance."

"In time you'll notice how our disparities outweigh the similarities." Her sister scraped up a smile and twirled her parasol. "Until then we'll take care you don't confuse us."

Naomi sucked in a sharp breath, sickened by the veiled allusion to their past. Her sister kept her claws sharp and tinged with more than malice. The attack seeped into Naomi's soul, stealing her joy at seeing Michael again. He didn't know the history behind Charlotte's seemingly innocuous comment, but he saw its impact.

The warm brown of Michael's gaze sharpened. "You're distinctly different, and I could never mistake one sister for the other."

⁂

"Never say never," Mrs. Blinman cautioned, casting her sister a meaningful glance. "As Naomi can attest, you wouldn't be the first."

Mike looked from Naomi to her sister and back again, reaffirming his conviction that no man with an ounce of sense could confuse these two women after a moment spent in their company. From afar, the resemblance might mislead, but certainly not up close.

He hadn't lied when he said he wouldn't have guessed Naomi to be older. Mrs. Blinman fancied herself a coquette, but those fancy frills and simulated smiles couldn't sweeten the bite beneath her comments. Her sham sophistication, as with any poorly laid veneer, aged her. In fact, the woman reminded him of his mother-in-law.

By contrast, Naomi's simple dress and fresh face didn't detract from her beauty. Like finely grained oak, she needed no adornment save what God granted already. If affectation aged her sister, Naomi's unadulterated loveliness seemed almost untouched by the time. *Forty years from now, she'll be every bit as beautiful.*

"Just as we dislike being thought of as interchangeable,"—Naomi spoke stiffly and with an underlying fierceness, unsettled by her sister—"you can't judge Mr. Strode by the mistakes of other men."

Her sister's smile grew more feline. "How silly of me, when it's so clear Mr. Strode has. . .distinguished himself with you."

She took the words and twisted them with her tone, implying

impropriety where there was none. Mike didn't like the way Naomi had gone pale early in the conversation and not yet regained her color. When she'd mentioned her sister, he'd gotten the idea the two weren't close. Now that he met Mrs. Blinman, he understood why.

"Mr. Strode distinguishes himself with everyone he meets." The green in Naomi's eyes sparkled with an emerald brilliance her sister could never match. "Aside from his work, he's unusually observant."

It didn't take heightened powers of observation to see that Mrs. Blinman wasn't pleased with the way the conversation was going. "Perhaps he is. Then again, you make things easier by refusing to style your hair to conceal that bizarre white streak of yours."

"Why would she ever want to conceal it?" Mike challenged.

"Most ladies do not flaunt their oddities." She sniffed in disdain. "You must admit, Naomi's coloring marks her as outlandish."

"Unique." He barked the word. "Refusing to hide who she is doesn't mean Miss Higgins flaunts herself. It means she's genuine."

"What I am," Naomi intervened while her sister spluttered, "is genuinely excited to meet your son. I see he's returning from his walk with Decoy and Dunstan. Looks like he's enjoying himself."

Mike nodded, taking a moment to switch gears. In a few moments he'd gone from happy homecoming to the sad news of Mrs. Nash and had been unable to relish his reunion with Naomi thanks to her catty sibling. Now he had to push all that aside and make sure Naomi took to Luke and Luke liked Naomi back. He swallowed against a stomach spasm, and Mike belatedly recognized the sensation as nerves.

Lord, You know the desire of my heart. You know I've sought Your guidance about Naomi, and now I seek Your assistance. The timing feels rushed, more now than when I left Hope Falls. But if it's right, if You've planned this path, please pave the way.

"Luke!" He called his son over, wishing Mrs. Blinman would flit away to offer the three of them a little privacy. No such luck.

"Yeah, Dad?" Luke came running up, stopping suddenly enough to raise a small puff of dust and make Mrs. Blinman take a step back.

"Son,"—Mike brought his son to stand in front of him and clapped his hands on the boy's shoulders—"I want you to meet—"

"Miss Higgins?" Luke burst out, eyeing the women in blissful ignorance that he'd revealed how much Mike talked about Naomi. Luke couldn't tell that Mrs. Blinman realized the significance of his ignorance any more than he could tell which sister was Miss Higgins. His brows knit. "I mean, one of you is Miss Higgins?"

"That's right." Mrs. Blinman swept in front of Naomi, who'd already started to come forward with her hand extended. She reached out one perfectly manicured hand and pinched Luke's cheek as if he were still a toddler. "Aren't you the most adorable little boy?"

"No." Mike heard his thought echoed by both Luke and Naomi.

"I am not little. Or adorable." Luke rubbed his reddened cheek, pulled his shoulders back to look taller, and gave Mrs. Blinman a well-deserved glower. "And I don't think you're Miss Higgins."

Mrs. Blinman looked indignant at the reaction. "Well, I never—"

"My sister never said she was Miss Higgins." Naomi nudged her sister out of the way with a touch more force than was absolutely necessary, and Mike had to hide his grin. She stooped down a smidge and held out her hand for Luke to shake. "And your dad never said what a strong grip you have! Nice to finally meet you, Mr. Strode."

Luke, visibly puffed up by the way Naomi addressed him, pumped her arm another time to prove his strength. "You can call me Luke."

"Thank you. Please call me Naomi." She returned his grin, and Mike started to relax. "Now, you have a very important decision to make, Luke. I know what your dad would choose, but this time it's up to you. Would you like to go to the diner for some of my friend Evie's cooking, or do you want to stop and see the workshop first?"

"Workshop!" Luke burst out without even thinking it over then laughed when Mike groaned and rubbed his stomach in a sad way.

"Tell you what." Naomi straightened up and held out her hand in invitation. "We'll go to the workshop while your dad saves seats."

"Deal!" Luke plunked his hand in Naomi's without reservation.

As the two of them left, Mike's heart swelled with pride and hope.

"She's good with children." Mrs. Blinman watched her sister go then turned with a sorrowful expression. "Such a pity she's barren."

THIRTY-EIGHT

"What?" Mike couldn't muster up the more polite, "Excuse me?"

"Unable to have children." Mrs. Blinman shook her head in a regretful sort of way but finished with a shrug. "Barren."

"Why are you telling me this?" Mike's astonishment swiftly turned to ire. "How could anyone know that when she's unmarried?"

"How do doctors discover any condition?" Another dainty shrug made her ridiculous parasol bob. "There are symptoms when women lack the ability to bear children, though I won't detail those signs."

No children. Mike suddenly understood this was the missing piece—the final detail as to why Naomi never married. A woman like that didn't resort to hiring a husband without several reasons, and she'd only revealed the least personal ones to him. That, more than the condition itself, gave him pause. *But why would she confide that to me when I'm one of the few men who haven't tried to court her? She'd have no reason to give me such intimate information, and it's not something she'd want to discuss under the best of circumstances.*

Again, he couldn't help but see the irony. Not only had he found the only two women who might "hire" him for a husband, but they happened to be the same two who wouldn't give him a child of his own blood. Leticia because she carried another man's baby. Naomi because she couldn't carry any at all. *But does it matter? Luke is the son of my heart, and while I wanted to give him siblings, he's fine.*

In the midst of muddling through his thoughts, he realized Mrs. Blinman had started talking again. In his opinion, she talked too much.

"It's the reason why Harry chose to marry me instead." She tilted her head toward a well-dressed man in conversation with Mr. Corning. "He originally courted Naomi, but when I finished school and came home from France, Harry decided I would be the wife he needed."

What kind of man would choose her over Naomi? The fact that she would consider taking her sister's suitor makes her a poor choice. Mike did his best to hide his incredulity, struck by the memory of Naomi's wistful expression when she told him she had no family left because her sister had gotten married. "Your husband originally courted Miss Higgins? Is that why the two of you aren't close?"

"Jealousy ruins relationships." She gave a dramatic sigh. "I came to Hope Falls hoping to mend fences, but I can see that it will not work. How can I blame Naomi for being heartsick over Harry?"

Her words packed a punch that left him reeling. Mike struggled to make his lungs work. "Are you saying that she still loves him?"

She blinked at him, eyes widened with surprise. "Of course, Mr. Strode! Her first love is something a woman can never forget."

I couldn't have heard that right. Naomi paused one step away from passing the workshop window. She rubbed behind her ears and waited.

"Say it again!" Clump urged. "I want to try to remember how."

"Oh, it's nothing special," Charlotte demurred. "You can say the same thing in English or German, since you're multilingual."

"Stuff sounds so much better in French," Bobsley proclaimed.

"All right. To say 'I have a noble bearing,' it's: *Saviez-vous que vouz avez le nez d'un cochon?*" Charlotte repeated the phrase that had stopped Naomi in her tracks.

It had been a long time since Naomi had used her girlhood French lessons, and Charlotte learned the language in its mother country, but she knew without a doubt her sister hadn't complimented Clump's noble bearing. She'd asked him if he knew he had the nose of a pig! Clump begged her to repeat it, but Gent said it was his turn. "Now, what was that thing you said before about my fine manners?"

"One moment." Charlotte issued a string of sneezes, and Naomi was glad to remember that her sister couldn't stay around sawdust for long. *"Vous êtes plus dense que les arbres que vous hacher."*

Naomi swallowed a surge of anger as kind Gent—whose manners trumped her sister's—carefully repeated that he was denser than the trees he chopped. Charlotte was systematically insulting her suitors and compounding the crime by teaching them to go around insulting themselves! If any of them remembered the words and repeated them to someone fluent in French, they'd be laughingstocks.

"Charlotte!" She thundered into the room, unable to hold herself back until her temper cooled. "A word with you, please."

"Naomi! I was just entertaining your beaus while we waited for you to get back from showing Mr. Strode and his son to their house." Slyly suggestive and innocent all at once, Charlotte made it sound as though she'd done nothing wrong—and that Naomi was inappropriate to want to see Luke's reaction to the house she'd helped ready for him.

"Outside, please." She gritted her teeth, turned on her heel, and listened as Charlotte sneezed her way out of the room behind her. Naomi didn't trust herself to speak—or the men not to overhear—until they'd passed the buildings used for temporary storage.

"What do you think you're doing?" she demanded once stopped.

"Filling in." Charlotte inspected her nail beds. "Providing amusement so they wouldn't stop to wonder at your interest in Mr. Strode. You really shouldn't abandon your suitors like that, Mimi."

"I didn't abandon anyone." Naomi narrowly kept from mentioning the way Charlotte and their mother abandoned her after one night's mistake. Even in her anger, she knew there was no comparison—her mistake made her unworthy of understanding. But her failures hadn't ruined her ability to understand the feelings of other people.

Charlote rolled her eyes. "Let's not quibble over word choice."

"No, let's." Naomi refused to let her sister off the hook. "Your words, to be exact. You will not insult any of my friends, my suitors, or any Hope Falls workers again—not in English or French."

"Don't get overexcited. It's not as if they knew what I said."

"*I* know." Naomi struggled to put her outrage into words. "Why do you think it's all right to mock people, whether they understand it or not? Maybe it's even worse if they don't know what you're saying because you're taking advantage of their trusting natures."

"You've been in the country for far too long, sister." Charlotte's eyes held a predatory gleam. "Don't mistake foolishness for trust. Trust should be reserved for after someone earns it."

"Why? Why should everyone have to go around assuming other people are unworthy when only a small percentage ruin things?"

"That percentage can create a lot of trouble, and you know as well as anyone that even the so-called good people misstep. The fact that your suitors extend such confidence to either one of us attests to their lack of wisdom. They've barely met me, and they certainly don't know you any better." Charlotte's taunts sliced into Naomi. Her sister possessed a talent for vicious truths. "Stop acting so high and mighty, Naomi. Don't pretend you're better than you are, and don't pretend your suitors are more than clodpolls."

Naomi slapped the wall with the flat of her palm, welcoming the distraction of its sting. "They're far more than you'll ever know."

"How can they be, when they know so little?" Charlotte countered. "Tell me, were you planning on being honest with the man you'll marry? Warn him beforehand he's taking on damaged goods?"

A few sentences, and Naomi needed to defend herself. Unfortunately, she didn't have much to say. "I've been praying about it, but I won't know until I choose the man. Obviously I'll need to tell him that I'm not innocent, but I would hope to find a husband who would want to know the entire truth and be able to forgive it."

Her voice grew fainter with every word because aloud they sounded every bit as ridiculous as she'd feared but had tried to convince herself otherwise. Charlotte laughed at her admission.

"Now who's the fool?" she spat. "No man wants to know the

entire truth about anything, much less hear how another man beat him to his bride. Besides, what makes you think you could tell him, even if you found so spectacular an idiot as to offer forgiveness?"

"I'd find the strength. He deserves to know. If I'm going to promise to honor a man for a lifetime, I would need to from the start." Naomi stiffened. "And forgiveness isn't idiocy. It takes an incredible amount of strength to forgive a wrong and keep loving."

"It's not your secret to tell." Charlotte's hands curved into claws. "Listen, you self-important chit. Why do you think I didn't denounce you the morning after we dragged you from my marital bed? Because news of your betrayal would taint Harry's reputation, too. Neither one of us should suffer slander and ridicule so you can seek absolution from whatever man you convince to take you as his bride."

With that, Charlotte huffed off, layers of skirts billowing like a ship with sails unfurled. There was no way of stopping her, so Naomi's future depended on Charlotte's ability to stop herself. Because as much as she hated to think of it—she now realized she'd been avoiding thinking of it—Charlotte made sense. Only their continued silence could protect the Blinman name and Naomi's reputation.

I can never be honest with my husband. Naomi sagged against the splintering wood wall. *He can never know the worst of me.*

THIRTY-NINE

The best part about coming back was waking up, knowing Luke was safe with him and they could spend the day with Naomi. He and Luke spent yesterday afternoon exploring first the town then some of the outlying forest to help his son settle in. Mike resisted his impulse to ask Naomi along—it was clear she and the other women needed some time to recover from Arla's death.

In spite of Luke's enthusiastic approval of the woman Mike "liked" so much, Mike needed the two people he cared about the most to get to know each other. And Mike needed to start waging his campaign to win Naomi's heart. He'd known he lagged behind the loggers, but her sister's revelation yesterday meant Mike wasn't just competing with the lumbermen; he was up against the memory of the man who'd hurt her.

It didn't help that the memory—and the man who'd made it—happened to be wandering around town. If Mike didn't have so much lost time to make up for, he might be tempted to run the fool to ground, ask him what he'd been thinking, and hold him accountable for making Naomi think she didn't deserve more than a hired husband. Lucky for Blinman, Mike would keep busy convincing her otherwise.

Besides, the man shackled himself to Naomi's sister. That should suffice as punishment until Mike got things squared away. He couldn't wait to get started. For the first time, he ate one of Miss Thompson's delectable breakfasts without noticing what she served.

Instead, he kept an eye on Naomi as she wove around the tables, bringing out platters of food and rounds of fresh coffee. He barely managed to keep track of the conversation but paid closer attention when Dunstan invited Luke to go fishing with him and Decoy that morning.

"Good time for trout," the hunter was saying. "And until my ribs are better healed, there's not much hunting I can get done."

Luke wriggled on the bench, unable to hide his excitement. "Can we go, Dad?"

"I don't know." Torn between his obligation to Naomi's workshop and wanting to make Luke happy, he hesitated. "I've been away from the workshop for days now. There's a lot to do."

"Please, can't we go together? You were gone a long time." His son hadn't blinked since Dunstan issued the invitation. His eagerness, and the reminder that Mike hadn't been able to spend time with him for a while, broke down Mike's protest.

"Lacey'll be keen to come along," Dunstan mentioned. "Might be easier to ask Miss Higgins to join us and make a trip of it."

"I'll ask her," he promised. When the diner emptied out, Mike edged off the side of the bench, told Luke he'd be right back, and snuck into the kitchen.

"No loggers allowed," came a curt order from the stove where Miss Thompson hovered.

"It's Mr. Strode," her sister corrected and offered him a welcoming smile.

"Is there anything you need?" Naomi bustled over with a steaming pot of coffee, worry in her gaze.

"You," he blurted out then quickly added, "if the workshop can wait another day. And Miss Lyman, too. Dunstan's invited us for a morning of fishing, and Luke's raring to go."

"You're hooked into it then." Naomi gave a gentle laugh as the other women rolled their eyes.

"Obvious pun." Miss Thompson shook her head. "You can do better than that, Naomi!"

"Well…" She pursed her lips for a moment as though considering. "I suppose I could have said that with Luke invited, he couldn't worm out of it—but on the balance I thought that one was worse."

"It is," Mike assured her. "Who wants to be likened to a worm?"

"Ah." Her smile widened as she teased. "So you'd rather be hooked?"

He couldn't find a suitable answer for that, and the sudden pause brought a blush to her cheeks.

"Oh, cut line!" Miss Thompson stepped into the breach and brought on a new round of groans.

"I think you should all go. With Dunstan out of commission, we don't get meat like we used to. The kitchen could use a bountiful catch of fresh fish."

"I didn't want to neglect our work either." *Our.* He liked saying it when it meant him and Naomi. Especially when he could still see the vestiges of her blush over talking about hooking him.

"Luke can help us make it up later," she said firmly. "Every boy should go fishing with his father—and it'd be criminal not to give him a special outing on his first full day in Hope Falls."

"I'm game." Miss Lyman pulled down a large wicker hamper and plunked it atop a table. "Braden plans to take his investors around a bit, so the Blinmans and Mr. Corning will be occupied."

This was sounding better and better—Mike hadn't even considered the idea that Naomi's sister and old love might intrude on the fishing trip, but he was heartened to hear they couldn't.

❦

"I wanted to join in the first time you told me about this place." Corning gestured around. "It sounded like a perfect business proposition."

"It should have been." Braden knew he needed to say more, to get the conversation rolling and pry information from his suspects, but the sight of the collapsed mine before him stole his speech.

Blinman's chortle made his hands fist. "Nothing's perfect."

"Oh, phoo! I'm standing right next to you!" The man's wife pouted prettily. Why the woman insisted on joining them on this trek escaped Braden's understanding, unless she was trying to avoid the morose tone in town. If that was her reason, she'd failed miserably. The mines were as much a grave site as the place they'd buried Arla.

"I said no*thing*, darling, not *no one*." Blinman backpedaled and swiftly changed the subject. "Though the mines seem an awful waste."

"Yes." *Of life.* Braden's eyes narrowed at Blinman's renewed interest. "It was a devastating loss of irreplaceable resources."

Blinman furrowed his brow. "Irreplaceable, you say? I wasn't aware that cave-ins could actually destroy a mine's ore."

"They don't." Corning took a few steps closer to the blocked entrance, squinting at the small opening they'd made to free Lacey and Dunstan. "Reaching silver is a dangerous and difficult business to begin with, and the collapse destroyed the access points."

Braden noticed that Corning mentioned only silver. If only someone mentioned the gold—that secret only he and Owens had known about—Braden could catch his killer. But no one whispered a word about gold or Draxley or Owens, and his time trickled away.

"Then it's not irreplaceable." Mrs. Blinman brightened. "It's just buried treasure! Would it really be so hard to go after it?"

"Yes." Braden kept from snorting in disbelief. Buried treasure? Did the flea-brained woman think a shovel could salvage things?

"Why?" Blinman's eyes narrowed. "They went in after the collapse and pulled you out. Didn't they shore up the cleared tunnels? Couldn't we get a team in there and work around the collapsed areas, go even deeper if that's what it would take?"

"You would send men into an unstable mine, directing them to dig into shifting rock and knowing they could die at any minute?" Braden eyed Blinman in disbelief then speculation. He hadn't considered that the killer might openly suggest reopening the mine, but he should have. The saboteur's greed couldn't be denied.

"Mr. Lyman!" Mrs. Blinman sounded shocked and affronted. "My husband asked about the supports and specifically mentioned working around the dangerous areas. How could you make such an accusation?"

"It was a question, not an accusation," Corning observed as he started up the uneven incline and gestured to the small opening. "And not a foolish one either. Like Harry mentioned, men have already gone back into the mines since the collapse. He most likely didn't realize they barely managed to unblock enough to get in."

Why is Corning defending Blinman? Granted, the man always had a peacemaker streak, but were they working together to reopen the mine?

"Surely that could be widened." Mrs. Blinman waved a dismissive hand. "That passage looks far too small for a grown man. I simply can't imagine why they didn't make it bigger in the first place."

Braden circled around until he had a clear view of both Blinman's and Corning's faces. He wanted to see their reactions as he said, "True. They made a much bigger opening after the first collapse."

Instant impact. Corning's brows jammed together in consternation. Blinman's practically disappeared into his hairline. Mrs. Blinman, who hadn't been facing them, whipped around fast enough to dislodge her silly little bonnet. Each one evinced surprise and hesitation but not a single shred of shame or guilt.

"Did you say 'first collapse'?" Corning scrambled down the rocks, away from the opening he'd been examining with such interest.

"Do you mean that the mines shifted again shortly after the first collapse because things were so unstable?" Blinman clarified.

"No." Braden didn't hide his anger. "A month ago the mines caved in again, this time trapping my sister and her new fiancé."

"But that's three months after the initial event!" Corning jumped down the final boulder and wiped his palms on his waistcoat. "Why would your sister go into the mines?"

Avid speculation lit Mrs. Blinman's gaze, conflicting with the practiced innocence of her tone. The woman probably hoped Lacey had been meeting Dunstan for a tryst and was looking for juicy gossip to spread around back East.

"Obviously they'd already considered reopening the mines." Blinman moved closer to his wife. "Perhaps the second cave-in will have made things more settled, and they can try again in the future."

"No." Braden said. "Those mines won't open again." And he was starting to worry that he wouldn't be able to unlock their secret.

FORTY

T he secret to catching fish is—" Naomi didn't get to finish her advice before Luke broke in.

"I know. Patience." He looked like it took a mighty effort not to roll his eyes. Luke didn't recognize the irony of his own statement.

"If you know the importance of patience," his father spoke sternly, "then you'd know that you're not demonstrating your mastery of the skill by interrupting Miss Higgins."

Luke's face fell. "Oh. Right. Sorry, Miss Naomi." They'd agreed yesterday afternoon when she showed him the workshop that "Miss Higgins" sounded too stuffy to keep using. The boy didn't know that Naomi made the decision partly because this way Michael wouldn't have to stop using her first name. It would seem a natural progression that wouldn't raise so many eyebrows if he slipped.

"No matter. You'll get plenty of practice today," she assured him. "That's always the second part of learning something. First you know it. Then you practice it. Then you master it. At least you're already over the first hurdle."

"Yeah!" Luke brightened and looked at his father. "Dad taught me. He says that patience is the secret to everything."

"Almost everything," Michael corrected with a grin. He shifted his gaze to meet Naomi's then added, "Every once in a while you find something special, and you don't want to lose it by waiting too long."

Her breath hitched at his intensity. A warm, swoopy feeling in her stomach made her almost giddy. Michael looked at her as if *she* was something special—and he didn't want to wait before letting her know it.

Perhaps he'd missed her company during his trip—the same way she'd missed him? The swoopy feeling intensified, and it took real effort for Naomi to pay attention to Luke's comments as they reached the bank of the stream where Lacey and Dunstan already laid out an old blanket.

"I asked Cora to join us," she told Lacey. "She said she might bring Dorothy along in a bit."

"Did you tell her Braden wasn't coming?" Lacey looked up from where she'd been tying a hook to her line. "She might be more keen to join us if she knew he wouldn't be."

"She knows." Naomi gave an absentminded wave and went to join Luke and Michael.

"Squishy." Luke palmed a handful of mud, closed his fist, and watched it ooze from between his fingers.

"A mite too squishy," Michael warned. "Worms like their dirt more solid. Let's move back a bit and try again."

Naomi grabbed the empty pail and shuffled up the bank a few steps then lowered herself into a precarious squat alongside the men. This time she picked up a clump of moist earth, rolled it between her fingers, and watched it crumble back to the ground as Michael proclaimed it a good spot.

Decoy bounded over to shove his muzzle into the small hole Luke started. The massive dog nosed around before pulling his head back, shaking back and forth, and sneezing all over the boy.

Luke's laughter held the high, joyful pitch of childhood as he reached out and hugged the wolfhound. "I think he's saying it's a good spot, Miss Naomi. Let's prove him right."

She decided to forgo rootling around in the dirt, preferring to keep them company while the boys tugged long, slippery worms from their snug mud homes. Naomi made sure to enthusiastically praise each and every find, with particular attention paid to size, color, and width of the various specimens Luke presented before dropping them into the bucket.

"Oh, a wriggler," she improvised, running out of comments on worm appearance. "If I were a fish, I'd definitely notice the way that one twists around."

"You know? I think you're right." Luke's hand veered away from the pail where he'd been about to drop the critter. "Better keep this and make sure he's the first one I use. I want to be sure and get a good start."

Naomi tried not to wince as he stuffed the wriggler into his back pocket but couldn't refrain from issuing a warning. "Whatever you do, do not sit down until you've put the bait on the hook."

"Right." Luke gave a solemn nod. "He won't wriggle if I squash him, and then he's no better than the rest."

Michael gave a snort of laughter, his gaze dancing with their shared merriment. "All right. That should be enough to get things going." He rose to his feet with an easy movement and held out a hand to help Naomi straighten up.

"All ready there?" Dunstan thrust poles at Luke and Mike. "Bait 'em up then. I sprinkled the area with crushed beetles already, so there should be plenty of prospects swimming around. Just keep calm and quiet, drop in the line, and wait for the tug."

"I've got my wriggler!" Luke's exaggerated whisper didn't pass for quiet, but no one reprimanded him. In no time at all, he'd plunked himself on the bank, leaned up against Decoy's furry bulk, and strung his line into the water.

"You look mighty pleased with yourself." Lacey sounded amused.

"Yep!" Luke squinted over at her, beaming. "I'm sitting in the shade with my dad, the world's biggest dog, and my new friend Miss Naomi. What more can a man want?"

"Not much." Michael settled himself next to Naomi, so close that the brush of his shoulder made her shiver. He looked at her with the same intensity as before, folding his hand over hers to adjust her grip on her own fishing pole. "This is just about perfect."

Thank You, Lord. Mike woke up the next morning with a smile on his face and praise in his heart. For a few moments he stretched out in his bunk and offered up his appreciation for Naomi, for Hope Falls, for the way Luke had taken a shine to both.

He grinned all through breakfast, even when some of the loggers attempted to engage Naomi in conversation. *Let them try*, Mike decided, feeling smug. *I get to spend the entire day with her while they're all out chopping down trees.*

In fact Mike was focusing so hard on how he'd arrange the day once they got to the workshop he almost didn't notice the rain pelting them when they stepped outside the diner. The cold, stinging drops made him prompt Luke to button up his coat, but Mike remained preoccupied with how he planned to spend the day. Just him, Naomi, and Luke—

And four merry woodsmen. Mike opened the workshop door to find the room filled to the rafters with the last people—aside from the Bainbridges and their lackeys—he wanted to see. The surprise stopped him cold in the doorway until Luke shoved his way into the room.

"Good morning, Naomi!" He dripped his way across the floor to join her near the stove. "What are you making? Can I make one, too?"

"Well, here's another one that sounds just like us." Bear Riordan raised a bushy red brow and grinned. "Lucky for you, Miss Higgins has a big heart and a bigger project for us to help with."

"Is that what's going on?" Mike moved to hang his hat on the peg by the door but found it—as well as those beside it—already occupied. "Have we fallen so far behind since I left Hope Falls?"

"We were behind before we began." Her easy smile made him wish twice as hard that their workshop hadn't been invaded by loggers.

"Since there's been a lot of summer showers, Mrs. Blinman wrangled us a way to keep busy and spend more time with Miss Higgins." The edge of Bobsley's tongue hung out the corner of his mouth as he focused on fine-sanding a miniscule wooden square.

"And it's fun." Clump looked up from where he crouched on the floor, an old cloth draped over an older crate and covered in tiny gray lumps of who-knew-what. "Salt clay is good, but I didn't know of it until Miss Higgins helped me make a batch a couple days ago."

"Clay?" Luke zoomed to look over Clump's shoulder. "Do you squish it into shapes and stuff? What are you trying to make?"

"Salt and water on the stove, cornstarch and cold water in a bowl, then mix it all together and knead it like bread." Naomi creaked open the steamer trunk at her side, tugged loose one of the drawers, and pulled out what Mike recognized as a vanity jar.

He watched in a combination of irritation and pleasure as Naomi handed it to Luke. Pleasure because she did such a wonderful job of including his son and making the boy feel important. Annoyance because apparently she'd done the same thing for a bunch of men.

"I keep mine in this powder pot because the lid screws on tight and keeps the clay from drying out. Why don't you look at the things in the Lyman Place house and choose something to make?"

"Sure!" Luke grabbed the crystal jar and hurried away. Instead of grabbing something as soon as he got there, he began taking inventory of everything in the dollhouse. He looked so serious trying to choose something to mold for Naomi that Mike smiled.

"Not the rocking horse," Clump cautioned. "That's what I'm making now, with the clay and snips from my bristly brush for mane and tail. I already finished the cat for the kitchen last time." Sure enough, he pulled out the tiny figure of a crouching cat, painted in black and gray stripes with little white-tipped feet.

"Nice work." Mike didn't have to like the way Clump cozied up to Naomi, but he believed in giving credit where credit was due. Then the idea struck him. If he found out what the others were working on, he might be able to help them finish. So they could leave.

"Hello, Strode." Gent perched on a three-legged stool, hunched over like an overgrown crow as he painstakingly chiseled at a small white block. The scent of lye stung the air when Mike drew near.

"Soap carving?" Mike tried to sound interested rather than disappointed. This was a task he could do nothing to hurry along.

"For marble busts." Gent straightened up and stretched before extending his work. "This is William Shakespeare. For the study."

Sure enough, Mike could make out the beginnings of a nose over The Bard's trademark goatee. In spite of himself, he was impressed by Gent's ambition and solid start. "Very creative, using soap."

"The shavings help discourage ants and other creeping things." Naomi carefully replaced the silver brush of her paste pot, her graceful motions making Mike wish lye frightened off larger pests.

He gave Luke an encouraging nod as his son settled down cross-legged by Clump's clay-working crate. Then he wandered over to where Bobsley sat, so closely sawing and sanding flattened blocks.

"I dunno if we're going to paint these or paste paper over the sides," the high climber commented. "Painting would be quicker, but Miss Higgins says that fabric makes them look more like real books."

"Books. Also for the study, I take it." Mike's heart sank. If Naomi wanted the shelves filled with books, he could expect Bobsley popping into the workshop every time a cloud crossed the sky.

"Well, first I made this here fur rug to go in front of the fireplace." Bobsley dug around in his pocket and produced a patch of fur half the size of Mike's palm, roughly cut to look like a bear hide. "I seen the one in the fancy house over there, so I caught a squirrel and set to making one for Miss Naomi. But she says there's really only room for one fur rug in a house, so I'm on to books."

"That'll keep you busy for a good while." He tried to sound hearty, but Mike heard the bitter note beneath his cheery words. It was glaringly obvious this wasn't the first time the loggers invaded the workshop, and he didn't like knowing they'd stormed the castle in his absence.

How much time had they spent with Naomi? And how much progress had they made while he'd been gone? The smile he'd hitched on his face slid off as questions mounted.

"Not as busy as Bear." Bobsley gestured to where Riordan sat, bent nearly double over a table littered with headless matchsticks.

"What are you making?" Mike's curiosity got the better of him, since he couldn't usher the intruders out the door anytime soon.

"Shutters." With a single blunt fingertip, Bear nudged one completed set across the rough surface of the worktable. The squared matchsticks, divested of their sulfur-dipped ends, had been fitted and glued at slight angles within a larger frame. The tilted edges looked remarkably like raised shutters, perfect for a dollhouse.

"That's impressive." He didn't try to pick one up—they might not yet be dry. "These will look even better after we paint the trim."

"They're all so creative and patient, working on these things." Naomi favored the entire room with a brilliant smile. "If you ask me, this dollhouse is shaping up to be something very special."

To a man, they agreed. Mike could tell that the men were all thinking along the same lines; a project with Naomi at the helm couldn't be anything less than extraordinary. A woman like her demanded the best a man could give, and they would work their fingers to the bone before admitting defeat. None of them were just working on dollhouse pieces. They were working to win the woman.

※

"I'm sorry to say that you'll be losing us, but we really must go home." Charlotte clasped her hands over her bosom as though sincerely wrenched at the prospect of leaving Hope Falls. Or as though she thought the town would feel bereft after her defection.

Sadly, Naomi didn't feel that way at all. She wouldn't have believed it, after the extremes they'd come through in the past, but the longer her sister stayed, the more strained things became. She'd breathe easier after Charlotte left. And as for Harry. . .well, Naomi long ago saw his betrayal in choosing her sister as a blessing. In spite of everything—or perhaps because of it—she didn't want him.

After a too-long pause, the men figured out that Charlotte expected protests and requests that she prolong her stay in town. Muttering and grumbling, they made a suitably incoherent response.

"Yes. I, too, need to be getting back to the office." Corning stood, but he didn't seem much taller than when he was sitting. "Rest assured that I will tell anyone who asks that the Hope Falls sawmill is a sound proposition and an absolutely worthy investment."

"Our stay here has been marked with sorrow." Charlotte regained the proverbial floor. She probably interpreted the men's restless shifting for regret at her imminent departure rather than a disgruntled signal that she should stop holding up everyone's dinner. At any rate, she didn't sit down so they could start eating.

"The passing of Mrs. Cash gave you reason to mourn, and I simply can't ignore the fact that now Hope Falls needs a reason to rejoice." She utterly ignored mutters over her mispronunciation of Arla's last name, instead flinging her arms wide as though to embrace everyone in the room. "So before we take our leave, I intend to put together a party. A sort of backwoods ball, you could say. I'll arrange for music and dancing and refreshments so we can all enjoy one final evening together. A very. . .special evening."

A chill of foreboding raised gooseflesh on Naomi's arms. The way Charlotte paused before saying "special" was cause for concern.

"Any dance will be special, since we ain't never had one before." One of the men lessened the room's expectant tension.

"Ah, but this one will be very special indeed." Charlotte's gaze sought Naomi's, and her smile held more than a hint of triumph. "You see, in but a few nights' time, my sister will reveal the secret she's been keeping from all of you. Or I'll do it for her."

Naomi's heart skidded to a stop. It didn't simply skip a beat; it jumped, sputtered, and ceased working altogether. *She can't mean it. What about her protests that the past would harm her and Harry?*

"See how shy she is?" Charlotte made sure every eye in the room took in the heated flush creeping up her neck like a mottled rash. "That's why she needs her sister to give her this nudge. If I don't do something before I leave, Naomi might never reveal which of you men she wants to marry. She's too afraid of insulting the others!"

Relief brought air back into her lungs and even more blood rushing to redden her face. *She didn't mean that secret. Charlotte's just being dramatic. This won't ruin me, it just. . .* Naomi's thoughts hitched as Charlotte gave her deadline.

"In two nights, my big sister will choose her groom!"

FORTY-ONE

"Who is he?" Lacey wasted no time demanding an answer. As soon as they shut the door to the house and sent baby Dorothy upstairs with her nursemaid, the women rounded on Naomi in curious indignation.

"I don't know." Naomi sank into a wingback chair and moaned.

"Why is your sister forcing your hand?" Evie couldn't sit, too agitated to do anything but pace the parlor. "We all agreed you'd have as much time as you needed to choose a husband. No rushing, and at least two of us need to approve your selection beforehand. Did Charlotte know this before she waltzed in and dropped her decree?"

"Even if she didn't know the particulars, she knew better than to do this." Cora sat on the settee, spine ramrod straight. "I say we don't go along with it. Why should any of us dance to her tune and let her play puppeteer with Naomi's future? It's idiocy."

Naomi cleared her throat, if not her mind. "It's already done." If she didn't go through with Charlotte's well-publicized plan, her sister might very well decide to reveal a more interesting secret. After all, Charlotte probably didn't trust Naomi to keep quiet, and Colorado Territory was such a long, long way from back home.

"She's right." Lacey retraced Evie's circuit. "Charlotte's whipped Naomi's fellows into an awful lather. If Evie or I hadn't yet selected our fiancés, we could circumvent this. As it stands, we won't be able to buy more time for Naomi to decide. The men will be insulted and up in arms if she balks now. And Charlotte knows it."

"She's very astute," Naomi admitted. "She played this well."

"I have a few other descriptions I'd use before 'astute' occurred to me," Evie harrumphed. "But why is she playing at all?"

"Isn't it obvious?" Lacey's nonchalance made Naomi worry anew.

"Is it obvious?" She winced at the quaver weakening her voice.

"Charlotte's jealous. She knows Harry chose the wrong wife, and by now Harry's had half a decade to realize his mistake. Braden's invitation threatened her—she came to make sure her husband didn't harbor feelings for Naomi." Lacey stopped pacing in favor of shredding the ribbons dotting her skirts. "Now she's making sure Naomi's solidly married, just in case Harry invests in Hope Falls and takes it into his head to come down for another visit!"

"Well, we all knew I'd have to choose one of them eventually." Naomi decided to lay out the facts and try to hide the doubts and protests thrumming through her thoughts. "And since I'm holding up your and Evie's weddings and drawing out the loggers' expectations, it couldn't go on much longer. At this point, I'll have to choose."

"It's all my fault." Lacey plopped down onto the settee with enough force to make Cora pop up before sinking back down. "If I hadn't convinced you all to run that accursed advertisement, Naomi wouldn't be trapped in this predicament. At the very least, I should have waited to announce my engagement with Dunstan until you'd had more time to get to know the men and make an informed decision!"

"Poppycock." Naomi snorted. "It's not your fault I joined the ad, and after your private adventure in the mines became so public—with the men seeing you in those pants!—you had to announce your engagement. Stop taking credit for my mistakes, and help me choose."

"I've always had a soft spot for Clump," Evie confessed. "If not for Jake, I would've chosen him. You know he'd work hard to be a good provider, cherish his family, and not take you for granted."

"Clump has a good heart." Naomi's own estimation of the sincere

German echoed Evie's sentiments almost exactly. But Clump didn't make Naomi's pulse pick up pace when he walked up, smiled, or spoke.

"So does Riordan. He's breaking up a fight or helping Granger every time we turn around. And you know a man that size can care for his own. You could do worse than a gentle giant," Cora advised.

"That's true, too. Riordan looks like a Goliath, but he acts more like a David." Naomi couldn't say that, for all his gentleness, Riordan's sheer size made her skittish. She couldn't marry him.

"Bobsley's too young." Lacey flatly refused to consider the flighty high climber with the good-natured grin. "Gent's too old."

"I wouldn't say that." *I might think it, but I wouldn't say it!* "He's extremely conscientious, always thoughtful and well-mannered."

"Excellent. Do keep him in mind if you ever decide to hire a butler." Lacey's wry tone made it clear that Naomi hadn't convinced anyone she considered Gent and his top hat to be a viable option.

"What about Mr. Strode?" Cora ran a palm over her face as though trying to wipe away the day's difficulties. "He's fairly new, but I think you've spent more time with him than any of the others."

"I like him." *I want him. I'd choose him in a heartbeat!*

Naomi ruthlessly reigned in her thoughts. Michael deserved a wife he could trust, and after her discussion with Charlotte, she owed her sister her silence. She couldn't tell him what she'd done, what kind of woman she was—even if she thought he'd overlook it.

The next words pained her before they were born. "But he's not one of the men who's courting me, so I can't consider him anyway."

"You don't have much time," Evie mused. "But if he's the one who suits you best, consider giving him something to think about."

"That's not a bad idea. Try persuading him. He might be more interested than you suppose." Lacey brightened. "Dunstan was."

"Thanks for the advice." Naomi forced a chuckle. "But I'll never be as persuasive as you. We're very different women, cousin."

You have no idea just how different, and I hope it stays that way.

"You have to change it." Cora circled the fingers of her left hand around her right wrist and hung on tight to keep them from fluttering around while she spoke. "Since you didn't make it to dinner last night and you're the supposed head of Hope Falls, you can stop Mrs. Blinman's attempt to bully Naomi. Say you'll help!"

"So that's why they didn't leave this morning?" Braden sat still for a moment, mulling over this new information. "When I left Blinman and Corning yesterday, they sounded bound and determined to be on their way. If the doctor hadn't slipped me some morphine yesterday afternoon, I would've been there last night to intervene."

"You can be there now," Cora urged. "While it's mainly about refusing to let Naomi be pressured into a loveless marriage, there's another reason why Hope Falls shouldn't be holding this dance."

She waited for him to mention Arla so she wouldn't have to speak around the lump that clogged her throat whenever she thought of her friend. But Braden sat there waiting for her to continue.

"Arla! She hasn't been gone for even a week," Cora burst out.

"I know." But Braden didn't look at all like he really understood how inappropriate this dance would be. He stared out the window into a distance only he could see. "So many deaths."

She waited for him to acknowledge Arla specifically, to snap to his senses and declare he'd look after his cousin instead of letting Naomi be sacrificed for the sake of some stupid advertisement. And when he finally did speak, his thoughts surprised her.

"There's a lot that's not fair, Cora. Mrs. Nash's death, leaving her child orphaned, Naomi needing to pick one of her suitors so fast. . . None of this is fair." He pointed out the window. "But it pales in comparison to the men who died in the belly of that mountain, buried alive by the greed of a man I've yet to catch."

"Draxley's dead." Cora didn't follow his reasoning and wondered whether Doc had snuck Braden another dose. Normally she'd say it served him right for pushing himself too hard, but right now she needed Braden to be able to think clearly and act strongly.

"I know." His arm fell to his side, fist clenched. "So's Owens. But what about the man who convinced Owens and Draxley to sabotage the mines? We don't know his name, so he escapes any justice."

"That's not something I can solve. I'm busy trying to figure out how to keep Charlotte from ruining Naomi's life—and you don't seem to care!" Cora pinched the skin between thumb and forefinger, refusing to start wringing her hands or pacing. She'd promised herself she'd stay strong any and every time she talked to Braden.

Braden swallowed and faced her. "I care, Cora. But Naomi's a grown woman who can choose her own husband. The men on that ridge beside Mrs. Nash can't hunt down their own killer, can they?"

Cora was about to tell him she'd come back after his medication wore off when something clicked into place. "The investors."

He nodded miserably, confirming her blossoming suspicion.

"You invited the previous investors because you hoped the saboteur would be greedy enough to show up and say something so stupid and so obvious we'd all know what he'd done?" Cora gaped at her fiancé in disbelief. "That's beyond far-fetched, Braden!"

"It was all I could do." He rubbed the back of his neck. "I thought I'd lost my last chance, but this dance gives me another opportunity to question Blinman and Corning. I can't cancel it."

Cora felt her pulse thud at the base of her throat and raised a hand to cover it. "What about Naomi? What about little Dorothy, who'll someday hear that Hope Falls threw a party days after her mother's death? What about what you owe the people who still live?"

"Like the Loathly Lady in your story, Naomi can make her own choice." Braden gave a weary sigh. "And what makes you think little Dorothy will stay in Hope Falls? Lawson might move on, you know."

"Not if I marry him, like he asked, so I can be a mother to Dorothy." For the first time, Cora spoke of the promise she hadn't meant to give Arla. "I assured Arla that I'd take care of her daughter, and Mr. Lawson can't do it alone. Dorothy will stay."

"You're adopting this child?" Braden sat up, exuding anxious energy. "And you didn't think to discuss it with me before now?"

"No. You're busy pursuing your own vendettas. Our engagement is dissolved, and you don't see fit to honor my friends. Why would I discuss any of my decisions with someone like that?" She couldn't keep the scorn from her voice. "If it came down to you or Dorothy, there wouldn't be any question. I choose the child, and I choose to keep my promise to a friend who deserved more from this town."

She left before Braden could summon a response. No argument he concocted now could change her mind. He wouldn't help Naomi, and Cora couldn't help Braden. He'd failed her for the final time.

∞

"You need more time." Mike didn't waste words when he finally got a moment alone with Naomi. He'd been trying to pull her aside since her sister's announcement, but she hadn't so much as stepped foot in the workshop since. The lumbermen abandoned all attempts at logging, keeping Naomi hopping with their final, desperate attempts to woo her. Mike pushed away his bitterness over failing to do the same. Now he had this one chance, mere moments before the dance began, to make her listen.

"We'll catch up on the dollhouse." Naomi's eyes, made even greener than usual by her verdant dance dress, looked tired. "With all the things the men have made, we can make up the time."

"That's not what I meant." He curled his fingers around her elbow, feeling the warmth of her skin through the thin fabric. "I meant you need more time to make the biggest decision of your life."

"Why?" She blinked at him, more remote than he'd ever seen her. "It isn't as though my options are going to improve or expand. I put out the advertisement; I've gotten to know the men who responded. The men are waiting. Lacey and Evie's weddings are waiting on me."

"Hasn't anyone told you you're worth waiting for?" He rubbed his thumb along the soft fabric, wishing he could touch her without any barriers between them. "I don't think there's a man in that clearing or a single one of your friends who'd disagree with me."

"Well, there's one." She gave a sad smile, and suddenly Mike knew, without a doubt, Naomi was thinking of Harold Blinman.

"Any man who'd let you go didn't deserve you to start with," Mike whispered fiercely. "If you can't see that, then I'm right. You need more time to come to terms with your past before you can promise any man your future."

Now Naomi's eyes sparkled, but they were wet with unshed tears. "What do you know about coming to terms with the past, Michael? Some mistakes, once made, color everything that follows."

"Only if you let them." He wasn't whispering anymore. "But if there's any part of you that still belongs to Blinman, you shouldn't accept another man. You know I'm right. Don't do this."

"What do you know about Harry?" She looked as surprised and wounded as if he'd slapped her across the face. "Why do you care?"

"I want better for you." He stepped closer and abandoned his attempt to talk sense into her without pressuring her further. Mike cupped her cheek in his palm. "I would wait for you, Naomi."

Longing flashed through her gaze, and her gloved hand rested atop his for a moment. She closed her eyes, and when she opened them, he saw only grim determination. She dropped her hand. "You shouldn't."

She rushed off into the night, leaving behind a half-heard addition. "You'd only find out that I didn't deserve it."

FORTY-TWO

Shaken by Michael's unexpected offer, hardly able to breathe while regret pinched her ribs like a remorseless iron cage, Naomi ached to tell him the truth. To see if he still thought she was worth waiting for or if he'd denounce her as the worst sort of woman.

She didn't think she'd like his answer, even if she could ask the question. Ringed with lanterns and pressed by the promises she'd made her sister and her friends, the dance floor held all the charm of a gallows. Each step felt leaden, her stomach swimming in her shoes. Naomi knew full well she didn't dredge up a smile for anyone.

Lord, if I'm not to be with Michael, why did You let him return my regard? I know my sins; I've confessed and repented. So why this torment? If he didn't want me, I could move forward with my plan to accept Clump. But how can I do that now, knowing Michael might feel the same way I do? Knowing that I can never find out because I'm bound by my promise to Charlotte and my own unimaginable past?

She managed to nod and murmur her way through a dance with Corning before her suitors queued up. The phonograph Charlotte dragged from the house sounded as scratchy and sore as Naomi's throat felt from swallowing back her tears. But the music played on, and so did the farce her life had become. Gent took her for the first dance.

Admittedly, she didn't pay close attention to what he was saying until she caught a smattering of French. The words acted like a cold dousing, dragging her forward to face the moment.

"I'm sorry." She concentrated on not tripping over his boots. For some reason, her movement seemed disjointed and surreal. "You know, my French is rusty. Would you mind repeating that for me?"

"Ah, that caught your attention." Gent beamed down at her through a particularly enthusiastic swirl. "Your sister said it would. I practiced all day to memorize the inflection. *Votre premier amour n'a pas que vous voulez, et pas plus que ces hommes.*"

Your first love didn't want you, and neither do these men. Naomi stumbled as the words hammered into her. Stunned, she barely held on and finished the dance. Luckily, Gent seemed pleased by her dumbfounded reaction until Bobsley cut in.

"Good evening, Miss Higgins." Stiff formality made the young man seem awkward—though, then again, that might be due to his jerky movements and abysmal dancing. For a while, it took all of their concentration to remain upright. But soon enough, he spoke in stilted French. *"Vous n'êtes rien, mais une salope skunk-cheveux."*

You are nothing but a skunk-haired slut. Naomi went stock-still at the denouncement, causing the well-meaning Bobsley to tromp on her foot. The mishap bought her a few moments off the makeshift dance floor, but even so the world seemed to be spinning around her.

"Pardon?" Riordan hunkered down into the seat beside her when Bobsley left to get her something to drink. "That's a wonderful color on you, Miss Higgins. And I wanted to tell you—"

"Wait. Did my sister teach you something special in French?" At his nod, Naomi closed her eyes and braced herself for his words.

"L'homme que vous mariez vous haïra autant que notre mère."
The man you marry will hate you as much as our mother.

"Well." She sucked in a sharp breath and tried to hold back the bile burning the back of her throat. "I hardly know what to say."

"Here's your milk, Miss Higgins." Bobsley pushed a cool glass into her hand, and Naomi gulped it down gratefully. The burning sensation receded, and she didn't feel in danger of being sick.

Until Clump joined them. Well-meaning Volker Clump led her back onto the dance floor, tromping her feet with his too-heavy tread and battering her heart with his "compliment." His German accent clotted the French pronunciation, but Naomi heard each damning word. *"Votre nuit de noces sera encore pire que celui que vous avez volé."*

At that, Naomi mumbled an incoherent apology and excuse then rushed from the dance floor. Alone in the darkness of the night, she broke into a run. Each step pounded out her sister's final curse.

Your wedding night will be even worse than the one you stole.

"You don't mean that." Cora stared at him as though he'd sprung from his wheeled chair and begun a series of handstands and cartwheels.

"I do." He wanted to reach for her hand but knew he didn't have the right. Instead he forced out the words lodging in his throat. "If you want to go and dance, I'll hold baby Dorothy for you."

She squinted at him and laid a cool palm against his forehead. "Are you feeling all right Braden? You're not acting like yourself."

"Good." He decided to be blunt since he wasn't much good with words anyway. "I've been acting like a horse's rear end for months."

"Well." She pulled her hand away, and Braden fought the urge to snatch it back. "That's new. Since when do you admit you're wrong?"

"Since every time I try to control something, it goes wrong." He looked at the white bundle she cradled in the crook of one arm. "She seems healthy and happy, and so do you. Motherhood agrees with you."

"Do you think so?" A hesitant smile lifted the corners of her generous lips—the first smile she'd given him since she told the Loathly Lady legend. "I constantly worry I'm not doing it right."

"That's my fault, Cora." His smile faded so she could see his seriousness. "I should have told you what a wonderful job you do, taking care of people. You have a comforting touch, encouraging smile, and just enough starch to keep things interesting."

"Oh." She blinked then ducked her head and fussed with the baby's wrappings. "That's. . .well, that's the nicest thing you've said to me since I came to Hope Falls. Which isn't saying much, Braden."

He bowed his head. "I know. I have a lot to make up for."

"Well, it would have been a very nice thing to say anywhere," she relented, still focused on the baby. "But why would you try to make up for your behavior? You were grieving the loss of your men, dealing with a lot of pain, and trying to protect all of us."

"And failing to treat you like a grown woman fully able to make her own decisions." Braden stated it outright. "If I have any chance of convincing you to reestablish our engagement, I'll need to prove that I realize what a treasure you are. No matter my struggles, I shouldn't have stopped cherishing the amazing woman God brought into my life. Cora, I'm sorry for the way I acted. I just hope you'll let me make it up to you someday."

Confusion flitted across her features. "Then why did you offer to hold Dorothy so I could dance with someone else?"

"Because I'm giving you the one thing every woman wants." He reached up and clasped her hand in his, unable to keep from touching her. "I'm respecting your choice—whatever it may be."

After all, respecting was a far cry from accepting, should she make the wrong decision.

She stayed quiet for a long time but didn't pull her hand away. Braden clung to it and the hope that she'd see the change God had been working in him since the day of the cave-in. He had a long way to go still, but he figured Cora already knew that. He'd taken a bad turn and gone a long way down it. Getting back to the place where they'd been before meant a return journey.

"You listened." She squeezed his hand, but Braden didn't think she realized she'd done it until he squeezed back. "Why now? What changed?"

"I'm done chasing things I can't change at the expense of the people I'm supposed to cherish." His voice sounded croaky, but at least he forced the words through. "You were right. I should have called this thing off. Naomi looks like she's about to burst into tears, the men are circling her like jackals, and I haven't gotten a single clue from Corning or Blinman about the mine collapse."

Her brows slammed together. "Don't blame yourself for not finding the saboteur." Her whisper sounded a bit hissy. "Just like you need to stop blaming yourself for the accident."

"I have." Something like peace swelled in his chest. Cora still cared—he could build on that. "But I do blame myself for losing you. I want to win you back, Cora-mine."

A ghost of the gamine grin she used to wear flashed across her face. "I won't stop you from trying."

"Good because someday not too far off I intend to get out of this wheelchair." Braden grinned. "It's the only way I can get back down on one knee."

A fleeting smile, the shimmer of tears, and Cora's expression grew shuttered. "Before you start thinking you'll reestablish our engagement someday, you need to know that I've discussed Dorothy's situation with Mr. Lawson. At length."

No! Braden couldn't speak, could only scream a silent denial. After all they'd been through, he couldn't have lost her to Lawson!

"I turned down his generous proposal, but he agreed it would be in Dorothy's best interests if we honored Arla's last request. As of today, Dorothy is mine. I plan to raise her as my daughter, Braden."

He reached out and tucked back the blanket obscuring the newborn's face. Dorothy wrinkled her nose and let out an agitated gurgle, flailing one tiny fist before settling back into sleep. "She's beautiful. Any man would be blessed by the pair of you."

Cora smiled again. "Did you have anyone particular in mind?"

Not thinking, Naomi's steps carried her along the familiar path to the workshop. She flung open the door, strode inside, and grabbed her apron as she always did. Then she realized what she was doing. Her legs shaky, she barely made it to the chair before the sobs slammed together in the back of her throat, cutting off her air.

Charlotte found her bent over, clutching the apron like a lifeline and gasping for breath. The tears streaming down her face made her sister look hazy, as if rubbed by a zealous eraser. "What do you want?" Naomi choked on tears and bone-deep pain.

Charlotte sneezed. "To apologize." Another sneeze. "What I did was awful, petty, and cruel, and I can't tell you how sorry I am, Mimi."

"I hate that nickname," she protested thickly. Somehow it symbolized the way Charlotte always disregarded her feelings. That made it something important. "Don't call me Mimi, and don't give me your apologies when you don't mean them. I understand that you hate me, and I understand why. Leave it at that and leave me be, Charlotte."

"No! You don't understand. How could you? I've been jealous of you my whole life. You got to stay home while they shipped me to another continent," Charlotte burst out. "Then when France became the home of my heart, they dragged me back to the States so I could see my big sister marry some well-to-do man from a distinguished family. I stole Harry because I wanted to prove that I could make Mama proud, too—that I was just as good as you are. But look how that worked."

"I'm not apologizing again," Naomi snapped, trying to hold on to her anger. She couldn't handle or help her sister's old hurts, but they seeped toward her heart. Didn't Naomi know how it felt to be sent far away? To feel second best to her sister? She'd never realized Charlotte experienced some of those same feelings.

Another sneeze and Charlotte squeezed her hand. "I'm not asking you to. I'm talking about how I failed. Harry married me so I could bear him an heir—and I haven't. One miscarriage, and no more."

Naomi's wall crumpled at the forlorn grief in her sister's voice. She reached out to stroke Charlotte's black hair, an awkward attempt to comfort the sister who'd become such a stranger to her. "That's not your fault. You're not a failure—Harry seems happy."

Charlotte said something but lost it to another round of sneezes. When she caught her breath, she said, "Can we go outside? It's a warm night—we can go for a little walk in the woods where no one

926

will interrupt us. I'm not ready to rejoin the dance."

"Neither am I." Naomi stood, still clutching her apron. It gave her hands something to do, a simple comfort she desperately needed. They walked side by side, slowly at first, both of them loathe to draw attention to themselves. When they reached the woods and Charlotte stopped sneezing, she started to walk more quickly.

"What's the hurry?" Naomi hurried after her sister, pulling up short when Charlotte stepped up a series of small rocks to look over the edge of a steep drop. Darkness blanketed the area, and the recent rains probably meant slippery moss scattered around those boulders. She hung back.

"Aren't you coming?" Charlotte turned around and beckoned.

"No. Why don't you come back down here?" Naomi suggested. "As I recall, it's a very long drop from up there. One of us might slip."

"Well that's fine." Her sister gave a sharp laugh and pulled something out of her pocket. Moonlight glinted off the barrel of the pistol she pointed toward Naomi. "Since one of us is supposed to."

FORTY-THREE

It wasn't supposed to be like this. Mike glared at each man who spoke to Naomi, reserving a special intensity for the ones who danced with her. The lucky ones who could put their hand on her waist and smile into her eyes while they swayed to the music.

Although, in all fairness, Naomi didn't seem as graceful as usual. Her movements seemed abrupt, jerky, and downright clumsy at times as she tripped over her partners' feet. Mike felt something akin to satisfaction at the idea she was as unsettled as he was.

"Shouldn't you be asking Naomi to dance, Dad?" Luke's anxious query made him look down. "Because you know lots of other guys are, and you don't have much time left to convince her to choose us."

Us. Mike's jaw clenched at his son's innocent comment. Luke already saw the three of them becoming a family. Mike wanted the same. But none of that did any good if Naomi didn't choose them.

"She looks kinda upset." Concern crinkled Luke's brow as they watched Naomi jump back from Clump and rush away from the dance area. He pushed up his sleeves. "All right, Dad. Now's your chance. You go follow her, and I'll take care of the guy who made her cry."

Mike caught his son by the back of the collar before the boy could go do something foolish. "You don't know what happened. Promise me you'll leave Clump alone. Trust me, he's a good guy." When he wasn't trying to steal Naomi for himself at least.

"Okay. So long as you go get her." Luke pointed toward the

workshop. "She went that-a-way, so you better get a move on!"

His son's eagerness made Mike want to cry and punch something all at once. It was his fault. He'd raised Luke's hopes along with his own. And, unless God intervened sometime tonight, both of them would suffer major disappointment before the sun rose again.

Mike approached the workshop in time to see a set of skirts disappearing around the corner. For a moment he hesitated. Naomi obviously wanted to be left alone—but it looked like she might be headed for the woods. The memory of the stuffed cougar she persisted in decorating stuck out in his mind. The forest was too dangerous to let her go wandering around unprotected. Especially at night.

Quietly, Mike crept around the side of the shop and headed for the woods. In the distance he could make out two figures. While relieved Naomi wasn't alone, the idea of leaving two women to wander the woods by themselves made him uneasy. He decided he wouldn't intrude—just shadow them close enough to keep Naomi in sight, far enough to give her privacy. She probably needed to talk through her choice.

The farther the women went into the woods, the closer Mike followed. Otherwise too much cover separated him. He'd be of no use if he had to scramble through thickets and bound over boulders. When the women reached a clearing—the edge of a cliff face really, Mike stayed behind in the shadow of the woods. The wind carried their conversation to him, and Mike realized Naomi's companion was her sister. He'd just started to wonder if he shouldn't leave them to talk things out when Mrs. Blinman pulled the pistol from her pocket.

Mike started forward but realized his presence might startle the woman into shooting. Even if he didn't startle her, the knowledge that there was a witness might provoke her to violence. Desperately he scanned the area for closer cover and found none. The trees where he stood provided the nearest foliage, and the closest rocks were situated on the cliff edge behind the women. For now he had no choice but to stay concealed and wait things out.

"What are you doing?" Naomi stared at the weapon, eyes glued to the one threat Mike never suspected—a danger he couldn't reach her in time to prevent. "When did you start carrying a gun, Charlotte?"

"Since the day I boarded the train for Hope Falls. The mountains are a dangerous place for anyone," Mrs. Blinman singsonged and cocked the pistol. "But they're particularly threatening to me. Harry never suspected why our cousin invited him and the other investors 'to inspect the sawmill,' but I suspected. Braden found out the collapse wasn't an accident, didn't he?"

Still hidden, Mike bit back a groan. He'd been so focused on getting Luke home, he hadn't bothered to question Braden's blasé explanation about those special invitations of his. Now that Mrs. Blinman said something, it made perfect sense. Had Braden Lyman been sitting beside him, Mike would have been tempted to do violence.

"It was you who sabotaged the mines?" Naomi sounded flabbergasted. "Why would you bother arranging a cave-in?"

"Money, you flea-brain." She gave a bone-chilling laugh.

"But you don't need it. You have Harry and a house and fine clothes—anything you want." Naomi twisted some fabric in her hands.

"Not anything," her sister snapped. "Harry won't take me home. After all I went through to marry him and get that honeymoon in France, I couldn't convince him to stay there. He forced me to come back to America, no matter how much I begged to go back home."

"I don't see how the mine collapse would change that." Naomi slid forward, the shift so slight Mike might have imagined it.

"Of course you don't see. You never did see what was right in front of your face." Another cackle. "I took Owens as my lover. When the mine struck gold, I convinced him to manufacture a false cave-in so we could buy the other investors out for next to nothing. Then he'd go back in with a new crew, reap the riches, and we'd be off!"

"But you didn't tell him you planned to kill Braden." Naomi

seemed to understand something Mike could only guess at.

"No. I arranged that with Draxley. Why split the profits and dodge suspicion if we didn't have to? But Owens, sentimental fool that he was, got himself killed by racing back to save our cousin. Not that it mattered. Sure enough, Braden lived." She grimaced in disgust.

"Most of us were glad about that." Naomi shifted again. "Now, do you want to tell me why you're pointing a gun at my head?"

"Because you, dear sister, are going to climb those rocks and fling yourself over the edge. I'll make sure everyone knows you couldn't stand the thought of marrying anyone other than Harry. Your mad, unrequited love has built for half a decade, and you snapped." The crazy woman snapped her fingers to further illustrate the point.

Slowly, Mike pulled off his boots and started edging out of the woods, making as little noise as he could manage. If Naomi planned to jump her sister, he wanted her to know he was there for her. He wanted to get as close as possible to the crazy woman with the gun. He saw Naomi's eyes widen when she caught sight of him, but otherwise she kept her calm. Better, she kept her sister talking.

"Why kill me?" Naomi scooted again, making Mike's breath catch. Could she be trying to grab her sister's pistol? "What's the point?"

"I'm your closest relative. Your shares in Hope Falls—and the mine—will come to the sister you so recently reunited with." Mrs. Blinman waved the pistol and adopted a sorrowful tone. "Imagine my devastation, after I worked so hard to help you find a husband of your very own, that you decided to end your life over my Harry."

It seemed like ages passed since Mike started creeping up the cliff side, cautiously balancing amid small, sharp rocks. He sent up a prayer of thanks that he'd thought to remove his boots—the rocks against boot heels would have given him away in a heartbeat. Finally, he'd gotten close enough to risk lunging at the lunatic.

But Naomi beat him to it. With a deft motion, she untwisted the fabric she'd been bunching and unbunching in her hands. She pulled it taught and flung the thing upward, diving to the side in a cloud of sawdust. Her sister started sneezing immediately, finger tightening on the trigger and sending a bullet ricocheting off the nearest boulder and back into the woods behind all of them.

When Naomi dove to the side, Mike lunged. He caught Mrs. Blinman around the waist, hand closing over the wrist holding the pistol. For such a tiny woman, she had a surprisingly strong grip. He had to slam her arm against the ground before she released it.

For a moment all three of them lay there, gasping for breath. Mrs. Blinman punctuated the silence with a few more sneezes before Naomi got to her feet. Without speaking, she refolded what Mike now recognized as her work apron—and the source of the sawdust cloud. He couldn't help but grin at her brilliant makeshift weapon.

"Sawdust sneezes," her sister wheezed. "Crude, but effective. I should have remembered how hopelessly provincial you can be."

"As opposed to being a scheming, lying murderer?" Naomi glared down at her sister. "If that's what passes for sophistication these days, then I'm well rid of it. Just as I'll be well rid of you."

"Not so fast." Charlotte's sneer made Naomi's blood boil. "You can't prove anything—and you know you have to let me go. Otherwise I'll tell the world my big sister's sordid little secret, won't I?"

"No." Naomi froze, fighting the now-familiar clench of fear. "No one will believe an adulterer, saboteur, and murderer."

"People believe the best story," her sister spat out. "If you turn me in, I'll turn out your dirty laundry. Imagine how the gossips would love it—they'll gleefully pick apart a whole family!"

"What is she talking about, Naomi?" Michael's deep, steady voice made her nerves flutter more than ever.

"Nothing." She rubbed the bridge of her nose, searching for a solution to this impossible situation. She couldn't let Charlotte go— Braden deserved to find justice for the mine sabotage. And even if he didn't, she couldn't live with herself if her sister went on to hurt some other person, family, or even an entire town.

But she couldn't stand to have Charlotte tell Michael what a despicable, lowly woman she really was. The look on his face when he saw her unmasked would hurt more than a thousand Harold Blinmans. *Why are you leaving it up to Charlotte?* A small, brave voice surfaced from deep inside her. *You can't set her free, and she'll hurt you if she can. Don't let old guilt give her new power.*

"On Charlotte and Harry's wedding night, Mama gave me hard liquor to steady my nerves. Everyone was talking about me, staring to see if I'd fall apart. Then there were the toasts. And the punch." She remembered the sensation of floating and tried to capture that same detachment. "I don't remember anything, but I awoke in Charlotte's bed the next morning—in place of the bride."

"I don't believe it. You would never, not in a million years. . ." Michael rubbed his forehead as though trying to push away the thought. "All that about a man mistaking one sister for the other. . . Do you mean your sister's groom never realized his mistake?"

"No. It can't be true. I would've known. . . ." Harry emerged from the forest, visibly shaken and staring at her as if he'd never seen her before. "Why would you say something like that, Naomi? Did you hear me coming and think I was eavesdropping? Because I wasn't. I came to find you and your sister since you'd been gone so long."

"She said it because it's true, and I'm going to tell everyone," Charlotte crowed. "You went to bed so drunk you didn't recognize that the woman wasn't your wife. It's a wonder you did anything to be ashamed of, in that condition." She gave a crude snicker.

"Why didn't I remember? Why didn't anyone tell me?" Harry went pale and looked as though he was going to lose his dinner.

"Would you have wanted to know?" Naomi steeled herself for the answer. "Would it have made any difference, or would you have helped them ship me off and get rid of any difficult questions?"

Michael kept his gaze locked on the ground, unwilling to even look at her. That hurt more than Harry's refusal to answer her.

"Michael." She whispered his name, pleading for understanding. "I didn't mean to do it. I didn't plan on it or want to. I don't even remember anything except becoming ill when Mama told me."

"Your hair," Harry burst out. "I would've noticed your hair."

"Mama and Charlotte took pains to hide the white streak that night." Naomi closed her eyes at the memory. "So I'd look young enough to maybe catch the interest of some other gentleman. Not that I was at the party for long—I got so confused Charlotte took me back to the family wing so I could go to bed and sleep away the fog."

"Wait." Michael's head jerked up from where he was pinning Charlotte's arms behind her and tying them together with the apron Naomi had passed him. "Your sister is the one who took you to bed? After she tried so hard to hide your hair?"

Naomi understood what he was suggesting, but her mind couldn't make the connection stick. Not until Charlotte rose to her knees and hissed at Michael. That's when she knew. Michael saw what she never had.

She bent down to stare her sister in the eye. "You did my hair so I'd look more like you. You kept giving me champagne and making toasts to get me tipsy. You took me upstairs and put me in your own bed. . . . I should have realized someone undressed me. The maids would have taken me back to my room if they found me there. Even a drunken groom would notice his bride wore a red dress instead of white!"

"Yes. Your shame and guilt kept you from asking too many questions or examining your memory too closely." Charlotte cackled. "How else was I going to fool Harry into thinking he'd married the young innocent I pretended to be? A little sleeping powder for you and lots of bourbon for Harry, some creative juggling, and voilà. Stained sheets the next morning to make my husband happy."

"I never stole your wedding night." Naomi sat on the nearest boulder, her knees unable to support her. Relief and rage at this revelation robbed her of any strength. "You stole mine."

"For all the good it did me." Charlotte snorted. "Harry turned out to be as useless as you, but the secrets do me no good now. I'll tell them to anyone and everyone if you turn me in for the mines and trying to make you walk over the cliff," Charlotte promised. "You and Harry won't be able to hold your heads up."

"The mines?" Harry looked confused, and Naomi knew he really had just joined the conversation. Quickly, Michael filled him in.

"No one will believe you." He echoed Naomi's earlier hope.

"Gossips love a good story." Charlotte jerked against the binding Michael made from Naomi's apron strings, unable to get free.

"I'll give them a better one." Harry's face filled with wrath. "A selfish, grasping adulteress who seduced a good man, sabotaged a mine, and tried to kill her own sister. When she failed, she went mad and her poor husband had to place her in an asylum, where she screams obscene stories from the mess of her mind."

"You wouldn't put your wife in an asylum—it'd be the sort of scandal you want to avoid." Her sister's bravado couldn't hide her fear.

"Better than the sort you'd create if everyone didn't dismiss your ramblings for insanity." Michael's face hardened. "And considering the things you've done, I don't question that you're insane. The asylum will stop you from hurting anyone else."

But there was nothing he could do to heal Naomi's hurts. He didn't know how to banish the haunted look in her eye as Harry took her sister away, condemned by her own evil madness to a life of misery.

"Do you think I could've stopped her?" The choked question brought him to her side. "If I'd fought harder with my parents so they never sent her away? Maybe I could've helped her...."

"No." Mike decided they'd bypassed propriety by this point and folded her into his arms. Her hands crept up his chest and locked onto his shoulders, hanging on as sobs wracked her small frame.

When they slowed, he slipped a finger under her chin and forced her to meet his gaze. "It's not your fault. Not Harry, not the wedding night, and not the mines. You've shouldered her blame for the past five years—lay that burden down, Naomi."

"She used me." Naomi winced. "But my mistakes paved the way.

No matter how guilty Charlotte is, I'm still a fallen woman."

"No you aren't!" His hands closed around her upper arms, making her stand straight and tall. "If Blinman didn't look so sickened by the whole thing and I didn't know your sister orchestrated the situation so skillfully, I'd be tempted to beat him to a pulp for taking advantage of an unconscious woman. No man has that right, and no woman should bear the responsibility for what was done to her."

"But I'm still responsible for letting Charlotte trick me, for being so morose I drank enough liquor not to notice her machinations. If I hadn't been so wrapped up in my anger over her and Harry's betrayal, I wouldn't have been vulnerable to her plans."

"Have you confessed those mistakes? Repented of them?" He almost missed the nearly imperceptible bob of her head. "Doesn't the Word say that if you've done that, He's faithful and just to forgive you and purify you from unrighteousness?" Another stronger nod.

"Then why, Naomi, do you continue to doubt your own worth?" He slid one hand up her arm, over her shoulder, and into her loosened hair. Mike let the silken strands slip through his fingers. He knew what he had to do next, and he dreaded it. But he couldn't expect her to be brave if he hid things from her. "You're not the only one who's needed that sort of grace. I know I did—and still do."

She tilted her head back and looked at him through half-lowered lids, apparently enjoying having him play with her hair. "I'm sure it wasn't anything so horrible."

"I didn't marry my first wife for love." Reluctantly he stopped toying with the texture of her silky locks. "I married for money."

Her eyes snapped open in shock. "Why did you do that?"

"I just said." Her surprise was almost comical. "For money."

"No. I meant why did you need the money?" she pressed him. "I know you. There had to be some very important reason to make such a sacrifice."

"You believe in me that much?" He had a hard time getting the words out.

"No less than you believed in me." Naomi reached up to thread her own fingers through his hair. "You saw in a second what I never considered because you were looking for an explanation while I was busy wallowing in blame."

"My mother had consumption, and she was dying a slow, painful death. Dad passed on not long before and didn't leave much of anything behind. I'd just sunk my money into my workshop with nothing left to pay for the doctors, medicine, and help to keep her comfortable until God called her home." He resisted the urge to lean back like a cat, pressing against those soothing fingers.

"See? I knew you had a reason. And even if you entered into it for the wrong reasons and struggled afterward, you got Luke." Seeing her smile, Mike reached up and pulled her hand down, clasping it against his chest. What was the old saying? In for a penny, in for a pound...

"Luke's the reason Leticia needed to marry in a hurry." Mike brought her other hand up so that he held both. "He doesn't know. I don't want him to ever know, but I won't hide things from you."

"I won't tell him." She looked down at their entwined hands then back up. "Now I understand why you were so horrified by my ad. It touched on a sore spot, didn't it?"

He tightened his grip. "That, and I couldn't figure out why such an incredible woman had such a hard time finding a husband."

"Now we know each other's secrets." She brushed her thumb back and forth across his knuckles, sending chills up his spine. "Do you still mean what you said before the dance?"

"Which part?" Mike found it hard to think at the moment.

"The part about how I'm worth waiting for?" She tried to duck her head, but he released one of her hands so he could tilt her chin back up.

"Absolutely." He looked into her eyes for a long moment then lowered his head for an overdue kiss. After several more, he pulled away and drew a ragged breath. "Just don't make me wait too much longer!"

EPILOGUE

Hope Falls, August 30, 1887

Luke grasped Decoy firmly by the collar, both hovering a respectful—or perhaps apprehensive—distance from the fidgety bunch of brides. The cheery notes of Gent's fiddle grew fainter. Soon they would fade altogether in the late summer sunshine—it was time.

"Ready?" Cora twitched her nose, trying to stop the telltale tingle of tears to come. *You can't fall apart before the ceremony starts!*

"One last time then?" Naomi reached out and snagged one of Cora's hands and one of Lacey's. Evie swiftly joined in and closed their circle. "Since we'll no longer be 'The Lovelorn Logging Ladies'!"

"I forgot one of the responses was labeled that way!" Lacey's giggle was punctuated with a suspicious sniff, and Cora knew she wasn't the only one struggling against swelling emotion. That in itself was telling. Lacey almost *never* cried.

"It's a good reminder of just how blessed we are." Evie's smile lit her whole face. "The music's ending—we'd best offer up some of our thanks."

"Dear Lord," Naomi began, and all four of the women bowed their heads.

Cora didn't close her eyes, unwilling to unleash the tears yet. She prayed along with the others all the same, cherishing the sisterhood they'd forged through sheer determination and difficult decisions.

"Thank You for the men we're about to marry. Thank You for the burgeoning success of our humble sawmill. We know we went about things wrong and struggled through those mistakes, but today we're reminded of how You can shape all things to Your will and for our good." Naomi paused for a moment, and her voice cracked when she continued. "But most of all, thank You for the sisters surrounding me. They are the family of my heart, even as we branch off into our own marriages. I pray we maintain that bond, and I pray that You use it to strengthen Hope Falls for generations to come."

"Amen." Cora joined the whispered chorus and groped for a handkerchief. Keeping her eyes open hadn't helped in the face of Naomi's prayer. The words echoed the hopes of her own heart too closely.

"You're gorgeous," she told her sister for the dozenth time that day after they'd all wiped their eyes and the final note of "Great Is Thy Faithfulness" faded away. "Let's make Granger goggle all the way down the aisle."

"Oh, Cora!" Evie gave a watery smile, took Cora's proffered arm, and they started forward.

Every man stood, and when the women reached the first row, Cora heard Volker Klumpf's order ring out.

"Hat's off to the chef!" At the words, every man swept his hat from his head and held it over his heart.

Evie's laughter rang out, joining Granger's deeper notes in a harmony that boded well for the marriage and set the tone for the wedding. The lighthearted gesture helped Cora gather herself, and she managed a heartfelt smile at Braden.

Because every step that brought her sister closer to her groom brought Cora closer to Braden. A bittersweet longing lodged in the back of her throat, and Cora barely managed to answer when the preacher asked who gave Evie away to be married.

Soon enough Evie would walk her down the aisle. Braden wanted to wait until he could stand through the ceremony, so today they stood as best man and maid of honor for all three couples.

As soon as the whoops died down for the new Mr. and Mrs.

Granger, Lacey started down the aisle. With her full skirts and long—at least for the Territories—train, she looked a vision. Normally Braden would walk her down the aisle, but there wasn't room enough for her splendor and his wheeled chair. Besides, he was standing as best man for each of the three grooms. So Dunstan and Lacey dredged up another escort.

Dignified and handsome, with touches of gray threading through his hair, Lacey's escort was undeniably dapper in his jaunty bow tie. Luckily, Decoy was also tall enough to cut an impressive figure as he led the bride down the aisle. When the preacher asked who gave Lacey away, everyone laughed at the wolfhound's single authoritative bark. His part finished, Decoy politely edged out of the limelight and sat at attention beside Braden's chair while his master pledged his troth.

But as wonderful as the wolfhound was, Cora believed Naomi's escort topped them all. Dressed to the nines in a top hat and tails, brandishing a silver-topped cane Lacey slipped him that very morning, Luke Strode looked every bit as proud and happy as his father. Arm stretched high to support the bride, he visibly counted the steps so he could, as he'd put it, "get it right for Mama Naomi."

When they reached the end of the aisle, he rose on tiptoe to kiss her cheek. Amid many female tears and good-natured male whoops, he took his place beside Decoy and beamed through the rest of the ceremony.

By the time the last couple said "I do," Cora had gone through all six of the handkerchiefs she'd tucked up her sleeves and her cheeks hurt from smiling so much. She gave each of the brides a hug for good luck while the loggers scrambled to form what they called "the kissin' queue," lining up to buss each bride on the cheek.

Cora threaded through the crowd, retrieving baby Dorothy from Mrs. McCreedy and feeling grateful for something to snuggle. The weddings were wonderful, and Cora knew Braden would be back on his feet soon, but the entire thing did leave an unmarried woman feeling a bit wistful.

Apparently she wasn't the only one to have that reaction.

"Well," Bobsley sighed to Riordan after they'd filtered through the kissing queue, "that's it. Last one's spoken for by the mill owner, so I reckon we'll be bachelors for a good long while yet."

Cora's heart twisted for them. She had Braden—the real Braden—to look forward to. These poor loggers had come up here looking for love and were sticking around empty-handed.

"Or maybe not." Clump joined the other two and pulled something from his pocket. As always, excitement increased his accent. His darting glance missed Cora as he rustled a battered sheet of newsprint from his pocket and showed his friends. "Haf you ever heard of mail-order brides?"

KELLY EILEEN HAKE
Mistakes, Love & Grace!

Kelly received her first writing contract at the tender age of seventeen and arranged to wait three months until she was able to legally sign it. Since that first contract a decade ago, she's fulfilled twenty contracts ranging from short stories to novels. In her spare time, she's attained her BA in English Literature and Composition, earned her credential to teach English in secondary schools, and went on to complete her MA in Writing Popular Fiction.

Writing for Barbour combines two of Kelly's great loves—history and reading. A CBA bestselling author and member of American Christian Fiction Writers, she's been privileged to earn numerous Heartsong Presents Reader's Choice Awards and is known for her witty, heartwarming historical romances.

A newlywed, she and her gourmet-chef husband live in Southern California with their golden lab mix, Midas!

If you enjoyed
Husbands for Hire Trilogy
Look for

The
Brides
of Chance

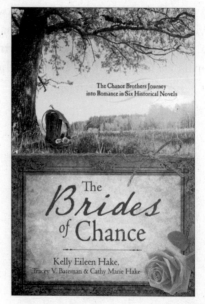